Will West

About the Author

MICHAEL LEE WEST is the author of *Mad Girls in Love, Crazy Ladies, American Pie, She Flew the Coop,* and *Consuming Passions.* She lives with her family on a farm outside Nashville, Tennessee.

Mad Girls in Love

Michael Lee West

HARPER

NEW YORK • LONDON • TORONTO • SYDNEY

HARPER

A hardcover edition of this book was published in 2005 by HarperCollins Publishers.

FIRST HARPER PAPERBACK PUBLISHED 2006.

Designed by Nancy B. Field

The Library of Congress has catalogued the hardcover edition as follows:
West, Michael Lee.
    Mad girls in love : a novel / by Michael Lee West.—1st ed.
        p. cm.
    ISBN 0-06-018406-X
    1. Southern States—Social life and customs—Fiction. 2. Women—Southern States—Fiction. I. Title.

PS3573.E8244M33 2005
813'.54—dc22
2004042371

ISBN-10: 0-06-098506-2 (pbk.)
ISBN-13: 978-0-06-098506-6 (pbk.)

06 07 08 09 10   ❖/RRD   10 9 8 7 6 5 4 3 2 1

for Ellen Levine

We need to know the writing of the past
and know it differently than we have ever known it;
not to pass on a tradition but to break its hold over us.

—ADRIENNE RICH

Mad Girls in Love

Prologue

A LETTER TO PAT NIXON

Dorothy McDougal
Central State Asylum
Nashville, Tennessee

Monday, October 17, 1972

Dear Pat Nixon,

I don't know if First Ladies read their fan mail, but I'm hoping this letter finds its way to your desk. I just didn't know where else to turn. And please don't be put off by my return address—I'm not crazy. In fact, I'm just as sane as anybody in Washington, D.C. But that's not why I'm writing. See, my nineteen-year-old daughter, Bitsy, is in a fix. A kangaroo court took her baby daughter away, and now the whole town is buzzing. I've enclosed copies of the Times-Picayune, Atlanta *Journal-Constitution, Nashville Tennessean, and the Crystal Falls* Democrat *to give you an idea of what's happened.*

First, let me just say that Bitsy isn't a violent person. She's never killed an insect, much less hurt a person. Well, that's not exactly true. When she was five years old, she accidentally swallowed a ladybug. I was frantic. I thought it might cause a tummy ache, but Bitsy didn't care about that. She was worried about that bug. Her eyes welled up, then she started to squall. I suggested that we throw a funeral—an in absentia insect funeral. It was real nice. But to this day, when Bitsy is outside, she's extra careful to keep her mouth shut. So you can imagine my surprise when I heard that she'd bludgeoned her husband. She used a frozen slab of baby back ribs, bought on sale at Piggly Wiggly for thirty-nine cents a pound.

I once had a lip-smacking recipe for baby back ribs—I'd be happy to send you the recipe. And speaking of babies, I remember when Bitsy was pregnant with Jennifer Leigh. Lord, her stomach was huge; I thought she was carrying twins, but the baby merely had a big head. All the Wentworths have gigantic skulls. Unfortunately, I got sent to Central State before my grandbaby was born, and I've only gotten to see pictures. Jennifer Leigh will be ten months old on October 31, and her head is a tad large but cleverly hidden by curly blond hair. She's got her daddy's pugged nose, along with his red facial moles. This, too, is a Wentworthian trait. Although Claude's mother, Miss Betty, will probably take the baby to a dermatologist in Nashville and get them burned off. Betty had Claude's moles burned off. She'd planned for him to get a nose job, too, but it looks like my daughter has done that for him.

Since the so-called crime spree, Bitsy has been living with my sister, Clancy Jane, who never liked me. But I won't get into that just yet. She reports that Bitsy can't stop crying, much less get out of bed. These are two things that will get you slapped into the insane asylum. The wards are full of women who are too sad to wash their hair or change their nightgowns. My hair is dry and crackly, but I'd wash it every day if they'd let me out of here. A mother should be allowed to comfort her daughter, even if that mother isn't right in the head. I always dreamed that we would live next door to each other and dress alike—I'm partial to cardigan sweater sets and open-toed sandals—and maybe we'd have our hair cut in similar styles. But it never occurred to me that we'd have mother-daughter nervous breakdowns.

This is where you come in, Pat—or would you prefer to be called Patricia? We mothers must stick together. (In addition to my daughter, I have a twenty-year-old son named Mack. Maybe Trisha would be interested in meeting him? He lost his leg in Vietnam, but he's real cute.) Anyway, I was wondering if you'd ask the president if the Supreme Court will hear my daughter's case. Or maybe Dick himself can make a few phone calls and smooth things over. I look forward to hearing from you.

Yours very truly,
Dorothy McDougal

P.S. Here is my recipe for baby back ribs. It will be a hit at White House dinners!

Dorothy McDougal's Bourbon-Soaked Ribs

7 to 10 pound rack of pork ribs (defrosted)
1 large white onion
½ cup brown sugar
2 tablespoon Dijon mustard
½ cup soy sauce
¾ cup bourbon
1 tablespoon Worcestershire sauce
⅛ cups apple cider vinegar
2 teaspoons fresh lemon juice
Salt, pepper, paprika

Mince onion. Into a large bowl, combine all ingredients and mix well. Season ribs with salt and pepper and a sprinkling of paprika. Set in baking pan. Pour sauce over ribs. Chill 8 hours or overnight. Using a charcoal grill, cook ribs for 45 minutes. Serves: 12.

Part 1

Bitsy

TO-DO LIST
OCTOBER 17, 1972

1. Get out of bed.
2. Or stay in bed and write down my side of the story.
3. Find an inexpensive (but smart!) lawyer.
4. Buy Summer Blonde to touch up my roots.

Notorious. That's what the *Times-Picayune* called me. And the Atlanta *Journal-Constitution* wrote, "Wicked Bitsy Wentworth looks like a blond Barbie—shapely on the exterior, but underneath the plastic is the razor-sharp brain of a teenaged criminal."

My name is Lillian Beatrice McDougal Wentworth—Bitsy for short—and this is my side of the story: It began two months ago on a hot afternoon in August. The day started out normal. First, I washed my baby's hair in the kitchen sink. Jennifer has quite a lot of hair for an eight-month-old, so it took a while. I wrapped her in a towel and we danced around the room. From the top of the refrigerator, the radio was playing Strauss's "On the Beautiful Blue Danube." Normally I would be listening to Neil Diamond, but ever since Claude and I had renewed our marriage vows—six weeks ago, to be exact—I was determined to improve myself. After all, Claude was a Wentworth, and his people have been cultured for the last hundred years. Which shouldn't be confused with buttermilk or bacterial cultures; I'm talking about sophistication. I'd tried to sound stylish by memorizing words from the dictionary, but sometimes I mispronounced the words, and Claude's mother, Miss Betty, would call me down. But I could stand to listen to classical music, as long as I didn't have to say the composers' names.

The baby stirred in my arms, sending up sweet gusts of baby sham-poo, and we waltzed to the other side of the kitchen, stepping through puddles of sunlight, which poured through the long windows. Jennifer laughed. It came from her belly and sounded a little like Phyllis Diller, but in a cute sort of way. After I fluffed the baby's hair and dressed her in a pink sunsuit, I carried her into the living room. I picked up a blanket and was just starting to play peek-a-boo, when I happened to glance at the clock. It was nearly three P.M., and Claude liked his supper on the table by five sharp. I put the baby in the playpen, hurried into the kitchen, and flung open the freezer door. All I could find was an enor-mous package of ribs. Hoping they'd defrost faster, I shoved the rubber stopper into the sink drain and turned on the water, then I tossed in the package. Next, I changed the radio station to one that played love songs. The Fifth Dimension was singing "One Less Bell to Answer," and I asked myself why men leave and what did fried eggs have to do with it?

From the living room, I could hear Jennifer banging on her toy xylophone—she sounded extra-talented to me—and then I grabbed the charcoal bag and a tin of lighter fluid. I stepped outside and hunkered next to the hibachi. It was too soon to light the briquettes, but I thought I'd get them ready. As I piled them into the bottom of the hibachi, I tried to remember my mother's recipe for barbecue sauce—did it call for honey or brown sugar? I couldn't ask because she was in a psychiatric hospital getting cured of paranoia and in no condition to exchange recipes.

The kitchen phone rang and I hurried back inside, skidding across the linoleum, my polka-dot dress swishing around my legs. I just love any-thing with polka dots, although gingham is awfully sweet, too. I grabbed the receiver and answered in my breathless Julie Christie voice, the one Claude liked. I'd copied it from *Dr. Zhivago.*

"Is Claude there?" It was a woman. I didn't recognize her voice, but it reminded me of sticky hot summer nights on my grandmother's old screened porch, mosquitoes humming in the damp air.

"No, but I'm expecting him any minute." I waved my hand, as if shooing a bug.

"I'm *sure* you are. Never mind, I'll catch up with him later." The woman laughed and hung up. I frowned, trying to place the voice. It hummed in my ear in dizzy circles. I wanted to slap it and draw blood. But maybe the caller was one of Claude's customers. He was a loan officer at Citizen's Bank where his daddy, Claude Wentworth III, was the president. People were always wanting to borrow money.

From the radio, Petula Clark began singing "My Love." I stared at the phone a minute. Then I dialed the bank. My love for Claude was deeper than the deepest ocean, and nothing in the world could ever change that love—unless he was up to something.

When the receptionist answered, I pinched my nostrils to disguise my voice. "May I speak to Claude Wentworth IV?" I put emphasis on the numeral, so the woman wouldn't put me through to Claude III, my father-in-law.

"I'm sorry," said the receptionist. "He isn't in his office this afternoon. May I take a message?"

"What do you mean, *not in his office*?" I cried in my real voice.

"He'll be here tomorrow," said the woman. Then in a more suspicious tone, "Who *is* this?"

I hung up and walked in a daze to the living room. I sank down into a teal blue plaid chair. I'd bought it at Goodwill, then Claude's mother had her upholsterer recover it in some of her leftover fabric. From this, I had put together a teal-and-white color scheme. Claude said he loved it. But then, he said a lot of things. If he hadn't been to the bank today, then where had he gone? Across the room, Jennifer had abandoned the xylophone and was busily fitting nesting cups together. She looked up and grinned—the spitting image of the Wentworths, with their high foreheads and curly blond hair. Then she tossed the cups into the air and screeched.

The phone rang again, and I sprang out of the chair, racing into the kitchen. As soon as I answered, the line went dead. Now I was worried. I had seen this happen many times on soap operas, and it meant one of two things, adultery or a contract killing. But usually it was the other woman. A hang-up call was the International Signal for Mistresses. Claude was rich enough to keep a woman, but he wasn't old enough. Although with his genes, anything was possible. I walked back into the living room and lifted my daughter from the playpen. "We're going to find Da-da," I told her as we headed out the door, but she didn't seem impressed. In the driveway, a hot breeze stirred the upper limbs of the hackberry tree. A wind chime clinked. The air smelled of stale suntan lotion. The source of this odor was the stained mesh chair on the side patio, where Claude often sunbathed. He was finicky about his looks, but so was I. It was the main thing we had in common, besides our precious baby girl. Only this morning, I had helped him select a tie that matched his blue linen suit, and he'd warned me that he might have to work late. "That's all right, honey," I'd said, trying to be a good wife. "I'll have you a nice supper ready when you get home."

Claude's black Labrador, a neutered male named Princeton, was stretched out in the driveway. He'd named the dog when he was applying to colleges. By the time the real Princeton had rejected him it was too late to give the dog another name. I stepped over the dog, then flung open the door to my powder blue Mustang and felt inside the baby's car seat, making certain that it wasn't too hot, the way Dr. Spock said to do. When Jennifer was strapped in, she squeezed her eyes shut and smiled, baring her rabbit teeth. For a moment my beautiful daughter looked just like Claude's mother.

First, I sped over to the bank, praying that the secretary had been mistaken. When I didn't see Claude's Corvette—white with an orange Go Vols! sticker in the rear window—I drove to the Mountain Air Motor Court and swerved into the parking lot, stirring up gravel dust. I circled slowly, hitting the brake each time I saw a squatty white car. The heat plus hysteria was making me queasy, and I could taste my lunch, a peanut butter and banana sandwich. If I'd known I was going to become a girl sleuth, I would have eaten something more soothing, like chicken salad on toast—that's what Nancy Drew preferred. I hoped that Claude was on the golf course with his daddy, slapping mosquitoes and drinking vodka tonics. But I had a feeling that he'd been up to no good.

Steering back onto the highway, I charged toward the Holiday Inn. I drove up and down that lot, too, but I didn't see a trace of Claude. I thought about stopping by my aunt's house for advice, but Clancy Jane had flown to Bermuda with Dr. Falk, her new husband. None of my relatives was in town. My father was on a church trip to Gatlinburg; my brother, Mack, was in Myrtle Beach with his wife, Earlene; my cousin Violet had gone back to college, and, of course, my mother was locked up.

Halfway down Town Creek Road, my car broke down. I steered off the road, tires crunching in the gravel. This had already happened twice this week; the engine would usually start if I just pumped the gas pedal. Jennifer twirled one finger in her hair and grinned. "Ta?" she asked.

I kissed the tip of her nose, then switched on the ignition. The engine whined, but it turned over. As I headed home, I thought of my "to do" list and mentally added *Get car fixed*. My daddy had bought me the Mustang when I'd graduated from high school—not that long ago—but the car, like my life, seemed to be falling apart.

When I pulled into my drive and saw the white Corvette, I couldn't help but laugh at my own silliness. We'd just criss-crossed each other, that was all. I unhooked Jennifer from the car seat. As we walked toward the house, something made me pause and touch the Corvette's hood. It was hot. Could it have gotten this hot just driving home from the bank? I took a deep breath and marched inside, trying to decide if I should confront him or just let it go.

When I stepped into the kitchen, the Eagles were on the radio, singing "Take It Easy." I glanced into the living room—Claude was reared back in the teal plaid chair, reading the Crystal Falls *Democrat*. I wondered if there was a hidden meaning in that Eagles song, warning me not to let the sound of my own wheels drive me crazy. But I couldn't stop myself from blurting, "Busy day at the bank?"

He didn't answer. Jennifer tipped out of my arms toward her father and opened her hands like starfish. Claude paid no attention and continued reading. I edged forward, trying to see what had captured his attention. Dr. Henry Kissinger was in Paris; a Venezuelan airplane had been hijacked and flown to Cuba; and Nolan Ryan pitched a no-hitter. I wished one of the headlines had given a hint to my husband's activities. I just wanted facts, no hysterics. However if Claude looked me in the eye and said, *Aspetti, confesso*, which was Italian, by the way, then I might go temporarily insane.

"Claude, honey. Can you put the paper down?"

With a sigh, he lowered the newspaper, the pages rustling. "Look, I'm really tired. I've worked my tail off today. Can you get me a glass of wine? After I relax, we can talk. I promise."

He was talking to me the way he talked to his Labrador. In a minute, he'd throw me a bone—anything to shut me up. I carried the baby down the hall, into the pink-and-cream nursery. My dog-eared copy of *Baby and Child Care* was lying in the crib, so I moved it to the changing table. Claude always laughed when I quoted Dr. Spock. I put Jennifer in her crib. She stretched out and stared up at me with her daddy's eyes. They were bluer than mine, and they seemed to say, Give it a rest, Mama. Go fold the laundry or something.

"Love you, Jennikins," I whispered, rubbing her chubby arm. "Take you a little nap."

I shut the door and stepped into the hall. On my way to the kitchen, Claude called out, "Honey, did you forget my wine?"

As I grabbed the wine bottle out of the refrigerator, I thought of the woman caller and got mad all over again. "Do you want it with or without arsenic?" I muttered. This was something my cousin Violet would say. She had all the brains in the family; and she'd warned me not to remarry Claude. But I'd watched her grow up fatherless, and I didn't want the same thing to happen to my little girl. I reached up, opened a kitchen cabinet, and selected a swirled green Fostoria goblet—wedding crystal that matched our Sculpted Daisy pottery. I had picked this out last year, right before our shotgun marriage. I'd longed for something blue, of course, but the jewelry store people said it was Miss Betty's pattern, so I knew it was in good taste. I sure didn't want to be like my mother. Her pottery had featured a great big ugly chicken. But now I didn't want to be like Claude's mother, either. Miss Betty kept a sterling flask in her Dior purse, and a bottle of Smirnoff in her trunk. Two weeks ago she was driving her Lincoln Town Car in the wrong lane and a policeman made her pull over. When he realized who she was, he got scared and let her go.

I glanced on the counter and saw Claude's wallet and keys. I started to reach for the wallet—the most likely spot he'd hide a motel receipt—but stopped when I heard his paper hit the floor. The chair creaked, then footsteps shook the cottage. A second later, he stood in the doorway, glaring at me.

"What did you just say?"

"Nothing, I was just getting ready to pour your wine." I moved away from the wallet and looked up into his eyes. I meant to ask him if he wanted cheese and crackers with his drink. Instead, what came out was, "Have you been with a woman?"

Claude blinked. "What the hell are you talking about?"

"A woman called here this afternoon."

"What woman? I don't know any women."

"She asked if you were home. Then I called the bank, and they said you'd taken the afternoon off."

"Well, yes," he sputtered. "To get a haircut!"

I glanced at his head. I couldn't tell if it had been cut or not. The blond hairs stood up like filaments, strands of fishing line. He kept his hair short to please his daddy. Chick Wentworth was president of the local Republican Club, and he was a staunch supporter of Richard Nixon. Mr. Wentworth even looked like his hero—the long, sloping nose, thinning hair, and stooped shoulders.

"After the haircut, I had errands," Claude said irritably.

"And they were . . ." I waved one hand, prompting him to continue.

"I don't have to account for everything." He frowned. Then, in a spiteful voice, he added, "In fact, I don't have to tell you shit."

"What about that woman calling the house?"

"Our phone number's in the book. I can't help who calls."

Well, he had a point. It occurred to me that I'd inherited my mother's paranoia. I took a few deep breaths, trying to calm down. The phone rang. I leaned across the counter and snatched the receiver. "Hello?"

Silence, then a click. I started to hang up, but Claude looked a little too cocky, as if he expected me to play Debbie Reynolds to his Eddie Fisher. So I decided to trick him. I rolled my eyes and thrust out the receiver. "It's *her* again."

Claude's eyes switched back and forth.

"Here, talk to her."

"No!"

"Suit yourself." I jammed the receiver against my ear and said, "Sorry, Claude won't come to the phone. He's chickenshit—"

"I am NOT!" He sprang forward and wrestled the phone from my hands.

"Candy?" he said. "Are you there?"

Candy? It was a perfect little name for a hamster, not a mistress. I knew a Candy McCall who worked at the appliance store, but she was a skinny platinum blonde who chain smoked, and besides, she was thirty years old. I had bought a refrigerator from her just last month. I couldn't see Claude falling for an older woman. Then I thought maybe he'd said Randy. Yes, maybe that was it. At least five Randys had gone to our high school, and any one of them might need a home improvement loan.

Claude gave me a sly look and said, "She's just a friend of mine."

"She?"

"Candy's a friend, that's all. It's not what you think."

I put both hands on my chest and cried, "How do *you* know what I think?"

"Because you're so obvious." He poured his wine then picked up the glass and walked into the living room. He settled into the plaid chair and reached with one hand for the newspaper. The subject was closed, Wentworth-style. He wasn't going to confess anything. I turned toward the sink and gazed down at the ribs. They still looked frozen, but I thought about cooking them anyway. If he broke a tooth on the rock-hard meat, it would serve him right. I imagined the woman calling the bank, saying, "Hi, I'm Candy. *Lick me.*"

The phone rang again, and Claude yelled, "I'll get it!" but I beat him to it. "Hey, Candy," I said in a peppy voice. "Or would you prefer if I called you Sugar Lump? I like that better, don't you? Or maybe you're not Candy. Maybe you're Taffy or Ginger." I forced out a laugh. "You know Claude—he's got something sweet in every corner of this town. Instead of dessert du jour, it's *girl* du jour. I just can't keep track of his sluts. Or should I say *les filles*? It sounds *so* much nicer, don't you agree?"

Claude ran into the room and lunged at me. We wrestled for control of the phone, and then I suddenly let go. He staggered sideways, gripping the receiver, then raised it to his ear.

"Candy?" he whispered. Then, more urgently, "*Candy? You still there?*"

As I studied my husband's face, my heart sped up. Whoever this woman was—refrigerator saleswoman or hooker—she was his lover. And I wished that I had never remarried him. My mother's sister, Clancy Jane, once said that Claude had little hope of becoming a decent human being, thanks to his spoiled, rich-boy upbringing. He slammed down the receiver, then beat his fist against the counter. On the window ledge, my favorite ceramic bunny—I have this really cute collection—fell over and broke. I wouldn't be able to glue it back. Its ears were shattered. I began gathering the broken pieces in my palm, holding back tears. It was just a rabbit, not my heart. Claude was still standing beside the sink. He reached into the water and lifted the package of meat.

"What's this?" His upper lip curled. "Pigsicles?"

I didn't answer. He dropped the package. It bobbed sideways.

"You need to get organized. I wanted to eat supper before my TV shows come on." He opened the cabinet and grabbed a fresh goblet. This was another Wentworth trait—they wouldn't drink out of a used glass, even if it was their own. Maybe Claude was this way with women, too. It sure was ironic that his favorite show was *Love, American Style*. Me, I liked *Bridget Loves Bernie*. The wine bottle gurgled as he filled the glass. Every afternoon his parents drank vodka martinis in their cherry-paneled den. By the time the maid called them into the dining room to eat dinner, the Wentworths were bombed, surrounded by empty glasses. And he was going to be just like them. He gulped down the wine, then got a new glass. I chewed my tongue, trying to control it. I knew I shouldn't mention the dangers of alcohol, but I couldn't stop myself. I gestured at his glass and said, "You've had enough."

"I'll drink the whole damn bottle if I please." He lifted his glass and took a long, deliberate swallow.

I wondered if he and Candy had opened a bottle of champagne. Then I blurted, "Go on, then, *be* just like your mother."

Claude's eyes narrowed. "I made a big mistake taking you back."

"Then why'd you do it?"

"For Jennifer's sake. But you aren't fit to raise my daughter."

"*Your* daughter? Just tell me one thing. Does having a girlfriend on the side make you a good parent?"

"I don't know. Look it up in Dr. Spock." He reached for another glass and filled it. "You're not worthy of me. Everybody in town knows about your family."

"They know about yours, too," I snapped. "Just visit any beauty shop in town, and you'll see—"

He threw the Fostoria goblet. It exploded on the floor, bits of green glass skittering over the linoleum. I felt something hot in my throat. Why, I could spit on this pug-nosed boy and burn him up. In ancient times, there probably weren't any fire-breathing dragons, just angry people with acid reflux. As I stared down at the wreckage, I thought of another insult.

"Go on, break another one. Miss Betty would."

"You bitch!" He grabbed my hair and dragged me to the sink, then shoved my face into the water. I felt it rush up my nose and I started to choke. I reached behind me for his face. My wet hand slid over his mouth. He bit down hard on my thumb. I opened my mouth to scream and sucked in water. I whipped my head from side to side, but he would not let go. Black spots swirled behind my lids, and my lips were going numb. Fighting to stay conscious, I pushed against the bottom of the sink. Then I felt the chain and grasped it, tugging on the rubber stopper. Water began to trickle down the pipe, but I felt how weak the suction was. Two seconds passed, then three. I'd never known what to do in an emergency, and this sure qualified as one. I'd drown before the sink emptied. My hands groped helplessly along the porcelain bottom of the sink, trying to get leverage. I touched the package of ribs. Then I grasped it firmly, dragged it up and out of the water, and swung it in a wide arc. I felt them smash into something rigid. The impact reverberated up my arms, but Claude didn't let go. I swung again. This time, his fingers loosened. I lifted my face out of the water and staggered backward. He was shrieking, his hands cupped over his nose. Blood trickled between his fingers. Behind me, the last bit of water gurgled down the drain.

"Bitch! You broke my fucking nose!"

He lunged toward the counter, and I brandished the ribs, ready to hit him again. He snatched up the stainless toaster, jerking the electrical cord from the socket, then lifted it. When he saw his reflection, he screamed. Then he threw the toaster. I tried to duck, but it grazed my forehead.

"You fucking bitch," he yelled, only it sounded like "futhin bith," because his lips and nose were swelling. He turned back to the counter, picked up the blender, and hurled it at me. This time I jumped out of the way; the blender hit the wall behind me and clunked against the counter.

"You'll wot in thail," he lisped. "My pawents'll see to it."

Afraid he might throw another small appliance, I gripped the baby back ribs to my chest and ran, leaving a trail of water behind me. Claude caught up with me and grabbed my hair, yanking me around. I tried to hit him with the ribs, but he lunged backward. His shoes skidded on the wet floor, and he let go of my hair. His arms whirled, then he fell. The back of his head cracked against the floor. I waited for him to get up and start cursing me, but he just lay there. With his eyes closed he didn't look dangerous.

"Claude?" I knelt beside him and gingerly nudged his hand. It flopped to the floor, giving me a full view of his damaged face. His nose was squashed to the left, and it had tripled in size. I leaned over, my wet hair swinging forward. Was he breathing? Oh, Lord, what if he was dead, or else in a coma like that poor Karen Ann Quinlan, wasting away in New Jersey? Her parents were seeking legal action to pull the plug. I shuddered, thinking of my own near-death experience.

Maybe he's just stunned, I thought. Maybe he'll wake up and want dinner. Hugging the ribs to my chest, I gave Claude's body a wide berth and hurried toward the door. On my way out, I grabbed a box of matches. In the backyard, a breeze was stirring the upper limbs of the hackberry tree, ruffling the crape myrtles, sending pink blossoms spinning through the air. I lifted one hand and touched my forehead. I wasn't bleeding, but a huge punk-knot was forming above my eyebrow. It occurred to me that I was acting peculiar—Claude wasn't in any shape to eat grilled ribs. But why not get them ready, just in case? I squirted lighter fluid over the charcoal. Then I lit a match. The wind gusted, and my polka-dot dress billowed, threatening to blow over my head. When I reached down to slap the hem, my match snuffed out. It was as if the wind was trying to warn me: *Don't do it, Bitsy. Don't cook these ribs.* But I couldn't stop myself. I lit another match and dropped it onto the briquettes. Flames licked upward, burning in a filmy, oily haze, and smoke billowed up into the sky.

Then I unwrapped the ribs. They hardly looked like a weapon, but then, I hadn't really committed a crime. He had tried to drown me. I'd hit him in self-defense. But this was Crystal Falls. The police were notorious for taking their time to reach a crime scene—usually nothing more than vandalism or public drunkenness. Even if I called them, they probably wouldn't get here for another hour, and by then my supporting evidence would be gone. My hair would be dry, the ribs thawed. The police would take one look at the boy on the floor, realize who he was, and haul me to jail. I wasn't overreacting, was I?

I closed my eyes and remembered how Miss Betty had cried at both my weddings. If her son was dead or comatose, she'd do more than weep: She would destroy my life. I tossed the meat onto the grill, orange sparks drifting up. I sat there for a long time, trying to figure out a plan. When the meat began to sizzle, Claude's Labrador suddenly darted out of the crape myrtles and sniffed the air. I threw the empty meat package at him. Princeton snapped it up, then trotted off. I stepped back into the kitchen, and the screened door clapped against the frame. Claude still hadn't moved, but he was moaning. Any minute now, he'd be coming around. When that happened, I didn't want to be here. In the last thirty minutes—or maybe it was only three?—the following things had happened:

1. I found out about the Claude-and-Candy affair.
2. He tried to drown me in the sink.
3. I accidentally broke his nose or maybe I'd killed him.

Until today, he'd never been violent. I'd known him since the first grade. He was my first and only love. And now I had permanently altered his profile. I walked to the sink and wet a tea towel. Then, kneeling beside him, I gently pressed the rag to his face. A fresh strand of blood, narrow as thread, curved out of his nose. It wove around the earlobe, under the jaw, down his neck. Normally I wasn't scared of blood—I mean, really, I'd survived childbirth, hadn't I?—but my hands began shaking, and I thought I might pass out. No, I couldn't do that. I had to be strong.

"Claude?" I cupped his cheek. I couldn't just let him lie here and bleed to death. I did love him, even with his shortcomings. I had come to believe that most men, including my own daddy, were devious when it came to sex—but good grief, there were worse things, like atomic warfare and bubonic plague.

"Open your eyes, sweetie," I said, rubbing his hand. "Talk to me, Claude."

From the nursery, Jennifer began to wail. I hesitated, torn between my daughter's tears and my husband's imminent demise. The baby let out another piercing wail. I got to my feet and started to step over Claude's body. Then I froze, remembering a high school football game. A big-shouldered linebacker had slammed into number 14, Claude's number. I'd watched with horror as the ball had flown out of Claude's hands into a defensive back's outstretched arms. Then the linebacker flattened number 14. A cheer rose up in the visitors' section. From the loudspeaker, the announcer called, "Fumble on the play. Recovery by Putnam County." Claude lay motionless on the field. A minute ticked by, and when he didn't get up, the coaches jogged over and helped him to his feet. As he limped to the sidelines, the home crowd had clapped. Later, in the backseat of his daddy's Lincoln Continental, he'd told me that he'd faked the injury to cover his error. "I should go to Hollywood," he'd said, and I'd agreed. I thought he'd be good either as a movie star or a politician, which were one and the same, if you asked me.

Remembering all this, I imagined his hand rising up, grabbing my ankle, and yanking me down. The baby screeched again, and I leaped over Claude and ran to the doorway. Then I turned. He still hadn't moved. The very least I could do was cover him. So I hurried down the hall, into our bedroom, and flung open the closet door. I ran my hands over Claude's suits, and the rows of color-coordinated shirts. Then I reached up onto a shelf and grabbed a stack of cashmere sweaters. I could vaguely smell his cologne, Canoe. *If I warm him up, he'll be all right,* I thought. *Please God, don't let him be hurt.*

From the nursery, the baby screamed again. Tucking the sweaters under my arm, I hurried out of the bedroom. I found my daughter standing in her crib, arms outstretched, chubby face streaked with tears. With my free arm, I lifted the child, cushioning her with the sweaters. Except for the distant humming of the ice box, the house was eerily quiet, but I forced myself into the kitchen. Claude was still on the floor, in the same position. His nose resembled a crook-neck squash. As I stepped closer, the baby twisted around, trying to see her daddy.

"Shhh, Daddy's sleeping. Let's don't wake him." I tried to press her little head against my shoulder, blocking her view. This was the sort of thing that warped babies, and I wasn't about to let that happen. Then I leaned over Claude and draped the sweaters over his chest as best as I could. My mind seemed to clear a little and I hurried over to the phone. Jiggling the baby up and down, I dialed Cox Funeral Home and Ambulance Service. When Mrs. Cox answered, I stammered, "C-come get my husband! He hit his head and won't wake up."

"Who are you?" said Mrs. Cox.

"We're at 508 T-Tarver Street. Please hurry." I hung up the phone and kissed my daughter's tousled curls. They smelled faintly of shampoo. Almost immediately the phone began to ring again. I had an idea it was the other woman, so I ignored it and gazed down at Claude. *Wait for the ambulance?* I thought, *or run away and hide?*

I carried Jennifer to the living room and set her down in the playpen. She immediately began to cry, but I had to get us out of there. I ran to the hall closet and pulled out a suitcase—it wasn't one of my blue ones, it was Claude's Gucci, a Christmas present from his family. But it would have to suffice. As I rushed around the house, hastily grabbing baby clothes, I found my *Webster's Dictionary* opened to the Ms. Before I closed it, I looked at a word: malefactor. *How fitting,* I thought. *The male factor.* But then I scanned the definition and saw that it meant criminal. That was an even better fit.

I slipped the dictionary into the Gucci, then zipped it. My plan was to stay gone a day or two, long enough for everything to simmer down. I didn't want to take Claude's Corvette—my name wasn't even on the title—but it wouldn't break down like my Mustang. I imagined my car stalling on a dark, foggy highway. I even imagined what the newspapers would say: *The blue 1972 Mustang was found abandoned on Cemetery Road. Police are still searching for the occupants, a teenaged mother and her tow-headed tot.*

After I slung the Gucci into the back, I strode over to my Mustang and got Jennifer's car seat. I fastened it into the Corvette then hurried toward the kitchen. Smoke wafted over the hibachi. I glanced down. The ribs were gone, although pieces of meat were stuck to the grate. I turned. Near the edge of the yard, Princeton dragged the ribs through the grass, leaving a greasy stain behind him. In the distance I could hear a siren. I ran back to the kitchen and grabbed Claude's wallet and car keys. Then I hurried into the living room to fetch my little girl.

Bitsy

OPTIONS

1. Return to Crystal Falls and tell my side of the story.
2. Keep driving.
3. Check into a motel, preferably in a cute city, and decide if I should do #1 or #2.
4. Stop making lists. I don't need to leave a paper trail for the police!

My mother's paranoia surfaced in me as I sped along the highway, and I began to think that a policeman was hiding behind every billboard. Once the Wentworths realized that I'd left town, taking Claude's baby and his Corvette, not to mention his Gucci, they would call the police. Miss Betty knew all the judges, and probably a few hit men. Oh, I knew what she thought of me. Years ago, when she'd remodeled her manse, she had let Claude decorate his bedroom. He'd just turned twelve, but he chose a circus motif: green grass cloth was pasted to the walls. Chintz curtains, printed with red and yellow balloons, were hung on the windows. A faux bamboo bunk bed was ordered from Nashville. Stuffed circus animals were strung up by their necks and hung from the ceiling with rope—a pleated, fabric-lined ceiling made to resemble a tent. The stuffed animals wore clothes—monkeys in jester hats and red vests, elephants in pantaloons, and tigers in tuxedos. It was colorful and cute, but totally unsuitable for a prepubescent boy. "Can't you pick something else?" Miss Betty had complained. "Price is no object. In fact, the more it costs, the better it'll look."

As far as Miss Betty was concerned, I was like that bedroom—a cheap, childish lapse in judgment, a passing fancy, something her son would outgrow.

Once I decided the interstate wasn't safe, I turned off at the next exit and began following Highway 70 toward Nashville. I drove through hilly towns named after flowers and trees. At dusk, I reached Crab Orchard, and I saw a woman in a yellow dress and chunky shoes step out of her house, carrying a tray to the carport where children were having a party. Floodlights burned on either side of the carport, and balloons streamed from the wrought-iron posts. I would have given anything to be this woman, to have her life, even though yellow wasn't my color. It brought out the circles under my eyes.

After Crab Orchard, the road twisted up a steep ridge. Past the dented guardrails, I could see a sheer drop-off, nothing but blue mist and the distant etch of mountains. From the valleys and river towns, lights twinkled up. Jennifer began smacking the seat with her baby bottle. Inside, Coca-Cola fizzled. Dr. Spock would not approve; no one would condone my actions. I myself didn't approve, but I couldn't think of another option.

I gassed up in Lebanon. While the attendant scrubbed the bug-spattered windshield, I pulled out Claude's wallet, counting the cash and shuffling through the credit cards. I didn't want to use his cards at all—it was against the law, and I'd done enough—but Claude only had three hundred dollars, and in my own wallet was not quite twenty. I gave the Esso man a card and forged my husband's name, my hand shaking so badly the pen slipped from my fingers. The clerk never glanced at my signature. If it was this easy to get away with fraud, then the world was in big trouble. Better the world than me.

When I reached Nashville, highway traffic was heavy, so I drove down shady streets, past houses with circular driveways, past white board fences where horses grazed in sloping pastures. In Bellevue, the highway curved, dropping off into cool, green darkness. I rolled my window down and the wind washed over my face, blowing my hair. The Corvette felt like a boat, and I imagined that I was riding waves instead of hills, the air pungent and salty. When I crested a hill, the lights of west Nashville reflected in the rearview mirror, then dropped off abruptly.

Mexico, I thought. *That's where I'll go. I can disappear in Mexico.* But tonight I had to at least reach Memphis. I was thinking of dying my hair, and Jennifer's too, maybe blue-black like Priscilla Presley. She was somewhere in Memphis, waiting for Elvis to come home and shoot out the television set. And if I wasn't mistaken, he'd cheated on her, too—with Ann-Margret, no less. I wondered how Priscilla had handled that, if she'd looked the other way or chased him around Graceland with a lethal weapon.

In Waverly, I filled up with gas again, then turned onto I-40, toward Memphis. Now the paranoia wasn't as bad. Besides, no one was looking for me and Jennifer. Not yet, anyway. If Claude died—and it was possible— then I would be a man slaughterer. But right now I wasn't a wanted woman. I was just a mother driving down the highway with her baby.

When Jennifer began to fret, I stopped at a restaurant in Jackson, one of those "all you can eat" smorgasbords. I put the baby in a high chair, rolled her over to a table, then grabbed a red tray and darted through the line. Normally, I never ate. I just picked at food. Claude thought that childbirth had changed my body, and it had sort of melted, like that soft Parkay margarine they showed on TV. Do not mess with Mother Nature, the ad warned. One time Claude gave me his mother's diet pills but I never took them, even though they were shaped like pink hearts. Claude worried about my figure, he said I was too short to eat. If it was up to him, I'd live on Dexedrine, Tab, and carrot sticks. But tonight I was stuffing myself. People glanced at me as I piled dishes onto the tray—roast beef, meat loaf, fried chicken, mashed potatoes. Then I saw baby back ribs, each one glistening in barbecue sauce, and I staggered backward.

"What's the matter, honey?" asked a woman with saucer-size earrings. "Are you fixing to faint?"

"No, ma'am. I'm just hungry." I kept loading my tray with dishes. Fried okra, macaroni, broccoli, corn muffins, chocolate pie. Maybe if I gained weight, the Wentworths wouldn't recognize me. I hurried back to my table and crumbled up the meat loaf for Jennifer, adding tiny bits of corn bread. The baby dug into the food, and I ate quickly, too. Pretty soon my empty plates shone with a greasy radiance. Before we left, I filled Jennifer's bottles with milk—according to Dr. Spock, babies need calcium or they get rickets.

I drove until I reached the Mississippi River, turning just before the bridge. The Peabody Hotel loomed in front of me. I had once made Claude promise that he'd bring me and Jennifer to see the ducks, but he was always in a golfing tournament. Or maybe he'd been up to something else.

In the hotel's parking lot, I handed Claude's keys to a valet and then unhooked Jennifer from the car seat. The valet followed me into the dark, air-conditioned lobby, past a three-foot-tall arrangement of gladioli and bells of Ireland. A pretty brunette receptionist smiled at the baby, then at me.

"I'd like a room, please," I said, fishing out Claude's American Express. It was stamped C. E. Wentworth IV, which stood for Claude Edmund, but if push came to shove, I'd tell a fib. I'd say it stood for Candy. I thought it was too bad that his initials weren't E. C., because then I could say my name was Eat Candy.

"Certainly," said the receptionist, glancing at the card. "Will there be anything else, Miss Wentworth? Or is it Mrs.?"

"I'll need a Portacrib," I said, trying to change the subject.

The woman looked at the card again, and my heart sped up. Trying to appear innocent, I glanced toward the open lounge, toward the fountain. It was famous for its ducks, but tonight it was empty.

"Enjoy your stay in Memphis," said the clerk, sliding the card across the marble counter. I snatched it up, then started to dash off, but the clerk called out, "Miss?"

I froze. This was it. Somehow I had been caught. I turned, ready to confess everything.

"You forgot your key," she said, holding it in the air.

· · ·

From the windows of my room, I gazed down at the lights along the river. The bridge reminded me of a carnival ride. Although I hadn't studied a map, I was pretty sure that Arkansas was the quickest route to Texas—and Mexico. I put my head in my arms, thinking of the mess I'd had left behind in Crystal Falls. And without meaning to, I was making things worse. I could now add credit card fraud to my catalog of crimes. Soon the people at MasterCard, Esso, and American Express would start looking for me—if they weren't already on my trail.

First, I needed to ditch the Corvette and replace it with a cheap, untraceable vehicle. I'd never bought a car—my blue Mustang had been a gift from my daddy. In fact, I'd never bought anything other than lipstick and Bobbie Brooks coordinates. If I paid cash for a car, would they make me sign forms? Ask for my driver's license? References? Just how much information would I have to reveal?

I moved away from the window and flopped onto the bed. I wasn't worried about waking Jennifer after the day she'd had. The coverlet was strewn with peach-colored flowers, and I buried my face in one. If only I were far, far away, living in an exotic place, a city that smelled of mandarin oranges and incense. Years ago my family and I had eaten at House of Fu in Panama City, Florida, and my fortune cookie had said: Swim with abandon into vast sea of life. I had prayed this would come to pass, even though I knew it wouldn't. Crystal Falls was hundreds of miles from an ocean. Not only that, it didn't even have a Chinese restaurant. Still, there was more to a town than thick yellow pages, and unlike some of the people in my family, I'd never felt the itchy urge to leave. I'd meant to stay put with Claude and our baby. I wanted to cook and sew and rearrange the furniture. And when I got old, I'd grow tomatoes. Great big ones that I'd enter in the fair.

Now it looked as if the fortune cookie had been correct. I wondered if I'd be safe living in Mexico. I couldn't drink the water and couldn't speak the language. It was too bad that I couldn't go to France. When I was younger, I'd taught myself to speak French. Claude had loved it, even when the phrases I'd whispered into his ear didn't make sense. He had encouraged my pursuit of foreign languages until I made a fool of myself at the Wentworths' annual Valentine's dinner. After two glasses of wine, I'd felt brave enough to speak a little French, and I asked the woman beside me to pass the beets, only what I said was "pass the dicks." The guests had burst into laughter, but Claude's mother spilled her wine. It was burgundy, and I cringed as the heirloom tablecloth turned dark red.

I got up from the bed and started poking around the room. I found a complimentary copy of the *Commercial-Appeal* on the dresser, and I opened it to classifieds. One advertisement caught my eye: '67 green Cadillac, grt cond, new tires, cheep.

I could just imagine what Miss Betty would say about this ad—any person who misspelled cheap was bound to drive a hard bargain. Throwing down the paper, I reached for the phone and dialed Violet's dorm room in Knoxville. I started to hang up, then Violet answered with a curt hello.

"It's me, Bitsy."

"Jesus Christ!" Violet cried. "Where are you?"

"It's better if you don't know."

"The Wentworths have been calling and raising hell. They're saying that you lost your mind and tried to kill Claude."

"No, it's the other way around. He tried to kill me."

"That's not what he's saying. He's sitting up in the ICU, cursing your name."

"ICU? So it's that serious?"

"Well, it's Crystal Falls, not Mass General. But never mind. You're in huge trouble. There's an APB out for you—they're calling this attempted murder, kidnapping, and grand theft auto. If you don't come back and tell your side of the story, you'll look guilty."

"But I'm not!"

"What happened, Bitsy? I thought you two were finally working things out."

"Well, we were, but I think he's been seeing another woman. We got into a fight, and he pushed my head into the sink. It was full of water. See, I was defrosting some baby back ribs? He intended to drown me, Violet. I couldn't breathe. So I . . . I hit him."

"And ran away. You little coward."

"But I can't go to jail. I can't leave my daughter."

"So you'll keep on running? Is this the sort of life you want for her?"

"No, of course not."

"Think of what's best for Jennifer."

"I am!" I cried. "Oh, Violet. Don't you see? No matter what I do, it'll be wrong."

After I hung up, I flopped back on the bed. Maybe Violet was right. Maybe I could call and explain everything to Claude's father—Chick was by far the most reasonable of all the Wentworths. I glanced at the bedside clock—it was almost ten-thirty. Had I left Crystal Falls only five hours ago? By now both Chick and Miss Betty had probably passed out, but with all the commotion, and with Claude being in the hospital, they might have stayed sober. However, if they were drunk, they probably wouldn't remember that I'd even called. It was a chance I had to take. I pulled the phone into my lap and dialed.

Miss Betty answered, her hello crisp and clear. I could imagine cigarette smoke curling above her head. I started to hang up, but her voice stopped me. "Bitsy?" she said. "Is that you?"

She paused and released a raspy, irritated sigh. In the background ice clinked in a glass. "It *is* you."

I opened my mouth to speak, to tell her that Claude had a mistress named Candy—Miss Betty just hated gooey names for women. I wanted to tell her that her son had tried to drown me, but I still loved him. Before I could put the words together, she said, "You are in trouble, young lady. I've engaged the top law firm in Nashville, and they have a whole slew of investigators. They will find you and my son's Corvette. And Bitsy, prison life may not suit you, but one thing's for certain, you'll look divine in stripes."

I hung up, chewing my thumb, wondering if Miss Betty's legal team had placed a tracer on the line. The entire conversation had lasted less than a minute, and that wasn't enough to pinpoint my location. I'd seen that on *Streets of San Francisco*.

I ran a bath and slid into the steaming water, then I shut my eyes. I wanted to clear my mind, but I kept seeing Crystal Falls. I pictured cedar trees growing along fencerows, the Appalachian mountains climbing up to the sky, my grandmother's house, yellow with bright blue shutters, the long, rusty screened-in porch, a white enamel bowl brimming with butter beans, a garden full of tomatoes, each one as big as a man's fist. I could see my grandmother's old housekeeper, Queenie; her dark hands had possessed a secret knowledge, they could draw lies from your mouth and the heat from your body. Brown hands with pale palms pressing against my small, flushed face. *You've got a fever, child. Where's that momma of yours?*

My mother was always rushing out of our red brick house to play cards, her charm bracelet jingling. But she'd always hurry back next door to Miss Gussie's porch. My mother was a wide-hipped woman, and when she sat down, the wicker chair creaked. Poor old Dorothy, trying to be helpful. Trying to make her mama love her. "Here, let me shell those peas for you, Mother Dear," she'd say, reaching for the enamel bowl.

Over in the red brick house, my father sat alone in the dark living room watching *Bonanza*. Mack, swelled with importance at being the only boy in the family, dashed through the sprinkler in our front yard, beads of water gathering in his white-blond hair. From Miss Gussie's porch, our mother, wearing pink pedal pushers and a Ship 'n' Shore blouse, would laugh and say, "Just look at that boy run. He could be in the Olympics." Dorothy wasn't insane then, and she had curly blond hair and a throaty laugh like Lana Turner. The most beautiful mother in the world.

I never thought our lives would change. It had shocked me when Mother and Daddy separated in the late sixties. Daddy only moved a few miles away, but it seemed farther. Or maybe that's further? I was never real good with grammar. He dated widows and the counter girls at his dime store. Lucky for him that Mother was locked up—separated or not, she wouldn't have cared for his new social life. Daddy had never been what I'd call a hands-on father, but I never dreamed he'd turn out to be a ladies' man. My brother liked women, too. Even though he'd lost his leg in Vietnam (and his metal prosthesis squeaked when he walked), the opposite sex still chased him. He and his second wife, Earlene, were crazy in love, and together they'd started a construction business. I hadn't gone to war, but somehow I'd damaged my life, and maybe Jennifer's, too. I sank down in the tub, and let the warm water cover my face, thinking of the moment Claude had tried to drown me. I'd never been that scared. But maybe I'd overreacted, maybe he hadn't meant any harm. What if he'd just been trying to scare me? If I'd waited one more second, he might have let go, and none of this would have happened.

The next morning, I called the Cadillac ad people. A child answered on the fourth ring. When I said I was calling about the ad there was a rustling sound as the child covered the phone. Then she hollered out in a musical voice: "It's about the c-ar."

A pause, then a gravelly voice hollered something back. The child resumed the conversation. "My grandmother's having a card party, but she said to come on out anyway. You can park in the street." She gave the address and directions, and I wrote them down.

On the way out of the hotel, I noticed a crowd in the lobby waiting for the ducks. I found a place near the elevators, and when the middle door finally opened, the ducks stepped out and waddled down the red carpet. Several people moved in to take pictures. Jennifer's small blond head turned and she pointed. Would she remember this? Would she remember the ducks climbing up the platform and then splashing down into the fountain?

A middle-aged woman smiled at Jennifer. "When I was her age," she told me, "my parents held my first birthday party right here at the Peabody, and I jumped into the fountain with the ducks."

"Oh, dear," I said, smiling. Jennifer began to whine, struggling to escape my grasp.

"After that, Mother put me in a harness." The woman's eyes clouded. "A leash! Don't ever do that to your little one."

"No, ma'am, I won't."

Jennifer flashed a haughty look at the woman and placed one hand on her tiny hip. I recognized whose genes *these* were, prissy and melodramatic, and I feared that my baby would grow up mispronouncing French and making flamboyant gestures.

Except for Aunt Clancy, who drank green tea and ate organic sunflower seeds, and my brainy cousin Violet, who dressed in fatigues from Army Surplus, most all the upper crust women I knew in Crystal Falls were fluffy. They all liked to spend a day at the beauty parlor, getting their hair teased and styled, nails buffed and polished. I have to admit that sometimes I put on way too much makeup, and it rubbed off on the necks of my blouses, an orange Cover Girl stain. I loved gold charm bracelets that clinked and rattled when I moved my hands. And several times a day I doused myself with Shalimar, my trademark fragrance. I was born a girlie-girl—that's not as wonderful as you might think—and it was in my genes. My mother used to say that people didn't realize how much *effort* it took to be fluffy. One could not achieve that look overnight.

While I waited outside for the valet to bring the Corvette, I tilted back my head and gazed up at the dingy buildings across the street. I didn't guess I'd ever see this town again, and it was a shame, because Memphis seemed a lot more southern than Crystal Falls. I wasn't accustomed to the humidity, but it made my Farrah Fawcett-Majors haircut curl up around my face—better than a home permanent. I could probably save a lot of beauty money by staying right here; on the other hand, if I lived this close to Crystal Falls, I'd have to spend a fortune dying my hair—and Jennifer's, too. I didn't think we'd look good as brunettes, not to mention redheads, so I made up my mind to keep on moving. I was still wearing the polka-dot sundress from yesterday, but the wrinkles were gone because I'd found an iron in the hotel closet. The Gucci suitcase was mainly filled with baby clothes, and for that I was grateful. I had bathed Jennifer in the sink, then buttoned her into a pale pink dress with ducks embroidered on the bodice. I could pick up a few outfits for myself at a thrift shop, or buy colorful muslin skirts in a border town.

The Corvette pulled up and the valet climbed out and held out my key. I carried Jennifer around the car and glanced down at the license plate. Below the numbers, in black letters, "Falls County" was plainly visible. Since my cash was limited—and I couldn't keep using Claude's cards—I wondered if I should keep the Corvette and just switch license plates; but if a cop pulled me over, I'd be in even worse trouble. Once he realized the car and tags were a mismatch . . . well, I'd just have to be cautious.

The person with the Cadillac lived at the end of Tulip Lane, a flat, heat-waved road. The house had columns, and the wood was painted a pinkish beige. Cars were lined along the street and in the driveway, and I remembered the card party the child had mentioned.

I stood on the porch and rang the bell. After a moment, a white-haired woman opened the door, and cool air poured out, scented with coffee and spice cake. The woman gazed at me, then grinned at the baby. "Well, hello there," she said with a broad smile. She was shaped like a teapot, round with one arm on her hip, the other extended, bent at the elbow. Her fingers clutched a lace napkin. Stray crumbs were gathered in the wrinkles around her mouth. A thin, redheaded child of about nine walked up behind her, peering at me. A constellation of freckles spilled over her small, pointed nose. From inside the house, I heard a woman shout, "I raised that bid already, you nitwit!"

"I called earlier about the car?" I said, shifting Jennifer to my left arm.

"Oh, yes!" She dabbed the napkin along her mouth, blurring the lace with red lipstick. She stepped onto the porch, pointing toward the driveway. "The garage is around back. I'll meet you there."

I walked around the house, the baby's legs bouncing up and down. The garage was also pinkish beige, with a weather vane attached to the roof. The woman came bustling out the back door of the house, gripping a key ring. The redheaded child followed, biting one of her braids. As the woman heaved open the garage door, heat flowed out, stinking of motor oil and freshly cut grass.

"Have you ever seen a hotter day?" the woman asked, dragging her hand over her brow. "All my poor little flowers are dying. But it's almost September, so I guess they don't have long to live anyway." She turned to the car, waving one hand. "Well, this is it, my mother's Cadillac."

The little girl had worked her way over to me. She reached up and tickled Jennifer's bare foot. "What's her name?" she asked, grinning a gap-toothed grin.

"Jennifer," I said. Then I winced. That wasn't too smart, was it? Giving out her real name.

"That's pretty!" The girl chucked Jennifer under her chin. "How old is she?"

"Almost eight months."

The little redhead turned. "Granny? Look at how the baby's smiling at me."

"I'm looking," said the grandmother, distractedly running one hand through her hair.

Jennifer let out a squeal and grabbed the girl's finger, babbling something with Ts. The woman started talking about the car, speaking with a loose vowels and consonants. I found myself entranced by her speech. I was more accustomed to mountain twangs, but her words sounded so pretty. I wanted to say, "Your speech is lovely." But I was afraid I might stir up a conversation—old people were so easy to get going—and I might slip up and reveal more information.

"Can I hold her, miss?" The girl turned her freckled face up to me. She had small brown eyes, rimmed in gold lashes. "I'm real good with babies. I hold them at church all the time."

"You can trust her," said the grandmother. "She's bony but strong. She opens all my pickle jars. Don't you, Alice Ann?"

The girl didn't answer. She kept grinning at the baby, making her eyes pop open wide.

"Well, all right." I eased Jennifer into the girl's thin arms. The baby leaned back and stared.

"Nee?" Jennifer asked, looking up at the girl, patting one of the red braids.

"She thinks I'm a knee." The girl grinned at the baby. "My name's Alice Ann. Say Alice Ann?"

"It was Mother's car," the grandmother said, jingling the keys. She gestured to the Cadillac. It was a bright bottle green. Not only did it remind me of a china parrot that Claude's mother had once kept in an ornamental iron cage, I thought it might attract attention on the highway.

"Mother thought she might travel," the woman continued while I examined the interior. "You know—discover America, like Lady Bird

Johnson used to say? We even had a luggage rack installed—see that shiny metal thing on the roof? It's ugly, isn't it? Mother thought so, too, and she never drove it out of Midtown a single time. It doesn't have but a few hundred miles. You can check the speedometer if you like."

"Odometer," called the child, bouncing Jennifer expertly on her hip.

"I can ne-ver remember that." The grandmother laughed and wiped perspiration from her cheeks, smudging her rouge. The sun glinted on her hair, turning it silvery at the edges. She stepped past me, giving off gusts of cigarettes, bourbon, coffee, and Miss Dior. I wondered if the little girl had placed the ad.

"It looks brand-new. Is it reliable?" I asked, touching the side mirror.

"Barely five years. And hardly ever driven," the grandmother said.

"She only went to the branch bank and Delchamps," the child added. "When she got sick, Dr. Peterson made house calls on her. Grandmama and me did all her errands for her."

"But not in *this* car," the grandmother said.

"We took it to Senatobia." The girl swayed back and forth, and Jennifer giggled.

The grandmother was waving her hands, trying to shush the child. When she saw me staring, she flushed. "She's making it sound like we went there all the time, and we most certainly *did not*. But there's the nicest Carter's baby outlet in Senatobia. You can pick up bargains. Didn't we find you a whole slew of clothes, Alice Ann?"

Alice Ann ignored her and kept talking to the baby in a sweet, high-pitched voice.

"And you're asking how much?" I asked the grandmother.

"Two hundred dollars." She ran one hand through her hair again. "It's worth a lot more, believe you me. Hundreds more, maybe even thousands. But it eats up the space. You see, I'm planning to turn this garage into an antique shop."

"I thought it was gonna be a playroom for me," said the girl.

"We'll discuss this later, Alice Ann," said the grandmother. From the house, a woman appeared in the doorway. She wore a gray uniform. "Miss Eunice?" she called. "We've got a disturbance inside. Mrs. Taylor and Mrs. Hill are fighting over cards again, and Mrs. Hill knocked over the punch bowl."

"Not Mother's bowl!"

"It didn't break, Lord knows why not, but planter's punch is spilled all over your floor."

"Oh, my heavens. If you'll excuse me," said the grandmother, turning to me. "I'll just be a minute. Alice Ann? You be nice, you hear?"

"Yes, ma'am."

The grandmother bustled off, climbing the stairs—right foot, right foot. Through the open door I heard a screech, followed by piercing laughter. Back in Crystal Falls, the Wentworths were renowned for their parties, and all of the social climbers in Crystal Falls longed to be invited, but they were cruelly shunned. My own mother, who was well-to-do herself, had never set foot inside Miss Betty's house—not even after I'd married into Claude's family.

I took a deep breath, thankful that I was through with all of that society nonsense, and turned to Alice Ann. "So, how old are you?"

"Ten." She grinned.

"Is this really a good car? I'd hate to get stranded on the highway."

"Which highway you talking about, miss?"

"No one in particular."

"Are you from Memphis?"

I shook my head. "So, it's a good car?"

"I guess."

"Why is she really selling it, then?"

"'Cause she needs the room for Odell's car. Odell's her new husband? He drives a Lincoln, and he hates for it to set out. Can I give Jennifer a cookie? I've got me one right here in my pocket. Sally made them for the party."

"Sally?"

"She's our cook. She can cook anything, even live turtles, but I've never eaten one." Alice Ann fished in her pocket and drew out a sugar cookie. Jennifer accepted it with two fingers, then scraped it over her bottom teeth.

Alice Ann turned to me. "She likes it. You better get the recipe from Sally. When I grow up, I'm getting out of here. I want to be an actress."

The girl's chatter was getting a little too friendly, and I was afraid of what I might say. So I stepped over to the car and traced one finger along the hood. Alice Ann cupped one hand under the baby's chin, catching the crumbs. "My grandmother's name's Eunice," the child continued. "But next week, she's sending me to a school in Arkansas. It's way up in the Ozarks."

"That should be nice." I squatted next to a tire, wishing I knew what to look for.

"It won't." Alice Ann frowned. "I'm trying to worm out of it. I *don't* want to go."

Still keeping my eyes on the tire, I wondered if the girl's parents were alive—it didn't sound like it. But maybe she'd been left with her grandmother the way Violet had been left with Miss Gussie that time Aunt Clancy ran away. Well, it wasn't any of my business, and besides, if I probed, it might make the little girl even chattier—or worse, she might cry. Alice Ann did not look like the weepy type, but I wasn't taking any chances. It was better to wonder about a person than to ask questions and stir up sadness. I had an idea that the child was like Violet—tough and silent, old for her years. The type who never volunteered personal information. There were still things I myself didn't know about my cousin and probably never would—especially since I had become a fugitive.

"Has this car ever broken down?" I asked Alice Ann. "Tell the truth."

"It never did on Granny. But Eunice was fibbing to you some." Alice Ann wiped a stray piece of cookie from the baby's chin. "She drove it now and then to flush out the engine. Odell says if you let a car set up, the tires'll go flat and the engine'll rot. Then you got to call Triple A."

"You know a lot about cars."

"Odell told me. He owned the dealership on Poplar, but he sold it last year."

"Where's Odell now?"

"Golfing. He can't take Eunice's card parties. They get rowdy. And they last for hours. So you might as well find you a shady spot and get comfortable. You're liable to be here awhile."

"I can't stay. I've got errands, so I'll just come back later." I reached for my baby. She rested her head in the curve of my neck.

"We'll be here," Alice Ann said. "Just don't take too long."

. . .

Before I checked out of the Peabody, I drew up a plan. First, I bought a map in the gift shop. Next, I called Eunice to ask if I could test drive the Cadillac, but Alice Ann answered. "I'll be there in an hour or so," I told the girl.

"I'll be waiting," she said.

After I hung up, I bent the credit cards until they broke. Then I flushed the pieces down the toilet, hoping it didn't clog the Peabody's pipes. Now, I had to figure out what to do with the Corvette. I needed to leave it in a place that wouldn't attract attention, where it would blend in with hundreds of other cars. A mall parking lot might work, but the airport would be even better. It was near Graceland, so after leaving the hotel I got onto the highway and started looking for signs. Jennifer began to fuss, pulling at her hair—the same thing my mother did when she was frustrated. I reached out and grabbed the baby's foot, hoping to distract her. "We're going to see airplanes," I said, trying to sound peppy, like Mr. Rogers. Jennifer responded by yanking out a fistful of hair. Then she lowered her fist and stared at the white-blond strands.

I angled into the lane marked Long Term Parking and pulled a ticket from the machine. The gate lifted and I drove into the lot. The humidity was intense, but I told myself to get used to a warm climate. In the heat-warped light, the vehicles in the lot seemed to sway as if the colors were melting. I parked next to a red Volvo, tucked the ticket behind the visor, then pushed the keys under the mat. A month from now, maybe longer, it would be noticed. By the time it was traced back to Claude, Jennifer and I would be out of reach.

As I got out of the car, an airplane passed over, stirring up a hot breeze. It smelled of fuel. I lifted the baby, who was still clutching the tufts of hair, seat and all, into one arm, then grabbed the suitcase with my other. I struggled across the shimmering parking lot, stopping several times to rearrange my load. The blistering wind snapped the hem of my dress, ruffling it above my knees, but I couldn't push it down. Jennifer was hanging on to the neckline of my dress, her head swiveling each time an airplane passed overhead.

"Ya!" she screeched, then opened her fist. The fine hairs were sucked up by the wind.

• • •

When the cab turned down Tulip Lane, the bridge players' cars were still lined up along the curb in front of Eunice's house. I paid the driver, feeling terrible about the miserly tip, and then lifted the baby into my arms and got out, pulling my suitcase and the car seat onto the sidewalk. Jennifer peered over my shoulder, watching the seat. "Ba-drang," she said gravely.

The cabbie gave me the finger and sped off, his tires squealing. Leaving the suitcase on the walkway, I grabbed the car seat with my free hand, dragged it up to the porch, and rang the bell. Once again, Eunice opened the door. This time, instead of holding a napkin, she clutched cards. The backs were printed with magnolia blossoms. Inside, laughter floated out, spiky and harsh. A glass broke and someone yelled, "*Whoops!*"

"You're back!" Eunice said gaily, fanning herself with the cards. Her curls bobbled up and down. "Alice Ann said you'd called again. In fact, she was playing in the garage, waiting for y'all to get here."

"Is she there now?" I glanced toward the driveway. "I'd like to tell her 'bye."

"Oh, honey, they ain't no telling." Eunice laughed. Then her face fell. "You didn't come back for the car? You came all this way to see Alice Ann?"

"No, I want it, but first I'd like to do a test drive."

"Yes, yes. That'll be just fine." A tinkly laugh drifted up from Eunice's throat. "You go on to the garage, sugar. I'll be out in a jiffy."

I stepped up to the garage. The door was still open, and a shaft of sun shone down on the Cadillac's hood, turning the metal a rich iridescent green. "Alice Ann?" I called. There was no answer. A mockingbird twittered from a branch, mimicking a cardinal. Eunice waddled down the back steps, right foot, right foot. She had ditched the cards and was clutching the keys to her chest.

"Did you find Alice Ann?" Eunice called.

"No, ma'am."

"Well, it's no wonder. She's *just* like her mother. Can't stay put. Gotta keep moving. But Alice Ann's real smart—she gets that from my side of the family. My son was a straight-A student. Alice Ann is so bright the teachers don't know what to do with her. She's a pint-size actress, too." Eunice rolled her eyes. "It's just the hardest thing in the world sometimes. Well, here're the keys, sugar."

"First let me see if the baby seat fits," I said, dragging it over to the passenger side.

"I was wondering what that was." Eunice pointed to the padded chair. "In my day, we let the children stand up. That's what I did with Alice Ann, and somehow she survived."

"Yes, ma'am. I just like to be safe is all." I shrugged. "Would you mind holding the baby while I buckle in the seat?"

"Hand the little darling right over." Eunice reached for Jennifer, making a clucking nose, then scooped her out of my arms. The baby watched Eunice's mouth, then she let out an indignant screech.

"My, she's got good lungs," Eunice said, letting Jennifer play with the keys. "Alice Ann had good ones, too. Lord, I'd be out in the yard, and I could hear her crying from her crib. Even now, when she gets mad at me, she has a fit. She'll scream until she gets her way."

"She's lived with you a long time?" I asked, reaching out to open the Cadillac's door. The door creaked open, and I set the baby seat inside. While I secured it with the seat belt, I breathed in the stale air, mothballs and dust and peppermint candy. I glanced into the backseat and saw a tartan blanket on the floor. I started to reach for it, but Jennifer began to whimper. I turned and held out my hands.

"I've had Alice Ann since she was a tiny girl," Eunice said, depositing the baby into my arms. "Her mother would drop her off and just disap-*pear*."

Eunice raised one hand and swirled her fingers in the air, as if demonstrating the capricious nature of Alice Ann's mother. "My son married himself a lowdown girl from the Gulf Coast. She said she was a stripper, but I don't know for sure. Well, you know how the young people are. They fall in love at the drop of a hat. After Alice Ann was born, my son got sent to Vietnam. His helicopter got shot down in 1967, the same year that Mother bought this Cadillac."

"I'm sorry," I said. It was on the tip of my tongue to tell about my brother Mack, who'd lost his leg in the Tet Offensive but I stopped myself.

"The Air Force *says* my son was missing in action, but his body was never found."

"What happened to your daughter-in-law?"

"Well, it's a sad story. One day she dropped Alice Ann off with a pink Barbie case. She was planning to head down to Biloxi and work as a Lord-knows-what. Then she waved good-bye and drove her car straight into the Mississippi River." Eunice's eyebrows slanted angrily and her cheeks flushed red. "On *purpose*, if you ask me. A witness said she never hit her brake. She drove through the railing. I just thank the Lord that she didn't have Alice Ann with her."

"Poor little thing." I shuddered.

"Just between you and me, she can be a rascal." Eunice laughed. "Now crank up that engine, dear. Take a spin around the block. Here's the keys. The big one is for the ignition, and the square one is for the trunk and the doors."

I strapped the baby into the car seat. Then I hurried around the Cadillac, slid into the driver's seat, and fitted the key into the ignition. The engine turned over on the first try. I didn't know anything about automobiles, but it seemed to run smoothly. Outside the car, I could hear Eunice chatting away. I glanced at the dashboard clock. If it was correct—nearly six o'clock—then I was behind schedule. I'd planned to drive south, straight through the heart of Mississippi. My plan was to reach Baton Rouge, Louisiana, before dark, but that city was 382 miles from Memphis. I'd be lucky to reach Jackson by nine o'clock.

"Actually, I don't need a test drive. I'll just take it," I said, reaching for my purse. I counted bills out of Claude's wallet and handed them over to Eunice.

"Are you sure?" Eunice looked shocked.

"Yes, ma'am. I've made up my mind." I continued to hold out the money, smiling up at the woman. "Besides, you need to get back to your party."

"Well, that's true." Eunice took the money, rolling it into a tight cylinder. "It's got new Bridgestone tires. And Odell just changed the oil for me. It shouldn't give you a moment's trouble. But I can't guarantee that it won't act up. It's been setting up a long time. But if you change your mind and decide you don't want the car—"

"I won't."

"Well, dear, I hope not. Because as far as I'm concerned, a deal's a deal," she said, suddenly all business. "Odell doesn't believe in giving refunds."

"I won't need one," I said.

"All right." She smiled and ran one hand through her hair, looking distracted.

"Please tell Alice Ann that I said good-bye," I said, shifting into drive.

"Oh, I will." She nodded. "It was so nice meeting you, dear."

I turned up the air-conditioning as far as it would go, then I put the car in reverse and pressed my foot against the accelerator. The car slowly rolled out of the garage. Eunice walked alongside it, like she couldn't bear to see it go. At the end of the driveway I stopped the Cadillac, opened the trunk, and threw in the luggage. I waved at Eunice again as I got back into the car then angled it into the street, and waved once more. Eunice was standing in the driveway, her hands clasped under her chin. She lifted one hand. Then I turned a corner and the woman dropped out of sight.

Bitsy

At dusk, on the outskirts of Jackson, Mississippi, I drove past a sign: You Are Now Entering Hinds County. At least the baby was sleeping; good, because the traffic was starting to get heavy, and that made me nervous. I glanced into the rearview mirror, and lights from an oncoming car swept into the backseat, shining onto the forehead of the little red-headed girl. The child's eyes cut to the mirror and met mine. I screamed, then stamped on the brake. The Cadillac skidded into the other lane. A car honked, and I grabbed the wheel and swerved back into my lane.

"Alice Ann?" I yelled, and Jennifer's head jerked up, eyes blinking open.

"Hey," Alice Ann said, waving.

"How did you *get* here?"

"I ran away."

"No, I meant, how did you get in this car?"

"Hid under this." She lifted the tartan blanket. "I'm wringing wet with sweat."

"Well, I'm taking you back," I said, switching on the blinker, guiding the car into the exit ramp. "Your poor grandmother is probably worried sick."

"I *won't* go." She scooted over to the door, grasped the handle. "I'll throw myself out."

"Let me slow down first," I said, trying to hide my panic. I suspected that she'd used this method before—the shock technique. When Claude Wentworth had been small, he'd controlled his mother by threatening to jump out of her Lincoln Town Car. Straight ahead, I could see a busy intersection. The traffic light turned yellow, and I patted the brake. I glanced at the car beside me, a yellow Studebaker, driven by a pretty brunette. Her hair was wind-tossed to perfection, and she wore tortoise-shell glasses. She frowned up at the traffic light, tapping one manicured nail on the steering wheel. I wondered if she knew how quickly her life could change. I wanted to roll down my window and tell her that a day or two ago, I'd been coasting through life with nothing but green lights.

The traffic light changed. I pulled into the parking lot of a hardware store and stopped the car. "All right," I said. "You can get out. Just be careful."

"You can't just dump me here," said Alice Ann. "I'm your new child."

"No, you're Eunice's child."

"She's too old to have a little girl." Alice Ann crossed her arms, narrowed her eyes. "But you're not."

"Alice Ann, do you know what kidnapping is?"

"Yes."

"Well, that's what the police will call this."

"I don't care." She poked out her bottom lip. "No matter what you say, I'm not going back. Eunice doesn't want me. Besides, she was going to dump me off at a private school."

"You might like it."

"I'll *hate* it. Nothing but c-r-a-z-i-e girls go there. The nuns make you wear uniforms and eat Cream of Wheat. It gags me." She reached and grabbed her throat, poking out her tongue.

"Crazy's got a y at the end," I said, "not an i-e."

"Who are you, my fifth-grade teacher?" Alice Ann rolled her eyes. "Look, Eunice hates me. You're doing both me and her a favor."

"Grandmothers don't hate their grandchildren."

"No? When I act up, Eunice goes outside, breaks off a thin willow branch, and switches my legs."

I tapped my fingers on the seat, trying to gauge the truth behind Alice Ann's escape. Way off in the distance, I saw glimmering neon arches, McDonald's, but I couldn't reach it from this road. I would have to get back on the interstate, fighting the traffic, and take the next exit. I shifted into drive and circled back the way I'd come.

"Where you going now?" Alice Ann began to bounce up and down.

"I'm driving to a restaurant," I said. "We'll eat supper, and then I'm calling Eunice."

"Fine, I'll tell her you kidnapped me."

"She'll know better," I said. "She saw me drive off."

"I'll tell her you knocked me off my bicycle and stole me. That you conked me on the head and threw me into the trunk. That you kidnapped me to babysit Jennifer."

"She won't buy that."

"She will, too," Alice Ann said. "That's not all. She forgot to give you the title."

I sucked in air, too startled to respond.

"There's more," she continued. "Your license tag says 274463X, Shelby County. Bet you didn't know that. And the tags expired last year. But don't worry. I fixed it up with shoe polish. I turned 1971 into 1972. Wasn't that smart?"

"Brilliant," I said.

"But I can't do nothing about the title." She leaned forward, her breath hot in my ear. "I sure hope your mind doesn't drift like Eunice's, or else I'll be calling the shots for you, too."

"I'm tempted to put you out of this car right now," I said.

"Do it." She folded her arms. "I don't care. I'll just hitch a ride. And if a policeman stops, I'll tell him what you did."

"I haven't done anything yet," I said, but I was already planning my telephone conversation with Eunice when I called her from McDonald's. Then I'd leave Alice Ann in the custody of the manager and explain how the child had stowed herself in the car. The minute Alice Ann opened her mouth, anyone would know she was a smarty-pants schemer. Then Jennifer and I would drive south. The more miles I put between myself and Alice Ann, the better. I could imagine the girl talking to the police, rattling off a description of the Cadillac, along with the tag number. In no time flat, I would be caught and dragged back to Crystal Falls. But I had to risk it.

Turning back onto the interstate, I peeked into the mirror. Alice Ann was staring out the window, humming "This Old Man," making every other word rhyme with kidnapped. I hated to steal a license tag, but it looked as if I had no choice. A tag could be switched in the parking lot of any Howard Johnson's. Although I couldn't leave the old one behind. That would make things too easy for the police. I could use a fingernail file to unscrew it. Now I was even starting to *think* like a criminal. And I didn't want this sort of life for Jennifer. My baby was supposed to grow up with girl friends and slumber parties, her own princess telephone in the bedroom. She would not only speak French, she would tour France, all the places I had only imagined. As the child of a kidnapper/murderess (not that I was either one), my daughter would be destined for a double-wide trailer—or, God forbid, a foster home.

I pressed my foot against the gas pedal, wishing the McDonald's sign wasn't so far away. From the backseat, Alice Ann said, "Uh-oh. A cop's on your tail."

I glanced over my shoulder, and sure enough, a blue light was filling up the rear window. Jennifer held out one hand, tried to grab it.

"See what happens when you go over the speed limit?" Alice Ann said. "That's against the law."

"Yeah? Well, it's a good thing. I'll just hand you over to the cop." I tapped the brake, steering into the gravel breakdown lane. Cars whizzed past the Cadillac, their taillights blinking red.

Alice Ann began to sing "This Old Man" again, making up the lyrics. "You don't have a tit-le. You will go-o straight to jail, where thieves and con men will pinch your tail—"

"Will you hush?" I cried. "Don't you say another word. Don't even open your mouth."

Alice Ann spread her lips apart with her fingers and opened her mouth as wide as she could.

In the side mirror, I watched the officer approach. He was tall and lanky, with a beaked nose. As he leaned over, peering into the car, heat lightning flashed behind him. The sky lit up with muddy clouds, then faded to black. A speeding ticket would prove that I'd been on this interstate. It would list the make and license number of the Cadillac.

"You were going sixty-two in a fifty-mile zone," he said, glancing at Jennifer, then back at Alice Ann. "That's not real wise, considering your cargo."

"Well, we're starving. I was just trying to make it to McDonald's." I laughed theatrically and rolled my eyes.

He reached up, tipped back his hat, and squinted down the interstate, toward the crooked row of neon signs. It looked as if a drunken farmer had planted them. Shoney's, Arby's, Best Western, McDonald's, Holiday Inn.

"We've just been driving forever," I said, and Alice Ann kicked the back of my seat.

"Where you good people headed?" He spoke with a deep baritone. I imagined him quizzing his daughter, if he had a teenage daughter, asking the girl why she'd missed her curfew. I tried to think of a nearby town, but this part of the country was foreign to me.

"We're just . . ." I paused. Behind the officer I saw a green sign, Hazlehurst 33 miles. "We're going to Hazlehurst," I said a beat too fast. I wondered if he'd seen my eyes shift behind him.

He had. From his car, the police radio crackled. "You got folks down in Copiah County?" he asked, shuffling one foot in the gravel.

I nodded, but I didn't think this was a state-trooperish question. Alice Ann began bouncing up and down. "Copiah County," she sang. "Elevation 479 feet. And the air is ever so sweet."

"You're a smart young lady." The officer smiled.

"A genius," I said.

The officer's smile faded as he turned his gaze on me. "All the more reason to drive careful, miss," he said, tipping back his hat.

"Yes, sir," I said, my voice squeaking.

"Your driver's license and registration, please?"

I blinked. Then I glanced at the glove compartment, wondering if Eunice had, by some miracle, added the registration. I leaned across the seat, pressing my arm against the baby's chubby legs, and clicked open the glove box. It was immaculate: a box of pink tissues, an oil change record, a folded map of Tennessee. In the backseat, Alice Ann giggled. I slammed the glove box, and sat straight up. I reached for my purse, but I couldn't find my wallet. And it had been there when I'd stopped for gas near Oxford. I knew it was illegal to be driving without a license and registration.

Alice Ann leaned forward, laying her freckled cheek against the back of my seat. She twirled one braid. "Mommy, you left your billfold in your other purse. It's got your driver's license and registration, and even the title. But Daddy can bring it to Hazlehurst when he comes."

She looked up at the officer and smiled, showing the gap between her teeth. "Please don't give us a ticket, sir. My Aunt Eunice just had herself a new baby boy and we're going down to help. That's why we're in a hurry. Isn't that true, Mommy?"

She lifted her braid and painted the side of my face. I tried to smile, but my lips were trembling. To hide the twitching, I covered my mouth with my hand and nodded. Jennifer cackled. She grabbed her foot and shoved it into her mouth. Then she gave the officer an engaging smile. "Please, sir," crooned Alice Ann, aiming the tip of her braid at him. "Give us *one* more chance. It's my fault she was speeding. I was being a brat. Boohooing and kicking the back of her seat. 'Cause I was starving. I'm always starving. 'Drive faster, Mommy,' I told her. I won't never do that again, Officer Nugent. I've learned my lesson."

I glanced at the patrolman's shirt—that was his name, all right, spelled out on his platinum badge.

"Where do y'all live?" he asked.

"Memphis," said Alice Ann. "Memphis, Tennessee. While we're in Hazlehurst, Daddy's getting a neighbor boy to feed the dog."

"What kind of dog you got, sugar?"

"Oh, he's the cutest thing! He's half pug, half Chihuahua. And real, real funny-looking. His name is Sneaky. Like some people can be?" Alice Ann leaned out the window. She grinned up at the officer, lifting her braid and letting it speak like a puppet. "Please, Officer Nugent. Pretty please? Let the nice people go. They'll be good. They'll drive *under* the speed limit."

The officer laughed and stepped back from the Cadillac. Then he pointed one finger at me. "I'll let you go, just this once. Now you drive careful. You hear me little lady?"

"Yes, sir." I nodded vigorously.

"Thank you," Alice Ann sang.

"All right, then." The officer gave Alice Ann a two-finger salute, then he walked back to his cruiser and climbed inside. After a moment the blue lights stopped flashing. I took a deep breath, then grabbed the wheel and shifted into drive. When the traffic thinned out, I touched my foot to the gas pedal, and the Cadillac shot out of the breakdown lane, onto I-55. Glancing into the rearview mirror, I saw that the trooper hadn't moved. Alice Ann leaned against the window, her arms propped under her head, and she resumed singing "This Old Man." Her voice rose up into the car, a child's voice, light and sweet. I drove cautiously, passing right by the exit for McDonald's. The singing abruptly stopped.

"Ain't we stopping to eat?" Alice Ann cried, turning to stare out the rear window.

"I'll stop later." I looked down at the speedometer. It hovered just below 55.

"At Hazlehurst, Mommy?" She began laughing, then she fell over sideways, slapping the seat. "Was I good, or was I *good*?"

"Terrific," I said. "Better than Shirley Temple."

"I saved you back there, so you better keep me."

"I'd rather keep a rattlesnake."

"I memorized Officer Nugent's badge number." She leaned forward again, hanging on to the back of the seat. "You get rid of me now, I'll tell him all about you."

"You don't know doodly about me."

"Oh yes, I do. *Lillian Beatrice*." She held up my blue vinyl wallet. I reached back for it, but Alice Ann scooted away. She perched on the seat, drawing her legs up to her pointed chin and popped open the wallet. "Relax, Lillian. Is it Wentworth or McDougal? You've got ID for both names. Isn't that illegal? Are you some kind of con man?"

"Do I look like a man?"

"Do *I* look like a child? Eunice always says that appearances can be deceiving. So, tell me. Why did y'all leave Crystal Falls?"

"Hand over my wallet this instant." I snapped my fingers.

"Won't do you any good. I already memorized your address. 214 Dixie Avenue. And the zip code is 38501. I'll bet somebody would pay me cash money to know your whereabouts."

"Nobody's interested in me," I said, hoping I wasn't showing my fear. This kid was smart, but deadly. "But I'm sure Eunice is frantic over you."

"No, she's not." Alice Ann began tossing the wallet in the air. "You're hiding something."

"Maybe I am. Maybe I'm a dangerous criminal."

"Sure, and I'm Art Linkletter."

"I might just stop the car and let you out."

"It's been done before, honey child," she drawled, "but I always come back."

"When we get to Hazlehurst, I'm calling Eunice. Aren't you worried about her at all?"

"Nope. Reach me that map so I can plot out our trip to Point Minette."

"Point Minette?" I blinked. "Where's that?"

"Your next stop." Alice Ann opened her shirt and dropped in my wallet, where it made a square bulge. "But it's getting dark. You better check us into a motel."

"What's in Point Minette?" I asked.

"Like I'd ever tell *you*."

"Well, you'd better. Because I'm going in the other direction."

"You were. But you're not now. See, my mama is in Point Minette and she's waiting for me."

"But . . ." I rubbed my forehead, trying to think of a delicate way to phrase this. "Your grandmother told a different story. She said—"

"Yes, yes, *yes*. I know what she told you, that my mama drowned in the river." She held up both hands, as if pushing them against an imaginary obstacle. "But they never found her body. I bet Eunice didn't tell you that."

"Er, no, but—"

"They *always* find a body, those river draggers. But they didn't find my mama's. And she wouldn't have crossed that bridge in the first place, because she was going in the other direction." The child lowered her voice, making it raspy. "'Honey, I'm heading down to Point Minette, Mississippi. I'm getting me a job as a stripper.' That's just what she said. It'll be real easy to find her."

"But . . ." I sighed, wishing I could leave her at a church, a note pinned to her dress, instructing the priest to call Eunice.

"If you're good, *I'll* be good," Alice Ann said, using her pigtail to swipe the back of my seat. "Do you understand?"

"Completely," I said. "But I still can't take you to the coast."

"You *have* to." She began pounding my seat. "I belong with my mama. I know what you're thinking, and it's a lie. My mama *is NOT dead!*" Alice Ann reached up to her face and brushed away tears. "She's *not! She's not!*"

"I never said she was. Eunice said it. Please don't cry."

"She's more alive than *you*," Alice Ann yelled. "And lots prettier. You better take me to her or you'll be sorry."

• • •

Around noon the next day, I parked the Cadillac in front of a pink brick building. Flying Cups & Saucers Café was painted on the windows in yellow paint, embellished with spinning Fiestaware. "I smell the ocean," said Alice Ann from the backseat. She yawned, stretching out her arms. Then her knees squeaked across the leather seat. "Is this Point Minette?"

"Mmmhum." I glanced out the window. Across the street were old buildings with wrought-iron balconies and hanging ferns. They had shops filled with inflatable rafts, folding chairs, and beach towels. At the end of the block, *The Poseidon Adventure* was playing at the theater. Most of the shoppers were women in cotton dresses and white sandals. Their children trailed behind, licking lollipops, their sun-streaked hair brushed into ponytails. I couldn't imagine a stripper picking this town. Not that I believed for one moment that Alice Ann's mother was alive. I looked back at the café.

"Well, let's go find my mama," said Alice Ann.

"I thought we'd get a bite to eat first," I said.

"All right, but make it snappy."

We got out of the car. I leaned over and lifted Jennifer into my arms. Alice Ann hopped onto the sidewalk, then she began taking exaggerated steps. I stopped in front of Flying Cups & Saucers and bought a newspaper, the Point Minette *Tribune*. Tucking it under my arm, I used my free hand to guide Alice Ann into the café. It was cool, smelling of fresh perked coffee, and ceiling fans stirred the green plants. A long counter was lined with glass domes—doughnuts, cookies, and pies. A grumpy-looking waitress sat on a stool there, drinking iced tea. She hopped down and seated us. Her dark hair was teased into a bouffant, and green eye shadow creased her lids. Pinned to her blouse was a name badge, Doris.

She helped me fit Jennifer into a high chair. "Get you ladies something cool to drink?" she asked in a weary voice. Then she reluctantly pulled out a green pad and a pencil.

"Just a Tab for me," I said, unzipping the diaper bag and pulling out a bottle. "Could I trouble you to fill this with milk?"

"Sure thing, hon," said Doris, taking the bottle. She winked at Jennifer, who was banging the high chair, then Doris turned her gaze on Alice Ann. "What for you, Red?"

"I'll have a cheeseburger, crinkle fries, chocolate milk."

"Everything on that cheeseburger?" Doris said without looking up from her pad.

"No lettuce, tomatoes, or onions," Alice Ann said. "And you better not forget it, either."

"Kids," said Doris, shaking her head. "Like my mama used to say, they're either a lump in your throat or a pain in your ass."

"You said a bad word," Alice Ann sang.

While we waited for the food, I opened the *Tribune* and began reading the classifieds.

"Are you looking for a job?" Alice Ann sat up on her knees, trying to read the paper upside-down.

"No. A cheap place to spend the night," I said.

"Just one night?" Alice Ann looked alarmed. "It might take a while to find my mama. And you're low on cash. I looked in your wallet."

"That wasn't nice." I stifled a yawn, wondering how much the child had guessed.

Doris strutted over with our drinks and plunked them down. "Y'all just passing through?" she asked.

"Yes," I told her, wondering if I could slip her a note, explaining Alice Ann's situation. I could wait until the child went to the restroom, then Jennifer and I could dash off.

"We're looking for a motel," said Alice Ann.

"Now let me see." Doris tapped her pencil against her pad. "There's a new one over on River Street. Nice but pricey. If you're saving pennies, then give Mrs. Finch a call. She's got a boardinghouse on the beach."

"Goodie," said Alice Ann, holding up her pale, freckled arm. "I can work on my tan."

Doris laughed and walked off.

"If you want me to be the mother," I said, leaning across the table, "then you better start acting like the child."

"I want to find my *real* mother." Alice Ann stuck out her tongue.

Forty-five minutes later we were standing on Mrs. Finch's front porch. It was a three-story house, towering over us like a wedding cake, white with butter-colored shutters. Shaggy roses were blooming along the steps, and red birds hopped in the ankle-deep grass.

"Are you sure this is it?" Alice Ann said.

"This is the address Doris gave me." I rang the ornate brass doorbell and it gonged out the first few bars of "Old Rugged Cross."

"Coming!" said a voice from inside, over the frantic barking of a dog. The door creaked open and a gray-haired lady smiled at us. A small black-and-white dog ran in circles, alternately sniffing and barking.

"You must be the folks Doris called about," the woman said, holding open the screen door with her gnarled hand. The little dog jumped up and down, his paws digging into the woman's purple housedress. "Stop that, Kenny," she scolded, but he kept on jumping and whining. "Don't mind him, he's acting plum crazy. I'm Mrs. Finch. Step right on in, y'all."

We walked into a dark hall that smelled of mildew. Kenny turned his wildness on Alice Ann, jumping on her knees. Mrs. Finch led us into a cheerless parlor. All the furniture was covered up with sheets. I sat down on what appeared to be a high-backed Victorian sofa, and a plume of dust curled up around my hips. Kenny scrambled over and laid his head on my knee, giving me a look of pure and utter devotion. He was all black except for a white circle around his right eye. As I petted his hard little head, I felt something inside my chest relax and uncoil.

Mrs. Finch prowled around the room, lifting the sheets and peering underneath them. The whole time she rattled off a list of things I should know. The rent was $25 a week, but she'd waive the deposit. Gas, water, and lights were included. Meals were not. The bathroom was a communal one, shared by the other boarders, but fortunately there were several other baths in the boardinghouse. All the downstairs rooms, including the large kitchen, could be utilized. While she prattled on, Kenny ran over to Alice Ann and licked her freckled hand.

"We've got a little community college, and I get a fair number of students. Most of them are waiting for an apartment to come available. My last boarder was an art major, and she painted her room deep purple. You'll be getting her old room."

"My cousin had a purple room," I said, and Alice Ann shot me a coy look.

"It's bright, that's for sure," said Mrs. Finch.

The baby in my arms, we walked in silence through the high-ceilinged rooms, with Kenny trotting behind Mrs. Finch. The dining room had scroll wallpaper and a long table with carved dolphin feet. Four of the chairs matched. The chandelier was full of glass doodads that hung down and caught the sun. She led us up a grand staircase with worn red carpeting. Kenny raced ahead, panting with the effort. He ran down the hall and stopped in front of a door. Mrs. Finch ambled over to him, fishing in her pocket for a key. Then she flung open the door. As I followed her into the room, I saw that the walls were much brighter than Violet's back home. They reminded me of an Easter egg that had soaked in lilac dye too long.

"Don't let this shade put you off," Mrs. Finch said. "You can paint it over if you like. But you will have to supply your own paint. I do have my limits."

"No, the purple's fine," I said quickly.

"Well, all right, then." Mrs. Finch smiled, and I thought the old woman might like us, just a little. While Kenny patrolled the hall, I opened a closet and peered inside.

"It's an old house," Mrs. Finch was saying, snapping her fingers at Kenny, "not much in the way of storage, but it has lovely views. That French door opens out onto a veranda. It's got steps that go down to the lawn."

Alice Ann turned the glass knob and peered out. I could see green wooden steps leading down to the yard, with camelia bushes at the base. There was a path to the beach, and a tall hedge grew alongside it. The path stopped abruptly, and the road began. Traffic drifted across the boulevard. Beyond the road, the beach started, and farther out, in the gray water, were whitecaps. Alice Ann reached down and scratched Kenny's head. The dog's lips pulled back, showing a rubbery blue edge, and his tail thumped wildly against the floor.

"We can stay here, I guess," she said, looking up at me. Mrs. Finch cast a quizzical glance in our direction. I put the baby in Alice Ann's arms, then unsnapped my purse and opened my wallet, counting out Claude's money. The green bills, which were mostly ones and fives, made a thick pile in Mrs. Finch's cupped hand, but she didn't seem to mind. She tucked the cash into her bosom.

"Welcome to Finch House," she said, and reached out to shake my hand.

After the woman left, Alice Ann spread out her arms and wheeled around the room. "It's a mansion!"

"Well, not exactly," I said, thinking of the Wentworths' estate back in Crystal Falls. A five-foot-tall black wrought-iron fence hemmed in their property, which was three acres near the downtown.

"We'll have to find a used furniture store and get a crib or playpen for the baby," I said, staring at the bed. It was a double, with a high, carved headboard. The chest of drawers had a cracked marble top, and pieces of wood were coming loose along the seams, but I could fix it with glue. Of course, to afford a crib and glue, I would have to find a job, and soon.

The next morning, I put on my polka-dot dress and stood in front of the spotted mirror, frowning at my reflection. The circles under my eyes matched the purple room.

"You look pretty," Alice Ann said, pulling Jennifer into her lap. "Where you going?"

"Job hunting." I reached down to straighten my wrinkled skirt.

"You need a black dress," Alice Ann suggested. "Blondes look more intelligent in black."

I laughed. "Where'd you hear that?"

"Mama was a blonde." Her brow furrowed. "*Is* a blonde."

"So where'd you get that red hair?"

"Nobody knows." Alice Ann shrugged.

"From your daddy?"

"No, Eunice says he was brown-headed."

"How do I look from the rear?"

"Like a brick shithouse," said Alice Ann.

"If I could afford to buy soap," I said, ruffling the girl's hair, "I'd wash your mouth out."

While Alice Ann entertained Jennifer, I filled out applications at restaurants along the water—they all needed cooks, but they were filled up on waitresses. Around noon, I emerged from a little tea shop, shaking my head. "They've got Ph.D.s waiting tables in there," I told Alice Ann. "In case you don't know, that's a fancy degree—"

"I know what it is. My mama told me."

"Okay, what does it stand for?" I shot her a dubious look.

"Please help, dahling?"

I laughed, thinking of my own mother's storehouse of malapropisms and mispronunciations: tuna was "albatross" and she called Chicago "She-CAR-go."

Our next stop had gas lanterns burning on either side of the door. Alice Ann asked if it was a funeral home, but I said no, that it was a fancy eating spot. I pointed to a gold plaque that was hammered into the brick wall. The Embers, it said. I pulled open a heavy wrought-iron door and we stepped into pure blackness. A man with hairy arms materialized out of the gloom, and Alice Ann dropped back, the baby in her arms, ducking behind a rubber plant. The man led me to a little red booth, half hidden by a lattice screen. When I leaned to the right, I could see Alice Ann squatting next to the plant, holding the squirming baby and trying not to draw attention, even though a mean-looking waiter kept passing by, giving her harsh glances. He disappeared through a door, and Alice Ann shot away from the rubber plant and across the room, hiding under a table with a long white cloth.

"What position are you applying for?" the man asked.

"I'll do anything—cook, wait tables, sweep floors," I said.

The hairy man just smiled. "Our salad chef is from New Orleans," he said. "And our pastry chef comes to us from the CIA."

My lips parted. *The CIA?* I couldn't imagine a little place like Point Minette having a spy cook the desserts.

"Most of our waiters have been here for five years or more," the hairy man added.

"Oh," I said, and my face fell. "I didn't realize."

"You might want to try Le Cordon Bleu. Tell Mrs. Bianchi I sent you."

We stepped out of The Embers into bright sun that smelled of cotton candy and turned down a narrow, brick-lined street where all the doors were painted bright colors. I stopped in front of a shop with a turquoise door. Then I reached down, pulled off my shoe, and turned it upside down. A tiny pebble fell to the sidewalk.

"We need to go back to Mrs. Finch's and tell her that we made a mistake," I said. "Maybe she'll give us back our rent. Even if she gives us half the money, it'll be better than staying here and starving to death."

"I don't need to eat," Alice Ann said, shoving the baby into my arms. "I'm getting fat as a hog. Don't make us leave, not yet." She skipped along the sidewalk and rounded a corner, then dropped out of sight. A moment later she let out an excited squeal. I tightened my arms around Jennifer and drew in a deep breath. Alice Ann sped back around the corner, her eyes shining with excitement. "I found the restaurant," she hollered, windmilling her arms. "Hurry!"

• • •

To celebrate my new job, we ate lunch at an expensive tearoom on a shady street. Miss Nina's it said on the sign. We really couldn't afford this treat, but at least I had a job. I was just a lowly cook's apprentice, but I had to start somewhere.

After lunch, we took the long way home, walking barefoot along the beach. The gulf was on one side, hotels and filling stations on the other, in between mansions, all of them built to resemble quaint cottages, with roses spilling over the fences. The sun was straight overhead, making the water glow with a strange radiance. Alice Ann said that angels were skimming over the surface, and their wings shed glitter. I just laughed. For all I knew, it might *be* glitter, because Point Minette was within spitting distance of New Orleans and the water was full of strange things that had floated up, coasters from Pat O'Brien's, plastic drinking cups, Jax bottles.

When the seawall ended, we cut over to the sidewalk. I lifted Jennifer high into the air. The baby giggled. We hurried past a stucco motel and an adjoining coffee shop, where tourists gazed through the plate-glass window. Next door, a condominium complex was under construction. I hated to walk past it because of the workmen. As we passed by, their cat-calls blended in with the screeching gulls.

"Will you wait tables or cook?" Alice Ann asked. "You never said."

She had fit her shoes on her hands like puppets.

"No, they're training me to cook. I'm starting out in salads, but I may work my way up to seafood." My polka-dot dress rippled around my knees and the baby reached down to grab it.

"Too bad they won't let you make cakes." Alice Ann began trudging through the sand.

"Don't step on any glass," I said. The wind kicked up my dress again, and when I reached down to smooth it, another gust caught the hem from behind, filling the skirt with air like a balloon around my hips. From the road, a man on a red motorcycle revved his motor, then yelled out, "Hey, you big-assed gal!"

I slapped the fabric with my free hand, desperately trying to deflate it. "I am *not* big-assed," I said through my teeth. But I really was. I just had this tendency for all of my weight to settle there.

Alice Ann stopped to watch. "I hate to be the one to tell you, but you are apple-butted."

A blue Datsun slowed down to stare, and a burly-necked man in sunglasses leaned out his head. "Hey, lady!" he shouted. "You! Blondie! I'll give you a free ride if you give me one! Whaddaya say?"

"Don't ever marry a Southern man, Alice Ann," I told her. "When you get grown, find you a nice man from New Jersey."

"I'm never getting married," Alice Ann said, skipping to keep up with me. "But I bet you will."

"No, I'm through with men," I said, turning back to look at Alice Ann. Her hair blew across her face, cobwebbing in her mouth.

"Don't be so sure," said Alice Ann. "When Mrs. Bianchi was showing you around, there was an oyster shucker looking you up and down. The one with the tattoo and a gold tooth."

"I'm not interested," I said. "I need a paycheck, not trouble."

We walked up the sandy path to the boardinghouse. Despite what Mrs. Finch had said about students, at the moment all the other boarders were women who had been abandoned by their men—death, divorce, disappearances at sea. It was a hotel for widows and I felt safe there. I could see the ladies sitting in metal chairs, sipping frothy pink drinks. They seemed always to be drinking something, or else sipping from bottles of cherry cough syrup. Kenny lay curled up in Mrs. Finch's lap. When he saw us approach, his ears perked.

"You, Lillian!" called Mrs. Finch. "Come have a cool drink with us."

"Another time," I said. "These girls need a nap. But thank you."

As we headed up the back stairs, I glanced back at the widows. I longed to join them, even though I wasn't much of a drinker, but in two seconds flat I'd be telling the women my life story, concluding with the afternoon I'd left town. I would tell them my real name and how Claude's mysterious absence from the bank had led to violence. I would describe the hibachi in detail, along with Claude's black Labrador, and the baby back ribs. But the very idea of a confession, even a drunken one, filled me with despair. I'd never thought of food—except for mayonnaise—as a murder weapon: potato salad incubating in a blue bowl, deviled eggs souring beneath a broiling summer sun. Now I saw danger everywhere. If frozen ribs could break a man's nose, then a frozen pound cake might crush a skull.

That night I lay awake in the boardinghouse, imagining a new kind of criminal, people robbing banks with frozen pork tenderloins, kielbasa sausage, or ears of corn. But my mind turned back to those brief days when Claude, Jennifer, and I had lived together as a family. In my mind's eye, I could almost see our little house brooding in the pitch-black darkness, and outside the fireflies would skim in the knee-high grass. The coals in the hibachi would still be burning, the feathery particles wafting in the night air.

A LETTER FROM DOROTHY MCDOUGAL

September 4, 1972

Dear Clancy Jane,

You should've told me about Bitsy. Imagine my shock, seeing my daughter's picture on the asylum TV. Actually it was Channel 5 News, and the anchorman, Chris Clark, called Bitsy a dangerous fugitive. I was sitting on a ratty day-room sofa, one that dated back to the Eisenhower administration, and I kept staring at the TV. Fugitive? *I thought. Then I made the mistake of hollering out, "She's no such thing! Why, she'd never break the law!"*

Two nurses ran out of their glass cubicle and grabbed my arms. The skinny one asked why I was yelling. I pointed to the TV. Bitsy's face was gone, replaced with a Mr. Clean commercial. "My daughter was on TV," I said. "I swear she was!"

"Calm down, Mrs. McDougal," said the other nurse. She reached up to adjust her red wig.

I tried to explain, but they began quizzing me. They asked the day of the week and the date, but I didn't know. It's easy to lose track of time in Central State. "It's September something," I finally said. Next, they wanted to know how long my daughter had been inside the TV. Hadn't they been listening? I rolled my eyes and said, "For the last time, her picture was on the news. They all but called her a criminal."

The nurses exchanged glances. "Not that sweet little blond girl who comes to visit?" asked the skinny nurse.

"You must be a tad confused," said the redheaded one. "It's unlikely that your daughter would be on the news."

"Well, she WAS," I yelled. The nurses signaled an orderly, who slapped me onto a gurney and rolled me down the hall into a green-tiled room. It was filled with masked people. Thinking this was a stickup, I raised my hands and told them I had money in my pocketbook. I told them to take it all, but please don't shoot. They held me down and glued wires to my head. I screamed for my son, for Jesus Christ, but the nurses wouldn't let go. All I could think of was Frankenstein, the mad doctor lifting Boris Karloff up into the skylight, into the crackling thunderstorm. Years ago I had paid good money to see that movie with my girl friends, but now I was living it. I was my own "Creature Feature."

Shock treatments are worse than pulling out your own eyebrows, worse than a home permanent gone wrong. The so-called treatment singed some hairs off my head and left bald spots. I thought the doctors would notice and think I might have mange, not hallucinations. They'd say I needed a veterinarian, not a psychiatrist.

They wanted me to admit that my daughter hadn't been on TV, that I was making it up. But I shouldn't have to tell lies. And I shouldn't have to get treatments that I don't need. If it keeps up, they'll just have to kill me. Well, maybe not. Before I leave this world, I'd like a guarantee that heaven will accept me. Then I'd have to see a menu. Here at Central State, the food is terrible except for desserts. So don't tell me the State of Tennessee isn't making a profit. God wouldn't be greedy and serve cheap food. Heaven must have little bakery shops full of praline cheesecakes, and cute little open-air markets with tropical fruits and frozen daiquiris. Everything's free, of course.

The doctors kept harping on my so-called TV vision. I got huffy and told them to call Channel 5 and ask Chris Clark about Bitsy. They didn't. They asked if I'd had other visions. "Just sugarplums," I said, trying to be cute. "And they dance in my head."

A big mistake. The doctors snapped their fingers and the uniformed orderly with the gurney came and whisked me back to the E.C.T. room. And now I'm having trouble remembering things. Like how to multiply and divide. But I know enough to be upset with you, Clancy Jane. Every bit of this could've been avoided if you'd had the decency to drive up here and break the news about Bitsy IN PERSON. I would appreciate it if you'd call them up and explain. I'd give you the telephone number, but it has been fried out of my brain.

Your sister,
Dorothy

Dorothy

Dr. Patterson's office was at the end of a long, green-tiled hall. When Dorothy stepped inside, the doctor was sitting at his desk, writing in a notebook. His black eyeglasses slid down to the tip of his nose. Dorothy leaned forward, ready to catch them, but somehow they stayed affixed to his nose. Dr. Patterson waved at a stiff-backed chair, and she sat down, folding her hands on her knees, watching him scribble away in the book. Their shrinking sessions always began with him asking the same question. "How are we today, Dorothy?" Like they were Siamese twins, sharing the same brain—or worse, sharing the same delusions.

The doctor shut the notebook. The chair squeaked as he swiveled around. "How are we today, Dorothy?"

"Pretty good," she said, repressing a smile. "Considering that I'm glowing in the dark."

"Glowing?" Dr. Patterson's eyebrows shot up.

"It's a joke," Dorothy said. Didn't he get it? Hadn't Patterson been the one to order the shock therapy? The doctor flashed a suspicious glance, then turned back to his desk and opened the notebook. He jotted something down. Without looking at Dorothy, he said, "I spoke with your sister this morning—Mrs. Clancy Jane Falk."

"I know her name." Dorothy nodded. At least *that* hadn't been fried out of her brain. Not yet, anyway.

"She cleared up the little misunderstanding about your missing daughter."

"*Little* misunderstanding?" Dorothy's right thumb twitched. It had begun after the last shock treatment.

"Mrs. Falk also mentioned your long-standing feud."

"She actually called it a feud?" Dorothy felt an urge to rub her eyebrows, but she couldn't because she'd plucked them out years ago. They'd never grown back—just her luck.

"Perhaps sibling rivalry might be a more accurate term." The doctor smiled. "How did it begin?"

Dorothy twisted her mouth to one side. "Didn't my sister tell you?"

"I'd like to hear your version."

"I see." She had copied this phrase from him, and she could tell that he didn't like it. But she couldn't worry about that, because her thumb was twitching again, much like a bank teller counts dollar bills.

"Have you forgotten?" Dr. Patterson cocked his head.

"No, it's just that I'm afraid to tell my side of *any* story. Look what happened to me the other day, when I saw my daughter's face on TV. Nobody believed me. And then y'all—"

"Yes, yes," the doctor said impatiently, "but I want to know your version."

"Fine. But it may take a few hours."

"Why don't you compile a list, itemizing your sister's positive and negative traits. And bring it to the next session."

"But I've got the list in my head. Can't we get started now? Her number-one bad trait is coldheartedness. But I won't start at the very beginning, which is the day Clancy Jane was born—that was in 1938, by the way, and it would be a very long story. Because all Southern women are born with the long-winded chromosome. I must have two of them, so I'll just speed things up. I'll start in 1953. Back then, I was a happily married woman with two children—Mack and Bitsy. She's the one I saw on TV? But my son is so much cuter. And sweeter. But anyway, in 1953, I was a twenty-one-year-old mother of two, and my sister was fifteen. Miss Everything at Crystal Falls High. Then she got mixed up with a hoodlum named Hart Jones. He was the captain of the football team. And he got Clancy Jane pregnant. They eloped. It nearly killed our mother."

"Yes, but I fail to see how that's coldhearted, and besides, our session—"

"I'm not finished—didn't I tell you it would take hours? You'd best cancel the rest of your appointments so you can hear me out. Anyway, Clancy Jane and Mother had a big fight. This was real unusual for them. Up to that point, they'd been close. So Clancy Jane and the hoodlum left town. I don't know where all they went. Seven months later, we got a postcard from Louisiana, saying that Clancy Jane's baby had been born. It was a girl, Violet. But we couldn't write back, because my sister hadn't put a return address.

"We didn't hear a peep out of her for five years. Mother was beside herself. She got real skinny. I tried to give her extra attention, but she'd just snap my head off. I guess her nerves were bad. I was upset with my sister for causing this. Anybody with a soul wouldn't let months and years go by without one word to her family. Then one day in 1958, Clancy Jane just turned up. A beat-up car pulled into the driveway—Mother and I lived next door to each other and we shared a big, old driveway. Anyway, the car had Louisiana license plates."

"That's interesting, Dorothy, but—"

"You're probably wondering if Clancy Jane was my mother's favorite? Well, she was."

"Dorothy—"

"And you're thinking that I felt slighted. It's true." She knew she was talking too much, knew he wanted to get away, but he'd asked for it, hadn't he? Or maybe this was a trap. Maybe this was a test to see just how crazy she really was. She put her hands over her mouth and said, "Just listen to me rattling on. Is this a bad sign?"

"No, Dorothy," said Dr. Patterson. "It's not bad. You have a lot of emotions churning inside. I'm developing a theory that you are terrified of not being loved. But we'll *have* to save this issue for our next session."

"Oh, phooey. We're on a roll."

"I know. But it'll have to wait. And don't forget to make a list of positives and negatives." He turned back to his desk and opened the notebook, signaling that their shrinking session was over.

Dorothy got out of the chair and started to leave. "Dr. Patterson?"

"Yes?"

"Now that you know the truth about my daughter, will they stop giving me shock treatments?"

"Possibly."

She blinked. Was this all he was going to say? Wasn't he going to offer her a consolation prize, like an extra dessert?

"Is there something else, Dorothy?" He stared at her over the rim of his glasses.

"No, I guess not."

"Good. Then I'll see you tomorrow, same time."

She walked back to her room and lay down on the bed. The nurses didn't like for the patients to stay in bed. No, they wanted you to play shuffleboard with homicidal maniacs—it was the truth. Some of the patients were criminally insane. It was all so tiresome. She shut her eyes. The shock treatments had blotted out much of her recent memory. If only it had burned away the past. 1958 was a little too clear. She could still see Clancy Jane drive up in that ancient black Plymouth. The window was down and Frankie Avalon's voice drifted out. The engine sputtered and died, and the music snapped off. The door creaked open and Clancy Jane stepped out. Her hair was longer than Dorothy remembered, and blonder. It was tied back with a blue chiffon scarf, but a few strands tumbled around her cheeks. She looked narrow-hipped and big-breasted in blue pedal pushers and a sleeveless blouse. On her feet were white sling-back flats. Dorothy had never seen anything so stylish in Crystal Falls.

The passenger door opened, and a little brown-haired girl hopped out. This had to be Violet, but she didn't have a look of Clancy Jane. The child had straight, dark hair and a sallow face. Her dress was yellow and wrinkled, and it hung below her knees. She was thin and wormy-looking, and she kept reaching down to scratch her ankles, which were covered in red scabs and welts. Next door a screen door slammed, and Dorothy looked away from the child. She saw her mother running across the grass, her arms open wide.

"I don't believe my eyes!" cried Miss Gussie. She grabbed Clancy Jane and they danced sideways. Then Clancy grabbed her mother's shoulders and steered her around the car, toward the little girl.

"Mama, look here," cried Clancy. "This is Violet, your grandbaby."

"Well, my goodness," said Miss Gussie. She knelt in front of the child, her hands clasped together. The child reached down and scratched her legs. "You're just so precious."

Clancy Jane's eyes met Dorothy's and she called, "Hey."

"Hi there!" Dorothy cried, and the last five years just dropped away. She opened her arms and said, "Get over here and give me a hug."

Just then there was a whirring noise above her head. She glanced up and saw a mockingbird fly across the yard. It made a beeline for her brand-new Coupe de Ville—pale yellow with a powder blue roof. The bird lifted its tail and splattered the windshield. Then it circled back, ready to drop another load. It was the fifth attack this week. And if it continued, Dorothy would be forced to carry an umbrella at all times.

The bird flew over to the Cadillac and perched on the hood ornament. It looked at Dorothy. Just last spring, the mockingbird had made a nest in the dogwood tree. The babies had fledged long ago, but the bird continued to guard her empty nest. Mockingbirds were mean and territorial—they would attack humans at the drop of a hat. Dorothy had read all about them in the *World Book Encyclopedia*.

From across the yard, Miss Gussie called up to the bird, "Aren't you a pretty little thing. See the birdie, Violet?"

The child tilted back her head but said nothing. Clancy Jane stepped up to Dorothy. If she'd noticed the bird—probably not; she never worried about anything—she gave no indication. The sisters embraced. Clancy's hair smelled faintly of soap, but her breath was sour and fruity, like old Mrs. Minchey's from down the street who had sugar diabetes. Dorothy gasped and shut her eyes. When she opened them again, she saw Miss Gussie and Violet walking across the grass, swinging their hands, chatting like two old friends.

"You look terrific," Dorothy said, pulling away from her sister. "How long will you be staying?"

"I'm not sure." Clancy Jane shrugged.

Miss Gussie was leading Violet next door, toward the screened-in porch. She glanced back at Clancy Jane and called, "Are you hungry? I've got a chess pie cooling on the counter."

"Famished," said Clancy Jane. She walked across the driveway, those pretty little shoes scraping in the gravel. Dorothy's stomach growled—she just loved her mother's pies—and she hurried after her sister. When she started up the back steps, Miss Gussie turned and said, "Let me get them settled, and then you can visit. Is that all right?"

"Of course." Dorothy nodded. She watched her mother go into the house and shut the door. Dorothy staggered toward her own yard. The g-ddamned bird swooped out of nowhere, flew over the Cadillac, and spattered the windshield, this time on Dorothy's side. Then it flew into Miss Gussie's walnut tree. Its chirruping sounded triumphant.

• • •

Dorothy sat in her knotty-pine kitchen and waited for the phone to ring. One hour passed, then two. She got up and made a two-layer cake, Betty Crocker's vanilla. The phone still hadn't rung, so she whipped up a batch of pink icing and began decorating the cake. In pale blue icing she wrote: "Welcome Home Clancy Jane & Violet."

She glanced at the clock. It was time to think about supper for Albert and the kids. She'd planned meat loaf, mashed potatoes, green beans, Jell-O salad, and corn bread. And of course that cake would be delicious. Didn't she have more than enough for Miss Gussie and them? She walked across the kitchen and called her mother. "Hi," she said. "It's me."

"I was just going to give you a call," said Miss Gussie.

"I'm about to fix supper. Would y'all like to eat with us? I'm making—"

"That's real sweet of you," Gussie interrupted, "but the girls are tuckered out. They're already in their nightgowns."

"Well, I could fix y'all some plates and bring them over."

"Could we just take a rain check?" Gussie paused. "You'll get to see them tomorrow. I promise. I'm looking at them right now. They've fallen asleep on the couch. They're my angels. Let me go watch them, and I'll see you tomorrow. Okay, Dorothy?"

. . .

The next morning, Dorothy and her children walked over to Miss Gussie's. Mack was tall for a seven-year-old, and he looked grown-up in his baby-blue Sunday suit and the plaid clip-on tie. Bitsy skipped ahead, her stiff braids hitting her shoulders. She was a year younger than Mack and wore a pale pink baby-doll dress. Dorothy was wearing a pink linen dress, cream spectator pumps, and the strand of pearls that Albert and the kids had given her last Christmas. She held an umbrella above her head, just in case that mockingbird was lurking in the trees.

"Who're we meeting again?" called Mack.

"Your cousin, Violet," said Dorothy.

"Why haven't we seen her before?"

A good question. Dorothy didn't have the answer. "Let's scoot," she told the kids. "Maybe y'all can take Violet into the backyard and play on the tire swing."

"I can show her how to climb a tree," Mack said.

Bitsy ran up the steps, her white patent leather shoes clattering. She started to open the screen door, but Miss Gussie's voice stopped her. "My, what a racket," said Gussie, frowning at Dorothy. "And what are y'all doing up so early?"

Dorothy reached around her daughter, opened the screen door, and herded the children inside. "It's nine o'clock," Dorothy said.

"Yes, I know what time it is, Dorothy," said Gussie. "And please lower your voice. You'll wake everybody up."

Mack stood close to Dorothy, but Bitsy threw her arms around her grandmother's legs. "Hi, Mith Guthie," she lisped.

"Where's the little girl?" asked Mack.

"Just come back later," said Gussie.

"When?" said Mack. Dorothy nodded. She'd been just about to ask the same question. Gussie didn't answer. She absently patted Bitsy's head and gave Dorothy a quizzical stare.

"Why are you holding an umbrella, Dorothy?" Gussie asked. "There's not a cloud in the sky."

"No, but there's birds," said Dorothy.

"Excuse me?" Gussie's eyes widened.

"A mockingbird is tormenting me." Dorothy lowered the umbrella and tucked it under her arm. Hoping to change the subject, she added, "I told the kids they could meet Violet."

"Well, she's dead to the world," said Gussie.

"Dead?" Mack gasped.

"No, no," Gussie said. "I just mean she's asleep."

"Maybe y'all can come over for lunch," Dorothy said. "I baked them a cake."

"We'll see." Gussie pursed her lips.

"Well, give us a call when you're ready." Dorothy took Bitsy's hand and steered her across the porch. Mack trotted behind.

"Oh, for heaven's sake," Gussie called. "Don't look so crestfallen, Dorothy."

"You said not to yell," Mack said.

Gussie placed one hand over her lips and nodded. "Sorry," she whispered. "I broke my own rule, didn't I?"

And my heart, too, thought Dorothy.

The children ran across the yard, but Dorothy lagged behind. The mockingbird shot out of a tree and swooped down. It seemed to pause in midair, right above Dorothy's head. She tried to open the umbrella, but the bird was too fast. It pooped on her head, then soared up into a pine tree.

"This is it!" she cried and shook her fist. "I've had it with you."

She hurried into her house, flung open the closet door, and reached for Albert's old BB gun. Then she headed back outside, gripping the gun and pumping the handle the way she'd seen Albert do. She paused in the driveway, looking up into the trees, trying to find that damn bird. She didn't see it but she heard it. She crept over to her car, and the bird plummeted from the walnut tree. She lifted the gun and fired, but missed. The bird flew back to the walnut tree and perched on a branch, twisting its head and laughing at her. That twitter sounded just like Clancy Jane. Dorothy raised the gun, took aim, and squeezed the trigger. The mockingbird fell out of the tree, and thudded onto the ground. A feather drifted in the air.

"*Well?* You had it coming!" Dorothy cried, her voice filled with despair. "I wouldn't of done it, but you egged me on."

• • •

The migraine had begun the minute she'd shot that bird, and by the time she'd thrown it in the trash, she was seeing double. Despite the heat, the bedroom window was propped open so she could hear the children in the backyard. She turned on her side, admiring her gauzy Priscilla curtains stirring in the afternoon breeze, sending dappled light on the pale blue walls.

From beneath her window, she heard children's voices. She lifted the cold rag from her eyes and raised up on one elbow, squinting into the crape myrtles. "Violet, you can't be Tarzan," Mack was saying. "*I'm* Tarzan. You can be Jane or Cheetah."

"I'm Jane!" Bitsy said indignantly.

"I ain't no monkey!" Violet yelled. There were scuffling sounds and cries. Then someone was wailing. It wasn't one of Dorothy's babies. That high-pitched and nasal cry had to belong to Violet.

"I'm telling!" the voice shouted.

"Crybaby," shouted Mack and Bitsy. Then she heard footsteps and a pummeling sound, followed by Violet's plaintive howl. Dorothy settled against her ruffled pillows and put the wet rag over her eyes.

Minutes later, her doorbell rang three times, in quick succession. Then someone began to beat on the door. Dorothy groaned and pulled herself up. Holding the rag to her forehead, she shuffled down the hall. When she opened the front door, Clancy Jane was standing on the porch, her face contorted. She was gripping Violet's hand. The little girl's face was splotched red and tears were spilling down her grubby cheeks. Sand was clotted in her hair. She looked up at Dorothy with brimming eyes and began caterwauling, with snot running out of her fat little nose. No one in their family had a nose like that, with an ugly bulb at the tip. All of the Hamiltons had straight, beautiful noses.

"Bitsy threw sand in Violet's eyes," Clancy Jane said, her chest rising and falling.

"I'm sorry," said Dorothy, rubbing her forehead.

"Is that *all* you can say?" Clancy Jane's voice shook. "Aren't you going to spank her?"

"Clancy Jane, please stop yelling. *I* didn't throw the sand. I've got a migraine headache and I just can't think straight." She glanced next door, at her mother's screened-in porch. It was empty. She just hoped it stayed empty. Because if Miss Gussie got wind of this fight, she'd swoop down on Dorothy.

"She could've blinded Violet." Clancy Jane grabbed her daughter's wide, tear-splotched face. "You can't let Bitsy go around attacking people."

"She's never had before," Dorothy said.

"Just look at her!" Clancy Jane kept squeezing Violet's face, distorting the features. "Why didn't you just get off your fat ass and stop the fight?"

Dorothy blinked. "Yes, I have trouble with my weight, but I don't appreciate you pointing it out. I don't want to fight. Just go back to Mother's."

"No, I'm staying here. You don't own this land. Our mother *gave* it to you and Albert."

"Yes, she did. It was a wedding gift."

"At least *I've* never taken anything from our mother."

Dorothy almost let that comment pass. It was a trap, a string-pulling trap; but she was still fuming over that remark about her being fat. However, the Bible said to turn the other cheek, and that was exactly what she planned to do. But she just couldn't hold back.

"You nearly broke Mother's heart when you ran off. She cried herself to sleep for two years. Anybody with a soul couldn't let months and years go by without one word to her family."

"I wrote after Violet was born." A tear dripped off Clancy Jane's chin.

"And didn't bother to give a return address," Dorothy said.

"I moved!"

"You could've written another postcard."

"Stamps cost money!"

Dorothy glanced down at her sister's feet and thought, *so do white sling-back shoes.* Then she glanced at Violet. The hem had come loose from the child's miles-too-big dress. "Anyway, you could have picked up the phone and placed a collect call."

"I didn't have a phone." Clancy Jane wiped her eyes.

"Let's drop this. I don't want to fight." Dorothy nodded at Violet. The child was rubbing her eyes. She looked so pitiful that Dorothy added, "And don't you worry, I will punish Bitsy. She can be too big for her britches. In fact, she's outgrown most of her clothes. Why don't we bring Violet inside and see if they fit?"

"I don't want your hand-me-downs!" Clancy Jane cried. "But then I guess you don't know any better than to offer them. You're used to getting the dregs, aren't you?"

"I just meant—"

"I don't care what you meant."

"I was hoping the children could get to know each other," Dorothy said.

"And look what happened!" Clancy Jane shook her head, the blonder-than-blond hair whipping back and forth. She snatched Violet's hand. "Come on, baby. We're going back to New Orleans."

She towed the child across the yard, through a rustling tunnel of for-sythias, then they bustled onto Gussie's screened-in porch and into the house. Dorothy rubbed her forehead, wondering how she could smooth this over. She'd be in the wrong—when it came to Clancy Jane, Dorothy had always been the villain. Gussie's screen door opened. Clancy Jane and Violet ran down the steps, clutching paper sacks with nightgowns dangling out. Miss Gussie hurried after them, calling, "What's the matter? Talk to me!"

Clancy Jane turned and pointed at Dorothy. Then she shook her head. Lord, what was she saying? Clancy Jane and Violet climbed into their car and backed out of the driveway, the tires spinning in the gravel.

"Please don't go!" Gussie cried. But it was too late. They were gone. Gravel dust was hanging in the air. Gussie jammed her hands into her apron pockets and marched over to Dorothy's side of the yard. "Why did you pick a fight?" she cried, stepping close to her daughter. Tears ran down Gussie's face, leaving streaks in her powder. "She said you were mean to her."

"The kids had a little tiff. And to make up for it, I just tried to give Violet some of Bitsy's old clothes."

"And did you?" Gussie's eyes flashed.

"Clancy Jane wouldn't take them. She got furious—"

"I don't believe it. Clancy doesn't have an ungrateful bone in her body."

"Well, she was insulted. But it's not a disgrace to get hand-me-downs," Dorothy said, then mentally added, *I've been getting them all my life.*

"It was probably the way you said it. Oh, I know how you can be, Dorothy. You've always hated your sister. And now she's gone. I may never see her or Violet again."

Dorothy's eyes filled. She didn't want to be Gussie's favorite, but it would be nice to put her head on her mother's shoulder.

Gussie wiped her eyes, then turned abruptly and headed back to her house.

"I'm sorry," Dorothy called. "Really and truly, I'm sorry."

Without turning around, Gussie lifted one hand and flipped it. She hurried onto her screened porch and slammed the door. Gravel dust floated between the two yards. Dorothy watched it float up into the trees, leaving a gritty film on everything it touched.

THE CRYSTAL FALLS DEMOCRAT
AND FALLS COUNTY NEWS
Vol. 99 * No. 82 *Since 1888*

POLICE SEARCH FOR MISSING TOT
Statewide Alert Issued for the Teenaged Mother

By Tim McCoy
Senior Staff Writer

Authorities have issued a statewide alert for a Crystal Falls woman who apparently bludgeoned her husband, Claude Edmund Wentworth IV, 19, and then kidnapped their daughter, Jennifer Wentworth, 7½ months. The tot hasn't been seen since August 19. Falls County Sheriff Jeremy Prescott said, "Right now we're concerned about the environment the child might be in." Prescott identified the mother of the tot as Lillian Beatrice Wentworth, 19, who is also being sought on three warrants: attempted manslaughter, auto theft, and theft of personal property, including credit cards and a designer suitcase. Mrs. Wentworth failed to appear in court on September 15, 1972, to answer the above charges.

See MISSING, page 3

MISSING
(Continued from page 1)

Though officials initially believed the pair was hiding in the area, credit card receipts have recently surfaced in Lebanon, Jackson, and Memphis, causing authorities to issue the statewide alert. "Because the mother has a history of insanity in the family, and because of some other things we've learned about her, we're very concerned about them," Prescott said. "The mother hasn't been acting rationally. She's a violent woman, capable of inflicting harm to herself and others. We feel like the child might be endangered."

Mrs. Wentworth is described as a blue-eyed blonde standing 5 feet, 3 inches tall and weighing about 120 pounds. She is believed to be driving a 1972 white Corvette bearing the license tag TNSTUD. Jennifer Wentworth is described as having blue eyes and blond hair, about 25½ inches tall and 16 pounds. She has a red mole on her right cheek.

"As it stands now," said Prescott, "we plan to take evidence to the grand jury on the mother, whether they turn up or not." He asked anyone with information regarding the child to contact the sheriff's department at 555-8262.

A LETTER FROM DOROTHY MCDOUGAL

September 15, 1972

Dear Bitsy,

    I don't know where to mail it, so I am sending this letter to 214 Dixie. I wonder where you are. Go for it, honey. I wish I had. One word of advice: Don't turn yourself in! If you go back, you'll end up wearing stripes or in a place like Central State. So do NOT let them find you. I know how Betty Wentworth thinks. I played bridge with that woman for twelve years, and her mind works like a squirrel trap. Chick drinks more than her, but he is more easygoing. Maybe it's because he plays golf all the time and the exercise relaxes him. But it could also be Valium. I'd always hoped that Claude would take after his daddy. I never dreamed that he'd turn into Miss Betty with balls. So you did the right thing, even though it will be hard to explain.

    If Clancy Jane reads this, I wish a plague of locusts on her head and in her yard.

    Your mother,
    Dorothy

    P.S. Claude ought to thank you for breaking his nose. It was pugged and ugly, and it's not like he doesn't have the $$ to get a new one.

Bitsy

It was my break, and Alice Ann and I were standing in the alley, getting some air and watching the shucker open oysters. Empty shells lay scattered on the ground. I'd been working here three weeks, and I'd learned that his name was Daniel. I didn't think he had a crush on me, but Alice Ann swore that he did. I just hoped she was wrong. When he opened oysters, his fleur-de-lis tattoo bulged. It looked homemade. I wondered if he'd served time in a penitentiary. The alley was cool, thanks to the shady banana trees that grew along the fence. The back door to the restaurant was propped open with a brick, and the smell of sauteed onions drifted out. From a transistor radio, an announcer read off the midmorning news with a lisping twang. *Henry Kissinger returned to Washington and briefed President Nixon on his eleven-day Asian tour . . . and in Munich the U.S. Olympic basketball team lost to the Soviets 51–50 in a controversial gold-medal match. The U.S. protested to no avail.*

The news was followed by commercials for Budweiser. I leaned against a crate and watched the shucker's muscles move, the fleur-de-lis twitching like a spider. Then I glanced into the kitchen and waved to the head chef, Joe, who wore a high, white chef's hat and kept a stubby cigar pinched between his teeth. The assistant chef, Manny, was chopping celery, wiping his face on his shoulder, and the new chef, Èmile, was shoving braided loaves into the ovens; Mrs. Bianchi, the owner, was sitting in her glassed-in office, a glass of tea beside her elbow. "Jesus," Manny said. "These onions are putting my eyes out."

I turned, blinking at a rusted car that skidded in the shells. It lurched to a stop and a pregnant woman climbed out, tears streaming down her puffy cheeks. She took a step forward, then reached into a purse, and pulled out a gun. First thing, she turned to me. A growl rose up in her throat and she pointed the gun at my head.

"You the one who been seeing my Danny?" The gun wobbled in her pudgy hands. Her wedding ring was fastened to her blouse with a diaper pin. It looked too small for her finger.

"I have not!" I cried.

"Ramona? Sweetheart?" The shucker grinned at his wife. "I been true to you."

It was the wrong thing to say. Her face contorted. "Liar, liar, LIAR!" Two purple veins throbbed on her forehead. "Why didn't you come home last night? I'll tell you why, because you was with *her*. And you know what I did? I lay up in our trailer, begging the Lord to let me die. That's right, Danny. Your pregnant wife, sweating in that trailer, waiting for God to strike her dead. And your little baby, too, Danny. Think about *that* for a goddamn minute. Meanwhile, you're having sex with a blonde. But I'm calm now. I see the light. I don't want to die, Danny. I want *her* to die."

Ramona squeezed her eyes shut and pulled the trigger. The top of a banana tree exploded. The green leaves shattered, pouring down on my head and shoulders. Alice Ann screamed and rolled into a ball.

"You no good slut!" Ramona yelped and took aim again.

"Don't shoot the child!" I screamed. "Run, Alice Ann!"

The shucker was creeping up behind Ramona. She saw him and tried to hit him with the butt of her gun. The commotion brought both chefs charging out the back door.

"Hey!" Joe yelled. Then he lunged ahead, rushing toward Ramona. She and the shucker were struggling, swaying back and forth. Before Joe could reach them, the gun fired again. I heard something whine past my ear. Then I felt hot pain. My hand flew up to my throat. My fingers came back tipped in red.

"Oh my *God!*" I said. "I'm hit!"

Ramona looked at the gun, then at me. The shucker jerked the gun from her swollen hands. "You stupid bitch!" he yelled, and a few drops of saliva hit her in the face. She made a fist, hit his shoulder. Joe rushed over to me, his big hands on my arm. "Let me see, Lillian. Come on, take your hand away. Let Joe see."

"Where's Alice Ann?" I said, pulling away from Joe, trying to find the child. Alice Ann was still crouched beside the banana tree. She opened her mouth as if to speak, but her lips seemed paralyzed.

"She's okay," said Joe. "She's just scared is all."

"Thank God," I said, closing my eyes. "Thank God."

"And you gonna be okay, too," Joe said. "The bullet grazed you. It's just a scratch is all, just a scratch." He took off his apron, pressed it to the wound, then glared at Ramona. "You coulda killed her!"

"Too bad I didn't!" Ramona tossed her head.

"It's a damn good thing you didn't, lady. Being pregnant won't keep you out of jail." Joe put one hairy arm around Alice Ann, dragging her over to me.

The shucker tucked the gun into his belt. His eyes flitted over to me. "I'm sorry about this. I don't know why she thought I was banging you."

"Because you was!" Ramona's face flooded with color. She raised her leg and kicked him square in the testicles. He screamed, then cupped his hands over his groin and dropped to one knee. Mrs. Bianchi shoved past the cooks and dishwashers who had gathered in the doorway to watch. She looked at the shucker, then she turned her gaze on me.

"Goddamn ruffians," she said through her teeth. "Danny, you're nothing but a swamp bug. Get off my property this instant. You, Blondie, you get out of here, too." She waved a dismissive hand at me, then nodded at Manny. "The rest of you, go back inside. We got a restaurant to run."

"But Mrs. Bianchi," I said. "This isn't my fault—"

"I don't want to hear it." The old woman made a fist and struck her palm. "You're fired. Get out of here or I'm calling the po-lice."

Joe squeezed my shoulder. "Hold pressure on that apron till the bleeding stops."

"In this kitchen this second!" yelled Mrs. Bianchi, pointing at the door.

"Go on," I said, pushing Joe with my elbow. "Don't get fired because of me."

"Hell, she won't fire me," he growled, but he shuffled away, avoiding Mrs. Bianchi's eyes. The cooks filed into the restaurant after him. Mrs. Bianchi spat on the ground, then closed the door.

Ramona glanced down at her husband, who was curled up at her feet. She sighed, rubbing her belly with the tips of her fingers. Then she cut her eyes at me. "First you steal my man, now you get him fired. I ought to shoot you between the eyes. You and your little bastard child."

"I'm *not* a bastard!" Alice Ann screamed.

"Oh, yeah?" Ramona tossed her head, snorted. "Well, that's good you got a daddy 'cause you gonna need him. Especially after I kill your mama. That's right, you little pussy bitches. Stare me down, but it won't change your future. One night, you gone wake up and find a knife to your throat."

"Don't listen to her," I said, pulling Alice Ann down the alley. We walked so fast our shoes stirred up a ridge of shell dust. My neck was hurting.

"I know a man, he just got out of Parchman," Ramona shouted. "He'll cut your hearts out. You and your girl's. Feed you both to the fishes!"

"What's Parchman?" Alice Ann gripped the edge of my apron, twisting it in her fingers. I was trying hard not to cry, but I could feel pressure behind my eyes.

"A prison," I said. "But don't worry. It's nowhere near Point Minette."

"I don't care. I'm scared. If that woman knows a bad man . . ." Alice Ann's throat worked up and down. She wiped her eyes with dirty hands.

"She doesn't know anybody like that," I said, reaching out with my free hand to pat the child's shoulder. My fingers were bloody. Alice Ann squirmed away.

"But what if she does?" Alice Ann looked up into my eyes. From the end of the alley, Ramona was still shrieking about pussy women getting their just deserts.

We slipped through the azalea hedge and got into the car. I pulled the apron off my wound and looked at it. My blood was bright red, and it hurt my eyes to look at it.

"It's not even suppertime, and you've already lost your job." Alice Ann crossed her arms. "Just take me back to Memphis. It may be boring, but at least nobody's trying to kill Eunice."

I ignored her and drove three blocks, then I angled the car down Oak Street. The boardinghouse was straight ahead and the widows were sitting in green metal chairs under the trees, sipping drinks. Mrs. Finch held Jennifer in her lap, letting her play with plastic keys, each one a soft, pastel color.

"I mean it," Alice Ann said. "Take me back to Eunice *right now.*"

"I can't leave town," I said. "Mrs. Bianchi still owes me a paycheck. We need that money. If you're scared, I'll push the dresser in front of the door."

"That won't stop them." Alice Ann crossed her arms, glaring at me.

"There *is* no them," I said. "That woman was lying."

"I don't care. If you don't take me back to Memphis, I'll call the police. I'll tell them your real name. I'll say you kidnapped me."

"Can we discuss this later?" I could see the old ladies gazing toward the car, sipping their drinks. "I need to wipe off the blood. We don't want Mrs. Finch and her boarders to get excited."

Alice Ann bolted from the car and ran up the back staircase. I glanced in the rearview mirror, assessing the damage to my neck. It was already trying to form a scab. One more inch, and I'd have been dead. I shuddered and stuffed the apron into my bag. Then I got out of the car. As I walked across the yard, I waved nonchalantly to the widows and sped up the stairs. When I opened the French door, I found Alice Ann throwing the thrift shop clothes I'd bought into paper sacks.

"Honey, don't be scared," I said. "That woman's not dangerous."

"Just leave me alone. I want my Eunice. I'm h-homesick."

"Let's get a good night's sleep, and tomorrow—"

"No, no!" Alice Ann stamped her foot. "We're leaving now, or I'm calling the police."

"Let me call Eunice."

"You are driving me home, and that's that." Without looking at me, Alice Ann grabbed two sacks and ran out of the room. Her footsteps pounded on the staircase. I walked out onto the veranda and looked down into the yard, watching the child run over to the Cadillac. I thought about calling her bluff. I didn't believe she would really go to the police.

"Where are you going?" Mrs. Finch called to Alice Ann, rising from her chair, the keys tinkling in Jennifer's hands. The other women were huddled together, watching the girl throw the sacks into the backseat.

"My grandmother died," answered Alice Ann in a clear, calm voice. "We have to leave right this instant."

"Oh, my stars," said Mrs. Finch, patting Jennifer's legs. "Are y'all leaving right now?"

"Yes, ma'am," said Alice Ann and glared up at me.

Suddenly I knew that she was fully capable of calling the police and stirring up a world of trouble. I had no choice but to drive the little psycho back to Memphis and pray that I never laid eyes on her again.

"Well, will y'all be back?" Mrs. Finch's forehead was wrinkled.

"No telling." Alice Ann shrugged.

"Be careful driving," called Mrs. Finch. "The road's full of maniacs these days."

I walked down the stairs, toward the old ladies. Alice Ann charged up past me. "You better pack your stuff," she whispered. I walked over to Mrs. Finch and lifted the baby into my arms. I drew in a deep breath. "I'm just so sorry," I said.

"Well, that's perfectly all right," said Mrs. Finch, glancing up at my neck. The other widows leaned forward and stared.

"Thank you for watching Jennifer. You've been awfully kind to babysit her and Alice Ann."

"She's a little angel," said Mrs. Finch. "I was proud to watch her. Now y'all be careful. Where is it that y'all are driving to?"

"Georgia," Alice Ann said, suddenly appearing behind me. She balanced the baby's car seat in her arms. She looked at me. "I've got your stuff all packed."

"That Alice Ann's like a miniature adult, isn't she?" said one of the boarders.

"Is her father alive?" asked another.

"No," I said, grateful that I didn't have to lie. I hugged Jennifer to my chest. From the corner of my eye, I saw Alice Ann running back up to our purple room. I was grateful that the widows hadn't commented about my bloody neck.

I hurried over to the Cadillac. The car seat was sitting in the gravel. I leaned over and strapped Jennifer in, then I lifted the seat. From the corner of my eye, I saw Alice Ann running down the steps, red pigtails flying. On the last riser, she tripped, and a sack of clothes went flying into the air.

The old women cried out. Alice Ann landed and didn't move. She lay motionless in the grass. I set the car seat on the roof of the Cadillac and hurried over to her. Squatting down, I whispered, "Are you hurt?"

"It doesn't matter." Alice Ann sat up, rubbing her scraped knee. Then she snatched up the sack, stuffed her underwear inside, and hobbled toward the car. She climbed into the front seat and began honking the horn. I picked up a blue shirt. The old ladies were watching, inclining their grizzled heads and whispering.

Alice Ann honked the horn again. Then she began to scream. I ran to the car, tossing the blue shirt onto the seat, next to my pocketbook, which resembled a butcher's bag. "Let's go!" Alice Ann shrieked.

My hand trembled as I stuck the key into the ignition. I started to back out of the driveway, but the widow women were scrambling out of their chairs, waving frantically. Alice Ann stood up on her knees and watched. Mrs. Finch was shouting, but I couldn't hear what she was saying.

"Something's wrong," I said, tapping the brake.

"No, it's not," screamed Alice Ann. She made a fist and beat it against the seat, denting the leather. Her cheeks reddened, and her eyes began to glow. "They're just stupid old ladies. Keep driving or I'll tell them everything."

I hesitated, glancing at the old ladies. They were scurrying toward the driveway.

"Don't you dare stop!" Alice Ann screamed. "They're probably after you for back rent. Drive."

She scooted toward me, knocking my purse to the floor, then slid down on the seat. Her foot crashed onto the accelerator, and the Cadillac shot backward crookedly out of the drive, knocking over Mrs. Finch's trash cans. Alice Ann sat up and tried to grab the gear shift, but I beat her to it. "Go!" she yelled, her eyes bulging. "Go, go, go!"

I shifted into drive, drove slowly to the corner, and turned onto Broad Beach Boulevard. Alice Ann screamed in my ear—"Faster, faster!" I gripped the wheel and focused on the road. The blue sky seemed to pour itself through the windshield, a vast, open space that seemed larger than the ocean. Alice Ann slumped beside me, her arms crossed over her chest. She began tapping her shoes together.

"How long will it take you to drive to Memphis?" she asked.

"All day." I didn't bother to add the dangers of my returning to Tennessee. I had little doubt what Alice Ann would tell her grandmother. "I was kidnapped," she'd say. "Taken in broad daylight." Eunice would call the police, give a description of the Cadillac, along with the license plate number, and I would be pulled over before I left the city limits.

I hadn't gone a block when I saw and heard a black-and-white police car zooming up behind me, blue lights wheeling, as it closed in on my Cadillac. The siren got louder. Alice Ann turned around, grasping the seat with one freckled hand.

"They can't be after us," I said.

"You were probably going too slow," she said.

The police car pulled up alongside the Cadillac. The officer was shouting and pointing at the roof of my car. I rolled down the window, stuck out my head. "What's wrong?" I hollered into the wind.

"Stop the goddamn car!" he screamed. "You got a baby on the roof!"
I stared at him, uncomprehending, then my mouth fell open. "Oh,
my *God.*"

Alice Ann sat on her knees, peering into the empty backseat. "You stupid idiot, you forgot Jennifer!"

FROM THE DESK OF CLANCY JANE FALK

Dear Dorothy,

    *They wouldn't let us see Bitsy until the hearing, and even then, she was
surrounded by two police officers and a court-appointed attorney. I sat in the
back of the courtroom with Byron, We had persuaded Violet to stay in
Knoxville, promising to keep her informed. However, Mack had insisted
upon coming along. He was seated next to me, and he kept shifting on the
bench, causing his trousers to hike up, revealing his prosthetic leg. For his
sister's hearing, he'd shaved off his beard, and he'd been allergic to the
aftershave—his chin and neck were pocked with red blotches. Every few
minutes he'd reach up and scratch, then nervously push his hair out of his
eyes. It was chin-length and wavy, several shades lighter than his sister's, from
working long hours in the sun.*

    *A little man stood up and said something about the State of Mississippi
vs. Bitsy Wentworth, case number 4152. The Wentworths sat on the other
side of the courtroom, looking smug as their attorney rattled off Bitsy's crimes:
assault and battery, two counts of kidnapping, forgery, fraud, grand theft
auto, and reckless endangerment of a minor child. The attorney didn't bother
to tell the truth about that demon child from Memphis, even though Alice
Ann had finally told the truth, that she hadn't been kidnapped, that she had
lied.*

    *The judge listened to Miss Betty's lawyers, then he listened to Bitsy's public
defender. I could tell that the judge wasn't impressed. He ordered Bitsy to sign
a legal document to relinquish her custodial rights to Jennifer. Then he told
her to sign another paper saying she wouldn't contest the divorce the
Wentworths were getting for Claude. Bitsy burst into tears and refused to
give up her baby. Then the judge threatened to hold her in contempt and
painted a bleak picture of the Mississippi prison system. Bitsy still wouldn't
sign. The judge leaned forward and told Bitsy and her lawyer to approach
the bench. Furious whispering commenced, with the red-faced judge talking
so fast spittle flew off his mouth onto the documents he kept waving. Bitsy*

bent over double, crying and crying. The judge kept on talking. I couldn't hear what he said. Finally Bitsy straightened up and reached for the pen. The judge slammed his gavel and the little old man stood up again and announced case number 4153, the State of Mississippi vs. Donnie Ray Weemus. Bitsy just stood there, staring up at the judge.

"You're free to go," he said.

In the back of my mind, I kept hearing Janis Joplin singing about her and Bobby McGee and what freedom meant.

We herded her into their car and left Point Minette that evening, driving on Mississippi backroads and then cutting over to Alabama. Her entire crime spree had lasted a month, but it seemed longer. Byron and Mack were silent all the way to Birmingham, but I kept asking, "Bitsy, why did you run away? What were you thinking?"

Bitsy was curled up on her side in the backseat and didn't seem to be thinking much of anything. Maybe it was the two Valiums she'd been given. I fiddled with the radio, but every station was staticky.

"Did you plan to stay on the Gulf Coast?" Byron asked. "And never see your family again?"

"If that's w-w-what it took to keep my baby," Bitsy said. Then she began to cry—big, wracking sobs that shook the whole backseat.

"At least you aren't going to jail," Byron said.

"Those goddamn Wentworths. Bringing in those Vanderbilt lawyers!" Mack said and hit the dashboard with his fist. "Bitsy never had a chance."

"And did you see Miss Betty?" I asked. "She was prancing around that courthouse like she was a member of the Royal Family."

Oh, I know all about that woman. Miss Betty might act like royalty, but her daddy used to sell shoes on the Square. Little Betty Stewart had come a long way. Or maybe she hadn't. Just a few hundred years ago her ancestors were painting their faces Smurf Blue and burning people alive in wicker cages. Now, of course, she wore Max Factor, but everything she touched turned to ashes.

Well, that's all for now. I will write again when I have more news.
Love,
Clancy Jane

LETTERS FROM CENTRAL STATE

October 17, 1972

Dear Betty,

Years ago we were friends—not the closest in the world, I'll grant you, but we belonged to the same bridge club and went on the same annual trip to Florida every single year. Also, we are Jennifer's grandmothers and this binds us in a special way. Because of our friendship and kinship, I am begging you to please let Bitsy see her daughter. If you're afraid of what'll happen, that Bitsy'll run off again, then send the police or the National Guard. But please don't come between a mother and a daughter.

Sincerely,
Dorothy

November 8, 1972

Betty,

My last letter to you came back in the mail—return to sender was scrawled on the envelope. I recognized your handwriting, that back-slanted block print you're so fond of using. Just for your information, I am not a bad penpal. I write regularly to Pat Nixon, and she NEVER sends my letters back. So I'm asking you one more time to please let Bitsy see our mutual grandchild. If you don't, it will warp her. Poor Jennifer is the one who'll pay for your selfishness. Do you realize that I myself have never laid eyes on Jennifer? But you don't hear me complaining. Never mind that YOU get to see her every day. A grandmother can't take the place of a mother. You can try but you will fail.

Dorothy

FROM THE DESK OF CLANCY JANE FALK

November 15, 1972

Dear Violet,

Thanksgiving is just around the corner. I will be so happy to see you. Here in Crystal Falls we've had one problem after the next. I drove by Bitsy's old house on Tarver, and it's been rented out to a family of five. I knocked on the door, told them who I was, and asked if they'd found any of Bitsy's things. They didn't know what I was talking about. I tried to reach Chick at the bank, to tell him that I would pay to have Bitsy's things brought over here.

It's not like she had a lot. But he never returned my calls. Later I found out that they'd hired movers to pack up her belongings and take everything to the dump.

The poor kid is shaky, like she's recovering from a near-fatal illness. Things really got worse for her when a packet arrived in the mail of all those papers she signed down in Mississippi. It just reopened the wounds.

When you come home, you might get a shock when you see Bitsy's room. Miss Betty returned all of the stuffed animals that we've been sending to Jennifer. I hid them in the upstairs closet, and then one day Bitsy opened the door and was hit by an avalanche. Pink and blue teddies came tumbling out. So now all those bears and stuffed poodles are on Bitsy's bed, and she sleeps with her arms around the big pink bear. She carries a little pink kitten—stuffed of course—around in her purse. It's her security cat. I'm wondering if it is a substitute for Jennifer. Or maybe she is regressing. I tried to look it up in Byron's textbooks, but I couldn't find a single mental disorder that centers around stuffed animals. Maybe you can think of one.

Byron says she's grief-stricken. I sure can relate to that. But even though Jennifer is alive, her absence must feel like a death. Maybe when you come home, we can take Bitsy on a shopping trip to Nashville. We've tried to shop right here in Crystal Falls but people were just too rude.

Well, so much for good Christian ethics. It's no small wonder that organized religion has turned me into an atheist.

Love,
Your heathen Mama

A LETTER FROM BITSY

December 30, 1972

Dear Jennifer,

Happy Birthday, honey. I can't believe you will be 1 year old tomorrow. I wonder how many words you're saying now, and if your hair is still curly blond and if you still remember me. In my mind's eye, I will be with you tomorrow. I hope you get lots of presents and I hope you like the stuffed panda. I'm sending this a day early so you'll be sure to have it at your party. I will always love you and you will always be my baby.

Love,
Mother

Part 2

January 9, 1973

Dear Dorothy,

The holidays were tough. Chick stopped by with all the letters and presents Bitsy had sent to Jennifer for Christmas & her birthday. Bitsy just cried and cried. The Wentworths are determined to remove her from her baby's world. And I fear they might succeed.

Last Sunday morning the temp. rose into the 60s, Bitsy and I went outside and sat in lawn chairs. It was chilly, but still possible for her to get some sun. She is so pale the veins beneath her skin are visible. This could be a vitamin deficiency. One day I kept track of what she ate—one strawberry, a teaspoon of soup, half a sugar cookie, and a sip of hot tea. Every bone in her face is visible. She has sworn off men and love. I told her not to be hasty, that she couldn't judge all men by Claude. But she just shook her head.

With or without a man, she still needed to do something with her life, so I sent off for an application to the Crystal Falls School of Cosmetology. I know you don't approve of such, but thought it was something she could succeed at. Plus she's always liked that sort of thing. All it takes to be a beautician is six consecutive weeks and a fondness for hair. I helped her fill out the application. But when it asked for a list of her hobbies, she wrote down "putting on makeup." I felt bad for her when she had to put a checkmark in the box that asked about a criminal record. The school sent Bitsy a rejection letter. I stuck it in an old Reader's Digest. No need for her to know about it. Next week I will drive her out to Central State so y'all can visit.

Love,
Clancy Jane

FROM THE CRYSTAL FALLS *DEMOCRAT*

CAFÉ UNDER NEW MANAGEMENT

—*From "Talk of the Town,"*
a column by Rayetta Parsons, June 1973

The Green Parrot Café will open its doors for noonday business, on June 6 at 11 A.M. Formerly the location of Velma's Diner, the café has done more than remodel the building. The café's new owners, Clancy Jane Falk and Zach Lombard, have overhauled the menu. Falk, a native of Crystal Falls, is the wife of a local physician, and she is interested in a healthy, wholesome cuisine. Lombard hails from Ithaca, New York, where he cooked at the Moosewood Restaurant. "I'm excited at the prospect of introducing Crystal Falls to international cooking," he told this reporter. For those of you expecting a meat and three, you might be disappointed with the café's selections, because the menu isn't typical Southern fare. Even if you aren't "into" faddish food, you will enjoy the "jungle motif" atmosphere, which is unique to this part of Tennessee. Ceramic parrots and stuffed monkeys dangle from the ceiling and peep out of the numerous potted palm trees. The vinyl booths have been upholstered in dark green. Ferns and Tarzan-like trees have been painted on the walls. If you look real close you can see parrots hiding in them. A stereo plays bird screeches for your dining enjoyment. On opening day only, the waitresses will wear parrot suits. However, Mr. Lombard emphasizes that the interior design has no bearing on the cuisine. "It's neither South American nor African, although the ethnic is certainly celebrated," Lombard said. "It's a sampling of many cuisines, including vegetarian."

The menu will include such exotic dishes as gazpacho, tabouli, and melted medley in a pita. A children's menu offers tofu nut balls, grilled cheese, and peanut butter and honey. All children's meals will be served with complimentary homemade animal crackers. The desserts include cheesecake with chocolate cookie crust, poppy seed muffins, carrot cake with cream cheese frosting, and Albanian chocolate mousse.

Bitsy

From the back of the café, I watched customers stream through the door, the bell tinkling above their heads. I was hot and tired, and I felt ridiculous. For the opening I was wearing a custom-made bird suit, complete with feathered headgear. I straightened my plastic beak, and wished Clancy Jane had named her café something else.

"You need to get out of the house," Aunt Clancy had told me when she'd gotten the idea to open a cafe. "You've sat around moping long enough. And I could use your help with my café."

"Do I have to?" I asked and swallowed hard. I kept hoping to hear from the beauty college but I never had.

"No," said Aunt Clancy, "but I wish you would. Nearly one whole year has passed since the scandal, and people have moved on to fresh gossip. So if you're scared of facing people—"

"I'm not," I said. I honestly didn't mind what people thought of me, but I was scared that I'd stir up gossip and lose all chance of winning back my daughter. After I lost custody, I stayed in one of Aunt Clancy's bedrooms for weeks, creeping downstairs for coffee and the morning paper. All the area newspapers had written about my troubles. "Kidnapped Tot Reunited With Frantic Relatives," announced the Nashville *Tennessean*. "Local Woman's Crime Spree Ends," asserted the Crystal Falls *Democrat*. My mug shot was on the front page—hair tousled, neck scabbed and bloody, mouth wide open. Now, almost a year later, I was still something of a pariah—my "P" word for the day.

Days before the café opened, I'd stopped by Noke's Butcher Shop to pick up cheese and spotted one of my bridesmaids from my first wedding to Claude, Kara Lynn Ketchum. I hadn't seen the girl since 1971, at a baby shower for Jennifer. She had given the baby a blanket, monogrammed W for Wentworth.

Kara Lynn was shouting at hard-of-hearing Mr. Nokes. "I want this," tapping the glass case, pointing to a sirloin roast.

"This?" Mr. Nokes held up baby back ribs.

"No, the r-o-a-s-t," shouted Kara Lynn. Her daddy owned the Buick dealership, and they kept their money at the Wentworths' bank.

"Eh?" Mr. Nokes wrinkled his nose.

Under the pink lights the meat looked plush and velvety. The butcher picked up the roast with his fat fingers and plopped it onto the scale.

"Hi, Kara Lynn," I said.

Kara Lynn turned and froze. "Bitsy," she said in a flat voice. "I haven't seen you in ages. I thought you'd left town."

"No, I'm still here," I said, stung by the harsh look in my former friend's eyes. We'd known each other since kindergarten. Kara Lynn turned back to the butcher. He was tearing off a strip of white crinkly paper. "That'll be all, Mr. Nokes. How much?"

"What?"

"I *said*, how much do I owe you?" She waved her pocketbook in the air. "Good grief, how MUCH?"

I rolled my eyes. So this was how it was going to be. Kara Lynn paid the butcher, then she collected her package and hurried toward the door without glancing at me. The door slammed and Kara Lynn hurried down the sidewalk.

"Next!" cried Mr. Nokes, even though I was the only customer in the shop. I stepped up to the case and told him I was from the Green Parrot. "I'm here to pick up the cheese," I said, carefully enunciating each word. Then, on impulse, I pressed a finger against the glass case, pointing at the baby back ribs. "And I'd like these, too," I added.

Now, huddled in the back of the café, I glanced down at my costume. My promise to help Aunt Clancy hadn't included wearing a feathered suit. I could hear the kitchen radio blaring out the midday news. Watergate, John Dean, Nixon, Vietnam. Aunt Clancy listened to the news, then hurried away. She wasn't wearing a bird suit. She was decked out in a long paisley skirt and a ruffled peasant blouse and lots of turquoise beads around her neck. She had always turned up her nose at the Bobbie Brooks separates I favored, preferring chic, hippie outfits that suggested journeys and far-flung places. Her closet was full of Indian muslin, Scandinavian sweaters, crocheted shawls studded with beads, sheer linen blouses with satin ribbons and eyelet trim. It occurred to me that her taste was as unique and colorful as the selections on the café's menu. She'd wanted the place to have an exotic decor, and in the weeks before opening day, we'd painted a mural—a dense jungle filled with monkeys, palms, and birds. Above my head, a ceramic macaw twirled from a length of fishing line. When the air conditioner was blowing just right, the way it was doing now, the bird resembled a vulture. Its underside had a large hole, just below the tail, which was unseemly for an eating establishment. Zach and Violet had hung a bird over every table, and when I saw the customers gaze up at them with horror, I knew what was on their minds. I told them to relax, those were china birds, not real ones.

From the kitchen, a bell rang, and the cook hollered out, "Pick up!" I sighed and reached for the plates, setting them in the crook of each wing. Trying not to breathe in the tofu fumes, I hurried toward the front of the café, whizzing past the plate glass window, where The Green Parrot Café was freshly painted. A real artist had done this, and each letter was formed out of green bamboo, trimmed in black; even I knew that didn't occur in nature. Scattered around the bamboo letters, the artist had embellished the glass with palm fronds and a larger-than-life macaw.

After the tables and booths filled up, it was standing room only. The waiting customers huddled on the sidewalk in groups of twos and fours, drinking complimentary cups of fruity iced tea while they waited for an available table. Even though the cafe was air-conditioned, the patrons kept opening the glass doors, letting in gusts of sweltering air. I patted my forehead with a paper napkin. It was getting hotter and hotter inside my suit. And if one more customer tugged my feathered tail, I might squawk. Well, not really. If I ever wanted to get custody of my daughter—or even regular visitation rights—I had to act ladylike.

I glanced around the dining room and spotted Violet. She was home for summer vacation, but today she was sashaying around the dining room in her parrot suit, her wings loaded with dishes. She seemed oblivious to the heat. Then again, it was difficult to tell what Violet was thinking. She passed by her mother, who was conferring with her partner, Zach Lombard. Aunt Clancy had opened the café against her husband's wishes. I wondered if Byron Falk might be jealous of Zach who was a hippie from New York State, with long brown hair which he tied back into a shiny tail with a piece of leather. Zach hadn't gone to Vietnam because he'd gotten a high lottery number. He was ten years younger than Aunt Clancy, but only five years older than me. But even if I was interested in finding me a man—and I wasn't!—he wasn't my type at *all*. Personally, I thought Zach was more interested in food than women. But Aunt Clancy said I was crazy. She liked him a little too much, however Zach didn't seem to notice.

"Miss, the soup's cold!" cried a bald-headed man just as Violet rushed by, juggling three platters. His hand grazed her feathers, and Violet stopped. "Life isn't perfect," she snapped. "Deal with it!"

The customer started to protest, but Violet zoomed off. As she passed by a booth, another outraged customer grabbed her suit and began to complain about his food. "Oh, I see the problem," Violet said in her know-it-all voice. "Gazpacho is supposed to be cold. Would you like something else?"

Before the customer could reply, a man with bushy eyebrows lodged a complaint.

"Ma'am? I didn't want mayonnaise on my burger."

"I'll be right back, sir," Violet called, hurrying to another table. Her eyes met mine, and I knew what she was thinking. In the weeds, the other waitresses called it. My cousin plunked down the plates and began sorting them, sometimes matching them up to a customer and sometimes not. I longed to be as careless as Violet—to say what was on my mind and not get in trouble. I tried real hard to get the details right, but already this morning I had made a grown woman cry over sour cream. Trying to soothe her, I'd said, "There's nothing worse than getting sour cream when you're not in the mood for it." The woman had responded by picking up her plate and smashing it to the floor.

"Miss?" called a man in a navy Izod shirt. "I ordered the mango chicken salad, but I'm not sure *what* you gave me."

"Oh, no. That's tabouli." Violet glanced around, then she snatched up the man's plate and switched it with the one in front of a woman at the next table. The woman held her fork in midair, a romaine leaf hanging down. She blinked as Violet plunked down the tabouli.

Turning back to the man, my cousin said "All set?"

"No!" cried the man, eyeing his plate as if Violet had given him the wrong brain, rather than the wrong food. "I can't eat this! She's already eaten some of my chicken!"

"I'll bring you another." Violet turned, her tail feathers shaking. The bald-headed fellow was holding up his soup bowl.

"Sorry?" Violet asked.

"Aside from being cold," shouted the man, tilting the bowl, "there's a hair in here, a curly black hair. Where did it come from?"

"I'm not sure," Violet said, "but I can assure you it's from somebody's head."

The man's mouth fell open, revealing a half dozen silver fillings. He gaped up at her. "I want to speak to the manager." he said, setting down his bowl. It clunked against the table.

"You'll have to stand in line," Violet said, nodding at the cash register, where a dozen folks were crowded around Zach. Clancy Jane was now waiting tables. Violet marched over to the next customers. Her pen was poised over the green tablet. The man had straight black hair, all whooshed back into a pompadour, and his female companion had a pretty face but her arms were fleshy.

"Hey," Violet said, peering down at the portly woman. If the woman smarted off, I was pretty sure that my cousin would respond with an insult—I could just hear her telling the woman that she would roast very nicely with a sprig of rosemary. Instead, Violet offered an uncharacteristically sweet smile.

"Ready to order?" she asked the woman, "or do you need a few minutes?"

• • •

One day, when the café had been open about a month, my daddy walked in. He blinked at the mural, squinting at the palm trees, monkeys, and macaws, as if to say, Is this compatible with nature? My arms were loaded with plates, so Clancy Jane greeted him. She smiled faintly and said, "Thanks for coming, Albert."

He glanced up, his eyelids fluttering. "Actually, I didn't come to eat. I came to see Bitsy."

"Certainly." Clancy Jane led him to a table beside the window, which was lined with prayer plants and pink geraniums, and hurried away. On the other side of the café, I had been watching this little exchange. Aunt Clancy and my father had not spoken in six years. His eyes were darting around the room, and he kept smoothing back his hair with one pale hand. He wore a wrinkled summer suit and a skinny tie that had gone out of style when LBJ was president. I walked over to him and kissed the top of his bald head, which tasted slightly salty. "Can I get you a nice glass of tea?" I asked.

"Er, actually—"

"Or maybe you want a full meal? Today's special is tabouli—just perfect on a hot day like today."

"Can you sit down a minute, honey? Please?" He gestured at the empty chair.

"I really shouldn't," I told him, but then I saw the disappointment on his face and I sat down. "What's the matter?"

His eyes looked old and sad. I steeled myself for the worst: Mack driving his truck off an embankment; Dorothy swallowing her tongue at the asylum.

"Well, it's like this, honey."

"Just say it, Daddy."

His cheeks turned pink, with little red veins stitched across them. "As you know your mother and I have been separated for a long time. And I guess I got lonely. See, I've met a lady? You may know her, Miss June Rinehart? She works at my dime store."

I nodded. Sure, I knew June Rinehart. The cashier at Daddy's dime store, a short perky blonde, her hair trained into a forties pageboy, with crimped waves and pin-curled bangs, which she fluffed out with a rat comb. She wore cotton housewife dresses that flared out like bells, the waists cinched tight with shiny plastic belts. Many a time I'd seen her peer into the little mirror over the scales—for a penny the machine would tell your weight and your fortune. June Rinehart never put in a penny. She'd just gaze into the mirror, teasing her hair and rubbing lipstick off her teeth. I knew for a fact that she'd started working at the Ben Franklin the year after my mother had been sent away.

"I want to marry her," said Daddy.

"But you're already married!" Soon as the words were out of my mouth, I cringed. All around me, the café had fallen silent. Several people were staring—the last thing I needed. In this town, you weren't supposed to shout unless you were at a football game. I just hoped nobody told the Wentworths about my little outburst.

Daddy folded his hands on the table. "But that's fixing to change. I've filed for divorce."

I shut my eyes for a moment. I had just gotten a letter from my mother. She'd been writing steadily ever since I'd lost Jennifer. Most of her notes advised me to rebuild my reputation, so I could take Claude back to court and reclaim my baby. This most recent note was packed with motherly advice, and I'd been touched. "I'm so happy that you are gainfully employed," she'd written, "even if it's with Clancy. Just don't scream at the customers. One of them might be related to a judge. You never know who's related to who in Crystal Falls."

"Please don't rush into this, Daddy."

"Your mother has been in Central State for two years," he said. "I don't think she'll get better. And don't forget, she and I had stopped living together long before she went . . . well, long before she jumped off the Ben Franklin's roof. I have a right to be happy. That's why I'm taking the divorce papers to her this afternoon." Daddy patted his suit pocket. Then he rubbed the hand over his brow, messing up his eyebrows. They stuck up crazily, like cat fur licked the wrong way.

I lowered my head, trying to sort my feelings. Thinking of my mother's letter again, I got teary-eyed.

"Oh, sugar," Daddy said. "Please don't."

I wiped my face. "She'll be devastated."

"Where'd you learn a big, old word like that?" Daddy smiled.

"On *The Young and the Restless*," I started to say. Because it was true. One couldn't learn everything in a dictionary. Then I narrowed my eyes. "Stop trying to change the subject. Think about Mummy. She's counting on the two of you getting back together."

Daddy's eyes widened and he leaned forward. "She said that?"

"No, not exactly," I said, wiping my eyes again, "but you've visited her every single Sunday for the past few years. You haven't missed a day. Surely that means you still love her. That you care."

"I do care. I will always care about your mother—well, in my own, special way I'll care. But I care about June Rinehart, too. Sugar, I didn't mean to fall in love."

"Can't you fall out of it?"

Daddy looked at me a moment. "I want to marry June. Your mother may be ill, but she understands matters of the heart."

"No, she won't. Not in a thousand years."

"Give her some credit. Dorothy's not a stupid woman. And Bitsy, honey, just because I'm divorcing your mother and moving onward with my life, it doesn't mean that I'll stop being your father."

"I know." I gave a short, jerky nod, and a tear hit the table. "It's not me I'm worried about, it's Mummy. You're all she's got."

"No, I'm not."

"Yes, you are. You're her whole world!" I cried. Again, everyone in the café stopped talking. Even the cooks were peeking through the kitchen doors. Violet and Aunt Clancy stood next to the cash register, whispering; Zach stood next to a palm tree, his eyes bulging. Even though the café hadn't been open long, I knew most of the customers, and they knew me. Little Bitsy McDougal, they called me, failing to add my married name, Wentworth. Little Bitsy McDougal, her daddy owns the five-and-dime, and her mama had a breakdown. They knew all about Aunt Clancy, too, and the customers left off both of her married surnames—Jones and Falk. They also knew about her dalliance with my daddy and how she'd abandoned Violet and run off to California with her no-good hippie friend, Sunny. People still whispered about Aunt Clancy taking Byron away from his wife and squandering his money to open this café. Crystal Falls was a town that thrived on knowing the most intimate, embarrassing details of your life. Nothing was sacrosanct. (A word I had memorized from the dictionary last week.) Me, I liked to keep a low profile—it was my only chance of ever winning back my daughter. Now the whole town would buzz about the McDougals and their long-awaited divorce.

Daddy ran his hand over his hair. "No, honey," he said, "I never was her whole world. Not to be cruel, but neither were you. Dorothy worships the ground your brother walks on. *He* is her world."

"That's not true." I was tempted to show him her letter, to prove that she loved me. To prove that he could be wrong. But suddenly I felt so tired. I just didn't have the energy to fight him. I stood up, and Daddy reached out to grab my hand. I pulled away, and my hand went flying back, smacking firmly into the shoulder of a man at the next table. His arm cocked upward, and a spoonful of curried fruit shot into the air, hitting the neck of a chubby woman sitting across the room. She stood up, lifted a peach segment from her throat, and then began to shriek. Zach rushed over to the lady, offering his handkerchief.

"Let me get you dessert—on the house," Zach was saying, his New York accent as strangely out of place as his food.

"Well, I don't want this canned fruit," said the woman, taking the handkerchief. "But I might like to try the seven-layer lemon marzipan cake."

"I can fix you a dessert sampler." Zach's beautiful dark eyes opened wide.

"I'm thinking." The woman tapped her chin. "I wouldn't mind. But could you put it in a doggie bag?"

"Certainly." Zach stepped backward, shooting me a murderous glance.

"Now look what's happened," I cried to my father. "And I've been trying so hard to be good."

"Well, I'm sorry. But I just didn't think you'd react this way."

"How am I supposed to act, Daddy?"

He was silent. Then he said, "I've already asked June to be my wife."

"And I'll just bet she said 'yes.'"

He blushed. "Miss Rinehart is a good woman. She sings in the choir at the Garden of Prayer First Born Church of the Living God."

"Isn't that the church of choice for rednecks?"

"Don't be so judgmental."

"But you're marrying a gold-digging Christian. Violet says they're the worst kind. Because they know not what they do—not a speck of insight into their own behavior." I broke off, putting one hand over my eyes. My cousin really had said that; but coming from me, it didn't sound smart and witty. I sounded like a crackpot.

"She's not like that." He swallowed, and his Adam's apple clicked. I stared at his lips, wondering if he'd kissed June Rinehart, and if she'd ever rubbed up against him in the storeroom. The very idea of my daddy being a sexual person filled me with embarrassment. Daddies weren't supposed to act that way.

"I can't help who I love, sugar," he said.

My chin wove. Then I spun around and raced into the kitchen. The cooks watched in mute horror as I stripped off my big apron. Then I began to twirl it over my head, around and around, until the heavy white fabric made a snapping sound. When I let go, the ties hit the chains of the pot rack, setting it to swaying. The cooks released a collective gasp. I could just imagine them on the witness stand, giving testimony about my temper tantrum. No, Your Honor, she's too crazy to raise a child. Jennifer is better off with rich alcoholics and woman chasers.

"Shit," said one of the cooks. "She's gone berserk."

"Not yet," Violet said, leaning into the kitchen. She lifted one eyebrow like Lauren Bacall. "But she's close."

I pushed open the back door, letting in a wedge of sunlight. Then I stepped into the alley, trying not to gag on the stench of coffee grounds and cantaloupe rinds. I heard footsteps and whirled around. I thought it might be Violet, but it was Aunt Clancy. "Get your ass back inside," she yelled.

"No." I shook my head. "I quit."

"You can't quit." Clancy Jane laughed. "This is a family restaurant."

"I'm bad for business," I said.

"Maybe you just need a break. Hey, I know what. Why don't you and Violet go on an errand? You guys can take a caramel cake to my beloved's office."

"What's the occasion? Is it Byron's birthday?"

"No, I'm just being wifely." She shrugged, then laughed. "That's what he seems to want. So to keep the peace, I'll give him a piece. Think he'll appreciate it?"

. . .

Byron's receptionist cheerfully greeted me and Violet. "My, that looks delicious," she said, eyeing the cake as Violet lifted it out of the box. I walked to the end of the hall and turned into Byron's office. Framed photographs were lined up on the edge of the bookcase, hiding the medical texts. I ran my finger over pictures of Byron's daughters, three blue-eyed blondes—two with dimples, one with braces. They didn't live in Crystal Falls anymore; they lived in Michigan with their mother. Byron never saw them.

Violet came up behind me and picked up a picture of Clancy Jane. In the photo, her mother was wearing turquoise leather boots and a long sweater. Her legs were small but curvy. Another picture, taken in a Las Vegas wedding chapel, showed Clancy Jane laughing and Byron hugging her from behind. Clancy Jane wore bell-bottom jeans and a gauzy white blouse with embroidered flowers. She had daisies pinned in her hair. Byron was wearing a striped golf shirt and shorts, and his nose was sunburned.

"They look happy," I said.

"Well, they're not," said Violet. "Come on, let's get out of here."

We played hooky from the café and drove straight home. Violet got out of the car and flopped down in the hammock saying she was dying of thirst. She had grown up to be a natural beauty—high cheekbones, thick lashes that didn't require mascara, but she'd never cared about her appearance.

"Can you fix us something cool to drink?" she asked. Then without waiting for an answer, she said, "Go make us some frozen margaritas."

"But it's the middle of the afternoon," I cried. "I don't want to be like Miss Betty."

"She doesn't drink margaritas, does she? Stop looking at me that way;

I'm parched. Go inside and crush up the ice in the blender. And don't put in too many ice cubes or it'll be lumpy. Cut you a fresh lime. Then look in the bottom cupboard and get the Triple Sec and tequila. Don't forget to put salt on the glasses. Use the giant brandy snifters, okay? But rub the rims with the lime wedge and roll the rims into salt. Not just regular salt, but kosher or sea salt—"

"I *know* how to fix margaritas," I said over my shoulder, then hurried into the kitchen before she could think of another command. My cousin would've made a good director. Or else a four-star general. Aunt Clancy always said that Violet had been this way since the day she was born. Personally, I thought college had turned her into a know-it-all. She was just a year younger than me, but she seemed older. Still, I couldn't fault her, because she was right most of the time. And I was mostly wrong.

I dug the Waring blender out of the cabinet and then ground up the ice, just the way Violet had instructed. Lord God, if Miss Betty could see me now, I'd never get custody of my daughter. I couldn't find but one brandy snifter. I held it up to the light. Violet had won it at the county fair; it had been a fishbowl with a blue fish swimming inside it. The rim squeaked as I rubbed it with the lime, then I rolled it in kosher salt. As I poured in the thick brew, I wondered how someone like Miss Betty—a closet alcoholic—could be considered fit to raise my child. Even though Claude had sole custody, I knew for a fact that Jennifer lived with his parents. And I was just worried sick that they'd set their house on fire with a cigarette or something.

I squeezed my eyes shut, then shook my head. If only I could get control of my imagination and stop thinking of what could go wrong. Besides, if I had custody of Jennifer, there was no guarantee that I could keep her safe. Just look what I'd done in Point Minette. At least the Wentworths hadn't left her on top of a car. I walked carefully into the backyard, past the gazebo, toward the hammock. After I sat down, I passed the huge glass to Violet.

"Don't I get my own glass?" She pushed out her bottom lip, then reached for the glass. "Hey, do you have any germs?"

"Honey, what I've got isn't catching."

"Are you still upset over your daddy?" Violet tilted the glass toward her mouth and took a greedy gulp.

"Yes." I nodded. "But not for long. Hurry up and pass me that glass."

Violet wiped her mouth, then held out the snifter. "I'm sure it's hard for you to understand, but even old men like your daddy have urges."

"I don't even *want* to understand." I grabbed the snifter and took a swallow.

"It might not even be sexual." Violet stretched out, wiggling her toes. "Maybe Uncle Albert needs somebody to take care of him. That's how his generation thinks. They need caretakers, not lovers."

"I don't think my daddy has . . . well, a private part."

"Then how'd *you* get here?" Violet laughed and punched me with her foot. "Listen, maybe he just wanted a good Christian woman."

"My mother went to church every Sunday."

"Yes, she went, but her thoughts weren't with Jesus." Violet sat up and took back the margarita. "Maybe he thinks he can dominate a churchy girl."

"Then he must be a fool. Have you *ever* seen a man dominate a Christian woman?"

"Well, not unless he had a whip in his hand."

"My daddy would never do that."

"All he'd have to do is quote Ruth—your people are *my* people, etc." Violet laughed. "He couldn't do that with your mother. Aunt Dorothy wore the pants in your family, and don't try to deny it."

"But look what happened." I ducked my head, and a tear hit my hand.

"Jesus, don't go to pieces on me!" Violet leaned forward, sloshing her drink, and patted my arm. "Hey, I know what. Let's ditch these home-made margaritas and go barhopping."

"You know I can't do that."

"But this is an emergency. Uncle Albert is marrying a ninny."

Finally we decided it was too much trouble to get up and get dressed. We just sat there, sipping the rest of our margarita, the sky darkening around us. Fireflies appeared, their yellow lights winking on and off, and way off in the distance, I heard neighborhood children playing kick the can. Byron's MG roared up the driveway. He hurried into the house, not even glancing in our direction. A minute later, Aunt Clancy pulled up in her Volvo. She didn't see us, either. As she walked up the back steps, Byron opened the door. He drew Aunt Clancy into his arms, and she giggled like a young girl. A long time ago she'd had a drinking problem, but she'd gotten over it. The café had helped. It wasn't easy being married to a doctor. But, then again, it wasn't easy being a Hamilton woman.

"Look at them, all lovey-dovey. Maybe they'll tell their story to *Ladies Home Journal.*" Violet snorted. "A marriage saved by caramel cake. Isn't that the stupidest thing?"

I didn't want to argue, so I said, "Mmmhum." Then I leaned back in the hammock and made a mental note to get that recipe.

A LETTER FROM CENTRAL STATE

July???, 1973

Dear Bitsy,

    I don't know the exact date because the TV is broken in the day room and without my shows, all the days of my life just run together. Also, Albert brought me a book to read, Jaws, *and I got so enthralled that I lost track of everything. But I have come up with an idea. I want you to start writing letters to important people, explaining your plight over Jennifer. I have written the First Lady, and I am seriously thinking of writing Jeanne Dixon, just to see what's in store for you. Also, I think you should write letters to Jennifer so she can get to know you. It's probably not a good idea to mail them, as she's too little to understand what all happened and besides, Miss Betty will just throw them away. Or else she'll accuse you of harassment. This can happen. A friend of mine here at Central State got accused of doing this—she was in love with her gynecologist and bombarded him with letters and even tried to kill him, so now she's weaving baskets with me. But you just keep writing letters to your baby because someday she will want to know the truth. Well, I've got to run. Here comes the nurse. She's mad at me because of a little incident the other day. One of the inmates, a geezer-sicko-schizophrenic man, tried to feel my breasts. So I just stuck him with my number 2 pencil, and now the man's going around saying he's got lead poisoning. Well, the point did break off under his skin. But a woman has a right to defend herself. And she's got a right to write letters.*

    Love,
    Mummy

A LETTER FROM BITSY WENTWORTH

214 Dixie Avenue
Crystal Falls, Tennessee

July 15, 1973

Dear Jennifer,

    You are too young to read this letter, but one day you will have questions, and I might not be around to answer them. So, no matter what your grandmother Wentworth tells you, I did not *give you up without a fight. Your daddy and Miss Betty wanted to put me in jail, and at the time I didn't think I could fight them in court. Now, of course, I know different. I*

don't have the money to hire lawyers, but I'm trying everything within my power to get you back. This is all I'm living for. No matter what happens, I will always love you. And one day you will find your way back to me.
    Love always,
    Mother

ROWAN, VAN CLEAVE, HARLOW, AND GRIFFIN, PLLC
ATTORNEYS AT LAW

600 First Avenue
Crystal Falls, Tennessee
PERSONAL & CONFIDENTIAL

July 30, 1973

Lillian Beatrice "Bitsy" Wentworth
214 Dixie Avenue
Crystal Falls, Tennessee

Dear Ms. Wentworth:
    All letters to Mr. and Mrs. Claude E. Wentworth III, Mr. Claude E. Wentworth IV, and Jennifer Wentworth ("CLIENTS") must cease immediately. If the harassment of CLIENTS continues, further action will be required.

Sincerely yours,
Arthur P. Van Cleave III

cc: Mr. and Mrs. Claude E. Wentworth III
Mr. Claude E. Wentworth IV
Mrs. Dorothy H. McDougal
Mrs. Byron Falk

A TAPED MESSAGE TO PAT NIXON

Dorothy Hamilton McDougal
Central State Asylum, Nashville, Tennessee

August 1 or 2, 1973

Dear Pat,

The nurses won't let me use lead pencils anymore to write letters. Instead they gave me this recording machine, and they promised they'd send you a tape. They're not supposed to listen to it, either. I just pray they don't. Maybe they think I'll unravel the tape and hang myself—I am not their favorite person. But never mind that, enough about me, I just thought I'd drop a line to cheer you up, what with your poor husband on the news every day. One minute he's signing a $769 million thingamajig—something about the cultivation of weapons, which surely can't be like the cultivation of orchids. The next minute, he's telling people to take their subpoenas and stuff them— I guess he wishes he'd never heard the word Watergate. Sometimes I wish I hadn't, either, because the hearings cut into my stories on TV.

Since my last letter, which you failed to answer, I've been keeping up with World Events. I may be batty, but I'm not stupid. In fact, some very smart people have been insane. Even a place like Central State has newspapers and televisions—we also get PBS—so I know what's going on with you and Dick in Washington. My own husband, Albert, isn't a Republican, and he isn't a psychiatrist, either. He doesn't know the first thing about women, and still he's a skirt chaser, and now I am stuck in this asylum. He put me here by the power of his signature. It was terrible, Pat. I can't help but call you Pat—or would you prefer Patty?—because I feel like I know you, even though we've never met. I think we'd like each other. We both are under the control of powerful men. Dick's got the Republican party behind him—or he did— and my psychiatrists apparently have the entire TVA at their disposal. All that electricity just for my benefit.

I don't know if you get PBS in the White House, but if you do, try to catch a rerun of their show on cats. It told all about the common tom cat and how he can sire dozens of litters a night. To reach a receptive female, he will risk unchained dogs and six lanes of traffic. And she will wait for him in the gutter. But if she's in heat and another tom gets there first, she will lift her tail and squat. Meow, she'll cry. "Mewowow!" If a cat has these needs, why not Don Juan? Why not Albert? Are humans and animals so very different? Maybe we aren't. I don't know. And I don't ask.

The doctor asks me to look at the inkblot and tell what I see. I see a penis the size of a thumb. Or maybe it's a thumb the size of a penis. I don't know. It could even be a chicken. Cock-a-doodle-do! This, I don't say. It's not very nice and, besides, you can't say what you think, whether you're in an asylum or a beauty parlor.

So I stare at the inkblot. After a moment, I say, "I see a cute little bunny. And over there, I see a flower." I do not mention the bee in the flower, much less the thorns and aphids. I do not mention the bunny's manly parts. They drag behind him in the lettuce patch. That's quite a large ding-dong you've got there, Peter Rabbit. I'm not sure if boy rabbits even have manly parts. But I don't ask, and I do not wonder.

I suppose you're thinking, How crude! *Well, let me explain. I've lost more than my social graces in this nuthouse. But as soon as I'm free, I will get them back. In no time flat, I'll be pouring tea for the church ladies. That is one thing about the good Baptist women in Crystal Falls—they will be nice to me, even if they don't like me. Not because they fear the wrath of God, but because they don't want people talking about them, saying they aren't good Christians.*

Pat, I've got to break off here, because the nurse is coming straight for me. But it's been a pleasure chatting with you.

Your friend,
Dorothy McDougal

The nurse told Dorothy that Albert was waiting in the visitors' lounge. Then she added, "Isn't that wonderful, Dorothy? Come sit at the nice card table with your husband."

Dorothy sat down, folded her hands, and nodded at Albert. The sun fell in diamond patterns over her arms. "They might call this a card table," she told him, "but they won't give us any cards because of the sharp edges. We can't play gin rummy in this joint. One of us crazies might slit their throat with the ace of hearts."

Albert flinched. He had bags under his eyes, but not one gray hair on his head. Dorothy lifted her hand and patted her hair, wishing the asylum had a beauty parlor. Her hair had turned completely white from the shock of being here. Maybe she could persuade Albert to smuggle in a bottle of Fanciful rinse.

"Hello, Dorothy," Albert said. "You're looking . . ." He broke off, as if searching for the right word. "Peaceful," he finally said. Then he reached into his jacket and pulled out a long blue folder. Dorothy thought it looked like what the AAA sends before you go on a trip. But on the front it said: Attorney at Law. Two things sprang to Dorothy's mind. One, he's hired a lawyer to get her discharged from this stinkhole asylum. Two, he's hired a lawyer to make sure she never got out. From the pained expression on his face, she figured it was the latter. Her first impulse was to jump on him, tearing his hair out by the roots, but she knew behavior like that would just get her sent to hydrotherapy or E.C.T. In a bughouse, you can't talk loud or do anything that will draw attention to yourself. A low profile is best on the mental ward.

"I know what you're up to, and you won't get away with it," she said softly, but she made a fist to let him know she meant business. "Why, I'll escape from this place. And I'll hunt you down. There's no place on earth where you can hide."

"Do what, honey?" Albert's hand jerked away from the blue folder as if it had stung him. One of the nurses glanced up from a chart she was writing on. Dorothy fixed her mouth into a smile. The nurse went back to writing. Albert looked distraught, more like the inmate. He kept running one hand through his hair.

"We haven't had a real marriage for seven years," he said, with a pinched look.

Dorothy's voice was pure ice, but she kept on smiling. "Don't give me that crap," she hissed. "What does our marriage have to do with my incarceration?"

Perspiration slid down Albert's forehead, and his cheeks turned slightly green, like he was on the verge of throwing up. Dorothy wondered fleetingly what the man had been eating without her to cook for him.

"When did you get this cruel?" Tears sprang into her eyes, but she quickly brushed them away.

"Sugar—"

"Don't you call me that!" Then she lowered her voice. "If this isn't cruel, wanting to commit me forever, then I don't know what the word means. I've been good. I've tried hard to get well. You signed papers on me once, and I forgave you; but I will never let you do it again."

"Wait a minute. Commit you? Where, sugar?" His jaw sagged, and his eyes blinked wide open.

"Here!" she cried, and the nurse looked up again. Dorothy gave her a big smile and folded her hands under her chin.

"Why, why . . ." Albert's lips parted.

"Close your mouth," Dorothy snapped. "You look just like a goldfish. A big, fat ugly one." And he did, she thought. He looked exactly like those fish he used to sell at the dime store, the transparent kind where you can see the doody inside, all coiled up like a watch spring.

"I'm confused." He rubbed the top of his head.

"As usual." Dorothy rolled her eyes.

"Calm down, Dorothy."

"I *am* calm."

"What's this about commitment?"

"It's what you're trying to pull." She glanced at his jacket, the ruffled papers peeking out.

"You've got it wrong, Dorothy. These papers in my pocket don't have a thing to do with keeping you here."

"No?"

"Absolutely not." He pulled out the blue papers and pushed them into her hands, and repeated that he wasn't trying to pull anything over on anyone. "I'm not trying to keep you caged. These are only divorce papers."

Only? Dorothy's throat tightened. She couldn't say the word, much less think it. I'll have to sing it, she thought, like Tammy Wynette *(d-i-v-o-r-c-e)*. "I'm going to faint," she cried to Albert, weaving back and forth. One thing she'd learned at Central State—if you act dizzy, like maybe your inner ear is acting up, the nurses will leave you alone. But it never fails to draw a man. She rose and veered to the left, and Albert's arms swung open, Johnny-on-the-spot, catching her as she pretended to fall.

Bitsy

Toward the end of summer, I began studying the L words in my dictionary, but when I got to "love," I skipped over it. I no longer knew what that word meant, you see. My daddy was in Mexico for a quicky divorce. My mother, in a rare lucid moment, told him to "go with God," and to just get out of her hair and into somebody else's. I drove up to the asylum to visit her, and while I was gone Aunt Clancy went to the Utopian Salon. She heard the ladies talking about Miss Betty, who was also a client. It seemed all she did was bad-mouth Jennifer's babysitters. She had gone through twenty-five women. Claude lived in their backyard—well, the pool house—but he wasn't involved with Jennifer at all, which didn't surprise me. Now the Wentworths were having trouble finding somebody who'd give up their lives and work twenty-four hours a day at minimum wage. Miss Betty had been forced to bring Jennifer to the salon. My baby was twenty months old—on the cusp of the so-called terrible twos. Aunt Clancy said the beauticians couldn't stop talking about what a spectacle it was. No one was allowed to reprimand her, and she ran around wild, eating anything she wanted from the candy machine, then slept when and where she pleased. It breaks my heart to think about how carefully I followed all Dr. Spock's rules.

The ladies also said that Miss Betty complained to anyone who'd listen that she was having to miss her bridge parties and soirees, and Chick couldn't play golf. Anyway, that was probably why they broke down and asked if Jennifer could stay with me. They were that desperate for a sitter. It was just for the afternoon, and when Miss Betty called, she stipulated (I knew I'd be able to use that word) that someone had to supervise me. Byron and Aunt Clancy said they would. I was desperate to bond with my child, but I didn't know where to start. I hadn't seen my daughter since that day in Mississippi. Not that I hadn't tried. Every day I drove past the Wentworths' house, but their yard was always immaculate and empty. There was no sign that a child lived there.

When Claude's father showed up at 214 Dixie, he was holding Jennifer in his arms. I restrained myself from rushing over and scooping her into my arms. So I just stood in the hall with Byron and Aunt Clancy. Jennifer was wearing pink coveralls and a tiny gold bracelet with a heart. She regarded me silently, a pacifier bobbing up and down in her mouth. She flashed me a disdainful look then buried her face in Chick's golf shirt. One small hand reached up and dislodged his white hat, which had Crystal Falls Golf & Country Club printed across the front.

Still holding the baby, Chick exchanged pleasantries with Byron, but refused to make eye contact with me or Aunt Clancy. Then he set Jennifer on the floor and headed out the door, promising to return in several hours. When the door slammed, Jennifer threw herself against it and began to screech. Two hours later, she was still hysterical. Aunt Clancy and I tried everything. We had desperately pulled out Violet's old Golden Books, and tried to read to her, but Jennifer tore the pages. Then she pushed the books aside, ran to the front door, and beat on the screen. "Papa," she wailed, her eyes on the empty street.

I raced into the kitchen, poured apple juice into a plastic sippy cup, then hurried back to the living room and offered the cup to my daughter.

"No!" Jennifer screwed up her face and slapped the cup from my hand, sending a comma of juice into the air.

"Ka-ka," screamed Jennifer. Then she grabbed her own hair and began tearing it from the roots just the way my mother used to do.

"Next it'll be her eyebrows," said Clancy Jane.

FROM THE DESK OF CLANCY JANE FALK

August 21, 1973

Dear Violet,

    I have tried to phone your dorm, but your roommate always says you're at the library. I know you've only been gone a week, but I miss you like crazy. Plus, the visits with Jennifer aren't going well. The moment Chick drops her off, she scoots under the sofa and hides until she hears his car pull into the driveway; then her round head pops out from the ruffled sofa skirt, the ever-

present pacifier stuck in her mouth, and she crawls out and runs to the door to fling herself at her grandfather.

Bitsy went to Albert's dime store, hoping to put some toys on layaway, but was told that Miss Betty had bought nearly every doll and Fisher-Price toy on the market. Since Jennifer will turn two on December 31, Byron thinks she's old enough to learn about nature. I do not mean the birds and the bees, but a gift that money can't buy, like the names of trees and birds and flowers. He said to think of it as intellectual training to combat the upbringing she's getting over at Miss Betty's. This is sad but true. That woman will try her best to turn Jennifer into a spoiled little WASP. Today, for instance, the baby showed up wearing an 18-karat gold bracelet, tiny diamond studs in her ears, and a child-size colorful Pucci outfit. I'm not kidding. Bitsy said that Mrs. Wentworth had probably paid her seamstress to turn all of her old dresses into jumpers and blouses for the baby.

Bitsy gets so angry about stuff like that. But she's lucky that the Wentworths are allowing these visits. Of course, they are just using her/us as babysitters, but it's a start. I am keeping a record of these visits to show the court how reliable we are when and if we take Claude to court. But I have to watch Bitsy. The other day she tried to accidentally-on-purpose spill grape juice on that Pucci. Bitsy is too impulsive, her own worst enemy. Byron says she's just immature for her age. And youth must be forgiven. Who knows? She might overcome her genetics—even though her parents are the King and Queen of Bad Judgment. But Bitsy has a smidgen of Miss Gussie in her. There's a chance that she will grow into a strong, interesting woman. Every now and then I see a glimmer of intelligence in her eyes. Of course, it could just be a reflection. She could very well end up selling Avon door-to-door. Although Mary Kay is more her style. Can't you just see her stepping out of a pink car, carrying a pink case, knocking on doors and doing makeovers, spreading skin creams and silliness wherever she goes? Well, somebody has to do it. Maybe she'll give us a discount.

Love,
Mama

Clancy Jane

Jennifer's visits were sporadic and revolved around the Wentworths' social calendar. One weekend, Chick brought the baby to Clancy Jane's house and mentioned that he had a golf game, and that Betty was playing bridge. "Take your time," said Clancy Jane, leading him to the front door. She and Bitsy had read up about nature at the library, and they couldn't wait to start showing things to the baby. They coaxed Jennifer into the yard, but when they started to put her into the stroller, she balled up her fists and began pummeling them. When they finally got her inserted, they walked at a brisk pace, which forced the baby to cling to the stroller's plastic tray, her blond hair floating in the breeze. After a while, Clancy Jane began to point out cloud formations, but Jennifer just pulled out a hunk of her own hair. They fast-walked around the block, then Clancy Jane started identifying birds, but when she looked down, Jennifer had fallen asleep. Bitsy suggested they give up on nature and just teach her the names of fingernail polish. They could use the colorful bottles lined up on Bitsy's dresser: "Cotton Candy," "Pomegranate," "Grape Kiss."

Bitsy couldn't name the presidents in order, but she knew the name and manufacturer of every lipstick and eyeshadow at Rexall Drugs as well as every shampoo and conditioner on the market. Not only that, she held definite prejudices. Prell was for boys, Suave was for penny-pinchers, and Breck was for babies. So it was no surprise that some people found her to be shallow and superficial. But she was also smart. She couldn't help being what she was—a mixture of Albert and Dorothy. Those bad genes were powerful and lasting—Byron compared it to skunk spray. When he said that, Clancy Jane just laughed, but it wasn't until later when she realized that he'd been referring to own her genes, too.

A LETTER FROM CENTRAL STATE

August 31, 1973

Dear Witch Betty,

Bitsy drove up to visit me today, and she's doing just fine and dandy, thank you very much. She happened to mention that her and Claude's divorce is final today. Guess whose else is, too? No, not mine and Albert's but Elvis and Priscilla's. I know this because I read it in the newspaper. It sure is funny that a famous man like him didn't try and keep Lisa Marie. He let Priscilla have her because children need their mothers. It's been a whole year since you stole my grandbaby. I'm keeping track. Don't be surprised if you get a letter of complaint from the White House.

Dorothy

Bitsy

Monday morning, on my way to work, I stopped in front of Marshall's Department Store and gazed into the display window. Miss Betty thought the store was tacky, but it was the only place in town that sold sandalfoot pantyhose. Also the Marshalls banked with the Wentworths, so Miss Betty was forced to buy coats, sweaters, and dresses there, which she promptly gave to her maids. She wouldn't be caught dead wearing anything but cashmere. But I thought Marshall's had gorgeous clothes and accessories, even though I could only afford to window-shop. To tell the truth, I was much more interested in pocketbooks than men. My heart was still frozen solid. I was pretty sure that I'd never find someone who'd love me, after all I'd done. But a pocketbook didn't care about my past. Especially if I bought it for someone else.

In the right side of the display, I saw a cute decoupaged purse with a wooden lid and a tiny gold clasp. The base, woven like a picnic basket, was painted to resemble a town. In black paint, the artist had printed *Strawberry Fields* on a street sign, *Norwegian Wood* on another. A church was called St. Paul's. Except for the Beatles references, I didn't know where this place was, or if it even existed. A discreet card showed the price: $59.99—a small fortune. The layaway policy at Marshall's was tougher than at any other store in town—they made you put down at least ten dollars, and I had only enough money for lunch. I could of course get free meals at the café, but I couldn't stomach the food. I knew that my aunt would adore this purse—the Beatles had disbanded three years ago, but she regularly played their old albums. Her favorite song in the world was "Strawberry Fields Forever." Her birthday had just passed, but this purse would make a great Christmas present.

So I decided I'd skip lunch. I marched inside and asked Mrs. Marshall if a five-dollar deposit would hold that purse. She shook her head and said, "Sorry, it's against store policy." Then she narrowed her eyes at me. "Besides, what do *you* need with a fine purse like that?"

"It's not for me," I explained, feeling my cheeks hotten up. I wondered if she was being hateful because of Miss Betty, or because she was just having a bad day. I went back to the café and drank a cup of coffee, stashing my lunch money in my pocket. I figured I'd have enough money for a down payment in two weeks.

Every day when I finished my shift, I paused by Marshall's window just to look at that purse. Sometimes I looked at it twice a day. I skipped lunch for two weeks, and when I'd saved twenty dollars—more than enough for a down payment—I hurried over to Marshall's. But the purse was gone. In its place was a half-dressed mannequin, wearing an Ali McGraw crocheted hat. Mrs. Marshall appeared in the window holding a fringed shawl and began draping it over the mannequin's torso. She glanced up at me and frowned. Hoping that it hadn't sold, I went inside and asked about the purse, explaining that I was prepared to put down a substantial cash deposit. "Sorry, but that purse was bought this morning. It was a one-of-a-kind," she said. "I've got one on order showing the streets and landmarks of Crystal Falls. How much can you put down?"

"I'll pass." I shook my head and thanked her, trying to hide my disappointment. A week later, I was sitting in Aunt Clancy's kitchen reading the *Democrat*. And I saw the Beatles purse on page six, dangling from the arm of Mrs. Cora Smith, a home economics teacher who was retiring that year due to Parkinson's disease. The home-ec students at Crystal Falls High had pooled their money and bought their teacher that pocketbook. Mrs. Smith was holding up the bag, a proud smile on her face. I smiled back at her.

· · ·

The next time Chick dropped Jennifer off—I believe he was playing in a golf tournament and Miss Betty was having a bridge party at her house—I took her into Aunt Clancy's garden. It was a lush, magical place, a hodgepodge of vegetables, herbs, and flowers. My aunt was off to the side, blending a mixture of smashed eggshells and dried blood, which she worked into the soil. She always said that her zucchini and tomatoes were so huge because they dined on animal matter. For blue hydrangeas, she hammered rusty nails under each plant. She left the pink ones alone. "My girls and boys," she called them. The garden was a good place for a child. While Jennifer picked an okra pod, I wove a story about Mother Nature, how she sent the sun and rain, helping the little vegetables grow. Jennifer didn't seem to understand. "Mama Wen'wurf," she said, holding out the okra.

"No, I'm your mama," I said. "Can you say mama?"

Jennifer violently shook her head. I leaned down to kiss the child—her hair smelled of sunlight and shampoo—the Wentworths weren't using Breck. Jennifer wiggled away and reached for an ear of corn. Her small hands closed on the shuck and she pulled it down, exposing rough, curly silk, and the delicate kernels, each one aligned tightly but imperfectly.

"Ewww," she said, pointing. I hunkered down and hugged her, but she shoved me away. Aunt Clancy's orange Persian darted out of a forsythia bush and scampered into the garden. When Pitty Pat saw me, he loped through the tomatoes, past the corn, over to me and rubbed against my legs. I scooped up the cat and cradled him.

"At least you love me," I told Pitty, then I felt foolish for talking to a cat and put him down. Across the garden, Aunt Clancy's head popped up.

"Don't be embarrassed," she called. "I talk to Pitty all the time. I call it chatting up the cat. He's a very good listener, you know. Better than husbands and daughters. Better than God. So keep on talking."

You are Cordially Invited
to Share in the Christ Sanctioned Nuptial Bliss of
Miss June Mae Rinehart
and
Mr. Albert Franklin McDougal
September 22, 1973, at two o'clock in the afternoon
Garden of Prayer First Born Church of the Living God
Old Nashville Highway
Crystal Falls, Tennessee
Reception Immediately Following,
Jesus Is Lord Reception Hall

"What is 'Christ sanctioned nuptial bliss'?" I asked Aunt Clancy, holding out the invitation.

"I don't know, and I hope I never find out," she said. She walked out into the backyard and began picking up green walnuts that had fallen around the gazebo. It was early September, and the days were getting shorter. But they still felt summery, all hot and hazy at the edges, without a hint that cooler weather lay ahead. The combination of the heat with Mother and Daddy's Mexican divorce had put me on edge.

I walked next door and found my brother in his kitchen, surrounded by pieces of paper—when he'd opened the invitation, he'd ripped it in half, then tore each half into teeny pieces. When he saw me, he ran one hand through his wavy blond hair. It was shoulder-length and he wore it loose. If you didn't know he was an ex-Marine, you'd never guess.

"Our daddy is a bastard," he said. His wife, Earlene, appeared in the doorway, wearing tight jeans and a halter top. She held a tube of lipstick and applied it without even glancing into a mirror. She'd stolen my brother from his Vietnamese wife, Sloopy, and his son, Christopher. They were living in California near her relatives. Earlene patted her cottony hair and struck a pose, holding the lipstick like a weapon. I knew for a fact that she flirted with Mack's crew when she thought he wasn't looking.

"What's that's mess?" She frowned at the shredded paper.

"My daddy's getting married," said Mack.

"Boy, he don't waste no time." Earlene rolled her eyes, then she sidled up to Mack and slid her fingers under his T-shirt. "I'd hate to be the one to tell your mama."

• • •

When Violet came home from Knoxville that evening, Aunt Clancy and I were in the kitchen, canning tomato-and-walnut chutney. Ball jars and lids were scattered along the counter. Steam floated over the black-speckled kettles. On top of the refrigerator, the little radio was tuned to NPR, and the announcer was giving a preview of upcoming selections. A minute later, the comforting sound of Debussy filled the room. Violet set down her suitcase and looked at the cork bulletin board. She squinted at the invitation. It was little more than a mimeographed sheet, blotched with purple ink.

Violet pursed her lips. "That's a hell of a name for a church. Obviously Miss June belongs to a cult."

"No, it's just one of those off-brand religions," I said, lifting the pot lid. Steam drifted up, clouding my vision for a moment.

"Are you going to boycott the grand event?" Violet asked me.

"I'd like to, but it wouldn't be right." I replaced the lid and walked over to the cork board. I reached for the mimeographed paper, then I smoothed my hands over it.

"Right?" Violet's mouth opened wide, revealing silver fillings in her jaw teeth. "Who cares about right?"

Aunt Clancy reached for her tongs, then held them aloft, as if she was getting ready to pinch somebody.

"I could never figure out your father." She waved the tongs. "He always seemed so . . ."

"Pussified?" Violet said helpfully.

"Exactly," said Aunt Clancy. She lowered the tongs and went back to fishing out the jars. "But it's always those silent, cowardly types who do the cruelest things," she added. "Serving papers to an institutionalized woman is about as low as a man can go."

"The quicky divorce was worse," I said and moved back to the stove.

"Is that even legal?" Violet yawned. "So you're definitely going to go?"

"Of course." I wiped my hands on my apron, leaving a curved red stain. "He's my daddy, no matter if he's marrying a weirdo."

"Well, I've seen her," said Aunt Clancy. "But I wouldn't call her a weirdo, she's just old-fashioned-looking."

"Uncle Albert always *did* have a tendency to select peculiar women," said Violet.

"I hope you're not including me in his harem," said Aunt Clancy, laying down the tongs.

"Why not?" Violet shrugged. "You were."

"For two seconds." Aunt Clancy laughed. "If that long."

"And here we are, six years later, still feeling the repercussions." Violet sighed. She picked up a tomato and balanced it on her palm.

"I wonder if my mother even remembers about you and Daddy," I said.

"It's hard to say what Aunt Dorothy remembers," said Violet, frowning at the tomato.

"It's those shock treatments. They wiped out her memory. Did you know the electrical impulses actually cause convulsions?" Clancy Jane's eyes widened.

I gazed back at her. Even though she was thirty-five years old—practically middle-aged—sometimes she looked young, with her small, turned-up nose and pouty lips. Her hair, which was freshly dyed by yours truly, was pinned into a loose bun, with a few tendrils hanging down. She wore blue granny glasses, which hid her beautiful eyes.

"Did I ever tell you about the girl I saw having convulsions?" Aunt Clancy asked me. "She was a little hippie girl on the Haight. She got hold of some bad acid. It happened in front of a head shop—her hands bent at the wrists, jerking under her chin, her eyes rolled back to the white. Her bladder let go and she peed on herself. A big puddle spread over the sidewalk."

"What happened to her?" I asked.

"I don't know. An ambulance took her away, and I never saw her again."

"Aunt Clancy, did you ever take acid?"

"You don't need to know every little thing I've done." Aunt Clancy smiled. Then she looked at her daughter. "Even Violet doesn't know everything."

Violet snorted.

"I'm famished." Aunt Clancy opened a cabinet. "Where did I put the Cheese Nips?"

"Stop changing the subject," said Violet.

"I will, if somebody'll change the radio station." Aunt Clancy wrinkled her nose.

"But it's Debussy," I said.

At this, Violet perked up. "You sure about that?"

"Yes." I nodded.

"And may I ask *how* you know?"

"The disc jockey just said it. You weren't listening."

"WPLN has disc jockeys?"

"Quit needling me. I'm just trying to improve myself."

"If you're looking for self-improvement, sweetie," said Aunt Clancy, "it'll take more than Debussy."

"I comprehend that," I said, happy that I'd slipped in a three-syllable C-word.

Aunt Clancy gave Violet a sly look. "She's memorizing words from your big, old *Webster's* now. Last week it was Cs. This week she's doing the Ps."

"What's today's word?" Violet smiled. "Prima donna? Princess?"

"Priapism," I said. Then I stuck out my tongue. "You don't really know me at all."

• • •

The church stood at the end of a country road. I parked my car and got out, listening to the cicadas shrilling from the weeds. *Run, Albert*, they seemed to be yelling. *It's not too late!* The church itself faced a weedy lot with a NO DUMPING sign nailed to a tree, but the order had been ignored. It was littered with a burned-up stove and a shredded La-Z-Boy recliner, the stuffing frothing out of the back. The sun glimmered on broken beer bottles, and a squalid smell rose up from a rusty metal canister. I wondered if my daddy was too smitten with June to notice the squalor.

I stepped toward the church, carrying a wedding gift in the crook of my arm. I had bought it at the hippie craft store on Constitution Street, a blue pottery bowl with dolphins swimming in a circle. It was signed on the bottom by a local artist. Violet said it was too bad I hadn't found a bowl with an old decrepit man standing next to a Jesus freak blonde. Mack hadn't bought our daddy a present. He was staying home with Earlene, watching a football game on TV.

The church was decorated with green balloons and streamers. I picked my way through them, following an old woman up the rickety steps. What this church needed was a Christian sugar daddy. Someone like Albert McDougal, ready to shower money on his bride's pet projects, such as whitewash and functional windows.

Inside, the heat was almost visible, causing distant objects, like the plastic cross over the altar, to wave and shimmer. Green crepe paper bows adorned every pew, and long curly strands hung from the ceiling. From the altar several dozen candles flickered, giving off a chemical stink. I breathed in the sickening odors of citronella, perfume, and perspiration. A baby wailed, but its mother made no effort to soothe it. A woman with crimped black hair took my gift, then gingerly set it on a table that was already sagging with packages. An usher with a ducktail hairdo popped out of a corner and offered his arm. "Bride's side or the groom's?" he asked.

The bride's side was overflowing, and I suspected that more than a few out-of-towners had been slipped into the groom's pews. As the usher led me down the aisle, I didn't recognize anyone except for Mr. Noonan from the Lion's Club. The back of his neck was wreathed in sweat, beads of perspiration trapped in the webs and wrinkles, seeping into his collar. Everyone looked somber, as if they were waiting for a tetanus shot rather than a wedding. Finally a chubby pianist in a wide green hat emerged from a side door. She sat down on the spindly bench, making the wood creak. Her fat fingers stabbed against the ivory keys and she began playing a clumsy version of "Promise Me." I thought of my first wedding to Claude. Big, fancy weddings didn't mean a thing, they just wasted money. If I ever fell in love again—and I didn't plan on it—I would elope.

Daddy emerged from a door and he took his place in front of the altar. He was joined by his best man, who bore a strong resemblance to June Rinehart: the same prominent teeth and wide-set, bugged eyes and fuzzy blond hair. I wondered if he was June's brother. Daddy and the man wore matching green suits, with green carnations pinned to their lapels.

The processional took an eternity: seven bridesmaids in kelly green gowns, clutching Bibles rather than bouquets; seven groomsmen, looking uncomfortable in their pale green polyester suits, which bore the telltale marks of Rit Dye. Next came a little redheaded ring bearer, dressed up like an elf. He seemed to be stricken with stage fright. His embarrassed mother got up and dragged the poor child up the aisle. The flower girl suffered from no such affliction. She had long black sausage curls and they bobbed up and down as she turned cartwheels down the aisle, spilling daisies and showing off emerald ruffled pantaloons. Finally an elderly couple, presumably the bride's grandparents, lurched down the aisle, clutching his 'n' her walkers. They were followed by the mother of the bride, who, escorted by an usher, waddled up to the front in an ice-green chiffon muumuu, which also looked homemade. A corsage was pinned to her dress. She was a tall, muscular woman, built like an armored tank, and the wooden floor groaned beneath her large feet.

Daddy turned, his eyes trained on the back of the church. His bride stood at the end of the aisle on the arm of her daddy, a bowlegged man with a tuft of white hair and black eyeglasses. As the music played, the duo lurched forward. June's gown stirred up the daisies. Her dress was pretty, ivory silk-satin with a high virginal neckline. Behind the tulle veil, I caught a glimpse of June's own black-framed glasses and little scrunched-up nose. The pianist stepped up her rhythm, and June moved a bit faster, as if towing her father. She had the air of a missionary eagerly striding on her way to the Amazon. Halfway to the altar, her heel snagged on her veil and she stumbled forward, a blur of high heels and tulle. She screamed, and her old daddy skittered left and sat down hard in a teenaged girl's lap. The piano music abruptly stopped. A collective gasp rose from the guests. The teenager pushed June's daddy out of her lap. The bride was lying motionless in the aisle. Then she lifted her head, her eyeglasses and veil askew. Daddy and the best man hurried to untangle the bride from her netting. Several teenage boys hopped up, offering their assistance. By the time they'd seated June's father with her mother, the bride was back on her feet. She took Daddy's arm, and the music started.

I was half-expecting the preacher to speak in tongues, or at the very least produce a live rattlesnake; but he cracked open a worn Bible and began to read from I Corinthians. In the background, the baby cried hysterically, but the preacher persevered, raising his voice. The baby wailed louder, then there was a muffled sound—a gloved hand striking bare flesh. The baby's cries broke off, replaced with a shuddering gasp. A second later the baby let out a blood-curdling scream. A young woman rose from the pew, clutching the squalling infant. She hurried into the aisle and ran out of the church. The cries faded, then ceased.

"You may kiss your bride," said the preacher. Daddy lifted June's veil and kissed her, nothing long and lingering, just a peck. The preacher cleared his throat and lifted his hands.

"Ladies and gentlemen," he said, turning the couple around, "may I present Mr. and Mrs. Albert McDougal!"

The reception took place in a stuffy building next door. On a wooden plaque, Jesus Is Our Savior was spelled out in silver glitter. There wasn't any real food, only mints, cake, and punch, all of it tinted in lurid shades of green. The church ladies doled out these refreshments assembly-line fashion. The lukewarm punch, ginger ale mixed with a block of lime sherbet, was sickly sweet. I could manage only a bit of icing. I set down my cup and plate, then worked my way to the end of the reception line, listening to snatches of conversation.

"What a precious wedding," said the pianist, straightening her enormous green hat.

"And that adorable flower girl!" exclaimed a lady with red hair and blue eyes.

Daddy spotted me at the tail end of the receiving line and stepped away from June, strode forward, and gave me an awkward hug. He smelled of mothballs and sweat, mingled with Old Spice cologne. "I'm so glad you came. I just wish you could've brought little Jennifer."

"The Wentworths won't let her ride in a car with me."

"Well, that's understandable." Daddy's shoulders sagged.

"It's what?" I squinted, wondering if I'd heard him correctly. If my own daddy thought I was a bad mother, then maybe I was. Maybe it was time for me to just give up and be satisfied with my life.

"Are you happy with your waitressing job?" he asked suddenly.

"You're changing the subject," I said. "But yes, I like working at the café. Aunt Clancy's a great boss."

"I'm sure she is." He smoothed back his hair. "Listen, honey, I've got something to say. I won't be seeing you for a while."

"Well, I guess not." I smiled up at him. "You're going on your honeymoon."

"Yes, we're going to Ruby Falls and Rock City. But that's not what I meant." He swallowed, and his bow-tie bobbed ever so slightly. "See, Junie and I are moving."

"Where to?"

"We're leaving Crystal Falls. I'm closing the dime store."

I just stared, shaking my head back and forth.

"That old Ben Franklin store just isn't making any money. So me and Junie are opening a dish barn on the outskirts of Gatlinburg. We might even sell souvenirs. Junie thinks we should."

"But . . . what about me and Mack?"

"Sugar, you know I love you and your brother. But sometimes a man's got to make drastic changes."

I kept on staring at him, trying to absorb the information. With Daddy in Gatlinburg and Mummy in the asylum, I was practically an orphan. "Well, this is drastic, all right," I finally said. "Does Mack know you're leaving?"

Daddy shook his head, looking down at me from the shadow of his eyebrows. "I was going to tell him, but he's not here. I was hoping you'd tell him."

"That's your job."

"Well, I guess so." Daddy rubbed the back of his neck. He looked old, with deep lines radiating from his eyes. Loose flesh hung in folds below his jaw.

"Oh, Bitsy. Don't look so sad, honey. It's not the end of the world. I'm not moving clear across the country. I'll only be a few hours away. And it's not like you're a little girl anymore. You're grown. And you'll be fine. Won't you?"

I gaped up at him. The question he'd just posed was imponderable. "Yes, I'll be fine," I said because that was what he wanted to hear. I reached down and took his hand, then I brought it up to my cheek. "I'm going to miss you, Daddy."

"I'll miss you, too, sugarplum." He glanced over his shoulder. From the reception line, June was frantically waving at him. He bent over and kissed me on the cheek, then he hurried off to join his bride.

Bitsy and Violet

Daddy's marriage left me with unstoppable hiccups. They began two nights after the wedding, awakening me from a fitful dream involving green bridesmaids with bell-pepper faces and string-bean-like fingers. At dawn the hiccups escalated, and I kept hitting my chest with my fist, struggling to breathe. To make matters worse, an unseasonable heatwave had settled over the mountains, and the temperature was edging into the mid-nineties. I couldn't eat or sleep; I could only converse in one-word sentences and desperate gestures.

In the middle of the fourth night, the hiccups made me pee the bed. I needed to take a bath, but I was afraid of waking up Byron and Aunt Clancy, so I crept down the hall to the bathroom and shut the door. Then I perched on the edge of the claw-foot tub, turning on the faucet, just a trickle. The door creaked open, and Aunt Clancy stuck in her head.

"Hey, you all right?" She yawned.

I started to tell her what happened, but a great big bullfrog croak popped out of my mouth. So I just shook my head and pointed to the soiled gown. As my aunt took in my wet spots, three wrinkles appeared on her forehead. "This is alarming," she said. "What if you can't stop hiccupping?"

"She will," said Byron, walking up behind his wife, yawning and rubbing his eyes.

"Maybe yoga will help," suggested Aunt Clancy.

"It's two o'clock in the morning," called Byron.

She ignored him and grabbed my hands and pulled me away from the tub, into the living room. We tried sun salutation and downward facing dog. But it didn't help. Finally she gave up and went into the kitchen to make tea. I took a hot bath.

Hours later I was still hiccupping when Mack and Earlene stopped by with a box of chocolate doughnuts. "Put sugar on your tongue," Earlene suggested, holding out a doughnut.

"Or let me frighten you," said Mack. "A bad scare's supposed to cure the hiccups."

"Forget those old wives' tales," said Byron, biting into a doughnut.

"Have you got a better solution?" Aunt Clancy asked.

"A Thorazine injection," Byron suggested, licking his thumb.

"But . . . isn't that the same medicine my sister gets at Central State?" Aunt Clancy asked.

"Yes, but it will stop intractable hiccups." Byron shrugged. "One shot probably won't hurt her."

"But it could?" asked my brother.

"Everything has risks, even hiccups." He reached for another doughnut. "I think Pope Pius got them and died."

"You're just full of good news," said Aunt Clancy.

• • •

By the time Violet drove up for the weekend, I'd been hiccupping for six straight days. She stepped into the kitchen and gasped when she saw my face. "Dear Lord, what's happened to you?" *Me,* I thought. *What about you?* Violet's hair was piled on top of her head, pinned into an elegant brown bun. She was rail thin, and with her large, dark eyes, she reminded me of Audrey Hepburn in *Breakfast at Tiffany's.*

I answered with a three-syllable squeak.

"She's got intractable hiccups," said Byron. He stood at the counter, going through the mail. He looked up as Aunt Clancy stepped into the kitchen. She ran one hand through her hair—she'd just dyed it ash blond—then she leaned up and kissed his forehead. Even though it was officially fall, she wore a summery red ruffled skirt and a white off-the-shoulder Mexican blouse. On her neck was a choker—silver crosses and jet beads made from old rosaries. Courtesy of yours truly, her toenails were freshly painted, Revlon's Raspberry Kiss. It had taken forever, because my hands were so unsteady.

"I know a cure," Violet said, blinking at her mother's nails. "Alcohol, consumed in vast quantities."

"What's with the hairdo?" Aunt Clancy squinted at Violet.

"She looks like Holly Golightly," I said, talking fast. The idea was to squeeze in as many words as possible in between the hiccups.

"This?" Violet dismissed the bun with a flip of her hand. "One of the giggly girls in my dorm was going to a fraternity dance, so she used my hair for practice."

"Oh, well that explains it," said Aunt Clancy. "I mean, it's not like you to doll up."

"No," Violet said. "It's not."

Mother and daughter stared. Clancy Jane was the first to look away. After a moment, she turned to Byron. "Honey, tell the truth. Will alcohol help Bitsy?"

"Look at it this way," he said, "even if it doesn't cure her condition, she'll be too drunk to care."

"Let's go," Violet said, grabbing my arm.

"Violet, you just *got* here," Clancy Jane cried. "And later *Sonny and Cher* will be on.*"

"But I have to try and help Bitsy," said Violet. "It'll do her good."

I violently shook my head. I didn't want to leave this house, not with my leaky bladder.

"But maybe you'll meet a cute guy," said Violet.

"Ha, I'm twenty years old going on eighty," I said, then hiccupped. I couldn't get a man in my condition. Even if I could, Miss Betty and her lawyers would find out and use it against me.

"Don't be silly," Violet scoffed. "It wouldn't hurt you to have some fun, date a few guys."

"I'm trying to rehabilitate my reputation, not drive it farther into the ground."

"Wow, you used a five-syllable word. You must have been studying R words."

"I resent that." I lifted my chin and hiccupped.

"Don't. I didn't mean any harm. I was just trying to shock you out of the hiccups." Violet winked.

"Didn't work," I said.

"All the more reason to go barhopping." She turned to her mother. "Hey, why don't you come with us, Mama?"

"I don't have hiccups." Clancy Jane walked over to the sink and began chopping green onions. She was making a vegetarian potato salad, which was a challenge, because she'd decided to go vegan. She'd blackballed everything from milk to mayonnaise. I was glad I had hiccups, because I wouldn't eat that salad if you paid me.

Violet pulled me toward the door, and we stepped out into the muggy afternoon. The air felt too hot and heavy to breathe. Other than the Vietnam War, all everybody talked about these days was the weather. A drought had struck the orange groves in Florida. Clancy Jane had pointed to the little television in the kitchen and said, "If you think *you've* got troubles, think of those poor citrus growers."

She'd threatened to do a rain dance if it didn't rain soon. I wondered if the heat could shock the hiccups out of my system. I lifted my hair from the back of my neck and wished I'd thought to brush it up like Violet's. Well, maybe not. No matter what I did, I looked more like Barbie than Audrey. I wanted to change, I just didn't know how. It was more complicated than pulling my hair into a sleek bun.

Violet strode ahead, her cork platform shoes scraping along the pavement. "You drive," she called, skipping past her Volkswagen, veering toward my old blue Mustang.

"Me?" I cried. "But I'm afflicted."

"Hiccups won't interfere with your driving."

"Well, they most certainly could," I said a little louder than necessary. "I might accidentally step on the gas."

"Please drive," Violet said. Then she whimpered like a puppy. "Please, please, please? I just drove all the way from Knoxville."

"Oh, all right. But you better wear your seat belt." I opened my door and slid into the baby-blue leather seat. It felt painfully hot, stinging the backs of my legs and my shoulders. I backed out of the driveway, then charged down Dixie Avenue, turning right onto Main Street. From the radio, Carly Simon was singing "You're So Vain." At the Square, I glanced at Citizen's Bank where Claude and Chick worked—well, if you called what they did "work." But the bank had a great sign. It flashed 98 degrees—4:57 P.M.

"Crystal Falls is way up in the mountains. It shouldn't be this hot," Violet complained. "But that goes to show how screwy this place is. I hate it here. I don't see why Mama moved back."

I pursed my lips and didn't answer. If it hadn't been for our grandmother's leukemia, Aunt Clancy might still be living out west, and Violet might have chosen a different college, maybe one in the east. I knew my own life wouldn't have changed one iota. I would still have broken Claude's nose and then run away. I would have lost my baby girl. And Daddy's marriage would probably still have given me hiccups.

The Hut was a popular drinking spot near the Cumberland River, offering backgammon, mixed drinks, and live bands. To reach it, I had to drive across the river, navigating over a high bridge. I hated that bridge and held my breath until I reached the other side. Once I was safely past that obstacle, I turned off the highway, down a rough-paved road. I cruised past the Rocky Top Concrete Plant, where statues of elves and flamingoes peeked out of a fenced-in lot. The road forked several times, but I knew the way. I drove beside a raspberry field, then turned down a gravel lane. Through the dust and haze, the Hut loomed up, a cinderblock building outlined in yellow Christmas lights. Every third one was burned out. The owner, Fred Harding, the ne'er-do-well son of a local optometrist, had hung a sign over the door, WELCOME TO VALHALLA.

"I'm surprised at Fred." Violet blinked at the sign. "I didn't think he was that smart."

"Just what *is* Valhalla?" I said, steering the Mustang into the gravel lot.

"You really don't know?"

"It sounds like a California wine." I hiccupped into my cupped palm.

"It was a beautiful hall where dead warriors drank wine from goat tits."

"I don't get the connection."

"After a few drinks you will," Violet said. "Come on. Let's get inside where it's cool."

"Just a sec," I called, digging into my purse. I pulled out a tube of lipstick—"Baby Lips"—and flipped down the visor. You just never knew who you'd meet in a place like the Hut. Maybe the man of my dreams, or maybe the devil himself. Surely to God they weren't one and the same.

I scrambled out of the Mustang and tottered across the gravel lot. I was wearing the same thing I'd worn all day—a blue-jean wrap skirt, sapphire blouse, and blue sandals. They were Candies with extra high heels, and my ankles seemed to bow. I stepped into the lounge, blinking in the smoky haze. Well, at least it was cool. I waited for my eyes to adjust to the darkness. More Christmas lights were strung up over the bar. Over to the right, the empty dance floor was illuminated by a revolving color wheel, the kind Mummy had once used on her aluminum Christmas tree. Now the colors flickered across the scuffed dance floor—red, green, blue, gold, then back to red. It was too early for the band, but a poster promised that Jerry and the Bottle Rockets would be appearing nightly through September.

I walked straight over to the bar and shoved in next to Violet, who'd struck up a conversation with Jeb, the bartender. He was a nice older guy with thick biceps who never called the police, even during knife fights. You could count on Jeb to keep your secrets.

"What you want, kid?" Jeb spread his hands on the counter.

From the other end of the bar, a man grinned at me. "Hey, cutie," he called, pursing his lips. "How do I say French kiss in French?"

Violet gave the man a dark look and said, "How about if I teach you to say 'kiss off'?"

The man cackled, then reached up and pushed back his hat. "Come over here and I'll teach you five ways to say peckerwood."

I leaned over the counter. "Jeb, I need a mai tai," I said, then hiccupped.

"Sounds like you've had one too many already," he said.

"Make that two," Violet said. She glanced over her shoulder and waved to a man in a red alligator shirt. I squinted, trying to place him. He wore tortoiseshell glasses, and his hair was dark blond and shaggy. As he hurried over to us, his cowlick bobbed up and down. His jeans were freshly ironed, and he had long, skinny legs. Violet's taste in men didn't run to hunks. Her old boyfriend, Laurence Prescott III, had been afflicted with a pinhead, and she had once spoken fondly of a cross-eyed boy. Violet had a theory that homely men were less likely to break your heart. I wasn't ready to test that theory just yet.

The guy wove through the crowd, heading toward the bar. As he got closer, I noticed that a slide-ruler was protruding from his hip pocket, as if he'd be called upon to solve an intricate math problem at any moment. He stepped up to Violet, and she playfully punched his shoulder. "Hey, Danny," she said.

"Want to play backgammon?" Danny asked Violet, straightening his glasses.

"Sure," Violet said. "Just let me get my drink."

I waited to be introduced, but Violet leaned against the bar and eyed a man in a cowboy hat. I wasn't used to Violet acting foolish around men, because it was usually just the two of us. Now Jeb walked up to the counter, holding two glasses. They were filled with luscious-looking red liquid. *My cure*, I thought, reaching for the glass. Violet grabbed hers and said, "I'll just be in the back with Danny, okay?"

I hiccupped into my glass. On the other side of the room, the jukebox began playing Three Dog Night. I gulped down the mai tai, then hastily ordered another. The bartender brought a drink and I tossed it down between hiccups. Jeb watched, shaking his head. When I held up my glass and ordered a third, he said, "Okay. *One* more. And while I'm fixing it, eat you some peanuts."

He parked a basket of nuts in front of me. I frowned at them. What if I hiccuped at the wrong moment and aspirated? I doubted that anyone here knew how to do CPR. I broke open a few peanuts and scattered the shells to fool the bartender. Aunt Clancy just loved nuts. "They're packed with protein," she'd say, sprinkling them on salads, tossing them casually over buttered asparagus, stuffing them into mushrooms. All the while preaching spiritual health, ecological awareness, the mysticism of legumes.

Jeb passed by and gave me a look that said You ain't fooling me. I just sighed. In the week that I'd suffered with hiccups, I hadn't been able to eat a bite, and my jean skirt was starting to feel loose. It was a damn pitiful way to lose weight. As soon as the hiccups went away, I was going to order a pepperoni pizza and eat the whole damn thing.

I heard giggles and glanced over my shoulder. From a booth, three girls were staring at me and whispering. With a jolt, I recognized them. They were known as the Three Sarahs—best friends, all with the same first name, set apart only by their looks—two blondes and a redhead— and their middle names: Beth, Lou, and Jill. After high school, they began working for the telephone company. It was amazing that they'd kept their jobs, because they had the kind of voices that escalated into hoots and shrieks, as if they were being tortured.

I could hear their whispering. A few phrases drifted over, *kidnapping, attempted manslaughter, lost custody.* I slid off the barstool and worked my way through the gloom, sipping my drink. I sidestepped the waitress, who looked old and tired, and I wondered if I myself would still be working at the Green Parrot when I was that age. Maybe it was time to move on, apply to a community college, learn a skill. But I'd been trapped by my own stupid choices, all of them made at age nineteen. I walked up to Violet's table. The funny-looking guy grinned. "She's beating me," he explained.

"That's why I don't play with her," I said in a cheery voice. Finally I was starting to feel the effects of the rum.

"That's not why." Violet turned her face up and smiled at her friend. "You know what, Danny? The real reason Bitsy won't play backgammon is she can't multiply. She adds everything on a cocktail napkin."

I wanted to hit her, but I was afraid I'd spill my drink, and I knew Jeb wouldn't give me another. "Stop picking on me."

"Relax, Ditsy. Have a seat," said the weird guy, and Violet emitted a shrill giggle, causing the Three Sarahs to lean out of their booth and stare.

"Ditsy?" I said. It was amazing how a consonant changed everything. The same for vowels. A while back, when I was studying the Ls in Violet's big *Merriam-Webster,* I'd come across labial and labile. I would hate to mix up those two words. Violet just loved to twist a person's name. She called me things like Itsy and Bitchy, resorting to Bessie when she was peeved. I fought back. "Calm down, Violent," I would say. "Don't get your panties in a wad, Violin."

A half hour later, we lurched out of the bar into warm air that smelled faintly of cedar. The sky was dusky blue, except for a swirl of burning pink clouds in the west. In minutes it would be dark. Danny stood in the doorway, backlit by smoky yellow light. "Y'all shouldn't drive," he called, sticking his hands under his armpits. He glanced up at the sky. "It's dangerous."

"We've done it a million times," Violet said, walking backward, grinning at him. Her jeans were tight, outlining her narrow hips. Her belt was studded with turquoise and silver, a souvenir from a trip to New Mexico back when Aunt Clancy had lived there. Several strands of dark hair had fallen from her upsweep, and she pushed them away. She had no idea that she was beautiful.

Danny frowned and rubbed his chin, brushing one hand over his hair, smoothing the cowlick for an instant before it popped back up. "It's still not safe. You just never know what's out there."

"Like what?" Violet lifted one eyebrow at Danny in a meaningful way.

"The cops," I said, eyeing my Mustang. "You know, he's right. Maybe we should call your mother."

"Don't be ridiculous." Violet shoved me toward the car. "We don't have far to go. We'll be fine."

"You drive," I called to Violet, holding up the keys. On the ring was a miniature rubber ducky, and it actually floated.

"No, you." Violet leaned against the Mustang and tilted back her head, looking up at the sky. It was getting darker by the second, and stars began to appear over the mountains.

"Hey!" somebody called from inside the bar. "Close the fucking door, man. All the air's blowing out!"

"Just be careful," Danny called. In slow-motion, he stepped back into the building and closed the door behind him, but I could see him looking out through its square window, his fingers spread on the glass.

"He seems fond of you," I said.

"No, he's just weird," Violet said. "He believes in little green men."

"Leprechauns?"

"Hell no, space men. Aliens."

"Seriously?" I glanced back at the bar. I could see Danny peering through the little window.

"Someday I'm going to live in a place where the temperature never goes above seventy degrees." Violet fanned herself.

I started to say me, too, then I held my breath, one hand rising to my throat.

"What's wrong?" Violet asked.

"I stopped hiccupping."

"See? I told you it worked." Violet flashed a triumphant smile. She ran one slender hand along her slicked-back hair, looking more and more Audrey-ish. "Where to next? The Tap Room? Or what about the Sheraton?"

"Let's go home and order a pizza, extra sausage and pepperoni. I'm starved."

As soon as I started the engine, I felt the full force of those mai tais. I peered through the windshield, and the road swayed. Gripping the wheel, I steered cautiously out of the lot, but I still managed to roll over a concrete curb. The car rocked violently, tossing Violet in the bucket seat.

"Hey watch out!" She reached for the dash.

"I *asked* you to drive." I tapped the brake and the car lurched to a stop. "You want to take over?"

"I'm more pie-eyed than you. Just get us home, Bessie."

"Then don't backseat drive, Violence," I shot back. Whenever I got scared, my voice climbed higher and higher; I was already petrified at the prospect of navigating over the bridge that spanned the Cumberland River. I had visions of plunging through the spindly green railing. Violet and I would break every bone in our bodies—if the crash didn't kill us outright, like it had done to Alice Ann's mother. I squinched up my forehead, wondering how that child was tormenting Eunice and Odell, or if they'd sent her to that school in Arkansas.

"Maybe if I shut my eyes," Violet was saying.

I hit the gas, and the tires spit gravel.

"Holy mother of God." Violet crossed herself; she wasn't even Catholic, she was nothing.

"I really think we should go back inside and call Aunt Clancy," I said.

"We're not calling anybody." Violet flipped one hand at the road. "Now drive the goddamn car or I'm going to pull out every bleached hair on your head."

"It is *not* bleached."

"Liar. I saw a Summer Blonde box in the trash."

"I'm not the only blonde in the house." I eased my foot onto the gas pedal and wondered if Danny was still watching. My Mustang had kicked up so much dust that the Hut's crazy Christmas lights were barely visible. I made a wide turn onto the gravel road, riding the brake. The car inched forward. There were no other cars, thank God, because I couldn't have handled the distraction. When I was drunk, I needed the road to myself. By the time I'd passed by the raspberry field, it was twilight, and the moon was hovering over the trees. The road forked, and I hit the brake. While the engine idled, I considered the options. I could turn left and be home in ten minutes, but I'd have to cross that damn bridge. Also, police cars liked to wait on the other side of the river. If they pulled me over, I would get a ticket or even thrown in jail—and the Wentworths would cut off my visitations with Jennifer, just as swiftly as they'd started them. If I turned right, I could avoid the police, but it was a dangerous route that hugged the river and crossed over not one but three dilapidated bridges. But that road was desolate and I could drive as slow as I pleased.

"What's the holdup?" Violet asked irritably.

"I'm trying to decide which way to turn."

"Jesus Christ, it's a road, not an entree at Howard Johnson's. Just pick one."

I hesitated a second more, then turned right. The road was so narrow that Queen Anne's lace brushed against the sides of the car, making a whuffling noise. Bugs hit the windshield.

"Dammit, I should've gone to the restroom before we left." Violet groaned. "I've got to pee something awful."

"Let me find a place to pull over." I pushed my face toward the windshield, but all I saw were weeds and potholes.

"I'm not going in the damn bushes. I might get chigger bites. So I'm just going to stick my little butt out the window and piss."

"Violet!" I drew back, horrified. "Men p-i-s-s. Girls tee-tee."

"Oh, don't be stupid. I've peed out of moving cars before."

"Not with me, you haven't."

"I've done it in Knoxville. All the coeds do it. Even the cheerleaders. It's more faddish than streaking."

"It's gross. What if you dribble some tee-tee on my car? Or *inside* my car. Just let me stop, okay?"

"Come on, loosen up. Be a part of the younger generation."

"I *am*."

"No, Bessie, you're stuck in the early sixties."

"I'm not the one with a Holly Golightly bun."

"It's a French twist, Bessie, not a bun."

"Don't call me that! And I don't want my car to smell like pee."

"It won't. I promise. Look, I know how to do this." Violet unbuckled her belt and peeled down her jeans. My cousin's buttocks were firm and round, and quite a bit slimmer than my own, even with my recent starvation.

"Quit staring. *Drive*," Violet ordered. She sat up on her knees and swiveled her nakedness toward the window. Gripping the roof of the car, she raised herself from her seat and leaned out, butt first.

"Now speed up," she said, her hair blowing out of the Audrey bun. "Hurry, unless you want piss everywhere."

"Thanks for the warning," I said, tapping my foot on the brake. Even when Violet was sober, it was difficult to reason with her. Once she made up her mind, that was it.

"You better pray this road stays empty," I added. "Oncoming traffic could lop off half your behind."

"Not unless it's going in the wrong direction." Violet was precariously balanced—her head and shoulders leaning into the car, her bottom jutting out, knees bent, her cork shoes pressing down on the armrest, denting the vinyl. Both hands clutched the roof of the car. She squinched her eyes shut, and two lines appeared on her forehead. Then she drew back her lips, showing small, crooked teeth. Individual droplets of urine blew out into the night air, pale yellow against the darkness.

"Ahhhh," she exhaled, and her mouth went slack with pleasure. Then she squealed. "Viva le fuck! Faster, Bitsy! I can feel piss blowing on my legs."

"Okay, okay!" I pressed my foot against the accelerator and the car shot ahead, the headlights carving out two tunnels of light.

"Perfect, just *per-fact*!" Violet whooped, then she pushed her butt farther out the window. "I'm just gonna air dry. God, this feels good."

I sighed with relief, thankful it was over. I looked away from the road and started to tell Violet to get back in, but before I could speak, the front tires hit a deep pothole. The force lifted me out of my seat, and the top of my head smacked into the car's padded roof. Then my body slammed down roughly, dropping me back into the seat. The headlights shone on the road—straight ahead were a dozen more huge potholes, and I was headed straight toward them.

Violet was still holding on to the roof of the car. She hadn't screamed, even though her mouth was open wide. I clenched the wheel. Then both tires plunged into another crater. Violet lost her balance and fell out of the window, arms and legs wheeling. Keeping one hand on the steering wheel, I leaned across the seat, trying to grab my cousin's ankles, but I was too late. Violet rolled off into the darkness. Stop the car, I thought. Find Violet, get help—in that order. I meant to hit the brake but the mai tais had disordered my brain, and I hit the accelerator. The car lurched ahead, veering away from the road, the headlights picking out weeds and saplings. Oak branches battered the windshield, and dried cornstalks crunched beneath the tires. I stomped against the brake. The car stopped abruptly, causing me to rise from my seat again, straight into the windshield. My forehead hit something cold and hard and then everything went black.

.   .   .

The headlights burned into the dark, shining through a curtain of oak leaves. I rose up, feeling dozy. Then I remembered. Violet was somewhere in the darkness. And I had to find her. My head throbbed as I scrambled out of the car, weaving back and forth in the tall grass. My legs felt rubbery, and it wasn't because of the Candies. The road was knotty, and I kept tripping into potholes. Twice I fell down and skinned my knees.

"Violet?" I called, then strained to listen. Nothing but the katydids beckoning from the weeds, harsh mating calls: *ch-ch-ch*. I heard the buzz of crickets, the deep, piglike grunt of a swamp frog. I had learned to identify them when Aunt Clancy and I were going to teach Jennifer about nature. I heard other, stranger sounds and I wondered what was out there in the dark.

"Violet?" I called again. A whippoorwill answered, the faint notes hanging in the air.

I heard a moan and whirled around, trying to sense the direction, but everything was black. "Over here," Violet cried weakly. "In the g-god-damn ditch."

"Keep talking so I can find you," I called. Despite the heat, I was shaking all over, and I could barely see where I was going. I staggered in the general direction of Violet's voice. I found her sprawled in a ditch. The remnants of her Audrey bun were hanging to one side. I didn't see any blood, but it was very dark.

"It HURTS!" Violet screeched. Then she looked at me. "Did you . . . hit . . . your . . . head or somethin'?" She spoke hesitantly, gasping between each word. "You're all . . . bloody."

"I am?" My hand flew up to my forehead. I felt something damp, then I looked at my fingers. They were smeared black. "Never mind me," I said. "Do you think you've broken a bone?"

"Hell, *I* don't know. Shit . . . get me outta this . . . ditch." Violet held up her other hand.

"Should I get an ambulance? What if you've hurt your head? *Is* it hurting?"

"No, no. My head is fine. Just take me home. It's my ass that's killing me."

Even in the darkness, I could see that Violet's shoes were still strapped to her ankles, but chunks of cork were missing from the soles. How badly was she hurt?

"Get me up," she commanded.

"You sure?"

"Yes!"

I gripped Violet's hand and pulled. She staggered to her feet, rising like something born from a swamp, still bloody from the birthing. Then she leaned heavily against my shoulder.

"You've got to see a doctor," I whispered. "We'll get Byron—"

"NO, NOT HIM!" Violet shrieked. "He'll just tell Mama, and I don't want her seeing me this way. She'll freak out."

"But you're hurt bad. You can't keep this from her."

"Just get me in the car and drive me home. You can sneak me upstairs.

All I need is a gauze bandage and some hydrogen peroxide. Or will that sting too bad?"

"We'll figure it out later," I said, trying not to alarm her. I had no intention of taking her home; I was taking her to the emergency room. I took a small step, but Violet didn't move. I started to cry out, thinking she might have died, then I saw the problem—my cousin was hobbled by the jeans around her ankles. Over our heads, I heard a nighthawk call out a harsh, nasal *peent!*

"Can I take off your jeans? I think you'll walk better without them." I glanced toward the car. It seemed far away, miles away. The taillights burned red behind a thick tangle of weeds.

"No, no!" Violet shook her head. "Don't touch anything. Just let me lean on your shoulder."

"Okay, but take it slow."

"Slow," Violet repeated dully.

"You're doing fine." I could taste those mai tais burning in the back of my throat. We staggered off the road, into Queen Anne's lace and trumpet vines, toward the car, toward the red taillights. Violet was solid muscle, heavier than I would have guessed.

As we approached the car, Violet's eyes widened. "Jesus, Bitsy. You ran off the road?"

"Just a little ways," I said, trying to sound comforting. In charge, in control. The kind of person you'd trust in an emergency. Or to raise a child. When we reached the Mustang, I opened the passenger door and guided Violet into the backseat, helped her to stretch out onto her stomach. Her silver belt buckle clinked as she settled down. The moon came out from a cloud and shone down on my cousin's buttocks. Oh, my *God.* She was torn to pieces. I jerked my head to the side afraid I'd be sick.

"This is all my fault," I said. "If I hadn't had those damn hiccups, we'd be sitting at home, watching *Friday Night at the Movies.*"

"No, we would not. We'd be watching *Sonny and Cher.* Stop kicking yourself and get your ass in the car," Violet said.

"I'm never going to drink again," I said. In the distance I heard the begging call of a screech owl.

"Oh, yes, you will," Violet said in a weary voice. I shut the door, then hurried around the car. I climbed into the front seat, and started the engine. When I shifted into reverse, the tires whined and spun helplessly.

"Stop giving it the gas," Violet called from the backseat.

I tapped my foot against the accelerator. The car rocked back and forth, caught in a little ditch, then it jolted ahead, rocking through the pasture, knocking down weeds and saplings. By the time I pulled up beneath the canopy at Crystal Falls Hospital emergency entrance, smoke was pouring from under my hood. I helped Violet out of the backseat. Somehow she'd managed to kick off her shoes and jeans, and I was horrified to see that she was naked from the waist down. She glanced up, squinted at the lights, then screeched, "No, no, I said no hospitals!"

I didn't have time to argue. I looked around for a sheet—anything to throw around her body. Her thighs were smeared with blood, blending into the dark, matted triangle of her pubic hair. It looked as if gravel was embedded beneath her skin, too. With my free hand, I unbuttoned my blouse and draped it over Violet's lower half. We veered toward the electric doors. The glass swooshed open, and we slogged through. A nurse walked by, holding a tray. When she saw Violet, she dropped the tray. Metal instruments clattered against the tile floor, scattering hemostats and scissors.

"Stop gawking and get a doctor!" Violet yelled.

·　·　·

I waited in the lobby. My blood-stained blouse had been returned but at least it covered my own nakedness. Tired-looking people, all of them dressed in summer clothes, were sprawled in the green vinyl chairs, staring up at the TV. *The Late, Late Show* was playing *From Here to Eternity.* Next to me sat a woman in lime green shorts and a purple halter top. Her shoulders were sunburned, the bosom sagging and wrinkled. I turned away, toward the plate glass doors, where an ambulance swung up, its red lights wheeling. Two medics hopped out, ran around to the back, and pulled out a stretcher. Another man ran alongside it, holding an intravenous bag in the air. The hospital's electric doors whooshed open, and the men bustled through, pushing the stretcher around the corner, through steel doors marked Medical Personnel Only.

The lady in the purple halter leaned forward, touching my arm. "Honey, did somebody beat you up?"

"No, ma'am," I said. "I was in a wreck. My cousin's being treated right now."

When Clancy Jane and Byron burst into the lobby, I stood up. So did the woman in the purple halter. "There's my doctor!" said the woman, waving at Byron.

Byron didn't seem to hear. He rushed to a window and rapped against the glass. A receptionist with teased brown hair slid open the window. Aunt Clancy stood behind him. She was still wearing the peasant blouse and the red skirt. Her hair was pulled back haphazardly with a leather clasp. She looked frightened, and she kept clutching Byron's sleeve like he was her seeing-eye man. He turned away from the window and put one hand on Aunt Clancy's arm, whispered something into her ear. He squeezed her shoulder, then he strode toward the treatment room, pushing open the metal doors.

"Sir?" the receptionist cried, poking her head through the window like a turtle. "Sir, you can't go in there."

"But he's a doctor," Aunt Clancy said, in the same tone she might have said, "But he's Jesus."

The receptionist's mouth formed a tight little O, and she withdrew her head. Aunt Clancy turned, scanning the faces in the vestibule. When she saw me, her eyes widened slightly. She stepped across the room, her red skirt swishing, then she grabbed my wrist and pulled me into an alcove. The woman in the purple halter leaned forward, watching.

"What happened?" Clancy Jane's voice sounded raspy, as if she'd been yelling at a football game. She scowled down at the bloody handprints on my blouse.

My head was throbbing again. I briefly closed my eyes, trying to figure out where to begin. The last thing I needed was a lecture on drunk driving—I knew we'd done wrong. "We were on our way home from the Hut, and . . ." I broke off, remembering my promise to Violet. "I had a wreck. And Violet got thrown from the car."

"Oh, *God.*" The veins stood out on Aunt Clancy's neck, and her cheeks turned pink. She glanced up at the ceiling. Through her teeth, she said, "Were you drunk?"

"Yes." I could feel tears burning in the backs of my eyes. My throat was closing. I swallowed again, wishing my hiccups would return so I'd have a reason not to speak. Aunt Clancy was waiting for me to continue. When I didn't, she said, "*Thrown* from the goddamn car." She crossed her arms over her breasts and began to tremble.

"I told y'all not to go. Didn't I?" Clancy Jane cried. "Well, how bad is it? Did she hit her head? Is she *paralyzed*? Is she conscious?" Clancy Jane's voice rose higher and higher. From the lobby, the whispering halted and people got up from their seats to stare. The woman in the purple halter gaped, as if fascinated.

"Now, don't panic, Aunt Clancy. She can walk."

"That's good, right?"

"I think so. She fell on her butt, not her head. The skin is all scraped off."

Aunt Clancy winced. She put her hand over her mouth and turned in a slow circle, her back hunched over. "On the way here, Byron said he hoped that she didn't have any internal bleeding," she whispered. Her eyes blazed with a strange blue light. One lid twitched. She reached up to rub it, but the minute her hand was gone, the lid began to quiver again.

"I hope she doesn't have that, too." I looked down at the floor, trying to sort out the dizzy patterns.

"What were y'all drinking?" asked Clancy Jane.

"Mai tais."

"Well, I can't think of a sweeter way to get drunk," she said in a bitter voice. "Unless it's pink ladies or daiquiris."

"They got rid of my hiccups."

"Great. I'll file it away in Mama's household tips box." Aunt Clancy extended one finger and wrote in the air. "A cure for hiccups."

That night, every inch of Violet's body was scanned and X-rayed, then she was transferred to a private room on the medical-surgical ward. Affixed to the door was a sign that said STRICT ISOLATION. The nurses explained that was to protect Violet from germs. All visitors were required to wear a gown and a mask.

"This is what we do for burn patients," said the nurse.

"But she didn't get burned," I said.

"No, but she's lost some skin, and she's vulnerable to infection."

Aunt Clancy and I stood outside the room. We couldn't go inside until the doctors were finished with their examination. Byron had called in several specialists and they hovered around the bed, shining lights on Violet's rear end. Outside, in the hall, the nurse gave me a shrewd stare. "How'd this happen, anyway?"

I shook my head, lifted my shoulders. Through the glass, I saw Violet's outline. She was lying on her stomach, a gauze tent draped over her buttocks, hiding the damage. Her eyes were closed. Byron came out of the room and put his arm around Aunt Clancy.

"She's real lucky. Not a single broken bone," said Byron.

"She must have a guardian angel," said Aunt Clancy.

Yes, I thought. The Tee-Tee Angel. Protected by the Goddess of Pee.

"Actually, she did," said Byron, turning to me. "Bitsy, thank God for you. Thank you for finding Violet in the dark and making her come to the hospital. You showed good judgment."

"I don't understand." Aunt Clancy's forehead squinched up.

"Apparently your bull-headed daughter thought she could patch herself up." He nodded at Violet's door. "She told me all about it. I'll fill you in later."

I kept on staring through the window. The praise was so undeserved. I felt ashamed.

"But I've got to know now," said Clancy Jane. "How bad is she hurt?"

"She's going to be fine," said Byron, looking into his wife's face. The door cracked open and another doctor stepped into the hall. Byron gestured at him and said, "Clancy, you remember Ron Fisher, don't you? The vascular surgeon?"

Aunt Clancy nodded and put two fingers to her lips.

"I know your daughter's condition seems alarming," said Dr. Fisher. "But it looks worse than it is. Her blood pressure is stable. No head injury. No signs of internal bleeding. She'll be fine—a little bruised and sore. And she may have a scar or two, but I daresay they won't show."

"Scars?" Aunt Clancy and I said together.

"If you've got to have a scar somewhere, the buttocks is the place for it," he said. "But she may have none at all. The main thing is, she's going to have a huge pain in the buttocks for the next week or two, but she'll recover."

He pronounced buttocks using both syllables. But-tocks.

"I'm not leaving her," said Aunt Clancy.

"Me, either," I said.

"I'll stay, too," said Byron. The three of us crowded around the window, staring at Violet as if we were watching a TV show, scared that we'd miss a crucial scene if we left for an instant.

• • •

The next morning I was awakened by a rattling cart. I opened my eyes and sat up, blinking at the tweedy sofas in the waiting room. They were empty. Sunshine pierced a glass wall, brightening the atrium. The light was too sharp and it hurt my eyes. I held up one hand, trying to block the dazzling brightness. I wondered if Aunt Clancy had gone to get coffee, or if Violet's condition had worsened. I started to get up but the room reeled to one side, and I slumped onto the sofa, holding my head in my hands. I didn't know if I had a concussion or a hangover, but it hurt too bad to move. After a while I drifted back to sleep. Almost immediately I felt someone shaking my arm. Looming above me was Aunt Clancy, holding two Styrofoam cups of coffee. She handed one to me.

"I just saw Violet," she said, taking a sip. "She's in a lot of pain, but at least she's sober. By the way, we had your car towed. It's in pretty bad shape."

From the hallway, I heard a rattling sound. A nurse was pushing a medicine cart, the wheels ticking against the tile. "I can see her again in eight more minutes," Aunt Clancy said. "You, too. The doctor said she can leave the hospital in a week. Of course, she's raising hell to leave now. She's got a whopping hangover—I bet you do, too—and she's busting a gut to get back to Knoxville."

"Will she be able to finish the fall quarter?" I asked.

"I sure hope so," said Aunt Clancy. "If she doesn't, she'll drive us all crazy."

Six days later, Violet was pitching a fit. "I demand to be discharged!" she yelled and raised her face from the sheet, glaring at the nurses. "I'm missing classes. I can't afford to get behind. I have a scholarship and I can't lose it."

I was sitting at the foot of Violet's bed, wearing a paper gown and mask, trying not to laugh; but I didn't fool my cousin, not for a second. "What's so funny?" Violet said crossly.

"You said behind." I smiled behind the mask, and Aunt Clancy's eyes crinkled in the corners.

"A subliminal slip." Violet turned on her side and winced. Since she was the patient, she didn't wear a mask. "Look, I'm not in the mood for any drunk-on-her-ass jokes. So don't you start."

"I won't."

Byron and the strange-talking doctor walked into the room, swathed in paper gowns and masks, and they said that Violet was in no condition to attend classes, or to involve herself in any sort of physical activity that required long periods of sitting.

"I'll stand," Violet said. "I'll buy a rubber doughnut. Bitsy had one of those after Jennifer was born. Didn't you?"

"Yes, and it helped," I said. "I can come to Knoxville with you. Drive you around. Carry your books. Hey, maybe we can drive over to Pigeon Forge and see Daddy."

After Byron, Aunt Clancy, and the other doctor left, Violet turned to me. "Honey, I love you. And you did the right thing bringing me here. But I don't want you coming to Knoxville. I've been taking care of myself for a long, long time. I got myself into this mess, I'll get myself out."

"But I could stay with you for a few days, just to make sure you're—"

"Bitsy, I'm a survivor. And besides, you wouldn't like Knoxville."

"Why not?" I asked, trying not to sound offended. But I couldn't help it. What did she mean? That I would embarrass her?

"It's faster-paced than Crystal Falls. And some of the girls are snooty and fashion-conscious. Oh, don't make a face. Shit, now I've hurt your feelings."

"No, no." I shook my head. "You didn't. It was just an idea. I understand how you feel."

"And how is that?" Violet's eyes widened.

"You love me, but you're ashamed of me. Your fluffy little cousin."

"Little? You're larger than life." She laughed. "In some places, you're too big for your own good."

"Rub it in, Violent," I said, patting my hips.

"I'm referring to your heart, not your ass." She grabbed my hands. "It's as big as a whale's."

ROWAN, VAN CLEAVE, HARLOW, AND GRIFFIN, PLLC
ATTORNEYS AT LAW

600 First Avenue
Crystal Falls, Tennessee

PERSONAL & CONFIDENTIAL

October 14, 1973

Lillian B. Wentworth
214 Dixie Avenue
Crystal Falls, Tennessee

Dear Ms. Wentworth:

  It has come to our attention that you were recently involved in risqué behavior, resulting in the personal injury of Violet Jane Jones. Therefore, all visitations with minor child, Jennifer Wentworth ("CHILD") will be discontinued until further notice. If you have questions, please contact this office. Under no circumstances are you to contact Mr. Claude E. Wentworth III, Mrs. Claude E. Wentworth III, or Mr. Claude E. Wentworth IV ("CLIENTS") or legal action, such as a restraining order, may be required. Additionally, all letters to CHILD and CLIENTS must cease or harassment charges will be forthcoming.

  Sincerely yours,

  Arthur P. Van Cleave III

The interdiction lasted not quite two and a half months, until Miss Betty couldn't find a babysitter, and she'd planned a big shopping trip to Atlanta. Chick called Bitsy and said he'd already called his lawyers and told them that the visitations could resume. When Chick showed up at 214 Dixie, Jennifer was wearing a black bouclé coat with a Chanel flower pinned to the lapel.

Bitsy knew something was wrong the minute she took Jennifer into her arms. The baby's cheeks were ruddy, her eyes glazed and shiny, and she was burning up. "Chick wait," Bitsy called after him, "this baby is sick," but he was already out the door. He climbed into his black Mercedes and drove off. Clancy Jane found the thermometer, and Jennifer had a temperature of 103.6. This was child abuse. Byron pressed his stethoscope to the baby's chest. He let Bitsy listen, too, and it sounded all crackly, like dry leaves. He said Jennifer had bronchitis and he'd call in some antibiotics at the Rexall, but that it might take a while for them to kick in. He was right. Jennifer woke up in the night with a tight, raspy cough. Bitsy carried her into the bathroom and turned on the hot water. Then she sat on the floor, the baby in her lap, and waited for her to fall asleep. By morning, Jennifer was beginning to breathe without struggling.

Bitsy was furious at the Wentworths, not to mention their lawyers. She complained to her aunt that the legal definition of unfit seemed to change to suit Miss Betty's schedule. A few more days without treatment, and Jennifer would have ended up in the hospital. That's what Byron had said. Bitsy started to fire off a letter to Arthur P. Van Cleave III, but Clancy Jane stopped her. "You'll only make things more difficult for yourself, honey."

"Can it get any worse?"

"Always," said Clancy Jane. "You've got too much on you. I think you need a little vacation. I can manage without you at the café."

So, the next weekend, Bitsy borrowed Aunt Clancy's car and drove up to see Violet, who was well enough to go barhopping. Under the black, twinkling stars in the Holiday Inn lounge, the cousins danced with traveling salesmen. Men from Tulsa, Cincinnati, Santa Fe, Mobile, Little Rock. Their accents were as varied as the mixed drinks they ordered from the bar—illegally, since Knox County was a dry county.

As they were driving back to the dorm, Violet said, "We should buy a wall-size map and stick colored pins in it."

"To keep track of the war?" Bitsy asked.

"No, to keep track of all the men we've danced with."

"I kinda enjoyed myself," Bitsy said, surprising herself. "Not that we could ever do this back home. Miss Betty would ruin me."

"Honey, she already has," said Violet. "But that's no reason to stop having fun."

A NOTE FROM BITSY

Dear Jennifer,

All the lawyers in Tennessee can't keep me from writing you. The problem is your grandparents' lawyers have forbidden me to mail you any letters. So your Great Aunt Clancy Jane bought me a carved rosewood box, and I'm keeping all my correspondence inside it. Then one day you can maybe read the letters and decide for yourself if I was a bad mother.

I love you,
Mama

~ Part 3 ~

Bitsy

The summer of 1974 marked the end of my celibacy. I owed it all to the new Winn Dixie. At the grand opening, I won a door prize, a free dental checkup, along with my choice of a complimentary tooth cleaning or one cavity filled. When it came to dentistry, my motto was: If it doesn't hurt, don't fix it. I guess I wasn't the only one with this philosophy, because down at the Green Parrot, I tried to give the coupon away, but nobody wanted it. Byron said he'd never heard of the dentist, Walter Saylor Jr., DDS, but he advised me to hang on to the certificate. I stuck it in a drawer and forgot about it, until the first week in June, when I got a toothache.

The wreck with Violet had totaled my Mustang, so I walked everywhere. Dr. Saylor's office was a squatty red brick building with casement windows. A breeze stirred the sign, making it swing back and forth, WALTER SAYLOR, DDS. I almost turned around, because my tooth had stopped aching yesterday, at the exact moment I'd made the appointment; but then I considered my finances and changed my mind. So I hurried inside—the waiting room was filled up—and I hastily wrote my name and appointment time on a pad. A gray-haired receptionist asked me to fill out a patient information form. I found an empty chair and propped the clipboard on my knees, scribbling out my name, date of birth, and next of kin.

Finally my name was called and I was led down a pink-and-brown tiled corridor that smelled of peppermint into a small room with a mural on one wall, featuring a waterfall, trees, and a rushing river. On the opposite wall was a glass block window. As I settled into the padded chair, which just happened to match the tile floor, I wondered why a dentist would need to obscure a view of the outside world and provide a fake one. I sure hoped it was to protect the patient's privacy rather than to hide barbaric techniques.

A drill whined in the background, and a heavy-lidded nurse put my chart in the door, then clipped a paper bib around my neck. Pinned to her chest was a white badge with her name spelled out in black letters, Patricia Eller. "Ma'am, I think I made a mistake coming here," I said, looking up at her huge forehead, which slanted like a shelf of rock, throwing her eyes into shadow. She resembled a Cro-Magnon, like the sketches I'd seen in Violet's anthropology textbook.

"Mistake?" She blinked. Her thick eyelids were dusted with turquoise powder.

"My tooth isn't hurting anymore." I started to rise from the chair. "So I'll just be going."

"Don't be scared, dear. Dr. Saylor is known as the painless dentist. Just sit tight. He'll be in here directly." She patted my arm, then turned on her heels and scurried out of the room, firmly closing the door behind her to block my escape.

I shut my eyes and listened to the piped-in music that wafted all around me. It wasn't old-fogey elevator music, either, but contemporary rock—Deep Purple was singing "Woman From Tokyo." After a long while, the drill stopped. I hadn't heard any muffled cries or outright screaming, so I began to relax. Finally the dentist stepped into my room, accompanied by the Cro-Magnon nurse. He looked old, at least thirty, and he had bushy red hair which was styled into a white man's Afro. His eyebrows were arched and wiry, setting off his pale, chalky skin—in fact, he looked as if he suffered from a serious blood deficiency.

"So," he said, glancing at my chart, "Bitsy Wentworth—is that Mrs. or Ms.?"

"Ms.," I said. "And I think I have a cavity."

"Alrighty." He picked up a long instrument with a round mirror at the end. "Can you open up wide for me?"

I shut my eyes and felt his fingers pull back my lips. "Hmm," he said, sliding the mirror along my gum, "not so bad."

"Rwelly?" I said around his fingers, and then I felt foolish.

"You have beautiful teeth." The dentist leaned closer, blinking at my incisors. "Did you wear braces?"

I nodded, but I was a little unnerved by his intense gaze. His eyes were brown with yellow slashes. He took the mirror from my mouth and then fixed me with a smile.

"Who did them?" he asked. "Your braces, I mean."

"Dr. Throckenberry," I said.

"He's retired."

"Yes, I know."

"I'd be more than happy to be your dentist," he said. "If you're a student—are you one?—anyway, I give students a discount."

"I'll bear that in mind," I said.

He fixed me with a broad smile and tapped his teeth. "Caps," he said. "But I didn't do them myself. Now, open up wide again. Good. Oh, that's just great."

He placed a long Q-tip against my gum. First, I tasted something sweet, then my mouth began to go numb. The dentist faced the counter and I heard the clinking of instruments. "I'm just going to put your tooth to sleep," he said, and the nurse held out a hypodermic needle. He grabbed hold of my upper lip, then I felt something sharp prick my gum; the doctor began to shake my lip back and forth.

"Does it hurt?" he asked in a concerned voice.

I managed to garble out a "nuh-uh."

"No?" he asked, and the nurse put a suction tube next to my tongue. It made a loud, gargling noise.

"Mmmhum," I managed to say. It looked like a dentist would know better than to strike up a conversation with an incapacitated woman. From somewhere behind me, a phone trilled. The dentist sighed, but he kept injecting medicine into my gum.

"Mrs. Eller," he said calmly, "would you please see who's buzzing me? And tell them that I'm with a patient."

"Certainly, Dr. Saylor." She nodded and stepped out of the room. Then he leaned closer.

"Would you like to have dinner and see a movie?" he whispered.

I wondered if I'd heard him correctly. Even if I had, I was afraid to answer, since the needle was still lodged in my gum, and the suction tube was slurping up Lord knew what. He seemed to sense my dilemma, and he removed the needle. Then he hovered over my face, the yellow eyes glowing.

"That's better, isn't it?" He lifted those crazy eyebrows. "So, will you go?"

This dentist was too mouthy for his own good. Once the word got around that he was hitting on the patients, he'd be ruined. I plucked the tube out of my mouth and held it aloft. "You're asking me on a date?"

"Yes, I guess I am," he said, looking sheepish.

"Can a dentist do that?"

"I don't normally. In fact, I've *never* done it. See, I'm going through a divorce, and I—well, I'm not sure what I thought. I hope I haven't scared you."

Scared wasn't half of it. My brow tensed up, and I focused at the wall mural, the water flowing endlessly into the river. Rod Stewart began to sing "It's All Over Now," from the *Gasoline Alley* album, which I recognized from Aunt Clancy's collection. As I listened to Rod, I tried to come up with a polite reply. I sure didn't want to make him angry before he filled my tooth. What if he hit a nerve? On purpose. I wanted to tell him that I was sorry, not to take it personally, but I just wasn't interested—not in him or anybody. All my energy centered around the café and the visits with my daughter. But then, I'd have to explain why I didn't have custody, and I wasn't in the mood to confess to a dentist.

"Thank you for the invitation," I began, rubbing my face. It was starting to feel numb and rubbery. "But I'm sorry, I don't date."

"Oh, oh." He looked surprised, then he nodded, as if he'd figured it out. "You're already involved with someone?"

"No."

"If you're not involved, then you're free to date me. Is that correct?"

"I don't think you understand. I no longer date men." I frowned. That didn't sound right, and I wondered if I'd only confused him more or if I'd made a faux pas.

"May I ask why?" he asked, his eyes bobbling.

"It's a long story." I glanced at my watch, a gift from Violet. It had a pink strap and Cinderella face, and her arms pointed at the three and the six. "And I'm in sort of a rush."

"I guess you stay busy, don't you? A pretty little thing like you." He paused, and I knew he was waiting for an answer. But I couldn't explain, and I decided not to try. He began to fiddle with his drill, fitting it with a new bit, or whatever it's called. It looked bigger than necessary, and my heart began to thud.

He glanced coolly at me and said, "Are you numb?"

"Excuse me?" I blinked. If he was asking if I'd become desensitized toward the male species, the answer was yes, but it wasn't any of his business. I thought back to the door prize and wished I hadn't set foot at the Winn Dixie.

"Your tooth," he said. "Is it numb yet?"

"Oh, that." I reached up, felt my face again. "I think so."

"Are you free this Saturday?"

"Actually, no," I said, and he looked crestfallen. So I quickly added, "I've got family obligations."

"All weekend?"

"Er, yes. I'm tied up both Friday and Saturday," I said. What I felt wasn't revulsion; it was more like the opposite of attraction.

"Are you free Sunday?" He persisted. "We can have breakfast. Or would you prefer brunch?"

He was bullying me. I shot him a disgusted look. Didn't he understand that no meant no? Maybe he was equally unclear about the meaning of yes. Wait a minute—that could be my excuse. "Sure, I'll have breakfast," I lied. Then I quickly added, "If my tooth isn't hurting, that is."

I promised to meet him Sunday morning at the Caney Fork Truck Stop, then he reached for the drill and began whittling away at my tooth, enamel dust wafting in the air. When I got home, I found Aunt Clancy in the garden picking green tomatoes, wrapping each one in crinkly paper. She looked as if she'd just returned from the café. She was wearing her usual funky garb—an embroidered cotton blouse and cutoffs. Around her waist was a fringed suede belt. In August, she would turn thirty-six, but she could pass for a much younger woman. Her hair hung past her shoulders, and it was tinted Dusty Blonde, the long layers melding together. As she moved, her earrings glinted in the late afternoon sun.

She'd certainly experienced many ups and downs, but you'd never know it from her calm, placid expression. Her eyes were large and luminous, a startling shade of blue. Her nose turned up slightly at the tip, dainty and regal—she was a natural beauty, the type that never showed her age. Her looks were more Old Hollywood than Crystal Falls. Violet always laughed when I compared people to movie stars, but today Aunt Clancy reminded me of Tippi Hedren in *The Birds*. Tippi with her hair down, minus the scarves, furs, and sunglasses—although Aunt Clancy would have looked stunning with those accessories.

"Where've you been?" She squinted up at me. "Your face looks strange."

"It's numb," I said, tugging at my lip. "I've just come from the dentist. And the strangest thing happened. He asked me out on a date."

"Before or after he filled your tooth?" Aunt Clancy laughed.

"Before."

"Isn't that blackmail? Date me, or I'll grind your teeth down to stubs!"

"That's what it felt like."

"But you said yes. Oops." She dropped a tomato, and it rolled between my legs.

I nodded.

"I just hope he doesn't have ulterior motives," she said.

"But he's a professional. He's taken oaths."

"I thought you said he was a tooth man."

"He is."

"The only oath he's taken is to overcharge for fillings and root canals." Aunt Clancy sighed. "Oh, Bitsy. I wish I had your innocence. You should hear Byron talking about the other doctors. Put a white coat on a man, and he acts like he's lord and master, in charge of his fiefdom. And you're an attractive girl."

"I have no intention of meeting him. But at least I got a free filling out of it."

"Is the dentist handsome?" Aunt Clancy reached for another tomato.

"Hardly." I laughed and sat down in the grass, tucking one foot beneath me. The summer light fell in long strips. Crape myrtles were in full bloom, sticking through the fence. "Plus he's got freckles and one thousand pounds of hair. It's orange, and real curly, like Abby Hoffman's."

"*Orange* hair?" Aunt Clancy's eyebrows slanted together, and she wrinkled her nose. "Well, does he *look* like Abby?"

"No. He looks like somebody dumped a bowl of sweet potatoes on his head." I laughed. "Oh, and he's got piercing yellow eyes."

"Like in *Rosemary's Baby*? What did you say his name was—Dr. Saperstein?"

"No, Saylor."

"They could be related. Both surnames begin with Sa." Aunt Clancy giggled. "I'd love to see a white man with an Afro in *this* town. Maybe he's got all that hair for a reason. Did you check his head for horns? Is 666 tattooed on his scalp?"

"I could meet him for Sunday breakfast and find out. 'Dr. Saylor?' I'll say, 'My Aunt Clancy thinks you're a devil, so will you kindly drop your drawers so I can make sure that you don't have a tail.'"

"Or forked tongue," said Aunt Clancy. "Is he married?"

"I think he said divorced."

"You *think*?"

"Well, he had a needle in my mouth at the time. But it's hard to believe that Dr. Saylor was ever married. He's too funny-looking."

"Yes, but he's a dentist. They don't need to be cute. If you go on this date, you better check him out. Because ninety percent of *all* men commit adultery. The rest of them die at puberty." Aunt Clancy held up a small Roma. "Will you look at this? It's too perfect to eat. It's like the perfect man. I'm just going to put it in the kitchen window and admire it."

Dorothy

In mid-June Dorothy McDougal was certified sane by the State of Tennessee. "Well, this is the day," the psychiatric nurse said. "You are finally getting to go home. Aren't you excited?"

"Nobody told me." Dorothy threw up her hands in disgust.

"You knew," said the nurse.

"I didn't either," Dorothy said, starting to get huffy.

"You've known for weeks," said the nurse. "If you're not ready to go, you can always stay another night."

Dorothy really had forgotten, but she was in no mood to argue. She hurried over to the phone booth to call her son, but he wasn't home. Neither was Bitsy or Clancy Jane. So she took a Greyhound bus back to Crystal Falls. A big mistake. The other passengers were scary-looking, and she was afraid to make eye contact. She caught a glimpse of herself in the window as she ran her fingers through her hair. Lord, she looked awful. Wrinkled and haggard, with bags under her eyes. Worse, every hair on her head was white and frizzed. Why, she was a dead ringer for Albert Einstein. And she was only forty-two years old. It wasn't fair to be young and look elderly. She brushed the frayed curls from her face. She used to be blond and pretty, a little on the heavy side, but stylish and pleasing to the eye. Once she got home, the first thing she planned to do was make an appointment at the Utopian.

Gazing out the bus window, she started to feel sorry for herself. If her family cared, they'd have been home when she'd called. The bus station was in a dangerous part of town. But that wasn't a healthy way to look at life. You had to overlook thoughtless behavior. "I don't forgive and forget," she had told her latest therapist, a bald-headed man with little John Lennon glasses. Underneath his starched white jacket, he wore normal clothes, Arrow shirts and Haggar slacks. "Do you want to be long-suffering and miserable, or lighthearted and compassionate?" the doctor asked, forming a steeple with his index fingers.

"Why can't I be long-suffering and lighthearted?" she'd asked, wondering if he was really a Pentacostal preacher.

"You can." He nodded. "But then I'd have to keep you here at Central State."

She'd tried her best to forgive, but it was the hardest damn thing she'd ever done. Breathing underwater would be easier than excusing the ones who'd put her here. And it wasn't just her family, either. Oh, she knew what people in Crystal Falls thought. If crazy old Dorothy ever gets released, she'll open a can of worms. Night crawlers, her daddy used to call them. They made good bait.

At the bus station, she bought an ice-cold grape soda and took a dainty sip. The man at the cash register was complaining about the weather. He said it hadn't rained in twelve days, and the five-day forecast promised nothing but hot, dry days. "I ain't seen you around here," the man told Dorothy. "Are you new?"

She had been ready for this; she'd planned to tell everyone that she'd been to a fat farm, only she wouldn't call it that, no indeed, she'd call it a rejuvenation spa. "Yes," she told the man. "I'm brand-new."

She walked outside, onto the bus station porch, and tried to get orientated. The streets in Crystal Falls had been named for the continents. A green metal sign said Africa Road. It was the old part of town.

Dorothy picked up her suitcase and began walking. She passed by Reggie Swain's junk lot, which was filled with wrecked cars. She saw a blue Mustang with Queen Anne's lace growing out of the hood, and she wondered if it was her daughter's. Bitsy had told her last September how she'd gotten hiccups and then totaled her car; with Violet in it, too. Dorothy had cringed when she'd heard about her niece's injuries, but the girl possessed those resilient Jones' genes, and she'd recovered with only a few scars.

Dorothy pressed on, her shoes scuffing in the gravel. She felt as if she were traveling into the deep heart of the Congo. The shade trees closed in around her, full of shrieking monkeys—hear no evil, see no evil, speak no evil. (But who really knew?) *In the valley of the shadow of evil* sprang to mind. Whoever wrote that wasn't joking, Dorothy thought. Why, they probably had lived in Crystal Falls. She wished that her house was located near Europe Street. Well, you couldn't have everything.

When she reached the intersection of Africa and Asia, she began to worry. Here, the shotgun houses began, with crooked picket fences and weedy gardens. The lack of rain had turned everything crisp and yellow. Several redneck teens loitered at the stop sign. They looked dangerous. Dorothy picked up her pace, moving through sunlight and shade. To scare away the teens, or any other potential muggers, she began singing hymns. *This is my sto-ry, this is my song, Praising my Savior all the day long.* She stepped over cracks in the sidewalk, *step on a crack, break your mother's back.* Well, her mother dear was already dead—Miss Gussie had been eaten up with leukemia and no one, not even Clancy Jane, had bothered to tell Dorothy. Miss Gussie had died before she could make amends. *I won't let that happen to me and Bitsy*, she thought.

She stopped walking, set down her suitcase, and wiped her face against her dress. It was boiling hot, even in the shade, and the crickets shrilled frantically from the trees. She puffed hard, sucking in the humid air. She hoped she wasn't walking her way into a heart attack. At the asylum, the doctor had said that exercise was good for crazy people—not in those words, of course, but Dorothy knew what he meant. Personally, she thought physical exertion was dangerous. She hoped her refrigerator wasn't empty, because she could use an ice-cold Coca-Cola, and maybe a can of mixed nuts, too. Over to the left, she saw hand-painted signs that said NO DUMPING! and MUSH MELLONS 4 SAIL. She reached for her suitcase and turned down a paved road that led up to the Square. Through the haze, she could see the faint outline of the courthouse and the statue of a fallen Civil War hero.

When she reached the Square, she passed a gray-headed man. Before she could stop herself, she winked three times. The man cringed, then sped off. His shoes clapped against the sidewalk. Dorothy turned around, the Nehi sloshing in the bottle.

"I wasn't *flirting* with you!" she hollered. "I've got a tic! And not the kind that bites!"

The man broke into a run, disappearing around a magnolia tree.

"Cracker," Dorothy said and heaved a sigh. She didn't know that gray-headed man, and even if she did, she wouldn't have winked on purpose. Her face had a mind of its own. She tried to stop it, but the harder she tried, the worse the winks got. At Central State, the doctors had given her some Psycho-Drano that ate away the nerves in her face. Unhappy with the results, the doctors had prescribed a different pill, but she kept on winking. "It may lessen in time," the psychiatrist had told her. "Then again, it might be permanent."

"I'll wink like this forever?" she'd asked, horrified.

"It's possible," the doctor admitted, "but it's a small price to pay for sanity."

Dorothy called it her winky-tinky smirk, but it manifested itself only when she was tired or jittery. As she walked around the Square, she winked three more times—the tics usually came in waves. When she finally turned down Dixie Avenue, her muscles began to relax. She lived four blocks from here. After being cooped up with lunatics, she longed for the privacy of her own house, where she could twitch and wink and watch her soap operas in solitude.

I am a lone woman, Dorothy thought. Alone and lonely. She was no longer Mrs. Albert McDougal. After he'd married his cashier—a winkless lady, no doubt—they'd moved away. Dorothy pictured her former husband, good old Albert with his sagging stomach and graying temples. Damn his soul, she'd been a good wife. But even in the Bible wives weren't appreciated. She often wondered how Lot had described his wife. "What a terrific woman. Why, she's a pillar in the community."

Every night at five-thirty sharp, Dorothy would set the kitchen table with her rooster dishes. She set out pork chops, mashed potatoes, lima beans, corn bread, and a chess pie for dessert. Oh, she could cook like nobody's business. She was a catch for any man. On Sunday nights she served Albert's favorite dish, hoppin' John, with a big pan of corn bread, and lots of sweet tea. She had kept a pretty house, a little messy in the closets, but you had to live. It just wasn't *fair* to lose so much, Dorothy thought. But she was beginning to understand that fair had never been part of the bargain. Life was tough, and you just had to hang with it.

Dorothy couldn't wait to see her avocado-green kitchen. She and Albert had built the house in 1951. It was a two-story red brick, ugly but interesting, with Gothic arches and butter-colored shutters. The house was next door to her mother's, who had died the very same day that Dorothy allegedly jumped off the roof of Albert's dime store. Well, you couldn't believe everything you heard.

By the time she reached her block, her dress was stuck to her skin, as if the cloth had melted.

She took one last sip of the Nehi, then squatted down and hid the bottle in an azalea. Stifling a burp, she walked along the sidewalk. At first everything looked strange yet familiar, and she kept blinking. At the end of the road, she saw a purple clapboard house with pale lilac shutters. Except for those shutters, which had witchy little half moons on them, and the color, of course, the house, her childhood home, looked exactly the same. In the old days her mother used to hire Preacher to repaint the house every few years. She used to say that she planned to leave orders in her will to paint it a different color every summer. Well, the poor thing hadn't been in her right mind when she'd died.

Dorothy hadn't been present at the reading of the will, but Albert had told her all about it. Her mother had left the family homestead to Clancy Jane and Violet. If only Miss Gussie had split it right down the middle, half for Dorothy, half for Clancy Jane. That was the fair thing to do. But she hadn't done it, for whatever reason, and the wishes of the dead had to be respected, dammit.

Shifting her eyes to the left, Dorothy started toward her old house, but it, too, had vanished. In its place was a squat building shaped like a cookie jar. The red bricks had been painted over with bright pink paint. And bottle-green shutters framed every single window. In the flower beds were plastic roses and sweet peas. Her eyes began to twitch, making it difficult to see. Then she realized this *was* her house. While she'd been locked up in the asylum, someone had gone around town painting houses, making it impossible for recently released mental patients to find their way home.

Why had they gone and painted her house pink? It looked like Pepto-Bismol. If someone was driving down Dixie and got heartburn, all they would have to do was stop at this house and lick it. After she'd gone away to Central State, Albert had mumbled something about Mack moving into her old house. He hadn't gone into detail, and she hadn't asked, but Dorothy knew that awful bleached-blond hussy was now married to her son. They had been dating long before Dorothy went bonkers. What was that girl's name—Darlene? Earlene? *Shar*lene? Something with a *lene* in it. Dorothy could just see them laying up in her house, rolling on the sheets she'd hand-embroidered, taking bubble baths in her very own tub and not even bothering to scrub off the ring.

Now, she stared at the house, praying that her son hadn't changed anything inside. Surely Mack hadn't repainted the master bedroom, where she and Albert had kissed good night for the entire length of their marriage. They always kissed the very second that Channel 2 news came on, with Larry Munsen, the weather, and sports (nothing much ever happened in Nashville). Oh Lord, her house had felt huge after everyone had left—first Albert, then Mack went to Vietnam, and Bitsy got married. No sooner had she gotten used to living alone that she went and had a nervous breakdown.

But it wasn't my damn fault! she thought. *My loving family stuck me in a mental hospital in November of 1971, and then forgot I existed.* Dorothy shut her eyes a minute, swooning in the hot sun. She walked crablike up the driveway. Mack was her darling, even if he had poor taste in women; but a Pepto-Bismol house was more than she could bear. It would draw attention to itself, and Dorothy did not like attention. She knew how people in Crystal Falls loved to put labels onto everything: This one was a cheapskate, that one was crazy, and *that* one lived in the Pink House.

As she stared, the lemon-yellow door opened, and a skinny bleached blonde stuck out her head. "Good God," said the blonde, shielding her eyes with one hand. "Mrs. McDougal? I don't believe my eyes!"

"Who are you?" Dorothy said. Well, this was a bald-faced lie; she knew exactly who this tart/hussy was, she drove a school bus, but Dorothy couldn't see it anywhere. Unless it was parked in back of the house.

"Don't you remember me?" The hussy was wearing white go-go boots, a red miniskirt with marabou trim, and a silver sequined halter top. And it was the middle of the day.

"Are you the maid?" Dorothy asked in an innocent voice.

"No, I'm Earlene. Mack's wife? Your daughter-in-law?"

"The last daughter-in-law I remember is Sloopy." Dorothy fixed the girl with an innocent look. Twice now, Mack had married very strange women. It was all so very unsatisfactory. She couldn't choose her children's spouses, but she damn sure didn't have to like them—or acknowledge them, for that matter. Earlene had an unsavory reputation, but it hadn't made one speck of difference to Mack. "She's electrified," he'd told his mother. "So was the bride of Frankenstein," Dorothy had replied.

"Mack divorced Sloopy a *long* time ago," Earlene said. "She and Christopher moved to California. Her sister lives there."

Dorothy pressed her lips together, refusing to comment, and so Earlene barreled on.

"Mack and I got married before you went . . . away."

"Sorry, I don't remember you." Dorothy rubbed the place on her forehead where her eyebrows would have been, then she turned her head ever so slightly, as if she were trying hard to remember. Yes, she could see that blonde just a-barreling down the highway, angling the bus around hairpin turns, the little schoolchildren huddled together, screaming for mercy, begging her to slow down.

"Hon, are you . . . all right?" Earlene looked frightened.

"I'm fine," Dorothy snapped. "How are you?"

"No, I just meant—"

"You want to know if I'm crazy?"

Earlene blushed.

"Well, I'm fine. Just fine and dandy. And I *do* remember you. I was just pulling your leg. You used to drive a big yellow bus."

"I sure did! But I gave that up. Now I drive a Cadillac." Earlene pointed to a white car with fins poking out of the brick garage.

"I'll just bet you do," Dorothy said under her breath.

"You look good, hon," said Earlene.

"You really think so?" Dorothy smiled. She was starting to warm up to Earlene—quite a lot, in fact. Even though she'd probably kept Mack from visiting Dorothy at Central State. It wouldn't have killed either one of them if they'd driven up a few Sunday afternoons. Well, never mind that. She gazed sideways at Earlene. "Where's my son?"

"Inside watching a baseball game." Earlene pointed. "I just fixed him a ham sandwich and a beer. Can I get you something?"

Dorothy edged up the path. Asylum food wasn't fit for consumption, and besides, most of the food at Central State ended up on the floor or smeared in the patients' hair. The thought of a civilian sandwich was mighty appealing. In fact, she hadn't tasted a ham sandwich in years. She could see it in her mind: stacks of glistening pink ham on toasted white bread, all slathered with mayonnaise, garnished with garden tomatoes and ice-cold crunchy lettuce.

"I could eat a little bite," Dorothy admitted, trying not to drool down the front of her dress. "While you're fixing it, you can explain why you painted over my bricks."

"It was Mr. Frank," said Earlene. "You remember him? Your old decorator?"

"What about him?"

"Well, it was every bit his fault," Earlene said. "Me, I wanted to paint it orange, but Mr. Frank said, 'No, no, no, Earlene. You *can't* do that!' He had his heart set on gray with crisp white trim—the New England look, you know. But we settled on pastels. I drew my color scheme from the petit fours at Ralph's Bakery." Earlene spoke in a confidential tone. In the sunny entry hall, she stretched her arms above her head, in a glamour shot pose. "Mack's a real hotshot builder now, Mrs. McDougal. But I guess you knew that? He's in county-wide demand. I pick out all the wallpaper and colors for his spec houses. That's why I done give up driving that lousy bus."

"I think I'll take that beer." Dorothy shuddered, and both eyes began to wink. "And don't bother with a glass, Darlene. I'll take it in the can."

"It's Earlene," said the blonde. "Earl-lene."

Earlene and Mack gave Dorothy the grand tour, inside and out. With rising horror, Dorothy saw, firsthand, how Mack had destroyed his family home, stripping it of its architecture and history. Not that there was a lot to begin with, but *still*. The blonde/hussy/tart probably put him up to it, but Dorothy didn't ask why, and she didn't dare to wonder. In the backyard, the color-coordinated flower beds were gone, replaced by a swimming pool with a blue bottom, and there wasn't a trace of ivy on the north wall. Her avocado-green kitchen had ceased to exist. The knotty-pine cabinets had been painted a deep fuchsia. Even the appliances had been colored to match. The floor had been ripped up—her pretty brown linoleum was gone!—and in its place were pink-and-white tiles, laid on the diagonal, forming a freakish checkerboard. Dorothy looked at the bay window, expecting to see her round cherry table with the captain's chairs. They were gone, too, replaced by a smoky-glass table on metal stilts. The plastic chairs looked uncomfortable, and the seats were upholstered in faux tiger stripes.

"You're welcome to live here with me and Earlene," Mack said, but he didn't look too happy about it. In fact, he looked downright distressed. Treacherous children, Dorothy thought. You suckle them from your breast, you wipe baby shit off their butts, and they can't wait to get rid of you.

"Me? Live here with you and . . . oh, I couldn't."

"Well, you can always go next door and live with Aunt Clancy. The room across from Bitsy's is empty."

Dorothy gaped up at her son. Didn't he know that living next door wasn't an option? Not after Clancy Jane had done what she'd done. An amused expression flitted across Mack's face. Except for that grin, which was totally inappropriate, he was the same boy she'd always adored. Unlike her house, which scarcely resembled its old self, Mack had stayed the same—blond and blue-eyed, with one leg shot off in Vietnam. Her Mack. She'd loved him more than she'd ever loved anyone. *This* was how he showed his thanks.

"You know that Clancy Jane and I don't get along," Dorothy said. "Besides, she's married. And I could never share a bathroom with a strange man."

"Hon, we've got a guest room upstairs, where Bitsy's old room used to be," said Earlene. "It's real pretty. Decorated in hot pink, the same color as the bricks outside. You're welcome to it."

Dorothy's cheek began to twitch. Somehow she'd been swindled out of two houses, one pink and one purple. Where will I live? she wondered, trying not to panic. *And with whom?*

I will not live amongst mine enemies, Dorothy thought, casting an involuntary glance at the purple house next door. She could see it from nearly every window, except on the north side. For years she'd spied on her mother and Clancy Jane, her mother's favorite, watching them dig in the garden, their heads inclined. It didn't help a person one bit, loving them too much. In fact, it probably weakened them at the core. The neglected ones always had bigger hearts, and they seemed better off.

No, sirree, Bob. She didn't wish to mingle with her sister, much less live under the same roof, even if Bitsy was there. Dorothy had always favored Mack—she just couldn't help loving him more than she loved Bitsy. The asylum doctors—oh, what did they know!—had said something about Miss Gussie being a bad role model. And when Dorothy had her own children, she'd followed in her mother's footsteps, picking Mack to be her pet. The doctors also said that Dorothy had never learned to get along with her mother or her sister, and therefore, she would continue to squabble with other women, including her own daughter.

The doctors had encouraged her to forgive and forget. She had looked at them, her eyes wide with astonishment. Forgiveness was a religious thing, not a psychological one. And she would forgive whom she g.d. pleased. Before Albert's defection, he'd been Dorothy's most faithful visitor. Which was a bit ironic, considering their marriage had ended after his debauchery with Clancy Jane. Oh, it hurt her head to think about it. Besides, she had more pressing matters.

Mack added, "You'd probably be happier with Bitsy and them than with me and Earlene."

Ungrateful little snipe. He didn't know the first thing about happiness, least of all hers. Dorothy wanted to seize him by the shoulders and shake him. Instead, she counted to ten, but it didn't help. She was still steaming. So she counted to twenty, thirty, forty. When she hit seventy, she felt calm enough to speak. "I'm staying right here," she said, looking up her at handsome son, this blond cover boy whom she'd made from scratch. He had her eyes, nose, and hair—well, her old hair, before the shock treatments had fried it. There wasn't a look of Albert in the boy. It was a miracle.

"Here?" Mack and Earlene cried together.

"Yes." Dorothy ignored her son's stricken face and her daughter-in-law's curled, defiant lip. "Now that we've got that settled, where's the guest room?"

A TAPED MESSAGE TO PAT NIXON

212 Dixie Avenue
Crystal Falls, Tennessee

June 17, 1974

Dear Pat,

I know you've been a nervous wreck, what with all your troubles with Dick, so I forgive you for not answering. But I'm home now, living in my brick house on 212 Dixie, so feel free to use this address for future correspondence. Only it doesn't feel like MY house anymore. When I got married to Albert, my mother gave us the land next to her house. This was way back in the early fifties, mind you. We hired a contractor and he let me choose everything. I picked red bricks. I'd planned to spend the rest of my days there, but Albert did what he did and I got slapped in the mental hospital. While I was gone, my son and his smutty old wife moved into my house. They hauled off my clothes, shoes, and knickknacks. Mack even threw away his OWN stuff—his old clothes, toys, and report cards that I'd saved. Well, to make a long story short, Mack knocked down walls, cut holes into the roof, and ripped up the wall-to-wall.

But you haven't heard the worst. My son's wife painted my house pink. The upstairs resembles a gymnasium, like the room where Jack Lalayne used to exercise on TV. It's just horrible, the worst thing I've ever seen. Well, I must admit that I like the ceiling windows. I can lay in bed and watch the moon float past. But I do NOT like climbing up the stairs every night. I have a bad leg from where I fell off the roof of Albert's dime store. And I do NOT like the way my room is decorated. My old cherry furniture has been painted burnt orange. The curtains are skimpy and came from Sears—orange and pink flowers. A hideous painted coconut head hangs from a ceiling hook, and its eyes follow me around the room.

My house has changed so much, I hardly recognize it. Somedays, I'll be walking home from town, and I'll go right past it, ending up on the next block. And when I creep around in the night, I bump into walls and knock over tables. My mind keeps slipping out of gear like a faulty transmission— half the time I can't remember if I've took my nerve pills. And you can't double up on those or you'll overdose. I'm convinced that's how Marilyn Monroe died, not that I have a fixation on her, I just feel pity. She had everything going for her but she just couldn't keep track of her pills.

Just the other day, Earlene gave me some envelopes to mail, and I set them down on my dresser and plum forgot. Earlene is my son's two-faced, bleached-blond wife. Not much more than a streetwalker if you ask me. Just like my slut of a sister, she stole my son away from his first wife. Mack has lost touch with his boy. Sloopy remarried and her new husband has adopted the boy. Earlene is thrilled, I can tell. She doesn't like any competition, even if it's a child, or a mother-in-law. She works like a man, driving tractors, hammering shingles, laying bricks. When my son met her, she drove a school bus, but now she helps him build houses in Shenandoah Estates. Once the houses are built, she turns them over to Century 21. She carries a fingernail file and a tiny screwdriver in her right hip pocket.

This is not to say she is all bad. She is just mostly bad. She keeps an immaculate house, I'll give her that. Gleaming floors, dust-free baseboards, sparkling toilet bowls. She has shapely legs, and she shows them off every chance she gets, but she doesn't cook. Fortunately, I am practically a gourmet chef because I got to watch Julia Child on Channel 8 at the asylum. So I began whipping up soufflés and omelets, but Earlene turns up her nose and drags Mack off to the Burger Barn. Every morning she lays his clothes out on the bed: socks, boxers, jeans, shirt, belt, cowboy boots. Several times a week she sprays his wooden leg with Pledge and puts WD-40 on the hinges. She sits on his lap and kisses his neck, and it just burns me up. It's vulgar. What mother wants to see this? Back to those envelopes Earlene asked me to mail. They turned out to be her and Mack's bills, and the City of Crystal Falls cut off our utilities.

Turning off an old woman's water supply is mean, especially if that old woman keeps caged birds. I have one canary who sets in his food dish and beats his wings. You can just imagine the result. It takes water to clean a mess like that. It made Earlene so mad that she made me get rid of my bird. I tried to tell this to the lady at City Hall, but she just said I had to pay my bills on time. I tried to explain about the envelopes and my bad memory, but she just gave me a stony expression. So I just begged her to make a notation on my son's account. Then I realized I might be confusing the woman a tad, so I backed up and explained the whole story, how I was living with Mack and Earlene and so on and so forth. She kept interrupting me, telling me that she just worked for the city, she didn't personally cut off the utilities.

But I can't make coffee or flush the toilet, I told her. Then when my son came down personally to pay the bill, you people took your sweet time turning back on the water. And when you did, guess what happened?

What? the girl said.

Air in my pipes.

The girl shrugged. She was young, about the age of Earlene, but not nearly as trashy. I just really don't like other women, all except for you. In fact, now that I'm out of the asylum, I'm hoping that I can come up to Washington, D.C., and have tea in the Blue Room. Or we could go to your private quarters.

I sure hope you don't forget to answer this letter, or I guess you'd call it a tape recording. It's terrible to be absentminded. Just the other morning I woke up and couldn't remember my daddy's face. He's only been dead twenty-six years, and you'd think I'd remember something of this nature, but my mind would not call back his face.

You don't have to be crazy to lose your mind. Although it could be hardening of the arteries or the medicine I'm taking. I sure would like to remember everything. It's important to know where you're going, but it might be even more important to know where you've been. At first I thought I might keep a family history for my children, but how could I explain what I was doing without them getting suspicious? If they think I've lost my memory, it's just a hop, skip, and a jump to thinking I've lost my mind. Then they'll slap me back into the asylum. I try to hide my confusion, like where I put the TV Guide, but it's a terrible way to live. It just occurred to me that your husband might have a memory problem, too. He might've erased his tapes and then forgot what he'd done. If you need me as a character witness, don't hesitate to ask.

Your friend,
Dorothy

FROM THE DESK OF CLANCY JANE FALK

June 19, 1974

Dearest Violet,

I haven't written because I've been busy helping Bitsy fix up a nursery for Jennifer. We picked Miss Gussie's old sewing room because it's sunny, then we peeled off the wallpaper. Bitsy went down to Sherwin-Williams and bought pale blue paint. We rolled it on the walls and even the ceiling. I thought it was too much blue, until Bitsy started painting clouds everywhere. Next, we hung gauzy white curtains over the double windows. We found a poofy, ruffled white bedspread and matching pillow shams in the attic, and Dorothy dumped them into the sink and dyed them blue. Byron and Mack painted the furniture white. I found a fluffy white rug at the remnant store. Bitsy's stuffed animals went into the bookcase, then she framed some old lace doilies and hung them over the bed. We did it for under $150, including the rug for $75. Bitsy has found her calling. Only I don't think a living can be made from decorating other people's houses. Mr. Frank has cornered the market in this town, and look what he drives—a beat-up Chevy van.

XX OO

Bitsy

I stood in the cereal aisle at Winn Dixie, trying to decide between Cap'n Crunch and Special K, when I saw a tall man staring. He had shocking red hair and freckles. It took me a minute to recognize him. *Oh, my God,* I thought. *It's him, Dr. Walter Saylor.*

"I know you." His eyes opened wide, showing the yellow irises. "Didn't I fill one of your cavities?"

"Mmmhum." *Go away,* I thought.

"Is it doing okay?" he asked, eyeing my brown plaid sundress—not my color at all, but it was a gift from Earlene. It had spaghetti straps and a built-in bra that made my teacup-size breasts seem larger.

"Fine," I said, thinking about our so-called breakfast date. I'd stood him up.

"I'm just doing a little shopping." He stared down into his cart. I looked, too. He had apples, lettuce, bread, liver loaf, Hellmann's mayonnaise. It was tempting to analyze people by the food in their grocery carts, but I resisted the impulse. These days, I was trying hard not to make snap judgments. Besides, normally my own cart was filled with strange items for Aunt Clancy and would lead someone to deduce that I suffered from a picky palate. Today, my cart was jumbled with soy milk, artichokes, flat-leaf parsley, yogurt, navy beans, chocolate syrup, vanilla ice cream, frozen puff pastry, blue birthday candles, a wheel of Brie, T-bone steaks. It was for Byron's thirty-eighth birthday, which was coming up. On that day, my aunt was actually serving meat and making a cake that called for a dozen eggs.

"I've been wondering about you." Dr. Saylor tossed a cereal box into his cart. "What was your name again?"

"Bitsy."

"Oh, right. Now I remember." He reached for another box. "I waited a long time for you at the truck stop."

"Sorry about that," I said, casting about for a convincing lie. Several came to mind, but I discarded them all. Honesty was another part to my self-improvement campaign. But looking at Dr. Saylor's downcast eyes, I just felt terrible.

"Well, you missed a good breakfast." He sighed. Then his eyes swept over my breasts, down to my feet, then back up to my face. "That's a real pretty outfit. You look like a fashion model."

I had the oddest feeling that I'd heard these words before—maybe on a deodorant commercial. "Flatterer," I said.

"I'm not. You're pretty enough to be a movie star. You're real hot-looking. In fact, I'm getting hot."

I frowned. It seemed wrong to discuss sexual chemistry in the cereal aisle of the Winn Dixie.

Dr. Saylor smiled, dropping another box of Raisin Bran into his cart. He glanced at me again, then picked up a box of Trix.

"You must be crazy about cereal."

"What? Oh, my gosh." He blushed, and began placing the boxes back on the shelf. "I don't know what's wrong with me."

"Well, it was nice seeing you, but I've got to dash off. My ice cream is melting." I pushed my cart forward.

"So's my heart." He laid one hand on his chest.

He was making me sick, so I tossed out a "see you later," and then hurried to the checkout line. I kept glancing over my shoulder, afraid I'd see Dr. Saylor bearing down on me, but he never appeared.

I dropped off the groceries at 214 Dixie, then Aunt Clancy sent me back to town to look for a telescope. She thought it might be a nice present for Byron. I went to Big K and Western Auto, but I returned empty-handed. As I turned up Aunt Clancy's curved walkway I saw a bouquet of yellow roses propped against the screen door. I reached for the white card.

Nice seeing you again.
Love, Walter.

The next morning, I started out the kitchen door, and tucked inside the screen was another large bouquet of roses—pink this time and still dewy from the florist's refrigerator. Despite Claude's wealth, he had never sent me flowers, except for proms, and my two wedding bouquets, which I myself had chosen. As I picked up the flowers, the green paper crinkled in my arms. A white card fell out.

Proof that I don't give up easy.
Love, Walter.

When I came home that afternoon, another bouquet of pink roses was propped crookedly against the screened porch. I took my time walking to the porch, halfway hoping the flowers were a mirage. They weren't. I picked up the bouquet, and a note drifted to the porch steps.

You haunt my dreams.
Love, Walter.

. . .

I was brushing Jennifer's hair when the doorbell rang. The baby knocked away my hand and raced to the door, screaming for Chick. But when I opened up, a two-foot-tall arrangement fell into the room, spilling water over the floor, along with red roses, carnations, and baby's breath. The water gushed over the card, which dangled from a long piece of red ribbon. I picked up Jennifer, to keep her feet from getting wet, then I reached for the vase. The water had blurred the ink on the card, but the message was clear.

I'm not giving up on you.
Love, W

With my free hand, I scooped up the flowers and marched to the end of the driveway. Jennifer grabbed a fistful of carnations and crammed them into her mouth. "No, bad flowers," I scolded, thinking she was too old to act this way. She screwed up her face and howled, as if she was in the habit of eating flowers at the Wentworths. Hooking my finger into her small mouth, I raked out the petals. She coughed and wiggled down, out of my grasp. On the ground she glared at me and defiantly held out one hand. Petals littered the small palm.

"Gimme!" Jennifer screeched. Then she stamped her small foot and pointed at the flowers.

"No," I said. "Bad flowers."

I dropped the bouquet into the trash can, then slammed down the lid. With a yelp, Jennifer flopped onto the driveway grabbing handfuls of her blond hair, tearing it from its roots—just like my mother. I glanced next door at the pink house and there she was, standing spread-eagle in the dining room window. Ever since she'd moved in with Mack and Earlene, my mother had amused herself by spying on me and Clancy Jane. The rest of the time she was cooking meals for Mack and Earlene. I waved and the curtain fell. A minute later my mother stepped out of the pink house. She wore baggy overalls and a red paisley blouse. And she had forgotten to paint on her eyebrows.

"Bitsy, what's going on? Is the baby hurt?"

"No, M—" I had been going to say, No, Mummy, but I broke off, my lips pursed around the word. I knew she liked for me to call her that. I made a *mmm* sound, but couldn't not push out the other letters without remembering how Claude used to taunt me, saying "Mummy" was a stupid name for a mother. It's true that whenever we'd fight, he'd try and make me feel ashamed. Maybe it did sound affected, as if I were trying to sound British. Maybe it was high time that I called my mother something else.

"No, Dorothy," I said, surprised at how good it felt to use her actual name. "She's just mad because I won't let her eat the flowers."

"You can't let a baby eat flowers."

I frowned, trying to think of a five-syllable word. "Jennifer ate them *intentionally*," I said.

"Don't be silly. Children don't eat plants unless they're starved."

Jennifer scrambled to her feet and threw herself at my legs, pummeling them with her fists. "Mine!" she growled.

"Well," Dorothy said. "You'd better calm her down. If Betty Wentworth finds out, she'll make a fuss."

Long ago I'd stopped following Dr. Spock's advice; I switched to Dr. Brazleton, who advised ignoring tantrums. I leaned over, trying to brush flowers from the child's pale blond hair. "A guy sent me a bouquet. I didn't want them," I told Dorothy.

"No!" Jennifer yelped. She reached up with one hand and messed up her hair. "Don't!"

I held up both hands in mock surprise and stared down at my child.

Once Jennifer had been a quiet and content baby, but she'd turned into a pint-size delinquent. "Can't you act nice?" I asked, and she violently shook her head.

"A guy?" Dorothy's wide, unpainted forehead creased. "Do I know him?"

"I don't think so."

"Go on, then. Be mysterious. But it wouldn't hurt you to have a boyfriend." Dorothy marched over to the trash can, lifted the lid, reached inside, and grabbed the bouquet. "Just *look* at these pretty things. Why, they're carnations. You should be thrilled. It's a *sin* to throw away flowers."

"Where in the Bible does it say that?"

"Isn't it in Proverbs?" Dorothy scratched her forehead where her eyebrows should have been.

"Yes, it's Proverbs," Dorothy continued emphatically. "I remember now. Waste not, want not. Or is that one of Benjamin Franklin's sayings?" Her blank forehead moved up and down. "Oh, you've just got me so confused, I can't stand it!"

Dorothy snatched up the flowers, and Jennifer let out another piercing scream. When I tried to pick her up she grabbed the neck of my blouse and yanked down, showing my garage-sale bra. Dorothy paid no attention to the child. She began talking to the bouquet.

"You poor little things. You're all bent. Well, I'll fix you up." She held out one hand to her granddaughter. "Come on, Jennifer. Dry your tears, honey. Let's take these pretty flowers into my house and put them into a vase."

Jennifer let go of my shirt and stuck out her tongue, revealing a tiny carnation petal. With her free hand, Dorothy grabbed the baby's chin. "Spit it out, honey."

Jennifer clamped her teeth and scowled up at Dorothy. "No!"

"Well, go on, then. Eat the nasty thing," Dorothy said. "But when you get a tummy ache, don't come crying to me."

Dorothy reached for Jennifer's hand. "Don't you worry. I'll take good care of her. And I'll get that flower."

"Good luck," I called, feeling a pang as I watched my daughter slip her hand into Dorothy's.

"I think she could be cutting a molar," said Dorothy. "I'll check her mouth real good."

"Maybe it's pinworms," I called.

"Well, I'm not checking her there. I'll let Chick and Betty deal with that." Dorothy glanced down at the child. "You don't look wormy to me. Not one bit."

Jennifer smiled, showing her bunny teeth.

"We'll have tea party, you and me," said Dorothy. "And after that, I'll let you jump on Earlene's water bed. Won't that be fun?"

"Don't spoil her, Dorothy," I called.

"I wouldn't dream of it," she said. "Why, that's the Wentworths' job."

. . .

Two days later, I opened the kitchen door, and five bouquets fell into the kitchen. Aunt Clancy stepped into the room, her eyes wide. "From the yellow-eyed dentist?" she asked.

"I'm afraid so. The house already smells like a funeral home."

"Or a wedding chapel," said Aunt Clancy. As she gathered the bouquets into her arms, five white cards dropped to the floor.

Each was inscribed with a single word in what I had come to recognize as Walter's crimped handwriting. I laid them out in a line, but they didn't make sense. *Call A Please Me Give.* I rearranged them.

Please Give Me A Call.

"Maybe you should," said Aunt Clancy. "I've been asking about him. He's an excellent dentist. At least, that's what my beautician said. According to Stella, he's got a reputation for being a painless dentist, not a womanizer."

"You talked about me at the beauty shop?" I cried.

"Well, *I'm sorry*, but it just came up while she was bleaching my roots. And I didn't talk about you in particular. I just asked who her dentist was, and when she said it was Dr. Saylor, I almost fell out of the chair. So I egged her on, and, honey, I got an earful. Do you want to hear?"

"No."

"Sure you do. He told the truth. He *is* separated from his wife. Her name is Fiona, and she's got a reputation for being pushy."

"They must make quite a couple. I've never heard of a dentist asking for a date with a patient—especially when he's just stabbed a needle into her gum."

"It's not ethical for doctors; I don't know about dentists. But Stella said he was very business-like when he pulled her wisdom tooth. And the lady in the chair beside me—she was getting a perm?—said that he barely spoke to her when he filled her eyetooth. So he must've been attracted to you."

"It wasn't mutual."

"No? Honey, it's been two years since you've been with a man."

"That's not long. Anyway, I'm just not ready."

"And when will that be?"

"When I get my life back together. Maybe then the right man will come along."

"The right man is a myth. Settle for the left. You don't want to lose your dating skills. Don't make a face—it happens. I've lost mine."

"But you're married."

"Barely. Anyway, Dr. Saylor might not be the man of your dreams, but can't you practice on him?"

"That wouldn't be very nice."

"Excuse *me*, Miss Congeniality."

"I want to concentrate on my daughter, on our visits."

"Yes, but you deserve a little fun. You don't want to wake up one day and find cobwebs in your vagina." Aunt Clancy opened a cabinet and selected a green McCoy vase, an old, elegant one shaped like a bouquet of hydrangeas. She turned on the faucet and filled it with water.

"After he's divorced, I might give him a call," I said, hoping to placate her.

"I know why you're this way. Because of what Claude did to you." She turned off the faucet and lifted the vase. "I suppose you disapprove of me, seeing as I took Byron from his wife and children. But he and his wife must have been miserable, or he wouldn't have taken up with me."

"Maybe *she* was happy," I said. "Maybe she assumed that Byron was, too."

"A fatal mistake."

"For whom?"

"Why, his wife, of course. I certainly didn't mean Byron or myself, if that's what you're asking." The vase looked intact, but within seconds a fine trickle of water began to leak from the base onto her hands.

She set the vase gently into the sink and lifted out the whole clump of flowers. Laying them aside, she said, "I can try and glue it back. Thank goodness I didn't put it on Miss Gussie's table. It would've left a white spot."

"It wouldn't have been your fault," I said. "If you didn't know it was broken, how can you be expected to fix it?"

"You can't." Clancy Jane's lips tightened, and she picked up a rose, the petals trembling. "That's the trouble, you just can't."

• • •

That weekend, Violet drove up from Knoxville. When she stepped into the kitchen she goggled at the vases lined up on the counter and the floor.

"Who died?" She leaned over to smell a coral rose. She wore green army fatigues and clunky boots, but her hair was swept into an Audrey bun.

"Bitsy's got an admirer," said Aunt Clancy.

"A florist?" Violet gave the rose one last sniff, then she jerked open the door of the refrigerator and poked her head inside. She pulled out a Sara Lee chocolate cake.

"No, a dentist," said Aunt Clancy, watching as Violet opened a drawer and removed a knife and three forks. "And don't include me in this sugar-fest."

"Oh, come on." Violet ripped off the plastic wrap. "Preservatives are *good* for us."

I told her to cut me a big slice as I walked over to the Welsh cupboard, grabbed three polka-dotted plates, and set them down on the table.

"So, tell me about this suitor who sent all these flowers," she said, serving the cake.

As Aunt Clancy told her the whole story, Violet fit a hunk of cake into her mouth and chewed vigorously, her dark eyebrows moving up and down. They were virginal brows—not a single hair had ever been plucked. Still chewing, she reached into the cake box and dragged her finger along the cardboard bottom, scraping up a hunk of icing. She put her finger into her mouth, then burped.

"I'm so glad you're home," I said, meaning it. I loved the way women were able to relax when no man was around. And these days Byron was always at the hospital, signing charts, recording discharge summaries. When he was home, he either fell asleep on the sofa or buried his face in a medical journal.

"What's this dentist's name?" Violet asked.

"Walter Saylor Jr.," I said.

Violet's eyes popped open wide. "Hey, I might know him. Does he have a harelip?"

"I didn't notice."

Aunt Clancy snorted. "How could you overlook a disfigurement like that?"

"I didn't say I overlooked it," I shot back. "I said—"

"It's not Bitsy's fault," Violet said, waving her fork. "If we're talking about the same Walter Saylor, he has a slight scar on his upper lip. I understand it's barely noticeable. I've never seen him. I don't understand why he'd be sending you flowers, Itsy. He's married. Or at least he *was* last summer. But he's a wife beater, so you'd be smart to steer clear of him."

"How do you find out all this stuff?" I asked. "Who told you?"

"Sources. Deep Throat," Violet said. "The Crystal Falls version."

"It's Danny, I know it," I said.

"That little pip-squeak?" Aunt Clancy smirked. "He doesn't know his ass from a hole in the ground. You said so yourself, Violet."

"I never said it was him. I said source*s*. That's plural. And my sources know a Vietnam veteran who painted the house next door to Dr. Saylor's. He heard screams."

I'd been cutting into my cake, and my hand froze. I hoped that Violet was making this up, trying to scare me. Unlike her mother, my cousin believed that a Crystal Falls man was the last thing I needed, and she was always begging me to go to the community college where I'd meet men and at the same time get an education.

"The painter heard screams?" Aunt Clancy asked.

Violet nodded.

"Quit eating." Aunt Clancy slapped Violet's wrist. "What kind of screams?"

"High-pitched ones," Violet said, her words garbled by cake.

"Could it have been the television?"

"The TV doesn't squeal, 'Please, Walter. Don't!'" Violet opened her mouth, showing a streak of black on her tongue, and shoved in another mouthful. Still chewing, she added, "Apparently the painter heard a great big crash, too. And the next day, he saw the wife in the backyard, wearing a floppy hat and sunglasses."

"What's that supposed to prove?" Clancy Jane asked. "Maybe it was a bright, sunshiny day."

"I thought of that, too. But according to the painter, it was overcast. Hey, are y'all through with this?" Without waiting for an answer, Violet began dragging her fork over the top of the cake, scooping up the icing. "The wife didn't need the sunglasses or hat *unless* she was trying to hide something."

"A black eye?" Clancy Jane suggested

"That's what the painter thought." Violet licked the tines of her fork. "The wife was wearing something long-sleeved too. Totally weird for a hot summer day."

The three of us fell silent. The only sound was Violet's fork scraping over her teeth. Finally Aunt Clancy said, "What about you? Are you still sleeping with that poet?"

"No, he left me for an art major, and I'm better off. He was messy and forgetful." Violet sniffed. "Men have two speeds, on and off. They aren't complicated. In fact, they're too fucking shallow."

"If you want depth, get a swimming pool," said Aunt Clancy, "but don't turn into a man-hater."

"Would you prefer me to be a man-eater?" Violet pulled the Sara Lee box into her lap. "Personally, I prefer cake."

"How do you eat so much and stay thin?" I asked.

Before she could answer, the doorbell rang. I followed Aunt Clancy into the front hall. She opened the door, and Donnie, the florist's gnome-like delivery man, held out two glass vases, both filled with tropical flowers—hibiscus, bird-of-paradise, and some weird, spiked things. I carried the vases back to the kitchen and set them on the table.

Violet stared.

Aunt Clancy touched the envelopes. "May I do the honors?"

"Be my guest."

"And the winner is . . . " She ripped open the envelopes and held up two white cards. One said CALL, the other said ME. A phone number was scrawled on the back of ME card. She handed it to me, saying, "You have to end this."

"Don't you dare call that wife-beating bastard," Violet cried, rising from her chair.

"But she can't keep ignoring these flowers. She's just got to be firm with him, and real, real specific, or he'll think she's secretly interested."

"Bitsy, don't listen to Mama," Violet said. "If you call, you'll only inflame him. Ignore him, and he will go away. Eventually."

"I hope you're right." Aunt Clancy pursed her lips.

I threw the cards in the trash.

"I'm still hungry," Violet said. "Let's go to the Square and get some ice cream."

We hopped into Violet's Volkswagen and drove downtown, looking for an empty parking spot near the ice cream shop. The radio was blasting out "What's Going On" by Marvin Gaye. We passed a man who was jogging down the sidewalk. Violet suddenly hit the brake and leaned toward the windshield. "Wow, look at him. He's cute."

The man was running past Rexall Drugs wearing shorts and a faded

Memphis State T-shirt with the sleeves cut out. He had long, muscled legs and broad shoulders with chiseled biceps. A faded bandanna was tied around his forehead, and perspiration was dripping off his hair, which hung around his face in dark orange ringlets. The wind caught his shirt and it blew up, showing a flat midriff and a hairy chest.

"Why, that's Dr. Saylor," I cried.

"Damn, what a body." Violet whistled. "Gee, he sure doesn't look dangerous. Even if he is, I can handle him."

"You?"

"Why not? God, my nipples are getting hard, even with that orange hair. But it'll blend in perfectly at the U.T. football games."

"If you can handle him," I said, "then so can I."

"Bet you wish you hadn't torn up that ME card!" Violet laughed, and Dr. Saylor ran around the corner and disappeared.

After supper, while Violet and Aunt Clancy did the dishes, I sat cross-legged on the counter, the phone book in my lap. Walter Saylor Jr. had two numbers, an office and residence. I dialed the home number before I lost my nerve.

"Who are you calling this time of night?" Aunt Clancy asked, dipping a glass into the sudsy water.

"The dentist," said Violet in a dreamy voice.

"What?" Aunt Clancy whirled around, slinging suds onto the floor.

"I'll explain later," said Violet, throwing down her drying rag and hurrying over to me. She hopped up on the counter and pressed her ear against the receiver. When Dr. Saylor answered, I said, "Hi, er, this is Bitsy Wentworth. The one you've been sending flowers to?"

"Oh! You got them."

"Yes, I did," I said in a bubbly voice, thinking of his legs.

Aunt Clancy set the glass in the plastic drainer and stepped over to the counter. I moved the receiver so we could all hear.

"Can you hold on a second?" he asked. "I'm in the hall, and I've just got to drag the phone into the bathroom."

"Hold on," he said. "I'm turning on the shower."

Violet put her hand over her mouth and giggled.

"Maybe I should call you later," I said.

"No, now is fine. It's just fine. See, I'm still living with Fiona—but not as man and wife. Fiona's my soon-to-be-ex? She wouldn't like it if I was talking on the phone."

"Oh." I made a face at Violet.

"Is he still getting a divorce?" Aunt Clancy asked.

"Shhh!" Violet hissed.

"I'm sorry, I shouldn't have called," I told him. "I was under the impression that you were separated—"

"I am. It's a long story. If you meet me for breakfast tomorrow, I'll explain everything."

While we decided on time and place, I heard a pounding noise. "What's that?" I asked him.

"It's Fiona," Walter said. "She's banging on the door."

In the background, I heard a gravelly voice. "Walter? What are you doing in there? And why do you need the phone? Do you need me?"

"No, Fiona. Just go away," Walter yelled.

"Walter?" cried Fiona. "If you don't answer me, I'm picking the lock. Walter?"

"Say *something*," I suggested. "Tell her you're fine."

"I'm fine," he called.

There was a moment of silence. It occurred to me that my husband had tried to drown me, and now I was encouraging a wife beater. Why did I attract these types?

In a loud voice, Fiona cried, "But Walter, honey, what's taking you so long? Are you talking to your mother again?"

"No, Fiona. I'm calling time and temp."

"I can give you that information," Fiona yelled. "Honey, if you're pooping then just say so. Did your diarrhea come back?"

"No!" Walter screeched. "I'm not your honey. I'm divorcing you, Fiona. So *go away*."

"I most certainly will NOT!" Fiona screeched. "I'm going to jerk out the phone if you don't come out."

I waited for an opening, then said, "Fiona sounds upset. We'd better hang up."

"Wait, not yet! Meet me tomorrow at the Caney Fork Truck Stop out on Highway 70," he said. "Is nine o'clock too early?"

"Fine, I'll be there," I said.

"Good, good!" Dr. Saylor said.

"What's good?" Fiona screamed. "What's going on in there, Walter? Open the door *this* instant, or you'll be sorry."

"I may have to spend the night in here," said Dr. Saylor. "So don't leave if I'm a little late."

After I hung up, Violet made a pitcher of margaritas, and we went outside and sat on the back porch, gazing up at the stars. It hadn't rained for weeks, and the City of Crystal Falls was threatening to ration water. Aunt Clancy stepped out onto the porch, carrying a portable radio. John Denver was singing "Annie's Song." She inched open the screen door, careful not to bump us, then eased down onto the step behind Violet and reached down for the pitcher.

"I wish it would rain," I said.

"Maybe we should dance," Violet suggested.

"I think I've forgotten how," said Aunt Clancy.

"It'll come back to you," said Violet, grabbing her mother's hand.

"Come on, Bitsy," they called. "Get your butt out here."

While John Denver sang about his lady, the three of us entwined our fingers, then raised our arms and began to sway to the music. Next door, the porch lights blinked on. Dorothy and Jennifer stepped out, followed by Earlene. "Y'all look ridiculous," Dorothy called.

"It's a dance," called Aunt Clancy. "Get over here. We need you."

"I most certainly will no—"

"Yes!" Jennifer began pulling Dorothy's hand. "Me dance too."

"Oh, for heaven's sake." Dorothy rolled her eyes. But she let Jennifer pull her down the steps and across the yard. I let go of Aunt Clancy's hand and took my daughter's. Earlene fit herself between Jennifer and Violet. Then we all turned to look at Dorothy.

Clancy Jane extended her hand. "I won't bite if you won't," she said.

"That's all right. I've had my shots." Dorothy took her sister's hand and the six of us began to move in a circle. "Now, dance and fill your minds with watery things," Aunt Clancy ordered. "Baths, rivers, dew, waterfalls, mermaids, fish, crabs."

"Frogs," said Dorothy. "Leeches."

"Runny noses," said Violet. "Amniotic fluid. Breast milk. Menstrual blood. Salt. Sweat."

"Shut up, Violet," Aunt Clancy told her, laughing.

"Thirst," I said. "Fountains."

"Drowning," said Dorothy.

"Floating," I said.

"Faster!" Jennifer cried, towing us along. Her laughter rose up into the air, a beautiful sound like a spoon tapping against fine crystal. "Dance, Mama," she said, tugging on my hand. "Dance."

. . .

It had just stopped raining when I pulled into the parking lot of the Caney Fork Truck Stop, a squatty cement building trimmed in green neon. Glancing in the rearview mirror, I smoothed back my hair. Today I had it swept up into a Grace-like twist and was wearing a blue floral dress with a low sweetheart neckline and puffed sleeves that I'd found at the junk store. On my feet were blue leather shoes with double ankle straps and high, thick heels. We'd all raided Miss Gussie's attic, finding a mother lode of vintage fashions—the latest fad for the fall of '74. But I was a little surprised at myself for going to all this trouble for a man who hid in the bathroom and who may or may not be a wife beater.

When I stepped inside the truck stop, he was leaning against a red SEAT YOURSELF sign looking crisp and collegiate in dark green corduroy pants and brown tasseled loafers. His white shirt was unbuttoned at the neck, showing a triangle of coppery hair and deathly pale skin. The hair, as always, was shocking. When he saw me, he smiled and placed his hand on my elbow.

"It's not the International House of Pancakes," Dr. Saylor said with an aw-shucks shrug. "But it's the closest thing we've got in Crystal Falls."

A haze drifted over the tables, cigarette smoke and grease, making my eyes water. Two truckers turned around and gaped, their mouths filled with scrambled eggs.

"Is this table okay?" Dr. Saylor asked, gesturing to a window booth, which looked out onto the weedy parking lot. The windows were spotted with raindrops. Instead of curtains or blinds, there was a philodendron growing over them, attached here and there with green thumbtacks.

"Mmmhum," I said, glancing toward the ominous cloud of smoke drifting from the kitchen toward the dining room. Not a single worker wore a hairnet—Aunt Clancy would croak if she saw this place. I scooted my hips across the booth, and Dr. Saylor sat down across from me. Despite the outrageous hair, he had rather delicate features. Today his eyes looked brown, without any yellow. I looked for his hairlip scar. It was pale and white and curved. Afraid he'd catch me staring, I dropped my gaze to the table. I could see tracks of a recent wiping on the Formica. In our window, the philodendron had been trained to fall in strips. The sun fell in long, slender bars, shining through the heart-shaped leaves.

"What an interesting idea," I said, reaching up, rubbing my fingers over a glossy leaf. As Dr. Saylor reached out to touch the plant, his hand accidentally bumped into mine. I gingerly traced my finger down the vine, away from his hand. I was relieved to see our waitress appear, her wide hips swaying. Her eyelids were daubed with green iridescent shadow. *Minnie* was embroidered on her left pocket. She plunked down two menus on the table.

"Coffee?" she asked Dr. Saylor.

He nodded. "Sure, I could use some. How about you, Bitsy?"

I smiled up at Minnie. "Fresca, please."

Minnie made a note and then drifted off. I lifted the menu, which was two faded mimeographed sheets, each encased in a cracked and yellowed plastic sheath. In ballpoint pen, someone had sketched a crude trout in each corner, its gaping lips about to bite into a hook that looked like Dr. Saylor's scar. The Green Parrot's menus featured printed calligraphy and a parrot logo. In addition to the menus, Zach had set up an oversize chalkboard where the daily specials were written out in pink chalk. The café was a perfect blend of cute and classy, trendy and traditional. Customers felt hip when they dined there. For the duration of lunch, they could be part of the counterculture without having to travel any distance or make any permanent changes in their diet, politics, or lifestyle. Not that most people in Crystal Falls actually thought about such things.

Minnie returned, holding a tray. She set down the coffee, a wisp of steam rising up, then my Fresca. With a sigh, she pulled from her pocket the same type of pad that I used at the Green Parrot. "Y'all decided yet," she drawled, "or do you need more time?"

"Give me one more minute, but you go ahead," I said to Dr. Saylor.

"Okay, then. I'll have the Trucker's Special."

I glanced down at the menu. The Trucker's Special offered pancakes, sausage, grits, hash browns, and four eggs, any style.

"How do you want your eggs, sugar?" Minnie asked.

"Sunny-side up, please."

"With extra toast for dunking?"

"Definitely." Dr. Saylor nodded.

"And you, ma'am?" Minnie smiled at me patiently while I studied the menu, searching for something that wasn't doused in two pounds of grease.

"Do you have salads?" I asked hopefully.

"Not really. Well, we have tuna." Minnie made a face. She leaned toward me and whispered, "*If* you like mayonnaisy things, that is. You ain't saving no calories, trust me. I'd get the omelet. My motto is, if you're gonna eat something fattening, you might as well eat something tasty. You know what I'm saying?"

I smiled and nodded. I liked Minnie's style. "Have you been waitressing long?" I asked her.

Before Minnie could respond, Dr. Saylor interrupted, "Just make that two Trucker's Specials."

"Oh, no." I shook my head. "That's too much."

"It's a bargain," said Minnie. "You get one of everything."

"We're not coming for the food, anyway," Dr. Saylor said, giving me a knowing look.

"Ain't heard that one before." Minnie raised her eyebrows and scribbled on the pad. "I guess you two are in love."

She bustled off, and Dr. Saylor propped his arm on the back of his booth. "My baby sister Jobeth used to work here," he said. "That's how I know about it."

"I'm a waitress at the Green Parrot Café." I touched the philodendron again.

"Well, I'll have to start eating lunch there." He smiled. The sun blazed through the window, shining through his Afro, making his scalp gleam. "When you aren't waiting tables, what're you doing?"

"I like to work in the garden with my aunt." I rubbed a spot on the table.

"I used to have plants. You know, ferns and whatnot. But I've been thinking that I'd like to study astronomy, learn the constellations."

"Yes, that would be neat. Do you have a telescope?"

"No, but maybe I'll get one." He leaned across the table and tucked a lock of my hair behind my ear. "So soft and pretty," he said. "I wonder what you'd look like as a redhead."

Awful, I almost said but stopped myself. I leaned back, and my hair slipped from his fingers.

"I'm sorry," he said. "I just can't seem to keep my hands to myself."

I let that pass.

"You don't feel comfortable with me, do you?"

"Should I?"

"Maybe you will when you get to know me better." He folded his hands. "Do you have any questions?"

About what? I thought. But I said, "Why did you and your wife split up?"

"We just did." His face turned red, and he looked down at his hands.

"Were you having an affair?" I thought this was probably the reason, because he'd acted pretty forward with me from the get-go.

"No, no! You've got me pegged all wrong. I'm not the type to run around. I mate for life."

"Maybe you still love her. Why don't you try and patch things up?"

"And risk death?" he cried. Several truckers turned around to stare.

"Fiona's a violent woman," he mumbled, his cheeks turning purple. "She beats me."

I blinked, wondering if I'd misunderstood. "You mean, like, she hits you?"

"All the time. Last night, she chased me with a hot spatula. I've got a mark to prove it." He glanced over his shoulder, then rolled up his sleeve, to reveal a square red patch above his wrist. I saw little dots, each corresponding to the holes in a spatula.

"She started beating me on our honeymoon," he said. "And she never stopped. But I never laid a hand to her. Not ever. Not that I'm expecting a medal or anything. But I put up with a lot."

I squeezed my hands together, remembering how Claude pushed my head into the sink, his fingers digging into my neck. And then I remember how I'd bashed in his face.

"But if she's so violent, why are you still there?" I managed to ask.

"Squatter's rights. She wants the house, and legally it's half mine. But I paid for it all."

Minnie was bearing down on our table, her arms loaded with trays. She began setting down plates in front of Dr. Saylor, rapidly covering the table's shiny surface: four sunny-side up eggs, ruffled strips of bacon, disks of sausage, buttery grits, hash browns, fried apples, biscuits, toast.

"Man, look at this." Dr. Saylor pursed his thin lips and whistled.

"Ain't it a beauty?" Minnie grinned, arranging plates in front of me.

"And it was fast, too," said Dr. Saylor.

Minnie grinned, as if she was personally responsible for the swift service. I wondered how long ago the food had been prepared.

"Y'all need some milk to wash it all down?"

"Bring us the whole cow." Dr. Saylor grinned at Minnie, then he turned his attention to the table, gazing rapturously at the food. I felt dizzy breathing in the greasy fumes.

"After all this, I won't be able to eat for a week," I said.

"Me, either." Dr. Saylor squirted catsup over his hash browns.

I lifted my fork, speared a sausage. A droplet of grease hit my plate. I still wasn't one-hundred percent convinced that he was telling the truth. From the corner of my eye, I watched Dr. Saylor digging into his eggs. Freckles were splattered on the backs of his fingers, way too many to count, and his nails were marred by white dashes and dots, like his body was sending urgent signals in Morse code. *Danger, Stay Away*. Or the code might have said: *Harmless, Free Roses. Take Advantage*.

"This food is de-licious," he said, shoving a forkful of hash browns into his mouth. A blob of catsup hit the front of his shirt, directly over his heart, neat as a bullet hole. "But it's not as good as El Toro's. Maybe one of these days, we'll go there, just you and me."

"Please don't take this the wrong way," I said, "but I'm afraid to go anywhere with you. You're still living with Fiona. What if she just cracks?" I snapped my fingers to emphasize my point, and he flinched.

"The only thing she'll crack," he said, a grim look crossing his face, "is a whip—across my back."

Clancy Jane

In a yard sale cookbook find, Clancy Jane found a recipe for a dish called Buddha's Jewel—tofu dumplings floating in a sweet-and-sour sauce, with mushrooms and water chestnuts. She ran to the cramped, cookbook-lined office in the back of the café to show it to Zach. He vetoed the idea, arguing that Buddha had *three* jewels, not one, and besides, the customers might confuse it with the "family jewels." She hadn't thought of that.

He suggested instead that they serve a tofu and spinach quiche, a big hit up north where he was from, and reached for *The Vegetarian Epicure*, volume I, by Anna Thomas. While he reverently thumbed through the index, Clancy Jane noticed again his gorgeous hands, and was glad she was wearing a wispy voile tunic over jeans and Violet's red shoes, each decorated with a leather rose. She moved closer to look over his shoulder at the recipe but told him she hadn't totally given up on Buddha's balls. He laughed and said she reminded him of his gutsy friends back home. Clancy asked him if Crystal Falls didn't seem like home now and his reply was, "I'm like Odysseus. I pine for Ithaca."

She started to ask if Odysseus was one of his friends up there, but was afraid he'd think she was prying, so she just asked him what Ithaca was like. Instead of answering he said he had something important to discuss. Clancy Jane could feel her heart tapping away, and wondered if he could feel it too. Then he asked how she would feel about expanding—opening the café for breakfast.

She realized no matter how long he had been there, he was right, he hadn't made this his home. She gently tried to explain that the folks in Crystal Falls love their grits and biscuits. But seeing his face fall she added that she guessed they could serve cheese grits. Zach wanted a hipper menu, of course. Omelets, blueberry waffles, spiced coffee cake, home-made jams. And flavored coffee.

Clancy Jane pointed out that they'd be working seven full days a week and would die of exhaustion. He just laughed and said not to worry, she'd get her beauty sleep. Then he pinched her cheek. *Would he do that if he wasn't attracted to me?* Clancy Jane thought. She thought he liked her, but he knew she was married, and of course there was the age difference—ten years was a bit much. He was probably smart not to add any more headaches to his life. But if he was older—or if Clancy was younger—they would have made the perfect couple.

Her mind filled with all the older women/younger men stories she had ever heard, she went home to break the news to Byron. She found him in the kitchen, reading a medical journal at the harvest table. It was the first thing in their house that been theirs as opposed to his or hers from previous lives. They had found it at an antique shop out in the country and it wouldn't fit into the Volvo, so they had tied it to the roof. When they got it into the kitchen, Clancy Jane had hopped on top of it, feeling the rough wood beneath her thighs, and held out her arms to Byron. When they started making love, she had feared that the table might cave in, but it remained upright.

Now Byron lowered his magazine, and she told him that she was thinking of opening the café for breakfast. He raised his eyebrows and said, "This is your idea?"

"Well, mine and Zach's," she clarified.

Byron threw down his magazine and got up from the table. Clancy Jane yelled after him, "Gee thanks for being supportive."

He shouted back over his shoulder, "I *have* been."

Clancy Jane's response was a tirade about how she couldn't sit home just waiting for him and that her work at the café was important, that food was a symbol of nurturing.

He laughed. "*Nurturing?* Did I hear *you* say *nurturing?* There hasn't been one egg in this house since we got married. But go ahead, feed omelets and eggs Benedict to the masses. At least someone will get to eat."

"That's not fair," she cried. "Are you forgetting all the eggs I put in your birthday cake? And what about that huge steak I fixed? God, your memory is short."

"I knew you'd say that," he told her and quickly left the room.

"I should've married a vegan," she said under her breath. "Maybe next time I will."

Bitsy

Aunt Clancy and I were sitting on the porch, having a sort of sad talk. I told her about my problem with Dr. Saylor. I wouldn't date him as long as he and his wife were living in the same house. Then she told me about how sometimes in the night she'd wake up and feel Byron's body next to hers and wonder how two people could be so close and yet so far away. She was just saying that food had driven them apart when a gray T-bird pulled into the driveway and Dr. Saylor got out, wearing cutoff blue jeans and the Memphis State T-shirt. He reached into the backseat and pulled out a long box. On the side was a picture of a telescope. I didn't like him being there but was glad for the interruption.

Once he was on the porch, Dr. Saylor glanced down at the box, then shifted his eyes over to me. "Hi, I hope I'm not interrupting anything," he said.

"Not at all," said Aunt Clancy. "You must be Dr. Saylor."

He nodded, and I quickly made the introductions. Then, even though I pretty much knew the answer, I asked, "What's in the box?"

"A telescope," he said. "I told you I might get one."

"It's super," said Clancy Jane. She got out of her chair, cracked open the front door and leaned into the hall. "Byron? Can you come here a sec?"

A minute later, Byron appeared in the doorway, holding *The New England Journal of Medicine*.

"This is Dr. Saylor," I said.

"The flower guy," Byron said. He and Dr. Saylor shook hands.

"And look what's he's brought." Aunt Clancy's voice was real high and bouncy.

"I could sure use some help putting it together." Dr. Saylor set the box on the floor and pulled off the lid. He pulled out an instruction sheet. "You got a Phillips screwdriver?"

"I wouldn't know. I'm not mechanically inclined," Byron said. "I'd only make things worse."

"There's a box of screwdrivers in the shed." Aunt Clancy headed toward the screen door. "I'll be back in a minute."

"That's okay, I'll go," said Dr. Saylor. "Just direct me to it."

Wow, I thought, tilting my head to one side, staring at Dr. Saylor's muscular legs, his frayed white socks peeking above his sneakers. *I may have underestimated this guy.*

·   ·   ·

The next evening he showed up again, holding a bouquet of pink tea roses and several boxes of Whitman's chocolates. Tucked beneath his arm were Little Golden Books for Jennifer, even though he'd never laid eyes on the child. I myself hadn't seen her in weeks.

"What are you doing here?" I bit the inside of my cheek, hoping I hadn't sounded rude. I was wearing black sweat pants that were covered in lint and a baggy T-shirt.

He answered by holding out the books—*Pokey Little Puppy, Ugly Duckling, The Gingerbread Boy, Henny Penny,* and *The Three Billy Goats Gruff.*

I started to thank him, but my throat had closed. Then I started to cry, big sobs. Aunt Clancy heard the commotion and came running into the front hall.

"Did I do something wrong?" Dr. Saylor asked my aunt. The tips of his ears reddened. "Is her daughter too young for books?"

"Oh, *no,* they're perfect," Clancy Jane said. "Bitsy loves to read. Did you know that she learns a word from the dictionary every single day? What's today's word, Bitsy?"

The pride in her voice made me cry even harder. "Umbrage," I said.

"So the books are okay?" Dr. Saylor asked.

"P-perfectly," I said, hugging the books to my chest. "Dr. Saylor, do you still want to take me on a real date?"

"Yes." He nodded. "More than anything."

"Then let's go."

"Now?"

"Just let me change clothes." I put the books on a table and laid my hand on his arm.

We drove to The Electric Circus—the only disco in town—and found a quiet corner. After two beers, I tried to explain why Jennifer didn't live with me. I glossed over the lurid details, especially the part about the baby back ribs. I'd expected a barrage of questions, but Dr. Saylor surprised me by saying, "You poor kid. You didn't deserve that."

Later we drove over to the Princess Theater to see *The Odessa File*. It was after midnight when we got back to my house. I took Dr. Saylor's hand and led him into the dark living room. We leaned against the wall and began to kiss, his hand moving roughly over my blouse. Then we inched our way across the dark room, stumbling over chairs. Dr. Saylor fell back onto the sofa, and I fell on top of him. He took my face in his hands and whispered, "I wanted you the first day I saw you," he said, his voice hoarse and creaky. "I just had to have you."

I wasn't sure if I believed him. To lighten things up I said, "I don't want to be your rebound woman," but he thought I was serious.

"No matter if you are, I can't let you get away." He rubbed my chin.

I glanced down at him. There was the godlike body, but then there were the teeth and hair. However, I admired his intelligence and his thoughtful ways. Once my heart had pounded for Claude's kisses. I had longed for his touch, and in the backseat of his father's Lincoln Continental, I'd eagerly surrendered my virginity. Just yesterday I'd been telling Aunt Clancy that I wasn't sure I could ever feel that way again. She'd looked at me a long time, then said, "Be glad."

Dr. Saylor must have misinterpreted my silence for indecision. His head was tilted back, the frizzy curls flattening against the sofa. He stared up at the water-stained ceiling, his eyes dilating. "You've got me all hot," he whispered, towing my hand to his crotch. I started to pull away. Sex on a first date would give him the wrong idea about me. Then I froze. Beneath the tented fabric, I felt him. He moaned, turning his head from side to side. Aunt Clancy was always talking about the sexual revolution—free love and women's liberation. A woman could enjoy a man, she was always saying, and she didn't have to be pie-eyed in love with him. Maybe I could do this, too. Maybe it was better to *like* a man.

His zipper made a whispery sound, then he kicked off his trousers and pulled down his cotton briefs, Fruit Of The Loom. The air was filled with a musky smell and it drugged me. "Let's get comfortable," he said, and he unbuttoned my dress slowly, taking his time. I held up my arms, and he pulled the dress over my head, then neatly folded it, set it on the floor.

Next, he pulled down my panties. I held still, passive as a child, feeling him lift my feet, one at a time. He took off the rest of his clothes then, laid them next to my dress, then drew me back down onto the sofa. Every worry and scruple I had ever possessed was driven out of my mind.

The next day Walter moved out of his orange house. After my shift at the café, I walked over to his office. Ignoring his employees' stares, he pulled me into his arms and blurted out that he'd taken a room at Sullivan's Motel, a seedy place that rented by the week. "I no longer live with Fiona. Now we can date right here in Crystal Falls," he declared, and his receptionist's eyebrows shot up. He picked up a lock of my hair, rubbing it between his fingers. "Just for fun, why don't you dye your hair to match mine?"

Before I could shake my head, he took my hand and said, "It would mean the world to me."

. . .

I made an appointment at the Utopian, the beauty shop where Aunt Clancy got her hair dyed. My beautician was Tina, a short, wide-hipped woman with a gap between her front teeth. Her eyebrows were tweezed into thin, upside-down Vs. Not a good sign, I thought, but I followed the woman to her station and sat down in a cushioned pink chair.

"Can you streak my hair a little?" I asked. "Just a subtle hint of red? But I want it to look natural, you know?"

"Honey, who don't want it natural?" Tina chortled, her fingers moving expertly over my scalp, parting hairs as if she were searching for lice. "Looks to me like your natural color's blond. A level eight, beige blond. People would *kill* to get this color. Pardon me for asking, but why would you *want* it red?"

"It's just temporary." I shrugged. "I plan to change it back."

"Hon, you don't understand. Getting your hair red is the easy part. Going from red to blond is another story."

"Even if it's just streaked?"

"Yes. Not to mention the damage you'll be doing to your shafts." Tina exhaled. She lifted a strand of my hair and gave it a doubtful look. "Just buy you a wig."

"Who sells wigs in Crystal Falls?"

"Well, you got me there. You'd have to drive to Nashville."

"Maybe you could just streak it a little."

"You sure are brave. Or else cracked in the head."

It *hurt* to get my hair streaked. Tina shoved a rubber cap, which was full of tiny holes, over my head, then tied the straps under my chin. She reached for a long, sharp object—it resembled a crochet hook or a dental probe—and started digging out strands of hair. While she pulled, I gripped the sides of the chair, tears streaming down my cheeks. I thought about the time I'd applied to cosmetology school, and how I'd recently, found my rejection letter tucked into a old *Reader's Digest*. That was probably a lucky break, because I didn't like how beauty parlors smelled.

Tina didn't seem to mind. She was exchanging mother-in-law stories with the other stylists, but I couldn't concentrate. Tina's voice droned on and on like an attic fan. After a while she filled a plastic bottle with orangy-red dye and squeezed it over the strands. Then, using her fingers, she formed the strands into stiff prongs until they fanned out all over my head.

In the mirror I thought I looked like the Statue of Liberty.

After my hair was shampooed, Tina led me back to her chair and began to comb me. I was in a pleasant daze, listening idly to all the gossip around me and wondering if perhaps the chemicals did more than relax curls and dye hair—they loosened tongues. Then I heard a name that brought me to full attention. Tina was talking with the squatty beautician in the next cubicle. "Don't look now but Fiona Saylor is getting yet another haircut."

The other beautician glanced toward the front of the shop and said, "That's the second time this week. I wonder what's wrong at home?"

"Ask Anita. She's been doing Fiona's hair forever."

My head swiveled around, and I saw a woman whose hair looked too short for styling. I watched, fascinated, as the beautician took an electric razor and shaved the back of Fiona's neck. The blade made a harsh scraping noise. The beautician ripped off the cape, waving it like a matador, and said, "Wait till Dr. Saylor gets a load of you! He'll call off that divorce."

"Oh, that. It's not for real." Fiona lifted her hand from the plastic cape and gave a dismissive flip, then reached back under the cape, fumbling for something in her lap. She pulled out her eyeglasses and pushed them onto the bridge of her nose, then she squinted at her reflection. "Oh, it's adorable," she said. "Walter'll just love it, I'm sure."

Wait a second, I thought. *Is Walter two-timing us?* I remembered how she'd yelled at Walter when he was in the bathroom and it was the same voice, just turned down several notches. Well, I didn't love her new hairdo. In fact it was not becoming to her tiny head. From behind, it looked as if a South American headshrinker had performed experiments. I kept watching in the mirror while she walked up to the counter, her long feet splayed outward. She wore thick boots, the type favored by deer hunters. As she moved, her shirt caught the light. It was blue denim, with FIONA spelled in shiny green and blue sequins. The shirt was tucked in military style, accentuating her hips, which bulged on either side. She heaved her pocketbook onto the glass case and pulled out a battered leather wallet. On her left hand, I saw a wedding ring. It flashed as Fiona counted out bills and handed them to the teenage clerk.

Then Fiona waddled over to the squatty Coca-Cola machine and stared at the selections behind the glass door. It was an old machine, with a round top. She studied the buttons—Orange Crush, Tab, 7UP, Coke. She inserted a dime and pressed the Orange Crush button, then moved back, her eyes on the chute. When the bottle didn't appear, she stepped closer, made a fist, and whacked the machine. Still no bottle. Turning around, she yelled at the beauticians, "It took my money again! Can you get it back?"

"Sorry, it's not our machine," said Tina. "I can't open it."

"Who can?" Fiona planted one hand on her hip.

"The Coke machine man," said another stylist. "And he lives in Nashville."

"He needs to come down here and fix this thing." Fiona leaned over, bending at the waist to peer up the chute. Then she stood up and kicked the machine a couple of times. The bottle rattled down and Fiona grabbed it.

She opened the door, the bell dinging above her head, and stepped out onto the sidewalk, sipping the Orange Crush. Anita shook her head. "She does that every damn time."

"One of these days she's going to break it," Tina said as she led me to the dryer.

"And when she does," said Anita, "I'm sending her the bill."

"She's so rough," said Tina. She lowered the lid and turned on my dryer, and the roar swallowed up the women's voices. I could see their lips moving, and I wondered what they were saying. Tina dumped a *Photoplay* and *Glamour* into my lap, then she walked toward the front of the shop and returned with another customer, an elderly woman with stiff hair.

Some time later, when I emerged from the dryer, my cheeks flushed from the heat, Tina began unwinding the rollers, revealing long reddish-blond strands. It resembled the licorice candy that the teenage cashier was eating.

"Oh, my *God*," I said, covering my mouth with one hand. My cry brought the other stylists. They gathered around me.

"I warned you," said Tina. "God in His wisdom knew what He was doing when He made you a blonde. Don't cry. I can fix it. I just can't fix it *today*, because I'm booked."

"It'll grow out," said another stylist.

"That's what I love about hair," said Tina.

• • •

One hazy afternoon in July, Walter took me for a drive. "I want to show you my old house," he said, steering his Thunderbird down the Nashville Highway. "I want to show you everything about myself."

When he said things like that I worried about not having told him the full story about me and Claude and the baby back ribs. So I just nodded. He angled off the highway, into Shenandoah Estates, turning right on Gettysburg Court, then left on Shiloh Avenue. Walter's house stood in a cul-de-sac. I thought about Violet's story of the screams coming from that house, and Fiona appearing the next day wearing sunglasses.

In my mind, I'd pictured it as sad-looking with crooked shutters, dead bushes, trash piled up in the driveway. A place with burned-out light bulbs, peeling paint, missing shingles. Instead, it was well tended. No overflowing trash cans. Zinnias bloomed from a flower bed. Aunt Clancy and I hadn't set out bedding plants. Of course, we didn't need any with all the roses Walter was still sending.

"It's just a shame that we can't live here." Walter's chin jutted out. He pressed his foot against the accelerator and drove to the end of the street, then he backed into a paved driveway, and cruised by Fiona's house a second time. A wooden sign next to the front door cheerfully announced Welcome to the Saylors! Round stepping stones curved past a forsythia bush. I caught a glimpse of a redwood deck at the back, and a kettle grill, the top portion neatly covered with black plastic.

"I seeded that lawn myself," Walter said. "I had to get a special shade mix, too."

"You did a good job," I said.

"It's not that I *begrudge* Fiona getting it," he said, casting one last glance at the house. Then he chewed the inside of his lip. "Well, I guess I do," he admitted. "I do begrudge her. I wouldn't be human if I didn't want what's mine. Not a penny of hers went toward the mortgage."

"You'll get another house," I said.

He pursed his lips and made a *pffft* sound, as if he were spitting out cat hairs. "I doubt it. She'll get so much alimony, I won't have a pot to piss in."

"I guarantee that you can find peace and happiness without a house," I told him.

"I sure could use some peace," he said, a slow smile breaking across his lips.

"You want to spell that last word for me?" I smiled.

"First, let's get out of here," he said, laughing.

. . .

Walter wanted me to meet his family, so a week later we drove way out into the country, toward a community called Hanging Limb. He turned up a gravel driveway that gave way to a rutted dirt road, then put his Thunderbird into park and dropped his right hand to my knee. "I want to tell you about my folks," he said. "Mama's a homemaker, but Daddy's a golf nut."

Walter glanced up at the house. It was clapboard, painted moss green, with black shutters. The lawn was littered with yellow golf balls. A pink chenille bedspread was airing on the porch railing. I was having trouble picturing a golf nut living here, but Walter's description of his mother seemed accurate.

As if reading my thoughts, Walter said, "He played golf all last summer. He'd set his alarm clock for five A.M. so he wouldn't have to wait in line to tee off. Mama stayed home and vacuumed. She doesn't even drive. You'll just love her. My sisters live here, too, so you'll meet them."

"How many do you have?" I asked. The way he said "my sisters" put me in mind of a harem, women with long flowing hair and jeweled belly buttons.

"Two. Lacy's the oldest, and Jobeth's the baby."

When Walter and I reached the front door, a woman's head popped out. It had grizzled hair and bright blue eyes. It let out a whoop, then the body it belonged to—surprisingly girlish in a red polyester pantsuit that showed off slender legs and a small waist—ran out onto the porch and drew Walter into her arms. She kissed his eyes, nose, and forehead.

"Stop it, Mama," Walter complained. "I can't breathe!"

Mrs. Saylor released her son and spun around. "You must be Walter's little girlfriend," she gushed, grabbing my hands. "We've been dead to meet you. His sisters will be out here in a minute. They're in the bathroom douching." She pronounced it DOO-shin.

I glanced at Walter, but he didn't seem to find anything odd about his mother's comment. He took my arm and led me inside. As I stepped into the living room, I smelled the biting aroma of apple cider vinegar, and my eyes began to water.

"Oh, look, Walter. She's crying!" Mrs. Saylor grabbed my hands again. "How sweet. She's tenderhearted, just like we are. This calls for a drink. Walter, take your girlfriend into the living room, and I'll be right with you."

Walter led me down a dingy hall with faded green wallpaper, past a heap of dirty laundry and a long pine bench. A cross had been carved into each side of the bench, and I realized it was a church pew, but I didn't have time to ask questions, because Walter was steering me into a paneled room. Here the air smelled of cigarettes and dirty feet. A golf tournament flashed on the portable TV. There were two vinyl sofas—one green, one tan, both of them ripped. Three recliners were angled in the corners. A stubby little man was stretched out in one chair. He had thick forearms, and his dome was bald and gleaming, surrounded by a thatch of graying orange frizz. He didn't even glance our way.

"Hey, Daddy," said Walter.

"Hold up!" Mr. Saylor barked. He leaned forward, keeping his eyes on the television. His ears resembled raw oysters. I gulped, remembering Point Minette. "He's on the thirteenth hole."

"Who is?" Walter persisted.

"Arnold Palmer, now hush!" Mr. Saylor cried.

Walter pressed his lips to my ear and said, "When he's not playing golf, he's watching it."

I nodded and glanced around the room again. I thought Walter had been a little too generous in his description of his mother. Wisps of dust hung from the ceiling. Large glass ashtrays were filled with cigarette butts. He led me to the tan sofa and we sat down, our thighs touching. I tried to move away, but he pulled me back. Since I didn't want the Saylors to get the wrong idea about me, I sat primly—hands in my lap, knees together.

On the wall behind Mr. Saylor, I noticed a framed print showing the Arc de Triomphe. I froze. Claude's mother had owned a similar picture—not a print but an oil painting. This wasn't a good sign.

From the hallway came the sound of a door slamming, followed by feminine laughter. A moment later, Walter's sisters appeared. They were strawberry blondes, with pale, freckled faces. One sister was tall and willowy, the other was short and curvy. They perched on opposite ends of the green sofa and smiled at me. Their teeth were sharp and tiny, like upholstery tacks.

A door swung open, showing a glimpse of a filthy kitchen—counters heaped with dishes and potato chip bags. Mrs. Saylor bustled in, carrying a tray. "Girls, say hi to Walter's girl," she told them, handing out Bloody Marys.

"Hi," the sisters said in unison.

"That's Walter's daddy over there," said Mrs. Saylor, nodding in his direction. She lifted her drink, the ice tinkling. "We call him Rooster, and he *does* kind of look like one. Rooster, turn off that TV and say hello to Walter's girl."

"In a minute. Arnold's putting." Mr. Saylor frowned.

Mrs. Saylor plopped down on the green sofa, bracketed by her daughters. I sipped my drink. The vodka tasted strong and bitter, the tomato juice weak and watery.

"Waltie, do you think it's fair that Fiona gets your house?" Mrs. Saylor gave him a sly look.

"Please don't start, Mama." He gave her a warning look.

"You're generous as the day is long. But if it was *me*, I'd kick her butt out of that house and make her get a motel room. The way you've had to do." Mrs. Saylor lifted her glass and drank half of her Bloody Mary, then she sighed and turned to me. "I just love vodka, don't you?"

"Yes," I said in a polite, eager-to-please voice. I'd only taken a few sips and already I was feeling giddy.

"Feel free to call me Wilma."

From the television came the sound of the crowd clapping for Arnold Palmer. Now Walter was sitting on the edge of the sofa, rooting and cheering.

Mrs. Saylor looked at her daughters and made a face, as if to say Boys will be boys, then shot a cautious glance in my direction.

"That's a lovely painting." I raised my glass, as if saluting the Arc de Triomphe.

"Yes, isn't it?" Mrs. Saylor's eyes shifted away from me, and she turned, gazing over her shoulder. "I don't know what it's a picture of—maybe Walter does. He gave it to me last Christmas. Didn't you, Walter? *Walter?*"

"What?" Walter's head swiveled.

"What's that a picture of?" Mrs. Saylor pointed.

"A place in Italy or Greece, I think." Walter squinted at the painting. "Or maybe Holland."

"My boy is so smart," said Mrs. Saylor. Then she thumped my arm. "How did you and him meet?"

"At his office," I said. I didn't volunteer any details, and neither did Walter.

"When you say 'at his office,'" Jobeth said, making quote marks in the air with her celery stick, "were you working there?"

"No, no," Walter said, and he put his hand over mine and squeezed it. "She came to get a tooth filled, and the minute I saw her, I fell head-over-heels."

Jobeth and Lacy stared at his hand and raised their eyebrows, but they didn't say anything.

"Bitsy, do you work anywhere?" asked Mrs. Saylor.

"The Green Parrot Café," I said.

"Her aunt owns it," said Walter.

"When's the wedding?" Jobeth asked Walter.

"That's a stupid question," cried Lacy. "He and Fiona ain't even divorced."

"She sure is cuter than Fiona," said Jobeth.

"And she's got a nice figure," said Lacy.

"How much do you weigh?" Jobeth asked me.

"Well . . ." I couldn't answer because I had no idea. The scale in Aunt Clancy's bathroom had a mind of its own. One day I'd step on it and the dial would swirl up to 138, the most I'd ever weighed, and the next day, it registered 122. I liked those days best. I was just about to explain when Walter jumped into the conversation.

"Jobeth, what's the matter with you? You shouldn't ask people their weight."

"But she's not fat." Jobeth shrugged. "She's just stubby."

"Fiona was huge," said Jobeth.

"No wonder. She couldn't cook nothing but fried chicken and banana crumb cake," said Jobeth.

"Can you cook, Bitsy?" Mrs. Saylor asked.

"Oh, yes, ma'am." I nodded.

"She was a home ec major in high school," Walter said.

"That'll come in handy," said Mrs. Saylor. "My daughters majored in cigarettes and sex."

Everyone but Rooster and me laughed. Jobeth wiped her eyes. "We done all right," she told her mother. "We ain't perfect, but we done all right."

From the television, a cheer rose from the crowd. Rooster catapulted from the vinyl chair, scurrying forward, planting himself in front of the old Motorola. "Y'all HUSH!" he yelled.

"Well, don't have kittens," said Mrs. Saylor, grinning at me. The Saylor sisters smiled, too. For a moment, I felt a warm acceptance.

"Shit," said Rooster. Then he blinked at his son. "Hey, I didn't see you over there."

"But you talked to me a minute ago," Walter protested.

"Was that you?" Rooster's eyebrows moved up. "Want to go hit a few balls?"

"*If* he has any balls." Mrs. Saylor laughed, biting into her celery stick. "I think Fiona took them."

"You might want to check, son." Mr. Saylor laughed, then winked at Walter. "Take it from me, sonny. These bitches will cut off your balls and leave you bleeding. And they won't bat one eye. They'll cut off your little woman's balls, too."

"Jesus, Daddy," Walter said, aghast. "Women don't have testicles."

"They do in this family," he said, clapping Walter's shoulder. "But I wish to God they didn't. Now, how about us going to hit a few?"

A TAPED MESSAGE TO BETTY FORD

212 Dixie Avenue
Crystal Falls, Tennessee

August 9, 1974

Dear Betty,

    As I watched your hubby get sworn in (not in person, on TV), I wondered if I should bother writing. You kinda look stuck up. Also, there's no way you'll be as much fun to write to as Pat. I know she must be a nervous wreck, but so am I. But just look what all I have to deal with: Earlene is an evil bitch from hell who doesn't cook. Just this morning, she hung up a sign on my kitchen door, Blessed Is the Mother Who Gives Her Children Wings to Fly. I just laughed when I saw it, but it hurt my feelings. Raising a child isn't so easy—you don't graduate them, pinning little wings to their collars. Currently she and I aren't on speaking terms. Last night I cooked my son a fine meal. It started off with bacon dip and pork rinds, then we had French onion soup (it was canned but don't tell anybody), followed by a tossed salad with French dressing and a pot roast that was so tender you could cut it with a spoon. For dessert, key lime pie—but it wasn't truly "keyed" as I had to use bottled Minute Maid lime juice. Earlene sat off to the side, painting her nails a vile shade of copper and not talking or eating.

    Even though you don't look so friendly, I was hoping we could correspond with each other, exchanging hints and ideas. Or just venting, as they say in psychiatric circles. I am thinking that it's harder being a mother than a first lady. In a few years, if your husband doesn't get reelected—not that he was in the first place—then you can go back to being a wife. But no matter how old or mean-natured your children get, they're still your babies. There might be an expiration date on mothering, but not motherhood. And there are certainly no wings involved unless you're an angel or a bat.

    Tonight I'm fixing Swiss steak, rice, English peas, sliced tomatoes, biscuits, and sweet tea, with pineapple upside-down cake for dessert. The pineapples were canned, but the tomatoes came from my sister's garden. Before it was hers, it was my mother's, and that should make it half mine, but Clancy Jane hogs the vegetables as if they're heirlooms. The ones she doesn't want she gives to me or else serves them at her hippie café, so she'll make a profit. My daughter, Bitsy, works at the café, and she lives next door with my sister. Clancy Jane snatches up everything, from tomatoes to people. She tried to steal my husband, and when that didn't work, she stole somebody else's.

Bitsy will be twenty-one years old in October. She has a daughter who is two who she lost custody of although it was her husband who struck the first blow. Bitsy's girl's name is Jennifer. I wished they'd named her after me but that's the way it goes. She visits now and then, and I have discovered something—I LOVE being a grandmother. What they say is true, it's all the fun and none of the responsibility. She just loves going up into my mother's attic and digging through the old clothes. I believe she is liking us better too. But she still runs to the door the minute she hears Chick's car pull into the drive. Chick is her rich, alcoholic, Republican-loving grandfather.

Well, I need to be running along, as I have supper to fix. Then I want to watch M*A*S*H* with my son. I could send you some samples of my cooking if you'd like. Just say the word. In fact, just say anything. I won't tell anybody your secrets if you won't tell mine. Is that a deal?

Your new pal,
Dorothy McDougal

It was early evening, the middle of September, and dry leaves blew across the lawn. Walter and I were sitting on my porch swing in the humid dark. He wrapped his arm around my shoulders. "I love you, Bitsy. I want to slay dragons for you."

I wanted to say something witty, something that would make him laugh, but I was still thinking about his family. He pointed up at the sky. "Look over there, way, way up. What's that really bright star?"

"Sirius?"

"You remembered." He kissed the tip of my nose. From the next street, a dog started barking. Then came the yowl of an alley cat. The dog let out a series of yips, followed by a keening wail.

"That poor old dog," I said, snuggling next to him. "Barking like that."

"Want me to go kill it?" Walter said, laughing and nuzzling my neck.

"Lord, no."

Walter reached into his pocket, and drew out a red velvet box. He creaked the lid open, revealing an emerald-cut diamond in a Tiffany setting. He reached inside, picked it out with two fingers, held it up. "Bitsy, will you marry me?"

Dumbfounded, I gazed up at him. I wanted to say *Just give me a minute. Let me look before I leap, I'm such a bad leaper. I'm so afraid of mak-*

ing another mistake. We had been dating hardly a month. His family was beyond weird. And he wasn't officially divorced; but his smile was so hopeful. All of these problems hummed in my mind. I shut my eyes, waiting for divine inspiration. If only God would step in and clear everything up. *Bitsy,* He might say, *Do you know the difference between love and need?*

No, Lord, I'd say. *I sure don't.*

Walter waved the ring in front of my nose, as if he were holding smelling salts. "Bitsy?"

"I'm just overwhelmed," I said.

"After we get married, I'm going to hire a lawyer, and we'll get your daughter away from your ex."

"You'd do that?"

"I'll do whatever it takes. I'm not stopping until Jennifer and you are back together. Now, give me your hand. That's a good girl." Walter slid the ring onto my finger. "There," he said. "A perfect fit."

Clancy Jane, Bitsy, Violet, Dorothy, and Earlene

The girls were giving Bitsy an all-girl engagement/Halloween party. Clancy Jane rushed around the dining room, her long velvet skirt sweeping over the floor. She pushed back the sleeves on her cowl-neck sweater—fashion simply wasn't compatible with life, she thought—and poured Tiki punch into a cut-glass bowl. She was putting the finishing touches on Bitsy's party. On the sideboard, she'd set candles inside carved jack-o-lanterns, and she'd draped orange crêpe paper around the chandelier.

From her new eight-track player, Crosby, Stills and Nash were singing "Just a Song Before I Go." Violet came into the room carrying Jennifer's box of magnetic letters. Dorothy was right behind her, carrying a platter of homemade Halloween cookies. She paused at the sideboard, smiling down at the cake. It was orange with black icing and had Congratulations Bitsy & Walter! scrawled across the surface. Next to the cake were baskets filled with Ritz crackers. Violet had set out assorted dips, leaving them in their plastic containers. Well, no wonder, thought Dorothy. That poor child had never learned the social graces. And she never would.

Dorothy started to ask her sister if she wanted her to put the dip into cute little bowls, but she was afraid Clancy Jane might take it as criticism. The girl might run a café, but at home she didn't know doodly squat. Empty bottles of Tiki punch were stacked underneath the table, beside an empty Mason jar. Dorothy had seen that jar before, beneath the sink in

Mack's house. She had thought it was Clorox, but he'd said, "Hell no, Mama, this is my private stash of pure grain alcohol."

"For rubbing your sore muscles?" Dorothy had asked.

"It's moonshine, Mama."

Now Dorothy set down the cookies and walked over to the punch bowl. She was determined to make small talk with her sister. After all, they lived right next door to each other, they should let bygones be bygones.

"This is the reddest punch I've ever seen," Dorothy said, wishing they'd dyed it orange to match everything else. She didn't plan to drink any of it, but she was hoping the others would. She just loved it when she stayed sober and everybody else got drunk. That was a nightly occurrence over at her house—or should she say Mack and Earlene's house? Byron was over there now, watching TV so the girls could enjoy their party.

"The punch is wicked," warned Violet, looking up from her cup. "It's got PGA in it."

"Want a sip?" Clancy Jane held out a cup, but Dorothy shook her head.

"Oh, go on, Aunt Dorothy," said Violet. "The PGA doesn't alter the taste or the color. It tastes like a regular punch."

Dorothy started to explain about her nerve pills and how they didn't mix with alcohol, but the front door opened and a woman hollered, "Yoo-hoo!"

It was Earlene. She breezed into the dining room, carrying a tray of finger sandwiches, which she set down on the table. She had taken black eyeliner and drawn a Liz Taylor mole on her right cheek. Despite the chilly weather, she was wearing a purple tube top and cutoff jeans and high heels. She looked very Halloweenish, a cross between a witch and a hooker. "The wind is kicking up something awful," she said, patting her hair. She looked at the women. "Where's Bitsy?"

"Upstairs primping," said Violet.

"Why?" Dorothy was startled. She touched her forehead, hoping she'd remembered to draw on her eyebrows. "Walter isn't coming, is he?"

"No, it's just us girls," said Clancy Jane.

Bitsy came down the stairs wearing a burnt orange velvet dress, one of her Goodwill finds. Her hair was swept up into a French twist, but the strawberry blonde streaks clashed with the dress, making her look more like Lucille Ball than Grace Kelly. When she stepped into the dining room, Clancy Jane started clapping. "Here's our guest of honor!" Earlene and Dorothy clapped, too, with Violet halfheartedly joining in.

When the noise died down, Violet looked up at Bitsy and said, "Gee, didn't you have an oranger dress in your closet?"

"I'm saving it for you," Bitsy said.

"Touché," said Violet.

"You better capitulate," Bitsy said.

"You're regressing," Violet said. "You're back to using C words? That's pitiful. I thought you'd be up to the Zs already."

"I'm not going in order, but this is my second pass through your dictionary, I'll have you know," Bitsy said. She sat down next to Violet, then held out her left hand and gazed at the diamond. She looked around the room, her eyes lingering on each woman's face.

"Y'all, am I doing the right thing?" she asked.

"You can't back out now," said Earlene. "You'd break that boy's heart."

"He's hardly a *boy*," said Violet. "Bitsy, honey, were you asking a rhetorical question or did you really want my opinion?"

"Both, I guess." Bitsy kept on looking at the diamond.

"Hey, Bitsy," Clancy Jane said, over her shoulder. "Right before I married Byron, I got cold feet."

"What happened?" Bitsy sat up straight. "What did you do?"

"That's obvious. She married him." Violet laughed.

"Hon, it's normal to have doubts," said Earlene. She lifted the Saran Wrap from her sandwich tray.

"I'd be scared, too," Dorothy said, "if I got engaged again."

"Don't hold your breath." Violet reached for a chicken salad sandwich.

"You don't know everything, Violet," said Dorothy. "You don't even know that it's tacky to serve dip in these plastic boats. I could get a man. But I just don't want to fool with one."

"What's wrong with plastic?" Violet asked.

"It's cheap. The *least* you could've done was scrape the dip into cut-glass bowls," Dorothy said. "When my mother lived in this house, she had hundreds of bowls. But I *never* see them. Where did they go?"

"A catfight's brewing," Earlene told Clancy Jane. "Hurry up and pass the punch."

"Coming!" Clancy Jane began ladling punch, then passed around the cups. Dorothy handed hers over to Violet.

"Cool," Violet said. She drained both cups, then she got an empty wineglass and slid it to the center of the table. Next, using the magnetic letters, she spelled out YES; on the other side, NO. "Enough of this speculation. Let us join hands and contact the living."

"Don't you mean the dead?" Dorothy whispered.

"It was a joke." Violet delicately placed the tips of her fingers on the base of the glass. The women gathered closer, elbows touching, and placed their fingertips next to Violet's.

"Concentrate, y'all," said Clancy Jane. She squeezed her eyes shut, and little wrinkles fanned around her eyes. Three lines appeared on her forehead.

"All right," said Violet in a low, sultry voice. Her eyes were downcast but not closed. "Does Walter worship the ground Bitsy walks on?"

"Worship?" Bitsy groaned, lifting her hands from the wineglass. "Don't ask it that!"

"It's my glass. I'll ask it whatever I please," said Violet.

"You sound ten years old," said Dorothy.

"No, that's how *you* sounded at ten," Violet snapped. "I'm sorry, Aunt Dorothy. That was mean. I'll go a little lighter on the punch."

"Worship, worship, worship," Dorothy was saying, ignoring her niece's comment. When it pleased her, Dorothy had the most amazing powers of concentration.

"Oh, all right." Bitsy sighed and put her fingers back onto the glass. It began to tremble, then it scraped across the tablecloth to NO, paused for two seconds, then sped to the other side of the table, to YES.

"Did y'all see that?" asked Violet, her eyes widening.

"Why can't it make up its mind?" Bitsy said.

"Maybe both answers are true?" Clancy Jane looked at Bitsy.

"You moved it," said Bitsy, jabbing Violet's elbow.

"I did *not.*"

"Maybe y'all's fingers slipped," suggested Dorothy. "Let's ask it again."

"But at least reword the question," said Earlene.

"All right. Just let me think a minute." Violet shut her eyes. Then she said, "Is Walter insanely in love with Bitsy?"

The glass trembled, then it lurched across the table, dragging the women's fingers along with it, forcing Earlene to rise from her chair and stretch across the table. The glass stopped at YES. Then it careened back to NO.

"See? I told you the damn stupid thing can't make up its mind," Bitsy muttered.

"It needs more information," said Violet. "Bitsy, tell us what Walter looks like naked."

"I've been wondering that myself," said Earlene.

"I haven't," said Dorothy.

"Ask the damn wineglass," Bitsy said. "I'm not telling y'all a thing."

"Is he skinny *all* over?" Earlene giggled. "And just where do the freckles stop?"

"Don't ask personal questions," Dorothy said. "It isn't becoming. Anyway, you've already got a man."

"Do I?" Earlene stared at her mother-in-law. Everybody in the family had urged Earlene to have it out with Dorothy, but Earlene would always shake her head and say, "I can't. She's his mother. He feels too guilty to straighten her out."

"Ask what you want. It's just us girls," said Violet, pouring herself another cup of punch. She didn't sip, she tilted the cup to her lips and poured the liquid into her mouth, like she was watering a rosebush.

"We don't need to ask the spirits," Clancy Jane said, raising her arms over her head, lifting her heavy dark blond hair. "From the look on Bitsy's face, he must be interesting."

"So are Andy Warhol paintings," Violet said.

"Honey, all men look good in the dark," said Earlene.

"And you should know," Dorothy muttered.

Earlene just laughed and said, "It's the truth. I'm not ashamed to say it, either."

"I've seen Walter Saylor's body and it's great," said Violet. "Don't look shocked. It was perfectly innocent. Bitsy was with me. It was a turning point in their relationship."

"No, the salami was," said Clancy Jane.

"I'm confused," said Dorothy. "First, you're talking about his naked body. Then you're talking about luncheon meat."

"It's a euphemism, Aunt Dorothy," Violet said, flashing a wicked smile, "for his *dick*."

"I just love salami." Earlene hopped out of her chair and skipped to the freezer.

"Girls, we've had too much PGA," said Clancy Jane. "Our spiritual auras are muddled. Let's get rid of the kiddie letters and play Voodoo Scrabble."

"Good idea," said Violet. It was her Scrabble game, dragged from the depths of her cluttered Volkswagen. When the women got together, they used the game in a variety of ways—sometimes they played Vulgar Scrabble, allowing only disgusting words. But they had to be a little drunker to play that version. Their favorite game was Voodoo Scrabble, spelling out words as if they were in a trance. All the letters were spread face up in the box, and the players could select what they wanted. There was only one rule: You had exactly ten seconds to spell your word—and make it fit into the others. While you decided, the other players timed you out loud—one-one-thousand, two-one-thousand.

Earlene walked back the table, holding a grape Popsicle.

"I don't remember how to play," said Dorothy.

"You'll pick it right up," Earlene said. She put the Popsicle into her mouth and sucked hard, her cheeks denting. "All you have to do is read between the lines."

"Give me some tiles." Violet fit a dip-drenched Triscuit into her mouth, then held out her hand.

"I'll start," said Clancy Jane. Without hesitation, she spelled out SEXUALITY in a horizontal line, her tiles clinking against the board.

"Man, that was lucky." Earlene finished off her Popsicle and biting down on the stick, she gathered up her tiles. "How do you spell *fellatio*?"

"If you've gotta ask," said Clancy in a Louis Armstrong voice, "then you'll never know."

"Speaking of which," said Violet, picking up an F, C, and K, fitting the tiles over the U in SEXUALITY.

"We should've asked the Ouija board if Walter and I will have any children," said Bitsy.

"Stay on the Pill," said Clancy Jane. "You *are* on it, right?"

"She takes Ovral," said Violet. "With the little butterflies on the case. I've seen it in the medicine cabinet."

"Keep taking it," said Clancy Jane.

Violet was looking at Earlene. Finally she said, "Hey, are you and Mack going to have a family?"

"I can't have kids, hon," said Earlene, crossing her legs. "The doctor says my tubes are clogged."

Dorothy's hand shook as she reached for a punch cup. Thank God for germs, she thought. On the other hand, a baby was exactly what Bitsy needed to make up for Jennifer. Bitsy had grown into a sweet young lady. She was just as curvy as Earlene, even though she didn't show off her body in a vulgar fashion. Walter Saylor was ugly, but his profession more than made up for his hair and eyes. Dorothy didn't like to brag—well, *not much*—but here lately she'd been going around town referring to the boy as Dr. Saylor, my daughter's fiancé. Sometimes she'd preface a sentence with "My future son-in-law, the dentist." That got people's attention.

"Any child of Walter's will have good health insurance. Dentists can afford the best," Dorothy said. "But it'll probably have his goat eyes."

"Actually, his eyes are kinda froggy," said Earlene.

"Y'all stop it!" Bitsy slapped her hand on the table, causing the tiles to jump. "He's good to me."

"Good in bed?" asked Earlene, "or good as in godly?"

"Good isn't a reason to get married," said Violet.

"I might be making a mistake," said Bitsy, "but I won't sit here and let y'all run him down."

"She's right, hon," Earlene said, picking up a tile. "Who knows? He might change Bitsy's life."

"Sugar lump, it'll take more than a man to do that," Violet said, not bothering to hide the sarcasm. She picked up a few tiles, spelling out ROMANCE. "Try education."

"College isn't for everyone," Clancy Jane said.

"It all depends on what you want out of life." Violet shrugged.

"I want a husband who reads the morning paper while I fry his bacon," Bitsy said.

"I'm confused," said Violet. "You want to be a personal chef? Wait, how 'bout doormat?"

"Doormat?" Dorothy and Bitsy said together, looking baffled.

"Fry his *bacon*? Scramble his eggs?" Violet shuddered. "Go on, then, *be* Donna Reed again!"

"Do not judge lest ye be judged," said Dorothy, stifling a belch.

"I just want to be loved," said Bitsy. "I want a man who's kind and honest."

"You want a *little* too much, honey," said Clancy Jane, but her voice was tender.

"I'm scared to death." Bitsy reached across the table, over the board, and grabbed Violet's hand.

"You don't have to be," Violet said. "Nobody says you have to get married right away. You can have the world's longest engagement."

"You really shouldn't offer advice," Clancy Jane said. "You've never been married."

"By the grace of God," Violet said.

"You'll probably end up with a well-educated man," said Earlene. "You could never be happy with a blue-collar guy."

Violet turned to her mother. "Don't you wish someone had talked to *you* about blue-collar men before you married my daddy?"

"No, indeed not," said Clancy Jane. "Then I wouldn't have you."

Violet's chin wove, but Clancy Jane kept on talking. "You were my anchor. Even when you were small, you held me together."

"Let's don't get into this," Violet said in a shaky voice.

"Hush, y'all. Look at the board," said Dorothy, busily arranging new tiles. "The oracle has spoken."

```
                    L
    G               O
    I N             V
    R O M A N C E
    L       A
    S       D
```

Fiona

On All Saints' Day, Fiona Saylor drove to Kmart, thinking about the Northern tissue sale. Despite the fact that Walter had filed for divorce, she still held out hope that he would return. Just in case he did, she wanted to be prepared. She had an idea that something was desperately wrong with his bowels, considering how much time he used to spend in the john, so when she heard about the sale, she'd hurried over to the store. She turned her cart up an aisle and came face to face with two of her nosiest nosy neighbors.

"Fiona!" cried Mary Sue Parks. Her hair looked freshly styled and she was wearing a red peacoat over black pants. "I'm surprised to see you out and about."

"Why? I haven't been sick." Fiona looked past Mary Sue, into the eyes of her other neighbor, Leslie Adams. She lived in a red brick split level on Appomattox with her husband and three loud children.

"I'm just so sorry," said Mary Sue, patting Fiona's arm. "I had no idea."

"About what?" Fiona blinked. She was starting to get mad.

"Why, the awful news," replied Leslie Adams, her large green eyes bulging.

"About Walter's engagement." Mary Sue leaned closer, watching Fiona's face. "Are you all right? You look pale, Fiona. Are you fixing to faint?"

"I'm fine, I'm *fine!*" Fiona said, pushing the woman's hands away.

"He's marrying a cute little strawberry blonde," said Mary Sue, obviously enjoying herself. "Petite, but curvy. I saw her at the beauty shop. She was getting a French twist. I think her name is Betsy. Or maybe Becky? Works at the Green Parrot Café? And she's got a little daughter, but I don't think the child lives with her . . ."

"I'd really love to chat," said Fiona, "but I'm in a rush."

"Well, wait a minute," said Leslie. "You and Walter haven't been divorced very long, have you?"

"We're *not* divorced," snapped Fiona, pushing her cart around the Northern tissue display. She broke away from the women and scooted her cart down another aisle. She rounded a corner, then shoved the cart as hard as she could. It wheeled crookedly, then crashed into a display of Nair hair remover. All of the jars tumbled to the floor. Fiona pressed her fingers to her lips, imagining unspeakable things. She knew every inch of Walter's body, the limbs all covered with springy orange down, the long, freckled penis hanging between his legs. She imagined a hand snaking up, tenderly cupping his genitals. The hand belonged to a goddess, a composite blonde with a face like Brigitte Bardot, breasts like Marilyn Monroe, teeth like Farrah Fawcett-Majors, and legs like Cheryl Tiegs.

She ran out of Kmart, into her car. If those women at Kmart knew about Walter's engagement, then the whole town knew. Still, she had to hear this straight from Walter himself. She drove across town, swerving from lane to lane, honking at slowpoke motorists. Five minutes later, she pulled up to his office, climbed out of her car, and ran up the sidewalk. The waiting room was empty. She strode past the goggle-eyed receptionist, an old, mothbally thing that Fiona hadn't seen before.

"Miss? Can I help you?" called the woman as Fiona stomped into the hall. Oh, she knew how she looked in her baggy blue jeans, the waist cinched with frayed clothesline. Well, Walter had taken all his belts when he left, and they'd fit her perfectly; he had also taken his Fruit Of The Looms, but she'd planned to buy more at Kmart.

Fiona found Walter in room 3, which featured a waterfall mural. He was bent over Mrs. Edward Crane, whose husband owned the hardware store. A new dental assistant looked up, an older woman with jowls.

When Walter saw Fiona, he froze. The drill stopped whining. Mrs. Crane lifted her head, and looked from Walter to the assistant.

"What are you doing here?" Walter spoke in a casual voice, but his pupils were dilating with fear.

"I want the truth!" Fiona stepped closer. "The truth about that woman."

"Who, me?" asked the patient, glancing at Walter.

"No, not *you*." Fiona began to tremble. She snatched up a tray full of instruments and threw it against the wall.

The assistant turned to Walter. "Doctor, should I call the police?"

"Not just yet," said Walter. He reached down and patted Mrs. Crane's arm. "Sorry for the interruption. I'll be right back." He pushed the drill aside, got up from his stool, and strode out of the room. Fiona hurried after him.

"All right," she said, grabbing his sleeve, yanking him back. "Start talking. Tell me about the strawberry blonde."

With her free hand, she began to punch Walter's head, her fist sinking into the red hair.

"Fiona, stop!" Walter put his arms in front of his face. "Stop! You're making a scene!"

"I want to know what's going on." She smacked him again.

"All right, all right." Walter turned pale. "I-I've met someone."

"So . . ." She stepped forward, her fists raised in the air. "It's *true* you're engaged?"

He nodded.

"But you're still married to me," she cried. Sure, they'd had spats—spatula spats, she called them, but nobody was perfect. Living with another person could try the patience of a saint. "This is bigamy!" she added.

"It's perfectly legal," he said. "I can be engaged to one person and still be technically married to another. I'm not breaking any laws."

"You might not have broken a law," Fiona said, her eyes filling, hands dropping to her sides, "but you've shattered my heart."

Walter stared down at the floor. Fiona stared, too. Long ago she had picked out those tiles, thinking they would hide dirt. And *this* was how he'd thanked her.

"You could've told me!" Fiona balled up her fists, preparing for a fresh onslaught. "But *no*. I had to hear about it at Kmart. Our *neighbors* knew before *I* did!"

"Fiona, I can't discuss this now."

She responded by raising her fist and cracking it on his head. He backed up, his orange eyes wobbling. "You're in a lot of trouble, Fiona. I'm filing a complaint against you."

"For *what*?" She spat out the words.

"Assault and battery. My office staff saw your little outburst. I'm getting a restraining order against you."

"It was self-defense!" she cried.

"No, it wasn't. This time, I've got witnesses." He rubbed his scalp. "I can feel knots everywhere," he added. "You're abusive, Fiona."

"You poo-poo head. You mama's boy." She reared back to slap him, then she froze and stared at her hand. She wanted to smack him but not in public. No, she would wait. She had time. She ran out of his office, down the hall, into the waiting room, past the startled patients. Then she hurtled out the door, into the chilly November afternoon. Thanksgiving was sometime this month, but there would be no family around *her* table, much less a husband to carve.

Down by the curb she climbed into her car, cranked the engine, and headed toward town. Well, she'd show him and that pigmy blonde. She swerved her car into The Utopian parking lot and hurried into the shop. She waved at Anita, who was giving a permanent to an elderly woman. "Did you have an appointment?" Anita called.

"No, but this is an emergency. I need the works," Fiona said. "Manicure, pedicure, and a new hairdo."

"Fiona, I'm swamped. Can you come back tomorrow?"

"Tomorrow's too late!" Fiona shrieked.

The laughter and gossip snapped off, and everyone turned to stare at her. "Please, it's life or death. You've just got to squeeze me in."

"I'll try." Anita frowned. "Just have a seat."

Fiona grabbed an armful of magazines and carried them over to a wicker chair. She flipped through the pages, staring at women with long blond hair. A long time ago, Fiona herself had been a sight for sore eyes. When she'd met Walter Saylor, she'd weighed only 140 pounds and wore a size 10; her hair was dark brown and stick straight. No small wonder that she'd attracted Walter. They got married the summer before he started dental school. Fiona had fought with her mother over her bridal gown. Her mother had picked out a dress that resembled a lampshade, and Fiona had wanted a simple A-line, no lace or seed pearls. Instead of a bouquet, she'd wanted to carry her pet rabbit, Mr. Moffett, down the aisle, but her mother had reacted as if Fiona had said she wanted to carry a stool specimen.

Her mother cried, "What will people think?"

Fiona shrugged. It wasn't as if the wedding would be featured in *Town & Country*. Walter's parents were so backward, they might have thought a bunny bouquet was chic.

On their Panama City honeymoon, Walter bought Coca-Colas from the hotel's machine, then he'd bring them back to the room and leave the half-empty bottles on the tables. It got worse when the honeymoon ended, and they moved to an apartment in Memphis. Every morning, before Fiona drove to her job at the bank, she spent ten minutes picking up Walter's empty Coke bottles. She began to notice white circles all over the tops of their nice Drexel furniture. "This has got to stop," she told him, pointing to the rings. "If you leave *one* more Coke bottle on the table, I'm going to throttle you."

One night, she was frying hamburgers and from the corner of her eyes she saw him put an empty bottle on the coffee table. She reached for a spatula, flipped the burgers, then walked out of the kitchen. She raised the spatula and lunged for Walter. He sprang off the sofa, into the hall. She chased him from room to room, her hot, greasy spatula making a whooshing noise. She had hoped the episode would force him to change his slovenly ways, but it seemed that Walter would rather get a beating than obey a woman. He continued to leave the bottles, and the rings on the furniture multiplied.

She had thought about moving out, but Memphis was an evil city. The paper was full of rapes, murders, muggings. No, she'd stay married and make him change his slatternly ways.

After they moved to Crystal Falls and he set up his dental practice, Fiona rarely saw him. But she was glad that he was drinking his colas elsewhere. She amused herself by watching the people next door, who were getting their house painted. The workers had beards and long hair and shot each other birds or else flashed the peace sign—they looked to Fiona like Charles Manson's family. She was afraid they'd stick a fork in her chest and write PIG on the walls. Then one afternoon she was in the bedroom and heard muffled footsteps on the stairs, each one saying, I'm coming to get you. From the night table, she picked up a silver fingernail file. "I've got a weapon," she called. "And I'm not afraid to use it."

When the man stepped through the bedroom door—dammit, she'd forgot to lock it—she screamed and ran at him, her arm jabbing like the mother in *Psycho*. *Whack, whack, whack.* Sweat was in her eyes, but she kept on stabbing. She chased the man all the way back into the hall.

Then he cried, "Stop it, Fiona! It's just me. For the love of God, stop!" Her vision cleared and she saw Walter. The shock caused her to take a step backward. Her foot missed the landing. Screaming, she plunged down the stairs, blackening both eyes and bruising her buttocks, arms, and legs. For a week, she was forced to wear sunglasses, long-sleeved blouses, long trousers, a floppy hat. It was summer, and she nearly burned up. Walter showed no remorse. He refused to discuss it with her, other than to say he was an abused man, and if she ever cut him again, or even used a fingernail file in his presence, he was going to call the police. But he never did. He was too much of a pussy.

Now Fiona was too nervous to sit in the beauty salon chair. She threw down the magazines, causing the girl at the cash register to stare. Fiona knew what that girl was thinking. *Divorce* meant the same as unwanted. There was a certain dignity to widowhood, but losing your husband to a bleached, brainless strawberry blonde was embarrassing—and she was certain that *all* blondes lacked brains and morals. Just look at Jayne Mansfield and Marilyn Monroe. And yes, she'd read in *Photoplay* that Jayne Mansfield was supposed to be a genius, but Fiona thought it was a lie. She didn't know what was worse—having your husband leave you for another woman or having him accuse you of assault and battery. Either way, she'd be ruined.

Glancing out the Utopian's front window, she saw a darkening sky, one that would make Bobby Vinton proud, blue velvet, soft and cushy as the robe her mother used to wear. Fiona was not fond of the color blue. After she'd whip Walter, the welts on his back and arms turned indigo, but he hid them from the world. In the hottest part of summer, he would roll down his shirtsleeves so no one could see. The bruises turned purple, fading into a sour, hateful yellow that lasted several weeks and seemed to mock her. *Hit me again,* the color used to say. *I dare you to hit me again.*

He would undress in front of her, and the marks seemed louder than any admonishment. *This, too, will pass,* she told herself. She marveled at the resilience of the human body. Every second it was working toward health, breaking down the spilled blood, reabsorbing the overflow, carrying it away to the lymph glands—the body's way of flushing its crap down the toilet. She had read all about it in Walter's books. He could have been a doctor if he'd wanted. He could have been a lot of things, including a good husband.

She got up from the chair and walked over to the Coke machine. She couldn't take it if Walter's blonde was a girlie sort of girl—perfume, hair bows, lipstick, ruffles, silk stockings, pink princess phone. "Pink!" she said, spitting out the word. Pink was worse than blue. It was a dainty color, and it smelled like a pussy. She dropped a coin into the slot and listened as it jingled down. She started to hit the Orange Crush button, but then remembered how it never seemed to work, so she punched 7UP instead and waited for the bottle to roll down the chute. When that didn't happen, she kicked the machine. Still, it would not give up the 7UP bottle. Somehow it reminded her of Walter, hanging on to his old habits, not caring if she was inconvenienced. Her face contorted, and she made a fist and began pounding all the buttons, then she grabbed the rounded top and rocked the machine back and forth. Behind her, the beauticians began to yell, but Fiona didn't hear what they were saying. She was getting into a rhythm, dancing with her rage. It just felt so good to manhandle something. She let out a war whoop and lunged forward. She wrapped her arms around the machine and it tottered, then fell forward, smack on top of her.

Walter and His Family

Clancy Jane was cleaning her house for Bitsy's wedding. It was scheduled for December 28, but Clancy had a bad feeling about it, because Walter was still legally married. According to Bitsy, the divorce would be final after Thanksgiving unless Fiona contested. Clancy stood next to her bed, struggling to flip the mattress, wishing she hadn't offered to throw a home wedding.

"Look, I'll plan everything, if you'll let me," she'd told Bitsy.

"I wish Jennifer could be the flower girl," Bitsy had said. "Think Claude would allow it?"

"Probably not, but it won't hurt to ask."

Clancy Jane had decided to use her living room for the ceremony—the fireplace would be a lovely backdrop. That room could hold twenty-five people, maybe thirty; and she'd get someone to play the ancient piano. A local violinist was also lined up for the evening. At Flowers by Joy, Clancy Jane ordered an arrangement for the dining table, potted poinsettias to set about, and hurricane globes with candles to stake along the driveway. For the bride's bouquet, she and Bitsy decided on three dozen red roses with crimped lace inserts, ribbons streaming down. Zach made up a menu: cheese straws, mints, strawberries dipped in chocolate, punch, and champagne. Finally, a three-layer traditional cake was ordered at Ralph's Bakery. This was a Crystal Falls tradition. You could not get married or have a birthday without one of Ralph's cakes.

Still struggling with the mattress, Clancy Jane heard the doorbell ring. She hurried downstairs, opened the door, and looked up into Walter's bloodshot eyes. "Is Bitsy here?" he asked, his teeth chattering.

"She's next door." Clancy Jane took a closer look at Walter. His eyes didn't seem right, and she wondered if he was coming down with a cold. "She'll be right back. You want to come inside and wait?"

"I don't know what to do. Oh, *God.* Fiona's *dead.* I never meant to cause this. I didn't." He began to shake all over. Clancy Jane was afraid he'd faint, so she pulled him inside the house and up the stairs to Bitsy's bedroom where she got him to lie down. As she pulled the gauzy blue curtains across the window, she glanced outside. It was getting dark. Soon the moon would be on the rise.

"Thank you," he said without opening his eyes. "Why did this happen? Is there a purpose to it?"

"Sleep," Clancy Jane said. She wanted to ask what had befallen Fiona, but Walter looked too distraught. "Just sleep. You'll feel calmer after you'd had some rest."

Walter stayed in bed, wrapped in a quilt, stirring only when Bitsy brought him chicken noodle soup and crackers, glasses of ginger ale, bowls of lime Jell-O. He slept all night and awakened the next morning in a pensive mood. He picked at his breakfast tray, a sick child's meal: a three-minute egg, toast, and tea.

"What an awful way to get my house back," was the first thing he said to Bitsy, after he'd explained about Fiona and the Coke machine. The next was, "I want to go over there. Maybe she won't haunt me if you're with me. You *will* spend the night, won't you?"

Bitsy hesitated. Only hippies and movie stars spent the night with a lover. No one in Crystal Falls would understand, except Aunt Clancy. "Let me think about it," she said.

"If you don't go," said Walter, "she'll get me for sure."

• • •

That night, Walter moved back into the orange split-level. While Bitsy helped him rearrange the bedroom furniture, the doorbell rang. Before they reached the foyer, the front door opened and Walter's mother poked her head inside. "Yoo-hoo, anyone home?"

She gave Walter a kiss and smiled at Bitsy, then she hurried toward the kitchen. Lacy and Jobeth stepped into the foyer, followed by Rooster. "God, I'm starving," said Lacy.

"Me, too," said Jobeth.

The sisters barged into the kitchen. Bitsy peered through the doorway. Drawers and cabinets were slung open, as Fiona's china and flatware was gathered. Jobeth dug into a chicken casserole that Fiona had apparently made earlier. Lacy opened the fridge and found a pecan pie in a bakery box. Meanwhile, Mrs. Saylor rummaged in the cabinet, pulling out a box of Mystic Mint cookies. They kept talking about Fiona and the awful way she'd died.

"I didn't invite them," Walter told Bitsy. "Maybe they won't stay long."

"I heard that," cried Mrs. Saylor. "Let's go, girls. We're not welcome. We just came to pay our respects to Fiona, but that's just fine, we'll leave."

On their way out, Lacy shot Walter the bird. He closed the door and locked it. Bitsy glanced back at the kitchen. Cabinet doors stood ajar. The cookie box—empty except for crumbs—sat on the counter, next to the gutted chicken casserole. The Saylors reminded her of locusts—they arrived in a swarm, ate up all the food, and then flew off.

．　．　．

Now that Fiona was gone, the Saylors were determined to reclaim Walter. Just as Bitsy had once felt their approval, now she sensed their dislike— eight thumbs down. They did not mention Fiona's funeral or Walter's wedding; in fact, they had stopped speaking directly to Bitsy. Mostly they referred to her as "Walter's girl," putting the same emphasis on the words as if they were saying "Walter's virus" or "Walter's tumor."

One Sunday they crashed into the split-level, and looked surprised to see Walter and Bitsy on the floor with Jennifer, who was visiting for the afternoon—Clancy and Byron had dropped her off. Walter was helping her build an elaborate Lego city.

"Who's this child?" Mrs. Saylor locked her hands under her chin and smiled.

"Jennifer, Bitsy's daughter," said Walter.

"What pretty eyes you have," said Mrs. Saylor, crouching down. "And what pretty hair."

Bitsy immediately thought of *Little Red Riding Hood*. As Mrs. Saylor leaned closer, brushing her fingers through Jennifer's white curls, Bitsy smelled bourbon. Rooster got down on the floor beside Jennifer and pawed the carpet like a bull, giving off gusts of whiskey. Then he began to bark and meow. Jennifer's eyes widened. She looked up at Bitsy, then she scrambled to her feet and flung herself facedown on the sofa.

"Quit scaring her, Daddy," said Walter.

"I thought I was funning her." Rooster's face fell.

Lacy clapped her hands together and smiled at Jennifer. "Come over here and see me, baby."

Jennifer gave Lacy an imperious look, eyebrows raised, nostrils flaring. Bitsy cringed. *She looks just like Miss Betty*, she thought.

"What's the matter with her?" Lacy frowned.

"She's tired," said Bitsy, reaching over to pat the child's shoulder. Jennifer scooted away, giving her mother a baleful stare.

"She might need a spanking." Mrs. Saylor rocked on her heels, dipping close to Jennifer. The child picked up a blue pillow and threw it at the woman. Mrs. Saylor yelped and ducked, and the pillow hit the Lego city, sending the red and white pieces flying.

The Saylor sisters laughed. "Hit 'er again," said Lacy, holding out another pillow. Jennifer scowled and pushed it away.

"In my day, children were kept in playpens," said Mrs. Saylor.

"She's not a baby, Mama," said Walter. "She's three."

"That's not too old for a pen," said Mrs. Saylor. "She looks like a handful."

"She's cute," said Lacy, sitting on the edge of the sofa. "Don't you think she's cute, Jobeth?"

Jennifer ran to the bedroom and slammed the door. Bitsy started to go after her, but Walter touched her arm. "Let her be," he said.

"He's right," said Mrs. Saylor. "You have to ignore temper tantrums."

"She's a spitfire, all right," said Jobeth. "But she *is* mighty cute. Her daddy must've been good-looking. Was he good in bed, too?"

"Cut it out, Jobeth," Walter said.

"I will *not*." Jobeth stuck out her chin. "It's not my fault that another man planted his seed in Walter's girl's womb."

"Don't say womb," said Lacy. "That's ugly. Say twat."

"I've certainly had lots of seeds planted in *mine*," Jobeth said, reaching for a tin of peppermints. "And I bet Walter's girl has, too."

"Bitsy," Walter said. "Her name is Bitsy."

Mrs. Saylor ignored him and said, "I will bet you that her you-know-what's been stretched to hell and back."

"Mine's as loose as the belt on a vacuum cleaner," said Jobeth.

"I bet Walter's girl's twat is too big for him," said Lacy.

"Don't you know it is," said Jobeth. "You could probably drive a Mack truck through it. Did you see the size of that baby's head? It's *huge.*"

Walter's eyebrows came together, and he stood up. "Jobeth, if you can't shut up, then leave. Besides, you can't talk. You've had a child."

"But its head was smaller," Jobeth said.

"Every vagina is different," said Lacy. "Anyhow, Jobeth's kid doesn't live with us."

"I couldn't help that, my goddamn boyfriend got custody," Jobeth cried.

"You gave it to him," said Lacy.

"Bitsy's child doesn't live with her, either," said Walter.

Bitsy cringed, waiting for them to quiz her, but Lacy kept on talking about vaginas. "All the women in *our* family have extra-small twats," she said.

"That's the truth," said Mrs. Saylor. "When I go for my yearly Pap smear, the doctor has to use a child-size specimen."

"It's *speculum,*" Jobeth corrected, rolling her eyes.

"You ought to know," Mrs. Saylor shot back. "You've had thousands of them stuck up inside you. Especially afer that truck driver infected you with—"

"We get your drift, Mama," said Jobeth, holding up her hand, her face turning red beneath the freckles.

"Well, you liked to *never* got cured," said Mrs. Saylor.

"Put a lid on it, Mama," said Jobeth. She turned to Walter. "Hey, you got any free samples to give us? Free toothbrushes, dental floss, Darvocet N-100s or Percodan?"

"Not here at home," Walter said.

"I don't need a toothbrush," said Lacy. "I need me a rich boyfriend. Don't roll your eyes, Mama. I need one bad. Walter, can't you fix me up with one of your dentist friends? I don't care if they're divorced, separated, or married."

"All the dentists I know are ready to retire," said Walter.

"I wouldn't mind being an old fart's sugar baby," said Lacy.

"Especially if he makes you his beneficiary." Jobeth laughed.

"Then you could buy me a new house," said Mrs. Saylor.

"No, I'm buying me a Corvette," said Jobeth. "Anyhow, Walter's the one who promised to buy you a house, not me."

"That's true," said Mrs. Saylor.

"Don't you worry, Mama," said Jobeth, patting Mrs. Saylor's leg. "We'll get you a fine house someday. Even if I have to whore and steal and write bad checks."

"If there was one dime left in our house, we'd all get a share," said Lacy. "If there was one cookie left in our kitchen, we'd break it up evenly. Everybody would get a piece."

"Don't be too hard on Walter," Jobeth told her sister. "He paid for your last two abortions. And you got to keep your extra-tight twat. That's the only thing men want, when it's all said and done."

"I'd hoped that his tooth degree would be our salvation." Mrs. Saylor sighed. "I told him this every morning after I crawled in his bed and woke him up with kisses."

This got Bitsy's attention. "You mean, when he was a baby," she said. All the women turned to stare, and Bitsy felt her cheeks hotten up.

"No, when he was married to Fiona. Sometimes he'd sleep over at my house, and I would bring him coffee in bed." Mrs. Saylor flashed a thin-lipped smile, obviously enjoying herself. "I hope you don't mind."

"Of course she doesn't mind," Walter said. "Mama, are you trying to stir up trouble?"

"Me? Honey, I'd ne-ver do such a thing." Mrs. Saylor's lower lip slid forward. "Ne-ver in a million, zillion years."

· · ·

After Thanksgiving, the weather warmed up and Clancy Jane went outside to rake leaves. They lay in deep drifts between her yard and Dorothy's. "Come and help me," she called to Bitsy, who was hiding in the kitchen.

"I would, but what if Walter's family sees us?" She was afraid to go outside, in case the Saylors should drive by and see her there. They cruised down Dixie Avenue several times a week, and if they spotted Bitsy in the front yard, they considered it an invitation to come in, opening the refrigerator, making fun of the food. Bitsy loathed and feared them the same way she loathed and feared black widow spiders—except she could not smash Walter's family with her shoe.

"Yes, I know they're horrible, but you shouldn't hate them, honey," Clancy Jane advised. "It will boomerang back on you. That's what hate does."

Bitsy smiled. "Aunt Clancy, you fear bad karma more than anything. Maybe this is a sign."

"Of what?"

"That I shouldn't marry him."

"The path to true love is never easy, baby." Clancy Jane pressed her forehead against Bitsy's. "Talk to Walter. He knows them better than anyone."

. . .

Lacy burst into Walter's office. She found him sitting at his desk, eating a butterscotch doughnut. He stood up abruptly, crumbs falling off his trousers. "I just hope you know how much you've hurt Mama," she cried. "We were a family long before you found Fiona or that other girl. It's her or us, buster. Who's it gonna be?"

"But I'm getting married in a few weeks," Walter said. He sat down so hard his chair rolled back and hit the wall.

"When did you get so stingy?" Lacy glared. "You were raised to share."

"Please don't start *that* again." Walter sighed. He was sick of the family motto, share and share alike. When he was in high school, stricken with cystic acne, Lacy used to sit on his chest, straddling him, and squeeze his pimples. After she'd mashed all of the bumps on his face, she'd roll him over and search his back.

Now Lacy glowered at her brother. "Pick one!" she cried. "Us or that girl."

"It's not right to make a man choose."

"Pick!"

"Her, I guess." He swallowed.

That afternoon, Bitsy began getting prank telephone calls. "Sorry, wrong number," a woman would say. Bitsy told Clancy Jane she recognized Jobeth's twang.

Sometimes a voice, plainly Mrs. Saylor's, would ask for First National Bank. "I'm sorry," she would say. "I must've dialed the wrong number. I can't see good anymore, ever since . . . oh well, never mind. Sorry if I disturbed you."

Whenever Byron or Clancy Jane answered the phone, the caller was silent for a few moments, then the connection would snap off. Although once, Clancy Jane distinctly heard someone hiss, "Bitch!"

"We've got to get an unlisted number," she told Bitsy.

"I'll do it first thing tomorrow," the bride-elect promised.

. . .

Walter was sitting at his desk, studying honeymoon brochures—he was keen on taking Bitsy to Niagara Falls, but they were getting married in the wrong season for that trip. He heard a knock at the door and when he glanced up, he saw his office manager. "Dr. Saylor, your mother's on the phone again," she said. "She says it's urgent."

"It's always urgent," Walter muttered, glancing at the phone. Line one was frantically blinking. He wearily switched on the speaker and said, "This is Walter. What do you need, Mama?"

"Well, it's about time," she screeched. "Why won't you take my calls?"

"I'm at work, Mama," Walter said. "I've got teeth to fill."

"I can't call you at home. And I can't call that little witch at her house, either. Y'all went and got un-listed numbers!"

"So it *was* you calling," Walter said. "Bitsy was right."

"Do not mention that whore to me!" hissed Mrs. Saylor. "I can play *this* game. We're getting us an unlisted number, too."

"It's all her fault." It was Lacy, on the extension. "She's got you by the balls."

"How can you turn on your blood kin?" cried Mrs. Saylor. "Ignor-ing us. Not caring if we live or die or have bad teeth—" She broke off, sob-bing into the phone. "And me, with bleeding gums. My mouth is falling apart, I tell you, and my son, the dentist, doesn't even care."

"I care, Mama."

"No, you don't!" Mrs. Saylor's whimpered. "I'm old and broke and I've got a toothache. Meanwhile you lay up in that house with that girl, drinking gin rickies. I am your goddamn mother. I brought you into this world. I fed you and diapered your ass. And I deserve a little respect."

"You deserve more than that," scoffed Lacy. "You deserve a brick house with an attached garage."

"He isn't giving me shit," said Mrs. Saylor. "It's all going to Walter's girl."

"Mama, just calm down. If your tooth is bothering you, come by the office. I'll check it out."

"Do I have to make an appointment?" Mrs. Saylor was all business now.

"No, Mama. Just come over any time."

"To your office or to your house?"

"To my office. That's where the X-ray machine is."

"You can't brush us off," cried Lacy. "We have a right to visit you anytime we want."

"I need my privacy," Walter said. "I've got a life."

"I've got news for *you*," said Mrs. Saylor. "You've got a family, and *we're* your life."

Bitsy

Crudités
Soup à l'Oignon Gratinée
Coq au Vin
Tart de Poireaux
Choux de Bruxelles
Haricots Blancs
Tart Tatin
Gâteau au Chocolat

We were in Byron and Aunt Clancy's living room helping them string colored lights on the Christmas tree, when Walter presented me with the crumpled sheet of paper. "I've drawn up a menu," he said.

"I'm sorry, Walter," said Aunt Clancy, lifting a tiny silver angel from the box. "Zach and I have already started freezing ahead. But if you want something special, we can serve it."

Walter blushed. "I was talking about another party. A family get-together."

"Family?" I asked, glancing at the paper.

"Yours and mine," Walter said. "A before-the-wedding get-together. In fact, we could have it here."

"*Here?*" I cried, a bit too loud. I was fed up with Walter's mother and sisters prowling around the house. Aunt Clancy fastened the angel ornament onto a branch, then she grabbed Byron's hand and they left the room. After they'd gone, I said, "That's not a good idea, honey. See, Aunt Clancy and I are still cleaning the house for the wedding, and a party will just make things harder."

"Then we'll just have it at my house," said Walter.

I laid the menu aside and picked up a red ornament. A get-together at

Walter's house for his family and mine? Not if I could help it. "Please don't take offense," I began, "but I'm not the party type."

"Sure, you are," he said. "Look, I know my family has given you a hard time. But I was thinking if we invited them to something, they might back down."

"Does it have to be a party?" I hooked the ornament onto a branch. "Couldn't we take them to El Toro?"

"It wouldn't be the same."

"Can I think about it?" I reached into the box and pulled out a tiny snowman ornament, so old, the color had worn off in places.

He reached for the menu and thrust it into my hands. "This is just suggestions for what to serve. Nothing's set in concrete. But I was hoping you could try something French since you speak the language and all."

I glanced at the paper—I didn't know what half the items were. A long time ago, Miss Betty had accused me of macerating all things French, whether it was a sauce or a delicate phrase, but whenever I whispered certain words to Walter, he swelled with pride. "My fiancée speaks French," he told all his patients. "She's a real classy lady." At night I would whisper *ma puce*, my flea, or *mon chou*, my cabbage, making it sound romantic and naughty. But when it came to cooking, I was an All-American girl.

"Will you do it?" asked Walter, the orange eyebrows moving up and down.

I looked at his menu again and sighed. "Won't you reconsider El Toro?"

"If that's what you want. But it would make me so happy if you'd impress them with the French food, French wine, and French talk." He picked up my hand and kissed the knuckles. When he looked up, I could see my whole future reflected in his eyes. And to some extent that future included his family.

"Say yes, Bitsy." He began kissing my other hand. "Please, please say yes."

"Oui," I said.

. . .

On the afternoon of the party, Walter stood on a ladder, stringing colored lights into the bare branches of his dogwood trees. I directed from the ground, saying, "Move left. No, higher, HIGHER!"

Then I ran back into the kitchen and pulled a casserole out of Fiona's old oven. My family hadn't been invited—at their request. I was dreading the dinner, having to make small talk with the Saylors and ignoring their jabs. I would have preferred to spend the evening curled up on the sofa with Walter, watching the original *Christmas Carol.*

Instead I was searching for ground cinnamon in a top cabinet. I found the spice mixed in with a stash of old medicine—dozens of plastic pill bottles. Valium, Nembutal, Demerol. FIONA SAYLOR was typed across each bottle. TAKE AS DIRECTED. I shook a Valium bottle. Maybe one might calm my nerves. My mother took it daily, and it seemed to help her. I dropped the bottle into my pocket and hurried back outside.

After the lights were hung, Walter dragged the ladder over to Fiona's wisteria arbor, where I thought more twinkly Christmas lights should go. "The best way is to just toss the lights higgledy-piggledy," I called up to him. "Coil them up like barbed wire and toss them. Yes, that's it!"

"It looks good." Walter rubbed his chin, his fingers rasping over the dirty red stubble. From the top of the ladder, he grinned down at me. "Hey, drill sergeant. Think I have time to shave?"

"You have time for more than that," I promised, returning his smile.

· · ·

I stood in the living room window, watching the road. A stack of Billie Holiday records was on the turntable and "You're My Thrill" was playing. I wore a black dress that I'd found at a garage sale, and Miss Gussie's pearls. Even though my hair was swept into a French twist, and it was bitter cold outside, my neck felt sweaty. My chin was red, as if I'd been repeatedly kissed by a man with a day-old beard. The culprit came up behind me and kissed my bare neck.

The Saylors's station wagon was turning into the drive, tearing up the gravel. It stopped next to Walter's T-bird. "They're here," I said, reaching into my pocket for the pill bottle.

"Hell, I broke a goddamn fingernail," cried Lacy, coming up the porch steps. She stared with horror at her right hand. "You got a emery board on you, Jobeth?"

Mrs. Saylor helped herself out of the station wagon. She wore a red pantsuit and red leather boots. A red pocketbook swung from one arm. Pinned to her lapel was a little jeweled Santa Claus.

Walter gave my hand a squeeze. "It'll be all right," he said. I wanted to believe him, but from the porch I could hear Jobeth saying, "Hell, yes.

I've got everything, even disposable douche." I remembered what Miss Gussie used to say before stressful social gatherings: "They can kill me but they can't eat me."

I silently repeated this, but the mantra held little comfort as Walter opened the door and I looked into those freckled, toothy faces.

"Hey, y'all," said Walter.

"Hey, yourself," said Jobeth.

I held out my hands to greet them, but Mrs. Saylor ignored me and silently eyed her son. She rummaged in her bag and lit a cigarette. "Something sure does smell good," she said.

"A glass of wine, anyone?" Walter asked. I had selected a nice pinot noir, a label that I'd once seen Mrs. Wentworth serve at dinner parties. So I figured it had to be the best.

"I knew you was gonna ask that," said Jobeth. "Dr. Hoity-Toity," she added.

"I'll take me a beer if you got one," said Lacy, stifling a burp.

"I don't think we do." Walter gave me a questioning glance, and I shook my head.

"I thought as much." Lacy sighed. "That's why we brought our own. We don't want nobody accusing us of freeloading."

"Rooster, baby," said Mrs. Saylor. "Run on back to the car and fetch the cooler."

"What kind of old-fogy music are you playing, brother? Damn, put on some Christmas carols!" Lacy punched Walter's shoulder, then she leaned over, plucked the cigarette from Mrs. Saylor's fingers, and blew a smoke ring. It floated over her head, toward the twinkling Christmas tree, circling the crêpe-paper angel, wrapping around her neck like a noose.

· · ·

While the guests drank Pabst Blue Ribbon, I hid in the kitchen, waiting for the bread to heat. I kept sipping wine and swallowing pills and listening to Billie. From the living room, the conversation flowed past me in icy waves. Most of it centered around Fiona, her pitiful death, and Lacy's former boyfriends—one was apparently a wrestler from Oklahoma, and another was serving time in an Arkansas jail for armed robbery.

"Waltie, you have bad taste in women, too," Mrs. Saylor said. "Speaking of which, have you seen Patricia lately?"

"Patricia?" Walter asked. "I don't know any Patricias."

"That woman who works for you," said Mrs. Saylor. "Patricia Eller."

"Oh. Her," Walter said. "Why do you ask? I see her most every day."

"I'll just *bet* you do," said Lacy. She and Jobeth giggled.

I peered out the kitchen door and saw Walter sitting in a brocade chair. He looked crisp and clean in a plaid shirt and festive green corduroy trousers.

"Bitsy ought to drop by your office sometime," said Jobeth.

Actually, I'd stopped by the dental office yesterday. I'd found Walter sitting at his desk, making notations on a chart. Patricia was standing behind him, gripping an armful of folders. He closed the chart, then held it up. Patricia immediately added it to her pile, then she hurried out of the room, giving me a polite nod. Walter laid down the pen, and opened his arms. "There's my girl," he said. "Come here and give me a kiss."

"Last time we dropped into his office," Lacy was saying, "Patricia was rinsing out her mouth. *If* you get my drift." She looked at her sister and both collapsed into giggles, pausing to make gestures with their mouths and hands.

"Girls, y'all are *awful,*" scolded Mrs. Saylor. "Maybe she just had bad breath."

"I'm not awful, I'm hungry," said Jobeth, cutting her eyes at Walter. "When we gone eat, babycakes?"

While Billie sang "Good Morning, Heartache," I pulled the homemade French bread, a gift from Zach, out of the oven. Dammit, I'd overcooked it. I set the pan on the counter, then dropped another pill onto my tongue and washed it down with wine. Taking a deep breath, I stepped into the dining room and beckoned my guests to the buffet table. "The plates are at one end, the silverware at the other," I directed, waving one hand. The gesture seemed exaggerated, and my tongue felt thick.

"Come on, children," said Mrs. Saylor, clapping her hands. "Kindergarten is starting."

The Saylors lined up, guffawing and rolling their eyes. Behind them, through the pocket doors, the Christmas tree glittered. Walter came up behind me, kissing the back of my neck. "Don't let them get you riled," he whispered. "It'll be over soon."

I nodded, wondering what his family was suggesting about Patricia Eller. I didn't like what I was thinking—not that I was a prude or a wimp—but the idea of Walter and Patricia . . . why, it was revolting. The woman was old enough to be his mother. Or maybe that was the attraction. I tipped back my glass and drank the last of my wine. I could feel the Valium working. Or maybe it was the wine. I didn't know and didn't care. Lurching into the kitchen, I picked up the bread and began to swing it like a club. Bits of crust flaked onto the floor.

Walter stepped into the kitchen. When he saw me swinging the bread, he blanched. "What's going on?" he asked.

"I'll tell you if you explain about you and Patricia. Quid pro quo, Waltie."

"There's nothing to tell. My sisters are trying to make you mad. Just don't listen to them." Walter looked up at the ceiling and shook his head. I wasn't sure what to believe, and the Valium wasn't making me one bit calmer. Giving him a long, contemptuous glance, I dropped the bread into a wicker basket. It made a decisive clunk. I picked it up and stepped around him into the dining room. Billie was singing "That Ole Devil Called Love." I watched as the Saylors descended on the table.

"Hey, what's this stuff?" Lacy pointed to a Pyrex pie plate. "It looks like a pie, but it sure don't smell like one."

The others leaned over to stare at the food—some in CorningWare, other on china platters—I had arranged on the blue-checkered cloth.

"A leek tart," I said, walking up to the table. *Bottled tranquility did not leave you tranquil*, I thought. It only made me slow and stupid and suspicious.

"Did you take a leak in it?" Lacy laughed.

"Not yet," I said. "But I'm considering it."

The Saylors gaped at me, trying to decide if my remark was meant humorously. I felt a rush of pity for them. When it came to culinary matters, the poor things had led chaste lives—vinegar douches notwithstanding.

"A leek is a kind of onion," Walter said, stepping into the dining room.

"Well, pardon my French." Lacy slapped her thigh, then nudged Jobeth. "And pardon yours, too."

"Tell them what everything is," said Walter.

"She may not know what's what," said Lacy. "*If* you get my drift."

"Walter's right," said Mrs. Saylor. "She better tell us what we're eating."

"I agree," said Jobeth. "A person has a right to know what's going into her mouth."

"How true," I said, feeling absurdly calm. I reached into my pocket, touching the medicine bottle, thinking of that song by the Rolling Stones, "Mother's Little Helper." Forget the music, I'd rather have Mick Jagger. I stared down at the table. Instead of the food I had painstakingly prepared, I saw Patricia Eller balancing on her knees, mouth agape. If this was an accurate vision, and I suspected it was, I owed the Saylors a debt of gratitude. I blinked and prepared to identify the dishes. Touching a Pyrex bowl, I said, *"Trou de cul."* Which, of course, meant asshole.

I pointed to another dish and said, *"Pourriture."* Rotting trash.

"Merde à mouche." Shit-fly.

"Chagatte." Pussy.

"Well, thanks a bunch," said Jobeth, rolling her eyes. "That *really* helped."

I moved along the table, pointed to another dish, and said, "Don't forget to try this—it's *fils de pute*."

"You're serving us a poot?" Rooster looked horrified.

"It must go with the pee-pee tart," Lacy said. "Excuse me—I mean fart."

"No, it goes with the music," said Jobeth.

"We just want to know what the hell we're eating," said Lacy. "You know?"

Jobeth grimly nodded.

"Otherwise we could have stayed home and ate hot dogs."

"Wilma never served me a poot in her life," said Rooster.

"Oh, I bet she has," I said. Suddenly I felt gay and buoyant.

"Is this some kind of joke?" Mrs. Saylor lifted her arm and briskly waved it over the table, as if she were an evil fairy casting a spell.

"I *told* Bitsy to fix y'all a feast," Walter explained. "*I* made up this menu. I specifically requested French food. So if you're upset, then blame me."

"Honey, we'd forgive you if you killed somebody," said Mrs. Saylor, her eyes filling. "Blood is thicker than piss."

"Oh, Mama." Walter put his long arms around her, his freckled fingers smoothing her wiry hair. "Please don't cry. It's just food."

"I can't h-h-help it."

Over by the table, Rooster lifted a Pyrex dish. It was filled with small green balls. "What the hell did you say this was?" he asked.

"Actually, I lied. That casserole is not *fils de pute*," I said. "In fact, it's not a casserole. It's brussels sprouts."

"Well, why didn't you just say so from the start?" Lacy giggled and wiped her eyes.

"I was wondering what stunk so bad." Jobeth wrinkled her nose.

I stepped over to the sideboard and poured another glass of wine. I drank it in three swallows. As the Valium collided with the alcohol, I felt both cheerful and careless. "My darling rednecks," I said in a grand voice, exactly like Mrs. Wentworth's. "*Fils de pute* means son of a whore, but I promise it doesn't taste like one. And *I* should know."

Lacy and Jobeth looked at each other and snorted. Walter came up next to me, his red hair bobbing, cheeks flaming, and he put his hand on my shoulder. "Honey," he said in a patient voice. "You've had too much to drink."

"No, I've just had a minuscule amount." I squirmed away from his grasp.

"What's minuscule mean?" asked Rooster.

"Look between your legs," Mrs. Saylor said, and her daughters dissolved into giggles.

"*Laisse-moi tranquille,*" I said, waving my free arm.

"Stop," Walter cried, spinning me around.

But I couldn't stop, I was on a roll. I pulled away from him, then stared into the blank faces of my guests. "I'm sorry," I told them. "Let me translate. I just said: 'You're annoying as shit! Leave me alone.'"

"Cut it out, Bitsy!" cried Walter.

"Did you tell Patricia to *spit* it out?" I asked.

"Uh-oh," Jobeth said. "I *think* a family tift is brewing."

"I believe the word is tiff," I said.

Jobeth slammed down her plate and turned to the others. "I ain't putting up with this parley voo shit. Let's haul ass and go to Lucky Lee's Smorgasbord on Highway 231. They'll be sure to have ribs."

"Barbecued ones," said Lacy.

"But not the kind that kill," said Mrs. Saylor, picking up her red pocketbook. Then she turned to her son. "By the way, ask Bitsy how she cooks baby back ribs. Ask about her first husband and what she did to him."

Walter opened the front door and said, "She didn't do anything to anybody. So just leave."

"She bashed her ex in the face." Mrs. Saylor patted her nose. "And that's the *real* reason she don't have custody of her child. Me and the girls have been asking around about her."

Lacy turned to me. "I guess you thought you'd pulled a fast one, didn't you? You never dreamed the gossip could reach Hanging Limb, Tennessee."

"Actually, it didn't," said Mrs. Saylor. "We had to ask around the beauty shops in Crystal Falls to hear the juicy stuff. Her ex had plastic surgery after Bitsy got through with him. A nose job. Be sure and ask her *all* about it, Waltie. Have a safe Christmas."

The Saylors hurried out of the house. Jobeth lagged behind. "We're real simple people," she told me. "If you'd served us barbecue and banana splits, we'd a kissed your feet."

"Maybe I don't want my feet kissed," I said, wishing I could shut up, wishing I hadn't taken that Valium.

"If you talked English," said Lacy, poking her head around Jobeth's, "we'd a kissed your ass."

"Tire-toi morpion!" I said gaily.

Walter shut the door after his family, then leaned against it, glaring at me.

"I am sorry, Walter," I began. "I was nervous about tonight, and I just don't know what came over me. Well, I guess I do. I drank too much wine. And I took some of Fiona's Valium. I found it in the cabinet—why was she taking it, by the way?"

"I didn't know she was."

"I may have taken too many."

"You can't blame wine and tranquilizers. I know my family's loud and tasteless, but I love them and you went too damn far."

"What about you? Were you getting it on with Patricia?"

"There's *never* been anything between me and her."

I looked up into his eyes. "But your sisters said—"

"They want to break us up." His orange eyebrows lowered. "What's this about your ex-husband? Did you smash his nose, or was Mama lying?"

"No. But I can explain."

"You actually *hit* him?" He backed up, his hands raised.

"I'm not like Fiona. It was self-defense."

"That's what Fiona used to say. Why didn't you just tell me? You had plenty of chances. I can't risk being hooked up to another abusive woman." He held out his hand, his fingers slightly curled. "I'm sorry, Bitsy, but the engagement's off."

I hid my left hand behind my back. "You said yourself that your family wants to break us up."

"Give it to me!"

"But I love you, Walter. We're getting married."

"Haven't you been listening? The wedding is *off*!" He crossed his arms like a football referee. Fumble! Pass intended for Bitsy Wentworth is *incomplete*.

"Let's just sleep on it, all right? Then, tomorrow, you can talk to Aunt Clancy. She'll explain about my first marriage." I tried to smile, but my lips felt rubbery, and I probably grimaced instead.

"I don't need to hear any more. I'm not getting in bed with a rattlesnake. Just keep the goddamn ring. It didn't cost all that much, anyway."

"But I want *you*, not the ring."

"Just leave, I want to be alone."

"Fine." I looked down at my finger, then twisted off the diamond. I grabbed Walter's hand, and he flinched as I fit the ring onto his pinkie. "A perfect fit," I said.

A TAPED MESSAGE TO BETTY FORD

December 22, 1974

Dear Betty,

I hope your Xmas turns out to be better than mine. The dentist (Walter Saylor) broke off his engagement to my daughter. She had turned cartwheels trying to please him. She has naturally blond hair, but when he asked her to be a redhead, she went straight to the beauty parlor and had it dyed. Anyway, after they broke up, she marched straight to the drugstore and bought a box of Miss Clairol, a level 8. Only it turned out muddy, and she had to go to the salon and get yet another color correction. I'm sure you understand—you being a blonde. Only her hair was too porous, not to mention damaged from all that dye, and it broke off two inches from her scalp. She took it in stride, but short hair doesn't flatter her round little face. My heart went out to her. Not only is she torn up over her romance, she's practically bald. So don't tell me that this isn't cosmic justice. First, Fiona has a beauty parlor disaster, and now Bitsy.

Of course, now that her love life is in shambles, I won't be able to get you a discount for your teeth. But if you come to Crystal Falls, I will cook you a delicious meal. Yesterday I baked a ham—the secret is to baste with Coca-Cola—along with macaroni and cheese and corn bread and turnip greens. A chocolate pie for dessert with a scratch crust. My food is better than what my sister serves down at the café and she no longer cooks at home. Most every night, Bitsy and Byron eat with me and Mack and that thing he's married to. I don't think my son is happy. He's got a beer bottle in his hand all the time now, even in the daytime. And I no longer hear their bedsprings squeak.

I'll just be honest—love troubles can drive a body to drink. I don't, of course, because it wouldn't mix with my medicines. My son just lays up watching Sanford and Son *or* Good Times, *then his head will tip over and he'll start snoring. But he wakes up the minute I change the channel to* Rhoda. *Well, I've got to sign off because the oven dinger just went off, and I don't want my cookies to burn. They are oatmeal raisin, and I've enclosed a few dozen for your dining enjoyment. Wish you were here,*

Dorothy McDougal

A NOTE FROM BITSY

December 30, 1974

Dear Mrs. Wentworth,

I am sorry for writing this letter, but I wasn't able to reach you any other way. What I'm wanting to know is, may I have permission to take Jennifer out to dinner at El Toro? My whole family will be going, too. I know it can't be on her birthday, but please let me know which day will work for you. I have enclosed a card and birthday presents from all of us. Will you please give them to her at the party?

Sincerely,

Bitsy

December 30, 1974

Dear Jennifer,

I just can't believe that you will turn three years old tomorrow. I am sending your presents a day early, so you'll have lots of goodies at your party. I miss you, and I hope we can see each other soon.

Love,

Mother

Part 4

TAPED MESSAGES TO BETTY FORD

January 15, 1975

Dear Betty,

For my 43rd birthday, my daughter fixed up my bedroom. In the old days, I just loved to redecorate. I'd call the designer and tell him what I wanted. But Bitsy beats him all to pieces. I told her my room was my own personal island in a Sea of Antagonism. Since green is my favorite color, Bitsy painted the walls key lime. Meanwhile, she put Mack to work, scraping that hideous orange paint off my furniture. The ugly Sears curtains came down and up went matchstick blinds from Pier One. Over these we hung filmy white sheers that stir in the breeze. We even bought a wicker cage for my canary, Frank Sinatra.

Then at garage sales Bitsy found a quilted bedspread patterned with giant palm fronds; two white lamps shaped like oriental temple jars; and an overstuffed chair that matched the bedspread. Then we went out to Mr. Peyton's greenhouse and loaded up on live plants. We bought a bird's nest fern, baby's tears, and a palm tree. I just hope I remember to water them.

When we got back, Mack had painted the furniture off-white. Bitsy talked him into buying me wall-to-wall carpet. When Earlene found out, her face turned red. She insisted on riding with us to the carpet store and she wrinkled her nose when I picked white shag. She did not go with me and Bitsy to the Starving Artist Sale at the Holiday Inn. We picked out a few beach scenes, then drove back home. Earlene told me to look in my bedroom, that she'd bought me a present. It was a green plant, a mother-in-law's tongue. Do you think she's hinting at something, or is she just jealous?

Love,

Dorothy

May 1, 1975

Hi, Betty,

It's me again. Dorothy McDougal from Tennessee. I have the most wonderful news. My niece Violet will be graduating with honors from the University of Tennessee, and she has applied to medical school. We are all going to Knoxville to see her walk across the stage, and then we are going out to dinner.

This is not to say that my life is trouble-free. My daughter hasn't had a date in seventeen months, two weeks, and six days. Except three months ago, a Purity milkman asked her out. They were going to the 7 P.M. movie. At 6 P.M. the milkman called and said he'd just heard that Bitsy was an attempted manslaughterer, and he was sorry, but he had to cancel their date. Bitsy just laughed and said she was changing her name to Lizzie Borden. But I am worried that she'll never find true love. She isn't a violent person. It just looks that way. She would make some man a good wife. If your cute son would like to meet her, please write. And just think—if they hit it off, we'd be in-laws.

Your friend,
Dorothy

A NOTE FROM VIOLET

June 17, 1975

Dear Bitsy,

Thanks for the bookstore gift certificate. I will put it to good use. I enjoyed seeing everyone in Knoxville. The graduation ceremony was so cool, wasn't it? I got accepted to Vanderbilt Medical School and U T in Memphis. Mama is pushing Vandy, but I just can't justify the cost. Part of that sentence isn't true. Spot the fib. Actually, it's too close to Crystal Falls. There, I've said it. I love my mother, but I long to live far, far away. So come September, it looks like I'll be singing the Delta blues. Please talk to Mama for me. She's got to come to grips with the fact that I'm grown. Otherwise she's going to make me feel guilty and end up pushing me even farther away.

My nickel.
Violet

Bitsy

Mack and Earlene invited Aunt Clancy, Byron, and me to go down to Center Hill Lake on the July Fourth, and we were about to step out the door when the phone rang. Aunt Clancy told Byron to ignore it, but, thinking it might be the hospital, he picked it up. It was Chick. Apparently he and Miss Betty were going to a fancy party at the country club, and they couldn't find a babysitter for Jennifer. Byron told him that we'd be more than happy to take her—talk about understatement—but we were going to the lake for the day and was it okay with them if Jennifer came with us. Chick had to confer with Miss Betty. After a minute, he said it was fine.

When we got to the lake, Earlene barged up to a family of five and asked if she could borrow a life preserver. The family seemed a little stunned, but they gave the jacket to her. I was going to put Jennifer into her swimsuit but when I looked in the diaper bag Chick had left us, which was actually a big, drawstring Vuitton purse, I saw they hadn't packed one, just outfits. Earlene wanted to borrow one from the family, but we decided just to improvise, so we took off Jennifer's shorts and let her swim in her panties and the big life preserver. She looked adorable, like a sea nymph, and had the best time.

Before we started for home, I returned the life jacket. I took off Jennifer's wet panties, stuck them in a plastic sandwich bag in the Vuitton, and put her into the dry shorts. She was tired out and slept all the way back home. Then, about fifteen minutes after Chick picked Jennifer and her bag up, Miss Betty telephoned, screaming that only a fiend would send a child home without panties, and that she was calling the police. Aunt Clancy tried to explain but Miss Betty wouldn't listen. She kept calling me hateful names, nothing unusual, but she even implied that Byron and Mack might be perverts. Now the Wentworths have cut off the visits again, but everyone says that won't last long because we're the only babysitters who'll put up with them.

A NOTE FROM VIOLET

October 15, 1975

Dear Bitsy,

I appreciate you and Mama coming to Memphis and helping me get moved in. The curtains look real nice, and I am enjoying all the groceries. Also, you were sweet to buy me a pet rock.

How is Mama doing? Do you know that she's calling me every day? She used to write all the time, but this is worse. It's driving me insane. I love her, but I got a phone to order pizza, not to chitchat. In order to study, I need peace and quiet. Please tell her I'm fine.

Violet

P.S. I haven't had a date since I got here. All the guys in my medical class are either married or something is wrong with them, like obsessive-compulsive disorder.

Violet Jones

It was Halloween, and Violet was stuck in the middle of a smoke-filled room in Midtown. It was a stupid costume party, but she'd refused to dress up. Her date was sitting on the kitchen counter, waiting for his turn at the bong. He wore a clown suit. What a loser. She grabbed her Army surplus jacket and wandered outside, jamming her hands into her pockets. On her way out the door, she stumbled against a tall, sallow-faced guy, who caught her elbow.

"I'm sorry, did I trip you?" he asked.

"I'm fine, thanks."

He let go of her elbow and stepped backward. Beneath the porch light, Violet noticed that he had straight brown hair, and quite a few cowlicks. He wasn't wearing a costume, either.

"I just can't take all that smoke," she said, gesturing at the door.

"Me, either." He looked at Violet and blushed. "I'm not much of a party animal. In fact, I was just leaving."

"What's your name?"

"Oh, I'm sorry." He extended his hand. "George Atherton. I'm a grad student at Memphis State. I'm writing a thesis on Hardy."

"Violet Jones," she said, shaking his hand. "I'm a first-year med student."

Someone inside the house yelled, "Trick-or-treat!" Violet noticed that George had gorgeous brown eyes and long lashes, like a cartoon giraffe. His face was round, and he had a rash on his chin, but she loved his shy expression. She started to ask how old he was, then someone burst out the door, yelling, "Happy Halloween, you ghouls!" Inside the house, someone tossed a handful of Hershey's kisses. She saw the candy fall around her date, who was kissing a petite blonde in a metallic miniskirt, with gauzy fairy wings somehow affixed to her shoulders.

"Do you have a car?" Violet grabbed George's arm.

"Sure." He nodded. "Do you need a ride home?"

"How about if we go to your place? That is, if you have a place."

"Yes, but—"

"Come on." Violet took his hand and dragged him down the porch.

He lived only a few blocks away, and when he opened his apartment door, an Irish setter bounded down the hall and jumped up on him. "Down, Beau!" he said. "Hey, where's your manners? We've got a guest. Say hello to, er, what was your name again?"

"Violet."

"Ah." George shuffled his feet, and his face turned red. "Would you like a late-night brunch?"

"Great." Violet followed him into the kitchen and sat on the counter.

"Do you like your eggs scrambled or fried?" he asked.

"Both," Violet said, amused. "I was raised by a vegan, so naturally I'll eat anything. I've never met a man who can cook—except Zach, of course."

"Zach?" With one hand, he broke eggs into a bowl.

"He and my mother own a café in Crystal Falls."

"Ah."

"You're a man of few words, George."

"Yes."

While he scrambled their eggs, Violet wandered around his apartment. It was cluttered, but she liked it, lots of books, threadbare Persian rug, frayed velvet chairs with goose-down cushions, and an old planter's desk, crammed with papers. She turned a corner and found herself back in the kitchen. During her absence, George had cracked open the long kitchen window, and delicious smells wafted over from Justine's Restaurant across the street. The dog loped to the window and pressed his nose through the crack, sniffing hard.

"It must be difficult living next to Justine's," Violet said. "Do you like French food?"

"I've never really had any."

"Me, either. Also, I never had a dog," Violet said, raking her fingers through the setter's extravagant red coat. His tail whipped back and forth against her legs. She leaned over and patted his head. "I bet you pant over all the girls, don't you, Beau?"

"Actually, you're the first," George said and two pink blotches appeared on his cheeks.

After breakfast—which was very good—he drove her home without so much as a kiss on the cheek. Violet promptly forgot about him until a week later, when he invited her to an M.S.U. basketball game. After they got back to his place, Violet curled up on the sofa and began playing with the dog. George sat across the room in one of the velvet chairs, his eyes shifting back and forth. Violet got up, walked over to the chair, and sat down in his lap. She leaned over, her dark hair falling between them, and kissed him. His lips were clamped together, and she tried to pry them apart with her tongue. With one hand she started unbuttoning her blouse. "I like you and you like me. So let's go to bed," she said between kisses.

"I'd rather we didn't."

"Why not?"

He started to breathe fast. "Violet, I'm—" He broke off. Then he licked his lips and started over. "I'm not a cosmopolitan man."

"But you read Hardy," she said. A smile started on her lips but it was instantly repressed.

"I don't date a lot. In fact, I don't date at all."

"Never?"

"No."

"Hey, you need Masters and Johnson, not me." Her hands trembled as she started to rebutton her blouse. He wasn't attracted to her. That was it. She slid off his lap.

"Yes, I probably do." He stood and began to pace, glancing back at her periodically. He seemed to be arriving at some sort of decision. "I don't know how to tell you this, but—"

"What?" Violet tried to appear calm, but horrific thoughts were filling her mind. Deformity. Arrested development. Undescended testicles. She frowned, trying to remember what the *Merck Manual* said about genital malformations. *If he says hermaphrodism,* she thought, *I want to see proof.*

"Well, see, I'm—" His round face seemed to swell.

"Just *say* it, George. I'm a medical student. It can't be that bad."

"I've never been with a woman."

Violet exhaled. She looked down at the floor, then back at George. "Is that all?"

"Isn't that enough?"

"We've got to fix this immediately." She walked toward his bedroom, flinging off her clothes as she went. She found a candle on the dresser and lit it. George was standing in the doorway, his hands pressed against the frame. The flickering light had tinted the air sepia, and she felt as if she were posing in a vintage photograph. *Couple Contemplating Intercourse* would be a fitting title.

"You're pretty," he whispered, then he gave her a bashful smile.

"Have you ever seen a naked woman before, George?" Violet cupped her breasts in her hands, trying to distract him from the scars on her buttocks. They weren't that bad but she didn't want to scare him.

"In movies but n-not in real life," he said.

She walked over and started unbuttoning him. He stepped obediently out of his jeans and boxers, then followed her over to the bed. It was walnut, with a high, carved headboard. The sheets felt crisp in Violet's hands, and smelled faintly of detergent. They lay there for several minutes, staring at each other. She felt his breath on her face. A virgin, she thought. This was going to be so cool. She reached for his hand and put it on her breast. He shuddered. Then she leaned over and began kissing him. She felt him tremble. Moving her hand down, she rubbed the inside of his thighs. When she felt his erection brush against her arm, she pulled him on top of her.

"Will you, ah, can you . . . oh, shit. " He grimaced, then collapsed, gasping for air. After a moment, he kissed her hair and whispered, "Sorry. I just couldn't wait."

"That's understandable," Violet said, glancing over at the night table. She wondered if he had any Kleenex.

"It is?" he asked in an incredulous voice.

"Hey, it's your first time. We'll keep trying until you get it right."

He drew back, his eyes rounded. "You think I ever will?"

"Oh, yes," she said, pulling him back down. "Absolutely."

Clancy Jane

Clancy Jane was sitting at the harvest table, writing a letter, when she heard a car roll up the driveway. She glanced up from her notepad and saw Zach Lombard's blue Toyota. He tooted his horn. Clancy Jane hurried to the kitchen door, opened the screen, and stepped out onto the porch. In the distance, thunder crackled.

"Hope I'm not disturbing you," Zach said, climbing out of his car. The wind tossed his ponytail, which fell midway down his back. He had studied Buddhism, and recently he'd lent her his favorite book, *The Narrow Road to the Deep North and Other Travel Sketches*, but she hadn't found the time to read it. She vowed to start it tonight. Maybe it would offer insight into his psyche.

"Not at all," she said.

"I've been visiting the Mennonites. I couldn't wait to show you the cool things I bought."

"You went by yourself?" Clancy Jane said, feeling a pang. She'd asked him repeatedly if she could tag along on his foraging expeditions. To hide her disappointment, she peered through the Toyota's windows at the overflowing boxes.

Instead of answering, he reached into the backseat, pulling out one of the boxes. "And it seems that I've returned none too soon. It's getting ready to storm."

"So, what'd you get?"

"Preserves. Strawberry, peach, plum, and apple jelly."

"Wow," she said, hoping she sounded enthusiastic. He headed toward the door and she propped open the screen as Zach passed through.

"But this box isn't for the café," he said, setting it on the counter. "It's for you."

"Why, how sweet of you." She smiled. "Stay and have a cup of tea. I want to hear about the Mennonites."

He glanced at his watch, then out at the sky. The wind was stirring the trees, and a few dried maple leaves drifted down onto the pavement. "I better not."

"I've got some tea leaves from Northern California," she said.

"They grow tea in California?" Zach smiled.

"No, it's Assam. My friend Sunny sent it," Clancy Jane said, filling the kettle with water. "She weaves lovely blankets on the Mendicino Coast. A boutique sells them for outrageous prices."

Outside, it began to rain. Clancy Jane set the kettle on a burner, switched the knob to high, then walked over to the cabinet. She paused to turn on the radio. Sergio Mendes & Brasil '66 were singing "Fool on the Hill." Not her idea of seduction music, but it did bring back 1968. As she pulled out mugs, she silently blessed the downpour, and the empty house.

"I wish we could serve afternoon tea at the café," Zack said. "Just the classics, of course. Scones, crumpets, lemon curd. Although I don't know where we'd get clotted cream."

"A stodgy English tea? That's so unlike you."

Zach didn't answer. His attention had shifted, and he was staring out the back door, as if mesmerized by the storm. Outside, water puddled in the driveway, filling up the cracks in the stone path. From the stove, the kettle whistled, and Zach glanced over his shoulder.

"I really shouldn't stay," he said. "I should get home."

"But you'll get soaked." Clancy Jane set down the tea tin.

"I'll make a run for it." Zach pulled up his collar. He started toward the door and she impulsively grabbed his arm.

"Don't go," she said. She looked up into his eyes. Behind her, the kettle was screaming, but she ignored it. One step closer, she thought, and he'll be within kissing range. She wanted to do more than kiss. He had to know it, she thought.

His eyes widened for a moment, as if she had pinched him. Then he stepped back. *He's appalled,* Clancy Jane thought. He held up both hands as if deflecting a blow. "I'm a big boy," he said. "A little rain won't hurt me. You worry too much."

Big boy? *This* was how he saw her—a nurturing, let-me-take-care-of-you sort of woman. She wasn't motherly—look how she'd botched it with Violet. It occurred to her that he was pretending. Maybe that was the Buddhist way. Her way was the fool's way. Now she couldn't even love him from afar, because, no matter how he was acting, he knew what was in her heart, and he was embarrassed for her. If only she could take it back, if only she hadn't been so grabby; but God, she hadn't been able to help herself.

"I have to go," he said and dashed out the door. The rain beat hard against his shirt. He leaped over a puddle, then ducked into his car. The Toyota swung around, leaving tire tracks in the damp grass, then sped down the hill, into the street, and off into the downpour.

. . .

The first week in December, Byron went to a medical conference in Kansas City, and when he returned, he felt as if he'd come back to someone else's house. First, he walked toward the back door and glanced up for the wind chimes; they were gone. Instead he saw several copper-eyed cats sitting in the trees. They gazed down at him as if he might be edible. The largest meowed. Byron wondered if Pitty Pat, Clancy's elderly Persian, had somehow replicated himself.

Byron hurried into the kitchen and started to holler for Clancy Jane, but stopped and set down his suitcase. He didn't recognize the room. Before he'd left, the kitchen had been pleasantly jumbled with plants and polka-dotted crockery. The Welsh cupboard had been packed with platters, dishes, and covered bowls, with mail tucked behind saucers, but in his absence, everything had disappeared but eight polka-dotted dinner plates. The counters were bare except for the radio. Heart was singing "Barracuda." Byron rubbed his eyes. Over by the sink, a crooked line of water bugs moved to the music, winding their way across the counter.

He walked into the hall, into the living room. Clancy Jane was lying on the sofa, a red afghan tucked around her, reading a hardback, a new translation of the Tao Te-Ching. Stacked beside her on the floor were *Zen and the Art of Motorcycle Maintenance* and *Large Sutra on Perfect Wisdom*. She looked at Byron over the book. "Hey, back already?"

"I'm thrilled to see you, too."

"How was Kansas City?"

"Fine. But what happened here?" He glanced around the room. All the pictures had been taken down, leaving nail holes in the Sheetrock. The matchstick blinds were gone, and through the windows, he could see early evening gathering under the trees. "Where are your wind chimes? And what happened in the kitchen?" He pointed over his shoulder. "Are you getting ready to redecorate?"

"No, I just got sick of the clutter." She set down the book and sat up, brushing her hair from her face. "Bitsy helped me box up everything."

"I liked it. It was pretty."

"We had too many possessions, Byron. Too much to worry about. Too much upkeep. So I pared down."

"Had?" Byron asked. "Did you say had?"

"I took a few things to Goodwill."

"Without consulting me? It's human nature to develop attachments to objects." He started to sit down, but a cat screeched and leaped over his shoulder, digging its claws into his shirt. He whirled around. "What the hell?"

"That's Jellybean," said Clancy Jane. "Someone dumped her off while you were gone."

"What about the cats outside, the ones in the trees? Do they have names?"

"Stella, Moksha, and Calcutta," she said.

"And where's Pitty Pat?"

"Hiding. He doesn't like the new people."

"Neither do I. Call the animal shelter."

"That's a death sentence."

"But you just said you wanted to pare down. If dishes are too much responsibility, what the hell are these cats?"

"Dishes are inanimate objects, Byron. These cats might have been humans in another life. I was just reading about something called samsara. In Sanskrit that means wandering from one life to the next. I believe Jellybean and the others might be doing that."

"You could have waited till I got back. I live here, too, you know." Byron started to sit down again, but he froze. The cushion was missing. He eased into the hollowed-out space.

"I didn't think you'd mind." Clancy Jane shrugged.

"Did Zach have anything to do with this?"

"Well, he let me borrow these books. We haven't discussed anything yet."

"But you will. Right?"

She didn't answer. Instead, she reached down and picked up Jellybean, touching her nose to the cat's nose. "Are you hungry, girl? Shall I pour you a saucer of milk?"

"What about me?" Byron cried. "I'm starved."

The next morning, Clancy Jane caught Byron spraying the kitchen with Raid. She ran over and knocked the can from his grasp. "Murderer!" she yelled.

"What's your problem?"

"Stop killing the ants!" She rushed over to the counter and pointed to an ant that was desperately trying to reach a crack in the Formica. "This could be a transmigrating soul, not just a bug crawling on the counter."

"Oh, fuck," he said.

"What we do in this life has a bearing on the next."

"Next what?"

"Life! Your next life. This ant could be your grandmother."

"Maybe it's just a bug, Clancy Jane."

.   .   .

Three days later, Byron broke out in welts and began sneezing. "If you don't get rid of those cats, I'll have to move out," Byron said, blowing his nose into a Kleenex. The trash can was filled with wadded-up tissues. "I've already spoken to an allergist. He says we should find homes for these cats."

"You probably just have a cold." Clancy Jane picked up a knife and began viciously chopping green onions.

"I can't breathe," Byron said. "You're killing me."

"Maybe you're allergic to onions, not cats."

"You don't understand, I'm suffering."

"No, *you* don't understand." She stopped chopping and waved the knife. "Those cats are involved in the cycle of rebirth. I am *not* getting rid of them. The humane shelter would kill them. And if I set them loose, they might get hit by a truck or bitten by a dog. It's bad karma."

"Fuck karma. I want those goddamn cats out of here."

"This isn't about allergies." She narrowed her eyes. "First, you hated my café, and now it's cats. Why can't I have a pet?"

"Pets, Clancy Jane. P-e-t-s."

"I can spell."

"You had Pitty Pat, and I didn't complain. But a fucking pride is something else."

"So, this is about your pride?" Clancy Jane yelled.

"I'm referring to a pride of lions." Byron shook his head. "As in pack of dogs, school of fish? Or is that over your head?"

"Oh," she said, feeling the heat rise to her cheeks, "*that* kind of pride."

"Right," Byron said. "Like you knew."

A TAPED MESSAGE TO ROSALYN CARTER

January 21, 1977

Dear Rosalyn Carter,

You don't know me from Adam—or is it Atom?—but I voted for your big-lipped hubby. I watched y'all on TV yesterday and it looked like his suit was straight off the rack. I don't know how he got a pretty little thing like you. Of course, a lot of people said the same thing about me and Albert—he's my ex-husband. A lot of people said, Dorothy, we don't understand how Albert ended up with you! I just guess it was my feminine wiles, not to mention my 36-D chest, but even worthy men go bad.

Which brings me to my point: how did you handle it when your Jimmy admitted to having lust in his heart? Did you go into shock? Did you first hear about it in Playboy, *or did he tell you beforehand? Walk up to you and say, Rosalyn, I've got the hots for a short-skirted tart? Somehow, I think* Playboy *was the first to know. Men don't spill their guts to a woman. Men lie. Men cheat. Rosalyn, don't be a fool. If lust is in the heart, you can be sure it's in the loins. Your Jimmy was all but saying that his pecker gets hard around pretty women. If he was a plumber, no woman would want him. I say this to comfort you, not to accuse the president of being ugly. If he'd ever done more than lust, you probably would have forgiven him. You might have cried and made him go to a Christian marriage counselor, but in the end, you would have stayed.*

I never got a chance to forgive my skirt-chasing husband. Albert divorced me while I was in a hospital, then he up and married a woman he worked with. Only he forgot to change his life insurance policy. I was his sole beneficiary. I guess it just slipped his mind—or maybe his mind slipped first—but that was lucky for me, because guess what? Last month Albert went sledding up in the Smokey Mountains—I just wonder where the heck his wife was—and he crashed into a tree and broke his neck. He had one of those policies that pays double if you die in an accident. The next thing I knew, I was rich. Woo-hoo! The wife pitched a fit and hired a hick East Tennessee lawyer who didn't know doodly squat. My lawyer had a Vanderbilt degree. So I got all the money. It's vulgar to say how much, but it's six figures. Not that I'm glad that Albert's dead. Well, maybe a little. Actually, he had it coming to him. He started out a prince but turned into a toad. Maybe I didn't kiss him enough, because he hopped onto another lily pad.

Now that I'm no longer living hand-to-mouth, I would like to make a contribution to the charity of your choice. Please write back and tell me which one.

Best wishes,
Dorothy

Violet
and Clancy Jane

Violet hadn't planned on coming home for Easter, but when her mother called, talking excitedly about her menu—instead of a traditional ham and the usual spring vegetables, Clancy Jane had bought a pig—Violet felt homesick.

"Mack's bringing over his domed grill, and we're going to smoke the piglet all day long."

"I thought you didn't eat flesh," Violet said, laughing

"I don't. But Byron does."

Since Violet wasn't quite ready to introduce George to the family, she came by herself. Besides, she'd already told her mother about the deflowering, and Clancy Jane had made cracks about blood on the sheets.

It was night when Violet reached Dixie Avenue. She pulled into the long driveway and her headlights picked out two figures huddled in the dark. It was Clancy Jane and Mack. They were watching smoke billow from the outdoor cooker. Clancy Jane smiled and waved. Her blue eyes looked unusually small and shiny, and her cheeks were red and fleshy, with jowls beneath her chin.

She hugged Violet then she turned back to Mack who was squatting down, feeding hickory wood into the grill, and said, "Like I was saying, the man may be a proctologist, but he doesn't know his ass from a hole in the ground." Clancy Jane tonged up smoldering charcoal bricks. She turned to Violet. "I'm referring to one of Byron's colleagues. He's a real butthole."

Mack snorted. A transistor radio sat on a metal table, playing "The Israelites" by Desmond Dekker and the Aces. Violet noticed that her cousin's hair was thinning, and he had a chunk of fat around his middle. She tactfully shifted her gaze.

"Where's Aunt Dorothy and Bitsy?" Violet asked. She didn't mention Byron because she was used to his absences.

"I wrote you a letter," said Clancy Jane. "They're in Cozumel."

"Together?"

"Well, they've got closer since Daddy died," Mack said.

"Albert's *dead*?" Violet cried.

"From a sledding accident," said Mack. "He crashed into a tree."

"I'm so sorry," Violet said. For the longest time, she hadn't opened any letters from home. When she wasn't dissecting cadavers, she was in bed with George. So far anatomy was her favorite subject.

"When Mama found out, she nearly fainted," Mack explained. By the time Dorothy McDougal had thought to inform Bitsy and Mack of their father's passing, the funeral was over and his remains had been laid to rest in a Pigeon Forge cemetery. "Then she nearly fainted again when she found out about him leaving her his insurance," Mack added.

"It was a $250,000 policy," said Clancy Jane. "But since it was an accidental death, she got double indemnity."

"I'm surprised that she isn't in Zürich," Violet said, "setting up a numbered account."

"She didn't keep it all," Clancy Jane said. "She gave $50,000 to Mack and $50,000 to Bitsy. The rest went into the bank. And I've got to give Bitsy credit. I thought she'd squander it. You know how she loves shoes and pocketbooks. But she bought a used Mustang and new set of tires. Then she bought CDs—but not at Claude's bank."

"Hell, I went hog wild," Mack said. "Me and Earlene bought his 'n' her motorcycles. And we took a few trips to Vegas."

"Bitsy signed up for a home study course," said Clancy Jane. "The Ha'vard School of Interior Design. Not to be confused with Harvard, of course."

"She always had a knack for decorating," said Violet.

"But not a knack with men," said Clancy Jane. "She isn't dating anyone. She studies all the time."

"Nothing wrong with that." Violet shivered. "Where's Earlene?"

"She's up in Monterey," said Mack. "Her mama's sick."

"These days, she's always sick," said Clancy Jane.

"Hope it's not serious," Violet said, blowing into her hands. "Burr, it's too cold out here for me. I'm going inside."

She stepped into the kitchen and was startled by the order. Her mother had never been terribly neat—in fact, she was a slob—but the counters were clean and empty, except for a tray of Fostoria goblets. Violet got a glass of water, then headed toward the living room. The gold velvet chairs were missing, along with Gussie's marble tables. No art hung on the walls except for a red floral Georgia O'Keeffe poster. Cats were lounging on the back of the sofa, and Pitty Pat was sleeping on Byron's console TV, one paw curled over his face.

She wandered upstairs, into her old room, and saw that her mother's austerity program hadn't reached there. She flopped facedown on the cherry spindle bed and smoothed her hands over the lilac comforter. Her bookcase was pleasantly jumbled with old textbooks and folders. The door to her closet was ajar, and she could see little plaid dresses that she'd worn in high school. Violet never had cared about clothes. She'd wear anything as long as it fit. She closed her eyes, and when she opened them again it was the middle of the night. She heard footsteps on the creaky staircase, followed by Byron's voice. "One more step, Mack. No, no, don't turn right. That's good, buddy. You're doing fine."

Violet got out of bed and hurried into the hall, blinking in the harsh light.

"Your cousin's too drunk to walk home," Byron explained, leading Mack down the hall. "I'm putting him to bed."

"Where's Mama?" Violet glanced into the hall, trying to see into their bedroom.

"Downstairs," Byron said, but he wouldn't look at her. "I'm sorry I woke you, Violet."

Mack's eyes fluttered. He looked at Violet and grinned. "Hey, cuz!" he said brightly. "I been drinking burning roses with your mama."

"Turn left," Byron said, steering Mack into the spare bedroom. Violet padded back to her room, changed into a nightgown, and got in bed. She switched off the light, lay back, and shut her eyes. No sooner had she drifted off to sleep when she was awakened by a crash. She sat bolt upright, straining to listen. There was nothing but silence, followed by a muffled groan, a woman's groan. She tensed her stomach muscles, waiting for Byron's footsteps, but the whole house was eerily quiet, except for the clicking of the furnace and wind blowing around the eaves. She threw back the covers and crept downstairs. Clancy Jane was sprawled on the kitchen floor, surrounded by broken goblets.

"Mama!"

Clancy Jane lifted her head. "I slipped."

"Are you hurt?" Violet crouched beside her mother.

"I don't know." Clancy Jane rubbed the back of her head. "I'm not cut anywhere, just a little stunned. But just look at my kitchen."

"I'll clean it later. Let's go upstairs." Violet helped her mother up.

"I'm not a bit sleepy," Clancy Jane said, then she reeled backward, throwing out one arm.

"Be careful walking through this glass," Violet cautioned, slipping one arm around her mother's waist, feeling ripples of loose flesh. She might not be eating meat, Violet thought, but she was certainly eating something.

"I don't need to sleep, I need to cook," Clancy Jane said. She took another step, her leg rising at an exaggerated angle. "I'm not sleepy in the least."

"Yes, I know," Violet said in a soothing voice, but she felt angry and frightened. She wished she'd stayed in Memphis. She and George could have eaten a turkey dinner at Morrison's Cafeteria, and she wouldn't have known that her mother was drinking.

When they reached the landing, Violet hesitated, blinking at Byron's shut door. She tried to remember if it had been open or closed. "Come on, Mama," she said, leading Clancy Jane down the hall to her own purple room. Violet helped her mother into the spindle bed, then she drew the covers up to her chin. Drunk people everywhere, she thought. Falling down drunk people.

"I'll just rest a minute," Clancy Jane said, her eyelids fluttering. "Just a minute is all I need."

Violet went back downstairs, found a broom and dustpan, and swept up all the broken glass. She saw where Clancy Jane had made a bar on the counter—bottles of scotch, bourbon, tequila, rum, tonic water. Cans of Coke and Canada Dry were stacked on the floor. Inside the refrigerator were long-necked bottles of Mexican beer and little bowls filled with maraschino cherries and sliced limes. An ugly voice inside of Violet said, *Throw it all out, Violet. Pour out every stinking drop.* If she did that, her mother would accuse her of being wasteful. Also, she didn't want to get her mother in trouble with Byron. From the looks of the kitchen, Clancy Jane had apparently turned against her dietary principles, and now she was courting Byron with food. A red velvet cake sat on a glass pedestal, next to a homemade fruitcake that reeked of whiskey. There were also three pies—chocolate, pecan, and lemon chess. The fridge held cartons of half-n-half, packages of bacon, and little parcels of smoked salmon.

She slammed the refrigerator door, then hurried back to her purple room. Lifting the covers, she eased into the bed and stretched out beside her mother, flinging her arms over her head. Clancy Jane was gently snoring, giving off toxic fumes of sourmash and tequila. Long ago, when they first came to live at Miss Gussie's house, Clancy Jane had pasted glow-in-the-dark stars onto Violet's ceiling. They had long since peeled off, except for a dozen or so that still gave off a faint, eerie light, incandescent at the edges. She was glad her mother's redecorating hadn't touched her room.

That night she dreamed that Clancy Jane was standing on the edge of an abyss, holding out her hand. "Can I come to Memphis and live with you?" her apparition asked. "No," Violet said in a sad voice. "I'm in love with George."

The next morning, she put two cups of coffee on a tray and carried it up to Clancy Jane. Then she slipped into the bed. She both loved and despised this woman with a fierceness that made her feel childlike. "Wake up, sleepy head," she murmured. "It's Easter, and I don't know how to cook."

"Oh, shit." Clancy Jane groaned, covering her eyes with one hand. "I hate the fucking holidays."

"We'll get through it. We always do."

"I smell coffee."

"I brought you a cup."

"You're a saint." Clancy Jane pulled up on her elbows. When she was settled, Violet placed the cup into her mother's trembling hands. Clancy took a bracing sip, then she leaned back against the cherry spindle headboard. "I guess you're wondering about last night," she said.

Violet looked away.

"I'm in trouble." Clancy Jane took another sip of coffee.

Violet reached for her own cup. Her mother was a binge drinker. A period of abstinence, sometimes a lengthy one, always ended with Clancy

Jane's nose in a wineglass. For Violet, when she was younger, each lapse negated a thousand days of sobriety.

"Aren't you going to say anything?" Clancy Jane asked. Pitty Pat leaped onto the bed and began kneading the covers. She reached out to stroke his fur. "I suppose I could blame Byron. He'd blame Buddha and my feline population."

"Mama, how many cats *do* you have now?"

"Eight. But they're indoor/outdoor. That's not so many when you think about it." Clancy Jane pursed her lips and blew into her coffee. "Personally, I think Byron's allergies are an excuse. I've had Pitty Pat for most of our marriage, but he never complained until now."

"What are you going to do?"

"I don't know just yet."

"Just don't pull a Bitsy and hit him in the head." Violet winked.

"Honey, if I won't kill an ant, why would I kill Byron?" Clancy Jane set her cup on her chest, then she stroked the cat. It began to purr.

"That's right, Mama." Violet patted the cat's broad head. "Let fate deal with Byron."

"You know what? I need a new life." Clancy Jane ran one finger around the mug's rim. "But that doesn't seem likely, so I'll do what all the other doctor's wives do—I'll buy something frightfully expensive."

"You'll never do that. You're not a spend-thrill, Mama."

• • •

Violet turned out to be right. Instead of squandering money, Clancy Jane decided to be miserly with her emotions. She began to ignore Byron, carrying on long, one-sided conversations with her cats. Then she decided to exclude him another way. She emptied the kitchen cupboards. And she stopped drinking. Not that Byron seemed to care. He just ate his meals in the doctors' lounge or with Dorothy and Mack. Clancy Jane spent long hours at the café, helping Zach with Sunday brunch. They installed a long buffet table with halogen lighting and steam that rose up, curling to the ceiling. She was careful not to stand too close, but she hadn't given up on him. Then he hired a harpist named Lydia from the Blair School of Music in Nashville to play on Sundays.

Clancy Jane stood next to the espresso machine, waiting for the milk to froth. She cut her eyes at Zach. He was standing next to the trompe l'oeil wall, blending into the painted fronds and primates, and his face filled with rapture as if entranced by the ethereal sounds. The harpist's fingers were crooked slightly, like a spider spinning her web. Her long black hair fell like a silk curtain over her shoulder. And Clancy saw he was going to fall in love with her.

After the brunch ended, Zach gave Lydia a green bottle filled with Ganges River water and a statue of Buddha. Clancy Jane locked herself in the restroom and bawled her eyes out. Finally she came to the conclusion that she was damn lucky to have him in her life. She could rejoice in loud arguments about global problems and passionate discussions about how supermarket chains are victimizing America. She could relish their debates over the virtues of buckwheat groats, the versatility of rice, and the nutritional values of falafel and mung beans. It was no crime to secretly love him. As long as she wasn't hurting anyone, what did it matter? She'd alienated Violet. She'd given up alcohol. Her marriage seemed to be dying. All she had were a few dozen alley cats and an infatuation with a younger man. But it was enough to keep breathing.

Bitsy

I was worried about Aunt Clancy. I asked Violet if she'd come home, but she told me no because she and George were going to New York and besides, she had no control over her mother's life. She pointed out that her mother hadn't batted an eye when she, Violet, had gone off to college in '71. That might be what Violet thought, but I remember when we'd helped Violet move into her Memphis apartment in the summer of '75. Aunt Clancy broke out in a sweat while hanging Violet's curtains; my cousin kept rolling her eyes, asking us when we'd be through.

I remembered that day so clearly. Once we pulled out of the apartment complex, Aunt Clancy had a meltdown. First she let out a shrill cry, then she began sobbing so hard that she couldn't drive. She had to pull off the road. Then she turned to me and said, "Don't get me wrong. I'm so proud of Violet. But the bottom of my world has fallen out."

"Memphis is only five hours away, and we'll come and visit her all the time."

Clancy Jane pressed her hand against her chest and said, "It just went too fast. I wish she was small again."

Then I said something unintentionally cruel. I said, "Why didn't you cry when she went to U.T.?"

Her bottom lip slid forward. "Because I didn't know what it meant. I didn't know that everything would change. The whole time Violet was in college she kept coming home. It was easy to believe that U.T. was no different than summer camp. That she would eventually come home for good. But now I know different. She will never again live with me fulltime. I have lost her."

We drove back to Crystal Falls. She cried most of the way. I knew just how she felt. But after we got home she continued to cry. Her eyes stayed red and swollen like she'd had an allergic reaction. I kept hoping that Byron would pull her into his arms and baby her just a little. But he never did.

I wanted to tell Violet not to be too hard on her, but I couldn't. She just wasn't in the mood to understand.

May 2, 1977

Dear Bitsy,

I'm back from NYC. George and I got caught in the downpour coming back from a restaurant. It was about 9 P.M. when we reached our hotel. We squeezed into a crowded elevator and the power went out. If we'd been alone, we might have enjoyed it. However, standing cheek-to-jowl with seven other passengers, most of whom were screaming in Italian, isn't my idea of fun.

BTW, Mama's suffering from empty nest syndrome. She needs to get over it.

Violet

Dorothy and I were sitting at Aunt Clancy's harvest table, pasting photographs of Jennifer into an album.

We'd just finished the next-to-last picture when the back door opened and my aunt ran into the room, trailed by three yellow cats. "Guess what? Byron and I might be moving." She reached down, scooped up a cat. "Isn't that groovy?"

"Moving?" I almost dropped the Elmer's glue bottle. "Where?"

"I found a dream house way out in the sticks, near the county line. It's near the Caney Fork River; I can hear it from the upstairs bedroom. We just left the real estate agent's office. Byron made a low offer, but the house has been on the market awhile."

"Not to burst your bubble, but there's no such thing as a perfect house." Dorothy's eyes moved around the empty kitchen.

"Well, this one is close to it," said Aunt Clancy. "It reminds me of the ranches in Northern California——wood, glass, and stone. With cathedral ceilings and a wraparound deck with a hot tub. It's got so many rooms I lost count. And sixty-nine acres. The view reminds me of the Rocky Mountains. Well, the baby Rockies."

"I thought you said it was like Northern California." Dorothy raised a faux eyebrow.

Aunt Clancy shrugged.

"Would the Buddha need that much room?" I asked.

"No, but Byron does." Aunt Clancy pulled out a chair and sat down. "Oh, I just love it. The kitchen has a wall of glass and looks out into the woods. Right now it's a little overdecorated. Too much wallpaper, too many colors. I'm hiring Mack and Earlene to do the painting."

"Don't ask Earlene," said Dorothy. "Unless you want a House of Ill Repute design scheme. You'd better get Bitsy to help. She has exquisite taste."

"I said I was hiring Earlene to paint, not decorate," said Aunt Clancy.

"What will happen to *this* house?" Dorothy asked.

"Violet owns half already, so I guess I'll deed my part to Bitsy."

"Well, isn't that generous." Dorothy pressed her lips together and reached for the Elmer's bottle. She squirted glue onto the back of a picture, then she slapped it against the scrapbook page. "I don't suppose you'll be taking any of this tacky old furniture with you."

"No," said Aunt Clancy, burying her face in the cat's neck. "Guess not."

Dorothy's eyes bugged. "Even your dishes and forks and whatnot?"

I just sat there trying to absorb the information. I hadn't even known that she'd wanted to move, especially to such a remote place. "I'm surprised that someone would build a dream house near the county line," I said. "No wonder it hasn't sold."

"When you see it you'll understand why I want it," she told me. "I'm only taking my clothes and Byron's. And this harvest table, of course."

"You're not taking Byron's television set? Or his La-Z-Boy?"

"Less is more. It is peaceful out there."

"It's none of my business, but Byron's never home," I said. "You'll be stuck in the country all by yourself."

"She'll have her cats," Dorothy said.

"Yes, I'll have my fur kids." She stroked the cat's head, then she set him on the floor. "I never dreamed I'd end up married to a workaholic."

"At least he's not an alcoholic," said Dorothy. "Because Mack is drinking way too much. And I blame it all on that tasteless hussy he married."

"We can't help who we love, Dorothy." Clancy Jane walked across the room and opened the refrigerator. She gathered green peppers into her arms, then crossed back to the table and dumped the vegetables onto the surface. One rolled dangerously close to the scrapbook. Dorothy snatched up the pepper, then set it down with a flourish.

"Can't you chop somewhere else?" Dorothy scowled at Aunt Clancy. "We're pasting."

"I won't get in your way." Aunt Clancy reached for a pepper and balanced it on her palm. "I'm fixing gazpacho."

"Doesn't Byron hate that?" I asked.

"Yes, but he hates everything from cats to cold soups." She began peeling an onion. "Y'all better leave the room, or the onion fumes might make y'all cry."

"I never cry," said Dorothy.

Byron's offer was accepted almost immediately, which made me wonder if the owners were desperate. Aunt Clancy perked up. I'd never seen her so happy and vivacious. Even though they hadn't closed on the house, she began to pick out a color scheme.

"I've narrowed the general color to ecru. The one I like is called Lace Napkin," Aunt Clancy told Violet, who drove home when she'd heard the news. "Bitsy likes Oyster Bisque, but I also favor Old Porcelain."

"I like Old Porcelain, too," I said.

Byron did not seem jubilant. The dream house was practically in the next county, and he would have a twenty-five-minute commute twice a day. He was sitting at the table, thumbing through a *New England Journal of Medicine.* Aunt Clancy walked over to him, nudging away the magazine. She spread an array of color chips on the table. "Sweetie, which one do you like?"

He shrugged. "They're almost the same."

"No, they're not. Are they, Bitsy? If you look closer, you'll see how different they are. I wish you'd pick one."

"Okay, okay." Byron glanced down at the cards. He tapped his fingernail on a square. "This one."

"Powdered Sugar?" Aunt Clancy's face fell. "Are you sure?"

"Pick what *you* want, honey. It doesn't matter to me."

"Well, it *should.* After all, it's your house, too."

Byron scratched his head, then he ran his hand over his face. He glanced down at the table, reached for the swatches. "Okay." He tapped one broad fingernail against the darkest chip, a muddy cream. "Here, I pick Old Porcelain."

"Oh, sure. I can *see* how much you like it, too."

"What do you want from me?" He scooped up the chips, held them out. "Are we fighting about colors or something else?"

Aunt Clancy's mouth fell open.

"You're a living contradiction," he continued in a cold voice. "No, you don't want *things*, yet you're dithering over colors. And you don't seem to have any qualms about taking on a thirty-year mortgage."

"I am not a contradiction. Sure, I have a lot to learn about Buddhism, but I think I know a little more than you."

"See, you're mad. I can't talk to you when you're like this." He got up from the table, strode across the room, and pushed open the screen door.

He was acting strange, as if suffering from a severe case of buyer's remorse.

"I'm not mad, *you* are," she called after him. He didn't respond. His footsteps clapped against the stone walkway, then dropped off, muffled by the grass. Aunt Clancy spun around, fanning her color chips.

"What do you girls think? Is Oyster Bisque too beige? Bitsy, come here a second, sweetie. You've got an eye for colors."

I craned my neck to see. "It's more of an off-white."

"If you ask me," Violet said, "off-white is hideous. You might as well paint the walls with Gerber's oatmeal."

"Hush, Violet. Pick a color, Bitsy. I trust your opinion."

"They're all pretty," I said.

"But which one?" Aunt Clancy held up the chips.

"Well, it's hard to know—the colors are never the same once you get them on the wall." I hesitated, then tapped my nail against Linen Napkin. "I'll bet this is gorgeous."

"Beechnut pablum, you mean," Violet said.

"Stop criticizing my taste." Aunt Clancy threw down the chips. Several cats shot out of the room.

"Oh, Mama, come back," Violet yelled. "It's just a *color*. If you don't like it, you can paint over it."

"They're all nice," I called. "Really, they are."

Aunt Clancy wouldn't answer. Silence filled the house, stirring in the corners like something poured. Violet and I stared at each other. "Mama's in trouble," she said. "She's drinking on the sly. I can smell it on her breath."

"Maybe this new house will help."

"Oh, it will." Violet rubbed a towel over a plate. "For a while. But it won't last. She'll just pack up her problems and take them with her. She'll chase off Byron, then she'll be left alone on that mountaintop. And she'll regret it. I think she loves him more than she knows."

"She acts like she hates him."

"That's the trouble. Mama doesn't know how to give love. She was brought up to take it."

I put my arms around Violet, drawing her close, the way I held my small daughter. We gazed out the window to where Byron was fiddling with Walter's old telescope. He pointed it toward the sky and bent over, one eye closed, searching for only God knew what.

FROM THE CRYSTAL FALLS *DEMOCRAT*

—from Mrs. Rayetta Parson's column, May 25, 1977, page 6

The wedding of Claude Edmund Wentworth IV and Miss Kara Lynn Ketchum is slated for July 4th at First Presbyterian Church. The bride-elect is the daughter of Mr. and Mrs. Hoyt P. Ketchum Jr. of Crystal Falls. She attended Tennessee Technological University, where she was a cheerleader and a member of Alpha Delta Pi. The groom is the son of Mr. and Mrs. Claude Edmund Wentworth III. The bride has been feted at a series of miscellaneous showers and luncheons. A rehearsal dinner will be held on July 3rd, in the Iris Room at the Crystal Falls Golf and Country Club. The Wentworth-Ketchum wedding promises to be the highlight of the midsummer nuptial season, with a festive red-white-and-blue color scheme. The event will culminate in a firework regalia.

Clancy Jane and Violet

It was eighty-six degrees in Memphis, the humidity so thick you could reach up into the air and stir it with your fingers, but Violet wanted a hot cup of tea. Her grandmother had raved about its curative effects, that it literally warmed the spirit. While she waited for the water to boil, Violet pictured her mother standing at the sink, filling her copper pot. As the water pattered against the metal, Clancy Jane would begin to hum. In this memory she did not look like a bad mother. But Violet knew better.

Her outlet had been academics. She had hoped that medical school would become the perfect Mama-buffer, because up close, Clancy Jane was too colorful, almost painful to the eyes, like peering at psychedelic op art. Even at a distance Clancy could get to her. Like late last night when her phone had rung, and even before Violet could say hello, her mother's voice had streamed out of the receiver. "So, are you roasting down in Memphis?"

In the background, Violet could hear cats meowing, and Led Zeppelin was singing about a hurting in their heart. Violet thought, *It can't compare to the pain in my ass.* "Why aren't you asleep?" she asked her mother, balancing an anatomy textbook on her knees. It was uncanny how Clancy always called the night before an exam. According to Bitsy's reports, Clancy Jane was becoming known as Catfucius. Violet politely asked how the felines were doing.

"A lady down the street complained about them," Clancy Jane was saying. "Well, I tried to be nice, but she started yelling. She threatened to buy a Havahart trap to snare my babies."

"But you'll be moving soon," said Violet.

"Not soon enough for me. Apparently someone pooped in the neighbor lady's tomato plants."

"Some*one*? Or some*thing*?"

"She implied it was one of my cats. I don't see how she could tell. I mean, there's no way to DNA cat shit. But she screamed at me, Violet. She said, 'Lady, if I want my vegetables fertilized, I'll buy Miracle-Gro.'"

"Well, it *is* good fertilizer," Violet said, trying to make her mother laugh.

"What can I do but keep them inside?" Clancy Jane cried. "Then Byron just complains about his allergies."

"Nobody's pur-rrfect," said Violet.

"Go on, join the club. Make fun," Clancy Jane said.

Violet sighed. When her mother got like this, there was nothing else to do but hang on and listen. She held the phone against her ear, thinking her mother was sounding more and more like Aunt Dorothy. They were sisters, after all. People will succumb to genetics, the same way madras will bleed.

Clancy Jane sighed. "I need a break from this horrid town."

"Yeah, I need to get away, too. George has next weekend off. He's taking me down to New Orleans for jazz and gumbo."

"Groovy."

"Nobody says groovy anymore," Violet chided.

"I'm not a lemming. I'll say what I want." Clancy Jane yawned. "So, how is old George?"

.   .   .

The next Saturday, while Violet was packing for the trip to New Orleans, she glanced out the bedroom window and saw her mother's car angle into a parking space. As Violet shut her suitcase, she felt something fall inside her chest. She cursed and ran to the front door as Clancy Jane climbed out of the front seat carrying a honey-colored Samsonite suitcase. She was wearing a baggy T-shirt printed with If You Don't Talk To Your Cat About Catnip, Who Will? When she saw Violet standing in the doorway, she waved. "What a pretty dress you're wearing," she called. "You look so *good* in purple."

Violet murmured an ungracious thank you and touched her silver earrings—a birthday present from George. Then she smoothed her dark hair. Earlier she'd washed it in beer and let it dry naturally, one of Bitsy's old beauty tricks. Halfway up the sidewalk, Clancy Jane abruptly stopped. "Is anything wrong?"

Violet shook her head.

"You don't look real happy to see me."

"Of course I'm happy." Violet touched the earrings again. "It's just . . . who's keeping your cats?"

"I bribed Byron. Why?" Clancy Jane looked at her daughter's earrings and her shiny hair. "You're hiding something."

"It's nothing sinister, Mama. George and I are going to New Orleans this weekend. Remember I told you that when we talked the other day?"

"You never told me." Clancy Jane's forehead wrinkled.

"Yes, I did."

"I'm so sorry. I guess I forgot." She swung her suitcase back and forth. A piece of blue fabric stuck out the side. "Do you want me to leave? I will. Just say the word and I'll go."

"You know you're always welcome. It might even do you good to get away from Kittyland. I'll give you an extra key."

"Thanks. I think." Clancy Jane walked up to the little porch and hugged her daughter awkwardly, giving off whiffs of chamomile tea and curry powder. Then she stepped into the small apartment, dropping her suitcase on the floor.

"Are there any decent vegetarian restaurants in Memphis? I'm famished."

"There's lettuce in the fridge." Violet gestured at the kitchenette. "I could fix you a salad."

Clancy Jane sat down on the sofa and crossed her legs. The bones in her knees were visible. "You know what? I should go. I don't feel welcome."

"What have I done now?"

"I don't blame you. I'd be mad, too, if *I* was leaving for New Orleans and my mother showed up. Do you remember when we lived there, me and you and your daddy?"

Violet crossed her arms but said nothing. She remembered those days all too well.

"I can stay in a motel." Clancy Jane scrunched up her face. "Can you recommend one?"

"Don't be silly. You're perfectly welcome to stay right here."

"Am I?" She gave her daughter a quizzical stare.

The front door opened and George poked his head inside. "Violet? Ready to go?"

"Almost," said Violet.

"You must be George," said Clancy Jane, rising from the sofa.

"Yes, ma'am." He stepped forward, tilting his head to one side. "And you're . . ."

"I'm Clancy Jane, Violet's mother."

"Ah." George nodded, then shook her hand. "You're much younger than I expected."

"What's Violet been telling you?" Clancy Jane laughed. "That I'm Old Mother Hubbard?"

"Oh, no ma'am." He blushed. "I just assumed it."

"Well, I *did* have her when I was quite young." Clancy Jane sat down on the sofa, curling one leg beneath her. Violet knew that posture; she knew her mother was getting ready to tell George everything about her life, starting with the time she'd jumped into Bayou LaFourche. Then she'd tell about Violet's father getting blown up in Vietnam, working up to her sojourn in California as a hippie, and continuing all the way up to her marriage to Byron and their upcoming move. Violet wouldn't put it past her mother to start chatting about virginity—it had been a mistake telling her about George.

Violet lifted a lace shawl from the back of a chair—it was one of Bitsy's famous thrift store finds. It was too hot to wear it in Memphis, so she wouldn't possibly need it in New Orleans, but it was so delicate and pretty, she wanted it with her. She threw it around her shoulders and turned to her mother. "I hate to run off, but George and I need to get on the road."

"Yes, we really should. Good-bye, Mrs. Jones," said George, his hand touching Violet's arm. "It was nice meeting you."

"Actually, it's Mrs. Falk, Clancy Jane Falk. Violet's name is Jones, and I used to be one, but I remarried a doctor? He hates my cats. I told him, 'I thought you liked pussy, Byron.' Sometimes I think he'd prefer to live in a condo. A catless condo, I might add."

Violet could see that her mother was getting started. "We really should go." She nudged George to the door.

"Wait, I've hardly talked to—what's your name again?"

"George." He glanced nervously at Violet.

"I'm sorry, I'm just so forgetful." Clancy Jane patted the sofa. "Come here, George. Tell me about yourself. What are you studying?"

George started to move toward the sofa, but Violet grabbed his hand and pulled him back. "He's going to be an English professor," she said.

"I'm a teaching assistant at Memphis State," he put in.

"Violet's real bright, too. But I guess you already noticed. She scored so high on her MedCat, they couldn't keep her out of medical school. But if you want big money, go into plastic surgery. That's what Byron always says. Although I expect that Violet could tell you more about the various specialties than *me*. I don't care how much or how little Byron makes, but I wish he had more time off. Maybe we could travel. I always loved New Mexico."

Violet cringed, knowing that the next chapter in her mother's saga was her years as a hippie.

"Well, you two kids run on," Clancy Jane said. "And don't worry about me. I'm tired from all that driving. And I'm a little depressed, too, but I'm not suicidal. Far from it. Although I do get that way from time to time. It runs in the family."

George turned to Violet and raised his eyebrows, as if to say, Is she always like this?

"'Bye, Mama." Violet took his hand and pulled him out of the door, into the steamy Delta afternoon. As soon as they reached the sidewalk, they took off running to his car, the lace shawl fluttering behind them.

Clancy Jane

Clancy Jane spent the weekend in her daughter's apartment thinking about love, trying to understand it. She had been a widow for five years when she and Byron met. This wouldn't have happened if she hadn't come home for Bitsy and Claude's wedding and found out about her mother having leukemia. She hadn't had romance on her mind then. Byron was Miss Gussie's doctor, and he was married. But then one day he'd stopped by to see his patient, and Clancy had invited him to sit in the kitchen for a cup of tea. He'd wanted to hear all about her so-called wild life in California and New Mexico, so she told him a few things.

She could tell he was fascinated, so she kept on talking. While Miss Gussie slept, helped along by morphine tablets, they drank green tea in the kitchen, their knees touching beneath the old white enamel table. He leaned over, took her face in his hands, and kissed her, a really good kiss. She slid her hands up and down his spine. Still kissing, they stood up and lurched backward to the counter. Her elbow knocked into the cookie jar. It was shaped like a pig and Miss Gussie used to say it might stop them from snacking. The pig didn't break but Byron pulled her away from the counter and pressed her against the refrigerator, dislodging all the colorful magnets. Then he shucked down his trousers, and lifted her up into his arms.

Sex with Byron had been metaphysical, two people occupying the same exact space at the same time. Still joined, they had danced across the room, colliding with the counter. Clancy Jane's head had banged against the knotty-pine cabinet, and she remembered crying out, not from pain but from pleasure.

If I could have one wish, she thought as she sat on her daughter's beat-up sofa, *I'd want Violet to find a great love—one that stays alive, without inflicting damage or swallowing her whole. Maybe it will be this polite boy. Maybe it will last forever.* She reached for the phone. Byron answered on the fifth ring. "I'm coming home," she said. "Keep the porch light on."

A TAPED MESSAGE TO ROSALYN CARTER

July 15, 1977

Dear Rosalyn,

I have moved back into my childhood home, and I wanted to give you my new address. It hurt to leave my son's house, but he is only next door. His trash-mouth wife Earlene is tickled to pieces. She pushed me out the door. And all this time I'd been doing her grocery shopping, cooking her meals, vacuuming her floors. I wanted to holler out, You'll miss all that I did. But I have learned to keep my mouth shut when people disappoint me. You have to let actions speak. Angry words get you nowhere. Silence isn't being a wimp. It's being smart. It took me forty-five years, some of which was spent in a mental hospital, to appreciate the power of the understatement.

Anyway, you can address all future correspondence to 214 Dixie Avenue, Crystal Falls, Tennessee. I know why you haven't been writing: Because that stupid Earlene was throwing away your letters. But that's just fine. She'll get hers one day. And all this time I thought you or your people were ignoring my mail—after all, Son of Sam wrote letters, too. But I'm not like that, I'm a sweetheart.

Fondly,
Dorothy McDougal

Clancy Jane and Byron

After the Falks moved into their house, they continued to fight over the decor. Byron wanted his La-Z-Boy recliner, Clancy Jane wanted sisal mats and tasseled pillows. When she set up a shrine to Buddha, Byron was annoyed by the incense. He couldn't breathe, couldn't find a place to relax. He was a man, he kept saying, not a monk.

Clancy Jane turned her back on his complaints and found refuge in her kitchen, baking bread and mixing daiquiris. The room was one wash of cream—marble counters, tile floor, white matchstick blinds. The appliances blended into the cabinetry and walls, which were painted Linen Napkin. The old harvest table stood in front of the windows, but there was no place to sit—she'd left the chairs behind at Dixie Avenue. It was a problem, but she believed that the universe would offer her a solution.

One evening, they decided to drive down to Crystal Falls to see a movie, but before they left the house, they began to argue. Clancy Jane was dying to see *Looking for Mr. Goodbar*, but Byron said he wasn't in the mood for anything heavy, and he begged her to see *Star Wars*. So they just stayed home. Byron went into the living room, piled the cushions onto the floor, and switched on the television. Clancy Jane hung out in the kitchen, making a pitcher of daiquiris and listening to her new Carly Simon album. She carried her drink over to the harvest table, then she got an idea. She found a saw and sawed off the table's legs. Then she stepped back to admire her handiwork and realized she'd made a mistake.

When Byron found out, his face contorted, the veins stood out on his neck. "Clancy Jane, what did you DO?"

"I'm just decorating," she said in a small voice.

"No, you're destroying. I can't live this way. I'm getting out of here." Byron left the kitchen and ran upstairs. She thought he was pouting until he came down with a suitcase in each hand and headed out the door. As she ran after him, her shoes kicked up loose gravel, and a dozen cats trailed behind her. She prayed that Byron wouldn't turn on them, call her the Pie-Eyed Piper or something. But she didn't have the heart to chase the animals away.

"Byron, wait," she called. "*Wait!* What did I *do?*"

"I loved that table," he said over his shoulder. "It was the first thing we bought together. How could you chop off its legs?"

"I didn't chop off yours."

He cursed and strode past her blue Karmann Ghia to his white MG. As he sped down the driveway, his taillights didn't blink a single time.

Clancy Jane waited for him to call. She spent hours on the back porch, staring down the long, twisty driveway, hoping she'd glimpse his car. When the cats rubbed against her legs, she poured cream into chipped Pyrex bowls and scooped out stinky cans of Friskies tuna and egg.

The cats were all she had left in the world—they were much more amusing than her human child, and considerably more attentive. Her kitties vied for places on her bed, chased each other through the house at daylight, slept on the dwarf dining room table, and left paw prints on the hood of her car. She gave them weird names—the little half Siamese was called the Prince of Wails, another was dubbed the Prince of Poop, because he was always in the litter box. According to Clancy Jane, her old Persian, Pitty Pat, was the ambassador for the other cats. In another life, Pitty must have been a demigod. Every morning at daylight, the other cats would gather in the downstairs hall then they would send the ambassador upstairs to Clancy Jane's bedroom, where he meowed until she got up. As she padded down the steps, Pitty Pat called to the others. They lined up by the kitchen door, tails crooked, waiting for Clancy Jane to open it. When Pitty trotted down the steps, into the grass, the others followed in his wake.

As Clancy Jane told this story—it was during a late-night long-distance call to Violet—she knew how crazy she sounded, and she began to worry. Cats didn't have ambassadors; they didn't manipulate human beings that way. Perhaps there was no such thing as reincarnation. What if she had emptied her life for no reason? She suspected that she might have slipped into a mild sort of insanity, the middle-age crazies—didn't it run in her family?

Now that Byron was gone, she understood the problem. He didn't hate her cats, he was jealous of them. Well, she *had* put them first. And while she demanded antiseptic conditions at the café, at home, if grapes spilled to the floor, she'd squat down and eat them. If one of the cats had diarrhea, and developed mats on its hind end, Clancy Jane would set the animal on the kitchen counter and press warm paper towels to its behind. Then she would patiently pick off the bulk of the offensive matter and finally trim the area with manicure scissors. "That's *so* gross," Byron used to say. "We prepare food on this counter." "*I* prepare the food, not you," Clancy Jane had told him without looking up from the cat's anus. "Anyway, it's not unsanitary. I worm my cats on a regular basis."

Once she was alone in the house, it did seem yucky, and she was prepared to admit it to Byron but she didn't hear a peep from him. Another week passed, and she began playing her old albums. She knew she was in trouble when she listened to "The Pusher" and counted how many times Steppenwolf said goddamn. In the bathroom cabinet, she found Byron's toothbrush and a half-used bottle of Lavoris, and sank to the tile floor. She actually missed him. The bastard had abandoned her, and here she was, crying over his damn toothbrush.

She didn't have the energy to work at the café, so she left everything in Zach's hands. One morning he called to go over the menu, and they began debating over the soup du jour. When she started to blather on about Byron, Zach cut her off by suggesting that she sell him her half of the Green Parrot. "Take the money and move back to Taos," he elaborated. "You've never been happy in Crystal Falls."

"Was it that apparent?" she asked.

"Yes," he said, and her heart sank. What was the point in staying? To watch Zach and his pretty harpist fall deeper in love? To hear people make fun of her cats?

"If you want the café," she told Zach, " it's yours."

Bitsy

When Zach told me the news, I drove straight over to Clancy Jane's house, my old blue Mustang bumping over the waves in the gravel road. I pulled around to the back and hurried up the porch steps. The door was open, so I stepped inside. As I moved through the stripped-down rooms, I could see my reflection in the wood floors.

I found my aunt in the living room, sitting zazen in front of the empty fireplace. Near the V of her crossed legs, incense burned in a brass cup. She was wearing a white kimono and her hair streamed down one shoulder. Her eyes were closed, palms balanced on her thighs.

I was afraid to say anything, lest I interrupt some weird Buddhist ritual, but it could have been witchcraft, for all I knew. Clancy Jane opened her eyes. Her face looked smaller and shrunken in. "Have a seat," she said.

Where? I wondered and glanced around the room. Sunlight rippled though the bare windows, moving on the floor. So I knelt beside her. "I just heard about you and Byron." The air smelled chalky, spicy, and it tickled my nose.

"Did he tell you, or did Violet?"

"No. Zach."

"I'm sorry, honey. I should've told you myself." Clancy Jane lifted one hand and waved it through the incense, stirring up gray ribbons. Her wrist looked small as a child's.

"But what happened? Zach didn't seem to know."

"Go see for yourself." Clancy Jane pointed toward French doors. "It's in the kitchen."

As I approached the French doors, I saw the old harvest table. Damask pillows were scattered around—nice fabric, too, beige backed in creamy velvet, with fat gold tassels. It looked like something from a James Bond movie, *You Only Live Twice.*

"As you can see, I altered it somewhat," called Clancy Jane. "But it doesn't look so bad, does it?"

"Why don't you come back to town with me and stay a few days?"

"I couldn't. It wouldn't feel right," Clancy Jane said. "Dorothy's filled the house with junk. I need space." She extended one thin arm, gesturing at the stark room.

When Clancy Jane and Byron had moved out of 214 Dixie, Dorothy had moved in with a vengeance. Magnets had returned to the refrigerator, holding postcards, memos, snapshots of Jennifer; I had arranged Aunt Clancy's brass cricket boxes on a shelf and fanned magazines on the coffee table—just the way I had learned from the Ha'vard School of Design. "I know it's jumbled at our house," I said, "but couldn't you stand it for one night?"

"No." Clancy Jane lowered her head, and her hair swung forward, hiding her face. "I've got all these cats to feed."

"We'll bring them along. It'll be like old times."

"That's not possible."

"Surely there's something I can do. Have you eaten? Do you need groceries? Tell me what to do."

"You can stop making a fuss."

"But I'm worried."

"I'm fine. Really I am." Her thin hand shot out to tousle my hair and remind me who was the grown-up and who was the child. "I don't need groceries. I just need to get my shit together."

When I left I drove straight over to Byron's medical office and demanded to see him *this instant!* The receptionist started to protest, but I dashed past her through the side door, into the hall. His rooms were cool and smelled faintly of Phisohex. A redheaded nurse cast a nervous glance in my direction. The receptionist came running up behind me. "Miss? I'm afraid you'll have to—"

"I'll be in his office," I told her over my shoulder. "Tell Byron that his niece is here."

The receptionist shrank back and I walked straight into Byron's office. It had been decorated by his first wife, and it was a masculine room, filled with books and brown leather. A lamp burned on his desk. Pictures of his three daughters were scattered on the bookshelves, but I couldn't find a single photograph of Aunt Clancy. What had he done with them?

Byron hurried into the room, his face flushed. "Is something wrong? What's happened?"

I immediately launched an attack. "How could you just leave Aunt Clancy? What's the matter with you?"

"Me?" Byron walked around his desk and sat down in the tufted chair. "Did she tell you about the table?"

"I saw it. It's not too bad."

"Not if you're a Munchkin."

"Byron, it's replaceable. Buy another one."

"It's a little late for that."

"Why, aren't you coming back?"

"Did she ask you to talk to me?" He leaned forward.

"No, she'd be furious. But I saw her today, and she looked awful. She's pale and thin. I don't think she's eaten in days."

He gave me a stony look.

Then I understood. "It's that nurse in the hall, isn't it?"

"No, no," he said emphatically. "It's the mangled table. It's no chairs, no social life, no red meat, and too many cats."

"She *loves* you, Byron."

"I love her, too."

"Then call her. Tell her you're coming home. You just admitted that you love her—"

"I can't live with her."

"What about the redhead? Is she next?"

"I already told you why I left." His voice was studiedly calm, he might have been speaking to a hypochondriac, someone who would not listen to reason. "And it had nothing to do with another woman. I was a faithful husband to Clancy. But I'm touched that you want to help her. It shows that you're growing into a fine woman, Bitsy."

"What did you do with Aunt Clancy's pictures?" I asked.

"Are they gone?" He turned back to the bookcase, his chair squeaking. He leaned forward, poking around his books. "No, I don't see them anywhere. But I'm glad you noticed. I didn't even know they were missing."

Violet
and Clancy Jane

Around midday August 16, 1977, Clancy Jane showed up in Memphis again. Violet barely had time to unlock her door when her mother barreled inside, hugging two sacks of groceries. "Let me in quick before I melt," Clancy Jane said. "Is Memphis always this hot?"

Without waiting for an answer, she rushed past Violet and stepped into the kitchenette. From one of the sacks, she began pulling out carrots, potatoes, onions, and canned beans. "I'm making you a nice pot of lentil soup," she said. "Would George like to join us?"

"He hates lentils. But, yes, he'll be coming over later." She wasn't going to address the question of seasonally appropriate food.

"I hope you know what you're doing," Clancy Jane said, opening a drawer and grabbing a potato peeler.

"About what?" Violet sat on a stool, her chin in her hands, watching her mother rinse the vegetables under a stream of water.

"Falling in love can be dangerous." Clancy Jane started peeling the carrots. Orange strips began to fill the sink.

"Come on, Mama. Talk to me. What's bugging you?"

"It's Byron." She reached for a potato and began viciously peeling it. "I miss him."

"I'm sorry, Mama. But you didn't want him."

"I did, too. I was in awe of his education. He was a doctor and I never finished high school. And he loved *me*. That just blew my mind."

"Why are you using the past tense?"

"Because it's past. And stop acting like an English teacher. Act like a daughter."

When the soup was gently bubbling, Clancy Jane wiped her hands on a towel. "Is there a liquor store around here? I'd like some wine with our soup."

"Take a right at the light and go three blocks."

"Aren't you coming?"

"Can't, I've got to study." Violet grabbed a textbook off the shelf and curled up on the sofa, pretending to read. If her mother hoped to use this apartment as her own personal heartbreak hotel—coming when she wanted, leaving when she pleased—then she was mistaken.

After Clancy Jane walked out the door, Violet waited five minutes, then she threw down the book and stepped outside. Her mother's car wasn't in the parking lot. The hot air smelled faintly of barbecue from the joint down the street. She was thinking of sneaking off for a pork platter, when a little girl walked by, pushing a bike.

"Hey," the kid said, "did you hear the news? Elvis croaked."

"Elvis Presley?"

"It's all over the TV," said the kid. "The King is dead. My daddy works at Baptist Hospital, and he says Elvis was taking a poop and died. He must've strained too hard."

The kid put one foot on the pedal and shoved off, her hair bouncing up and down.

When Clancy Jane drove up, Violet was still sitting on the front porch. She watched her mother climb out of her Karmann Ghia, then curve up to the sidewalk, hugging paper bags to her chest.

"I bought a burgundy," she called. "I don't know what vintage, and who cares. It was marked down twenty-five percent. And I also bought a—"

"Didn't you hear the news?" Violet stood up.

"What news?"

"Elvis died. We've got to turn on the radio. Give me your keys."

"Dead? Oh, *no!*" Clancy Jane held out the keys. Violet snatched them and ran down to the car. When the radio clicked on, Violet twirled the dial, stopping on WMSU. A disc jockey was saying, "It's true, Memphians. Elvis Aaron Presley, dead at the tender age of forty-two."

"I feel like I've lost a boyfriend!" Clancy Jane sat down abruptly on the curb, the paper sack resting between her knees. In the car, Violet turned up the volume, and the announcer's voice boomed through the parking lot. People stepped out of their apartments and gathered around the car.

"Is this for real?" asked a guy with long brown hair and small green eyes.

"Has it been confirmed?" asked a girl with frizzy hair.

"It's true, guys," Violet said.

"But there's gotta be a mistake," cried the guy with green eyes.

On the curb, Clancy Jane began rocking. At first Violet thought her mother was moaning. The crowd stepped back, and a few people murmured, "What's wrong with her?"

"Elvis," someone answered. "He just bought the farm, man."

Clancy Jane's voice began to rise, loud and strong and mournful, rising up into the muggy afternoon. It sounded so pretty, Violet turned down the radio.

"Is it 'Amazing Grace'?" a boy in cutoff jeans asked.

"No, it's 'Can't Help Falling in Love,'" said the guy with green eyes.

More and more people were drawn from their apartments, attracted by Clancy Jane's singing. When she finished one stanza, she barreled on to the next, and when she ran out of words, she began to hum. A huge crowd was gathering around her. Violet climbed out of the car and made her way toward her mother. Clancy Jane was singing about fools rushing in and crazy old humans who can't help loving each other.

Then everyone began to sing, their voices rising and falling.

From the corner of her eye, Violet saw George's red car turn into the parking lot. He got out, then stared. Holding Beau by his leash, he threaded his way through the crowd. The people stepped aside to let him pass. The Irish setter looked up at them and whined, his lips waffling. George tugged the leash so hard that Beau stood up on his hind legs and bawled. "Violet, did you hear the news?" he asked when he got to her side.

"Shhh," Violet said, holding his face in her hands. "Mama is singing."

Clancy Jane

September 15, 1977
Dear Byron,
We were together for almost six years. I hope you'll remember the good
times, not just the bad. I'm willing to try again if you are. Please call.
Love,
XX OO

Now that she'd broken the silence, Clancy Jane had to follow the rules of love and wait for his reaction. She had an idea he'd call; at least, she hoped he'd call—or write. Once a day she trekked down to her mailbox. It stood at the end of a twisty gravel lane. The Long and Winding Road, she called it. Finally she opened her box and found a letter inside—it was typed, no stamp or postmark. She ripped it open, sending tiny pieces of paper spinning into the air.

Dear Clancy Jane,
Meet me tonight at El Toro Restaurant at 7:30 P.M. and all will be
explained.
Byron

She called his office twice, but each time a youthful voice explained that Dr. Falk couldn't come to the phone. Both times Clancy Jane left messages. Then she called Bitsy and said, "Help. I'm meeting Byron for dinner at El Toro. What should I wear?"

"A little black dress," said Bitsy. "Do you even have one?"

"No."

"Well, I've got several. I wear a six, but you've lost weight, so you're, what, a four?"

"If you say so."

"I'll be right over."

"Bring shoes!" cried Clancy Jane.

"But I wear a six and a half and you're a seven and a half."

"I'll grease my feet with Vaseline."

Bitsy set her makeup case on the counter. It was a three-tiered, top-of-the-line tackle box given to her last Christmas by Mack, Dorothy, and Earlene—Dorothy herself had thoughtfully filled it with cosmetics from Wal-Mart and Rexall.

Bitsy made Clancy Jane sit, then she went to work, moving in a blur. Blush, lipstick, nail polish, mascara, smoky eye shadow. She swept Clancy Jane's hair into a loose twist, picking out tendrils in strategic places. She'd brought along a black dress, sleeveless with a plunging neckline. It showed off Clancy Jane's collarbones and her bouncy breasts. Bitsy dampened cotton balls with Shalimar and stuffed them into Clancy Jane's bra.

"I haven't worn one of these in years," Clancy Jane complained, tugging at the straps.

"Hush." Bitsy picked up a can of Aqua Net. "And close your eyes."

After the hair spray settled, Bitsy held up a mirror. "Well, what do you think?"

"Oh, my God." Clancy Jane inhaled. "Bitsy, you're an artist. You missed your calling. You would have made a dynamite beautician."

Bitsy pressed her cheek against Clancy Jane's and whispered, "Good luck."

At six forty-five, Clancy Jane stepped into the restaurant, tottering in Bitsy's too-small black high heels and walked up to a lectern. A slew-eyed hostess in a prom dress asked if she had reservations. "Yes, Falk, party of two." Clancy Jane reached up, patted her hair.

The hostess gave Clancy Jane a wide-eyed look, then she glanced down at her book. Her hair was curled up like a shepherdess's. All she needed was a ewe and a staff.

"Anything wrong?" Clancy Jane asked.

"Did you say Falk?" The girl glanced up, her forehead wrinkling.

"Yes. My husband will be along any minute."

The girl tapped a pencil against her lip as she stared at the reservation book, then she shrugged. "Would you like to be seated?"

Clancy Jane nodded. Her eyes hadn't yet adjusted to the gloom, and she stumbled after the hostess. The girl seated Clancy Jane, then handed her a padded faux-leather booklet with a blue tassel. A swarthy, foreign-looking waiter materialized from the shadows. He lit the candle with a flourish. Clancy Jane ordered a glass of house burgundy. She didn't think Byron would care if she started without him.

She glanced around the room. At a table near the windows, a man with dark hair and graying temples caught her attention. He was facing in the other direction and his shoulders were partially obscured by a Ficus benjamina. The shoulders looked familiar—broad yet rangy. And that swoosh of hair, expertly combed to hide the bald spot.

It was Byron. He was sitting at the best table, with a 180-degree view. Poised across from him was a redheaded woman, her face illuminated by the flickering candle. She rested her elbows on the table, smiling and nodding at something Byron was saying. With one hand, she flipped back her long, straight hair.

Clancy Jane reached down, lifted the red candle, and blew it out. A small stream of smoke drifted into the dark air above her head. From the neighboring table, a couple shot her a disapproving look. She ignored them and gazed at Byron and his date. He held out a forkful of cheesecake and slid it into her mouth. Then she fed him a spoonful of mousse. In their entire marriage, Byron had never fed Clancy Jane a crumb. Food had been a source of tension between them, a bone of contention, you might say. She glanced away as the waiter set down the wineglass, its contents swaying dangerously. His dark hands hovered over it, as if commanding the liquid to settle down and behave. While he bustled around her, she recognized the redhead. She was a nurse at Byron's office.

Clancy Jane drank the last of her wine. Byron looked smitten. She didn't have a chance of winning him back. The foreign-looking waiter appeared and asked if she was ready to order.

"No, but I'd like a screwdriver." Clancy Jane squinted up at him, hastily wiping her eyes. Whoever had put that leter in her mailbox had meant to cause irreparable damage.

She stole another look at Byron's table; he was handing his credit card to a waiter. This was a real bummer, the worst bummer in the world. Clancy Jane leaned back when the waiter returned with her screwdriver. Without hesitation, she picked it up, draining the glass in four noisy gulps. Then she held it out, exhaling loudly. The waiter's eyes bugged slightly.

"Another," she said, feeling lightheaded. "On second thought, just bring me two."

"Anything else?" he asked.

"How about that man over there?" She closed one eye and pointed. "Right *there*."

The waiter gave her a helpless look.

"Forget the man," Clancy Jane said, waving her other hand dismissively. "Just bring those drinks."

The waiter fled, and Clancy Jane turned her attention back to Byron's table. They were rising from their chairs. Clancy Jane felt her temper rising. Stop, she wanted to cry. Come back! The redhead stepped around a rubber plant, and Byron's fingers grazed the small of her back. It was an inconsequential gesture, yet it told Clancy Jane everything she needed to know. If they hadn't already slept together, they would soon. It was time for Clancy Jane to get on with her life.

She didn't wait for the drinks. Instead, she threw a wad of cash on the table and stood up, veering toward the private bar, through an upholstered door with a porthole. Even the walls in the El Toro Club were padded, like something you would see in a lunatic asylum.

"Screwdriver," she told the grizzled old bartender.

"Yes, ma'am."

She glanced sideways at the smooth-faced man beside her. He was peering gloomily into a glass of beer. His straight brown hair flopped onto his forehead. Mechanical pencils protruded from his shirt pocket, and he wore thick horn-rims. When he saw Clancy Jane staring, he straightened up. "Hey, aren't you Violet's mother? Violet Jones?"

"Why, yes," she said. The bartender slid a large glass in front of her.

"It's so nice to see you," the boy said. He grabbed her hand and pumped it enthusiastically.

"And you are . . . ?"

"Oh, I'm sorry. Daniel Walker, but everybody calls me Danny. I went to U.T. for two years. Violet and I would've graduated together, but I had to drop out. Want to play backgammon?" he added, grinning.

• • •

Danny had been working at the Sunbeam plant ever since he'd flunked out of U.T. He worked the day shift, maintaining the machines. When his shift ended, he rode his bicycle to Clancy Jane's house in the country—a ten-mile trip, with steep hills. She was grateful for the privacy of her mountain, because if she lived in town, people would think she and Danny were lovers, and they most definitely *were not*. There was nothing romantic between them. True, they drank a lot, and he often fell asleep on the living room floor; but she thought of him as a child.

Apparently her family did, too. "Isn't he a little young?" Mack said, when he stopped by one night for a beer. Danny was out in the yard, looking up at the stars with Walter's old telescope. A tortoiseshell kitten jumped into Mack's lap and meowed.

"The same thing could be said about Byron's girlfriend," Clancy Jane pointed out. "I saw them at El Toro a few weeks ago, and after his date finished eating, he had to burp her." Then she told Mack about her evening at the steak house, starting with the mysterious letter and ending with Danny.

"You ought to show Byron the letter," Mack said.

"I threw it away. Did I mention that a deputy drove up here the other day and served divorce papers?"

"Son of a bitch." Mack slapped his leg. "On what grounds?"

"Irreconcilable differences." Clancy Jane laughed. "What about irreconcilable redheads?"

"Well, don't rush into anything with this crazy boy. I know you're hurt, but take it easy." Mack's eyes narrowed. "Do you think Byron was seeing her on the sly while y'all were still together?"

"No." She shook her head. "But I almost wish he had."

"Why?"

"Because he left me for no reason."

· · ·

Grateful for Danny's company, she took him in like another stray, feeding him endless bowls of vegetable broth. He was small-boned and frail, even if his thigh muscles were overly developed from riding his bicycle. He lived on quaaludes and salted peanuts, which he kept in his trouser pocket. He had seen every episode of *Star Trek,* and he had an unusual interest in films like *Forbidden Planet* and *Close Encounters of the Third Kind.* Also, he suffered from allergies, and he sneezed whenever Clancy Jane's biggest tom cat, Mephistopheles, jumped on his chest and began kneading.

One night while they shared a marijuana cigarette, he put his hand on Clancy Jane's shoulder and told her that she was in danger. She thought maybe he was referring to her single status, living alone in the country, but it turned out he meant something vastly different.

"Aliens are among us," he said. Behind his thick eyeglasses, his pupils were dilating.

"Yeah?" Clancy Jane said, inhaling smoke, holding it deep inside her chest. She thought he was referring to Vietnamese refugees.

"The Vellagrans have us under constant surveillance," he said.

"Who?" Clancy Jane said, sputtering smoke.

"The Vellagrans," he said, surreptitiously glancing over his shoulder.

"Excuse me?" Clancy Jane stared at the joint, wondering if he was refer-ring to her diet. Vegans and Vellagrans sounded awfully close. Or maybe she had gotten some tainted marijuana. Sometimes it could induce paranoia.

"They hail from the planet Vellagra," he explained. "It's somewhere on the edge of the Milky Way. I've been wanting to tell you, but I had to make sure you weren't one of them."

To protect her from Vellagran rays, which were apparently as powerful as the magnetic beams on *Star Trek*, Danny taped Clancy Jane's attic win-dows with a triple layer of heavy-duty Reynolds Wrap, explaining that it would block the rays. From the outside, the windows looked like a church-bound casserole. Next, he sealed up the second-story windows and was making his way downstairs when Clancy Jane stopped him.

"That's enough," she said. "I need sunlight and fresh air."

"You like to live dangerously," he said and retreated to the attic, where he had situated Walter's old telescope aimed out a peephole in the foil. Danny turned the attic into a command post. He drew a crude diagram of the solar system that featured a close-up of each planet just on the edge of the star-strewn Milky Way, and beyond, clumps of galaxies, which he painstakingly labeled in black India ink. Every night he stood out in the backyard, looking up into the night sky, mistaking airplanes and weather balloons for mother ships.

Clancy Jane didn't know what was wrong with him. A bad diet, but she also suspected paranoid schizophrenia. She dug out Byron's *Merck Manual* from where she'd packed it away. Danny had every symptom of schizophrenia except auditory hallucinations. Still, she was lonely, and his craziness was more amusing than frightening. Their odd alliance might have continued indefinitely, if one night she hadn't suggested they sit in the hot tub. "Come on," she said, pulling two thick towels from the dryer. "It'll relax you."

"We'll be sitting ducks out there for the Vellagrans!"

"I'm not a happy woman, Danny. If they want my body, and the life that goes with it, then they're welcome to it."

She strode out the back door, onto the deck, letting the screen bang behind her. When she reached the hot tub, which was built into the plank floor, she began to undress. The night air felt silky and cool as she eased down into the bubbling water. Above, the moon drifted between clouds. She shut her eyes and tried not to think of the few times she and Byron had enjoyed this tub. Now she grasped the spout and her body floated up to the surface.

Danny stepped onto the deck, holding a bottle of tequila. He glanced furtively at the moon, then at her.

"I'm still here," she said. "I guess the Vellagrans have business elsewhere."

"You don't know the risk you're taking," he said hoarsely. He lifted the bottle to his lips. Tequila ran down his chin.

She raised her right hand. "Pass it down here, buddy."

He squatted at the edge of the tub. As he handed her the bottle, the tips of their fingers touched. Her breasts floated just beneath the surface. After a minute she handed up the bottle, giving him a view of naked flesh. "Funny, but I've never heard of waterborne abductions. They always seem to occur in the woods."

"That's true!" He took another drink and started walking toward the tub. "I'm coming in."

"In your clothes?"

"Oh, right." He set the bottle on the edge of the tub, yanked off his shoes, and pulled off his T-shirt. Then, turning his back to her, he stepped out of his jeans and underwear. Before Clancy Jane got more than an impression of white buttocks, he clasped his hands over his groin and spun around. Curly brown hairs protruded through his fingers. Then he slipped into the water.

She swam toward him, her feet skidding on the bottom of the tub. Then she noticed how he was staring. What if he thought she was in league with the Vellagrans? He might push her head under the water and hold her down until she stopped flailing. He lunged forward, sending a sheaf of water over the tub, and fell on his knees in front of her. He clasped his arms around her waist.

"Hey," she said.

He pulled her down and silenced her with a kiss. She tried to push him away, but he seized her wrist and shoved it down between his legs. She felt something the width of a celery stalk, but only half as long. It occurred to her that *he* might be a Vellagran. She wrenched away from his grasp and surged through the bubbling water, trying to climb out of the tub. He grabbed her arm. "Hey, don't rush off," he said and fell on top of her, pinning her against the steps.

"I'm not rushing, I'm—"

His mouth closed over her lips and nose, as if he were giving her artificial respiration. She felt him grope between her legs and insert his finger. She gripped the sides of the tub, desperately trying to stay above the churning water. He blew air into her mouth, and once again she was reminded of CPR. *One-one-thousand, two-one-thousand, three-one-thousand.* He was still probing with his finger. Then she felt his hands on her waist—*both* of his hands. So if it wasn't his finger down there, what in God's name was it? She began to struggle for air, and the boy, apparently mistaking her movements for passion, began to gasp. He groaned, and pushed hard against her.

"God, that was good," he said, panting. He rolled off, and the celery stalk floated between his legs.

Oh, my God, she thought. *That's what a Vellagran's penis looks like.*

"Was it good for you, too, Mrs. Falk?" He gazed up at the stars. "I sure hope the Vellagrans didn't see."

At the mention of aliens, she sobered a little. She scooted to the far end of the hot tub, then climbed out rather ungracefully and reached for the tequila bottle.

"Don't leave just yet," he called. "I'm just getting revved up."

• • •

That night a possum crawled into an electrical transformer, plunging the entire county into darkness. Danny was still outside, and he began to scream for Clancy Jane. Still feeling woozy from the tequila, she made her way to the deck. Danny was wild-eyed.

"It's an alien plot. They want to distract us," he yelled, pointing at the sky. "So they can abduct us. Without any lights, they can do what they want."

"I don't see anything." Clancy Jane looked up. The moon was hovering over the trees. The air smelled of pine needles.

"Listen," he whispered.

She was just about to tell him to leave, that she'd had enough, when she heard faint rumbling. At first, she thought it might actually *be* a spacecraft, but then four National Guard helicopters chugged across the sky, stirring the trees beneath them. They flew over her land regularly, and she always cursed them for waking her up.

"Man, it's a fucking invasion," Danny was saying.

"No, it's not," she said. The helicopters were making a grinding noise, and the windowpanes began to rattle. Danny began to jump up and down, his tiny penis swaying. "They see us!"

"These aren't aliens, they're just National Guard," she said.

"No, these are *black* helicopters!" he cried.

"Now hold on just a minute," she said testily. "These helicopters fly over here once a month. It's the goddamn Guard!"

"No, it's *them*." He strode to the edge of the deck. "And it's high time I faced them. So don't you worry. I'll protect you, Mrs. Falk. I'll throw up a smoke screen and make them abduct me instead of you." She could still hear the helicopters, way off in the distance. Danny hurried down the steps, then took off running across the meadow. Clancy Jane opened the door to go in, then glanced over her shoulder. Danny stood poised against the sky, as if he might heave himself into it. "Over here!" he cried. "I'm the one you want."

A TAPED MESSAGE TO ROSALYN CARTER

December 28, 1977

Dear Rosalyn,

 I am writing to thank you for the Kodak Christmas card of you, Jimmy, and the kids. I am impressed that you can send cards and still find time to buy presents for everybody. I am dead to know what you got your mother-in-law. Lord, that woman looks like she'd be hard to deal with. Earlene thinks I am difficult. She didn't like what I gave her for Xmas. I gave her a copy of Jamaica Inn *that I found at a tag sale. Earlene lied and said she'd read it, but when I quizzed her, I found out that she'd only seen the movie.*

 My son just sat there and didn't say a word. But if Earlene lies to me, she will lie to him.

 I gave my daughter a pretty black pocketbook from the Episcopal rummage sale, and she hugged and kissed me. We get along real good these days. When Bitsy was little, I never dreamed that she'd turn out to be a good daughter, but she is so kind and easygoing. We didn't get to spend Xmas with her little daughter, Jennifer, as her other grandparents have taken her to Hilton Head. They won't be back until January. But we are leaving up the tree and keeping all her presents—exactly ten—crowded under it.

 Anyway, thank you for the card. I will treasure it.

 Fondly,

 Dorothy

Part 5

POSTCARDS FROM BITSY

May 2, 1978
Princess Hotel
Montego Bay, Jamaica

Dear Dorothy,

Thank you again for this lovely graduation present. It's so pretty in Jamaica. When I come home I'll be rested and sunbaked, and ready to find a job with my decorating degree. I bought Jennifer a pearl bracelet and a seashell one. I wish I could give her the stars and moon.

Your daughter,
Bitsy

P.S. I've sent a card to Jennifer too. I hope they let her get it.

May 3, 1978
Princess Hotel
Montego Bay, Jamaica

Dear Jennifer,

I just got here and already I'm missing you like crazy. You'd like it here except for the food. They serve a lot of curried goat, which tastes awful. I have bought you some cute gifts.

Love,
Mother

May 4, 1978
Princess Hotel
Montego Bay, Jamaica

Dear Violet,

Today I walked on the beach and some island guy tried to sell me a marijuana cigar. I told him to go away, that I was a missionary. He told me that I should try a different position. Ha-ha. At first I was real scared, but then it hit me—I've never been anywhere by myself! Not in my entire life. That's sad. Now it's time for me to kick up my heels and have fun. I went to Ocho Rios with a tour group and climbed a waterfall. Everybody held hands, making a human chain. There are some cute men here on vacation, but I'm scared to talk to them. On the way back to Montego Bay, I got to see a wild pineapple growing beside the road. So far, I've signed up for a Jeep tour of Cockpit Country and a hot-air balloon ride. But this afternoon, I'm relaxing by the pool. I can't come home without a tan.

Love, Bitsy

Bitsy and Louie

A bee dropped out of the sky, emitting a halfhearted buzz, and landed on a martini glass that lay crooked in the sand. The bee rested on the rim, wings flicking, and began a slow counterclockwise crawl. I straightened my sunglasses and watched the insect, wondering how a bee could be attracted by the bitter remains of a martini, especially when the island was full of sweeter offerings.

Yesterday, on the way back from Ocho Rios, the tour driver pulled off the road and pointed out a pineapple plant. Another passenger, a man with curly black hair and deep-set eyes, smiled at me. He wore a red Izod shirt, white shorts, and flip-flops, but his cultured voice suggested a mansion back home filled with children and a beautiful wife, so I just brushed him off. Later, at the hotel swimming pool, I saw him again. Treading water in the deep end, we exchanged superficial information. His name is Louie DeChavannes, and he is a cardiovascular surgeon from New Orleans.

"I'm recently divorced—for the second time," he told me, swimming closer. "Do I sound dangerous?"

He did. I flashed what I hoped was a mysterious smile, then swam over to the ladder, got out of the pool, and climbed to the high diving board. Below, in the blue water, the doctor was swimming laps, a perfect American crawl. I waited until he reached the shallow end, then I dove into the pool. When I surfaced, the doctor paddled over to me. "You look like Aphrodite," he said. "Would you have dinner with me?"

We ended up skipping dinner. In fact, we never left my room. We undressed recklessly, and somehow overturned my perfume. The next morning, we ordered room service. Croissants, papaya, jam, and honey. Thick island coffee. To escape the overwhelming odor of Shalimar, we ate on the private terrace, which overlooked Montego Bay and a small sandy strip of land where a uniformed guard patrolled with a German shepherd and a double-barreled shotgun.

"You're a Libra to my Scorpio," he said. "And a graduate of Harvard?"

"Ha'vard School of Interior Design," I mumbled biting into a croissant. It made me feel guilty to mislead this man. I felt even worse indulging in pastries when the locals seemed malnourished. The beggars were waiting at the edges of everything, chasing after the tour vans, holding Coca-Colas and cigarettes up to the windows. Louie seemed to feel no such qualms. He snapped up his croissant, then licked the flakes from his fingers.

After we finished eating, he carried me to the bed and kissed the concave space between my breasts, then moved down to my stomach. "The Shalimar has to go, baby," he said.

"Shalimar?" I said dreamily. "Why?"

"It's unworthy of you." He moved his kisses up to my shoulder, then higher and higher until he reached my neck. "You need to wear Bandit. It's rumored that Garbo loved that scent. She was a goddess, and so are you. A goddamn goddess."

. . .

May 6, 1978
Princess Hotel
Montego Bay, Jamaica

Dear Violet:

Two days ago I met Louie DeChavannes. I can't begin to pronounce it right, so don't even ask. He's been married at least twice, but now he's divorced. He does open-heart surgery at Oschner Hospital in New Orleans. I'd first caught his attention on a tour bus. But we got better acquainted in the hotel swimming pool. More later.

Your cousin,
Bitsy

We stopped by the concierge's desk and booked a day trip to Negril Beach, the supposed heart of hedonism—a mere ninety minutes away from the hotel on bad roads. When the tour van arrived, we found a seat in the back. The other passengers filed in: a blond couple, dressed in matching blue plaid shorts, who spoke in British accents; newlyweds from Missouri who sat in front of us and French kissed; two talkative women in straw hats and ceramic fruit jewelry. They passed a roll of peppermint Certs, urging all passengers to take one. There was also a stocky girl with a shaved head and lovely blue eyes who kept firing questions at the driver. He responded by turning up the radio. Nilsson was singing "Coconut."

Negril was the sort of place where no one dressed for dinner, although the nicer restaurants and bars had signs posted: NO GANJA—NO COCAINE. We went to the most popular place, Rick's, where locals and tourists gather to watch the sunset. I was wearing a white fishnet shift over my black bikini, but no one even glanced in my direction. It was such a relief to fit into a place, to not have anyone point at me and whisper.

The waitress seated us on the terrace. I ordered a lobster salad and Chardonnay; Louie ordered a lobster tail and champagne. I wasn't sure what he was celebrating—the end of his vacation or the end of our fling. In a few days we'd be leaving this island. He'd go back to New Orleans and I'd go back to Crystal Falls. But I wasn't sad. I'd learned a few things on this trip—that I could travel alone and take a lover and not freak out. Over his shoulder, I could see the sun dropping down into the water with alarming speed.

When it disappeared, turning the water a ruddy pink, the diners stood up and applauded.

Louie was looking just beyond the cove, to the cliffs, the rocks backlit by a tangerine sky. There was still enough light to see swimmers moving like ants across the cove's white sandy bottom.

"I'm going," Louie said, pulling off his shirt. Then he reached into his trunks' pocket and pulled out his wallet and room key. He dropped everything on the table.

"Where?"

"To dive in. Why don't you join me? Put our stuff in your beach bag."

"But if I go, who'll watch the bag?" I looked up at him.

"I guess you're stuck with it, Beauty."

"Beauty?"

"Just an endearment. Hey, do you mind if I go by myself?"

Yes, I *do* mind, I wanted to say. Absolutely. Sit your handsome self down and drink your drink. But Louie had already kicked off his shoes and was heading along a red-sand path to the cliff. "Don't hit your head on the bottom," I called. "I bet there's not a single neurosurgeon in Negril."

From the depths of the terrace, a voice yelled, "There's not!"

Two tables over, a man grinned at me. "He's pulling a Zelda," he called in a Yankee accent. He was balding, with a paunch. I gave the man a blank look.

"Zelda Fitzgerald?" the man continued. "The mad wife of F. Scott? One night on the Riviera she jumped into the ocean, a thirty-foot dive at *low* tide. Later she leaped into the fountain in front of the Plaza Hotel, but that must have been anticlimactic."

At the next table, the British woman said, "Your husband must be a risk-taker."

"He's not my husband," I told her.

"Too bad," said the Zelda man. "Leapers make life exciting."

I watched Louie climb to the top. A blond man jumped first, curling into the fetal position just before he struck the water. When he surfaced, he let out a war whoop, then swam over to the metal steps. High above the lagoon, standing on the ledge, Louie appeared to contemplate the blue water. From below, one of the scuba divers—a woman with long red hair—spit out her regulator. "Come on, beautiful," called another, a long-limbed blonde, her breasts squeezing out of her wet suit.

I got up and moved over to the rail. I expected Louie to give a thumbs up, or at least a wave, but he kept his eyes on the water. He swung his arms over his head and inhaled. Then he bent his knees and sprang upward. He fell straight down, knifing into the water with hardly a splash.

When he didn't immediately surface, I gripped the rail and peered over the edge. He was swimming underwater, but he wasn't alone. The women divers circled him. Two minutes went by, then five. I realized that he wasn't coming up, that he was down there having a party, sipping from their air tanks. Behind me, a champagne cork exploded; I turned, and the waitress held out the spewing bottle. I could hear the tinny sound of exploding bubbles. I thought my heart might burst.

"Cheers," said the waitress.

May 10, 1978
Montego Bay, Jamaica

Dear Dorothy STOP:
I've tried to call but nobody is ever home STOP I have decided to stay
an extra week STOP Having fun STOP Don't worry STOP
Love Bitsy STOP

. . .

May 20, 1978
MGM Grand Hotel
Las Vegas, Nevada

Dear Violet,

Louie and I got married this morning, and I am officially Mrs.
DeChavannes. Isn't that the greatest news? I haven't met his mother yet, and
I'm scared to death. She has two big houses, a summer place in Pass
Christian, Mississippi, and a regular one in Alabama. I know you probably
think I got married on impulse, and in a way I did, but I've never met a
man like Louie. He's a world traveler and knows about wine and music, but
he's not snooty about it. We're going to buy a house in New Orleans and fill it
up with babies. I'm thinking this is my chance to do things right this time. I
hope Claude will let Jennifer visit. I bought her the cutest pocketbook, which
I'm sending to Dorothy. I am so happy! Louie is taking me on a real
honeymoon—to Paris, France. Isn't that the most romantic thing you've ever
heard of? I know how Grace Kelly must have felt when she met Prince
Rainier. Not that I am like her at all—I don't even have a passport. But I'm
getting one.
Love,
Bitsy DeChavannes

P.S. Excuse the letter. I've tried to call both our mothers umpteen times
but can't get through. They're probably worried sick. I know how you hate to
talk on the phone, but will you please give them a buzz?

P.S.S. I just remembered, Aunt Clancy and Byron also got married in Las
Vegas, so maybe this will be a family tradition.

P.S.S.S. Please tell your mother to mail my old rosewood letter box. She
will know where to find it. I will send the address later.

May 25, 1978

Dear Jennifer,

I hope you like the little pocketbook. I bought it at the cutest boutique here in Las Vegas. The bracelets are from Jamaica. I have married the most wonderful man. His name is Dr. Louie DeChavannes, and he can't wait to meet you. I will be moving to New Orleans, Louisiana, but don't worry, I will explain everything later on the phone. I hope you will be able to visit. I love you very much and say a prayer for you every night.

Love,
Mother

Dr. and Mrs. DeChavannes

We were invited to Louie's mother's house on Mobile Bay. A few miles past the Grand Hotel, he turned off the road and stopped in front of an imposing iron gate set in a high stucco wall, the old brick showing through in places. The black wrought iron was decorated with what looked like a donkey, with words spelled out under it in curlicues. It appeared to be a coat of arms, but I wasn't sure. Louie's window zipped down and he reached toward a metal box, punching in numbers. The smell of pine needles and salt water blew into the car. I was worried about meeting my new mother-in-law, Honora DeChavannes. If she was anything like this elaborate gate, then I was in trouble.

"I can't make out those words." I squinted at the gate. It made a whirring sound then creaked open. I thought *ane* might mean ass, but I couldn't remember. Since the incident with Walter's family, my French had deteriorated.

"It's a long story." Louie sighed and drove on through. A paved road twisted off into the pines. "First, you have to understand that Mother isn't ostentatious. But she married into a family that was. You should've seen the old gate. It was encrusted with gilded fleur-de-lis and big DeCs."

As Louie drove, he explained that his grandmother, old Mrs. DeChavannes, had named the house Chateaux DeChavannes. After her death, the house had passed into Honora's hands. "My mother never bought into the pretension of my father and his family. So, when the gate needed replacing, she devised a new escutcheon," Louie explained. "She came up with *chauve*, which means bald and hairless. *Ane* means ass, as in donkey, but it also has the same association as in English with fool. One of her artistic friends designed a symbol—a bald, dumb-looking donkey—to be used like the lion and unicorn of England. That's what's on the gate."

"What does it mean?"

"As far as Mother could tell, my daddy's family must have been the French equivalent of tenant farmers, with just a bald mule to their names, and they added the 'de' to try and class themselves up."

I nodded, trying to appear nonchalant, but my heart was pounding. Louie's mother sounded brilliant and whimsical, but what if she turned out to be like Claude's mother? I looked out my window and saw five peacocks strolling under the live oaks, dragging their plumage.

"Not much farther," said Louie. The road curved, and the house came into view. It was three stories high, beige stucco with red roses growing up the walls. Louie parked his Mercedes in a circle drive, under the shade of a live oak.

"Baby," he said, reaching across the seat and patting my hand. "I've got to tell you a little about Mother. She collects people. All kinds of people. Some of them are down on their luck, and some are quite gifted. Musicians, artists, burned-out movie stars, ex-junkies. They all end up at Mother's."

"She sounds kind."

"Yes, she's kind," Louie said. "But she takes it to extremes. She's also direct. You'll know in two seconds if she likes you."

As we walked toward the house, I brushed my hands over my pink floral skirt—which suddenly seemed too short and garish. We stepped under a rose trellis and walked past a fountain. "See that statue?" Louie asked. "It's Circe, pouring poison into the water."

"Circe?"

"An enchantress from the *Odyssey*, with a penchant for turning men into animals," he explained. He pulled me around a curved path, where we passed a marble chessboard, scaled for human-size pieces, the black-and-white squares denting the St. Augustine grass. I squeezed his hand. He was eight years older, but a thousand years wiser. I prayed that my good luck would continue, that he would love me forever.

The path swept up into a series of rounded steps, which led to another wrought-iron gate, festooned with more donkeys. In the sagging branches of a live oak, a brilliant blue peacock called out, *Eee-yah!*

"Honora's guard dogs," Louie said, laughing. He nudged the gate with his knee, and it swung open. I had never seen a yard like this before, except in magazines. I looked up. The trees blotted out the sky, and moss hung from the trees. "Is this the front of the house?" I asked.

"Yes, but we're going around back."

I tucked my polka-dot handbag under my arm, hoping it wouldn't show. If Louie had really grown up in this mansion, then he must have been spoiled rotten. The last thing I needed was another Wentworth.

"I've got to give Mama credit," Louie was saying. "She's done her level best to turn the old mansion into a gigantic country house. She added striped canvas awnings one year, and a screened-in porch the next. If she didn't love sunbathing so much she would have filled the swimming pool with dirt and plant trees and made another garden."

Straight ahead, the walkway opened up into an enormous brick patio, where an L-shaped pool sat in deep shade. Dotted here and there were Grecian urns, each one spilling ivy and pale pink flowers. The iron furniture looked regal, burnished green chairs and chaise lounges with brass claw feet. At the far end, sheathed in trees, stood a cabana, its front door invitingly ajar. Baskets of fuchsia, the petals dripping red and purple, swayed back and forth in a breeze that smelled of chlorine and honeysuckle. Through the Spanish moss, I saw a pier jutting out into the choppy waters of the bay.

"Home sweet home," Louie said in an ironic voice. He waved one hand. "Come on inside, I'll fix us something cool to drink."

We stepped through French doors into a sunny kitchen, with peach and white tiles, creamy marble counters, copper pans hanging from the ceiling. A cast-iron pot bubbled on the stove, filling the room with the smell of stock and the seasonings. Tea towels hung on a rack, each one embellished with Honora's donkey. The kitchen had four ovens, two gas stove-tops, with a total of twelve burners, two side-by-side refrigerators and two dishwashers. The Green Parrot didn't have this much equipment, and the café fed hundreds every day. I wondered if my new mother-in-law was a gourmet cook, or else entertained on a grand scale.

"Mama?" Louie shouted. He looked at me and shrugged. "I can't imagine where she's gone."

"In here," a woman called. I followed Louie into a glassed-in room off the kitchen, filled with plants and oil paintings. An attractive brunette set down a brass watering can and stepped over to Louie. She looked to be in her mid-fifties, and her hair was pulled back into a sleek bun. She wore beige slacks and a black turtleneck, the style favored by Jackie O. Across the room, two women and a bald-headed man sat around a glass table, smoking cigarettes. The table was littered with ashtrays and empty margarita glasses, and it wasn't even lunchtime.

"Darling," said the brunette, kissing Louie's cheek. "I see that you've brought Bitsy. My, she *is* lovely. You didn't exaggerate."

"The last girl he dragged here had green hair," said a middle-aged blonde, lighting a cigarette.

Dragged? I thought, wondering if the word had been directed at me.

"A hideous shade of green," said the bald-headed man.

"But hadn't she fallen into Honora's pool?" asked a woman with sharp green eyes and a chin-length bob.

"I'd forgotten all about that," said the blonde. "She smelled poignantly of chlorine."

"She positively *reeked* of it," agreed the bald-headed man.

Louie turned in my direction. His smile was blinding, almost too happy. "Hey, baby, come meet my mother and her pet vultures."

"First, let me give her a hug." The thin brunette smiled and embraced me, giving off gusts of a delicious perfume. Then she pulled back, her eyes wide and unblinking. "Darling, I'm so sorry I wasn't out front to greet you. By the way, I'm Honora."

I felt tongue-tied. But I saw exactly where Louie had gotten his good looks, the dark, slanted eyes and high cheekbones. Honora pulled me over to the glass table and began making introductions. "Y'all, this is Bitsy, Louie's bride. That cute little blonde number over there is Desirée, and the green-eyed vixen is Gladys. The bald creature is Merrill."

"Creature?" Merrill gave Honora a withering stare. "Have I been demoted?"

"Never." Honora took the cigarette from Merrill's hand and touched her red lips to the filter. Exhaling smoke, she said, "Guess who's living in my guest room?"

"There's no telling, Mother."

"Isabella. She's camped out upstairs with her Yorkies." Honora sighed, then she turned to me. "Isabella D'Agostino, the actress? Have you seen her movies?"

"Nothing but film noir," sniffed Desirée.

"Hush, Desi," scolded Gladys. "You're just jealous."

"Better Honora's guest room than mine," said Merrill.

"Well, she's got twelve," Desirée said.

"And *all* the rooms are occupied," said Merrill.

"All?" Louie's eyes widened. "Mother, how many people are living here?"

"You mean, this week? Six at the moment," Honora said, giving the cigarette back to Merrill. "But it fluctuates. Isabella requires two bedrooms, of course. One for herself, and one for the Yorkies."

"They're just using it as a lavatory, I'm afraid," said Gladys. "You'll need to fumigate when Isabella leaves."

Honora ignored her friends and stretched her arms above her head, then walked over to the French doors and flung them open. The pool glowed with an eerie green light. "I might take a swim," she said. "But what I'd really like is a kilo of Beluga caviar. Can't you see it, ladies? A gold can surrounded by crushed ice. A silver platter glinting in the light, full of toast points and maybe some latkes."

"A mother-of-pearl spoon," said Gladys.

"And a tall, blond butler with buns of steel," said Desirée.

"We're not normally like this," Honora told me. She held out one arm, her skin gleaming in the light.

"No, usually you're worse," said Louie, kissing his mother's cheek.

"Oh, poo," said Honora, pinching his cheek. "You're a fine one to talk. Now, fix your darling wife a drink while I show her around."

FROM THE CRYSTAL FALLS DEMOCRAT

—*"Who's Who & Who's Where," a column by Rayetta Parsons, page 3,*
August 10, 1978

Claude E. Wentworth IV and his bride, Regina Henley Wentworth, have just returned from a wedding trip to Hilton Head, South Carolina. The couple were married in a private ceremony at the home of Mr. and Mrs. Claude E. Wentworth III on August 1, 1978. They will reside in Crystal Falls, where Claude Wentworth IV is the new president of Citizen's Bank.

Clancy Jane

Clancy Jane set a pot of lentils on the stove, then turned up the heat and wandered into her empty living room, her footsteps echoing. She dragged the tasseled pillows over by the windows to a patch of sunlight and lay down. She only meant to close her eyes for a minute, but the bleating smoke alarm jolted her from a long, torturous nightmare involving Byron and the redhead.

The house was filled with a billowing black cloud, stinking of charred lentils. She scrambled to her feet and ran to the phone, which was sitting all by itself on the far end of the room. After she called 911, she hurried to the kitchen, flinging open doors and windows as she went, calling to her cats. Through the smoke, she thought she saw flames. A cat shot between her legs. Covering her mouth with one hand, she batted smoke with the other. Then she grappled for the cat-shaped oven mitts, which hung on a hook beside the stove. She'd bought them in Pass Christian when she went to Bitsy and Louie's reception. Fitting them over her hands, she lurched toward the smoking pot. God, the burned lentils smelled awful, it was enough to make her give up beans forever. She grabbed the handles and ran out of the kitchen, down the porch steps, into the backyard. When she reached the honeysuckle vine, she heaved the pot. It clunked against a tree. Then she staggered back to the porch and sat down, her head in her hands. She kept calling to her cats until she was hoarse, but the little bastards had gone into hiding, under beds and in closets. Only a few stragglers hunkered in the bushes.

She was still sitting on the steps, dazedly watching the smoke drift out the back door, when she heard the siren. A minute later, two fire engines roared up her driveway. The firemen hopped off the trucks, with hatchets and hoses, and marched into her house. One of the firemen stopped and touched Clancy's shoulder. He was tall, way over six feet, with dark bushy hair and intense blue eyes.

"Ma'am? You all right?" he asked.

"Yes. But my k-kitchen is ruined." Her teeth were chattering; she couldn't make them be still. "I was c-cooking lentils, and I t-threw the pot into the honeysuckle. Over there."

She pointed toward the woods. The fireman nodded.

"You sure you're all right, ma'am?" he asked again.

She nodded. It had been a long time since anyone had asked that question.

"Don't you move," he told her. "I'll be right back."

"I'll be here," she said, hugging herself. After all, where would she go?

·   ·   ·

As soon as her kitchen was functional—she needed new appliances and the ceiling had to be repainted—she called the fireman and invited him for supper. When Tucker O'Brien stepped into her house, he was carrying a six-pack of Budweiser. Clancy Jane led him into the kitchen and shoved the beer into the new side-by-side refrigerator. She slammed the door and turned and smiled. He was tall—much taller than she'd remembered. "Supper should be ready in about—"

He silenced her with a kiss. Rough, callused hands slid up her cotton blouse, tickling her skin. His hair smelled of shampoo, with an underlying scent of smoke from a warehouse blaze earlier in the afternoon. They undressed all the way to her bedroom, littering the polished floor with jeans and shoes and undergarments. The mattress was on the floor, centered directly beneath the ceiling fan. They sank down.

Later, during supper, Tucker sat cross-legged beside the harvest table. "How many inches off the ground is it?" he asked Clancy Jane.

"Oh, about six," she replied. "Are you uncomfortable?"

"No, I'm just fine. Would you hand me another slice of bread, please?" He ate three helpings of vegetarian lasagna and half a loaf of honey nut bread. Then she threw tasseled pillows onto the living room floor and stacked records on the turntable. There was a click and a whoosh, and the Stones began singing "Time Is on My Side"—Mick's definitive song of love, sex, and retaliation.

Tucker brushed his hand over her cheek, and she thought, *What if he turns out to be a loser?* Then she thought, *So what?* Even if he turned out to be wonderful, she wasn't sure she could stand that, either.

"This room sure is big," he said.

"An illusion. If I had furniture, it would seem smaller." She drew her legs into a half-lotus position.

"Why don't you have any? Did it get smoke-damaged?"

"No, I'm studying Buddhism, and—"

"Boo-*what*?" He gave her a blank stare.

"Some people think it's a religion, but it's more a philosophy of life. Anyway, I'm trying to reduce my fondness for material objects. I'm a long way from Nirvana." She held up her wineglass. "See? I still drink."

"Where's Nirvana?"

"It's the goal Buddhists aim for."

"Tell me about it." He stretched out on the pillow, crossing his long legs. Thrilled to have a captive audience, Clancy Jane began to talk rapidly, her voice rising and falling. He would nod, pausing to interrupt her now and then for clarification. For all his small-town ways, he seemed to understand everything, except the concept known as All Is Suffering. That took a bit of explaining. When she finished, Tucker glanced around the empty room.

"You might be onto something," he said. "People do get wrapped up in stuff. Cars and boats and TV sets."

"Yes!" Her eyes widened. "Exactly."

"When I'm putting out fires, you wouldn't believe what the folks beg me to go after." His eyes met hers. "Can you teach me it? This Buddhism?"

"I'd *love* to." She clasped her hands.

"Damn, I can't wait." He grinned and tugged a lock of her hair. Just for a moment, Clancy Jane was reminded of Mack. He was always starting sentences with damn. It was a way of talking favored by Southern punks. Not that Mack had started out that way. Over the years, he'd lost what little polish Dorothy had inflicted upon him, and the moment she was locked up, he'd fallen under the spell of Earlene and her bawdy ways.

"How old are you?" she asked.

"Twenty-eight. Is that too old, too young, or just right?" When she didn't answer right away, he picked up her hand, rubbed her knuckles. "What?"

When she was seventy-one, he'd be fifty-eight. Was that so terrible? Well, maybe not for her, but chances were they wouldn't be together two weeks, much less two decades. She tilted her head, smiling up at him.

"I'm thinking that this empty living room is perfect for dancing."

. . .

During a late-night phone call to Violet, Clancy Jane said, "I'm madly in love."

"With the fireman?"

"Yes, and I swear he is *the* one. When he put out the fire in my kitchen he lit another fire in my heart."

"Oh, Mama. That's so lame."

"He's real tall and muscular, like the lumberjack on Brawny paper towels."

Violet laughed.

"We went camping last weekend, and he didn't complain once about the nuts and fruit I brought along. I put some frozen pepperpot soup into a cast-iron pot and we cooked it over an open flame. His best friend Joe is the fire chief in Crystal Falls. And he's got a houseboat on Center Hill. They cruised by our camp site and we swam out to the boat. We just had a ball."

"I'm glad for you, Mama. You deserve to be happy."

"Yes, it's about time. But wait—I haven't finished telling you about a house that burned up. Tucker went in and rescued a cat. He breathed air into its little lungs and saved it. Then he brought it to my house. We named it Cinders. He's got a singed tail and whiskers, and his meow is so pitiful—it's real hoarse."

"Just what you need: another cat." Violet laughed again.

"There's always room for one more. And you know something else? Now that I'm teaching Tucker about Buddhism, I'm able to see where I went wrong. How I went to extremes."

"You mean your no-frills decor?"

"Exactly. I'm a middle-aged woman, not a monk with a begging bowl. If I have a sofa set and a dresser for my underwear, it won't undermine my journey toward Nirvana. Besides, I won't make it there in *this* lifetime. It's like Tucker said, getting dog-drunk is probably worse than having pictures on the wall. So we gave up beer and wine, and now we just drink iced tea with lots of lemon."

"Get out of here," Violet cried in an incredulous voice.

"I'm thinking about selling this house and buying a little cottage in town. Oh, Violet. You've just got to meet him."

"Bring him to my wedding," Violet said.

"Your—oh, my God!" Clancy Jane squealed. Her voice echoed in the empty house. She began jumping up and down, and the phone cord twirled like a jump rope.

"Calm down." Violet laughed. "It's not till next summer. You've got plenty of time to find a dress."

"My dress! What about yours? Oh, my gosh. My baby's getting married. Remember how much fun I had planning Bitsy's wedding to Walter Saylor? Maybe you can come home—bring George, of course—and we'll pick out flowers and music and cake."

"We've already done that."

"Oh?"

"George and I want to have the wedding in Memphis. The reception will be at the Peabody."

Clancy Jane began untangling the telephone cord. After a moment she said, "Are you having bridesmaids?"

"No. And I barely agreed to a wedding. But George's mother would've been disappointed."

George's mother? Clancy Jane winced.

"Mama, you still there?"

"Mmmhum."

"You're not mad, are you? Please tell me you're not mad."

"Mad? No, I wouldn't say that." Clancy Jane lifted her chin, determined not to be annoyed. "I've never been to the Peabody. Should I rent a tuxedo for my honey?"

"Honey?"

"Well, at my age, boyfriend sounds pathetic." Clancy Jane laughed.

"You can always call him your significant other. And no, a tux isn't required."

Bitsy

In November, I discovered that I was pregnant, and Louie began searching for the perfect house. His requirements posed a challenge to every real estate agent in New Orleans—he wanted something old and elegant, preferably in the Garden District. Our latest Realtor was a stocky woman with short red hair, cut in a sharp elfin V around her ears. Today she'd taken us to see a grand, if run-down, house off Pytrania Street, an elegant beige stucco with dark green shutters. It had a hipped roof and ornate trim around the eaves. The columns were a curious mixture of Ionic and Corinthian, and along the back was a screened-in porch. I knew all these terms from my interior design course. In the backyard, I glimpsed a messy crape myrtle hedge and a striped hammock hanging between two trees. It reminded me of the one back in Crystal Falls where Violet and I used to drink and discuss men.

Louie took my hand and together we explored the yard. It was large and shady, with live oaks, banana trees, and a hulking forsythia hedge. The real estate agent herded us inside and repeated her litany: five bedrooms, five-and-one-half baths, swimming pool, pavilion, beveled glass doors. She pointed to the chandeliers and pier glass mirrors. "They were taken from a turn-of-the-century brothel."

Louie went upstairs to check out the bedrooms, but I stayed behind. Just off the dreary dining room, I opened a door, thinking I'd found a closet, and saw a porcelain sink, etched with rusty stains, and a crooked toilet that made a gargling sound when I pushed the lever.

"It needs a lot of work," the Realtor said, coming up behind me. Then she glanced up at the ceiling, as if tracking Louie's footsteps. "But Dr. DeChavannes likes it. I can tell. And I understand you're an interior designer—well, this house is a designer's dream."

"Or nightmare," I said with a laugh. "Actually I was hoping for something smaller."

"I probably shouldn't even say this," the Realtor said in a cozy, conspiratorial tone, "but a long time ago, I showed Dr. DeChavannes and his first wife an old mansion. Just a few blocks from here, I think. Or maybe it wasn't his first wife. How many times has the doctor been married?"

I chewed the inside of my lip while the agent barreled on. "Anyway, Dr. DeChavannes loved the house and she hated it. I think her name was Shelby? They ended up buying a house by the golf course. She liked modern, I guess. The doctor had his heart set on a grand old house." The agent paused. "I guess you know she just sold it? The golf course house, I mean. And for a steal, too. She must have been desperate. Bad memories can make a seller do crazy things."

This woman was good. I turned away and headed up the curved staircase. Each riser gave off an indignant squeak. On the landing Louie grabbed my hands and pulled me into a sunny room that faced the garden.

"How about this for the nursery?" he asked.

I stood in the center of the room, in a wedge of light. The windows looked into live oaks, and through the branches I saw chips of blue sky. I could paint clouds on the ceiling and walls. And we could put a bookcase on the left, the shelves loaded with dolls. I just knew I'd have a girl. According to my calculations, my due date was around the end of July. "Can we get it finished in time for the baby?"

"I'll move heaven and earth." Louie kissed my hands. He seemed so happy, so eager to please, but I couldn't stop worrying. This house demanded an elaborate lifestyle, one far more extravagant than even the Wentworths enjoyed. The idea was alarming. Wealth hadn't brought Miss Betty any pleasure—her designer suits notwithstanding—so I had no reason to believe that it would enhance mine.

"Let's make an offer." Louie kissed my neck.

"Are you sure?" I asked.

"Positive."

I thought it might be haunted and I almost blurted, "Let's keep looking. Surely we could find another house, one that pleased us both."

As if reading my thoughts, Louie said, "I know it looks awful now, but I'll call the best architect in New Orleans. But if we get into the renovation and change our minds, no problem. It's not irrevocable."

Few things are, I thought.

From the Mercedes, I watched my husband at the front door of his ex-wife's new house. It was a weathered, little shotgun that jutted out on the bayou: Shelby DeChavannes's replacement for her five-thousand-square-foot contemporary over by the golf course. Shelby finally opened the door, wearing baggy jeans and a T-shirt. Her blond hair was twisted into a sloppy bun, anchored by yellow pencils. Their little daughter, Renata, shot out. Shelby caught the child's hand and pulled her back for a good-bye kiss. Then the woman glanced toward the car, fixing me with a wild-eyed stare. Shelby had refused alimony, didn't want a dime from Louie. Child support went into an account for Renata. Shelby was writing bad checks all over town. Apparently the floating house needed constant repairs; it was taking a financial toll. Worse, the move had forced Renata to change schools, upsetting her so much that she'd walked into a glass door and broken out her front tooth—a permanent one—requiring a root canal and a porcelain cap.

"Was Shelby always like this?" I'd asked Louie after Renata's last visit.

"No," he'd said, his voice full of despair, as if he were speaking of a priceless object he'd mislaid and had no hopes of recovering. I shot him a look but asked no more questions.

Today Renata was wearing faded red shorts that were several sizes too large, giving the child a knock-kneed look. I was reminded of Alice Ann. Every time Louie and I went to visit Honora at her summer house in Pass Christian—which was near Point Minette—I was always tempted to drive down the highway and see if Finch House was still standing, but I was afraid of stirring up ghosts. With Walter Saylor in mind, I'd confessed everything to Louie, but he had found my past quirky and humorous, and for a while he'd referred to me as his little criminal. Now, it was never discussed.

The pregnancy made me lightheaded and queasy, but I was determined to prepare a home-cooked meal for Renata. The kitchen in Louie's bachelor apartment was no larger than a coat closet, but the window over the sink had a lovely view of Lake Pontchartrain. I asked Louie what he wanted for supper. He thought a moment and said, "Fried shrimp."

"And you, Renata?" I asked.

"I don't eat on weekends," she said. Her face was gaunt, the fine bones painfully visible through her pale skin.

"Never?" I asked, and Renata shook her head, her pigtails whipping from side to side. There really was a spooky resemblance to Alice Ann.

At dinner, Renata only nibbled at the shrimp and hushpuppies, but later I caught her in the kitchen, making a potato chip and Dijon mustard sandwich. "Honey, let me fix you something good," I said.

"This *is* good," Renata insisted, biting into the sandwich. She chewed fiercely for several seconds, her teeth crunching on the chips. "When me and Mommy move in with Granny Honora, we can see Daddy *all* the time. And I won't have to put up with *you* anymore."

Renata stuck out her tongue. It was stained yellow, flecked with tiny chips.

Dorothy and Louie

In early January, when Dorothy learned of her daughter's troubled pregnancy, she locked up her house and drove to Louisiana. Bitsy was in her first trimester, and her cervix was starting to prematurely efface and dilate, so her obstetrician had ordered bed rest.

Dorothy drove with the window rolled down. Her silk scarf, green with blue parakeets, flapped in the wind, catching the attention of every truck driver on the road. She honked and waved. For her last birthday, she'd gotten herself a makeover at Merle Norman. She'd bought two bags full of cosmetics and face creams, then driven over to the Utopian, where her hair was artfully cut, dyed, and styled. Since she didn't have any clothes to go with her new look, her next stop was Karen's Consignments, where she found just what she wanted. More than a few outfits had come from Miss Betty's closet, all size twelve, and they fit Dorothy to a T. Then she took off for New Orleans.

Bitsy and her new husband had just moved into an old mansion in the Garden District, and the remodeling had apparently brought on the obstetrical woes. Fortunately her husband was one of the leading physicians in New Orleans, and he knew all the best ob-gyns, so Bitsy couldn't have been in better hands. Dorothy just loved having a doctor for a son-in-law, and she went around Crystal Falls referring to him as "the heart surgeon," or simply "the doctor." It was lots better than a dentist. Sometimes she'd preface a sentence with, "My son-in-law, the cardiovascular physician." That got people's attention.

. . .

When Dorothy pulled into her daughter's circular driveway, she saw a bunch of scary-looking men on the roof. And some gangster types were painting the porch. Dorothy got out of the car, and the hammering stopped. All of the workmen-convicts turned to stare as she reached into the backseat, grabbed her suitcase, and scurried onto the front porch. The door was wide open and she hurried inside, praying that those workmen-convicts weren't rape-stranglers.

She found Bitsy lying in the middle of a four-poster bed, which was reputed to have come from the childhood home of Margaret Mitchell—a wedding gift from Louie's mother. "Dorothy!" Bitsy cried, pushing up on the pillows. She waved a limp strand of hair out of her face. "Thank God you're here."

"I drove like a maniac," Dorothy said. "Where's Louie?"

"At the hospital."

"How have you stayed in bed, what with all these . . . horrible men running around?" Dorothy touched her daughter's face. The cheeks seemed rounder, as if they'd been slightly inflated. Already she was fattening up.

"Oh, Dorothy. They're not horrible. They're craftsmen."

"Well, whatever." Dorothy shivered. "But what about you? Any more spotting?"

"Not a bit. The bed rest seems to be working." Bitsy picked up a black remote control and pointed it at the television set. The screen flicked on. "Even though I am getting tired of watching soap operas."

"You poor thing," Dorothy said, her ears perking up. "Which ones?"

"The Young and the Restless," said Bitsy. "But I'm getting hooked on *Guiding Light.*"

"Then we'll have a good time. Those are my favorites, too." Dorothy perched on the edge of a blue silk chair. She tried not to look at her daughter's messy room. On the floor, books were piled hip-high, mostly decorating guides and childbirth manuals. An empty box of Wheat Thins was being used as a makeshift trash can. Dirty teacups were lined up on the fireplace mantel. Dorothy leaned over and ran her hand along the windowsill; her fingers stirred up long tendrils of dust. She decided to speak to Louie about hiring servants. Soap opera people rarely had maids, but somehow their homes were stylish and immaculate. If only real life could be that way.

Later, while Dorothy prepared lunch in the half-renovated kitchen, she decided she'd alphabetize the canned goods. Next, she planned to scour the bathrooms, which had been grossly defiled by the workmen. It would probably take weeks to hire a housekeeper, so Dorothy decided she'd bring order, serenity, and cleanliness to her daughter's bedroom—crisp linen, fresh air, the furniture wiped down with lemon Pledge. After Louie got home, he drove her to the Winn-Dixie, where she bought cleaning supplies and nourishing food. Dorothy wanted that heart surgeon to know that Bitsy came from fine people. People who knew how to take control of any situation and make it better.

• • •

Louie watched his mother-in-law prance down the hall. From behind, Dorothy had wide hips and slightly humped shoulders. During his years as a physician, he had observed that mothers and daughters tended to age similarly. His own father, the late Dr. DeChavannes, had refused to marry Honora until he'd set eyes on *her* mother. Louie's first wife, CeeCee, had descended from a clan of Alabama brunettes who believed that a woman aged according to the skill of her beautician—a good colorist could knock off as many years as a plastic surgeon. Louie's second wife, Shelby, came from a long line of Louisiana beauty queens. What Louie remembered best about Shelby's mother was her hair—it turned blonder every year until it eventually acquired the texture of sphagnum moss. Last month, when the woman had died quite suddenly, she had been completely bald.

When he'd heard the news, he'd driven over to Shelby's floating house, to offer his condolences. Shelby had fixed him a glass of whiskey, then she fell into his arms. "Poor Mama," she wailed. "I can't bury her until I find a wig."

Louie had rounded up not one, but two human-hair wigs. During the wake, he and Shelby had broken away from the crowd, which had included his mother, his daughter, and his pregnant wife, and Louie had followed Shelby upstairs, into the casket display room. She'd kicked off her heels, then climbed into a "tall man's" coffin and stretched out on the faux silk cushion. Louie had unbuckled his trousers, then climbed into the casket.

Later, all flushed from lovemaking, he returned downstairs to his wife and daughter in the chapel. He had picked up Bitsy's hand and kissed her palm. "There you are, Beauty," he said a little breathlessly. "I've been looking everywhere for you."

"Well, I've been right here." Bitsy smiled at him. He noticed a softening around her edges; her lovely cheekbones were obscured by flesh. Still, she possessed an iridescent beauty that seemed to come from the baby. He had sworn to himself that he wouldn't let things start up with Shelby.

Days later, his resolve faltered. He kissed his new wife good-bye and drove across town to Shelby's house, his path as straight and unwavering as a homing pigeon's. He climbed into Shelby's bed, the mattress creaking beneath his weight. Then he pulled Shelby into his arms. Her hips arched upward, taking him deep inside her, he knew she was about to come; she had a way of shaking her head from side to side, eyes closed, crying out his name, *Louie Louie*, over and over until it brought him to the edge. Her lovemaking was familiar and soothing, and he told himself that it wasn't adultery. He was just caught in a transition. But the transition had reactivated an old problem: insomnia. Guilt had always produced sleepless nights.

Louie hoped Dorothy's arrival would give him more time to spend with Shelby. But his squatty little mother-in-law turned out to be a tyrant. She ordered him to take her grocery shopping, and he gritted his teeth as he pushed the metal cart, trying to appear interested in the differences between kinds of kale and winter tomatoes. When they got home, she insisted that he help put their purchases away. When that was done, she placed a dust mop in his hand and told him to push it over the dusty heart-of-pine floors.

"Anything else?" He raised his eyebrows. "Shall I defrost the freezer? Wash the baseboards?"

"I had no idea you were this marvelous," Dorothy said. "You're a prize. You don't have to do any of those things just yet. But I would just love for you to chop an onion. I thought I'd fix you and Bitsy some of my famous spaghetti. Do you like Italian food, Louie?"

She pronounced Italian with a hard I. Louie nodded, then selected a large Vidalia, carried it over to the chopping block, and pulled out a French knife.

"Be sure to chop it real fine," Dorothy called. "It's criminal to make spaghetti with big, old hunks of vegetables."

"Yes, ma'am," he said, nodding. He raised the knife, then hacked the onion in half. The truth was he was guilty of crimes his mother-in-law hadn't even begun to suspect. Lying to one wife, lying with the other— what could he be thinking? Well, at least he could chop onions. His mother had trained him well.

A month passed. Bitsy would not hear of hiring servants, so Dorothy continued to direct Louie. Under her supervision, he scoured the toilets, rearranged the linen closet, and swept the front porch. The household chores kept him too busy to see Shelby. On Valentine's Day, he stopped by her house. She met him at the door. "Already tired of me?"

"No, I swear I'm not."

"Prove it," she said, crossing her arms over her breasts. She was wearing a black see-through nightgown. "Renata's at your mother's house. So spend the night with me."

"I can't, I've got to get home and vacuum." He hadn't meant to say that. He cringed.

Shelby's lips tightened. "You never vacuumed when *we* were married. Wow, you must really be smitten by that little blonde."

He didn't know how to respond, so he just stood blinking on the rickety dock, clutching his offerings—Elmer's Gold Bricks, Shelby's favorite candy, and calla lilies.

"No, I actually feel sorry for you. Poor Louie. His wife is sick and can't fuck him. So he vacuums floors. I don't need this shit. So either you commit to me, or it's over." She lifted a hank of blond hair and studied the ends. They resembled frayed platinum wires—Shelby was her mother's daughter, after all. She looked very tired.

"What do you want from me?" he asked.

"Our old life back." She put her hands on his face, and he felt his heart fold in half.

. . .

It was late when Louie walked into his own house, depressed and empty-handed. He was met at the door by Dorothy, who grabbed his arm and hissed, "Where's the candy? The flowers?"

He reeled backward, wondering if she'd been spying on him and Shelby. "What are you talking about?" he blustered.

He walked past her into the kitchen, alarmed when he realized she was following him. Maybe Shelby had gone crazy, called Bitsy, and confessed their affair. Well, no, it wasn't really an affair, just an encounter. He opened the Sub-Zero, pulling out a bottle of chablis.

"Put that back," Dorothy scolded. "I need you to drive me somewhere."

"Now?" he said.

"Yes, now! You forgot flowers!" She threw her hands up in the air. "You forgot candy!" Dorothy crossed the kitchen in two steps and yanked the wine bottle from his hand. "It's Valentine's!"

"Christ!" He slapped his forehead.

"All the florists are closed by now," she said, "but if you hurry you can still find candy at Walgreens. And a *card*. Oh, whatever were you thinking, Louie?"

* * *

In sleep, Bitsy looked wary. Her forehead wrinkled, and she threw one arm over her head, clenching her fingers. Louie's insomnia surfaced. Pulling back the sheet, he eased out of the Margaret Mitchell bed, down the dark, squeaky stairs. Through a maze of rooms, all destined to be gutted, he threaded his way into the kitchen. Opening the silver door of the Sub-Zero, he blinked when the light hit his cornea. Then he saw how his mother-in-law had decorated the inside of the refrigerator—celery sticks standing in striped glasses, brown eggs in a wire basket, the gourmet mustards lined up on a silver relish tray. She had also thoughtfully sealed the leftovers in tinfoil, which meant he had to open every single packet to see if it was what he craved.

He decided on the cold hamburger steak. Then he unwrapped the French bread, sliced it at an angle. He slathered both pieces with mayonnaise, catsup, and Dijon. Next he slapped on romaine, jalapeño cheese, sprouts, and roasted red peppers. When he was finished, he'd wreaked havoc on both the kitchen and the refrigerator art, but he'd made one hell of a sandwich. With his free hand, he picked up the phone and dragged it into the dining room. Then he sat down on the floor, the phone in his lap. His molars crunched down on the romaine, and the pepper jack burned his tongue. In Shelby's bed, they had feasted on chocolates and tequila poppers—a jalapeño marinated in tequila, then stuffed with cheese, battered, and deep fried. She answered on the fourth ring, her voice sleep-drenched.

"It's me," he said.

"God, what time is it?" Shelby yawned.

"I don't want it to be over, Shel. Please, talk to me."

"I am." She yawned again.

"Can I come over tomorrow?" He pulled the phone over to the window and gazed into the trunk of a live oak. Beneath the streetlight, there was a camilla bush loaded with buds.

She was silent. Then she said, "No. You'd better not."

"Let me see you." He squeezed his eyes shut. "Please?"

"Your wife is pregnant, for God's sake. Since you obviously don't have a conscience, I'll use mine. Besides, I've got a hair appointment tomorrow."

"That's unfair. My heart's in the right place."

"But your dick isn't." She yawned again. "Good-bye, Louie. Really, good-bye."

"Wait!" he cried turning away from the window, toward the kitchen. "Don't hang up. Please. I've got to see you." There was a figure in the doorway. He froze, "Bitsy?"

"No, it's Dorothy," came the voice.

"Oh, God," he heard Shelby say, and the line went dead. Very softly, without making a sound, Louie hung up the phone. He drew in a deep breath, and tried to smile at his mother-in-law. Her face was stony, and her eyes were cold. He stepped forward, tripped over the cord, and fell, skidding on the hardwood floor. The phone flipped over, making a trilling sound. His right hand landed on and flattened the sandwich.

"Are you all right, Louie?" Dorothy folded her arms.

"I was talking to a patient," he said.

"A patient," she echoed. "At this hour?"

"Yes."

She stared down at him.

"A lot of my patients work odd shifts," he said. "A doctor never gets any rest. You know how it is."

"No, I don't." She stared at him for a long moment. Then she glanced back into the kitchen. Along the counter were open jars, a knife smeared with Dijon, the foil packages all ripped open.

"You've made a mess," she said. "And I'm afraid you'll have to clean it up yourself."

. . .

Dorothy returned to the guest room and stretched out in the iron bed, listening to her heart crank out a wild, irregular rhythm. *Damn him, damn his soul to the bottom of hell.* Her door stood open, and every sound was magnified by the darkness—her own raspy breathing and her daughter's soft murmur, the mattress squeaking as Louie slid into the marriage bed. All over the house the pine floors popped, and the kitchen appliances made whirring sounds. She pulled up the quilt, shivering. She had no idea that New Orleans got this cold in February. In five months, the Lord willing, Bitsy's baby would be born. And Dorothy couldn't breathe a word of what she'd overheard to her daughter, not one word. Because her daughter's hold on this pregnancy was tenuous. Because the phone call proved nothing. Because life would go on, and all Dorothy had to do was keep her mouth shut. She closed her eyes, remembering all he'd said on the phone. "Please," he'd begged the other woman. "I've got to see you."

If Albert were alive, he'd punch Louie in the mouth, even though Albert himself had wandered during their marriage. Men and their cheating little hearts. It was enough to make an old woman's blood pressure rise. It was enough to make her heart throw a clot. She decided she would say nothing; she would hold her tongue but remain secretly watchful. She was pretty sure that Louie was counting on her silence. He didn't strike her as the sort of man who leaped headfirst into a confession. Men did as they pleased, especially doctors—back home in Crystal Falls, all the physicians had swimming pools and mistresses. Only the Lord knew what Byron had done behind Clancy Jane's back. But at least he'd never got a swimming pool. Her own mother used to say that men were vulnerable to affairs during a wife's pregnancy, but Dorothy had a different theory—men were prone to infidelity *all the time*. They were genetically programmed to spread their sperm around, even if the stupid things had undergone vasectomies.

Dorothy just couldn't stand anyone hurting her child; but a mother could only do so much: make tea, wash the windows with vinegar water, sweep every speck of dirt under the rug.

A LETTER FROM CLANCY JANE

March 2, 1979

Dearest Violet,

Byron and the redhead broke up. I knew it wouldn't last. Apparently he'd caught his little darling kissing the twenty-two-year-old washing-machine repairman. To Byron's way of thinking, a kiss isn't all that far from a screw. He called to cry on my shoulder and mumbled something about getting together for dinner. I hid my glee and offered false pity, even though I told him I was involved with someone else. Man, that gave me a rush.

Tucker sends his love.

XX OO

Bitsy

Shortly after April Fool's Day, my mother-in-law stopped by my house with a bottle of Dom Perignon. She wore a brown tweed suit, and her dark hair was pulled back with an Hermès scarf—the colors in the scarf complementing the tweed. She carried a Chanel bag, and a manila envelope was tucked under her arm.

"I'm so glad to see you up and about," she told me, kissing the air beside my ear. Her perfume smelled spicy, fruity. "I know you're just thrilled to be out of bed."

"Yes." I smiled down at my bulging abdomen.

"And I love how the house is coming together." She turned around in the foyer, and her diamond earrings caught light from the chandelier. She handed me the bottle. "You'll learn to love this—well, after the baby's born. When are you due?"

"July thirty-first."

"That's a stifling hot month to have a baby, but thank God you've got central air. Is Louie just beside himself over the baby? Is he home, by the way?"

"No, ma'am." I said. "He'll be in surgery most of the morning."

"Good. That gives us time to chat."

We stepped into the large, rectangular living room and stopped in front of a French credenza that Louie and I had bought in the Quarter. "Oh, this is lovely," Honora said. "And your draperies are divine. Are they Cowtan and Tout or Brunschwig?"

"Cowtan and Tout," I said, a little surprised.

"But isn't that fabric only available through interior designers?"

I decided not to mention my diploma from Ha'vard.

"I bought that darling Osborne & Little fabric I have in one of my guest rooms through my dear friend, Sister DeBenedetto. She's not a nun, in case you're wondering. She's the leading designer in New Orleans. We were roommates at Newcomb a thousand years ago. Why don't I just bring Sister by one afternoon? You'll love her—and her fabrics."

Honora walked around the room, prattling about Sister and the antiques the two of them had brought back from Normandy. I nodded politely and tried to seem interested. I put the champagne bottle on a burled table and laid a protective hand over my stomach. I thought I felt something move—a foot? When my mother-in-law paused, I jumped into the conversation. "Please don't take this the wrong way, but I've been looking forward to decorating the rest of the house myself. It's a long way from being finished, but I want to take my time."

Louie's mother gave me a shrewd look. "Oh, I didn't mean for Sister to *do* your house. Rather, I thought you might work *with* her one or two days a week. After the baby's here, of course. Perhaps she'll take you on as a junior partner or something like that. She's got the sweetest shop on Royal? I'm only saying this because a job might help you cope with Louie's long absences. The boy is a notorious workaholic. Well, I guess you already know that."

"Yes, ma'am, I sure do," I said. The notion of working in the French Quarter held a bit of charm, but I knew that once the baby arrived, no power on earth—even the lure of a famous designer—would make me leave home.

"I know my son." She frowned. "I'm afraid it won't get any better."

"No, ma'am. Would you like some coffee?"

"Bourbon, if you've got it." She sat down on a jade damask sofa, so new the tags were still attached. She lifted one and made a small, approving noise. "This room is gorgeous. Your taste is exquisite. You'll *love* working with Sister. Have you done anything with the master bedroom?"

"Not yet."

"One word of advice," she said, laughing. "Never put a man in a room with a flowery bedspread, or he'll feel compelled to prove his masculinity. I'm speaking from experience, you understand. Louie's father was a bit of a rogue."

"I've asked Louie to pick out the bedroom colors and fabrics," I said.

"You clever puss."

While I poured the drink, she set the envelope on the coffee table. I

wondered what was inside—fabric samples? Legal documents? We chatted a bit more about Sister and her famous clients: a British rock star; a
TV chef; a former Miss America. Then Honora began talking about one
of her house guests, Isabella D'Agostino. "Back in the sixties, she was a
Hollywood star who specialized in playing rich, spoiled bitches. She co-
starred with Rock Hudson, James Garner, and Doris Day. After her career
dried up, she came to the Coast and I introduced her to the wealthiest
man in Mobile, Dickie Boy McGeehee. He died, and Isabella moved into
one of my guest rooms to spend the weekend, and she's been there off
and on ever since."

She set her empty glass on a coaster and lit a cigarette. Then she
reached for the envelope and spilled out Xeroxed papers. "I hesitate to
show you these things when you're expecting a baby," she began, "but I
didn't know what else to do."

I leaned forward and read a headline—FUGITIVE IN CUSTODY, KID-
NAPPED CHILDREN REUNITED WITH LOVED ONES. I felt something drop
inside my chest, and I sank back against the pillows.

"W-who sent those?"

"Some anonymous troublemaker—there wasn't a return address or a
postmark. The evildoer left the envelope in my mailbox."

I nodded, feeling tears burn the backs of my eyes.

Louie's mother stared down at her cigarette, smoke drifting above her
fingers. "Darlin', I hate to ask, but does Louie know?"

"Yes." Tears slid down my cheeks. "Everything."

She gave me a long, penetrating look. "Do you know who'd want to
cause you trouble?"

I shook my head, but offhand I could think of at least eight prime sus-
pects, all drawn from the Wentworth and Saylor clans. Although it could
have been a disgruntled diner from the Green Parrot, or one of my former "friends." Still, I couldn't imagine any of them driving down to
Mobile Bay and putting the clippings in my mother-in-law's mailbox.

She leaned forward, smoke curling above her head. "Did you really
kidnap those children?"

I began in a halting voice to tell her the story. When I finished, she
blew a smoke ring and said, "You know, I remember it vaguely. A young
mother was caught with her baby on the roof of her car. I was actually in
Point Minette that whole fall—it was seventy-two, right? I was going to a
chiropractor. It's such a sweet town, isn't it? I must have passed by that

boardinghouse a hundred times. Did you know it's been turned into a bed and breakfast? The old woman sold it to a man from Charleston, and he's fixed it up. Just a darling place. I never dreamed—"

She paused and I finished the sentence. "Dreamed you'd end up with a criminal daughter-in-law? I'm so sorry. I should have told you myself. You must be disgusted."

"No, no. You didn't let me go on. I was *going* to say that I never dreamed our paths would cross. You know me, I'm partial to damaged women. I take them in."

I did know that. Shelby DeChavannes and Renata had been living with Honora for the past month. Whenever Louie drove to Point Clear to fetch his daughter, he went alone, and my imagination had gotten the best of me. Not that I had any proof. It was just a feeling. I looked up at Honora and said, "I'm probably overstepping myself here. And I know it's none of my business, but I've got to know something."

"Yes?" She leaned forward, brown eyes alert. Smoke drifted over her head in a comma.

I folded my hands and squeezed them, hard. This wasn't going to be easy. I was definitely prying, and my mother-in-law wouldn't appreciate it. "Does Shelby still love my husband? Does she want him back?"

She looked startled. She stubbed out her cigarette, then lit another.

"I'm sorry," I said. "I shouldn't have asked." Calm *down,* I told myself. Hadn't she just said that she was drawn to damaged women? With Aunt Clancy, it was cats. And my mother-in-law also had an enormous collection of designer handbags. Violet had once said there was a fine line separating collectors from compulsives. I myself walked that line, because I shared the handbag fetish, and Louie was spoiling me with outrageously expensive shoes. When my feet began to swell, Louie would just take me down to Maison-Blanche and buy me more in larger sizes.

"Nonsense. You have every right to know." Her mouth slanted downward. "My son can be such a naughty boy—just like his father. So when Shelby asked if she and Renata could stay with me, I was happy to oblige. And it was a good thing, because Shelby has been suffering from a terrible depression. But . . . can I speak candidly?"

I nodded.

"When I first met you, I hadn't the foggiest notion about your earlier . . . escapades. And even though I liked you very much, I thought you were probably an opportunistic little piece of fluff who'd snagged my son. Louie can be quite dense when it comes to women. I honestly thought—oh, it doesn't matter what I thought. Right at the time you came into Louie's life, he and Shelby were on the verge of reconciling. He'd invited her to Jamaica, but Renata came down with a bad cold, and Shelby wouldn't leave her. And then Louie met you."

I flinched.

"He didn't tell you?"

I shook my head.

"I'm not surprised." She paused and blew another smoke ring. "Do you know what? I believe that it's time for Shelby to move on with her life. In fact, I know *just* the man for her. I'm a terrible plotter, but I *do* mean well. Never mind all that. I owe you an apology. I was too quick to judge you, and I'm sorry. You've got more spunk than Louie's other wives. Did you *really* break your ex's nose and knock him unconscious?"

"Yes. With frozen baby back ribs."

"Oh, dear. Well, from what you say, he had it coming to him." She smiled and lit another cigarette. "But you and I will get along splendidly."

"Yes, ma'am."

"Please, call me Honora." She rose from the sofa, walked over to the fireplace, and tossed the clippings onto the empty grate. Then she dropped her cigarette on the papers. "Now," she said. "May I see the rest of what you've done with the house?"

FROM THE *TIMES-PICAYUNE*

—May 21, 1979

Ms. Shelby Stevens DeChavannes and Randolph Filbert Van Dusen III were married on May 21, 1979, at two o'clock in the afternoon at the home of Mrs. Honora DeChavannes in Point Clear, Alabama. Reverend Dale Newbury officiated. Goldie Hawn served as matron of honor in absentia and James Caan served as best man in absentia. The bride's daughter, Miss Renata DeChavannes, served as flower girl.

Guests included Mrs. Honora DeChavannes of Point Clear, Alabama, and Pass Christian, Mississippi; Mr. and Mrs. Randolph Filbert Van

Dusen Jr. of Brentwood, California; Isabella D'Agostino-McGeehee of Beverly Hills, California, and Point Clear, Alabama; Senator and Mrs. James "Bubba" Bradent of Baton Rouge, Louisiana; Dr. and Mrs. Chaz Breaux; Dr. and Mrs. Martin Addison; T. S. Talmage; Beverly Shantrell; Dr. and Mrs. Jordan Theroux; Mrs. Vernon St. Clair, all of Point Clear, Alabama; Dr. and Mrs. James DeChavannes, of Pass Christian, Mississippi; Dr. and Mrs. Niles DeChavannes, of Gulfport, Mississippi; Miss Mary Agnes DeChavannes, of Pass Christian, Mississippi.

After a honeymoon in Tuscany, the couple will reside in Malibu, California, where the groom is an executive vice president at Van Dusen Films, Inc.

Clancy Jane & Violet

Violet Jones and George Abernathy
Invite you to their Wedding
on June Twenty-Third
Nineteen Hundred Seventy-Nine
at Seven o'clock in the evening
First Unitarian Chapel
Memphis, Tennessee
Reception following at Peabody Hotel

In lieu of gifts, please send a donation to
The American Psychiatric Foundation

Violet walked down the aisle wearing a white silk shantung pantsuit, culled from the bargain rack at Rich's Department Store. She reached up to adjust her floppy straw hat—a last-minute find at Goodwill Industries, complete with a rumpled grosgrain ribbon and old-fashioned veil. She and George had decided no bouquet, bridesmaids, or best man and no schmaltzy piano music. Looking over her shoulder, she nodded to a guy with long black hair, whose hand was poised over a rather elaborate PA system. He pushed a button, and Queen began to belt out "Crazy Little Thing Called Love."

A side door opened, and the groom stepped out, followed by the minister. Both men had chosen unorthodox clothing—George wore faded jeans and Earth shoes, the minister a black, floor-length cape. Violet strode toward them, stopping beside each pew for a little tête-à-tête with friends and family. A guy in a white intern's jacket kissed her cheek and handed her a long-stemmed rose. When she reached the DeChavannes's pew, Violet lifted the rose and, in the manner of a fairy godmother waving a wand, tapped Dr. DeChavannes on the head; then she hugged Bitsy, exclaiming over her cousin's frothy blue chiffon maternity dress. When she reached the front of the chapel, she gave the thumbs-up signal to Dorothy, Mack, and Earlene, then she smiled at her future in-laws. George's parents didn't respond. His father looked stonily ahead; his mother pressed both hands over her nose and mouth, her fingers forming a tent. She appeared to be either praying or hyperventilating.

Violet stopped beside her mother's pew. She made a fist and socked Tucker's arm, then grabbed Clancy Jane's hand. They walked to the altar and faced the minister. He opened *The Book of Common Prayer* and said, "Who's giving this chick away?"

"I am," Clancy Jane said, steering Violet toward George.

Violet reached into her pocket, pulled out a crumpled paper, held it aloft, and read an Edna St. Vincent Millay poem. George's turn was a little more lively, having elected to recite Carl Sandburg from memory. Instead of promising to love each other, they pledged to give each other room to grow, with "no ties that bind." The minister smiled and said, "You're hitched. Dig it?"

· · ·

Clancy Jane had wanted a room with a romantic view of the Mississippi River, but the window looked out onto a gravel roof and the other half of the Peabody Hotel. Tucker went down to the front desk and sweet-talked the clerk into switching them to a room just below the penthouse. Clancy Jane opened the draperies. The dark water appeared oily under the lit-up bridge. How did they change the burned-out bulbs? she wondered. The river made her think of that old song by Creedence Clearwater Revival. She pulled off her clothes, trying to cool off, and threw herself onto the king-size bed. Then she looked at Tucker. He was a pretty man, his dark hair cut short, in the armed-forces style. He wore a St. Christopher's medal around his neck. All the firemen did, he said. It would keep him safe.

He crossed the room and climbed on the bed, his right knee between her legs. His medal swung back and forth, brushing against her breasts. She tugged on his belt, pulling him closer. He moved on top of her. Proud Mary keep on rolling, she thought. Rolling down the river.

"I love how we fit," he said.

"Are you comparing me to the ill-fits in your life?" Clancy Jane traced her finger around his lips. "Short women whose little heads didn't quite reach your chin? Or tall ladies with real long necks, and you'd climb up on them like a fly crawling on a calla lily?"

"You're an original, Clancy Jane."

"Do you know how much I love you?"

"Yes" he said. "But keep on telling me."

Bitsy

The clock radio clicked on, and the room filled with Jimmy Buffett's voice. He was singing "Changes in Latitudes, Changes in Attitudes." Keeping my eyes closed, I began to sing, mixing up the lyrics, changing latitudes to lassitude. The baby kicked, as if lodging a protest. "I'm sorry, darling. Your mama can't carry a tune," I whispered. Then I slid my leg over to Louie's side of the bed, finding nothing but cold linen. *This is a sign*, I thought. *Empty bed, empty heart. He is leaving me. He is running off with a flat-bellied woman.* I suddenly flashed back to the scene in the alley behind Le Cordon Bleu in Point Minette.

I sat up, looked out the window. It was going to be another hot July afternoon in New Orleans, one hundred degrees, no rain in the forecast. Last week, during the sonogram, my doctor had pointed to the screen. "The fetus is in breech position, too late for him to turn."

"Him?"

"See? There's the penis." The doctor pointed. Then he'd moved the wand lower. "But over here, your placenta is too low. It's not a previa, so don't get alarmed, but it's attached very low on the uterine wall. Better get Louie mentally prepared for a C-section." Get *Louie* prepared?

From the kitchen, he was calling me. "Bitsy, are you coming? We're going to be late."

"One second!" I threw back the covers and climbed out of bed. I didn't want to be late for Honora's birthday party in Point Clear. I hurried in the bathroom and yanked a black maternity smock off a hanger, then flung it over my head. The dress smelled of perspiration and perfume—Robert Piaget's Bandit. Inside the maternity smock, the aromas were suffocating, and I began to panic. The more I struggled, the more tangled I became. With a desperate shove, I pushed my head through the opening. When I saw my reflection in the dresser mirror—the gargantuan belly, the navel pushed out like a valve on an inner tube—I grimaced. The dress was still bunched up around my neck, resembling a frilled Elizabethan collar, and my queen-size pantyhose were tight and glossy from the strain. I pulled the dress down, painfully mashing my breasts. My hair was carelessly braided down my back, and short strands had escaped, frizzing around my temples. In disgust, I flipped one hand at the mirror, then reached along my back, groping for the zipper. I grabbed it, sawed it up and down, wincing as the zipper rasped over bare skin.

Louie stepped into the bedroom and I gestured to the back of my neck. "Sweetie, can you zip me?"

Our eyes met in the mirror. "It's going to be hot this evening," he said, giving my long-sleeved dress a doubtful look. "Can't you wear something cooler?"

"No." I shrugged. "After this baby is born, I'm going to burn this dress."

"Oh, Bitsy." He squeezed me. "It's just one afternoon. You'll get through it."

● ● ●

The hummingbird thermometer on Honora's patio registered ninety-one degrees. As we stepped around the swimming pool, I saw a blonde in a frilly green dress sitting on the diving board, flicking cigarette ashes into the water. Her long hair was artfully streaked several shades of blond, and was tossed back over her shoulders.

"Who is she?" I whispered.

"Mrs. Dickie Boy McGeehee."

"That name sounds so familiar. Didn't she send us a silver tureen when we got married?"

"If she did, it was probably one of Honora's. Mrs. McGeehee lives in one of Mother's bedrooms."

"Why haven't I met her?" I asked.

"Darling!" The blonde waved at Louie, then climbed off the diving board, showing a flash of thigh. "Come over here and give me a kiss. I haven't seen you in ages."

We walked around the pool, toward the deep end. The blonde opened her arms wide, and Louie stepped into them. She kissed his cheek, leaving behind a pink smudge. Louie reached for my hand and said, "Isabella, have you met my wife?"

"No, I haven't had the pleasure," the woman said, smiling. "But I've heard about you, dear. All *good* things, of course. Aren't congratulations in order? I understand you're expecting another little DeChavannes? How utterly thrilling."

"Where are your Yorkies?" Louie asked.

"Honora made me shut them up in a room." Isabella turned to me. "Would you mind terribly if I borrowed your handsome hubby for a moment?"

Before I could reply, Isabella took Louie's hand and pulled him toward Honora's gazebo, which was nestled in the live oaks. Louie gave me a helpless look as he stepped inside. I lifted my braid off my neck, then eased into one of the wicker chairs. The cushion made a whooshing noise, like escaping gas, and I hoped Louie and the blonde hadn't heard. The afternoon sun was slanting over the azaleas, and the air was buzzing with midges. I remembered a time when I'd cultivated the sun. Violet and I would stretch out in the backyard on a quilt, with a bottle of homemade suntan lotion, a mixture of baby oil and iodine, which gave our skin a golden hue, even if it tinted our palms orange. In those days, my body was hard and lean; I never thought one second about growing old. "Age isn't ugly," Miss Gussie used to say, with a shrug. "It's just age."

The French doors opened, and Honora poked out her head. She looked elegant in a sleeveless beige linen dress with a double strand of pearls around her neck. "Bitsy, you're going to flambé out here. Come on inside and have some birthday cake. I'm afraid I've already blown out the candles."

Through the French doors, I could see into the dining room. In the center of the polished rosewood table was a floral arrangement—bells of Ireland and wild sea grasses. On the far end was a massive sheet cake, decorated like a nine-hole golf course, with miniature tees, fairways, and greens. Honora was an enthusiastic golfer, and a present to herself stood off to the side—a new set of Patty Berg clubs nestled in a Louis Vuitton golf bag.

I rose from the chair, bracing my stomach with one hand, casting a furtive glance toward the gazebo. "Some woman has shanghaied Louie," I complained.

"Oh, that's just Isabella D'Agostino." Honora squinted. "Dickie Boy McGeehee's widow? I've mentioned her haven't I?"

"How did her husband die?"

"It was his liver. Dickie Boy's drinking was legendary—and that's saying a lot. He didn't look terminal till the end. But then, he'd never looked healthy. Anyway, at the funeral, Isabella wanted a closed casket, but Dickie Boy's mama had a fit. So they laid him out on pale gold satin, which clashed horribly with the jaundice. But he left Isabella with a net worth over two hundred million."

Out in the gazebo, Isabella laughed at something Louie was saying. She crossed her legs, and the green dress rode up past her knees. Despite her beauty, she was way too old for my husband. I started to relax. Then Honora said something that sent my pulse racing.

"I love her to death, but don't let Louie linger with her," Honora said, then she guided me into the house. Gifts were piled up on the sideboard. Louie's uncles—the DeChavannes males— were holding court around the punch bowl, flirting with Honora's friends from Point Clear. Uncle James was a leading neurologist on the Gulf Coast, and he had aged gracefully, the way brunet men so often do—a light misting of gray around the temples. Uncle Nigel, known to everyone as "Boo," was a general practitioner. He was recovering from a face lift, and his eyes were still a little swollen and slanted like a Chinaman's, but the bruises had faded. His face looked taut and shiny.

To the women, who begged to see his scars, he complained, "Had to get off my Coumadin before the surgeon would touch me." Honora's friend Desirée, in spiked heels and a black dress, pranced into the living room. "Welcome!" Honora cried. "I thought you were still in Scotland."

"And miss your party?" cried Desirée. "Lord, I saw enough sheep to last me a lifetime."

"Did you meet any titled chaps?" asked Uncle James.

"No, but I saw a Kerry blue terrier with undescended testicles."

"Did you bring him back?" asked Boo, laughing.

"Honey, I've already got one man without balls. Do I need another?"

•   •   •

At twilight, I stepped out into the backyard, looking for Louie, and spotted him at the edge of the pool, sitting on a blue lounge chair, directly opposite Isabella. Their heads were inclined, their knees touching. They looked up, saw me approaching, and broke apart. I suddenly thought about when Violet had read Casanova's memoirs—twelve volumes of relentless womanizing. Now I wondered where I could find a copy so I could read it myself.

On the drive home, I aimed the air-conditioning vent between my legs. "What was going on out there?"

"Where?" Louie's forehead wrinkled.

"Don't play dumb. With you and that actress. Y'all were a little too cozy."

"You're getting upset for no reason, and it's not good for the baby." Louie lifted one hand from the steering wheel and rubbed the back of his neck. "It's supposed to rain next week. Maybe it'll cool things off."

That night, I lay next to Louie, watching a *National Geographic* rerun. It was soothing to see Jane Goodall cavort with her chimpanzees. Somehow Jane had found love in the wilds of Africa. And she was especially close to her mother. When the show ended, I climbed rather gracelessly from the bed, trying my best not to disturb Louie, and lumbered into the kitchen. My feet were painfully swollen, and I had to creep slowly. I opened the French doors and stepped out onto the patio, past the swimming pool, into the garden. The air was still uncomfortably warm, but the grass felt cool and damp against my toes. I squatted down, legs splayed rather awkwardly, and began to pull weeds.

I worked until dawn, and I was still working when Louie, leaving for the hospital, poked his head out the back door.

"You been up all night?" he asked, jingling his car keys.

I nodded, then flashed a look that said *I can't help this. Please don't harass me.*

"You look a little puffy. You feeling all right?"

"I'm fine, Louie. I'm just having trouble sleeping."

"Then let me drive you to the beach tonight. I'll make you a pot of gumbo."

"And you'll stay the whole weekend?"

"I'll need to make hospital rounds, but that's no problem. I'll just drive back and forth."

During the sticky hot, interminable morning, I thumbed through my dictionary, then stretched out on the living-room sofa and pondered the conundrum of love. An answer eluded me the way sleep had.

At midday I got dressed and drove the long way to my doctor's office. When I checked in at the desk, the nurse waved me into the hall. I stepped on the scales, and they rattled. The nurse clicked her tongue with disapproval. "You've gained five pounds in one week!"

"That's impossible. I haven't eaten anything but salads."

"Scales say otherwise, dear."

The nurse led me into a windowless room with fuchsia wallpaper. It was a hideous shade, the color of mashed fruit. I could almost hear the buzz and hum of flies. The nurse wrapped a blood pressure cuff around my arm. The bulb made a whooshing sound, and my arm began to ache. The nurse's thin eyebrows shot up.

"Your pressure is way too high. We don't need it going up any more," she said in a stern voice.

"Well, *I* didn't do it," I snapped. True, I might have eaten a little cheesecake, but my vital signs were totally beyond my control.

"Slip off your panties, dear, and climb up on the table," said the nurse. "Dr. Savat is going to be so upset."

The nurse stepped into the hall and shut the door behind her. The overhead fluorescent light crackled. I swayed, then reached out and grabbed the table, steadying myself. *Slip off your panties, dear.* Those words suddenly struck me as obscene. *Not unless you take yours off first.* The raspberry walls were making me wild and reckless. Any minute now the doctor would come into the room and make small talk while he squirted ice-cold jelly onto my stomach. Then he would push the ultrasound's wand over my abdomen. I'd love to tell him the truth about having babies. It *hurt* to have a watermelon inside your body. I thought of that Led Zeppelin song, the big-legged woman, the juice running down her legs.

Still holding on to the table, I shut my eyes, tried to ignore the nausea. Pink dots swirled behind my lids. I needed rest, not another damn ultrasound in this hideous room with its pink and sour and boiling hot walls. I felt an urgent need to see Louie, to put my head on his chest. Maybe we could drive down to the beach right now. I lurched toward the door. When I reached the Mercedes, I cranked the engine. The air conditioner came on, giving off a musty smell, with the hint of sun and new leather. As I drove across town, the nausea vanished, and I began to crave a sirloin steak salad with crumbled bleu cheese. Or fried shrimp with lots of cocktail sauce. I turned off St. Charles, toward Louie and his beautifully decorated office—he'd given me carte blanche, and I'd gone out of my way not to choose any color associated with heart surgery—red might have scared off the patients. Hadn't Dr. Savat's wife more sense than to choose womb-colored paint for his examining rooms?

Suddenly the road seesawed, and instead of four lanes of traffic I saw eight. As I turned into the parking lot at Oschner, I rolled over a curb. The tires shuddered, and the baby beat its little fists in protest. I found the medical arts building and circled it twice. I parked the Mercedes in the shade of a magnolia, its branches studded with blossoms, each one the size of a dinner plate. "Lunch," I thought, feeling those fresh five pounds dragging behind me.

Heaving myself out of the front seat, my legs splayed like an old woman's, I stood up, weaving slightly. It was difficult to move my wide, bloated feet, but I shuffled forward, tilted backward like a penguin. Several pedestrians stepped aside to let me pass. When I entered the air-conditioned Medical Arts building, my vision narrowed. Red spots churned in the air. I felt light-headed, and I placed one chubby hand against the wall and waited for the dizziness to pass. After a minute my eyes adjusted to the dim light, and I headed down the corridor with its swimmy green walls. What wife had picked *that* color? I stumbled ever so slightly—not a stagger but more of a dance, the pregnant woman's dance. The elevator was out of order, but Louie's office was on the second floor, so I climbed a flight of wide stairs. When I reached the landing, I was breathless and dripping wet. I staggered into a windowless corridor. This would shock the hell out of Louie, I thought. Since I'd gotten pregnant, I'd rarely stopped by his office. I entered a door marked PRIVATE and stepped into the hall.

I heard Louie's laughter before I saw him, heard the stereo system that I'd artfully hidden in his bookcase tuned to an FM station playing an old Tina Turner song. I knew Louie's laugh as intimately as I knew his smell. Then I heard a feminine twitter, high-pitched and rhythmical, like a laying hen. I wanted to stop and turn around, but the weight of my body propelled me forward, around the corner, into Louie's office, where a frizzy-haired blonde wearing a short white nursing uniform sat on his desk, her long, lithe legs crossed and swinging. She seemed full of herself, in love with herself. On Louie's desk—carved mahogany from an outrageously expensive shop on Royal Street—was a Pepsi can and a half-eaten muffuletta sandwich, resting on a sheet of waxed paper that was scattered with olives and capers. Lipstick on the bread, lipstick on the Pepsi can. But nothing on Louie's collar. The girl's head turned, the laughter still bubbling from her lips—a bow-shaped little-girl mouth with ice-pink lipstick. Louie was laughing and smiling, too. Then his eyes swept past the girl, and he saw me. He stood abruptly, his chair rolling behind him, bumping into the bookcase. The girl sat straight up, back arched, and tossed her hair.

"Sweetie," Louie's voice was curved, a question mark hanging in the air. The girl turned to face him, eyebrows raised expectantly, as if she wasn't certain whom he was addressing.

"I came to take you to lunch," I said, pushing back my sweaty hair. "But it looks as if you've already eaten."

"Have a pickle," said the girl, her eyes going to my stomach. "Don't pregnant women crave pickles?"

A drop of sweat ran down into my eyes, and I wiped it away. The blonde made no effort to move. Her voluptuous hips were planted on a stack of charts. I put my hands somewhere in the vicinity of my own hips and tipped my pelvis forward. I was one heartbeat away from asking this blonde to leave; but all of a sudden I felt sick. I fought an urge to spit on the floor or maybe on this blond hussy. It was a short distance from the doctor's desk to his lap; once she was in his lap, she was on her way to his bed.

I saw my future with a cruel clarity. In six years I would be fattened up by another pregnancy or maybe one too many steak salads. The portly wife, presiding over parties, passing a tray of cheese straws, making excuses to the other wives, "I didn't mean to puff up like this," I'd say. Yes, I could see myself slipping into a position of vulnerability, looking the other way, waiting for Louie to grow up and stop fucking other women.

"I'm Bitsy DeChavannes," I told the woman. "And you are . . ."

Before the woman could answer, Louie said, "This is Tiki. She's just filling in."

"Tiki the temp. As in time and temp?" I forced out each word. Push harder, the doctor would say before too long. Go ahead, rip yourself wide open.

"We were going over some charts." Louie flicked one hand at his desk. "They need my signatures."

"You can't do that yourself?" I asked.

Louie's face reddened. It took a lot for this man to blush. Extreme anger or embarrassment, hot tubs, sunburn, physical exertion, too much wine—and fear. He was growing ruddier by the second, and I stared him down, waiting for him to speak. From the stereo, Tina Turner eloquently asked "What's love got to do with it?" She was answered by three million years of biology. "Breed," it whispered. "Perpetuate the species, pass on your DNA."

The blonde tossed her head and stared straight into my eyes. "Can I get you anything in particular? A glass of water? Sandwich?"

"All I want," I said, facing the girl, "is for you to get your ass off my husband's desk."

Louie glanced nervously at the blonde. "The conference is over, Tiki."

Conference? I thought.

Tiki uncrossed her legs. Then she scooted off the desk with excruciating slowness, making her white skirt ride up higher, then without looking at me she pranced to the door, leaving a wake of Emeraude. Louie wouldn't approve. The smell was making me woozy, and I pushed loose strands of hair away from my face. My hand felt heavy and smelled of soil. Women on his desk, women with pretty legs, women who smell good enough to eat. After Tiki's footsteps faded down the hall, Louie turned to me. "She's only temporary."

"Like a twenty-four-hour virus, I hope," I replied, not bothering to hide the venom. I leaned toward his desk, picked up part of the muffuletta. "You shared this with her?"

His chin jutted forward and his lips protruded, his most sullen expression. His eyes darted back to his desk. "Good God, Bitsy. It's just food. We didn't *plan* it or anything. She just stopped by to ask about the charts, and she was fixing to eat lunch, and she asked me if I wanted some."

"Some . . . *what*?" I was still holding the sandwich.

"She's harmless." Louie lifted his shoulders.

"Like a sand shark?" I dropped the sandwich, scattering Genoa salami onto his desk.

"Don't worry. She won't be here next week."

"No, but someone just like her will."

His forehead puckered. "I didn't do anything. Why do you persist in staying upset all the time? Never mind, it's your *hormones*."

"No, it's you."

"Just go home and try to calm down."

A bearded man with round eyeglasses passed by Louie's office. A stethoscope was coiled around his neck. I couldn't recall his name, but I knew he was Louie's new partner—he was supposed to be on call every other weekend. So far Louie's workload hadn't lessened.

"Bitsy, you look haggard," Louie said. "Why don't you go home and put your feet up? I'd drive you home, but I've got patients scheduled."

"Can't your partner see them?"

"He's got his own patients." He picked up a strand of lettuce from the desktop, holding it aloft. *One of these days*, I thought, *it will be a pubic hair.*

"Fine. I'll leave." I stepped out into the hall.

"Get some rest," he called after me. "I'll see you tonight. Then we'll go to the beach, okay?"

I turned. "I might just go by myself."

"I wish you'd wait," he said. "But I know how you are."

"No, you don't," I said, shocked that he'd even consider letting me drive all that way alone. I didn't want to go without him—didn't he know that?

"Call when you get there safely," he said.

Without bothering to respond, I spun around and walked down the hall. Thank God this pregnancy was portable. Otherwise, I'd have left it behind. Actually, most of the weight had settled *in* my behind. I waddled into the parking lot, climbed into the Mercedes, cranked up the air conditioner, turned up the radio. The Doobie Brothers were singing "What a Fool Believes." As the chilly air blew around my face, I felt like a fool, but I wasn't sure what to believe anymore.

I drove on old Highway 90, and when I passed through Slidell, I remembered that Jayne Mansfield had died on this road, and even though she'd been buried elsewhere, beneath a heart-shaped headstone, her ghost might still be lingering in the kudzu. I didn't wish to join her, so I drove below the speed limit, ignoring the impatient motorists who honked then zoomed around me.

The minute I pulled up to our shingled white cottage, with its peaked, witch-hat roof, I knew I'd made a mistake. My feet were swelling, and my head ached. I felt a strange pounding in my ears, and I wondered if it meant my blood pressure was rising. I turned the car around and drove back to New Orleans, feeling like Hera coming down the mountain, sniffing Zeus's trail.

Several hours later, I pulled up in front of my house and parked next to Louie's black Jaguar. I rubbed my eyes. The pink dots had returned. I got out of my car and waved to our next-door neighbor, Mr. Harkreader, who was watering his potted ferns. From my backyard, I heard splashing, and I walked toward the sound. It was early evening, but the air felt heavy and hot. I just wanted to lie down with a cold rag over my eyes. When I reached the patio I glanced at the pool. A long-limbed naked woman was swimming underwater, blond hair fanning behind her, a stream of bubbles curving over her head. Sirens, I thought, dumbstruck. Sirens in the pool, sirens below sea level. Her head shot out of the water, and I recognized the face. It was Tiki, the hussy I'd seen on my husband's desk. Louie stood beside the wrought-iron bar, wearing blue swim trunks. Ice cubes rattled as he stirred a pitcher with a long silver spoon. A pile of fresh mint leaves lay stacked on the bar. How dare he make that home wrecker a julep with my mint.

The pool sweep sent up a jet of water, pattering on Tiki's bleached head. I stood with my mouth open, breathing in chlorine, bourbon, mint, and coconut suntan oil. My Chanel pocketbook, a gift from Honora, hit the brick pavers, spilling out lipstick, Rolaids, keys. Louie, reaching for a mint sprig, saw me and dropped the pitcher. The crystal exploded on the pavers. The girl was in the center of the pool, treading water.

"Bitsy?" Louie said in a strangled voice. His eyes rounded in alarm. "Honey, listen. This isn't what you think. She doesn't mean a thing," he said, waving one hand at the girl. "Honey, wait!"

Weight broke the bridge down, my mother used to say. I felt a cramp low in my spine and my uterus tightened. I staggered back to the walkway and hurried around the house. The pink dots caused me to walk into a banana tree. The leaves made a whuffling noise and I clawed my way free. Again, pain knotted in my back and stomach. I somehow made it to the driveway, but halfway to my car, I fell. The ground felt surprisingly hard and I threw out both hands, trying to protect my baby. From a long way away I heard Mr. Harkreader yell. Then he was looming above me, shouting my name.

"My baby." I clutched his arm. "Don't let anything happen to my baby."

Mr. Harkreader's head moved, and I saw Louie hobbling over to me. Satisfaction. That's what I felt when I saw that his right foot was pouring blood. I was glad he'd stepped on the broken glass. Louie's face was contorted, and it was impossible to know the source of his pain.

A TAPED MESSAGE TO ROSALYN CARTER

July 25, 1979

Dear Rosalyn,

I am writing to tell you that my daughter lost her baby after she found a naked woman in her swimming pool. My son drove me down to New Orleans, but by the time we arrived, the doctors had already done an emergency C-section and Bitsy was still in the recovery room. Louie was pacing in the hall, his shirt untucked, tears streaming down his face. On his foot was a bloody bandage. I couldn't feature what had happened. Then his mother took me aside and explained about the swimming pool lady. Then she said that Bitsy had been sick with swelling and high blood pressure. And her womb split wide open and cut off the baby's air supply. If you ask me, it wasn't blood pressure that brought this on, it was my son-in-law's philandering. I wouldn't be surprised if he was a Republican. This is not to say that all conservative men are liars and infidels, or that they don't have the People's interests at heart. My son-in-law is probably a Republican because he's filthy rich and wants tax cuts. Come to think of it, he wants too damn much. I wanted to slap him down but he just looked too distraught.

I was wondering if you could write to my daughter, just to cheer her up and maybe give her some pointers about men. The President is just crazy about you, I can tell. So you must have some secrets. I've enclosed my daughter's address in New Orleans. Don't worry if she doesn't write back. She's out of her head with misery, and her husband has taken her to recuperate at the beach and I'm taking the nursery apart.

Yours truly,
Dorothy McDougal

A NOTE FROM HONORA DECHAVANNES

August 11, 1979

Dear Bitsy,

I'm sitting on your front porch, trying to decide if I should ring your doorbell and possibly disturb your rest, or if I should just leave a note. So here I am, writing on the back of a Rib House menu. My dear girl, I know your heart is breaking, and you're facing difficult questions about your marriage, but I felt the urgent need to offer you a little advice about wayward husbands.

Long ago, my friend Desirée—she's a doctor's wife, too—made up a Rule of Three. One affair is a fluke. Two might be wild oats or even misadventures. But three means a pattern is forming. You are probably too stunned to make decisions right now, but it behooves you to decide if you love him enough to forgive his transgressions—and look the other way when his eye wanders, as it surely will. Living with an unfaithful man takes a toll. It hardens the heart. You might consider building a life of your own—and I still recommend Sister's shop in the Quarter. If you are "out in the world," which is filled with all sorts of gorgeous people, you will keep your sanity.

Now for the hard part: If you decide to leave, then go. Do not look back. You'll need distance, and lots of it. Otherwise he will try his best to squirm back into your good graces, and be forewarned, he has many tricks at his disposal. If you decide to stay, then be prepared. Finding him in flagrante will be a way of life. Whatever you decide, I want you to know that I am here for you. I'm on your side. When you're feeling stronger, I do wish you'd come up to visit. I'll teach you to play bridge—and we'll have a long talk about my son.

All my love,
Honora

A NOTE FROM BITSY

September 19, 1979

Dear Violet,

When I woke up from the anesthesia, I saw Louie's dark head pressed into the hospital mattress. His shoulders convulsed, causing the IV bottle above my head to sway back and forth. I knew then I'd lost the baby. Dorothy was sitting across the room, her head bent over a needlepoint canvas. Come home with me, she kept saying. Then she told me that the whole time I'd been on bed rest, Louie had been dillydallying with Shelby—to what extent, no one knew. My mother threw down her needlepoint and lit into him. She said: Don't you pee on my head and tell me the roof is leaking.

She couldn't understand how I could think about returning to him after I'd caught him with a naked woman and then miscarried. But I don't believe the shock brought on the labor; I am to blame for not taking care of myself. Dorothy said, don't waste your life on this man. Come back home with me. I know you love him, but he will do it again. His mother sort of said the same thing.

I asked the nurse for a dictionary and I turned to the Fs and looked up the definition of forgiveness. I'd ached for it after I lost Jennifer. In those days I had a childlike belief that atonement would lead to absolution. But it didn't. Then it occurred to me that if I expected to be forgiven, then I must forgive.
    Love,
    Bitsy

A NOTE FROM VIOLET

9/25/79

Louie:
    Yes, I know she's back. Just remember that if you give in to your every desire, then you will be left with nothing of value.
    My nickel,
    Violet

Part 6

A TAPED MESSAGE TO NANCY REAGAN

February 25, 1981

Dear Nancy,

That sure was a nice suit your husband wore to the Inauguration. Yours wasn't half bad, either. I have been reading all about you at the beauty shop, and it's a relief to have a First Lady who doesn't get along with her own children. I know you've been criticized for being too close to Ron, but I admire what you've done. Children leave, but husbands are supposed to stick with you. And they generally won't if you put the kids first. That was a lesson I learned too late.

Since you and I have family strife in common, I was hoping we could console each other with letters. Oh, and by the way—where do you get those cute little suits? I think they'd "suit" me. Ha ha.

Regards,
Dorothy McDougal

A LETTER FROM BITSY

800 Pytrania Avenue
New Orleans, Louisiana

March 1, 1981

Dear Violet,

Louie has decided to take a leave of absence from his medical practice. He rented a stone house in England, in a village called Stow-on-the-Wold. The house comes with a gardener, housekeeper, and several acres full of sheep. We'll be leaving the country on July 7. But first we're flying to Tennessee to spend a few days with Dorothy. I would love to see you before I go, but I know your schedule is chaotic.

You won't believe this, but I myself am a working woman. I took a job with Honora's friend, Sister—she's the designer I told you about—and we've been refurbishing several gorgeous old homes off St. Charles. Sister's a talented woman, and I'm lucky to be her assistant, even if her work habits rival Louie's—Sister puts in eighteen-hour days. We've racked up scads of frequent flier miles going back and forth to Atlanta. I've been so busy that I put the renovation of my house on hiatus. Actually, I'm relieved. It was getting harder and harder to work up any enthusiasm over Bombé chests and granite countertops. These things are lovely, no doubt, but in the end, they're just stuff. When you read this, you'll probably fire off one of your famously cryptic, one-line letters saying I'm depressed. But don't. I'm not. I'm just getting philosophical in my old age.

    Your evolving cousin,

    Bitsy

Jennifer Wentworth

Jennifer came home from Grandparents Day at Crystal Falls Elementary School and threw herself on Miss Betty's floral chintz sofa, wailing that she was the only child in Crystal Falls who didn't have a family. She raised her head and glared at Grandmother. "You forgot me!" she growled.

"I thought it was *next* week," said Miss Betty, wringing her hands.

"It was today," yelled Jennifer, pushing away from the sofa. "I'm through with you. I want to see my other grandmother *this instant!*"

"That's not a good idea," said Miss Betty.

"It is too." Jennifer crossed her arms and glared.

Miss Betty sighed, opened a chest, and pulled out a thick pile of newspapers. She set them in front of the child. The papers were curled and yellow, and the dust made Jennifer sneeze, but she didn't let this deter her from reading all the juicy stuff. On the top paper, the headline blared: DERANGED HOUSEWIFE JUMPS OFF DIME STORE'S ROOF. A smaller headline read: DEATH AVERTED BY FLOODED STREET. Underneath was a grainy black-and-white picture of Dorothy being carried away on a stretcher, the paramedics wading through surging water. Her hair was wild, and she appeared to be screaming. Behind her was the courthouse square, flooded by Town Creek.

The other papers weren't about Dorothy, they were about Jennifer's mother. Jennifer traced her finger under each word, keenly aware of Miss Betty's watchful gaze. Her grandmother was always saying that it was a blessing that Jennifer hadn't grown up around *those people*. It was a godsend that the child didn't remember her atrocious babyhood. Yet her grandmother seemed hell-bent on re-creating it for her. "She left your father for dead," Miss Betty cried, thumping one of the newspapers. "She put you on the roof of a car and then drove off. You came within an inch of dying."

Miss Betty held up two fingers, a tiny space between them. "Do you still wish to see Dorothy?"

"Yes!" Jennifer said, then screamed.

"Oh, all right." Miss Betty stiffened. "I've no idea what brought this on. Surely not my absence at Grandparents Day. Did you know that Dorothy never really liked Bitsy? She preferred Mack. So why on earth would she like *you*?"

"Because she does!"

Miss Betty yelled for Papa Chick and told him to hurry up and take Jennifer over to the crazy house—her pet name for 214 Dixie Avenue.

"Come on, sugar." Papa Chick stood in the doorway and waved his arm.

Jennifer grabbed the top newspaper from the stack and shoved it under her shirt. "I'm ready," she called in a sweet voice. "I'll be right there."

Later, when she showed the paper to Dorothy, all her grandmother would say was, "The baby back ribs were frozen, not barbecued—at least not yet. It must've been your daddy who got that rumor started."

After this visit Jennifer whined to visit the crazy house. She was doing it to annoy her paternal grandmother. In fact, she preferred the luxury of the elder Wentworths' home on Jefferson, with its gated driveway and manicured lawn that stretched the length of one city block. There she could do what she pleased, and the maids gave her anything she wanted. "Poor little motherless child," they'd say when Jennifer passed through the room. She was fatherless, too, but everyone seemed to overlook that. Her daddy was preoccupied with his new family: His third wife, Regina, had recently given birth to a cone-headed daughter.

Two weekends a month, Chick drove her three blocks to her daddy's house, a Victorian with a picket fence around it. In the spring, red tulips flopped through the slats. There was a pool in the backyard, surrounded by another fence, and off to the side stood an elaborate swing set—this belonged to Jennifer's half-sister, Millicent Ann, who was only a month old. On a visiting Saturday, when Jennifer stepped into the house, the air smelled of dirty diapers and Lysol, and her stepmother was yelling at her house-keepers. "I'm having a formal dinner party in *five hours*," Regina shrieked from the head of the stairs, "and I want this dawdling to stop. Open some windows, make this house smell like a garden."

Jennifer was standing in the marble entry hall, holding a pink Barbie suitcase. She loved it when the maids poked fun at Regina, who hadn't lost the weight she'd gained during her pregnancy. Most of it had collected in her hips and thighs. They called her "Miss Regina" to her face, but when she was out of earshot, she was dubbed "Big Mama Woo Woo."

Jennifer set down her suitcase and followed the women into the dining room. They let her help polish the silver and set it out in precise patterns on the polished table. Jennifer had learned party planning at Miss Betty's knee, and she loved setting out the crystal salt dishes with teeny tiny doll-size spoons beside each. She was just placing the last one when Regina swooped into the dining room, her cheeks flushed.

"When did *you* get here, Jennifer? Oh, never mind. Just run on outside and play. I can't think with you standing here!" Regina rubbed her temples.

Jennifer snatched up her Barbie suitcase and hurried out to the back porch, one of those old-fashioned ones, deep enough to hold an entire set of wicker furniture, including a glider. She unzipped the suitcase, took out her paper dolls, and arranged them beneath the glider. From inside the house, she heard her half-sister's screech, followed by footsteps. Jennifer wanted to love her new sister, but her daddy and Regina were always slobbering over it. She abandoned her dolls and wandered into the kitchen. The caterers had started to arrive. Outside, the wind began blowing, sucking up Jennifer's play pretties, blowing them off the porch toward the swimming pool. Regina ran into the kitchen, over to the door. "I just pray it's not going to storm—" She broke off, staring at the paper dolls, whirling in the air. She turned, her eyes narrowed, and grabbed Jennifer's hand.

"How did your dollies get out there?" Regina's forehead wrinkled into a hard V. Her fingers tightened, the nails dug into Jennifer's flesh. "Just *look* at this! What will my guests think? Don't you *ever* make a mess like this again." Regina shoved open the kitchen door and slung Jennifer onto the porch. "Get out there and clean up your mess. Do you hear me?"

"Yes, ma'am." Jennifer poked her thumb into her mouth.

"And get that dirty finger out of your mouth," Regina snarled. From upstairs, the baby began to wail. "Now look what you've done! Oh, you miserable little rat. I can't *wait* till your father gets home and sees what you've done."

The next day, when Jennifer returned to her grandparents' house, she rushed to find Miss Betty in the sunroom and rolled up her sleeves, pointing to the nail gashes. "Regina did this," Jennifer wailed. "I want my real mother. If you don't let me see her, I'm showing Dorothy these marks. And *she'll* take Regina to court."

Within ten days Miss Betty had made the arrangements for Jennifer to fly down to New Orleans.

Jennifer loved exploring the DeChavannes's house. When they weren't having parties, the dining room was dark and quiet, as if it was recovering from a long and difficult illness. But it was still a beautiful room, with the pale blue silk draperies, streaked with lemon, surrounding deep bay windows that looked out into banana trees, and the ornate wrought-iron fence in the distance. Upstairs, her mother had turned a small bedroom into a closet. It smelled of powder and expensive perfume. Jewelry hung from a pegboard, and wall-to-wall shelves were crammed with shoes and pocketbooks—the purses were gifts from Louie's mother. Jennifer sat on the floor, examining each bag while Bitsy described its features and events where it would be appropriate. What Jennifer especially loved to do was go to the racks, which were crammed with sparkly party dresses, and press her face into the fabric, breathing in her mother's smell.

Bitsy was an interior designer, and she worked two days a week with a famous woman called Sister. The famous woman had helped Bitsy dress up her dining room—the table was longer than Regina's, or Miss Betty's, for that matter, with sixteen chairs and a lovely organdy and lace cloth that skimmed the floor. Her mother had explained the different fabrics, urging Jennifer rub them between her fingers. When she grew up, she wanted to be a designer, too.

After that visit, when Jennifer returned to Crystal Falls, she spent more and more time with Dorothy. She craved the stillness of a summer evening on her grandmother's old porch, where the lilacs smelled like an old woman's neck, and the iced tea glasses didn't need coasters and none of the fabrics matched. She could spill blue fingernail polish on the floor or a cherry Coke and no one screamed or blanched. Jennifer spent many rainy mornings in Bitsy's old bed, listening to water pouring out of the overflowing gutters. She wondered if her mother had heard this, too. After breakfast, she would push a pen into her grandmother's hands and dictate letters to Bitsy, the way she'd seen her grandfather do at the bank. She wanted to know about her mother's parties, her favorite wines and floral arrangements, and if she'd ever thought of matching her dress to the tablecloth. In due time, Bitsy's answer would arrive, her handwriting difficult to read, and Dorothy would have to translate. Bitsy listed the food in haphazard order, mixing appetizers with dessert, the entrée with the soup.

Jennifer begged to visit New Orleans again, but the Wentworths, plotting to keep her in Tennessee, had enrolled Jennifer in ballet classes.

"I can take ballet in New Orleans," Jennifer argued.

"You just can't go, and that's *that*." Two spots of color flashed on Miss Betty's cheeks.

"I'm going to visit my mother. And *you* can't stop me."

"Let her go for a week, Betty," Chick said.

"Two weeks," the child pleaded.

"Ask your father," said Miss Betty. "You'll be seeing him this weekend."

At dinner with Regina and her daddy, Jennifer broached the subject of a New Orleans visit. "No, absolutely not," said Claude, shaking his head. "You can't ruin your grandmother's plans."

"Has your mother invited you?" Regina spoke up.

"No, but—"

"Then she doesn't want you," said Regina, spooning mashed potatoes into the baby's mouth.

"You don't want me, either," Jennifer cried. "You just want the baby."

"Don't be jealous," said Regina.

"I'm *not*."

"Lower you voice," hissed Claude. "The maids will hear."

"I hope they do!"

"If you say *one* more word, little lady," Claude warned, "I'm taking all your dolls to the Salvation Army."

"Take them," she said bravely, even though her voice shook.

"All right, fine." Claude pushed his chair back and strode out of the room.

"I didn't say one word, I said two," she called after him.

Her stepmother's fork was frozen in midair, a limp strand of asparagus hanging down.

"What are you staring at, Vagina?" Jennifer's eyes glittered.

Regina put down her fork and reached for her napkin to blot her pale mouth. "You may leave the table," she said.

Jennifer ignored her and reached for her glass of tea.

"Why, you *little* . . ." Regina's nostrils flared.

On her way out to the door, Jennifer leaned over Regina's plate and spit a mouthful of tea.

"I'm telling your father. He'll ground you for a year," Regina said in a choked voice.

"You aren't my boss," Jennifer said. Then, in a faint whisper, she added: "Vagina breath."

"Claude? *Claude?*" Regina cried. "Take her back to your mother's *right now!*"

"Go ahead, tattletale," said Jennifer. "But I'll be here long after you're gone."

Bitsy

Before we left for England, Louie called up Claude and asked if Jennifer could go with us. "We'll be there several months, but if you'd prefer, she can visit for two or three weeks."

"I'd prefer that she stay right here."

"England will be cultural for her," Louie said in his soothing, doctorly, I-know-what's-best voice. Claude shot back, "She's just a little girl, for God's sake. She can't cross the Atlantic without an escort."

"How old is she now? Nine? She can fly over with us," said Louie. "We'll put her in first class going back."

"Are you crazy?" Claude cried. "A house in Florida, I can understand, but England is too far away."

Louie began to protest, but I knew he was wasting his energy. For all the Wentworths' small-town grandeur and their wealth, they had never set foot outside the continental United States. Their idea of a luxury vacation was a week in Destin or Hilton Head, or a shopping trip to Atlanta.

In early July, Louie and I stopped off in Crystal Falls to visit my family. Aunt Clancy invited us for lunch, but Louie said it sounded like a girl thing and that he'd stay home and nap. So Dorothy and I climbed into her old station wagon and took off for Aunt Clancy's mountain. We drove past a sign that said Cat Crossing, then parked at the top of the hill. When we stepped out of the car, a dozen felines scattered through a grape arbor, past trees where wind chimes dangled from the branches. A black cat with three white paws ran over to me and rubbed against my legs.

"Damn thing probably has worms," Dorothy said, giving the animal a withering look.

White Adirondacks were lined up on the deck. The front door stood open, and as we passed to the kitchen, we saw furniture—floral sofas and chairs, a bookcase crammed with pretty rocks and albums. In the middle of the kitchen stood a long pine table, its legs intact. Clay pots, overflowing with herbs, were lined up in the sunny window. On top of the large refrigerator, a green-eyed cat sat on its haunches, watching.

Aunt Clancy was standing next to the sink with her hands on her hips, shaking her head at Violet's asymmetrical haircut—jaw-level on her right side, and three, maybe four inches shorter on the left. "What happened? Did you leave the beauty shop before the beautician was finished?"

"Quit harping," said Violet. "It's purposely uneven."

"Violet!" I cried. "I didn't know you were coming!"

"It was a surprise," said Aunt Clancy. "Ladies, please have a seat."

Violet yawned and said, "Where's Earlene?"

"Who knows?" Dorothy lifted her shoulders. "She *said* she was helping her mother hoe the garden. Isn't that funny? The 'ho' is hoeing. Personally, I think she's having an affair. How about you and George?" Dorothy pulled out a chair and sat down. "Is the honeymoon over?"

"Not yet. We're blissfully happy." Violet smiled into her cupped hand. "He's one in a million."

"What's your secret?" I asked, sitting down between my mother and Violet.

"I've no idea." She shrugged. "In fact, I try not to analyze it too much."

"I'm glad for you." I grabbed my cousin's hand and squeezed it.

"And proud," put in Dorothy. "My own niece, a future head shrinker. Now if I can just talk Jennifer into being a lawyer, we'll be set."

The ladies fell silent. Jennifer had been invited, of course, but Miss Betty had offered a feeble excuse. A vein throbbed in my right temple as I watched Aunt Clancy set down a blue glass platter full of tea sandwiches laid on the diagonal: cucumber, pimento cheese, smoked turkey, and egg salad. She went back to the counter and returned with more platters. Zucchini bread was piled up on a milk-glass dish. Arranged on a crystal plate were bakery petits fours, the pink icing dusted with sugared violets. EAT ME was written on each in white icing.

"So, how's the decorating business?" Aunt Clancy asked.

I laughed and told them how, since joining Sister's design firm, I was not only privy to the finest antiques in town, I got to hear the dirt on the créme de la créme of greater New Orleans. All our clients seemed to be politicians' and physicians' wives. I launched into a story about an influential allergist who'd given his wife an infection. I finished up by saying, "So the doctor brought home Flagyl."

Violet laughed and said, "Flagyl is specific to trichomonas."

"Is that what you get from eating raw pork?" asked Dorothy.

"No, it's a sexually transmitted disease," said Violet. "But go on, Bitsy. What happened?"

"Apparently the wife refused to take the pills until the allergist agreed to tell the truth. He insisted he'd been faithful, acting as if the infection had just occurred spontaneously—a virgin birth of germs, so to speak. And the wife said, 'Look, you can lie all you want, but I've got a fulminating infection, and I didn't get it from a toilet seat. You have been fooling around with pond scum.'"

"The moral of the story is this," said Violet. "If a man sticks his dick in a whore's butt, ask for antibiotics, not a confession. After all, you're not his priest. You're his wife."

Violet's language appeared to agitate Dorothy, and she interrupted with a comment about the rabbits in her garden and how they were eating the lettuce. Then she began complaining about the price of store-bought lettuce, and followed up with a long, chatty recipe for seven-layer salad. I smiled into my cupped hand. Listening to my mother was like stepping through the looking glass, trying to keep up with the White Rabbit.

Dorothy popped a captioned petit four obliviously into her mouth. Aunt Clancy set down an enormous brandy snifter filled with strawberries. She parked a bowl of whipped cream beside it. I knew that my aunt still avoided animal products, and I was deeply touched by this concession until Dorothy leaned over, her mouth full of cake, and whispered, "What if it's poisoned?"

The copper kettle began to howl, and Aunt Clancy walked over to the stove. "How is Louie?" she called. "Is he being good?"

"He better be," said Dorothy.

"And if he's not?" Violet lifted one dark eyebrow.

"Then he'll be singing in the Viennese Boy's Choir," said Dorothy. "I'll make sure of it."

"Isn't it Vienna Boy's Choir?" Violet smiled.

I was glad the conversation had gone off on a tangent. It was difficult for my family to understand why I'd taken Louie back. But all they had to do was listen to Billie Holiday. Billie understood the crushing weight of bad love. When Billie sang "Ain't Nobody's Business If I Do," she was telling the world to go fuck themselves.

While the tea steeped, Aunt Clancy set out mugs with Drink Me written on the sides in gold Magic Marker. She looked happy. I wondered if she and the fireman would get married or if they were content with the status quo.

"Claude ought to let Jennifer go with you guys," said Violet.

"He's not," said Aunt Clancy.

"Maybe he's scared for her to fly across the Atlantic," said Dorothy. "I know *I'd* be terrified."

"Well, she's nine years old," said Violet. "Nowadays the courts are letting children of divorce make up their own minds about where they live and with whom. And the Wentworths have done their best to prevent Jennifer from loving you, Bitsy. They keep seeing this tiny little light in her heart, maybe it's no bigger than a fingernail clipping, but they're scared it'll grow. So they try to annihilate it. But if you stamp out everything in a heart, what's left?"

We fell silent.

Finally Dorothy patted Violet's head, jostling the asymmetrical hairdo. "You may not know it, but you got your high I.Q. from me."

·　·　·

Our flight was scheduled to leave at 10:45 A.M., nonstop from Nashville to Chicago. According to the itinerary, we would spend most of the day languishing at O'Hare, then catch the 7:43 P.M. British Airways flight to Heathrow. When we boarded the plane in Nashville and found our seats in the first class cabin, the stewardess, a perky brunette with freckles scattered across her cheekbones, offered a choice of complimentary beverages. Louie interrupted her litany. "Do you have champagne?"

"Yes!" she said brightly. "Shall I bring two glasses?"

Louie nodded and kissed the tip of my nose.

"I love honeymooners," said the stewardess with a smile.

Louie gasped, then he sat bolt upright. His eyes were fixed on something in the aisle, past the stewardess.

"What's wrong, honey?" I grabbed his hand, then followed his gaze. Another stewardess was coming toward us, holding by the hand a little blond girl.

"Jennifer!" I sprang out of my seat, the top of my head grazing the overhead bin. As I stumbled into the aisle, I knocked into a gray-headed man with a leather briefcase. I profusely apologized, then squeezed past him. Jennifer blinked up at me, then took a cautious step forward.

"Your daughter's tickets," said the stewardess, handing me a packet. "I'll stow her suitcase."

Those tickets couldn't have weighed more than a few ounces, yet they rooted me to the floor of the plane. I had a million questions, but I didn't know where to start or whom to ask. The last thing I wanted to do was alarm Jennifer. Maybe someone in the family had abducted the child, then spirited her off to the airport.

"Is anything wrong?" The stewardess looked alarmed.

I shook my head and squatted beside my daughter. "Baby, how did you *get* here?"

"Daddy," Jennifer said.

"And you're going to England with me and Louie?"

She nodded again. The stewardess was starting to look desperate. I knew we were blocking traffic, but I couldn't move.

"Can we let these passengers by?" the stewardess asked, eyeing the congestion. People were backed up to the cockpit. I leaned over and kissed Jennifer's head, smelling shampoo, and led her up the aisle to where Louie was standing. I told my daughter to stay with Louie, that I'd be right back. He took Jennifer's hand and guided her to our seats. When I reached the front of the plane, another stewardess charged in front of me, blocking the doorway with her arms. Behind her, the metal steps plunged down to the pavement. I peered over the stewardess's shoulder to where I had spotted Claude on the edge of the tarmac, his hair blowing in the wind.

"I'm sorry," snapped the stewardess, "but you can't disembark."

I leaned across the woman's outstretched arm and lifted my hand into the air, feeling the wind push against my palm, and yelled, "Claude? Over here!"

When he heard my voice, his head swiveled around, straightened up, and he took a tentative step forward. A man with earmuffs shouted something into his face and pushed him back. Keeping his eyes on me, Claude spread his arms up to the sky and shrugged, as if to say *I can't explain it.*

· · ·

Once we were in the Cotswolds, Jennifer became sulky. "When's it gonna stop raining?" she asked Louie, dragging her finger through a half-eaten egg salad sandwich. We'd only been here a week.

He thought a moment, then shrugged. "How long is a piece of string?"

"What does string have to do with the rain?" She frowned.

"Pretty much everything," he said.

"I don't like it here," she said.

Louie lifted an ironic eyebrow and said, "Would you prefer a trip to Opryland next summer?"

"Of course she wouldn't. Don't be silly." I unfolded a map of Britain and began plotting day trips. The next day we took the train to London and took a taxi to Westminster Abbey, where we walked over the graves of the poets.

"It smells funny in here," Jennifer said, tugging on my hand. "Can we go? Please?"

Late that afternoon, we bought tickets for a sunset boat ride along the Thames. Most of the sightseers were seated, but Louie insisted we stand at the rail, our coat collars turned up against the biting gusts. He tried to point out landmarks, but Jennifer wasn't interested. She kept pulling my coat.

"Mother, what time is it in Crystal Falls?" she asked over and over.

"I don't know, baby," I replied each time.

"Guess," Jennifer finally said. "Just take a guess."

"It's eleven A.M.," Louis answered without even glancing at his watch. The boat was drifting past the House of Commons, where people were gathered on a terrace, drinking white wine in fluted glasses. One man raised his glass and saluted the boat. In the distance, Big Ben chimed. I counted six gongs. Which meant it *was* eleven A.M. in New Orleans.

"Isn't this fun?" I asked my daughter.

"It's cold," Jennifer said, jumping up and down. "Burr!"

The boat made a U-turn, and a gust of wind lashed my legs. Jennifer leaned against me. I unbuttoned my coat and pulled her inside.

"Better?" I asked.

· · ·

Away from New Orleans, Louie seemed untroubled, placidly buying seedlings at the nursery, waiting in line at the butcher's for a leg of lamb, chatting with the postmistress while buying stamps. "This is your element, isn't it?" I asked him one day—it wasn't a question, really, more of a wish. It was *my* element. I felt utterly at peace in England—and safe. But we were far, far away from Louie's world.

"Sure," he answered as he shook out the *Guardian*. "But I'd sell my soul for a cup of shrimp gumbo."

"I prefer cock-a-leeky," I said, eyeing him carefully.

"Darlin', I can't wait to show you the world."

"Don't you like it here?"

"Well, I like the concept of tea," Louie said after a moment.

"Didn't you love those pink and green meringues we bought yesterday in Bath?"

"And the funny thing is," he continued, as if I'd never spoken, "you don't often see an overweight Brit."

"I'm sure they're around," I said, trying not to look at my bulging thighs. I'd already gained two kilos, if those rusty old scales at the cottage were to be trusted, but the bulk was well hidden beneath woolly sweaters and long tartan skirts.

"There's a lesson here," Louie said. "Americans eat too much. And we're far too sedentary."

"I certainly am." I patted my lumpy hips.

"We'll take a walk later." He stretched out on the houndstooth sofa, signaling that it was time for his nap.

A LETTER FROM STOW-ON-THE-WOLD

July 28, 1981

Dear Dorothy,

We made a special trip to London today just so we could stand with the adoring British subjects and see Prince Charles and Lady Diana get married at St. Paul's. The streets were clogged with taxis and Rolls-Royces. Lady Diana arrived in a Cinderella carriage, her veil balled up against the windows. I bought you a Charles and Diana commemorative plate and some tea towels. Quite a few Americans were wedding guests, including Nancy Reagan.

I am loving the country life. Our garden is full of white hydrangeas, each blossom large as a cauliflower plant. Pink climbing roses cover the stone walls. Tomorrow we're having tea at a pub called Passage to India. I guess you can tell how much I love it over here.

I hope you remembered to watch the Royal Wedding. We were there somewhere in the crowd.
   Love,
   Bitsy

Louie said that Dartmoor was England's last bit of wildness. It looked awfully desolate to me. I remembered Violet reading *The Hound of the Baskervilles*, and getting so scared she'd had to sleep with the lights on. As we drove through Devon, a mist rose up and engulfed the car. Louie hunched over the steering wheel, driving slowly down the two-lane road. Jennifer began whining from the backseat. "What if you drive off a cliff?"

"Anything's possible on the moor," Louie said. As we neared Princetown, the mist cleared a bit, and the prison loomed up, ethereal and eerie. "It was built for Napoleonic prisoners of war," Louie said. "Americans were put here during the War of 1812. But now it's where England keeps sex offenders. There's a pub down the way. Shall we stop?"

"Lovely," I said, eyeing the prison. It seemed to fall back into the whirling fog.

We parked the Land Rover on the street, then walked toward the Prince of Wales Pub. A light, chilly rain started to fall, and my teeth were chattering when we stepped inside. Jennifer and I took a seat next to a spitting fireplace, while Louie stepped up to the bar and ordered two pints and a Coca-Cola. Then he began chatting with a pair of grizzled gentlemen.

"How long before the fog clears?" Louie asked them.

One lit a cigarette and said, "Could be minutes. Then again, could be days."

"Last summer, three prisoners escaped. Two were found on the moor," said the other man, scratching his beard. "They're still looking for the other one."

"Fell into a bog, most likely," said the first man. "Or he could've been pixie-led. It's common for travelers and convicts alike to lose their way on the moor."

At this, Jennifer stopped rubbing her hands and sat up straight. "What's pixie-led?" she asked the men.

"Some say pixies are the souls of unbaptized children. But whatever they are, they're bent on doin' mischief. They mislead travelers like yourselves, luring them with fairy lights. The poor chaps get turned around. And they're never seen again."

"Do the pixies eat them?" Jennifer leaned forward.

"No, lass. They deceive them. Any person who loses his way is considered to be Pixie-led."

Jennifer's eyes rounded as he began telling the old legends—fog, rain, convicts, pixies, and phantom hounds. One of the gentlemen glanced in my direction and advised me to take care if I should decide to visit the W.C.—apparently it was haunted by the spirit of a womanizing monk. Then he turned to Louie and warned him to be cautious on the drive home.

"Be on the lookout for Harry Hands," he said.

"Who's he?" Jennifer asked.

"Why, it's not a he," said the man. "It's two ghostly hands that appear from nowhere, and they seize your steering wheel and cause you to wreck." Then, nodding at the window where the fog was inching its way down the cobbled street, he issued another warning about the pixies. "But if you see one, turn your petticoats inside out, and off the imp will go."

"Show me a pixie." Jennifer pointed at the window where the fog was swirling. "Get me one right now."

The old men laughed and said, "What would you do with it, lass?"

"Why, I'd put it in my suitcase and take it home. Then I'd turn it loose on my stepmother," said Jennifer.

Jennifer complained on the way to Stonehenge too. She kicked the back of Louie's seat and demanded that he turn the Land Rover around *this instant.* Louie reached for my hand, gave it a squeeze, and then glanced back at Jennifer, lowering his dark eyebrows.

"You should try out for soccer," he told her. "Here, they call it football."

After he'd parked the car, we walked toward a tunnel, where a tall, gawky guide was speaking French to a large group. Her voice echoed, exotic and lyrical. Jennifer lagged behind, distracted by an elderly woman walking an unruly Cairn terrier. When the dog saw Jennifer, it strained toward her at the end of its braided lead.

"I wish *I* had a doggie," Jennifer whined, kneeling beside the terrier, stroking his stiff coat. She looked up at the woman, her eyes filling. "Can I buy him from you?"

The woman shook her head and clucked to the dog. Together they trotted out of the tunnel and disappeared into the crowd. Louie was pawing through the bins, looking for English-speaking headphones. He grabbed two, then hurried over to me.

"After we leave here," he suggested, "let's have tea in Salisbury."

"I don't want tea," Jennifer said, her voice rising. "I hate tea, and I hate scones."

"You can get a sandwich and a Coke," I said, reaching for my daughter's hand. "Come on, let's see Stonehenge before it starts raining again."

"I don't want to see any stupid rocks!" Jennifer crossed her arms over her chest and stuck out her chin.

"They're not stupid," I said in a cajoling tone.

"Oh, yes, they are!" Jennifer lowered her eyebrows.

Louie had been watching this little exchange, and he touched my arm. "It's useless to reason with a child," he advised. "It never works with Renata. I'm sure she wouldn't like Stonehenge, either."

I'd never spent more than five consecutive days with my daughter, so we'd never had time to work out the tenets of discipline, much less the secret language that all families develop. Louie had one with Renata. Without speaking a word, all he had to do was raise his eyebrows in a certain way, and Renata knew she was about to get a spanking. That's what I needed, a look that said "Keep this up, and you'll be in trouble."

"If you want to see Stonehenge, now is the time," Louie told me, holding out the earphone, "because I'm not coming back."

I pushed aside the gadget. I'd already read about the stone circle, and I wanted to sit down in the grass and imagine the ancient rituals.

"She'll be all right," Louie said, glancing over at Jennifer. The child had planted herself against the tunnel wall and was watching us with a venomous expression.

"You sure?"

"Positive."

Louie took my arm and we walked out of the tunnel, up a steep, paved grade. Behind us, Jennifer began to scream, her voice echoing in the burrow. The French tour guide stopped talking and stared, along with everyone in her group. An Asian couple drew back, their eyes rounded in horror. A teenager with spiked green hair gave Jennifer a thumbs-up, and in a Cockney accent, said, "Let 'er rip, wench."

"I hate it *here*!" Jennifer shrieked. "I hate *you*. I want my daddy!"

"Keep walking," said Louie, towing me along. In the tunnel, the screams had reached ear-splitting decibels.

Startled tourists were emerging from the tunnel, glancing back at Jennifer as they turned up the steep incline.

"Funny that she chose to scream," Louie said, leading me up the path. "It's the one form of communication that speaks all languages and dialects. They probably think we kidnapped her."

When he said "kidnapped," I flinched and stopped walking. Louie kept on, oblivious. Behind us, Jennifer's screams snapped off suddenly. A minute later she raced up the path, her face red and puffy, her cheeks stained with tears.

"You left me!" she said in an outraged voice. "Somebody could've snatched me! I hate you!"

"Jennifer, stop it," I said.

"No!" With a sharp little cry, she charged forward and pushed hard into my stomach. I fell backward and hit the ground.

"That's enough," Louie told Jennifer. "No more out of you today."

"You can't tell me what to do." She stuck out her tongue.

After I caught my breath, Louie helped me to my feet. I grabbed her arm and said, "Don't you *ever*—and I mean *ever*—shove me again."

Jennifer tossed her head. "You can't spank me. Daddy said so. Only a parent can do that."

"I am your parent."

"You're not!"

"Yes, I *am*." I turned away from my daughter and husband, then I started up the path alone. The huge boulders came into view, larger than I'd ever imagined, and I just stood there, the wind whipping through my hair, unable to look away, even for a moment.

FROM THE CRYSTAL FALLS *DEMOCRAT*

—*September 9, 1981, page 4*

NEW COFFEEHOUSE SLATED
FOR GRAND OPENING!!

The Java Hut will open for business at 1244 West Broad Street on September 18, 1981. The proprietor, Clancy Jane Falk, says she will be serving cappuccino, espresso, and plain old coffee, too. A dazzling array of desserts will be featured, including local favorites like coconut cake, cinnamon coffee cake, apple strudel, key lime pie, turtle cheesecake, and

Mississippi mud, to name a few. Bins of whole coffee beans from Kenya and the Kona coast will also be featured, to be sold by the pound, along with coffee grinders, decorative mugs, and flavored syrups. Business hours are Monday through Friday, from 7 A.M. until 2 P.M.

A LETTER FROM CLANCY JANE

September 12, 1981

Dear Bitsy,

Thanks for the tea towels and the picture book. I'm glad you got home safe and sound from England. I haven't seen Jennifer, or your mother, for that matter. Violet is settling into her psychiatric residency in Virginia, and I haven't seen her either. She will be studying Commonwealth crackpots for the next three years—just the sort of activity she loves. George snagged a teaching position at a college in Richmond, and he plans to work on his Ph.D. I'm glad everything is so good for them. I sent an announcement to the Crystal Falls Democrat. Violet would never think of broadcasting her accomplishments. I just don't know what made her so closed-mouthed.

Oh, by the way, Zach and Lydia broke up, and now he's going with a woman MY age who bakes baklava for a living. If I can find a refrigerated glass case—a cute revolving one—I will start selling some of her pastries in my coffee shop. I will also be selling cat-theme mugs. These are made by Kelly Lane, a local potter. Tucker is putting up display shelves so I can attractively display them. You know, I didn't believe that it was possible for a man and a woman to live together for any length of time without resorting to anarchy, but Tuck and I never seem to tire of each other. We just fit together in every way. But I'm still too superstitious to even think about marriage.

Love,

XX OO

A TAPED MESSAGE FROM DOROTHY

September 26, 1981

Dear Bitsy,

Mother's old bamboo is in full bloom behind the garage. I've been calling and inviting people to come over and cut some. It makes the prettiest floral arrangement. Clancy Jane's florist friend had a fit over it. Speaking of my sister, her coffeehouse opened, and I stopped by to show my support. Her brew is too stout and bitter for my taste, but she had oodles of customers. She is selling handmade pottery mugs, each one shaped like a cat. One of her new hippie friends has a kiln and makes the mugs for practically nothing. I helped Clancy Jane display them on shelves. I wish the pottery woman would make dog mugs. Well, that's food for thought.

    Love,
    Dorothy

A LETTER TO NANCY REAGAN

October 1, 1981

Dear Nancy,

    I wonder if you have any sisters and if so, how do you get along with them? I have a sister, and she's very hard to love. Clancy Jane is a hippie and a vegetarian, and I worry that she might be a Communist. She does not like you or Ronnie. She hates your "Just Say No" campaign, and you know why? Because she's into drugs. Yes, I have seen her funny cigarettes with my own two eyes. She had a party last week and didn't invite me and we were just starting to get along. So I'm guessing that she was up to no good. If you want to send the DEA down to investigate, I'll give you directions to her house.

    I wouldn't have even gone to her damn party, but the least she could've done was invite me. I guess she doesn't want me around her friends because I might act up. See, years ago I had mental problems but I'm not nearly as paranoid as I used to be. But try and tell that to my sister.

    Your friend,
    Dorothy

Dorothy
& Her Son

Earlene McDougal shocked everyone by running off with a Century 21 Realtor, a member of the Million Dollar Club. The note she left Mack blamed his drinking and his mother. Mack went into a tailspin. He set up aquariums in every room of his house, just so he wouldn't have to be alone. Next, he installed an electric putting green in the long hallway. When that failed to improve his mood, he painted his wooden leg Day-Glo green, then he broke it all to hell riding a go-kart. With the insurance money, he bought a new leg, the most expensive model at the medical supply store.

Mack didn't like his new leg, and he didn't like living without a woman. God dammit, he missed Earlene. She had always taken care of him—kept the books, sent out and paid the bills, stalled or sweet-talked for him. With her gone he was too depressed to work. He neglected his contracting business, and blueprints gathered in the corners of his office. Sometimes the rubber bands snapped and the pages rustled to the dusty floor, where they remained untouched. No one would hire him, and he was reduced to odd jobs—painting porches, unclogging drains, repairing screen doors. Shit work that no respectable contractor wanted.

Since life wasn't worth living—not without a woman, anyway—Mack drank himself into a nightly stupor. His eyes turned yellow, and his hair began to fall out. On the rare occasions that Bitsy talked to him—usually when she couldn't catch Dorothy at home—he would rant incoherently. He swore that Earlene was sneaking into his house, drinking his beer and eating his food. He'd tell long, drunken stories about how he was stalking the blackbirds that crapped on the roof of his house. He described to Bitsy how he'd sit patiently in his truck, a loaded shotgun in one hand, a beer in the other, waiting for the birds. He said when he saw one swoop toward his house, he'd scramble out of his truck and lift his gun; but the birds would always scatter into the trees before he could take aim.

"I'm worried about you," Bitsy would tell him, but she never offered to come home and straighten out his life. He might have starved if Dorothy hadn't cooked him three square meals a day. She came and went through his kitchen door with her own personal key. He hated to complain about her coming and going because, in addition to the cooking, she washed his clothes, changed the linen, mopped the floors, and poured flat beer down the drain. She kept hinting that they'd be better off living together, either in Mack's house or Miss Gussie's, but he wanted his house to himself. He liked to go honky-tonking and hook up with skinny bleached blondes, women who reminded him of Earlene, but he'd take anything he could get.

. . .

On Columbus Day, when Dorothy was walking her new Pomeranian puppies, enjoying the crisp morning air and minding her own damn business, she found a half-naked man curled up beneath Mack's glider. The puppies began to growl, and the little male tinkled on the man's shoe. Then she saw the front door open, and two skimpily clad blondes stepped out. One of them was holding a baby.

Dorothy gathered up her dogs, went straight home and suffered her first dizzy spell. Rather than call Mack, she called 911. Byron Falk admitted her to the hospital and ran tests, while Mack sat at her bedside, sipping beer from a Dixie cup and flirting with the nurses. Dizziness of unknown origin was Byron's final diagnosis, a polite way of saying it was an emotional problem. Mack drove his mother home from the hospital, settled her in her own living room with a can of Diet Coke and a Subway sandwich, then he took off, saying he'd like to stay and keep her company, but he had a hot date with a nurse.

"The curvy one or the bottle blonde?" Dorothy asked.

When he told her it was the blonde Dorothy shut her eyes, and the room began to sway. "Oh, dear," she gasped, but Mack just hurried out the door, leaving his mother to fend for her poor little self.

The next afternoon Clancy Jane stopped by with apple strudel and a thermos of Kona coffee. She found Mack in the driveway, shooting at the blackbirds, surrounded by empty Pabst cans. Clancy took one look and said, "Mack, you look horrible. Buddy, what's wrong?"

"Nothing." He shrugged. "I've just been messing around."

"You've got to stop drinking."

"What's the point?" He shrugged. A bird tore out of a tree and made a beeline for his roof. He lifted the gun and fired. Next door, Dorothy charged out of her house, her arms swinging back and forth. She brightened when she saw her sister. "Why, look what the cat dragged in!"

"I brought strudel," said Clancy Jane, glancing down at the beer cans. "Mack, honey, your liver can't take this abuse."

"You leave his liver out of this," Dorothy said, lumbering over. She snatched the strudel from her sister's hands. "Worry about your own. Speaking of liver, I have the *best* recipe for pâté."

A LETTER FROM CLANCY JANE FALK

December 15, 1981

Dear Bitsy,

Thank you for inviting me to New Orleans this Christmas, but Tucker and I have big plans. We promised Sunny—you remember my old friend?— that we'd have Xmas dinner with her. Last year she left Mendicino and came back to Crystal Falls to open a boutique. She sells carvings from Madagascar and rugs from Morocco. She has a loom where she makes her own rugs, too. The name of her shop is Magic Carpet Ride. Anyway, Sunny and I are cooking the holiday meal at her house—and guess what? It's not 100% vegetarian! That's right, I'm eating meat again. Of course, Tucker will be there, along with Zach and his new girlfriend, Helen, a die-hard vegan. A new friend, Laura—the first atheist in Crystal Falls—will be joining us. Laura is a florist, and I sure hope the church people don't run her out of business. We get together every Friday night and discuss art, music, politics. I haven't heard a peep from Violet, but I know she's busy studying people's brains. I hope you and Louie and Dorothy and Mack have a nice get-together.

Peace and Love,
Aunt C.J.

Dorothy

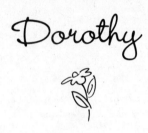

A centerpiece of white Christmas tulips dominated the DeChavannes's dining room table. Dorothy wondered if they were artificial, so she bent over to smell them. No, they were real, all right. She straightened up and stepped into the kitchen, where her daughter was rushing around. She wanted to say, "Stop, let's sit down together and talk. Tell me how you're doing."

Dorothy thought Bitsy looked peaked. Her cheekbones were more prominent, and her pretty black dress, which appeared to be silk, fell in loose folds around her hips. After her vacation in England, Bitsy had gotten chubby. The recent weight loss didn't suit her, even though skinny was all the style now. The young girls starved themselves or else stuck fingers down their throats. Not that Bitsy would do that. Dorothy hoped the weight loss was due to dieting and not Louie's extramarital antics. Although it could be due to Jennifer—after that horrible trip to England, the child had turned against her mother and stepfather.

Dorothy wondered when her daughter would have time to sit down and chat, but the girl was too busy. Over Bitsy's protests, Louie had hired a chef to cook the family dinner, but a rather famous photographer had just dropped in—with seven friends. The hired chef took Bitsy aside and hissed, "You told me it was dinner for four!"

"It's twelve now." Bitsy patted the chef's shoulder, her hand crinkling his white uniform.

"But they're uninvited," stammered the chef.

"No, just unexpected," Bitsy said. "But quite welcome. I'll just set eight extra places."

"Jesus, Mary, and Joseph!" The chef began to smite his forehead. "That will solve nothing! Christ, there's not enough food!"

"I have three dozen eggs in the refrigerator. We can serve omelets. Oh, come on now. Don't look so glum. I'll help you."

"Omelets for *Christmas?*"

"We'll throw in some red and green peppers." Bitsy opened the refrigerator. "And we'll make turkey salad. The food is secondary to the company."

Dorothy gripped a Pomeranian in each arm. Ever since her days in Central State, she'd despised the smell of cooked eggs. If crazy had a smell, it would definitely be egg. At the island, the chef began hacking into the turkey breast, and Bitsy started to make the salad dressing. Dorothy would have loved a room like this, with garlic braids hung from a wrought-iron pot rack, and glazed Italian pottery arranged just so in the cupboard. On the desk, a brandy snifter was filled with matchbooks, and each one had foreign words on the cover. Next to what Bitsy called a "prep-sink," a dish held tiny French soaps, each one infused with a different floral scent. At the opposite end of the kitchen, a door opened into a climate-controlled wine room with wooden racks in the ceiling to hang glasses.

"Can I help y'all do anything?" Dorothy asked, as the chef eyed the little dogs. Dorothy wasn't sure, but she had a feeling that he wanted to use them to fill out the menu.

"Thanks," Bitsy said, "but we've got it under control."

Relieved, Dorothy explored the sun-filled rooms. Her shoes sank into thick Persian rugs, their patterns intricate as stained-glass windows. The entry hall was dominated by a beveled glass door with a fanlight. A long, carved table stood against the wall, holding three dozen white gladioli in a crystal vase. In the dining room, Dorothy picked up a dinner plate and turned it over. Wedgwood. How boring. It wasn't festive or Christmasy. Back home, she was collecting pieces of Naif, a Villeroy and Boch pattern. She had first spotted the dishes at Borden's Jewelry, and the colorful scenes on the dishes had mesmerized her. She longed to live in a place like that, where everyone in town decorated the Christmas tree and skated on ponds, their bright knit scarves floating in the snowy air.

She moved to the back staircase, looking at the black-framed photographs hung there in pleasing patterns. Pictures of Bitsy and Louie on all their travels. Dorothy recognized some landmarks from movies on TV— the Eiffel Tower, the Arc de Triomphe, London Bridge, the Acropolis. She even recognized Michelangelo's David. Others were unfamiliar, like the one showing Bitsy and Louie backed by an enormous, snow-capped mountain. It looked dangerous and exciting. The wind was blowing Bitsy's hair, and Louie was smiling. Behind them, footsteps dented the snow, leading up a steep path.

Since her marriage to Dr. DeChavannes, Bitsy had grown worldly and capable. *She gets her talents from me,* Dorothy told herself, although she knew better. Still, those gladioli in the entry hall haunted Dorothy—why so *many*? And why place them in a room where guests would only see the arrangement in passing? It reminded her of Miss Betty's house, the way she always showed off at her bridge parties.

Dorothy felt a jolt of irritation at her daughter—irritation at *all* women who knew how to put a spin on life. Although she would never admit it, she lacked this talent. The pretty side of life was beyond her. It wasn't financial, either, because Albert's insurance policy had left her wealthy. It was some intangible thing.

"I can't get comfortable in this house," Dorothy whispered to her dogs. In the den, she passed a down-filled sofa, noticing that the flowers in the chintz matched the flowers on a needlepoint pillow. Dorothy sat in a Louis XIV chair, covered in plaid moiré silk. She put her dogs down, but they whimpered and stood on their hind legs, begging to be held.

"I just can't find a cozy spot," she told them. What she meant was, I'm afraid I'll hurt this pretty fabric. Sometimes my bladder leaks when I laugh too hard, and even a Depends won't hold it in. I'm afraid I look out of place on this moiré silk. I don't fit into my daughter's life. Not one thing in her house resembles anything that I have in Crystal Falls. She has moved beyond my reach.

After the meal, Dorothy accepted a snifter of brandy from Louie in the living room. Then she sat down on a striped loveseat. Her Poms danced around her legs, their foxy faces desperate. "Oh, all right," she said and scooped them onto her lap.

Bitsy passed a tray of chocolates and cheesecake fingers, which the chef had hastily assembled. Dorothy sipped her brandy. The more she drank, which couldn't have been more than a thimbleful, the louder she talked. The photographer and his friends listened politely. Mack stood up and lumbered over to the mirrored armoire that had been turned into a bar. He reached into a silver bucket and pulled out a wine bottle, the ice cubes clinking. After he poured the remains of a two-liter bottle into his glass, he stepped back, as if admiring the bar. At home, he kept his wine jugs on the kitchen floor, but here in New Orleans, Bitsy did everything right.

On his way back to the chintz sofa, Mack interrupted his mother. "Mama, they don't want to hear about how you dyed our Easter outfits to match—Daddy's included. They don't want to *hear* about the secrets of Rit Dye."

"Slow up with the wine, Mack," Bitsy warned.

"But it's the holidays." He tottered back and forth, and the Poms leaped to the floor and ran under Dorothy's legs for protection, peeking between her wide, muscular calves.

"Don't spill that on Bitsy's rug," she told her son. Then, with a nervous laugh, she turned to the guests. "My son doesn't normally drink this much."

"The hell I don't," said Mack.

"I cook supper for him every night," Dorothy continued, her voice rising. "But do *I* get any thanks?" She drained her brandy with a flourish. "No, I do *not* get any thanks," she continued. "Mack just eats and runs. He's a slam-bam-thank-you-ma'am son."

"Oh, Dorothy, *really*," said Bitsy.

Dorothy cringed and stared into her empty glass. It was the brandy talking. The photographer and one other guest laughed. The others shifted in their chairs, looking uncomfortable. "That's very kind of you to cook for him," said the photographer, a handsome blond fellow with a laconic grin.

"It's all a mother can do," she said, batting her eyes modestly. Not that she was flirting or anything. The photographer wasn't her type. She glanced surreptitiously at Bitsy, who was glaring. Dorothy raised two fingers to her lips and turned them back and forth, as if locking her lips with an invisible key.

Across the room, Mack tossed down wine and tried to engage one of the photographer's friends in a conversation. "My ex-wife could drive a backhoe good as any man," he was saying. Then he began to weep. "She was a looker, and flexible. She could throw her legs plumb over her head."

"Was she a gymnast?" asked the photographer's friend. He had a Swedish accent that Dorothy had originally mistaken for Russian. *Well*, she didn't know; he sounded to her like the people on the ice skating shows.

"No, she was just real good in bed," Mack explained. "Yeah, she was a flexible little gal. *And* she didn't have no body odor."

"Why, that's just plain silly." Dorothy rolled her eyes. "Everyone has a body odor."

"Not my Earlene. She never smelled bad a day in her life."

"Where's Louie gone off to?" asked the photographer. "Is he hiding from us?"

"He's in the library, talking to Renata. She's in Italy with her mother and stepfather." Bitsy held out the dessert tray while the Swede studied the offerings. He selected a truffle and slipped it into his mouth.

"It's so sweet of Louie to take time from his party to call his daughter." Dorothy popped a truffle into her mouth and bit down. Still chewing, she added, "Speaking of daughters, have you heard from Jennifer?"

"No, but she usually writes after the first of the year." Bitsy's shoulders stiffened.

"She's too busy to send you a Christmas card?" The candy bulged in Dorothy's cheek. "She got a Princess Di haircut. But it's a little too much fringe near her face."

"I'm sure it's lovely."

"No, it's not." Dorothy set her empty glass on a leather-topped table, then she straightened her blouse, which had slipped to the side. Damn frilly ruffles made her look fat. "I sure appreciate the cards you and Louie send me every year," she continued. "A card means you care. And so do phone calls. The more the better."

"Mama, you sound like a commercial." Mack opened another bottle of wine. "Reach out and touch someone."

The photographer stirred in his chair. "Bitsy, I was hoping to see your lovely mother-in-law again."

"Honora's spending the holidays in Australia with friends," Bitsy said.

"Australia's lovely this time of year," said the photographer.

The group fell silent.

"Jennifer's lucky," Mack said, stifling a burp. "How many kids her age have a daddy who's a bank president, and a granddaddy who's—"

"Would anyone care for anything else?" Bitsy interrupted.

"Hey, you didn't let me finish," Mack shouted. "I was telling everybody how Jennifer's granddaddy is chairman of the board at that goddamn bank."

Bitsy ignored her brother and turned to the photographer. "We're not exactly a Norman Rockwell painting," she said.

"No, but Hieronymous Bosch is interesting, too." The photographer's eyes crinkled in the corners as he smiled.

"Are you talking over my head?" Mack lowered his eyebrows.

"I don't believe we were talking to you," said Bitsy.

"Quit changing the subject." Mack poured more wine into his glass. "You're just pissed because Jennifer didn't like England."

"We'll discuss this later," Bitsy said in a tight voice.

"Why? You got an appointment at the mall to have your nails done? I want to discuss it *now*, goddammit."

The photographer and his friends exchanged uncomfortable glances.

Mack lifted his glass and fixed his sister with a belligerent stare. "You don't need another drink," she told him.

"Hell, I don't need another golf club, either, but that don't mean I won't buy me one." He grinned at the Swedish man. "Hey, buddy. You play golf?"

"Let me fix some coffee," Bitsy suggested.

"I don't want no goddamn coffee. I want some more wine." He drained his glass, poured another, and limped over to Bitsy. "You ought to try a little. It might take that snarl off your mouth."

Two splotches of color appeared on Bitsy's cheeks, and she cast a help-less glance at Dorothy.

"Go on and say it," Mack shouted, swaying from side to side. Wine sloshed out of his glass and dribbled onto the floor. The Poms bolted forward and began sniffing the rug. "You think I'm a dumb ass."

"No." She looked down at the dessert tray and bit her lip. "But I'm worried that you're an alcoholic."

"What the fuck!" Mack's face contorted.

"Please, let me fix you some—"

Mack tossed his wine into Bitsy's face. She staggered backward, and the tray she was holding clattered to the floor, spilling chocolates across the rug. As the photographer and his friends stood up, the Pomeranians began to bark.

The Swedish man picked up the tray and set it on a table. The frantic barking brought Louie into the room. He stood in the doorway, his fore-head wrinkled. "What's going on?" he cried.

"Don't you mess with me," Mack said.

Louie hurried over to Bitsy and whipped out his handkerchief. It was monogrammed, LdeC. *Just like Rebecca de Winter*, Dorothy thought with a shiver. Louie tenderly wiped Bitsy's face and the front of her dress.

"There," he said in a soothing voice. "That's better. What happened, Beauty?"

"I'm afraid her brother doused her in wine," said the photographer.

Louie whirled around, his eyes narrowed.

"She had it coming," Mack said.

Dorothy quickly sized up the situation. Her son-in-law was three inches taller than Mack, and outweighed him by thirty pounds. Also, Louie didn't have a wooden leg and wasn't drunk. She raised her hand, trying to signal her son to sit down and shut up.

"You barbarian." Louie spoke in a hushed, furious voice. He clenched the handkerchief in his fists. "I want you to leave."

Mack looked at Dorothy. She held his gaze. *Fix this yourself,* her eyes said. *I've had enough.*

"But it's Christmas," Mack said. "I ain't had dessert yet."

"Pick one off the floor and go," said Louie.

"You can't kick me out. I'll whoop your ass if you try."

Louie grabbed Mack's bony shoulders then started dragging him across the room. Mack's shoe came off, exposing a plastic foot. It snagged on a Chippendale chair and creaked, but Louie didn't slow down.

"Oh, my *God,*" cried the photographer. "What's wrong with his foot?"

"It's fake," said Dorothy. She stood up, brushing away tears, and stepped over to her daughter. "I'm so sorry," she whispered, pressing her cheek against Bitsy's hair. "I just wanted to spend some time with you, honey. I just miss you so much."

"I know it," Bitsy said. "I miss you, too."

Dorothy gave Bitsy another squeeze, then she snapped her fingers at the Poms. She was hoping Louie might forgive Mack's outburst and let them stay, although it didn't seem promising. Bitsy looked stunned, and Louie was on his knees, picking up chocolates and fighting off the dogs who were trying to gobble them first. Still, it was Christmas, and families should be together, no matter if wine gets tossed and people's shoes get pulled off.

"Mama? Get your purse, we're leaving." Mack got off the floor, snatched up his shoe, and hobbled toward the entry hall. "Hell, I ain't never coming back," he yelled, then looked over his shoulder. "Mama? You coming?"

"Please say you're sorry, Mack. Ask for forgiveness."

"Why? I ain't sorry one damn bit. Hell, I think he broke a hook on my foot." He pointed at Louie. "I hope you've got homeowner's, because I'm sending you the bill."

He stomped outside, Dorothy and the Poms scuttling behind. When they reached Mack's truck, a red Ford with a double cab, he insisted on driving, but Dorothy wouldn't let him. She stood on her toes and gently put her dogs into the backseat. The truck was high off the ground, and she had to drag herself into the front seat. She gripped the steering wheel and waited for her son. He took his time settling into the passenger seat. Dorothy glanced back at the house. Bitsy was standing in the doorway. The front of her dress had a large stain, and her mascara was smeared. The dogs scrambled to look out the side window, their nails snicking against the glass.

Dorothy pushed her foot against the gas pedal, speeding past ostentatious houses with gaudy wrought-iron trim, wondering how she could have given birth to such different children and why her holidays always turned out so poorly. But they did every single time. Oh, it just wasn't fair.

Part 7

TAPED MESSAGES TO NANCY REAGAN

January 12, 1982

Dear Nancy,

You still haven't acknowledged my letters and tapes with at least SOME sign. Mostly, the other First Ladies sent pictures or Christmas cards, but I haven't heard a peep out of you. But I will give you another chance. Please write.

Fondly,

Dorothy

June 16, 1982

Dear Nancy,

Well, it's been quite a while, but you haven't written. I don't think you're going to. I wish you would, because I need advice. I'm worried about my daughter. She may not ever have another baby because she is the busiest decorator in New Orleans. As you well know, babies and careers don't mix. The least you could do is have your secretary send me autographed pictures, but no, you can't even do that. All you study about is wearing those silly suits and dieting so you can be "tiny." Ha. Looks to me like you've got a thyroid problem. Better get it checked before your eyes pop out of your head.

Sincerely,

Dorothy McDougal

June 30, 1982

Dear Mrs. High and Mighty:

Today the mailman made me sign for a huge box. When I saw that it was postmarked Washington, D.C., I nearly passed out. I tore that box apart looking for a note, but you didn't have the courtesy to send one when you returned all the letters and tapes I've been sending. You probably think I am a crackpot like that awful boy who shot your husband. Well, you're wrong. I wouldn't hurt anybody, not physically or mentally. Although once, I did kill a bird. It was very cruel of you to hurt my feelings by returning my letters. You will not be getting MY vote again.

Sincerely,

Dorothy McDougal, Letter Writer Extraordinaire

A POSTCARD FROM CERNE ABBAS

July 12, 1982

Dear Violet,

Honora, Sister, and I arrived in London four days ago. We rented a car and ended up north of Dorchester at the Cerne Abbas Giant. It's 60 meters tall, a Picasso-esque object d'art that was carved into the chalk hillside back in the Bronze Age. Notice on the postcard that the giant is anatomically correct, although the phallus and testicles are definitely not to scale. Some say it was a site for maypole dancing; others say it cures barrenness. The prudish Victorians called it "The Rude Man," and covered up its manly parts. But, as you can see, it was returned to its original state. On May Day, the Giant points directly at the sun as it rises over the hill. That would be worth seeing one day.

In the car park, we took turns photographing each other—backlit by the hillside, hands raised as if cupping the Giant's genitals. Later we stopped in the town of Cerne Abbas for tea, and Honora bought a clock. On its face is the Giant's figure, with a penis for the second hand.

Love,
Bitsy

Dorothy

Dorothy woke from a troubling afternoon nap, and as she lay thinking about it, realized it was a memory of something that had really happened back in August 1938, when she was six and Miss Gussie was pregnant with Clancy Jane. In the dream it was a hot and dry afternoon, and Miss Gussie was towing Dorothy down the sidewalk. Miss Gussie stopped abruptly in front of Borden's Jewelry where a set of china had been cleverly arranged on a length of royal blue velvet. She pulled Dorothy into the store. Miss Gussie picked up a teacup, setting it on top of her big stomach. A clerk walked over, "Isn't it pretty?" she said "It's Spode. Queen Mary picked it out last year, so it's called Queen's Bird."

Dorothy reached for a saucer.

Then, in slow motion, she dropped it. The saucer hit the tile floor and broke into two wedges—the bird's head on one half, its body on the other.

"Dorothy, no!" her mother cried. Then she seemed to collect herself and put her hand on her daughter's wet cheek. "Don't cry. It's just an old dish. I'll pay for it," Gussie said. Then she picked up another cup and saucer and smiled at the fuming clerk. "Actually, I'll take this one, too. So my little girl can have something pretty."

Dorothy had shaken her head, her hair whipping back and forth. She wasn't rejecting the gift, exactly, but she knew her mother didn't have the money for one cup and saucer, much less two. "No," she'd cried, "put it back. I don't want it." She could see how her mother's hand had trembled as she set down the cup. They had waited for the clerk to wrap the broken one and then walked home.

All these years later she remembered her mother's smile, her mother's hand on her face, walking home in silence, the broken Spode rattling in the paper sack. Clancy Jane was born a few days later, and everything had seemed to change. But now, she had no doubt that her mother had loved her. She wished she had just taken her portion, taken what her mother had offered, then everything might have been different.

And then Dorothy thought, *When I got married and had my babies, I repeated the mistake that I thought my mother had made. It's a wonder that Bitsy didn't hate her brother—or hate me for loving him to excess. But she didn't. I want to be like my daughter. I don't particularly want to be like Clancy Jane, but I don't mind being her sister. Well, not much.*

She threw back the covers and shuffled into the dining room, then rummaged in Miss Gussie's old corner cupboard until she found the Spode teacups. Lord knew how they'd escaped Clancy Jane's Zen house-cleaning rampages. Dorothy gingerly fit a cup into a saucer. She stared at it a long time. Then she found a box, drove to the post office, and mailed the cup to her daughter.

A NOTE FROM CLANCY JANE

August 20, 1982

Dearest Violet,

Dorothy came over yesterday, carrying a gift-wrapped box and a card and a store-bought cake. I had completely forgotten it was my birthday. When she's not paranoid, she's almost pleasant to be around. Inside the box was a pillow she'd needlepointed, with sunflowers in each corner. In the center, she'd stitched:

I Smile Because You're My Sister
I Laugh Because There's Nothing You Can Do About It.

XX OO

Clancy Jane

Clancy Jane wasn't in the mood for grocery shopping. She hated being around the masses, and their squeaky little carts filled with junk food and chicken breasts, for their shitty little families. She walked up to perfect strangers and said, "That food you're buying—it's poison. Don't you know that you're killing yourself?"

The people looked at her as if she were crazy. Clancy Jane stared back—she wasn't the transgressor, *they* were the ones screwing up, eating the wrong foods, going about their lives in this stink-hole town. They were clueless about the evils of white sugar. Hell, Christianity was just as bad as red meat. Well, it was. Still, if Tucker asked her to cook a steak and eat it, she wouldn't hesitate. Not that he'd ever ask, of course.

She drove home with her cartons of yogurt and her bags of brown rice, and then she called Violet to complain about small-minded southerners who were hell-bent on waiting for the Second Coming. "I feel like saying to them, 'Second *coming*? Surely you don't mean multiple orgasms?'"

"Mama, stop," Violet cried.

"When did *you* get religious?" Clancy Jane sighed. "I shouldn't call you up and whine."

"Whine? Try blasphemy. I'm really worried about you. I'm sensing that you have a lot of pent-up rage. You should let it out."

"What the hell are you talking about? I'm happier than I've ever been in my life."

"Seriously, you're repressing a lot of rage, and it's all mixed up with sadness. If you don't let all that out, you'll never find happiness."

"You sound like a Hallmark card. I'm in love with Tucker. I have no use for rage or sadness. And you'd better stop shrinking me or else."

A LETTER FROM DOROTHY

February 4, 1983

Dear Bitsy,

I heard on the news that Karen Carpenter died today. She starved herself to death. So I hope you're eating right. A little extra weight never hurt anyone. Also, I bought me another cute little Pomeranian puppy. I named her Emma. She is orange and sassy and should keep me busy. One day soon I hope to start breeding and selling dogs. I believe I can turn a profit.

Love,
Dorothy

A LETTER FROM JENNIFER WENTWORTH

July 25, 1983

Dear Mother,

I went to see Valley Girl, *and it was totally awesome. I want to move to California, like, tomorrow. But my dad and Regina will never leave this town. Grandmother is taking me shopping over the summer vacation, and that will be totally bitchin'.*

Love,
Jen

P.S. Call me Jen now, okay?

Bitsy

For no reason at all, Louie gave me a Harry Winston bracelet and a set of T. Anthony luggage, then we jetted off to Ireland for sixteen days. We drove up from Shannon and stopped for the night on the Connemara Coast. After a not-so-Irish dinner of spring rolls and salad, we wandered down to the windy, rocky shore to look at the stars. The tide was out, and rocks stretched off into the darkness. I leaned against Louie, the damp wind whipping around us. We sank to the grass, and begun making love. Seduced by Irish whiskey on Irish soil, by a dark-eyed man from New Orleans. Afterward, Louie reached for my hand and together we walked toward the lights from our hotel.

It was Louie, never me, who planned these excursions. He had a world map that covered one wall in his study. With each geographic conquest, a new pin would appear on the map. After Louie toured a place, he felt a sense of completion, as if he'd achieved a goal. During a guided expedition to the Galápagos Islands, Louie turned to me and said, "Well, that was exciting. No need to come back."

He'd made a similar comment while driving a Jeep through the outback of Australia, pausing now and then to snap photographs of the monitor lizards that glared at us from the red rocks. "Isn't this great?" he'd said. "Everybody should do this once." Coming back down the steep, olive-strewn path from the Acropolis, I'd stopped to feed feral cats bits of beef jerky. Louie had put his arm around me and said, "It doesn't get any better than this." But he didn't want to revisit.

On our fifth day in Ireland, we stopped at the Waterford factory, then drove over to the Ring of Kerry. It was too foggy to take pictures, so we found a pub and drank Guinness until the weather cleared. After my second pint, I slipped my arms around Louie.

"I love you, Beauty," he said, kissing my hair. "No matter what happens, you've got to remember that."

"What's going to happen?"

"Nothing in particular, Beauty. Except that I'll always love you."

A POSTCARD FROM IRELAND

August 29, 1983

Dear Jen,

Yesterday we kissed the Blarney Stone, and Louie said he hoped it wouldn't turn me into a chatterbox. On our way down the spiral staircase, I lost my footing and would have tumbled down if I hadn't been clutching the rope. It was very narrow, and crowded. Several turns below us, a woman got stuck—someone said her hips were too wide, another said it was vertigo. The poor thing was hysterical, and her cries echoed up the stairwell. When we finally got down, we walked over to the Blarney Mill. I bought you the most gorgeous sweater and a plaid blanket that you can take to football games. Tomorrow we're heading up to Dublin.

Love,

Mother & Louie

. . .

Louie and I were in the kitchen making gumbo. While he chopped celery, we chatted about the French Quarter townhouse that I was helping Sister renovate. "I wish Sister would let up. She's been working you too hard," he said. "Maybe I'll shanghai you, take you down to the coast for the weekend."

"I'd love that." Leaning across the counter, I watched him chop celery. He had long, slender fingers, like his mother, and I loved the way he expertly slid the stalks toward the French knife. I'd seen TV chefs do it the same way. When the celery was sliced, he changed the angle of the knife and began dicing it.

"Are you still going to that auction tomorrow?" he asked.

"I really should. But it's in Mandeville, and the bidding could go into the evening. You know how I hate crossing the Pontchartrain after dark."

"Don't worry, Beauty. Just give me a ring when you're ready to come home, and I'll send a limo."

But it was afternoon when I was driving back from Mandeville, and I decided to swing by Louie's office to show off a Limoges tureen I'd bought. I glanced in the rearview mirror—my hair was pulled into a severe knot, and Louie preferred it down. So I took a minute to remove the pins and brush out my hair.

The office was dark and quiet, except for a shaft of light spilling from beneath his door. Just before I opened the door, I had a sickening feeling of déjà vu. But Tiki was long gone, and my beautiful husband had reformed. I grasped the knob, pushed open the door. A bottle of Dom Perignon was on Louie's desk. A naked woman was sitting in his leather chair, holding a plastic glass.

I had purchased this particular bottle a month ago, and it had been chilling in our Sub-Zero refrigerator ever since, waiting for Louie's birthday next month. That son of a bitch had stolen it. Hadn't he noticed the red bow tied to the foil wrapper? Too bad I hadn't affixed it to his . . . never mind, there probably wasn't enough ribbon in the world to hog-tie that man. I saw this with a sickening clarity.

Heaped on the other chair was his Gucci suit, a lovely gray silk sharkskin that he'd bought in New York last spring. I had helped him select the lavender shirt to wear with it. Now the naked woman reached out with one hand and snatched the suit jacket, clapping it over her breasts.

"Gray isn't your color," I told her, calmly setting the tureen on the desk. Then I picked up the champagne bottle, corked it with my thumb, and began to shake it vigorously. I could feel the pressure building. The bathroom door opened, and Louie stepped out. "Have I caught you at a bad time?" I asked in a conversational tone. Louie's nostrils flared in and out, and his eyes widened. "I guess I have," I said, not waiting for him to answer. I released my thumb and sprayed champagne over the lovers.

"What a waste," I said, dropping the bottle at my husband's feet. On my way out the door, I glanced nonchalantly over my shoulder. "By the way, dear. I won't be cooking supper tonight. You might wish to order takeout Chinese."

Je me démords, I thought, slamming the door behind me. My heart was thumping, but I kept on walking. Behind me, Louie's door opened and he yelled my name. I ignored him. I was letting go, giving up.

I drove back to our stucco house and hurriedly packed two suitcases, taking care to grab a memento—a Spode teacup that my mother had given me and my old rosewood box that held all of my letters to Jennifer. I drove to the airport and caught the next plane to Atlanta. While I stood in line at the Delta ticket counter, I kept glancing at the monitor, studying the departure list. At first, I thought I might try living in Paris but I really only knew a few phrases of French and didn't need the added stress of a foreign language. So I jetted off to London, the city of Shakespeare and Dickens and Jack the Ripper, not to mention Henry VIII and all of his frustrated women. As I waited to board, I felt like a refugee—not from an oppressive, third-world government, but from love and my own checkered past.

During the long flight, I put on the earphones. Elton John was singing "Blue Eyes." Louie used to say that was my song. I switched the channel to hard rock. Somehow I fell asleep and dreamed that I was living in an English country house. Stained-glass windows, portraits of dukes, dark Jacobean furniture, a secret garden and secret passageways.

Pushing my cart through customs, I suddenly realized that I didn't know a soul on this side of the ocean. I hadn't even read Henry James. I glanced over my shoulder. If I turned around now it might create a scene with the customs officials, so I decided to wait patiently in line and then work my way back to the departure lounge. Although I had been through Heathrow many times, suddenly it looked dated, trapped in the Mod 1960s. Everything was brown and shabby. Even the air felt old and oppressive, almost difficult to breathe; then I realized the air was full of smoke—the British were all puffing on cigarettes.

Why, of all places on earth, had I picked London? A mood like mine needed Barbados, not Britain. And why should I leave home? I hadn't broken any vows. I pictured myself as a gay divorcée in Florence. Well, I didn't speak Italian, either. And I could be a single woman anywhere, even in New Orleans. Then I remembered what was waiting for me there, Louie and the home wrecker; but no, the woman wasn't in our home—yet—and besides, Louie had wrecked our home.

If I returned to New Orleans, he would renounce the woman in a showy, dramatic way. Louie was marvelous at reconciliations. He was the best. Anything you want, baby. Two weeks in Paris, chinchilla coat, BMW. Once, he'd given me a bouquet of sweetheart roses and dangling from the card was a three-carat diamond in a swirled platinum setting. Love for sale, that was his mantra. But it wasn't going to work this time.

"Next!" called the customs official.

I squared my shoulders and pushed my cart over the yellow line. I handed my passport to the man and he stamped it with a flourish. Without glancing up, he said, "Welcome to London."

Bitsy and Letters from Home

I checked into the Rubens Hotel and walked around London in a daze. I kept thinking that Louie would try to find me. The city wasn't at its best in late October, and for ten straight days, I never once saw the sun. It was dark when I woke up, which was unsettling, and then the sky would lighten a bit, gray at the edges, plunging into darkness by midafternoon. I began to wonder if I was suffering from that new condition, Seasonal Affective Disorder.

A week later, I moved to a bed and breakfast in Mayfair, a white row house with black wrought-iron railing. My room overlooked the garden, and I spent hours curled up in the window seat, contemplating my dilemma. Maybe Louie could get help. Or perhaps I was the one who needed to change. I could try and fix whatever was wrong. But no, I was through with Louie. I couldn't go back.

I made a pact with myself to stick it out for at least six weeks, and if I was still miserable, I'd reevaluate my situation. But until then, I simply could not feel sorry for myself. Next, I phoned my mother and made her promise not to tell Louie where I'd gone. "He's called here every day," she told me. Then she wanted to know about the other woman, and how I'd sprayed her and Louie with champagne. "Oh, I wish I could have done that to your father," she said.

After I'd settled into the Mayfair house, the landlady, Mrs. Sturgis, invited me for tea. She perked up when she found out that I was a designer. "My dearest friend is looking for someone freelance. She has a rather dreary flat not too far away, in Green Park. Might you be interested? Actually, I know several people who are looking for designers—if you're talented, of course, and if the price is right. In fact, this place could use a little remodeling. Perhaps we could work something out—no rental fee in exchange for your services. Would that interest you, my dear?"

It certainly would. I rang up Mrs. Sturgis's friend, and made an appointment to stop by her flat. We walked through the dark rooms, and I felt discouraged. This flat reflected my mood, and I was afraid I might only add to the gloom. All the walls were gray, and the windows were hidden by heavy draperies. We stopped in a glass conservatory, which the owner, a middle-aged attorney, or whatever the English called them, had filled with attic rejects. "What would you do with this flat?" she asked. I thought a moment, then I said, "Your colors need updating. Jewel tones are all the rage, but they'd be too dark. I see yellow walls in your bedroom, and maybe the living room, too. I'd pull down the draperies in every room, especially in the conservatory. The views are too lovely to hide."

She hired me on the spot. I threw myself into floor plans, colors, and fabrics. For a while, I stopped thinking about my problems, but as the news of my separation spread through the family, I was bombarded with letters. My mother's notes were fragrant with her drugstore perfume. Aunt Clancy's notes were speckled with cat hairs. I couldn't bear to throw them away, so I stored them in the old rosewood box. Once a week, I sat on the floor and spread the letters around me. I'd put them in order and reread every single one, finding comfort in the voices from home.

. . .

October 22, 1983

Dear Beauty,

I didn't know where to mail this letter, so I forwarded it to your mother. I am assuming you're in Crystal Falls, even though she denies it. Please, Beauty—I beg you to give me one more chance. I'll do anything you want. I'll hire all male nurses. I'll have my pecker removed. I will be waiting for your phone call. I have so much to tell you.

Your loving husband,
Louie

October 28, 1983

Dear Bitsy,

As much as I hate what Louie has done, I wish you hadn't run off like

you did. I read in the paper that one of the cabinet ministers over there
resigned in DISGRACE after his pregnant mistress revealed all. They usually
do. I will try and call you again tonight, but I hope I don't get the time zones
wrong.
  Love,
  Dorothy

                                                        October 30, 1983

  Dear Bitsy,
  The reaction to acute stress is called "fight or flight." It's a survival
mechanism. You put up a good fight for your marriage. It didn't work. So
this time, you flew away. I'm proud of you. I always knew you were a strong
woman.
  Love,
  Violet

                                                        November 1, 1983

  Dear Beauty,
  I am worried about you. Please write just to let me know you're OK. I am
seeing a psychiatrist. He says I am depressed and gave me a prescription for
Elavil. I know you must be thinking that I was unfaithful because I didn't
love you, but that's not true. You are my life, my one true love.
  All my love,
  Louie

                                                        November 17, 1983

  Dear Beauty,
  You've been gone for four weeks, two days, twelve hours, and thirty-three
minutes. I haven't heard anything from you, not even a postcard, and I'm
starting to worry. Are you all right? Please call or something.
    This morning I poured a cup of coffee and walked out into your garden. I
sat down on the bench and tried to pull myself together. It is nearly
Thanksgiving and your roses are still blooming. I am taking this as a sign
that your love for me is just as enduring. I remember when you planted those
bushes. You were kneeling, and a streak of black dirt was smeared across your
cheek. As I watched, my heart began to pound. And I took you inside and
laid you on the bed and told you how much I loved you. I still do. I always
will.
  Love,
  Louie

December 7, 1983

Dear Beauty,

I thought I was having a heart attack today. I started having chest pains and tachycardia. When I got to the emergency room, my pulse rate was over 150. On my way home, I was listening to the radio and heard about an airplane crash in Madrid. Thank God you didn't go there. Or did you? Please give me a sign. I'm falling apart without you.

Love,

Louie

January 1, 1984

Dear Mother,

Thank you for the totally awesome cashmere sweater. Even Grandmother liked it. But my favorite was the camouflage outfit. Where did you find it? Grandmother called all over the place, but every store was sold out. I gave my dad a new putter, and he thought it was way cool. I gave Regina a vomiticious red velour robe but she hasn't taken it from the box. She stays in her room all the time, crying and watching soaps. Are you, like, going to divorce Louie or just stay separated? If you stay in London, can I come and visit?

Here are my New Year's resolutions:

1. I will sponsor a child in Somalia or Ethiopia for less than 60 cents a day
2. I will quit spying on people
3. I will stop slicing up Regina's Estée Lauder lipsticks with razor blades.
4. I will open doors for the crippled and smile at retards.

Love,

Jen

TO MY VALENTINE

February 14, 1984

Dearest Beauty,
My heart will always belong to you.
Love,
Louie

April 1, 1984

Dear Bitsy,
Your mother and your aunt have closed ranks and will not disclose your
address to me or Louie. I don't blame them. Louie told me his side of the
story, and it was too sordid to be a lie. The girl on his desk was a
pharmaceutical rep for Eli Lily; her name is Danita Hollaway.
I don't mean to defend him, darling, but he swears that this woman had
been throwing herself at him for a long time. She just wore him down. I
don't know why he put everything on the line for a woman that meant
nothing. But I do know that he loves you. I have never seen him in such
torment. He is a shattered man. Please find a way to reach him. At least let
him know you are still alive.
Love,
Honora

May 4, 1984

Dear Beauty,
We met six years ago today. I know you're living over in England because
I got a letter from your solicitor. I do not want a divorce. I've done horrible
things, and if I could undo them I would. But I can't. All I have is the
future. Please call, so we can figure this out. I promise I won't start bugging
you with calls, or hop on a plane and show up on your doorstep. But I want
you to hear me out.
By the way, I'm still having tachycardia and chest pains.
Love always,
Louie

May 20, 1984

Dear Beauty,
Happy anniversary. I will always love you, kid.
Your husband,
Louie

September 11, 1984

Dear Mother,

I am, like, so totally excited. A local writer came to our school and talked. I might like to be a writer. That would be way cool, and I wouldn't have to leave home. On the other hand, I love dressing up, and I might want to work at a majorly cute boutique. Somebody asked how much money a writer made. The woman fell out laughing. I raised my hand and asked how she got her ideas, and she said I wet my finger and stuck it in a light socket. Well, her hair did look fried. But I just thought she'd given herself a home permanent. My teacher gasped and told the writer to leave. Then she told the class to never try that! For the rest of the period, she made us write a paper. Here is mine.

What I Did on My Summer Vacation
by Jennifer Wentworth

I spent the summer strolling on the salty, smutty sand. It was like so awful and so awesome all at once. The stinky smelling sea swept squalor over my shoes. "Ewww!" I cried. I hate to go barefoot due to the filthy shells, seaweed, and pond scum. But I love the ocean. Talk about awesomosity. The stupid sunbathers brought their chairs and coolers and striped towels to our private beach, ignoring the totally awesome signs we'd posted. They stuck umbrellas into the solid sand and smeared themselves in suntan oil. They were so bogus. They didn't supervise their kids. My grandmother started to call the police, saying she'd paid hundreds of thousands of dollars for this beachfront property, but before she could dial, the sturdy seagulls swooped down and shit on the strangers. That was, like, total Ewwness, which is not to be confused with sheep. Ewwness is a state of Ew and pertains to all things Ewwie. I laughed when the trespassers screamed and scattered. I was, like, slap me or something.

October 26, 1984

Dear Beauty,

The Brits transplanted a baboon's heart into 15-day-old human infant. I wish I could transplant forgiveness into yours. You've been gone one year and nine days.

Love always,
Louie

November 6, 1984

Dear Bitsy,

Well, it's election day here in the States. I have enclosed a taped message that I'm sending to Nancy Reagan, not that she deserves one. Hope you are staying warm.

Love,
Dorothy

Nancy,

I wasn't going to contact you ever again. BUT I changed my mind. I was eating chocolate and watching the election results. Well, well, well. Your man won by a landslide today. Now you will have oodles of $$ to buy another suit for yet another swearing in. Well, I have to run. It's time for another Godiva truffle. Yes, I admit it, I'm a chocoholic, but don't YOU expect me to Just Say No.

Very Insincerely,
Dorothy

January 2, 1985

Dear Bitsy,

We had a real nice Christmas. I just loved the tartan scarf and the shortbread. Clancy Jane gave me The Official Preppy Handbook, *and I'm enjoying it. I gave her cat slippers and a T-shirt that says "To Err Is Human, To Purr, Feline." I hope you liked the blouse. I got it at a ritzy-fitzy garage sale, but it still had the price tag attached. Your mother-in-law sent eight huge boxes filled with your clothes, shoes, and pocketbooks. Let me know what you want me to do with them. It's time for me to go and watch* Moonlighting. *I am dying for Bruce and Cybill to boink.*

Love,
Dorothy

January 12, 1985

Dear Mother,

Thank you for the awesome dictionary. I haven't had time to look up any big words because of what's going on at home. Grandmother and Chick think I'm a total mall chick. They wanted me go to Hilton Head for the holidays, but I'm in love with Patrick Little and needed to stay here. Regina like totally locked me in my room and called me a juvenile delinquent. She can eat shit and die. Please come and get me. I have NOTHING to do but read back issues of Seventeen.

Love,
Jennifer

May 10, 1985

Dear Mother,

My dad and Regina are getting a divorce. I told you. Grandmother is thrilled. She's taking us to the Caribbean for Memorial Day. Now maybe you and him can get together. I like a boy in my class, Sammy Wauford, but he likes Debbie Tickner, who wears clothes from Kmart.

Love,

Jennifer

May 12, 1985

Dear Bitsy,

Your mother broke down and gave me your address. I just returned from New Orleans. Louie collapsed at his office with an apparent heart attack. It turned out to be indigestion. He is such a sniveler. I completely understand why you are going ahead with the divorce. You can't sit still while the rest of time is passing by on the winds.

Don't fret—I won't give Louie your address. But do you mind if I pass it along to Sister? She asks about you all the time, and she knows quite a few designers on your side of the Atlantic. So if you're planning to stay in London, she can point you in the right direction.

Love,

Honora

June 4, 1985

Dear Mother,

School is out for the summer, and I am so totally bored. I went over to see Dorothy, and she got mad when I told her that The Official Preppy Handbook was a gag. I was like oh my God. Then she nearly fainted when I told her that George Michael is gay. She is always listening to that song, "Careless Whisper." She asked how I know so much, but I really don't. I sure was wrong about my dad. He wasn't too sad over Regina because he sat me down in his study and told me that he wanted me to meet a woman named Nicole. They met at the golf course. So I guess you and him won't be getting remarried after all. Next week, Grandmother and Chick are taking me to Hilton Head. I'd rather go to California and see real Valley Girls.

Love,

Jennifer

June 15, 1985

Dear Bitsy,

I haven't heard from you in a while, so I thought I'd send you a little taped message. It's so much nicer than a letter, don't you think? I invited my *widowed neighbor, Mr. Stump, to supper. I served him fried chicken, green beans, Jell-O salad, mashed potatoes, biscuits, and apple upside-down cake. The next morning, the phone rang, and it was him. He complimented my cooking and wanted to know if I had any leftovers. Well, I'd never heard of anything so bold, but Mr. Stump is from Indiana, and they are crude up there. So, I told him that I was sorry, all I had was a tiny bowl of mashed potatoes. He said he'd be right over.*

The nerve of that man! I may spit in those potatoes, even if they were exceptionally good. The secret is to add lots of REAL butter and sour cream. It will be a cold day before I serve another meal to Mr. Stump.

I hope you are enjoying your decorating jobs.

Love,

Dorothy

June 21, 1985

Dear Bitsy,

It's Solstice Day. How cool it must be to live near Stonehenge. I wanted to send you Violet's new address. At the end of the month, she and George will be moving to Boulder, Colorado. She has joined the Mountain Arts Medical Group. George will be doing research at the University of Colorado. My coffee shop is doing great. For July 4, Tucker and I are going to a party on Joe's houseboat. I wish I could have this man's baby, even though I have reached an age where I don't like children. Next month I'll turn 47, and the only eggs I have left are probably deviled.

Love,

XX OO

July 5, 1985

Dear Bitsy,

I tried to call, but I keep getting your machine. The most horrible thing has happened, so before you read any further, you might want to sit down. Yesterday, Clancy Jane and Tucker went to a houseboat party at the lake. The generator went out, and Tucker tried to fix it. Bitsy, he got electrocuted. I brought Clancy Jane to my house and gave her a pill. I called Byron, but got his answering service. They said he was on a vacation. I just bet he's not alone. So I called Zach and he came right over. He talked to her about the cycle of rebirth. But I just can't imagine Tucker coming back as a cat.

Honey, I've got to stop writing now. Clancy Jane is getting hysterical, and I need to give her a pill. I hope you like your new decorating job.

Love,

Dorothy

September 19, 1985

Dear Bitsy,

Thank you so much for wiring the flowers. They were real pretty. I'm sorry you couldn't make it back for the funeral, but Dorothy explained that you were moving to a new apartment and couldn't leave. I am sorry that it took so long for me to write, but I haven't been myself. Here is what happened that night. Three couples were on the houseboat, and we'd just taken a midnight swim. Tucker swam up behind me and said, Boo! Then he laughed and told me we had some important things to talk about. I asked him what, but he just smiled and said, You'll see, you'll see.

When we climbed up the ladder, everything was pitch-black. The electrical current was on the blink, so Tucker began fiddling with the generator. Somebody went to get a flashlight. Be careful, baby, I told Tucker, and I felt a chill. The lights blinked twice, followed by a crackling sound. Tucker looked like he was dancing, then he fell overboard. I screamed for help, then dove into the water. It was warm and dark, and somehow I caught his wrist. But he was so heavy, the weight of him just pulled me down. From the surface, I heard a splash and saw arcs of light, but I didn't let go.

I thought I might touch bottom but someone uncoiled my fingers—I couldn't see who—and I fought them off. Another person grabbed me from behind and shoved me toward the surface. When I came up, people were shining flashlights in the water, and one of the guys was swimming underwater, searching for Tucker.

At dawn, the police divers brought Tucker to the surface. It took three more to lift his body onto the boat. I asked everybody who'd pulled my hands off Tucker, but no one would admit it. I wish they'd just let me go.

Since Zach is the only other Buddhist in town, he helped me plan the service. We handed out candles to the mourners and told everybody to light them. Then we formed a line and walked out of the funeral home. We stood out in the darkened yard. Then Zach told everybody to blow out their candles one at a time. When we got to the last candle, which was Zach's, he said, "When one flame is extinguished, another is ignited." And he touched his candle to mine and lit the wick.

It would be nice to think that, at the precise moment Tucker died, another life began. But did it get his soul? I don't think so. I think he achieved Nirvana whether he meant to or not. He knew how to give love and to receive love, and if that's the only lesson any of us ever learn, then it's more than enough.

Love,

XX OO

October 15, 1985

Dear Mother,

I hate school. The eighth grade sucks. I've got a mean teacher and she is loading me down with homework. My dad is drinking all the time, even at breakfast. He fell down and hurt his back, and now he is taking pills that make him see double. Grandmother is so upset she had to check into the hospital. I will end up in an orphanage. Please come and get me.

Love,
Jennifer

October 20, 1985

Dear Mother,

Dorothy came over and took me to her house. She said you'd called her and explained what was going on. She has got another freaking dog, and it's peeing all over the house. I'm, like, gag me with a spoon. I shut myself up in your old bedroom to get away from it. I hate to tell her, but her house STINKS. Plus between the dog yapping and the walnuts falling from the tree and hitting the roof, I can't sleep. Do you have an English boyfriend? Or are you still pining for Louie? I myself have given up on boys. Here in Crystal Falls, I have few to pick from. I don't want to end up married to an electrician. I would prefer a doctor or a politician.

I'm moving to another room.

Love,
Jen

November 2, 1985

Dear Bitsy,

You may not remember me but I am the Wentworths' housekeeper. I worked there when you were married to Mr. Claude, only I was much younger. I just finished reading your letter to Miss Betty where you asked if Jennifer could visit you in London, England. I think it would be a nice idea. She will be out of school for Thanksgiving. But first, let me explain what is going on around here. Mr. Claude is at the Betty Ford Center, and the Wentworths flew out there to keep him company. I am staying here at the house with Jennifer. I don't expect to see Miss Betty until after Christmas. She would not like for Jennifer to go anywhere, but the child is just beside herself. No matter what they say, I know you love Jennifer. And I am willing to take this risk. Please feel free to call and let me know about the travel plans.

Sincerely,
Bernice Calhoun

November 25, 1985

Dear Dorothy,

This is what Mother bought me at Harrod's:

1. A purse
2. A silver keychain
3. A pink raincoat, pink umbrella, and pink Wellingtons, which are boots.
4. Fur mittens
5. Assorted gloves
6. Lip gloss
7. Two Journey albums

Mother lives on the roof of a tall, beige building. The English word for apartment is flat. Whatever it's called, it sure is vomiticious. Every time I want to go outside, I have to get into the teeniest elevator you've ever seen. It's called a lift and only holds three people. The only decent room in her flat has glass walls and a glass ceiling. A door opens onto a porch with a bench, and you can look down into the park. It has ewwie views of buildings. The Queen lives in one, but it's not so great. Last night the electricity, or whatever, went off and everything went dark. Mother and I went out to the roof porch and sat on the bench. Then it hit me that I only had a few days left, and then I'd have to go back to Crystal Falls. I burst into tears and told her that I didn't want to leave, that I would miss her too much. She started crying, too. We hugged each other for a long time.

Love,
Jennifer

A LETTER FROM CLANCY JANE

December 28, 1985

Dear Bitsy,

Christmas was such a bummer. Violet is living in another state, and you live in another country—all because of the men in your lives. And if it isn't a guy screwing things up, it's National Holidays. Why are there so many? I wish that Christmas only came every other year. I refuse to be manipulated by merchants, refuse to put up a tree, stockings, or mistletoe. Zach gave me a ceramic nativity scene that featured dogs. The Wise Men consisted of a German shepherd, black Lab, and a golden retriever; a white poodle took Mary's place, and Joseph was represented as a bassett hound. A tan chihuahua took Baby Jesus' place in the manger.

The nativity scene is cool, but it didn't lift my spirits. I'd tried so many outlandish things over the years. ROLFing, EST, Buddhism, transcendental meditation. Nothing has worked except good old-fashioned love. But I'll never have that again. I will never get over Tucker.

Last night I drifted off to sleep and dreamed I was moving through the trees, my shoes stirring up fog. A man built just like Tucker stepped out of the haze. I could smell him—ashes and soot mixed with man-sweat. He lifted one hand and waved and turned back toward the fog. I called for him to wait.

He stopped walking and glanced over his shoulder. It was Tucker. He wasn't dead. He'd come back. I ran as fast as I could and jumped into his arms, and he swung me around. Pushing his hair off his forehead, I said, "Do you know how much I love you?"

"I ought to," he said. "You've told me enough."

That was when I woke up and started crying. A long time ago, Violet had accused me of not knowing how to love or how to experience rage. She called me passive-aggressive.

I tried to remember the first moment I'd ever felt pure fury. Not in my childhood—Dorothy had been the one to have tantrums and rampages. I'd sailed through my formative years without ever raising my voice. I hadn't had to—Miss Gussie had raised hers, yelling at Dorothy on my behalf. Nobody ever got a chance to make me mad until I married Violet's father and he died before I could punch out his lights.

So, maybe I didn't know how to deal with anger. I tried a visualization technique. I squeezed my eyes shut and tried to summon it, conjuring rage the way I drew wild cats from the woods with bowls of half 'n' half. It didn't work. It only made me feel tired. But Violet was wrong about one thing—I do know how to love.

Anyway, I hope your Christmas was better than mine.

Love, Aunt Clancy

A LETTER FROM JENNIFER WENTWORTH

January 1, 1986
New Year's Day

Dear Mother,
Thank you for the Christmas and birthday presents. Last night during my birthday party, my dad got, like, totally drunk. Nicole poured all the liquor

down the drain, then she caught him in the pantry drinking Triple Sec and feeling up the caterer who's name is Gwen, and she has enormous breasts. Nicole told Gwen to please set out a fresh batch of cheese straws. I don't know what happened after that, because Nicole made me go back to my guests.

When everyone had left, Nicole chased Gwen out into the driveway. Then she found my dad passed out on their bed and she took a strip of electrical tape and pressed it down over his mouth. Next she pulled the sheet over him like she was tucking him in, but then she took a giant staple gun and pegged him to the mattress. He started to wake up, and she took an empty tequila bottle and knocked the hell out of him. He screamed for help, but Nicole kicked the door shut. I totally felt his pain. Now my dad is in the hospital and he looks awful, like, Ew Ew Ew Squared. And Grandmother got Nicole put in jail for assault and battery. She is also filing for divorce on my dad's behalf. Her lawyers will let her do anything.

Love,
Jen

March 5, 1986

Dear Bitsy,
Please call. I need to hear your voice. I am so lonely without you.
Love,
Louie

June 2, 1986

Dear Bitsy,
Thanks for helping me locate a Thomas Pink shirt for George. It's for his thirty-second birthday. I'm seeing seven patients a day, four days a week. I charge out the ying-yang. The money is great, but sometimes I wonder if I'm helping anyone. I never dreamed it would be this way. George says not to think about it, or I could become existentially depressed. I'm extremely proud that you've carved out a life in England. You have real courage.
Love,
Violet

May 20, 1986

Dear Bitsy,
We may not be married but it's still our anniversary.
I love you,
Louie

October 15, 1986

Dear Bitsy,
Happy birthday, Beauty.
I still love you with all my heart.
Love,
Louie

December 15, 1986

Dear Mother,
Here is my totally awesome Xmas gift list:
Dad—personalized golf balls
Gwen (my dad's new girlfriend)—Chanel No. 5
Grandmother—assorted coffee beans, coffee grinder, espresso machine
Chick—cigars
Mack—Jack Daniels and a tool box
Dorothy—blue velour robe, Godiva chocolates
Dorothy's Dogs—jeweled collars
Great-Aunt Clancy—umbrella printed with cats
I left off your name because your gift is a major surprise. I didn't get Aunt Violet anything because I never hear from her. Is she still alive? I will be 15 on New Year's Eve. For my birthday, Grandmother is giving me a huge party at the club. Hope it's better than last year's.
Love,
Jennifer

February 12, 1987

Dear Mother,
I'm sorry I haven't written sooner, but I have been totally busy. Thanks for the present. It's snowing, and school let out at ten o'clock in the morning. That was way cool. Gwen is so bogus and talks to me like I'm her girl friend, not her lover's daughter. This is what she said today: "It's hard to be sweet when Claude sleeps with anyone who'll spread her legs. He's made me into a joke. Why, I can't get a decent haircut in this town because he's slept with all of the beauticians."
And all this time, I just thought she had, like, real shitty hair.
Love,
Jennifer

August 2, 1987

Dear Mother,

I will start the 10th grade in September. Grandmother and I flew to Houston and a limousine took us to the Galleria. It's like, oh my God. The driver followed behind us, carrying our Saks and Neiman Marcus bags. Every now and then, we'd have to wait while he ran out to the limo to stash everything. He got a little huffy, and I told him to, like, take a chill pill. Grandmother bought from the new Valentino collection. Here is what I bought:

1. Gucci shoulder bag
2. Lace gloves
3. Lace hairbands
4. Green Laura Ashley dress with poofed sleeves
5. Puffy 18 kt heart pendant
6. Louis Vuitton wallet
7. A new Madonna album
9. Oversize pink knit sweater
10. Danskins

More later.

Love,

Jen

December 15, 1987

Dear Bitsy,

Mack and me went to the movies and saw Fatal Attraction. *You are so lucky that none of Louie's tarts were insane. But now I am worried that one of Mr. Stump's old girlfriends will take revenge on me. Yes, we've been seeing each other, and I'm scared. I can just imagine walking into my kitchen and finding one of my Pomeranians sticking out of a bubbling pot. Tomorrow I am calling a locksmith. Then I am giving Mr. Stump an ultimatum: Stop playing the field!*

Love,

Dorothy

December 22, 1987

Dear Mother,

I am staying at Dorothy's this week. She put up her totally faux Xmas tree this morning. She pulled out a box of grody ornaments, including some that I'd made in elementary school. When she finished, her bratty boy dog, Rebel, peed all over the tree. I miss you.

Love,

Jen

January 11, 1987

Dear Bitsy,

The Gulf Coast isn't the same without you. Just the other day I was cleaning my handbag room, and I found a vintage Jackie O Gucci. May I send it to your mother? Louie is still brooding. I've never seen him go this long without taking up with a woman. He only has himself to blame. I hope the Brits are giving you the respect and love you deserve.

Love,
Honora

May 12, 1988

Dear Bitsy,

My poor little friend, Mr. Stump, was standing on his back porch and tripped over his shoelaces. He fell into the flower bed and broke his neck. It didn't kill him but he stayed in the hospital for a month. Then his daughter came and took him home with her. He wasn't a real boyfriend, but I sure do miss him. Speaking of such, Earlene has left the Million Dollar man for a filthy rich widower in Knoxville. He is nearly 79. Now Earlene is driving a brand-new Jaguar. But she still has that platinum blond hair and could pass for a hooker. I just pray that she won't come sniffing after Mack,

Love,
Dorothy

May 20, 1988

Dear Bitsy.
Happy Anniversary. I won't give up, so you'd better call.
Love,
Louie

December 9, 1988

Dear Bitsy,

I'm so excited that you're flying home for the holidays. And I LOVE your idea of having an early birthday party for Jennifer. Clancy Jane says she'll bring the finger foods and coffee, and Mack is going to smoke a turkey and a Boston butt.

I'm counting the days,
Dorothy

January 10, 1989

Dear Mother,

It was way cool seeing you. I loved all my gifts. I'm sorry that I missed the party, but when it started snowing I was like no way, this isn't happening. So, when my friends said they were going sledding, I had to go. It was awesome. I got a spiral perm and my driver's license. I want my own car, but my dad is yelling at me to slow down and going totally Chuckie. I just ignore him and turn up the volume on my cassette deck. I am listening to it now. Roxette is singing "It Must Have Been Love."

Take care,

Jen

P.S. You guys need to remember to call me Jen, okay?

January 22, 1989

Dear Bitsy,

Here is a copy of a tape I sent to Barbara Bush. Do you think I sound kooky?

Love,

Dorothy

January 22, 1989

Dear Barbara Bush,

I haven't contacted a First Lady in years, but I'm hoping you and me can become friends. For one thing, we are dead ringers for each other. Same fluffy white hair and gracious smiles, except I am lots thinner. My niece, Violet, is also married to a man named George, and he is good to her, but not real family-oriented. He likes to snow ski and go white-water rafting. He was that way even before he and Violet moved to Colorado—nothing but weirdos out there. They are neither Democrat or Republican but Independent. They're also childless (I suspect a low sperm count). I understand that they voted for Ross Perot, who looks like the rat in Fantasia. I am not surprised at their politics. My niece is an atheist and she goes to Africa by herself to do free medical work, but I can't imagine what she does over there—she's a psychiatrist. Although I thought headshrinkers was something they had a lot of over there.

Yours forever,

Dorothy McDougal

February 5, 1989

Dear Bitsy,

All morning I've been wearing the cardigan that you left at Christmas. It still smells like you. I'm freezing to death. It turned bitter cold overnight. The temperature dropped into the teens, and my pipes froze. Mack tried to fix it. He used a blowtorch and I was scared that 214 would go up in flames. Mack turned on the upstairs faucet, and when the pipes thawed, the water filled the sink and flooded the bathroom. Water poured through the ceiling, into the dining room. So now I'm fighting with the insurance company. I think your poor brother has damaged his brain. They say that alcohol will actually KILL brain cells. It's a wonder that he has any left.

Love,
Dorothy

May 21, 1989

Dear Bitsy,

Another anniversary—I wish I knew your address. I would fill your flat with blue boxes from Tiffany's.

Love,
Louie

December 8, 1989

Dear Mother,

Guess WHAT? We're going on a Christmas trip to Switzerland next week!!!!!! We go from Nashville to Atlanta to Zurich. So I will get to ride on three planes going and three coming back. I was hoping we'd get to stop off in London, but it's too much out of our way. But I was thinking we could still meet somewhere, maybe in Lucerne. I know it's late notice, but maybe if you look at the itinerary, which I had to STEAL, we can figure out a way to meet without Grandmother finding out.

My fingers are crossed!
Jen

Jennifer and the Wentworths

Jennifer and her grandparents arrived at the Nashville airport, and Miss Betty had handed over their passports and travel documents at the Delta ticket counter. She turned to Jennifer and said, "Isn't this exciting?"

Then the Delta agent, a square-built woman, looked up. "There seems to be a problem," she said. She opened Jennifer's passport and held it up.

"What's wrong?" Miss Betty leaned across the counter and blinked at the passport. "I know she doesn't resemble that picture, but it was taken in 1984. So of course she looks completely different now, but it's her."

Jennifer produced her license and school ID card and handed them to the agent hoping they would prove her identity. The agent just looked puzzled and said, "That's not the issue. I know it's *you,* honey. You look just like the picture. The problem is that your passport will expire while you're abroad."

"And this means?" Miss Betty raised her eyebrows.

"She can't leave the country," said the agent.

"Give me that." Miss Betty snatched back the passport and peered down at the dates then started screaming. "But the goddamn thing hasn't expired *today*," she cried. "It expires on December thirty-first, and we're coming home January fifth. So there can't be much of a problem."

"I'm sorry," said the agent.

"This is so silly," Miss Betty said and turned to her husband. "Chick, give the girl a hundred dollars so we can get on our way."

The ticket lady began shaking her head.

"Three hundred?" Chick asked and laid his fat wallet on the counter. "Five? Don't stare at me, girl. Tell me what you want."

"Are you *bribing* me?" the agent asked.

Miss Betty exploded. "We would never condescend to bribe a lowly peon such as yourself. Don't take it out on me just because you're trapped in a dead-end nine-to-five job. I can't help it that I'm wealthy. I can't help that I'm going to Europe. It's not *my* fault that you've never set foot out of this country."

"Apparently you haven't, either," said the agent. "If you had, you would've known that Miss Wentworth's passport was about to expire—a big no-no in the jet set world."

"How dare you. I demand to see your supervisor."

At this, Jennifer's hopes went up.

"With pleasure," the agent said, picking up the phone.

Miss Betty turned to Chick. "We should call George Bush. After all, we're the biggest contributors in Falls County, if not all of Tennessee."

"Yes, but Senator Gore might have more clout," Chick said.

The Delta supervisor walked up. The ticket agent, Miss Betty, and Chick all began talking at once. At the other counters, people were staring. Jennifer shrank back, trying to make herself invisible. The supervisor picked up the passport and looked at it, then when Miss Betty paused to catch her breath, the man said he was terribly sorry, but Delta couldn't issue the transatlantic tickets. However, all wasn't lost. He asked the ticket agent to step aside and began punching keys on the computer. He told them they could fly down to New Orleans that day and the next morning could take a cab to the passport agency. Then either that night or the next—depending on what flights were available—they would be able fly to Switzerland. So far so good until he told them the rest: they would have to fly on standby, which meant they'd forfeit their first class seats.

"I will forfeit nothing!" Miss Betty cried.

The supervisor ignored her and squinted at the computer screen. "You can take Flight 211 to Atlanta, and then Flight 1145 to New Orleans. But, because these flights are last-minute, it will cost one thousand dollars extra."

"Just for the New Orleans tickets?" Chick asked.

"Yes," said the supervision. "You can always get credit for your transatlantic and go another time."

"You fool, price is no object," Miss Betty yelled. "But time is of the essence."

Now we're on our way, Jennifer thought. The supervisor held out her passport, and she snatched it up and dropped it into her handbag. Miss Betty had suddenly calmed down and was asking the agent if her and Chick's passports were in order.

When the supervisor admitted they were, and it was just Jennifer's that was the problem, Miss Betty whispered to Chick. He shoved hundred-dollar bills into Jennifer's hands and told her to call a limo.

"Why?" Jennifer asked.

Meanwhile, Miss Betty was sorting the luggage and directing a man to lift the Wentworths' Louis Vuitton bags onto a conveyor belt. The supervisor pushed the tickets into Chick's outstretched hand. Then they headed for the gates.

"Where do you think you're going?" cried Jennifer.

Miss Betty turned. "Darling, you really can't expect us to give up our trip. That wouldn't be right, would it?" She blew Jennifer a kiss and trilled over her shoulder, "Go on back home, and I'll bring you back a Cartier tank."

Thank God for the lady at the Hertz desk. She hadn't had enough money to break Jennifer's hundred, but she had a dime for the pay phone. She couldn't call her father. Claude was at the Betty Ford clinic again. He had stopped drinking, but they couldn't make him stop taking Percodan. So Jennifer called Dorothy, who told her to sit tight and not to talk to any perverts, that she and Uncle Mack were on their way. Jennifer took the escalator up to the gift shop, where she spent Chick's money on fashion magazines, stuffed bears, and candy. At the checkout, the clerk said, "Gosh, so much. Are these gifts?"

"No, they're all for me," said Jennifer.

"You sure are lucky," said the clerk.

"Yeah," said Jennifer, grabbing another stuffed bear and tossing it onto the counter. "The luckiest girl in the world."

TWO NOTES FROM DOROTHY

March 30, 1990

Dear Bitsy,

I hope everything is fine in London. I read the Nashville Tennessean *just to keep track of the weather over there, and I noticed that it was raining. So I have enclosed a cute umbrella. Also, a letter that I want you to read.*

Love,

Dorothy

COLUMBIA BROADCASTING SYSTEM
51 W. 52 STREET
NEW YORK, NEW YORK 10019

March 25, 1990

Dear Mrs. McDougal:

Thank you for contacting CBS. We appreciate your plot suggestions for The Guiding Light. *We are constantly seeking new material for the Josh and Reva storyline. Your idea of cloning Reva is, even for us, a bit far-fetched, but we will keep it in mind. However, once an idea is submitted, it becomes the exclusive property of CBS. Again, thank you for your interest. I have enclosed per your request an autographed photograph of Kim Zimmer.*

Sincerely,

James P. Calhoun, Editorial Assistant

May 21, 1990

Dear Bitsy,

Guess what? That's right, another anniversary. I wish you'd call. I am a different man.

Love,

Louie

June 14, 1990

Dear Mother,

I'm sorry I didn't get to spend any time with you at my graduation. But you know how it is with all those awesome parties to go to. My dad gave me $10,000 and a first class ticket to Atlanta. But I just LOVED the beige dress you gave me. I will wear it to college this fall. I was accepted to Tennessee Tech, but Grandmother talked me into attending Falls Junior College, which

*is only two blocks from her house. I want to major in fashion merchandising
and then move to Italy and maybe work at Gucci or Versace. Falls Junior
College doesn't offer this degree, so I will eventually have to transfer to a
bigger school. I checked out the dorms and they are dinky, so I'll just live at
home and drive back and forth. Chick bought me a bitchin' white BMW
convertible so I can start college in style.*

Love,

Jen

October 14, 1990

Dear Mother,

*Thanks BUNCHES for showing up at Parents' Weekend. Dad's gone
back to Betty Ford, and my grandparents are so upset they've gone to Hilton
Head. Even Dorothy couldn't come. She was at some stupid DOG show. The
one time I really and truly need you, and you let me down. I was the only
person there without a family.*

Jen

November 22, 1990

Dear Mother,

*It would be so awesome if you'd send size 10 Doc Martens for my new
boyfriend ASAP. His name is Luke Vantrese, and he's a business major at
F.C. Those are strange initials for a college—haha. Send size 6 Wellingtons
for me, as damp weather is in the forecast. I would prefer an earthy color as
it will hide the dirt.*

Jen

January 2, 1991

Dear Mother,

*Thank you for the perfume and the pocketbook. Luke didn't give me a
ring like I thought he would. In fact, he broke up with me. He said I was too
spoiled and crazy to make a good wife. I told him HE'D never make a good
husband because his dick is too small.*

Love,

Jen

March 22, 1991

Dear Bitsy,

*Thank you for the lovely birthday present. I can't believe that I'm 37.
Inside, I still feel 16. But George and I decided that we'd better try and have*

a baby before it was too late. After all of my conflicts with Mama, I just didn't think I'd make a good parent. But I think I'm ready now. I want you to be the godmother.

Love,
Violet

May 21, 1991

Dearest Beauty,
Come back to me. Give me one more chance. Or at least send your phone number. I have so much to tell you.

Love,
Louie

June 14, 1991

Dear Bitsy,
I have called and called, but you're never home. So I had no choice but to send this Air Mail. Before you read any further, take a deep breath. Two days ago, Jennifer was driving down South Maple with her girl friends. They rounded the curve and slammed into Mr. Raymond Fowler, who was pushing his lawn mower across the street. Jennifer lost control of the BMW and drove into a tree. Her girl friends were bumped and bruised, but Jennifer was thrown from the car. The angels must have been with her because she didn't die. All she got was a fractured skull and a broken wrist. Poor Mr. Fowler was pronounced dead at the scene.

The Wentworths smoothed everything over. Somehow they kept it out of the newspapers. They paid for Mr. Fowler's funeral, too. I heard that they gave the Fowler family hush money. Mack said this was vehicular homicide, and that in order to do what she did to that poor man, she must've been flying. I told him that she has been speeding down this path ever since she flunked herself out of college and Chick made her a vice president at his bank.

Tell me what you want me to do.

Love,
Dorothy

June 21, 1991

Bitsy:
Claude told me that you've been calling. And there's no need. Jennifer is perfectly fine. I don't know where you are getting your information, but she doesn't drive recklessly. Chick and I taught that child how to drive years ago. And if you continue to spread these lies, you will be hearing from my attorneys.

Elizabeth Wentworth

TELEGRAM TO BITSY

July 8, 1991
For the last time stop calling and writing. STOP Jen won't get letters. STOP
Do not come. STOP Jen not in Crystal Falls. STOP
Elizabeth Wentworth

July 14, 1991

Dear Bitsy,

Mack and I will meet you at the Nashville airport. But don't expect to see Jennifer. The Wentworths weren't lying—they really did whisk her out of town. I will try to find out where. See you soon.

Love,
Dorothy

August 2, 1991

Dear Bitsy,

Despite the stressful circumstances, I so enjoyed visiting with you and Dorothy. It was like old times. All we needed was Earlene and Violet and the Scrabble board. I wish you could've found Jennifer. Could the Wentworths have taken her to California? You know how crazy they are about Betty Ford. They probably have a wing named after them. I will keep firing letters to the Wentworths, so Jennifer won't doubt that we love her. Dorothy says she's been writing up to ten letters a day.

Love,
XX OO

August 6, 1991

Dear Bitsy,

I have thought about the situation with Jennifer and the Wentworths, and I've decided that they're all crazy. Actually, they could be suffering from folie à deux, *or in their case,* trois. *This is a shared delusion, a kind of contagious psychosis, shared by two or more persons living in close, intimate contact. A dominant personality imposes his (or in this case* her*) delusions onto the more passive members of the group. The cure is separation, but that doesn't seem likely. If you need me, I'm here.*

Love,
Violet

A TAPED MESSAGE FROM DOROTHY

September 6, 1991

My darling daughter,
I can't bear to tell you this on the phone and there is nothing you can do anyway. Jennifer is back. I found out that she was put into Cumberland Heights, that new psychiatric hospital next to the bowling alley. I ran into her at the Winn-Dixie and hardly recognized her. She was wild-eyed and skinny, and she had a cigarette in her hand. She said, "Oh, hi, Dorothy," like she saw me every day and nothing out of the ordinary had happened. She told me she was just fine except she was in a real, real bad mood. I tried to tell her that you've been sick with worry, but her eyes went dead. I could tell that she wasn't listening. I thought to myself, This is the saddest thing in the world. You have lost each other twice.
If I can do anything, let me know, and I will try my best. Meanwhile, I will continue to spy.
Love,
Dorothy (a.k.a. 007)

September 16, 1991

To My Biological Mother:
I almost died. You didn't care. After my accident you never wrote. You never called. So now you are like dead to me. These are all the old cards and letters you ever wrote me, the ones when I was a baby. I don't know why I saved them. Throw them away. Use them to start fires.
Grandmother took me to a therapist who says that YOU are the reason I'm fucked up. Your bad decisions set the tone for my life. So thanks bunches. My life is in total shambles. And don't try and say that Grandmother and Dad prevented you and me from developing a relationship. If you'd really loved me, you would've found a way.
I am 19 years old. I don't need a mother anymore. If I do, I've got quite a few stepmothers to choose from.
Jennifer

Bitsy

I called Violet to ask if she could explain why Jennifer was acting so hostile. My cousin said she couldn't imagine a legitimate therapist saying those awful things. She went on to explain about how our relationships with our mothers are critical to who we become, and affect all other relationships. Then she told me to stop blaming myself. That in this case Miss Betty seized that role, so if anyone is to blame, it's her.

Violet laughed and said that even at her age she hesitates to call her mother because all she talks about is her coffee shop and her hot flashes and irregular periods. Violet said that Aunt Clancy is going through Menopaws.

I hung up and walked into the conservatory, leaning my cheek against a glass pane. Violet's voice was still in my head. I missed the days when we'd all been together. Despite all of my troubles, that era had been a sort of golden age. And it would never come again.

July 11, 1992

Dear Mother,

I am working the 12-Step program, and I can't seem to get past #8 and #9 where I'm supposed to make a list of all the people I've harmed. Then I have to make amends to them. So, I forgive you, okay? Meanwhile, I am waiting for God, or my Higher Power, or whoever, to remove my shortcomings. I wish I'd meet the right guy.

One Day at a Time,
Jennifer

November 3, 1992

Dear Bitsy,

My Pomeranian had 2 puppies. I plan to sell them for a small fortune, not that I need it. I have enclosed a copy of a note that I sent to Barbara Bush since you enjoy reading my letters so much.

November 3, 1992

Dear Barbara,

Today I voted for your hubby, and I almost had second thoughts. I wondered if I should have voted for Clinton. Well, he is cute. Al Gore's not too shabby, either, and he's from my home state, even if he doesn't talk real Southern. I suppose that's Tipper's influence. Despite that, I might have voted the Democratic ticket just to see what they'd do with health care, but what finally tipped the scales was Hillary's cookies. Maybe it's just me, but they looked store-bought. I would appreciate having your recipe. I'll be staying up all night, watching the election results.

Your friend,
Dorothy

January 21, 1993

Dear Bitsy,

Here is a tape that I sent to Clinton. I hope you won't get mad that I bragged on you.

Love,
Dorothy

A TAPED MESSAGE TO BILL CLINTON

January 21, 1993

Dear Bill,

As I watched you on TV tonight, I admired your tie and wondered if Hillary had picked it out.

Even though I am too scared to fly over the ocean, I know you're not. Didn't I read somewhere that you went to school in Oxford? Or maybe that's the kind of shoes you wear. I am bad to mix up men's fashions and their education. But if you ever go to England on a diplomatic mission, feel free to look up my daughter. She is an interior decorator—a pretty darn good one, too. She is the favorite of the ritzy-fitzy set, with country houses, horses, and hounds. Her clients are evermore inviting her to parties, and they send a *limousine to pick her up. If the parties are far away, they'll send a private plane. You would like her lifestyle. In fact, y'all might run with the same crowd. Bitsy has decorated for a friend of a friend of Diana, Princess of Wales.*

She's a blue-eyed blonde, a dead ringer for Gennifer, except younger— and more discreet. I wish you were my son-in-law. Not that I'm hoping anything will happen to Hillary—but my daughter has no business living over in England, and she would make you a fantastic First Lady.

Fondly,
Dorothy McDougal

A NOTE FROM LOUIE DECHAVANNES

May 21, 1993

Dear Beauty,
This is my last letter, kid. I love you—always will. If I don't hear from you soon, I'm giving up.
Happy anniversary,
Louie

For days I kept his letter propped on my burled walnut desk, wondering if I should answer or just let it go. I didn't regret England for a moment but he had written faithfully for nearly a decade—this was impressive, considering his attention span. Not that I'd become dependent on those letters. I wasn't exactly leading a solitary existence. My friends were always introducing me to darling men, and I enjoyed their company immensely, but I never allowed myself to care. Every important relationship in my life had been damaged in some way—my mother, my daughter, my lovers. So I could not—would not—risk loving someone that deeply.

Each time I passed my desk, I picked up Louie's letter. It wasn't his threat of giving up on me, but his shaky handwriting that had gotten my attention. I had an image of him—all withered and stooped as he bent over the stationary, his fingers stiff and gnarled as they gripped the pen. Finally, I sat down at the desk, took out a sheet of paper, and began to write. But I couldn't find the right tone. I preferred to read a letter than to write one, especially one this important. In minutes, my trash bin filled with crumpled paper.

Dear Louie,
~~Don't be a quitter. Here's my number. Give me a call sometime.~~

I tore that letter up, threw it into the bin, and started over.

Dear Louie
~~Why don't we talk?~~

I ripped up that letter, too. Then I grabbed another sheet and hastily scribbled my phone number. Before I could change my mind, I folded the paper in half and slipped it into the pocket of my cardigan, a lumpy, old thing I'd brought from 214 Dixie Avenue. I started to make tea, then I happened to glance at my watch. I had promised to meet my friend Rosamund at Waterstone's, where she was promoting her latest children's book. Rosamund was a tall, angular blonde who bit her nails to the quick and chain-smoked. I'd decorated her Kensington flat last year, and while we were very different, we'd become friends, despite her irritating habit of dragging me to book signings and parties, introducing me to eligible writer-friends—not my sort of chaps whatsoever. In fact, just last month, she'd insisted I attend a publishing party in Bedford Square, where I'd met her editor, a young, blond fellow named Ian. I tried to be cordial, but privately dismissed him as too young.

Hoping the outing to Waterstone's might clear my head, I dashed out of my flat and caught a taxi on Picadilly. When I reached the bookstore, Rosamund was nowhere to be found. Instead of my friend, I found her editor sitting on the floor, reading *The Secret Garden* to several dozen children. I sat down with the kids, mesmerized by his voice, the elegant flat As and blurred Rs. After he finished, he stood up and the children swarmed past him. I started to leave, too, but he called, "You're Rosamund's friend aren't you?"

"Right." I extended my hand, surprised that he'd remembered.

"Nice to see you again." He gripped my hand and gave it a firm shake. "Once again, Rosamund's gone missing. I was left carrying the can, wasn't I?"

"You were splendid." I loved how the Brits added a rhetorical "wasn't I" to every sentence.

He muttered thanks—which came out sounding like *tah*. "I noticed it stopped raining," he said, glancing out the window. Wobbly sunlight shone down on the damp street. "Do you care to take a stroll?"

We stepped out of the bookstore and headed toward a pub Ian knew just off Charing Cross. The clouds washed low, and it began to rain again. "It's *throwing* it down," Ian said, handing me his umbrella. Then he stepped away to hail a cab. I slid one hand into my cardigan pocket, trying to warm up. A cab pulled up to the curb. When Ian turned to open the door, I started to close the umbrella, but I couldn't get the lever to work. I pulled my hand out of the pocket and my letter to Louie flew up and caught wind. I started to run after it, but then I saw that Ian was waiting. I gave the letter one last glance. It drifted over a phone booth, then caught an updraft and landed on an awning. I hurried over to Ian, and he helped me inside the cab. It smelled faintly of tobacco, but it wasn't unpleasant. Ian gave the pub's address to the driver—"four one treble six." Beads of water clung to his hair and his raincoat. The driver sped off, jolting me against Ian's shoulder. It felt rather nice—solid, familiar. I smelled his cologne—bay and spice and something else. Ian smiled down at me and said, "Sorry about that."

But I wasn't sorry. Not one bit.

. . .

October 15, 1993

Dear Bitsy,

I can't believe that you're 40 years old today. And our little Jennifer will turn twenty-two years old this New Year's Eve. You know how I like to buy ahead, so I got her a cute Dior evening bag from the Episcopal Church rummage sale. I have missed you so much. I'm sorry I couldn't get to London last summer, but I have all these dogs, and it's just so hard to travel.

Love,
Dorothy

January 3, 1994

Dear Bitsy,
Sit down before you read this. I have enclosed a newspaper clipping.
Love,
Dorothy

FROM THE CRYSTAL FALLS DEMOCRAT

Section F, Living, January 3, 1994

Mr. Claude E. Wentworth IV announces the engagement of his daughter, Jennifer, to Pierre Armand Tournear, of Atlanta, Georgia. Ms. Wentworth is the granddaughter of Mr. and Mrs. Claude E. Wentworth III and Dorothy Hamilton McDougal and the late Albert McDougal. A 1989 graduate of Falls High, Ms. Wentworth attended Falls College. She is employed at Citizen's Bank as a vice president.

Mr. Tournear is the son of Mr. and Mrs. Thurmond Tournear of Marietta, Georgia. He briefly attended Kennesaw College and is currently employed at The Gap in Buckhead, Georgia.

The nuptials are slated for May 15, 1994.

Dorothy

After Dorothy mailed the newspaper clipping to Bitsy, she called her granddaughter to complain about not having been told. Jennifer's response was to tell her to take a chill pill. Then she said, "I totally feel your pain, Dorothy. But I WAS going to tell you."

Dorothy couldn't think of a reply. She was sure Miss Betty had made Jennifer keep it from her. Nothing was enough for that woman. Not only had the lofty title of Grandmother been claimed by that old witch, but Dorothy didn't get to have a special name, and that irritated the hell out of her.

"Are you going to tell your mother?" Dorothy asked. "Or shall I?"

"Dammit, stay out of my business," Jennifer cried. "If you tell her anything, I'll personally send someone over to break your legs."

"I promise," Dorothy said. "But it sure is funny that you always cash your mother's checks but fail to return her phone calls."

"Stop meddling. Get a hobby."

"My family is my hobby." Dorothy paused, then quickly changed the subject. "Where did you meet the Frenchman?"

"Pierre isn't French. He's from Georgia."

"Well, that's a relief."

"Oh, forget it. Just tell me Mack's tuxedo size."

"Why?" Dorothy perked up. "Is he going to be an usher?"

Jennifer just snorted. "No, I want to make sure he dresses appropriately." Then she said to make certain that he ordered the tux this week.

"What's the rush?" Dorothy asked. "The wedding isn't till May."

"I just want to be organized."

To Dorothy she sounded just like the crazies on Sally Jessie. Obsessive-compulsive brides cracking up on national TV. As if reading her grandmother's mind, Jennifer said, "Make SURE that you tend to Mack's tuxedo. Or better yet, just give me his measurements, and I'll order it."

That night, Dorothy went over to Mack's house and rifled through his closet, pulling together all his sizes. She wrote them down on an index card then she handed the card to her son, and told him to please call his niece and give her the information, that she was having fits over the tuxedo.

Mack cracked open a Budweiser, sucked up the foam, and told her to handle it.

Dorothy reached for the portable phone and punched in her granddaughter's number, then shoved the receiver into Mack's hand. As he recited his sizes to Jennifer, his face turned pink. He was almost bald, a pale, blue-eyed, bald-headed man with purple bags under his eyes, not to mention a sour yellow complexion. *If his liver is shot,* Dorothy thought, *I will give him mine.*

Mack's forehead puckered and he said, "Inseam? Mama didn't give me one."

He held out the receiver, as if gripping a live copperhead. Jennifer was yelling, "I have never *heard* of someone not knowing his inseam. What kind of throwback *are* you? Listen, if you want to come to my wedding, you'd better get your sizes in order."

Mack hung up the phone and scowled at his mother. "This is *your* fault. You didn't give me a fucking inseam."

"No," she told him. "But God did."

Part 8

Bitsy Wentworth DeChavannes

High above Green Park, in a drafty, rooftop conservatory, my heirloom Spode cup lay shattered on the floor, spilling Lung Ching tea over the stones. I was feeling pretty shattered myself. In my lap was an engraved invitation to the wedding of my twenty-two-year-old daughter. I'd known about her engagement; I'd even been expecting this invitation. Still, she had managed to shock me. I put on my reading glasses, then reached for the card.

Claude Wentworth IV
requests the honor of your presence
at the wedding of his daughter
Jennifer
to
Pierre Armand Tournear,
on Saturday, the Fifteenth of May,
at half after six o'clock in the evening
nineteen hundred ninety-four
Hammersmith Farm
Crystal Falls, Tennessee
Reception immediately following

R.S.V.P.

The R.S.V.P. had been X'd out in green ink; but it was the phrase "wedding of his daughter" that had sent my teacup flying.

The heat rose to my face, and I fanned myself with the invitation, inhaling the faint scent of Boucheron. The fragrance evoked Jennifer, a small-boned, delicate woman with fierce blue eyes, her blond hair savagely cut into wisps that curled, Caesar-like, around a pale, broad forehead. We hadn't spoken in months, not since our last long-distance squabble, which had begun with a disagreement over the pronunciation of Hermès, and ended with her slamming down the phone. I'd tried to reach her, but she wouldn't answer my calls or letters. When it came to fashion, my daughter was up to date, but in all matters concerning me, she was merciless.

Still fanning myself, I rose from the chaise and stepped over the wreckage. I slipped a John Coltrane CD into the machine, and as "Lush Life" began to play, I calculated the time in Tennessee, then grabbed the phone and dialed my daughter's number before I could change my mind.

"Hi," I said, and my stomach lurched.

"Oh, it's you." She paused. "I suppose you're calling about the invitation."

"Yes." Cradling the receiver between my chin and shoulder, I stepped over to the French door and pressed my forehead against the rain-pelted glass. A straggly arm of laburnum stretched over the lower half of the rooftop terrace. It reminded me of the wisteria in my mother's garden. In a few weeks it would be blooming and bees would hum over the flowers. I had once foolishly pictured myself and Jennifer relaxing on the terrace, sharing a pot of jasmine tea and a platter of cress-and-egg sandwiches.

"Ecru is totally classic. Don't you love the pearl filigree?" Jennifer's voice suddenly turned girlish, rising and falling with excitement. "Wait till you see the napkins and matchbooks. And my dress is, like, oh my *God*. It's Vera Wang. A mermaid dress in oyster duchesse satin, and the veil is to *die* for. The tiara was made from Grandmother's old Van Cleef & Arpels choker."

"I can't wait to see it," I said, trying to sound impressed, but I was distracted by the felicitous association of "grandmother" and "choker."

"And for the wedding," she continued, "Pierre's wearing a black tailcoat, white pique shirt with a white pique vest and bow tie. Ditto for the groomsmen and ushers, but with different boutonnieres. But you might know all of this if you lived within driving distance. Or even if you *called* once in a while."

"I have tried. Your machine always picks up." I shut my eyes and pressed two fingers against the lids. I started to ask if she'd received her birthday present—I'd sent it months ago—or if she'd read my letters. Not that it was important. Maybe I should let it go. One part of me was determined to rise above petty squabbles, but another part, the part I got from my mother's family, demanded justice.

What came out was, "Why was my name left off the invitation?"

Jennifer released a long, stagy sigh. "I *knew* you wouldn't understand."

"It leaves the impression that you don't have a mother."

"Have I?"

La Belle Dame Sans Merci, I thought and started to hang up, but with the receiver halfway down, I stopped. If I broke the connection, I would be severing one of the last fragile strands between us.

"Look, I'm sorry if you're upset," Jennifer was saying. "I sent the invitation as a courtesy. I don't expect you to come. That's why I crossed off the R.S.V.P."

"Of course I'll be there," I said, breathing in faint traces of Boucheron, laburnum, and Lung Ching tea. "I wouldn't miss it for anything."

"Why not? You skipped my childhood. Look, do us both a favor and disregard the invitation. Just stay on your side of the ocean, and I'll stay on mine. But if you feel like sending a gift, I could use a Portmerion saucer. Unless you'd care to splurge on a teapot or a platter. My pattern is 'Botanic Garden.' Harrod's should have it."

I heard a decisive click and the line began to buzz. I continued to hold the receiver, hoping that it was a mistake, that I would hear my daughter's voice. Then, with one trembling finger, I punched redial. While the line rang, I prepared the words in my mind. *Jennifer, there's so much you don't know. I'm not a villain, just a flawed woman who loves you beyond all else.* But Jennifer was either ignoring her phone, or she'd left her house. I closed my eyes, hoping the answering machine would pick up, so I could at least leave a message. It didn't. Finally I hung up.

While "Seven Steps to Heaven" played in the background, I gathered the pieces of the broken cup. How strange that it had survived fifty years of upheavals in my grandmother's life, and half as many in my own—including my hurried escape across the ocean—without so much as a chip, then finally succumbed to my own clumsiness.

On my way to the trash bin, I stopped beside an arched window, with its soothing views of the park. *I will too go to that wedding,* I told myself. *I'm not giving up without a battle this time.*

Through the window, I saw people rushing down Queen's Path carrying umbrellas, huddled beneath raincoats. A decade ago, when I'd arrived in London, I'd panicked when the BBC weatherman had cheerily predicted rain for ten straight days. Now, all these years later, the rain was still falling. Down on the path, a punk with green hair approached an elderly gentleman who brandished his umbrella. The punk seemed unimpressed and hurried down the path. The park had once been the site of duels, but now it was used as a shortcut from Piccadilly to Buckingham Palace. Not too far away, on Eccleston Place, my much-younger lover, Ian Maitland, was probably working in his gloomy publishing office, surrounded by galleys and FedEx envelopes. I was expecting him for tea. I imagined what he might say about my row with Jennifer. He would probably point out that "disinvited" wasn't a word, but I couldn't think of another one. "Uninvited" didn't fit, either, because I *had* been invited.

As I contemplated the etymology of the word *invite,* I wandered into the kitchen, set the kettle onto the stove, and turned up the flame. In the living room, on the CD player, John Coltrane had been replaced with Luther Vandross, who was singing "A House Is Not a Home." To Luther, a chair was a chair, but I had to disagree: I was an interior designer, and I spent my days selecting fabrics, colors, and textures. Ian, who collectively dismissed my clients as "the Penelopes, Cynthias, and Daphnes," had been surprised when he'd first seen my flat. He'd been expecting Osborn & Little, but instead he'd found worn slipcovers, lumpy cushions, overflowing bookcases, and a hodgepodge of woods and periods. It seemed to me that objects seldom brought peace of mind, but I kept my opinions to myself. It wasn't my place to define another person's happiness. So, whatever my clients wanted—whether it was a Russian antique or Flemish tapestry—I worked hard to find it.

The phone warbled its two-note British ring. Thinking it might be Ian, I skidded across the polished floor and picked up the receiver. I was just about to say something provocative, when I recognized my mother's voice, high-pitched and nasal, with just a touch of hysteria. "I hope it's not the middle of the night over there," Dorothy said. "I tried to figure the time difference, but I couldn't remember if I counted forward or backward. Whoever dreamed up the time zones ought to be hog-tied. There's no need to s-p-r-e-a-d time. It's not butter."

"It's forward." I wondered if my mother was pacing while she talked—all of Dorothy's telephones had twenty-foot cords, and she prowled around the house with the receiver tucked beneath her chin, while she used her shirttail to dust Hummels and bird figurines.

"Your daughter just called me," Dorothy said.

"And?"

"You've got every right to be upset over that invitation, but at least you got one. Of course, she *says* mine is on its way. But I don't trust her. It's those Wentworth genes. Claude's people come from crocodiles. Thank goodness Jennifer inherited your prettiness and my sweetness."

I let that pass. My daughter possessed all the sweetness of an unripe persimmon.

"She offered to have the invitations reprinted," Dorothy rushed on, china rattling in the background.

"But they've been mailed."

"You know what, honey? You need to *drop* this. So what if your name was left off? You've got the birth certificate to prove that you're the mother."

"Haven't you heard?" I laughed. "Claude is Jennifer's mother *and* her father."

"Don't be bitter, honey. It won't do you a bit of good, trust me. I cornered the market on bitter. Besides, I know what's wrong with you. It's the change of life. Your estrogen is out of whack. When I was forty-one, I didn't have a single hormone left in my body," Dorothy went on. "I'll bet your estrogen is on *E*."

"I won't be forty-one until October."

"I know when your birthday is," Dorothy said. "You're a Libra, the sign of Air. Although you act like a Pisces. A fish out of water." Dorothy's voice turned strident. "You've just got to come to the wedding and show those Wentworths what you're made of. Pack your finest outfits, okay?"

"Outfits? I need more than one?"

"There's the rehearsal supper and the wedding," Dorothy said.

I wondered if I had time to dash over to Aquascutum or Jaeger, but alterations might take forever. My friend Caroline knew fashion designers from St. Martin's and the Royal College of Art, but she was hiding out in northern Italy with a famous (and very married) rock star.

"You've missed all the teas and bridal showers. Actually, I missed them, too. The post office keeps losing my invitations. At least, that's what Jennifer claims."

"She's utterly gormless." I set down my teacup—a chipped Wedgwood I'd found in the cabinet—taking great care to place it in the exact center of the saucer. "It means lacking sense."

"Then why didn't you say that in the first place?" Dorothy's voice began to rise. "England has plumb ruined you. Why, you can't even talk like a normal Southerner. Why don't you use words that I can understand?"

"Like incurable paranoid schizophrenia?"

Dorothy gasped.

Damn, I hadn't meant to say anything hurtful. I started to apologize but the line popped, then went dead.

Dorothy and Jennifer

After Dorothy hung up on her daughter, she walked out onto her screened-in porch and sat down in the glider. She wondered if a dizzy spell might be coming on—she always got one when she fussed with her children, or if Mack tried to bring home a girlfriend. Worked like a charm, too. She glanced out into the yard. This morning, the weatherman had said the temperature might climb to seventy-five. Dorothy was wearing Gap jeans, the cuffs rolled up past her ankles. Her T-shirt said BLOOM WHERE YOU ARE PLANTED, which gave her a chuckle because it was so absurd. It made her think of funerals. The dead weren't buried so much as planted, encased in pricey caskets. These days, the only flowers at the cemetery were store-bought.

She ran a hand over her hair, smoothing the fuzz. Her eyebrows had been hastily drawn with a black pencil. She was big-boned and blond, her muscles hard beneath the wrinkled skin. Her facial tics had long since stopped, but another problem had taken their place: She was growing a small hump on her back. *Redbook* said it was a calcium deficiency. If this was true, her bones were on the verge of snapping to pieces. When she'd showed the lump to Byron Falk, he'd prescribed a medicine to squirt up her nose, which seemed like malpractice. She was hunchbacked, not allergic.

Rocking back and forth, she stared through the screen mesh, trying to see what was coming up in the flower beds. In a few days the irises would bloom en masse, as Bitsy would say. The citizens of Crystal Falls took special pride in their iris beds. After the blooming season, the women would begin to "divide and multiply," which sounded Biblical, but it was a gardening technique. The women dug up their irises, separating the rhizomes into Y-shaped pieces. Using a sharp knife, they cut chunks away from the mother rhizome, making sure each section had at least one bud and one root. Then they would replant the rhizomes. Personally, Dorothy thought the procedure was more like "divide and conquer," because the ladies liked to sequester their plants, irises in one section, daffodils in another, nothing mingled together. However, the whole process of separating the babies from the mother rhizome wasn't too different from sending a child out into the world: neither could be accomplished without some type of severing.

In the old days, the Hamilton graveyard had been only a short distance from the house, and Dorothy had thought the land was haunted. She remembered squatting next to the tombstones, trying not to shiver, while Miss Gussie divided and planted rhizomes on graveyard day. She put a yellow iris beside each tombstone. Now, of course, the field was a subdivision. In the early '70s, Mack had inherited the land from Miss Gussie, which made up for years of slights. Well, it made up a little. He had moved the family graves and divided the land into teeny yards and built Hamilton Place. Once in a while, in one of the yards, an iris managed to punch through an expanse of crabgrass. This seemed miraculous, as if her mother, and all the women before her, were having the last word.

Dorothy stepped off the porch, into the yard, and paused beside the perennial beds. This time of year they were a mess, because the weeds were shooting up. She leaned over, snatched up a clump of God knows what. It might have been volunteers from the privet hedge, or even marijuana. When Clancy Jane had lived here, she'd been a dope fiend. She probably still was. Dorothy sniffed the weeds. A few seconds later, she felt strange and prickly. She couldn't remember if she'd taken her pills this morning; but then she never could.

What she needed to do was weed those beds. Yard work was satisfying—she just loved raking, mowing, mulching. It toned her muscles and calmed her mind. She was in darn good shape for a sixty-two-year-old woman. Although lately, the arguments with Jennifer and Bitsy had made her agitated. And now Clancy Jane's weeds had set off charley horses in her arms and legs. Nothing but pins-and-needles. Her hands prickled, the fingertips throbbing. Byron had diagnosed her as having panic attacks, but he was crazy. In case he hadn't noticed, she was no longer a mental patient, and she was entitled to have illnesses just like a normal woman. But no, he kept on prescribing brain pills. She took enough medicine to control the moods of a small country—Liechtenstein or Andorra. When Bitsy and Louie had been married, they'd sent her postcards from their vacations, otherwise Dorothy wouldn't have known about such places. Dorothy kept them pinned to her refrigerator with magnets, or stuffed them around the mirror in her living room. The picture cards had outlasted her daughter's marriage—and to such a nice man. Years ago, if anyone had told her that Bitsy would not only be living alone, but outside the continental United States, Dorothy would have laughed her head off. Then, after Bitsy up and moved to London—actually, fled was more accurate—Dorothy had phoned the girl daily, begging her to return *immediately*.

"Leave the man, not the entire *country*," Dorothy had begged. Louie DeChavannes was one of the most gifted cardiovascular surgeons in New Orleans and the biggest liar in Louisiana. Bitsy had felt an urgent need to place distance between Louie and herself, and (Dorothy suspected) also from her outrageous relatives back in Tennessee. But mainly, the girl had left because of Louie's philandering.

"He can be a one-man woman," Dorothy had protested.

"Don't you mean *one-woman* man?" Bitsy had said. "And no, he can't."

Now Dorothy's lips felt numb, and she patted them with her fingertips. She wondered if she should take a Valium; then again, she might need a Lasix. Or maybe she'd already taken them. Oh, it was such a bother trying to remember this pill, that pill. Jennifer was always making smart-aleck comments about the amber bottles lined up in the kitchen window. Sometimes after her granddaughter left, the Valium bottle was empty. Well, never mind, that was *all right*. Jennifer had inherited her nerves from Bitsy and Clancy Jane, but the hoity-toity airs came straight from Betty Wentworth, and maybe just a bit from Bitsy, too. Personally, Dorothy would rather have panic attacks than pomp.

Out in the yard, her Pomeranians began to squabble when an old striped alley cat, a descendant of Clancy Jane's pride, strutted past them. Earlier this morning, she had tethered the dogs to her clothesline, using swivel hooks to prevent snarls and tangles—she needed to get a patent on that idea, it would sell like hotcakes. The dogs ran back and forth, barking and growling, the metal hooks zipping along the rope. The male rose on his hind legs, which were no bigger than the barbecued hot wings from the Piggly Wiggly, and clawed the air with his front paws. The alley cat trotted down the path, his tail crooked at the end, ignoring the uproar.

"Quit that," Dorothy told the Pomeranians. She and Mack had taken

the dogs to training classes at the fairgrounds, one at a time, and the hard
work had paid off. The dogs settled down and began to pant. Dorothy
leaned over and started yanking out weeds—they looked like privet
branches. The Poms watched her, their beady eyes glimmering with intelligence. Then, two pregnant females began squabbling over a Nylabone—
they were like human women fighting over a man. The five-pound bitch
bit the three-pounder's tail, dragging her down the length of the clothesline. Dorothy planned to sell the puppies for three hundred dollars each.
The name of her kennel was "Dorothy's Darlings," and she advertised in
the back of the AKC *Gazette*, featuring adorable photographs—
Pomeranian puppies in teacups and little red wagons. And if people
called her a puppy miller, she'd sue. She'd already put a warning in her ad:
"I don't have a kennel! These puppies are home-raised with love." And a
clothesline, she thought, chuckling to herself. Truth be told, she'd rather
raise dogs than children. Dogs didn't ask if you'd had your pill. They didn't
ask for a g.d. thing except a pat on the head and a bowl of Eukanuba—
Dorothy served hers Small Bites, ordered special from the Co-op.
Though her Poms occasionally pee-peed on the floor, they'd never
crapped on her. Which was more than Dorothy could say about humans.

She pulled up another privet branch and then paused to watch her dogs
bounce up and down, play-fighting and sniffing each other's behinds, then
she leaned over the flowerbeds and poked her head into a patch of bloomed-
out peonies that her mother had planted way back in 1936. Most of
Dorothy's people were dead, buried in Crystal Falls Memorial Gardens, and
she made a point of keeping flowers—not artificial!—on the graves. She
wondered who, if anyone, would tend to her grave after she was gone. She
hoped Mack would bring a push mower, or maybe plant a few tulip bulbs,
but that didn't seem likely. Grave-tending was woman's work, and there were
no women in the family left around here, save Jennifer and Clancy Jane.
Somehow, Dorothy couldn't see those two picking up a trowel.

Her family was dwindling, and it saddened her. She was the only one
left at 214 Dixie—thank goodness Mack was next door. Yes, everyone
was gone, but they'd left things behind. Stuck way back in a drawer, she'd
found Bitsy's old perfume bottles, still smelling of Shalimar, and Clancy
Jane's love beads. In the tip-top of a kitchen cabinet, she'd pulled out
Easter candy, hardened and cracked. It broke her heart to think that
objects outlasted people.

From the street, she heard the revving of an engine. She recognized the sound and rose up on her tiptoes, holding one hand over her eyes. Jennifer's red BMW rolled up the steep driveway, setting off another round of barking. Her granddaughter hopped out of the car and strode up the walkway, toward the kitchen door, her high heels clicking on the cracked pavement.

"I'm in the garden," Dorothy called, waving the privet branches. The fat female Pom—Dorothy couldn't bear to call her a bitch, it was just too derogatory—made a perfect bow-wow bark, but the others sounded as if they were gargling with battery acid. Jennifer spotted her grandmother and headed toward the garden. The sun glinted on her short blond hair—a Mia Farrow haircut, Dorothy called it, although Jennifer had never seen *Rosemary's Baby*, much less reruns of *Peyton Place*. She always thought Dorothy was referring to someone she'd known in the mental hospital. Today, Jennifer's hair stuck up in all directions. She'd done this *on purpose*. Dorothy had seen the girl squirt mousse into her hand, then scrub it over the razor-shorn locks, letting it dry higgly-piggly.

Normally when the girl visited, she was decked out in outrageously expensive clothes, and she annotated each item for Dorothy's benefit, from the designer to the price. Today the girl was dressed like a punk funeral director: a short black skirt, black hose, ruched ivory top, and a black denim jacket. Not too much eye makeup. Tiny pearl studs in her ears, a discreet gold ring in her nose. She had a pierced belly button, too, although it was thankfully hidden under the top, along with a heart tatoo on her left shoulder. In the heart's center were tiny black letters: CHIC. These days, her hero was Courtney Love, whom she uncannily resembled except for the Mia haircut.

"You won't be wearing black hose much longer," Dorothy called. "Memorial Day is nearly here."

"It's weeks away." Jennifer frowned at the Pomeranians, who kept lunging toward her, causing the clothesline to bow. "Those are the worst-natured dogs I've ever seen," she added and stepped around the yipping animals, making faces at them. One Pom started rolling in the dirt, and the pregnant females fell on each other in a death lock, biting each other's furry throats.

Dorothy whirled around, facing the dogs, and screamed, "Leave it!"

The dogs froze. "There," Dorothy said with a nod. "That's better."

"They don't understand a word you're saying," said Jennifer.

"Yes, they do. They're just not used to strangers." She glanced toward the clothesline. The dogs had settled down, sniffing each other's bottoms, their lips drawn back, tongues coiled like elf toes.

"I'm a stranger?"

Of course, you are! Dorothy thought. *You're flat-out peculiar.* Although, she had to give the girl credit—her black shoes were magnificent. Dorothy knew good leather when she saw it. She decided that Jennifer wasn't as pretty as Bitsy. Her features were Wentworthy—her nose was pugged, just like her daddy's used to be before it got broken, and her square jaw was Miss Betty's made over.

"I didn't mean that, honey," Dorothy said. "We just don't get a lot of guests."

"Are you saying that I should visit more?" Jennifer pawed the grass with her pretty little shoe, in an unconscious imitation of the male Pomeranian, who was stamping his paw, snorting like a pint-sized bull. "We talk on the phone all the time," Jennifer added.

"Yes, you're real good to call." Dorothy nodded at her granddaughter's shoes. "I love your pumps."

"These?" Jennifer kicked out one leg. "Manolo Blahnik."

"I *thought* so," Dorothy lied. Truth be told, she didn't have a clue, although the name rang a distant bell. She wasn't familiar with shoe designers, even though Jennifer always brought over stacks of old fashion magazines, instructing Dorothy to study the fine print. And she'd looked at every single page. She never used to care about labels—she'd only minded if a dress made her look fat. But she liked to keep up with fashion so she'd have something in common with her granddaughter.

"You haven't mentioned my Birkin." Jennifer lifted the boxy handbag: black leather with a gold padlock. "It's Hermès. Four thousand dollars. A gift from Grandmother Wentworth. She was on a waiting list. I just got it last week."

"That's almost as much as a first-class ticket to London," Dorothy said. Jennifer's obsession with fashion seemed like a desperate bid for attention, and also one-upmanship. She seemed to be saying, *Look at me, Mother. I like what you like, only I can afford it.* Dorothy had seen a case just like this on Sally Jessy.

"I'd rather have a Birkin." Jennifer opened the bag, revealing an impossibly chic jumble—sunglasses, Louis Vuitton wallet, tube of Estée Lauder "Jungle Red" lipstick, tin of Altoids, thick stack of invitations.

Dorothy thought she saw condoms; a whole strip of them, each little square attached to the next like travel-sized Polident tablets. Although it might have been snacks, Fruit Roll-ups, or hermetically sealed teabags. Before Jennifer shut her bag, Dorothy thought she spotted a T and a J on the foil.

"Stop looking at my stuff." Jennifer slung the bag over her arm. "I don't look at *yours*."

"Count your lucky stars. You'd get snakebit," said Dorothy. Her granddaughter reminded her of someone—not Clancy Jane, not Miss Betty, but her own self. A thousand years ago, Dorothy had been a ring-tailed tooter.

"I wish Mother could see my Birkin. Remember that horrible fight we had about the pronunciation of Hermès?"

Dorothy made no comment. She'd heard this story before. Bitsy and Jennifer had agreed the "H" was silent, but they'd been divided about the "s" and the "è." Bitsy had pronounced it "Air-mess"; Jennifer had insisted it was "Er-Mays." Bitsy had pointed out that she'd recently heard the proper pronunciation in the Paris boutique, and Jennifer had demanded to know why her mother could jet off to France and not the U.S.

"I *have* been there," Bitsy had said. "In fact, I was in Atlanta last summer buying fabric for—"

"You were *that* close, and you didn't even call?" Jennifer had cried.

"I tried several times," Bitsy said.

"You didn't leave a message."

"Yes, I did."

"My answering machine *never* malfunctions."

"Maybe you accidentally erased it?"

"You could've at least called Dorothy, or even Clancy Jane, but no, that was too much trouble."

When Dorothy had heard about Bitsy's secret trip to the States, she'd sided with Jennifer, and the two of them had gleefully indulged in Bitsy-bashing. For a time, Dorothy and her granddaughter had seemed to bond. Jennifer began phoning late at night, and they'd complain about Bitsy for hours, dredging up her peccadilloes, obsessing over her shortcomings. And they had so many to choose from—why, Bitsy's flaws were as plentiful as the weeds in Dorothy's garden. She had forgiven her daughter—she always did—but Jennifer had been less magnanimous.

Now, Jennifer rubbed the Birkin, her fingers leaving smudges over the leather. "I can't stay long today. In fact, I'm late for the bank. But I have a quick question."

Dorothy prepared herself for a lecture. When it came to her grand-daughter, there was no such thing as a quick question. And lately, every single time the girl came over, she nagged Dorothy about her wedding attire. That was what she called it: Attire.

"But you haven't even given me a kiss," Dorothy said.

"Not now, Dorothy." Jennifer stepped backward. "You're filthy. What's that in your hands?"

"Privet hedge." Dorothy held up the weeds.

"Well, throw it away." Jennifer waved one hand. Her nail beds were inflamed and ragged. *What would make a woman gnaw her own hands like that?* Dorothy wondered. Especially one who was a slave to fashion. What quirks lay beneath her privileged upbringing? Personally, Dorothy thought her granddaughter had been indulged with one too many shop-ping sprees and bikini waxes. Dorothy knew *all* about that procedure, and she thought it was ridiculous. In her old age, she'd grown to like body hair. And why endure *pain* to get rid of it, especially when it didn't show? Jennifer swore it was the latest trend, but Dorothy had no intention of surrendering a single pubic hair.

"I hope you're wearing gloves for the wedding." Dorothy picked up her granddaughter's hand.

"I'm getting acrylics."

Dorothy dragged her eyes away from those horrible nails and studied her granddaughter's petite frame. Why, she was almost the size of a whip-pet or Italian greyhound—two breeds Dorothy wouldn't own if you paid her. She circled her fingers around Jennifer's wrist. "Have you had break-fast?"

"God, no." Jennifer pulled her hand out of Dorothy's grasp.

"But you're too thin. Let me fry you an egg. Or would you prefer poached?"

"My wedding gown is a size two. One egg, any style, and I'll have to find a seamstress."

"But I know you drink coffee. I've got a fresh pot in the kitchen."

"I'll get a cup at the bank."

"Not like mine. I buy my beans from Clancy Jane. Your mother loves how I make coffee." Dorothy began to chatter about the differences in beans, then she gave Jennifer a recipe that called for coffee. While she talked, she excitedly waved her hands, and the Pomeranians scrambled to their feet and started barking. The male began to yodel, and Dorothy snapped her fingers. "Sit! All of you!" she bellowed. The dogs eyed each other warily; they skittered in agitated circles before reluctantly perching on their furry tails. The male gave a disgusted snort and showed Dorothy his teeth. The dogs looked miserable, like prisoners let out for exercise, but they didn't flinch. They kept their butts down and their beady little eyes trained on Dorothy, waiting for the next command.

"I didn't come here to discuss recipes," said Jennifer. "I don't even like to cook. What I came to ask is, have you decided what you're wearing to the wedding festivities?"

"Not *this* again." Dorothy looked up into the trees. "For the last time, I'm wearing suits. One to the rehearsal and one to the wedding."

"I just hope they're dressy. Can't you buy a gown?"

"But they're designer suits."

"And did you buy them for my wedding, at a department store, or at a garage sale?"

"I'll have you know that I found a Gucci blouse at a yard sale last month," Dorothy said, bristling. Nobody but *nobody* was allowed to mock her bargain hunting. "Just for the record, I'm wearing a St. John to the rehearsal and a Chanel to the wedding."

"Can I see?"

"You'll have to stop by the dry cleaners." Dorothy averted her eyes. Actually, her suits were hanging in the hall closet. They had once belonged to Miss Betty, and her fat shoulders had ripped holes in the armpits.

"Don't you have anything more elegant?"

"What's more elegant than Chanel?"

Jennifer shrugged. "What color are they? I really need to know."

"For the corsages?" Dorothy said, perking up.

"No, so you won't clash with Grandmother Wentworth's ensemble. Or with Pierre's grandmothers' gowns." Jennifer glanced coolly at Dorothy's jeans and T-shirt. "It will be *just* like you to wear some putrid color. I have to make sure that you don't."

Dorothy lifted her chin, feeling a surge of defiance. Then she rubbed her forehead. Just for meanness, she ought to wear her latest garage sale find, an orange chiffon dress, tea-length, with Nine West pumps that were dyed-to-match. At this same sale, Dorothy had also bought a lime silk suit with square rhinestone buttons, and matching shoes and a darling bag trimmed in parakeet feathers and faux peridot—more like a pet than a purse, deliciously whimsical and unique. The hostess of the garage sale had been Dorothy's size—that was how she liked to think of those events, little soirees with hostesses who didn't give a rat's ass how long you stayed; although Dorothy just dropped in, made the rounds, and then flitted off to the next sale/soiree.

"Afraid I'll show up in a gold lamé pantsuit?" Dorothy lifted one eyebrow, unaware that it was smeared to her hairline, making her resemble a drugged clown.

"You wouldn't do that," Jennifer said, but her eyelids flickered when she stared at her grandmother's forehead.

Dorothy shrugged.

"Look, I've got enough to worry about." Jennifer planted her feet wide apart on the grass, her arms tightly folded, hands tucked into the armpits of her denim jacket. "Have you talked to Mother recently?"

"I have." Dorothy repressed a smile. There was no way in *hell* that she'd tell this mean-spirited child a single word that Bitsy had said. Her old psychiatrist had called her a control freak, but he didn't know doodly-squat about mothers and daughters, much less haute couture. He'd worn mismatched socks, but that had been his wife's fault. It was up to the woman to dress a man.

"And?" Jennifer leaned forward.

"It's quaint how you call her Mother. It just sounds so sweet and old-fashioned," Dorothy said, trying to stall. "I haven't gotten *my* invitation, by the way," she added. "I hope it's not lost in the mail."

"I've got one right here." Jennifer opened the Birkin, pulled out an ivory card. "Read it and tell me if *you* see anything wrong."

Dorothy took the card. It was pretty, no doubt the most expensive design at the bridal shop. When she read "his daughter" she glanced up at Jennifer.

"No, her name isn't there, and I'm *sorry*. But she hasn't been interested in me lately." Jennifer turned her face up to the budding Catawba tree. It was crawling with worms, the best fishing bait in the world.

"She's more than interested," said Dorothy. "She *loves* you."

"Stop defending her. The woman is, like, totally focused on herself."

"And you're not?" Dorothy pursed her lips, wondering if she should speak her mind or keep quiet. One of her favorite needlepoint sayings came from Will Rogers—"Never miss a good chance to shut up." But after all the psychobabble at Central State, she'd learned a few things about human nature—maybe not about her own, but self-analysis could be dicey—and she was eager to share them.

"Oh, Dorothy. You just don't understand."

"Maybe not, but why don't you call her? Tell her you're sorry—"

"No way." Jennifer gave Dorothy a withering look. "If anything, *she* owes *me* an apology. When I was a baby, she almost killed me!"

"But she didn't. You can't persecute a person for what *might* have been. Why are you dredging up this ancient history?"

Jennifer lifted both hands, ran them over her head. When she stopped, her hair looked like it had been chewed by a Rottweiler. "I just can't please my mother. Everything I do is wrong."

"It's not a matter of pleasing her, Miss Fussy Britches. It's a matter of not hurting her."

"She's not hurt. She's *pissed*. There's a difference."

Dorothy looked up into her granddaughter's eyes, searching for some tiny shred of compassion. She saw nothing but self-pity, a child hell-bent on making the world pay for every real and imagined slight.

"When did you get on *her* side?" The veins pulsated in Jennifer's pale, thin neck.

"I'm on yours, too."

"Sorry, you can't have it both ways."

"I can have it any damn way I please."

"Then I don't want your support. Give it all to *her*." Jennifer whirled around, charged across the grass. The dogs began to bark, claws scrabbling the dirt.

"Oh, honey, wait. Don't run off like this."

Jennifer hurried down the driveway and climbed into the BMW. As she drove off, Dorothy kept patting her chest, trying to catch her breath. Perspiration ran down the sides of her face. When she wiped it off, she couldn't feel her left cheek. And her left arm was numb, too. The sensation lasted a few seconds, then it was pins-and-needles again. She reached up to push back her hair. It was slick and damp from where she'd been sweating. Well, no wonder with a temperamental granddaughter like Jennifer. Thou shalt have no other mothers before you, she thought. If thy eyebrows offend thee, pluck them out. Pluck the whole g.d. thing. Get a freaking Brazilian wax job—if they can do it *down there*, then brows should be a snap. By damn, she'd cut Jennifer out of her will. She'd leave everything to the American Kennel Club before she'd let one dime of her money into Betty Wentworth's hands. The old hag would just squander it on Birkins and St. Johns.

A wave of dizziness forced Dorothy to her knees. Panic attack, my foot. Byron didn't know what he was talking about. He was too busy keeping his bright-eyed girlfriends entertained. The latest one resembled a younger, slimmer Clancy Jane, but she wasn't a vegetarian. Dorothy had seen them buying groceries together at Kroger, their cart filled with chicken breasts, pork tenderloin, sirloin steaks, even sugar-cured bacon. All the crap that Byron forbade his patients to eat. "Animal fat will raise your cholesterol," he always said. Meanwhile, *he* gorged on hens and hogs and underaged women. Dorothy wondered if his girlfriend got bikini waxes or if she let it all hang out.

Her head was throbbing—not real pain, just a dull ache. Nothing a Tylenol wouldn't cure; but you couldn't take too many of those or you'd ruin your liver. She warned Mack all the time, "Don't take Tylenol if you've been drinking." She didn't really love him the most. Motherly affection couldn't be measured and doled out like paregoric. If only love could be dispensed equally. Or, at the very least, according to body weight. But no, God had left it up to the mothers, not the pharmacists. "Figure it out yourself," He might have said, rushing off to more important events, like the X-rated problems in Sodom and Gomorrah, or the crap tables in Las Vegas. And the clueless mothers did the best they could, offering a dribble to one child, drenching the other, when perhaps it might have been better to pour the excess onto the ground.

Bitsy

At twilight, Ian Maitland dropped by my flat, holding a bag of scones. "My God, you're already in your flannels?" He laughed affectionately. He had straight, dark blond hair, which was quite thick and springy, and he combed it away from his forehead. His sharp jaw and dimpled chin was a bitch to shave, or so he claimed. I took his hand—Ian had great hands, an editor's hands, a man who thought with his fingertips as well as his brain.

"Yes, but wait till you see what's underneath." I led him down the narrow hall and gave him a recap of today's events. His response was a quote. "'Marry in May, live to rue, Aye,'" he said, pulling a scone from the bag. "It's a Scottish saying. Mary Queen of Scots married the Earl of Bothwell on May 15, 1597. It's an ill-omened month for lovers."

"It certainly boded ill for *her*," I said and reached for a raspberry scone—my favorite. Ian frequently showed up on my doorstep with pastries and a small jar of Devonshire cream, ever since I'd admitted a fondness for British tearooms.

I fell into the bed, dragged the covers up to my neck, and smiled at Ian. He was unabashedly sweet and earnest, and he was quite gifted as a lover; but on this particular afternoon, I had another motive for staying beneath the covers: a cold front had moved in overnight, and I was freezing. London wasn't the coldest place on earth, but it certainly wasn't the warmest. My bed was a massive, hideous construction from Queen Victoria's reign, and I had fortified it with at least a dozen woolen blankets, and one rather frilly duvet, yellow and pink, strewn with sweet flowers, but it was deceptively warm, packed with thick down filling.

"Having a lie-in, are we?" He sat on top of the duvet, trapping me beneath it.

"I've just been thinking," I said. "The omission of my name on that invitation is just a prelude. When Jennifer has children, I'll be shut out of their lives, the way I was shut out of hers. Claude will be both the grandmother and grandfather."

"Don't fret, love." Ian touched my cheek. From the CD player, Dolly Parton began singing "Little Sparrow." Behind him the arched windows were raised several inches, and a nippy wind stirred the lace curtains and howled in the fireplace.

"Do you have any silver bullets?" I asked.

"Whatever for?" Ian's eyes widened.

"To shoot the werewolf in my attic." I tried not to smile, but my lips twitched in the corners. I lifted one hand from beneath the duvet and traced my finger along a vein in his hand. How lovely to be a platelet in his bloodstream, traveling though every inch of his body. He moved his hand under the covers, lifted my gown, and touched my bare stomach. I held my breath when his fingers slid over the bumpy scar that began at my navel and ended above my pubic bone. "Still cold?"

"I crave warmth."

"I thought you craved grits and pecans."

"An electric blanket would be lovely," I said wistfully.

"Then you shall have one." He kissed the tip of my nose. Last December, I had taken to my bed with a cold, and he'd fed me tea and cock-a-leeky soup, explaining that British foods were calculated to thwart the chill. As he read passages from *Ivanhoe,* I closed my eyes and drifted on the curve of his voice, wondering if he was the last of his kind, a nurturing man, or if I'd awaken in the morning and discover that I'd been hallucinating.

. . .

Morning sunlight trickled into the bedroom. The windows were cracked open, and the chilly air smelled of hyacinths. Earlier I'd made a pot of tea and had gotten back into bed. Now I was sitting cross-legged in a nest of feather pillows, drinking Earl Grey tea, listening to Dolly Parton sing "I Get a Kick Out of You." Ian was stretched out next to me, his eyes closed; but his nose kept twitching, so I knew he was awake.

I lifted my teacup. This bedroom was my favorite spot—largely due to Ian, of course. Last night we'd gotten dressed and dashed over to the Hard Rock Café for burgers, then we'd raced home, skipping through the park. The bedroom floor showed evidence of our haste: Ian's shirt and pants. My lacy undergarments from Agent Provocateur. A black high heel lay upside-down beneath a tufted chair, in the exact spot I'd tossed it, the toe pointing to an empty bottle of Drambuie.

The wind stirred the curtains, and I shivered. "I'll never adjust to this climate," I said.

This got his attention. He opened his eyes, lifted his head from the pillow. "It's *only* been, what, ten years? Give it another decade or so, love. It's taken us Brits eons." In a dry, humorous voice, he added, "If you crave an inferno, go to Italy, preferably in July. I should take you to the Hotel Monaco in Venice. Stunning views. However, you'd love the pool at the Cipriani."

"I can't wait that long," I said, my teeth chattering. I leaned toward the night table and set down my teacup—a rather ugly pattern by Royal Doulton. "Perhaps I should dash over to Marks and Spencer and buy another blanket."

I burrowed beneath the covers and turned on my side. Ian curled up behind me, rubbing his chin against my shoulder. "You *are* positively frozen. You need a long weekend in Nice."

"I need longer than a weekend. Besides, aren't we going to Ireland?"

"Nice is warmer."

I imagined myself drinking cafe au lait at an umbrella table with Ian, feeding croissant crumbs to the wrens and staring off into the faint blue hills, the country of bad-tempered Cézanne. I remembered a hot, dry summer in Aix-en-Provence—Louie in a café drinking wine, watching me shop in an open-air stall, holding up a long, plastic-wrapped strand of sachets. We'd been apart longer than we'd been together. *Stop*, I told myself. If only these unwanted thoughts could be driven out of my mind by force. I sat up abruptly, dislodging Ian's hands, then slapped my pillow, using a little more strength than necessary. Ian reached out and caught a drifting feather. God, this man was beautiful. Even his gestures were thrilling. I traced my finger around the dimple in his chin. This was feeling far too good. And that was always the prelude to doom. I admonished myself to be cautious, to remember that the McDougal-Hamilton women had notoriously bad luck with men—excluding Violet, of course; and how my cousin had managed to escape this fate was a conundrum—one of the old C words I remembered learning from that battered *Merriam-Webster*.

Another breeze ruffled the curtains, and I said, "I smell hyacinths."

"No, darling," said Ian. "It's ginger. You're breathing in fumes from The Suntory."

I pictured the Japanese restaurant on St. James's Street, and my stomach growled. "You would have to mention food," I said, scooting off the bed. "I'm dying for more tea. How about you?"

"That would be lovely." He reached out to grab my hand and pulled me back for a kiss. Then I hurried into the chilly sitting room. My bare feet scuffed over the thick Persian rug as I stepped past a peeling, burled chest. I paused by the CD player, replacing Dolly with Miles Davis. Poor Dolly, she'd been singing love songs all night. It was time to give her a break.

In the kitchen, I filled the kettle, set it onto a burner, and turned up the flame. While I waited for it to boil, I glanced at a chrome rack where two towels hung crookedly—Mary Queen of Scots on the right, Elizabeth I on the left. The two queens appeared to be having a staring contest. Had they ever been this close in real life? According to Ian, the two monarchs had never met. There was a crease in Elizabeth's towel, right over her heart. Poor Bess had never known her mother. And, despite historical gossip, she might never have known romantic love. This was either the worst tragedy of her life, or her greatest blessing. The Queen of Scots was a love junkie. From her end of the towel rack, her head miraculously restored to its rightful spot, she stared contemptuously at her virgin cousin. "Hypocrite," I told her. Then I felt foolish for talking to a tea towel. From the left, Elizabeth watched with a bemused expression, as if to say wine, women, and song was the tip of the royal iceberg.

I'd purchased the Queen of Scots towel in Edinburgh last October; but I'd bought Elizabeth I several weeks ago, while on holiday in Bath. Ian had teased me when I'd squeezed into a gift shop, working my way past a group of tourists in front of the cathedral. "You'd best hurry," Ian had said, amused. "The souvenirs are going fast."

Now, rubbing my hands over Elizabeth, I wondered if these purchases *proved* something. I wasn't sure what, exactly—that I enjoyed tea towels? That I loved to shop? Tea towels were popular because they were easily folded into the bottom of one's suitcase, and upon return to the United States, there was nothing to declare. Maybe that was all I was doing, collecting mementos, things that would not require extra room in my luggage if I ever left this island.

Not that I was planning to move. Despite the weather, I loved England. Standing on my toes, I opened a cabinet. The wood was painted the color of clotted cream, with dish racks above a long, glossy expanse of black granite counters. When I'd first moved to the UK, I'd designed this kitchen for Lady Agatha Sykes, a well-to-do solicitor, who later moved to South Africa. When she asked if I'd be interested in looking after the flat, I'd jumped at the chance.

All these years later, I was still officially looking after her place. I reached into a cabinet and pulled out cups and saucers patterned with cabbage roses, along with an old china pitcher shaped like a cow. I set everything on a tray. The kettle still hadn't boiled, so I opened a tin of orange-rind biscuits and scattered them onto a plate. The citrus smell reminded me of the summer that Jennifer had visited me in New Orleans and she'd come down with a cold. I'd had nursed the child back to health, feeding her hot tea, chicken noodle soup, and orange-marmalade cookies. Long after Jennifer returned to Crystal Falls, I found myself making "sick child" trays for Louie.

I brought the tea back to the bedroom and Ian scooted up in bed. During my absence, he had lit a candle, even though the room blazed with light. I slid the tray onto the night table, poured his tea, and set two biscuits on the saucer. Across the room, a gust of wind rippled the curtains, and I turned my head, as if listening for something. The noises of London never ceased to enchant me—they still sounded quite foreign, and I liked that jolt of strangeness; but sometimes I could hear music from another flat, and it sounded like the blues and jazz in the French Quarter. Those sweet, sad, heavy voices always filled me with an unspeakable longing.

Dorothy

A TAPED MESSAGE FROM DOROTHY MCDOUGAL

Dear Tipper Gore,
You are the first Second Lady that I've ever written to. For the last
twenty-two years, I have been corresponding with First Ladies. However,
when Hillary came to the White House, I switched tactics and wrote to her
husband. Now, I have selected you. Also, I don't live far from Carthage, so I
expect you to write back. And I've got a lot of questions. First, I want to
know what makes your marriage tick. By the way, I was married to a man
named Albert, but he turned out bad. Sometimes I think that choosing a
husband is as risky as choosing a watermelon. You have to cut it open to see
what you've got. Don't take that the wrong way. I used to be in a mental
hospital, but I'm not dangerous—

Pain shot through Dorothy's head, and she stopped writing. Rubbing her temple, she wondered if she had a brain tumor. More likely it was the stress of Jennifer and Bitsy. Truth be told, Dorothy never missed an opportunity to brag about her daughter. Several years ago, she had been shopping for dog food at the farmer's Co-op, when she'd run into Walter Saylor Jr., Bitsy's old flame. Dorothy had noticed his thinning hair, and his red beard was tinged with gray. His muscles had degenerated, and he had a potbelly. "Well, hello, Mrs. McDougal," Walter had said. "Whatever happened to Bitsy?"

"Didn't you know? She's living in London—that's in England, you know," she added. "I sure do miss her. But did I mention that she's an interior designer? Her clients send her all over the world."

"I'm real happy for her," Walter said, his eyes slanting downward. He told her that he was still practicing dentistry. Apparently he'd never remarried and was living with his mother and sisters. Dorothy told him goodbye, then hurried down the aisle. But she really did wish him the best.

Normally she didn't believe in wishing, she believed in *taking action*. And that was why she'd mailed her copy of Jennifer's wedding invitation to Louie DeChavannes. Yes, it was wrong, but she'd taken guilty pleasure when she'd written out his address in her spidery handwriting, crossing out the printed RSVP information and inserting her own telephone number. She hoped Louie didn't suspect anything. He *was* a brilliant man. And he still sent her Christmas cards, accompanied by a floral arrangement for her dining room table—a table always set for two, since her daughter rarely made it home for the holidays. She wondered if Jennifer didn't want Bitsy at the wedding or if Claude had egged her on—or maybe his new girlfriend was causing trouble.

Dorothy's blood pressure began to rise—or, at least it *felt* like it—when she thought of Claude's latest girlfriend, Samantha Cole-Jennings. You couldn't keep a secret in this town, Dorothy thought, because it usually ended up in the Crystal Fall's *Democrat,* strategically placed on the society page. In recent weeks, Dorothy had seen pictures and write-ups about the parties for Jennifer—bridal teas, kitchen showers, luncheons. In every g.d. picture, standing front and center with Jennifer was Claude's woman. Dorothy had to give him a little credit—Samantha wasn't a vamp or a debutante but somewhere in the middle. And she wasn't too young, either, like his last victim. In the society page pictures, Samantha had a round, pretty face and curly, dark blond hair. Dorothy had asked around, and she'd found out that Samantha came from a middle-class family right here in Crystal Falls—the type the Wentworths looked down on. Samantha's daddy was an insurance agent, and the mother worked in medical records at Crystal Falls General. But she was a far cry from the ritzy-fitzy gals that Claude seemed to favor.

From Dixie Avenue, she heard a revving noise. Then Mack's white truck rolled up his driveway, a thick blacktop that Albert had installed in the '60s, when he was still her Albert, still a family man. Dorothy could hear loud music booming from the truck, something about a watchtower. She prayed that her son wasn't a closet Jehovah's Witness. Rising from her chair, she scuttled off the porch. By the time she reached the sidewalk, the music had abruptly stopped. Mack had already climbed out of his truck and was limping toward his house.

"Mack?" she hollered, scuttling crablike across the yard. Her son didn't acknowledge her. He strode ahead with his uneven gait. "You, Mack!" she called again, shrieking his name so loud that a bird flew out of the maple tree.

Mack froze. Then he turned around. His face contorted, and he cursed under his breath. She just made him so fucking mad. Couldn't even take a *shit* without her knowing. She'd chased off Earlene, and now she had him where she wanted him. Hell, all his life she'd been his protector, his cheerleader, his nutritionist, his tormenter, and his personal assistant, all rolled into one. He was her whole world, but she wasn't his. *Hell, no,* he thought. *I ain't no mama's boy. I'm as manly as they come.*

As Dorothy stumbled over, pushing back that wild hair, Mack wanted to bolt. Once, he had accidentally touched her hair, and it had felt so gross—like a rusted Brillo pad, with little prickly things sticking into his fingers—he'd wanted to scream. Today she'd stuck teensy butterfly barrettes all over her head. As he stared at the plastic butterflies, he felt a pang. Poor old woman, she couldn't help it, she thought she was cute. He forced himself to smile.

"I've got your supper ready," Dorothy said, edging toward him, perspiration dotting her forehead. Despite the butterflies, she looked haggard, with deep pouches beneath her eyes. "I fixed a pork roast and mashed potatoes. And I steamed some broccoli, too. If you eat enough broccoli, you'll never get cancer. I read that in *Woman's World.* Oh, and I've got strawberry shortcake for dessert, if you give me a minute to cap the berries and whip the cream."

"Ain't got time. I got to mend your fence so your shitty dogs won't escape."

"Don't call them names. They're practically your brothers and sisters."

He shuddered, then tugged his Budweiser cap over his eyes and hobbled up the driveway, toward his garage, Dorothy's old garage. Every damn thing he owned, except for his Ford truck, had once belonged to her. She was still giving him things. Mostly it was junk from garage sales, but she acted like she'd bought him a Bass boat and not some shitty weed-eater that she'd got for two dollars. *What the fuck, she meant well,* he thought as he slogged up the driveway. Cooking his supper, running his errands. And he didn't really mind some of her fussing. In fact, his life would be perfect if she would just give him a little privacy.

Dragging his artificial leg behind him, he hobbled over to the little refrigerator—Earlene had bought him that—and grabbed an ice-cold Bud Lite. The beer splashed against the back of his throat, cold and soothing. In a minute, maybe his hands would stop shaking. He was not an alcoholic, hell no, get the fuck out of here; and he wasn't handicapped, either. What the hell, everybody had a flaw. Some you saw, some you didn't. Ain't nobody perfect.

He finished the beer, but his hands were still trembling, so he reached into the fridge and pulled out another can. He drank it with the refrigerator door open, frosty air curling around his leg. It just felt so nice; but if he stayed here, Dorothy would catch him. He glanced over his shoulder, peering out the garage. He couldn't see his mother, but he felt her presence. In a minute she'd holler and tell him to be careful, not to hurt himself.

"Be careful," she called from her side of the yard. "Don't *hurt* yourself."

He ignored her, the way he always did, and went about his business. When he reached the fence, he set down his toolbox and took another swig of beer. Reaching into the box, he fished out a vise grip and hooked it onto the broken board. In the old days, Earlene had been his assistant. She'd hand him tools and nails, wipe his forehead, give him a kiss, little sips of beer—all of this had been done without him asking, mind you, she'd just done it. She'd acted like she was a nurse and he was a hotshot surgeon. Just thinking about her made his eyes water, and when he reached up to wipe his face, he somehow caught his finger in the vise grip. The beer can went flying, shooting out a geyser of Bud Lite. He yelped, and his eyes bugged out, Jesus *Christ*, it was the worst PAIN he'd felt in years. Worse than Viet Fucking NAM! Using his free hand, he tried to loosen the clamp, but it was stuck. He tugged—big mistake—and felt the flesh ripping. He threw back his head and cursed. His finger was twisting off at the joint, he could feel bones and ligaments tearing. Did they make prostheses for that? Might as well get one for his dick, too, one of those penile implants with a pump. He hadn't woken up with a hard-on in years.

A drop of blood splashed onto the fence the way it had splattered to the ground in Vietnam. Hump a few klicks, nail some dinks, drop that napalm, chop off your leg for Uncle Sam. He started flailing, slapping at the vise grip. He could die hooked to this fence, and she might never think to look down here. Then a year or two later, she'd take them dogs for a walk and just happen to look at the fence and see his skeleton hanging there. She'd scream and fall down, setting them goddamn dogs loose. They'd have a pissing contest on his bones. Man, that wasn't right.

He let out a scream. From the corner of his eye, he saw Dorothy running toward him, her frizzy hair lifting and falling. "Mack!" she cried. "Are you—"

"Goddammit, Mama," he bellowed and squeezed his eyes shut.

"Oh, Lord," she said, looming over him.

"Shit." He cracked open one eye. All he could see was hair and those horrible drawn-on brows. "Can't I even have a accident without you getting in my FACE?"

"You'll need a tetanus shot," she said, ignoring his outburst. "Should I call 911? Tell me what to do."

"You can get the FUCK outta here!"

Her face creased, like he'd slapped her. She turned around, pulling a tattered green sweater around her shoulders, and veered off toward her yard. Halfway to the forsythia bushes, she stumbled, then swayed from side to side. From deep within her throat, she made a growling nose, like she was trying to answer her bratty dogs. They were locked inside the house, barking their fool heads off.

"Mama?" he called, starting to get a little worried. She wouldn't answer, she just staggered back and forth. Hell, was she crying? She fell to the ground—kerplunk! That was just what it sounded like, a ker and a plunk. He waited for her to get up, but she just sat there. If she was fooling, he was going to be mad. Momentarily forgetting his trapped finger, he started to move toward her, but the fence jerked him back. The pain shot up his arm, but he couldn't worry about that now.

"Mama?" he hollered again. Hell, she was just pretending. She did that sometimes when he was mean. "Mama? Stop funning me, now."

On the lawn, Dorothy lay motionless, dandelion fluff blowing all around her. A breeze stirred the dogwood branches, setting the forsythias to swaying.

A bird flew over the forsythias, over the fence, and shit fell into Mack's open toolbox. He cursed again, then bent closer to look at the vise grip. It reminded him of those woven Chinese toys that his daddy had once sold at the five-and-dime. Mack had loved those things. He'd trick Bitsy into putting a finger into each end, and then he'd sit back and watch her try to break free. The harder she struggled, the harder it gripped her finger. Then she'd start crying, and he'd go fetch the scissors and hold them over her head.

"This won't hurt a bit," he'd say. "You won't feel a thing."

Bitsy

The phone rang, jarring me from a dream where I'd been flying above Stonehenge. With part of my mind still circling the megalithic ruins, I reached out in the dark, my hands clumsily groping on the bedside table. Patting the base of the lamp, my fingers slid upward until I found the switch. I winced at the sudden light and lifted the receiver.

"Hullo?" My voice sounded thick and drowsy. Through the open window, I heard Big Ben faintly gong three times.

"Bitsy?" It was my brother.

"Mack? What's wrong?"

"It's Mama." His voice broke. "I didn't mean to wake y'all up. It's eight o'clock in Crystal Falls."

"What about Dorothy?"

"She fainted out in the yard. I rushed her to the hospital and everything. The emergency room doctors didn't know what's wrong, but Mama says it's a stroke."

Stroke, I thought, and drew my knees to my chin. "So, she's . . . conscious?"

"Mama never did have much of a conscience. She just did as she pleased—"

"Is she able to talk?"

"Oh, hell yes. Awake and raising hell, as usual. But she keeps asking for you. She says she wants to say good-bye one last time. I hate to say it, Sis, but you might need to come home. I know you're all in an uproar about Jennifer's wedding, but what if Mama up and dies? She sounds so pitiful."

"I'll try to get a flight out tomorrow—well, I guess it's already tomorrow." I paused, thinking that my mother had solved the problem of whether or not I'd go to the wedding.

"I can't meet you at the airport. I can't miss any more work." He paused. "I'm real sorry. There's nobody else to call, I don't reckon. I know you're fighting with Jennifer, so maybe you can get Clancy Jane to fetch you. But I don't think she drives to Nashville anymore. She says the traffic is too bad."

"That's all right. I'll rent a car at the airport."

"Good idea. You always did know the right thing to do."

"No, I didn't," I said grimly.

"Well, I'll see you when I see you. You can stay at Mama's—if you can stand them dogs."

After I hung up, I stared blankly through the darkened windows. I was desperately trying not to cry, but my chin wove, and then my face crumpled.

My hair fell into my eyes, and Ian pushed it back. It was a shameful length for a woman my age. Like most middle-aged women, I'd lived long enough to inspire both flattery and criticism, sometimes from the same person, *in the same breath*. But I wasn't ready to cut my hair.

"Tell me what's wrong," Ian said.

"It's my mother. It's either a stroke or a dizzy spell. I need to go home. I was going anyway for the wedding. Oh, Ian—what if I can't find a flight?"

"Don't fret, we'll get you there, even if you have a layover in Paris or Amsterdam." Ian sat up straight and gave me a penetrating stare. "Shall I go with you, darling?"

His question seemed eager and forthright, and I knew the worst possible thing was happening. I was starting to care too much. Maybe it was best that I was leaving. "I'll be fine," I said and scooted off the bed. I flung open the closet door. Standing on my toes, I pulled a suitcase from the upper shelf and swung it to the floor. I'd better pack for Jennifer's wedding, too. Even if Dorothy *had* suffered a stroke, Jennifer was unlikely to postpone the ceremony. Reaching deeper into the closet, I haphazardly pulled out a long pewter skirt, strewn with abstract flowers, and a black georgette top, off the shoulder. The coloring was odd, but attractive. I also grabbed a lilac, floor-length Oscar de la Renta and the silver slingbacks I wore with it. Then from behind the shoes I pulled out the rosewood letter box I'd been lugging around for the last twenty-two years. I privately called the box My Side of the Story.

"Please, stop packing," said Ian. "Come over here and let me hold you."

Just before I moved away from the closet, my hands closed on a lumpy sweater—Louie and I had bought it for Jennifer years ago in Ireland, at the Blarney Mills, to be exact. It was pale blue, threaded with green, featuring white lambs and a single black sheep. Some years ago, my daughter had been so furious that she'd FedExed the sweater to my flat, with a note that had said, "This is too 'Gidget Goes Hawaiian' for my taste. You probably bought it for yourself, so I am returning it. Wear it when you go to Stonehenge."

Now I pressed my face into the wool, thinking that a woman could cross the ocean but she couldn't escape who she was or the people she'd left behind.

Ian took the train with me to Heathrow, until just outside Terminal 4, where a uniformed man was checking tickets and passports. "Sorry, mate," he told Ian. "You'll have to stop here. Only ticketed passengers beyond this point."

"I won't be a moment," Ian told the man. Then he put his arms around me. "I wish you'd change your mind and let me come with you," he said, lifting my chin. "Say yes, and I'll take the next available flight. Or do you have it in hand?"

"No, thank you. I'll be fine." I stood on my toes and kissed his cheek. Behind us, the passengers were stamping their feet, shifting their carry-on baggage.

"Hurry it up, love," called a woman with tight blond curls, a child in each hand. "Some of us have planes to catch."

I touched Ian's chin, my hand lingering for a moment. Then I set my own carry-on—which was crammed full of the old letters and clippings—on the conveyer belt. It surged forward, through black plastic strips. A woman sitting above the machine peered into a screen.

"Move along," the uniformed man told me, waving his hand.

Ian spun me around and kissed me. It caught me by surprise, and my hands hovered by his head for a few moments, then my fingers brushed over his hair. It was a long, damp, passionate kiss, and when he finally let go, the passengers clapped. Ian's cheeks reddened, but he saluted them, flashing a dimpled grin.

"Can we go now, love?" called the blonde, and several people laughed.

I stepped backward, still looking at Ian. I lifted my hand.

"Call me," he said.

"If she doesn't," the blonde said, laughing, "*I* will."

When I reached my gate, the first class passengers had already boarded, and a long queue was forming by the door, spreading out in a crooked S. The interior of the 767 resembled an egg carton, the blue seats cupped and waiting, wedged into a miserly space. Both aisles were blocked with people stuffing luggage into overhead compartments. A stewardess worked her way down the aisle, slamming the bins, calling out, "If you can't find an available compartment, we'll be happy to check your baggage."

I found my seat on the last row, which meant sitting bolt upright for the next seven hours and forty-five minutes. But I was grateful to have a seat at all. Ian had pulled strings for this flight, called in favors. So I squashed my bag into the overhead bin, then sat down, my knees brushing against in-flight magazines and safety brochures.

A man with a brown moustache sat down beside me and began pawing through an enormous leather bag, bringing up cough drops, nasal spray, eye drops, and a thick paperback titled *Free From Allergies*. In front of me, a heavyset woman was getting settled, shifting from side to side. I stared at the telephone, which was imbedded into the back of the seat, but quickly discarded the notion of calling my daughter. It was four A.M. in Tennessee.

My seatmate squirted Afrin into his nostrils. I set my watch to Central time and thought about Dorothy. If she'd really suffered a stroke, and it was altogether possible, then it might be some time before I could return to London.

After the plane took off, the heavyset woman sighed deeply and reclined her seat, pushing it into my lap. Beverage carts began rattling down the aisles. Over the droning engines, announcements were made about safety, movies, duty-free shopping, and meals—a peppered trout-and-celery salad, braised beef, or chicken mango korma. I found my pillow and a thin navy blanket, then tried to arrange myself in the cramped space.

Thirty thousand feet above the Atlantic, the plane lurched. I awakened just in time to see a wine bottle fly off the beverage cart and roll down the aisle. Another thud lifted me into the air, as, from the galley, glass shattered, followed by a muffled scream. I heard a ding, and the seatbelt light turned on. An attendant lurched up the aisle, her hands braced against the overhead bin. My ears popped as the plane changed altitudes. In front of me, the heavyset woman frantically signaled the attendant. Someone else cried, "Are we crashing? Into the *Atlantic*? Mother of God, I can't swim."

"It's air turbulence," the attendant said in a monotone. She might as well have said, *Benign tumor.* "Fasten your seatbelts, please. Fasten—"

The plane shuddered, and light bounced through the half-closed windows. The attendant tripped over my seatmate's legs. Then the plane dropped. Oxygen masks fell down, swinging back and forth. The cabin began to shake, and the overhead bins popped open. Several rows up, a Louis Vuitton Last Chance satchel fell, flinging lacy bras over the seats. When my carry-on bag fell into the aisle, it scattered letters and clippings, then the plane dropped again, and, just the way they say, my whole life began to flash before my eyes.

Dorothy

When Dorothy woke up, her sense of time was disjointed. She wasn't sure where she was, but she suspected that Mack had either sent her to a spa or had slapped her into another asylum. She glanced at the window. The blinds were drawn, so she couldn't tell if it was day or night or if there were bars. From a far-off place, she heard a television playing the theme song for *The Young and the Restless*. When she'd been a girl, she'd known all the Cole Porter songs; now she kept up with rock and roll, but in her heart of hearts, she preferred soap opera music. It was just so soothing, even if the story lines were depressing. It was a mystery why she liked TV shows that promoted desperation, lunacy, and backstabbing, not to mention vitamin deficiencies—but she ate them up. Personally, she thought the daytime actresses were way too skinny. Dorothy just bet they all took laxatives. What was wrong with a little flesh? Dorothy had survived mental illness and a bad personality, but she'd always eaten three square meals a day, and when she felt the need for regularity, she took Metamucil.

Women in white uniforms padded in and out of the room, asking Dorothy if she was comfortable, if she needed anything. She hoped they were hotel maids. "Water," Dorothy croaked. "Or a glass of champagne, if you've got it."

"Champagne?" The maid-woman looked shocked.

"Isn't this the Holiday Inn?" asked Dorothy hopefully.

"Hardly," said the maid-woman. "You had a panic attack, Mrs. McDougal. You are in Crystal Falls General. Don't you remember?"

"You're not the maid?"

"I have a bachelor's degree in nursing, Mrs. McDougal." The nurse drew herself up.

"Sorry. I'm just a tad confused." Dorothy rubbed her bald forehead.

"Try and relax," said the nurse, tucking the sheet around Dorothy's shoulders. "I'll be back in a minute with your water."

After the nurse left, Dorothy glanced around the room. A panic attack? No, that couldn't be right. She had been dizzy, and she'd acted a little dramatic. One of these days she'd push herself into an actual stroke. She wondered if she should pick out her coffin before somebody else did, like Mack—God love him, he was a sweetheart, but he had wretched taste.

Bitsy

Flight 1279 made an emergency landing at Shannon Airport. The PA system crackled and the pilot announced that the plane needed a "bit of work," including a fuel valve for the third engine. He said that the maintenance crew was looking for a spare part; if one couldn't be located, an alternative would be found.

The woman in front of me stood up and said, "What does *that* mean? Are they going to put us in rafts? Whenever I take my car to the dealership, it always comes back with a new problem. What if that happens now? Just how good are these Irish mechanics? They could all be on drugs, or in the IRA."

The stewardess, who was squatting in the aisle picking up my letters, glanced at the woman and said, "Ma'am, try and relax. Would you like some pretzels?"

"No," said the woman, "but I'll take a Xanax."

"Ma'am, I can assure you that the pilot won't fly this plane unless it's safe. He has a family."

"Well, so do I." The woman turned to me and added, "I'm never flying again. Will you?"

"Yes," I told her, shoving letters into my bag. At least with air travel, I was willing to take risks. Three hours later, a valve was located and installed, and the plane took off. It was the smoothest flight I could remember.

• • •

It was dark when I angled the rental Jeep up the driveway. The headlights swept over the two houses, one pink, one purple. I looked up at Aunt Clancy's old house—now Dorothy's. A chain-link dog fence ran the length of the yard. In the grass, the headlights reflected against metal pie plates, which appeared to be littered with dog chow. Wind chimes jingled in the trees, and a rusty metal glider—one from Miss Gussie's era—was angled beneath the hackberry tree. These old items comforted me in a way that I could not explain. Despite the circumstances, I was delighted to be home.

I glanced next door. Mack's security light illuminated the bricks that Earlene had long ago painted pink. The paint had worn off in places, making the house look as if it was shedding its skin. I climbed out of the Jeep, pulled my luggage from the back, and walked toward Dorothy's house. The screened porch was full of shadows, but I knew every nook and cranny. I clicked on the light and found the key under the mat. Mack had left a note taped to the front door.

> *Dear Bitsy,*
> *If you get here after 7:30 PM, I'll be sleeping. I've got to be at work early.*
> *Mama is in the hospital, room 314, but she'll be getting out day after 2-morrow. Byron ran a bunch of tests but every damn one came back normal.*
> *Whatever is wrong sure ain't physical. I hope I didn't make you come home 4 nothing. C U 2-morrow.*
> *Luv,*
> *Mack*

On the other side of the door, I heard frantic barking. I hesitated, then let myself in and shoved my bags into the hall. The air smelled of over-cooked meat and burned corn bread. Five Pomeranians charged toward me, barking and dancing on their hind legs.

"You're fine little watchdogs, aren't you?" I knelt down to pet them and peered into the living room—it hadn't changed since my last visit, except for another layering of clutter. The green velvet sofa still stood against the long wall with the rectangular Italian mirror hanging above it. All around the mirror's frame, Dorothy had crammed letters, newspaper articles, and photographs. I recognized my own handwriting on dozens of postcards, and I had a sudden vision of standing in front of a rack in Mont-St.-Michel, choosing the prettiest card to send my mother.

I hurried past a glass case filled with Hummels and dog figurines, then paused beside a bookcase that was jumbled with scrapbooks. A photograph protruded from one and I pulled it out. It was a picture of me and Louie posing in front of the Basilica of St. Nazaire at Carcassonne. It had been taken in 1982, the year before I'd left him.

I shoved the picture back into the book and stepped into the kitchen, thinking a cup of tea might revive me. The counters were jumbled with cereal boxes, Cheetos bags, jars of dog biscuits and rawhide chews. Folded paper bags were jammed into every crevice. A twisted sack of flour sat on the counter, next to an open jar of Coffee-Mate. Fine white powder was scattered over the green Formica. How long had Dorothy been living in squalor? I didn't know if I should start cleaning or just buy a can of Raid.

I lifted the tarnished copper teakettle and filled it with water. Inside the refrigerator, I found a carton of two-percent milk. I glanced at the expiration date—eight days ago. After pouring the milk down the drain, I searched in the cabinets for tea bags. In my mind I could hear Dorothy accusing me of being wasteful, lecturing about calcium deficiencies and humps on the back. She had never paid attention to expiration dates.

"I'm a child of the Depression," Dorothy would say. "It's sinful to waste anything."

I glanced at the green wall phone, with its ancient rotary dial. Behind the phone, numbers had been written onto the wall in red ink. Jennifer's number was scrawled in my mother's spiky script, next to ones for my old house in New Orleans and my flat in London. It was three in the morning over there—too late to call Ian; but Jennifer was probably still awake. I placed my hand on the receiver, hesitated for a moment, then dialed. Jennifer answered on the second ring.

"Hi, honey. It's your mother. I just got into—"

The line clicked in my ear. I replaced the receiver, then walked over to the counter. Standing on my toes, I opened a cabinet door and grabbed a pink mug with Happy Mother's Day 1977 written on the side. I remembered that spring—Claude had begrudgingly allowed Jennifer to visit the day before Mother's Day, and I'd taken my daughter to the Hallmark store to buy Dorothy a gift. We had decided on a mug, and the clerk had let Jennifer pick out the paper. I had watched my daughter lean over the counter, her frilly dress bunched up around her legs, showing ruffled panties. She'd lifted one tiny finger and had pointed at the purple foil. "Give me that one," she'd commanded in Claude's mother's voice.

I reached for the phone and dialed Jennifer's number again. "Wait! Don't hang up," I cried, talking fast, trying to get out all of the facts before my daughter hung up again. "Dorothy's in the hospital."

"Oh, my God. What is it?"

"I'm not sure, exactly." It was the truth, despite Mack's note. "I just got to her house."

"You're *here*? In Crystal Falls?"

"Yes."

"You *flew* in from London?"

I started to say, *No, rowed,* but I stopped myself. "Yes, I flew in from London to Altanta, then took a commuter plane to Nashville."

"It must be serious for *you* to come."

"She's my mother," I said. "I don't have a spare."

. . .

The next morning, I was sitting on the screened porch with Byron Falk, drinking coffee and listening to robins fussing in the trees. Byron's hair was mostly silver, grained with fine strands of brown. He was Clancy Jane's age, fifty-five, but according to Dorothy, his latest girlfriend was a year older than Jennifer.

"Dorothy looked good last night," I told him. "I got to the hospital after visiting hours, but the nurses let me stick my head in. She was complaining about the food."

"She's back to normal—if such a thing exists for your mother. The CT and MRI showed nothing. I even ran cardiac tests, just to make sure it wasn't her heart. Every inch of her body has been probed and scanned. I believe this was another panic attack."

"What a leg-pull," I said. "But I was coming back anyway for Jennifer's wedding."

"Yes, I got an invitation," he said, tapping his spoon against the green saucer. "And I saw her picture in the paper. She's pretty. Are you two still at odds?"

"Of course. We're like Kilkenny cats," I said. "That's an Irish legend about two cats. They fought each other so savagely that nothing was left but their tails."

Byron threw back his head and laughed. "You should tell that story to Clancy Jane."

I smiled and stirred sugar into my coffee. Then I stared down at my hands—so much like Violet's, and Dorothy's. I laid down my spoon and smoothed out the wrinkles in my dress. I'd found it in an upstairs closet.

"Didn't Clancy Jane have a dress like that?" Byron asked, his brow furrowing again.

"This *is* hers." With two fingers, I pinched the fabric. "She left it behind when you guys moved."

Byron lowered his gaze. He lifted his cup, took a sip of coffee. I wanted to say, Why didn't you fight for your marriage? Didn't you love her? But this was none of my business. Byron was free to love anyone he pleased, although I wished he still loved Clancy Jane. But men could be unforgiving when it came to the Hamilton women—Albert, Claude, Byron—even old Walter Saylor Jr.

"We'll be running more tests today, just to make certain that I haven't overlooked anything," Byron was saying. "I'll know more by this evening. But I don't expect to find anything. I'm sure she'll be able to go home tomorrow. Dorothy's a tough old bird. She claims to be sixty-two, but she seems much younger. She's got a few good years left." Byron smiled. "Her health problems are minor."

"To her they're not problems," I said, "they're solutions."

. . .

An hour later, I stepped into Dorothy's hospital room and found her sitting up in the bed, yelling at a technician. "I felt that—ouch! Stop sticking me!"

"I'm sorry," said the technician. "I'm almost finished."

Dorothy was wearing a gray hospital gown, one shoulder of which was splotched with a rusty stain. Through gaps in the gown, circular white patches were visible on her chest, recording her heartbeat, sending the patterns to a little monitor, which hung from the ceiling. On the screen, a white dot skipped up and down like the pinpoint on *Name That Tune*.

I can name that tune in three notes.

I leaned over the bed and kissed her cheek. "I talked to Byron this morning. He says you can leave soon, maybe tomorrow."

"I hope so. I feel like I'm in China getting acupuncture." Dorothy swatted the technician's hand. "I *said* stop that!"

The technician sighed and began packing up her equipment. Dorothy reached up and touched my hair. "I know you didn't mean to come home this soon, but I'm glad you did. We've got to start planning what we're going to wear. Oh, we're going to have the best time. It'll be just like the old days, won't it?"

． ． ．

At the sound of my key in the back door, the Pomeranians charged into the kitchen, skidding across the linoleum. When I stepped inside, hugging a bag of groceries, they followed me around the kitchen. I poured fresh milk into a pan, set it on the burner, and then rummaged for a spoon. Stuck in the back of the drawer was an engraved invitation to my father's second wedding, the paper darkened with age, crinkled in the corners. I'd heard that June McDougal had remarried and moved to Texas.

I shoved the invitation back into the drawer. The milk was ready. I poured it into a mug, then looked for a place to sit down in the living room. Sipping my milk, I glanced at my watch. It was six P.M. in London. Ian was probably at a pub. I longed to smell him on my hands, to press my head into the crook of his arm.

The phone rang, and I hurried back to the kitchen and snatched the receiver. It was Jennifer. "I know you're here and everything, but I haven't changed my mind. Feel free to skip my wedding. I don't need you there."

I shut my eyes, tried to collect my thoughts. I loved her, but I would not be a martyr to that love. "Why do I feel like I'm in a kangaroo court?" I said. "No matter what I do—or even what I *don't* do—I'm guilty."

"That's not my fault." Jennifer sighed.

"Your aunt Violet told me something a long time ago, and now I'm going to tell you. I don't love you because I *need* you, my darling. I need you because I love you."

"Whatever that means. Thank God that *she's* not coming to my wedding. I don't need any more psych-bullshit. Look, do what you want. You always do. You can come to the wedding or stay away. I'm hanging up now. Oh, one more thing. If you've brought me a wedding present—and you probably didn't—just leave it at Dorothy's house."

． ． ．

The next morning, I prowled through the upstairs. During my last visit, I'd tried to get rid of some of the junk, but Dorothy had stopped me. "Where are you going with that Waterpik?" she'd asked, raising her fake eyebrows.

"To the trash. It's broken."

"It's *not*. If you jiggle the cord, it'll work just fine."

This was my chance. I sorted until I heard a noise downstairs. The dogs started barking and then a door slammed. My brother's voice echoed up the stairwell. "Sis? Yo, Sis!"

"Up here," I called.

Mack climbed the stairs, left foot, left foot, his artificial leg hitting each riser. The Pomeranians couldn't climb the stairs, and they began to whine. Mack limped down the narrow hall and poked his head into the messy room. "Aunt Clancy would shit if she could see her old house."

"Has anyone called her yet?" I asked.

"What for?"

"To tell her about Dorothy. And to see if she's coming to the wedding."

"Don't look at me, Sis." Mack peered into the vanity mirror, wiping one finger down the grimy surface. Then he stared at his blackened fingertip. "I'm tired of Mama's spells. One day, she'll have a real one. I don't think she's been taking her medicine like she should of."

"She probably hasn't." I stood up, brushing my hands together. "She's let the house get out of control."

"Well, shit. What else is new?" Mack shrugged. "I try to avoid the upstairs. I don't go no farther than the kitchen."

"We ought to clean it while she's in the hospital." I lifted one arm, gesturing at the bric-a-brac stacked along one wall, and cardboard boxes overflowing with out-of-style clothes.

"We'll need us some wheelbarrows."

"A lorry would be better."

"I used to know a girl named Laurie. I wonder if she's still around. I could give her a call."

"No." I spelled it. "That's what the British call trucks."

"Well hell, I can't imagine what kind it would be," he said, "with a prissy name like that."

Clancy Jane

Clancy Jane slouched on her sofa, eating lo mein and spareribs from Peking Chinese. With a greasy finger, she flipped the remote control from HBO to Home Shopping Network. A big-breasted blonde was selling Loma's Self Tanner, not a stain, not a dye, yours for only $23.95. What a rip-off. She tuned to the music channel, Aaron Neville and Linda Ronstadt were singing a duet. Their voices melded together, entangled like lovers.

A noodle fell on Clancy Jane's robe, a recent catalog purchase. It had come with tuxedo cat slippers. She reached for the noodle and ate it. A striped kitten, Jellybean IV, stopped washing his face to stare, as if to say, Your manners, my dear. Clancy Jane's mountain was a halfway house for felines. She had abandoned Buddhism for the Tao of Meow. The empty spaces in her rooms—and there weren't many—were filled with kitty kitsch. Mugs, night-lights, tissue holders, trivets, pillows, and teapots. Her Volvo sported a bumper sticker that said: My Cat Is Smarter Than Your Honor Student. In her everyday conversations, she sprinkled phrases like cat's pajamas and catnaps. If people thought she was crazy, they were probably right. Violet called it feline mania, but she contributed to the fetish. Every Mother's Day, she dutifully sent a Laurel Burch plate, which Clancy Jane proudly displayed in her brand-new reproduction Welsh cupboard.

During her hippie days, she'd scoffed at gray-haired ladies who kept cats. Actually, she'd scoffed at just about everything. She picked up a rib, bit off a chunk of glistening fat. These days, Clancy Jane preferred meat to vegetables. She also preferred strangers to family. Her friends were selected from Crystal Falls' avant-garde community and they understood her need for solitude. Her years in the New Mexico commune had prepared her to live in a self-contained environment—baking bread, preserving vegetables. The Java Hut brought her into contact with everyday people, and it wasn't always pleasant, but the minute she drove up the mountain to Cat Crossing, a peaceful, easy feeling washed over her, just like in that old Doobie Brothers song. Her mountain was more of a steep ridge, but it was high enough to have its own climate. In the past few weeks, she'd awakened to a dusting of snow, and when she'd driven down to Crystal Falls, it was sunny and springlike, with people walking around in short sleeves.

Jellybean's ears swiveled, and a few seconds later, a car rumbled up the long gravel drive. Still holding the rib and lo mein carton, she ran over to the window. A white Jeep was moving ahead of a dust cloud. Her heart began to thud, and she wondered if the car's owner meant to do her harm—maybe he was a cat burglar. She looked at the sparerib, wondering if she could use it as a weapon. Bitsy had. And it would make a good headline: BURGLARY FOILED, VICTIM CREDITS CHINESE FOOD.

Clancy Jane watched as the car stopped. The door opened, and a pretty blond woman climbed out. The cats ran to the foot of the staircase. They hated strangers. But this wasn't a stranger. Clancy Jane leaned closer to the windowpane. This was her niece. She stuffed the rib into the carton of lo mein and set it on the coffee table. Then she wiped her hands on her robe. When she started toward the door, the cats bolted up the stairs, their claws snicking on the wood, and just for a moment, Clancy Jane felt like hiding, too. But she couldn't. If Bitsy was home, there was trouble, and it probably had something to do with Jennifer's wedding. Clancy Jane had followed her great-niece's parties in the local paper thinking they seemed like episodes from a serial novel.

Clancy Jane and Bitsy greeted each other like long-lost Alpha Delta Pi sisters. "You'll have to excuse the mess," Clancy Jane said, pulling away from Bitsy. "I haven't had time to clean. I went to a yoga class this afternoon and stopped by Peking Chinese for takeout. Would you like a sparerib?"

"No, thanks, but could I have a cup of tea?"

"I'll just put the kettle on," Clancy Jane said, squeezing Bitsy's hand. "I'm thinking of redecorating my house. Are you familiar with feng shui? Well, I'm thinking of doing that. Although in this house, I might should call it fang shui."

Bitsy laughed and hugged her aunt. "I've missed you *so* much."

Later, sipping her tea from a yellow mug shaped like a cat, Bitsy asked about Violet.

"I haven't heard a peep. She'll never change," said Clancy Jane. "Do you know that her favorite movie is still *Lawrence of Arabia*? Each time she sees it, she gets an urge to go camping. Did you know that she still carries a Swiss Army knife in her purse? Lucky for her that George is so outdoorsy." As Clancy Jane chattered, her face lit up. "They just bought a new house. I haven't seen pictures, but Violet says it's glass-and-wood, with entrancing views of Boulder. I wish they didn't live so far away. I wish for too much, I guess." She rolled her eyes and laughed. "I'm starting to sound like your mother. How is she? I haven't seen her in weeks."

"At the moment she's subdued. Or should I say drugged? She's in the hospital. Just a dizzy spell. Byron called it a panic attack. He's her doctor."

"I haven't seen the man in years. You'd think that he'd buzz by my coffee shop once in a while. But he can drink his coffee wherever he goddamn pleases. So, Dorothy is all right?"

"Physically."

"Well, nobody's perfect. Or, as Violet says, purrfect." Clancy Jane smiled, the skin around her eyes wrinkling. "Speaking of perfection, how is Jennifer?"

"You mean Bridezilla?"

Clancy Jane rolled her eyes again. "You'll have to tell me *all* about the wedding. All of the vile details."

"You're not coming?"

"Sweetie, I didn't get an invitation."

"Don't feel bad. I *barely* got one, and even then it was revoked. But you are planning to come, right?"

"Forget it, I'm not a gate-crasher. And I've gotten reclusive. I prefer cats to people." She gestured at two kittens who were creeping from beneath a chair. When Bitsy turned to look, they dashed across the room and climbed up the floral draperies, their claws hooking into the fabric. "I'd just as soon stay on my mountain. When I'm alone, I actually meow to them. And they meow back. I wouldn't admit that to anyone but you." Clancy Jane reached out and touched Bitsy's hair. "Have you ever noticed that craziness tends to run in our family? And we've got man problems, too."

"We're in good company," Bitsy said. "Madame Butterfly, Sylvia Plath, Elizabeth Taylor."

"Anna Karenina." Clancy Jane rolled her eyes. Then she smiled again. "So, tell me about Bridezilla. I want to hear *everything*."

Dorothy

The doorbell rang, setting off a cacophony of barking. Dorothy, freshly released from the hospital, called to Bitsy, "I'll get it!" Pushing her Pomeranians back with her leg, Dorothy cracked open the door and stared into her granddaughter's kohl-rimmed eyes.

"Well, it's about time," said Jennifer, striding past her grandmother. She was wearing ripped jeans and a hideous bomber jacket, olive satin that turned her eyes a strange, muddy blue. She shrugged off the jacket, showing the label to Dorothy. "Yohji Yamamoto," Jennifer said. "Eight hundred fifty-five dollars."

"I wish I had your job." Dorothy shook her head, silently adding, *But I'd wear Givenchy, not Yamamoto.*

"You haven't noticed my shoes." Jennifer lifted one foot, causing the Poms to scatter.

"You haven't asked how I'm feeling," Dorothy said. She ran one hand through her hair. "But I'll tell you anyway. I had me a little fainting spell, but no need to worry. Although it *could* be my heart. I just got out of the hospital. Your mother brought me home this afternoon."

"Well, are you feeling better?"

"Not really." Dorothy sighed. "My get-up-and-go is gone."

"It hasn't gone too far, because you cleaned up the living room." Jennifer turned in a circle. "It looks . . . sort of good."

"Your mother did it," said Dorothy, lowering her voice to a whisper. "But God only knows what she threw away. I'm afraid to ask."

"Is she here?" Jennifer glanced around the room.

"In the kitchen," Dorothy said. "Making tea. I think she smuggled it in from England. Want some?"

"No, thanks. I can't stay. I have to meet Pierre."

Dorothy shuddered. She wouldn't name a basenji Pierre.

Jennifer looked toward the kitchen, where Bitsy was slamming cabinets and clinking china. "The reason I'm here is I need to borrow some of your pictures if you have any. See, Daddy is having a video made for the rehearsal dinner. It kinda shows the story of my life. And they're doing a parallel one for Pierre. The video man called today and asked for more pictures. I was hoping you'd have a few of me."

Annoyed by the tone in her granddaughter's voice, Dorothy lumbered to the bookcase and picked out an album. On the first page was a photograph of Bitsy, posing at her baby shower next to a plastic stork. She was wearing an orange smock and maternity pants. Dorothy hastily turned the page, where there was a picture of a newborn Jennifer. "This must've been taken through the window of the hospital nursery," Dorothy said, pulling the picture out of the plastic sheath. On the back, the photograph was dated and annotated in Bitsy's loopy, girlish handwriting: "December 31, 1971, My New Year's Eve Baby!"

"I didn't realize you had these." Jennifer pulled the album into her lap and kept turning pages. The baby pictures ended abruptly in the fall of 1972. In 1974, the photographs resumed. Under the first pictures, in trembly script, Bitsy had written "Jennifer, age 2." A later picture showed Jennifer dancing in the front yard with Clancy Jane and Violet, all three of them holding hands and laughing. On the back, Bitsy had scrawled: "Doing the rain dance, Jennifer, age 4."

"There's lots you don't know," Dorothy sniffed.

Bitsy appeared in the doorway holding a wicker tray. She blinked at her daughter's satin jacket and tight jeans, the cropped hair. The nose ring, in particular, was shocking. "Jennifer," she said a little breathlessly.

"Hi, I'm just getting some pictures." Jennifer glanced at her mother then turned to Dorothy and held up the album. "Can I take it? I see several pictures that'll be perfect for the video."

"Well, I suppose," Dorothy said, looking up at Bitsy. "Just as long as you promise to return it."

"Actually, I'd like to take all the albums."

"Just be careful," Dorothy said. "We'd sure hate to lose them."

"I won't." Jennifer tilted the book, pointing to a photograph where she was holding a wide-mouth bass. "This will be awesome."

"That was your first fish." Dorothy beamed. "Your uncle Mack took you fishing at Center Hill."

"Funny, I don't remember." She studied the caption beneath the picture. Jennifer, age 5. She turned to a picture of herself blowing out six candles on a cake, surrounded by two generations of Hamilton women. "We had your birthday party a week early that year, because the Wentworths were taking you on a trip to Hilton Head."

"How come I don't remember any of this stuff?" Jennifer pursed her lips. "Traumatic memory loss?"

Bitsy and Dorothy exchanged glances. It was an awkward moment, and Dorothy jumped right into the middle of it. "Now that we're here together," she said. "I think it's high time that we all sat down and talked about that."

"I told you, Pierre is waiting." Jennifer gathered the albums into her arms and scrambled to her feet. She started for the door, but her grandmother stopped her.

"Not so fast," Dorothy said. "You get your little butt back in here."

"I can't. I'm seriously late. Look, I'll call tomorrow, and we'll set up something. Okay?"

She hurried out the door, onto the screened-in porch. Dorothy walked over to the window and parted the curtains. "She better return my pictures," she whispered to herself, "or I'll hire me a hit man."

Bitsy

After Dorothy went to bed, I called Violet, bringing her up to date on the latest Hamilton-McDougal misadventures. "I didn't get an invitation, either," she said.

"This is so strange," I said. "Why would Jennifer leave out one whole side of her family? Are we that awful?"

"Do you *really* have to ask? You're practically an ex-con. Dorothy's a little cuckoo, but I think her eyebrows are what's more worrisome to Jennifer. Not to mention Mack's artificial leg. And, of course, Mama's reputation was never the best. But I'm really pissed at Jennifer. She could have sent me an invitation. I'm no slouch. And my husband is a tenured professor."

"I talked your mother into coming, invitation or not."

"So?"

"Even Byron will be there."

"Now *that* should be interesting. In fact, I'd hate to miss it. Let me check my schedule. I've got it right here. Hold on a second." Violet paused. In the background paper rattled. "Okay, let's see . . . no, I can't make the rehearsal dinner. But the wedding's a possibility if I can get a morning flight."

"It isn't till seven P.M."

"Too bad Jennifer didn't run off to Vegas. She could've picked the chapel where Mama and Byron got married. Or yours with Louie. Then, after the thrill wears off—and with Jennifer that should take only about two days—they can get a divorce right there."

"I can't wait to see you," I said. "I've really missed you."

"Me, too," Violet said.

. . .

A dazzling spring morning in Crystal Falls. Sunlight blazed through the café curtains that hung crookedly in Dorothy's kitchen. In the center of the table was a platter of lemon poppy seed muffins. Beside the platter was a vase of pretty yellow weeds. Dorothy reached for a muffin, and her Pomeranians danced around her chair. Across the table, I lifted the tea bag from my mug, then gently squeezed it.

Dorothy glanced at the window, then ran one hand through her hair and said, "Your daughter's here."

I put down my mug, transfixed by my mother's gesture. This was the same one that Jennifer used when she was vexed.

"I wish she'd call before she pops in," said Dorothy, hastily buttoning her pink muumuu. "It's not eight A.M. yet, but she'll walk in here dressed to kill. Fix your robe, Bitsy. Your titties are showing."

The Pomeranians began to yip, and the back door swung open. When Jennifer breezed into the kitchen, the dogs hopped excitedly around her legs. "Stop it, you monsters!" Jennifer stamped her foot and lifted her briefcase, threatening to crush one of the dogs, but they wouldn't back off. She looked helplessly at her grandmother. "They'll ruin my hose. And I'm already late for work!"

"Sit!" Dorothy pointed at the dogs, and they scrambled under the table.

"Wow, they're *so* obedient. Just like Uncle Mack." Jennifer smirked, then brushed one hand over her pinstriped jacket. She kicked out one leg, showing off skyscraper heels. "Like my shoes?"

"You might start with a simple hello," said Dorothy, biting into a muffin.

Jennifer ignored her grandmother and glanced at her watch. "I can only stay a minute. But I need to clear something up about the rehearsal dinner *and* the wedding. We need to get in synch."

"Do you mean s-i-n-k," Dorothy asked, wiggling her eyebrows, "or something else?"

"I don't have time for jokes," Jennifer said, turning to me. "Let's discuss wardrobe. I don't know what you're planning, but I'm wearing Prada to the rehearsal."

"Name-dropper," said Dorothy, pinching off a piece of muffin and tossing it under the table.

"My shoes alone cost . . . well, you don't need to know." Jennifer looked down at her feet. "It would just make you ill. And since I'm obviously nauseating *some* people in this room, I won't mention the designer."

"But isn't the rehearsal on top of a mountain?" I asked, thinking she'd ruin those Pradas.

"So's the wedding, in case you've forgotten," Jennifer said. "But the rehearsal dinner is at the country club. It will be formal. So *do* dress accordingly, and that goes for both of you."

Dorothy smiled, flashing her teeth, where poppy seeds had gathered along the gum line. "We aren't nitwits. You can rest assured that I know what formal means."

"There's a difference in very formal evening, formal evening, and semiformal evening," Jennifer continued.

"Will my hot pink muumuu do, honey?" Dorothy asked. Beneath the table, the dogs began to growl. "Listen to that. Aren't they cute? I ought to make a tape and send it to Letterman."

"Can't you pay attention to anything but those dogs?" Jennifer cried.

"Don't be jealous." Dorothy reached under the table, snatched a Pom, and plopped it on her lap.

"Oh, forget it." Jennifer ran one hand through her hair, causing it to stand up like a rooster's tail. "I've got a thousand problems. The bridesmaids' gifts haven't arrived, and Tiffany's swears they were shipped two weeks ago. Plus, Sharper Image screwed up with the usher's presents. It's just a mess."

"Anything I can do?" I reached for my mug.

"You can write a check and pay for your half of the wedding," Jennifer said.

I spit out a mouthful of tea, and the Poms started to bark.

"Just kidding." Jennifer raised one thin eyebrow, looking eerily like Dorothy. "Although if you were still married to Louie, I'd expect you to pay half—not because Daddy needs the cash, but on general principle. But I know you don't make any money with your decorating business, so you're off the hook."

I started to say something, but Dorothy caught my eye and shook her head.

"God, Mother. Your hair is awful." Jennifer reached out and hesitantly fingered one of my curls. "You've got gray all over. You really need some highlights. And while you're at it, get it cut. It's *way* too long. Either wear it up—and not too poofy—or get it cut and styled."

I picked up a lock of hair and studied it. "There's not so much gray."

"Then you must be blind. It's there, trust me, and it adds ten years." Jennifer touched her own shorn locks. "And your eyebrows . . . you really should get them waxed. Make an appointment at the Utopian. It's the nicest salon in Crystal Falls. They're doing the entire wedding party."

"Even the men?" Dorothy held up her hand, hiding her broad, unpainted forehead from Jennifer.

"Well, yes. Some of them have unibrows." Jennifer sighed. "I don't want the wedding pictures ruined, so Pierre talked them into it. They're having pedicures, too."

"Don't let the gossips hear. They'll think you're having a toe-suckers convention instead of a wedding," Dorothy said.

"Very funny." Jennifer flounced out the back door.

"If she trips," Dorothy said, "we'll be going to a funeral, not a wedding."

. . .

Later, when I stepped into the living room and found Dorothy whispering into the phone, I told her to stop making clandestine phone calls. "I know you're talking to Jennifer," I added.

Dorothy hung up so fast the phone jangled. "I wasn't talking to her," she said, refusing to meet my eyes.

"Who was it then?"

"None of your beeswax. I have a life. With people that you *don't know about*," Dorothy bristled. "Can't I have any privacy?"

"I thought you wanted me here more often," I said.

"To visit," Dorothy said. "Not spy. But you know what? Sean Connery is my idea of the perfect man. Who's yours?"

Ian, I thought. Since I couldn't speak frankly to my mother about men, not without receiving an extensive cross-examination, I just shrugged. "Stop trying to change the subject," I finally said. "Tell me who you were talking to."

"It's a surprise," said Dorothy. "That reminds me. I've made the cutest little present for Jennifer. I want you to look at it and tell me what you think."

Dorothy opened the pantry, pulled out a plastic bag, and reached inside. She held up a pink-and-purple needlepoint pillow that said Headquarters of the Fashion Police.

"You made this?" I reached for the pillow.

"Mmmhum," said Dorothy, pulling out another pillow that said Gone to the Dogs.

"I know clients who would adore these," I said, bending closer to examine my mother's work. "Do you have any samples that I could take back with me?"

"Back?" Dorothy's forehead puckered.

"To London," I said.

"That's what I thought you meant." Dorothy sighed. "Even when you were a little baby, you couldn't stay put. But I'm all for global travel if these pillows sell. Why, I might have a second career. I wonder if it'll be more profitable than raising Pomeranians?"

. . .

At daybreak, the phone rang. Thinking it might be Ian, I scrambled out of bed and dashed into the hallway to answer it. "Mornin', Mother," said Jennifer in a cheery voice. "I'm just leaving for my morning run, but I wanted to remind you about the rehearsal at Hammersmith Farm. It's tomorrow night at six o'clock sharp."

"Got it," I said.

"And please make sure that Dorothy dresses appropriately." Her unspoken admonishment hung in the air: *And you, too.*

"I'll do my best." I stifled another yawn.

"Is Mack coming?"

"To the dinner, yes," I said. "But not to the rehearsal."

"Have you seen what he'll be wearing?"

"No."

"Can you find out and call me back?"

I lifted the curtain and looked down into my brother's driveway. The white truck was parked in the azalea beds, crushing several bushes. "No," I lied. "He's gone. I guess he's at work."

"He's probably with a hooker. But never mind," said Jennifer. "Is anyone else coming to the dinner? Clancy Jane? Violet? I didn't invite them because I figured you would."

"They're only coming to the wedding."

"That's a relief. Because I really hate to keep giving Pierre's mother these shifting numbers. Reservations were made months ago, and it's really embarrassing."

I was on the verge of saying something unflattering about Pierre's mother and her shifting numbers, but I managed to hold back.

"One more thing, Mother," Jennifer said in an edgy voice. "And it involves Daddy's girlfriend. I want Samantha to be seated in the grand-mother's row. With Dorothy. Do you mind?"

My heart began to pound. Tears sprang into my eyes, and I brushed them away. "Perhaps you should ask Dorothy," I said, "since this involves her."

"You sound upset."

"No, no. I'm fine. Just sleepy."

"Pinch yourself and wake up. This is important. If Samantha and Daddy were married, she'd be sitting in the front row with *you*," Jennifer said. "She's really been there for me, you know? And I just owe her this honor."

I'm sure you do, I thought. Jennifer wasn't being cruel, just plain stupid. Dorothy had mentioned that Claude's third ex-wife, Regina, would be attending the ceremony with their daughter. And the second wife, my former bridesmaid, had been invited, too. The addition of a girlfriend—especially if she was seated in a place of honor—might touch off an uprising. Which would be lovely, actually. Jennifer and her mothers.

"Hey, you still there?" Jennifer asked.

"I was just thinking . . ." I said, feeling the devil take hold. "Why don't you just put Samantha in the front row with me?"

"You . . . don't mind?" Jennifer asked in a suspicious tone.

"Not at all."

"Well, okay." Jennifer paused. "I will. And thanks."

"You don't have to thank me, dear," I told her.

.   .   .

Dorothy was getting her hair done at the Utopian, but I drove to Fabulous Fred's on the Square. I skipped the pedicure and eyebrow waxing, and asked the stylist, who resembled Cher—long black hair parted down the middle and Cleopatra eyes—to take off several inches. "You're gonna look so *good*," she said picking up her scissors. I shut my eyes and wished I'd had my hair cut in London—world-class salons were within walking distance of my flat.

After a while, the stylist said, "Okay, sugar. You can look."

I cracked open one eye and looked into the mirror. I didn't recognize myself. My hair was layered, just hitting my shoulders. I hated to admit it, but Jennifer had been right. "I love it," I said.

"I've got time to put on a rinse," the stylist said. "You're too pretty to have so many gray hairs."

"No, thanks," I said, rising from the chair. "I've earned them."

On my way home, I stopped by the jewelry store and bought a Fitz & Floyd tureen. It was large enough to hold all the letters I'd brought from England. Also, I threw in a gift certificate. When I got home, I began having second thoughts about the letters, and I went to my mother for advice, and to show her the tureen.

"She ought to treasure them," said Dorothy. "Hopefully they'll knock some sense into her head. But the tureen is so pretty she may never remove the lid and find the letters. I wish we could see all her wedding gifts, but they're at Miss Betty's. Jennifer said they're spread out on card tables in the billiard room. She'd promised to take some Polaroids so I could see, but I guess she got too busy. Speaking of which, you and I have work to do."

We spent the afternoon pulling together our costumes. I hung the glittery purple Oscar de la Renta gown on the back of the kitchen door to drape out the wrinkles and held up the strappy silver heels. "What do you think, Dorothy?"

"You'll look like a princess." Dorothy sighed. "If only I had something dressier. I guess my suits will have to do."

"They're perfect for a woman of your vintage," I said. "You'll be lovely."

The Pomeranians were scattered around the kitchen, some resting on the linoleum with their hairy legs stretched out behind them; others rooting for crumbs. It was a balmy night in the high seventies, and the back door stood open. The smell of wisteria drifted into the room.

I had just picked up a bottle of fingernail polish, to hold against the purple gown, when the phone rang. I barely glanced up. Dorothy said hello, then cleared her throat and held out the receiver. "It's somebody named Ian? He sure does sound spiffy."

I set down the bottle with a clunk and took the receiver. "Ian?"

"Darling," he said. "How are you?"

"It's nice to hear you." I hugged the phone and began to turn in a circle, winding the cord around my body. Only the British could turn a two-syllable endearment into an erotic paragraph out of a D. H. Lawrence novel.

"I've missed you so," he said. "That's why I rang. I've booked a flight tomorrow morning. My aeroplane should land in Atlanta around three P.M., or thereabouts. I've never been through customs there, so I don't know how long it will take."

"You're coming to Atlanta?" I chewed my thumb, wondering if I could somehow arrange to meet him.

"Only for a layover." He paused. "I'm coming to see you, darling."

"Here?" I sank back against the counter.

"Tell me straight away if I'm being intrusive."

"No, no. I'm over the moon."

My mother was over by the door, fluffing out the purple gown. She didn't appear to be listening, but I knew better.

"I shall arrive in Nashville tomorrow evening. How close is Crystal Falls to Nashville?"

"Two hours. I can pick you up."

"And miss your dinner? It's just not on. I've hired a car."

"A limousine?"

"No, I believe it's called Hertz." Ian paused. "I'll ring when I arrive. I've taken the last available room at the Holiday Inn."

"I'll have my cell phone," I said. "Call if you get lost. I'll come and find you."

"In that case, I might manufacture a crisis. I've packed my ancient tuxedo."

"It's not ancient," I said. "It's lovely. And I can't wait to see it on your gorgeous body."

"Bitsy?"

"Yes?"

"I'm crazy about you. Simply mad on."

Again, I glanced at Dorothy, who had stopped fooling with the gown and was looking more horrified by the moment.

"I know you are afraid," he continued, "but my darling, not all love ends tragically, does it?"

The question was typically British: he didn't expect an answer, and that was lucky for him because I wasn't prepared to give one.

When I hung up, Dorothy started. "All right. Who is Ian?"

"He's a book editor," I said. "I'm trying not to love him, but it's damn hard."

"Oh, my stars." Dorothy sat down hard in a chair, her legs sticking straight out, and the dogs began to growl.

"What's wrong?" I hurried over. "Are you dizzy again?"

"No, no." Dorothy impatiently flipped her hand. "It's just . . . Well, I didn't know about this Ian fellow. I'm afraid I've done something behind your back."

"What?" I froze.

"You're going to be furious." Dorothy ran a hand through her hair. "Do you remember the secret phone call?"

I nodded.

"Well, don't pitch a fit, but . . . I've invited Louie to the wedding."

"Well, you'll just have to call and uninvite him."

"I thought you said uninvite wasn't a word." Dorothy fixed me with an innocent look. "Anyway it's too late. He's in town. He arrived this morning, while you were out shopping. He's—"

"He's here? In town? What a cock up."

"That better not be a foreign curse word," Dorothy said. "I am your mother, and the Bible says you can't talk mean to me. Anyway, Jennifer said it was perfectly all right for Louie to come. After all, he was her step-daddy."

"A blip on the radar," I said dryly. "Thanks for asking *me*."

"You're welcome." Dorothy gave me a cunning look. "It might do you good to see him again."

"So we can catch up on old times?"

"Don't be cute. You can put him next to that English fellow and do a side-by-side comparison. I like to do that with cantaloupes."

"These are men," I said. "Not melons. Besides, I don't want to see Louie."

"Well, you're going to. Not at the rehearsal, just the wedding. You know how he appreciates fine wine and food. He'll get a kick out of Jennifer's very formal, five-course meal."

"He just *better not* be at my table," I said.

Dorothy blinked.

"*Dorothy?*" I cried. "Is he?"

"It's possible," Dorothy said. "To tell the truth, it's a great possibility. In fact, he's seated between you and me. But if we get there early, I can do a quick switch-a-roo with the place cards."

"Just pile on the agony."

"Well, I'm sorry. But I didn't know about this Ian person. *You* didn't even know he was coming. And besides, you need to face up to the fact that Louie was your big love."

"You make it sound like a one-time event."

"Isn't it?"

"I hope not," I said.

"You're such a optimist," Dorothy said. "But don't worry. Just act ladylike and everything will turn out fine. That's what *I'd* do."

The Wentworths and the McDougals

When I turned up the road to Hammersmith Farm, we were still arguing about Louie. It was early evening but the sun hadn't set, squeezing its last bit of light into the deep bowl of the valley. I parked the Jeep far away from my daughter's BMW; then I gathered up the skirt of the long purple gown and arranged it over my arm. Across the pasture, at the base of a dirt path that led up the mountain, a U-Haul truck was parked at an angle, and men were unpacking folding chairs and carrying them toward the hilltop where a white tent had been erected for tomorrow's ceremony. From a distance, the workers resembled picnic ants.

I stuffed my cell phone into my evening bag. Sunlight glanced off the Swarovski crystals, sending reflected sparks across the lap of Dorothy's St. John. "You look lovely. " I smiled.

"Thank you." Dorothy brushed at the skirt. "I bought it at the thrift shop. The clerk said Miss Betty had just brought it in. We both wear a size twelve. Wonder if she'll recognize it?"

"I doubt it. You always look original."

"That's because I am," Dorothy said.

A dark green Jaguar turned into the pasture and pulled up in front of my rental Jeep. Chick, wearing sunglasses and a lightweight blue windbreaker, climbed out of the Jaguar. He looked like Freddy Kruger, I thought. All that was missing was a ten-inch fingernail. He walked around the car and opened the passenger door. Miss Betty extended one pale hand. As she rose, her chin-length hair didn't move; it looked as if it had been shellacked. She was wearing sunglasses, too, even though dusk was gathering in the trees. Her frock was simple, a black sheath, with a cashmere sweater tied casually over her broad, fleshy arms. I looked down at my dress, then glanced over at Dorothy. Another car pulled up and three young women hopped out, each one wearing a cotton sundress.

"Wasn't this supposed to be ultra-formal?" I asked. "Or did I misunderstand the assignment?"

"You didn't misunderstand anything." Dorothy's mouth tightened. "But maybe Jennifer meant we were supposed to dress *down* for the rehearsal, and then go back home and dress *up* for the dinner."

"There's not enough time." I glanced at the dashboard clock. "The dinner starts in thirty minutes. That's barely enough time for the rehearsal."

Chick and Miss Betty were walking across the pasture. Miss Betty was wearing sensible black flats but she still seemed to be having trouble navigating. I wondered how I'd manage in evening sandals. A pasture required Wellies, not Giuseppe Zanotti slides—silver ones, at that. What had I been thinking? I knew the terrain in Tennessee, both geologically and emotionally, and I should have come better prepared.

A white Saab parked in front of the Jeep. As the people emerged, I saw a sockless man in brown loafers and two young women in splashy cotton skirts and denim jackets. A silver Mercedes angled up and Claude got out wearing a pale yellow shirt and navy twill trousers. He'd gotten beefy. His neck was burned red, and wrinkles fanned out from his eyes—the curse of all committed golfers. His blond hair, or what remained of it, was sprinkled with gray. When he turned to the side, I thought his nose looked rather beaked. The passenger door opened and a chunky blonde climbed out, wearing a black sleeveless dress. On her feet were low-heeled pumps. *Whatever happened to Candy?* I thought. Perhaps he'd eaten her.

"That's Samantha Cole-Jennings, Claude's girlfriend," Dorothy said. "She's been in the paper a lot here lately, what with all of Jennifer's parties. The two of them are the *best* of friends. It just makes me sick to my stomach."

From up on the hill, beside the path, Jennifer waved to her father. She was wearing a pink shift dress and pointy-toed brown flats. I stared through the windshield. "*That's* a sixteen-hundred-dollar Prada dress?"

"It looks like a Kathie Lee from Wal-Mart," Dorothy muttered. "And her shoes are straight out of *Snow White and the Seven Dwarfs*."

"So? I look like a female impersonator."

"Yes, you do," Dorothy said, "but a gorgeous one."

With my mother's help, I managed to reach the hilltop without ruining my shoes. Several caterers rushed past us, holding cane-back chairs. Near the tent, three workmen were putting the finishing touches on a fountain. "It's supposed to pump out champagne," Dorothy said. "Jennifer told me that it's modeled after a fountain in Disney World."

"Actually, the original is in Paris, in the Place de la Concorde," I said. "They used to execute people there—death by guillotine."

"Well, don't tell Jennifer," warned Dorothy. "She'll call you a party pooper."

Stacked all around the fountain were boxes with André on the sides. Dorothy gave the boxes a dubious glance. "How will they get all that champagne into the fountain?"

"One bottle at a time?" I said.

"Don't be cute," Dorothy replied.

In the center of the tent, which was large enough for a circus, workmen were laying down black-and-white marble tiles, forming a checkerboard that was reminiscent of the one in Honora DeChavannes's yard. All around the tent was an expanse of thick, cushy grass. It had been freshly cut, and the air was pungent with a sharp, sour smell. "It's sod," Dorothy explained. "Jennifer said the gardeners unrolled it like it was a Persian rug. You can still see the grids between each square."

As I approached the tent, a gasp rose from the guests. Miss Betty began whispering furiously into Chick's ear. The bridesmaids, in their thin cotton dresses, twittered behind their hands. The dumpy blonde standing beside Claude lifted her chin and smiled in triumph at Jennifer. A middle-aged woman with a Martha Mitchell bow in her hair rushed over, holding a clipboard.

"For those of you who don't know, I'm the wedding planner," she said. "Which one of you is the mother of the bride?"

"I think it's the lady in purple," said a smiling young man with curly hair. He pointed to me.

"Oh?" The wedding planner's eyelids fluttered for an instant, then she extended her hand to me. "If you'll just step over here, Mrs.—?"

"Bitsy," I said.

"Well, I guess we're ready," said the planner. "First, let's get the wedding party assembled."

Jennifer, refusing to look at either me or Dorothy, turned sharply and made her way to the ushers and bridesmaids, who resembled the cast of *Falcon Crest.* She was followed by the curly-haired boy who'd referred to me as the lady in purple. Like the other young men, he was wearing a white T-shirt and chinos. "The fiancé?" I wondered out loud, my eyes going to the man's bare ankles, then up to his face. His thick, brown, curly hair fell past a pointed chin. His eyes were dark chestnut, almost black. And I could smell his cologne—Bvlgari Pour Homme—the same fragrance Louie had favored.

Dorothy told me yes and that she'd seen him earlier in Wal-Mart wearing flash-mirrored sunglasses. This evening, the glasses were gone, and he kept winking at the maid of honor, a brunette with dangly earrings who appeared to be enjoying the attention.

"Did you see that?" Dorothy whispered.

"Yes. Don't you wish we hadn't?"

The wedding planner lined up everyone in order, assigning ushers to me and Samantha, after making sure we were content to share the same row. Next, the woman paired ushers with Pierre's mother, a chubby woman with a round, pretty face. She was wearing a lemon chiffon dress and lots of diamonds—apparently she'd gotten the assignment wrong, too. Finally the planner got to the grandmothers. Then she explained to everyone how they were to enter and exit their rows.

Dorothy glanced up at the darkening sky and sniffed. "It looks like rain."

"Oh, don't *say* that," said the wedding planner. "That would be horrid, wouldn't it?"

"Ghastly," Dorothy agreed.

. . .

The rehearsal took almost an hour. It was seven o'clock when we reached the country club and found Mack, who was standing under the canopy. Two bridesmaids came around the corner and almost bumped into Dorothy. One of the girls, a Heather Locklear look-alike, profusely apologized, then, eyeing Mack, said to her friend, "Gee, the clean-up crew is early."

The other girl, a dead ringer for Madonna, rolled her eyes and laughed. "Looks like the janitor's got a gimp leg."

"He looks creepy," warned Heather. "Hold on to your pocketbook."

"It's a handbag," Dorothy called out. "Not a pocketbook."

The girls turned and stared. "Excuse me?" said Heather.

"Only sixteen-year-old girls carry pocketbooks." Dorothy sniffed. "Don't you read the fashion magazines?"

The bridesmaids made faces at each other, then flounced off, leaving the McDougal clan alone on the sidewalk. Mack swept open the door and said, "Ladies first."

Dorothy stepped into the brightly lit lobby, but I hesitated. I hadn't set foot in this country club since my own rehearsal dinner back in 1971.

"Hey, Sis. You coming?"

"Sorry." I smiled at Mack and stepped through the door. We caught up with Dorothy outside the ballroom. Dorothy straightened Mack's lapels, then brushed the sleeves of his jacket. "I had to force him to buy this navy suit," she said. "But doesn't he look handsome?"

I said he did and kissed his cheek.

"Wait'll you see my tuxedo. It's got one hell of an inseam." He winked. "Now, where's the bar?"

"Take it easy, honey," Dorothy warned.

"Hell, I'm fucking middle-aged," Mack said, laughing. "Leave me alone."

"Your liver is middle-aged, too," said Dorothy, reaching up to brush lint from his shoulders. "Besides, it's rude to guzzle up free liquor. Don't you *dare* have more than two drinks. Your sister's already made a fool of herself tonight wearing the wrong dress."

Mack looked me up and down. "She looks pretty damn good to me." Then his forehead wrinkled. "Does Jennifer have something against purple?"

"She has something against Bitsy," said Dorothy.

We entered the ballroom. The same twinkly strobe light still dangled from the domed ceiling, turning in a counterclockwise direction. While Mack went to fetch our drinks, Dorothy dragged a chair over to a corner and sat down. I began to wander through the crowd. I spotted Claude's ex-wives standing on opposite sides of the bar—wife number two was glaring at wife number three, and number three was frowning at Samantha. Somehow they had managed to crack the dress code.

Then I found Mr. and Mrs. Tournear—the hosts of the dinner. I intended to speak to them at the rehearsal, but they had disappeared before I could get to them. They were not standing in a queue, greeting their guests, as I had expected, but were huddled against the wall, sipping their drinks. Pierre's mother kept glancing from her yellow dress to the rest of the casually dressed women. Pierre's father towered over his wife, and I idly wondered if he'd bought his black suit at the Big and Tall Man's Store. I took a deep breath, walked over to them, and introduced myself.

"Oh, yes, I saw you at the rehearsal," said Mrs. Tournear. She looked up at her husband. "Didn't we see her, honey?"

Pierre's father nodded but made no comment. Mrs. Tournear squeezed his arm and said, "I nearly ruined my shoes traipsing across that pasture. I wish Jennifer had warned me."

An awkward silence fell, until I desperately reached into my old store-house of Southern platitudes. This kind of talk was a skill I had honed during the years with Louie, attending carnival clubs and receptions. At first was I worried. It was a language I hadn't spoken in years. Fortunately it came right back. It helped that Pierre's mother knew the lingo, too, and in minutes we were discussing the versatility of toile. Soon Mrs. Tournear impulsively threw her arms around my neck, giving off heady gusts of bourbon and Escada perfume, begging me to call her Tonya.

I returned the hug, and promised to visit Atlanta real soon. "You're just delightful!" my new best friend gushed, and I was just a little sad that I now lived around the quietly understated British, with their passion for decorum. The only difficult moment came when Chick and Miss Betty stepped up to the Tournears. Chick's eyes were glassy and unfocused. Miss Betty smiled, her lips cemented in the corners. Her eyes were tilted into oblivion, the skin taut from one too many lifts.

"Well, isn't this a *nice* party?" Miss Betty said, focusing somewhere above Mrs. Tournear's head. She turned to me and in a thickened voice added, "I don't believe we've met."

"But this is Jennifer's mother." Tonya Tournear looked startled.

"She was just teasing," Chick said, squeezing his wife's arm. "Weren't you teasing, dear?"

Miss Betty's eyes rounded, then she tossed her head and turned in a queenly way, as if to acknowledge another guest, but bumped into a table. She steadied herself, teetering slightly, then descended upon the bridesmaids, saying, "Thank you all for coming."

Tonya Tournear grabbed my hand and said, "Can you believe that our children'll be married in less than twenty-four hours?" She began to weep. Then she laughed and swept her fingers under both eyes. "Oh, I promised Pierre that I wouldn't cry, and here I go. Tomorrow, I'll have to take a Valium. Not that I'm upset or anything. Well, maybe a little. It *is* sort of stressful. You know what I mean, Bitsy?"

"Yes." I squeezed her hand. "I certainly do."

· · ·

I joined Dorothy and Mack in the buffet line. Steam drifted over the stainless vessels of creamed chicken, whipped potatoes, shriveled green peas. At the far end of the table, wedges of pecan pie, still icy from the freezer, were lined up. The crowd closed in, gripping their plates like steering wheels.

"It looks like leftovers from Rotary Club," whispered Dorothy. "But I bet they jacked up the price for Pierre's family."

Claude went by, refusing to make eye contact with any of us, but Samantha stopped in front of me. "Your dress is, wow, a real showstopper," she said, arching her eyebrow. With one hand she reached out and grabbed Claude's arm, yanking him back. He glanced at me, then turned his gaze on Samantha.

"How sweet of you to notice." I smiled.

"She bought it in London," Dorothy piped up.

"Well, it's just so eye-catching," Samantha said. "Isn't it, baby?"

Claude muttered a terse, "Nice to see you."

Nice to see me? Was that all he could say after twenty-two years?

Apparently so. His jaw tightened, then he put his hand on Samantha's shoulder and said, "They need us at the head table, honey."

They crossed the room to take their seats at the table with Pierre's parents and grandmother. We found our places at the far side of the room. I was seated between Mack and Dorothy. A middle-aged couple who introduced themselves as Samantha Cole-Jennings's aunt and uncle were already sitting.

Toward the end of the meal, the lights were dimmed and a waiter rolled out the large-screen TV from the bar. Claude walked up to a podium and grabbed the microphone. His eyes flat and shiny as he strutted back and forth holding up a video tape. I remembered the time he'd brought Jennifer to the Nashville airport so she could fly to England with me and Louie. Even though Jennifer hadn't liked the UK, I would always be grateful to Claude for allowing her to come. "I'd like to direct your attention to the screen. I've put together a little video commiserating the lives of Jennifer and Pierre," he said.

Commiserating? Even Dorothy had picked up on the gaffe.

"The boy is pie-eyed," she whispered.

After a bit of fumbling, the video was crammed into the VCR. Background music started up, Barbra Streisand singing "The Way We Were." First, there was a photograph of a newborn Jennifer, then it faded into a photograph of a newborn Pierre. The pictures whizzed by, those misty memories of Pierre, Jennifer, Claude, Miss Betty, Chick, and Claude's second and third wives. Not a single picture of the way Jennifer and I were. Not a single picture to show that Jennifer *had* a biological mother. Dorothy leaned over and pinched my arm. "What happened to all those snapshots that I loaned Jennifer?"

"Shh," hissed Samantha's aunt, shaking her finger. When she turned, Dorothy stuck out her tongue.

On the TV screen, Jennifer's picture appeared. She looked to be five or six. Her small face was split into a smile, and she was holding up a fish. Everyone in the room said, "Awwww!" and someone shouted, "Daddy took his little girl fishing. How darling!"

"That's *your* fish, Mack," Dorothy said, nudging him. "Quick, stand up and tell them."

"I don't give a rat's ass," he said, reaching for his wineglass.

"Shh," hissed Samantha's aunt.

"Hush yourself," Dorothy snapped. "They can't reinvent history."

"They just have," said Mack.

• • •

The video ended with an engagement photo of the couple, then the toasts began. At first, they were lighthearted, and somewhat comical, but as the evening dragged on, they became increasingly long-winded and maudlin, fueled by endless bottles of house champagne and chablis, which kept materializing on the tables. At one point Miss Betty stood up, weaving slightly, and said, "I wish you all the love and happiness that Chick and I have had." Then she reached behind her, groping for her chair, and sank down.

Dorothy whispered, "That's more like a curse."

Chick staggered to his feet and raised his glass. "Pierre, I'd like to offer the three rules of marriage: Never tell her she's wrong, never call her frivolous, and never, absolutely *never* tell her she looks fat, even if she asks."

The audience laughed, and several paunchy older men stood up and clapped.

Samantha rose from her chair, her right hand lingering on Claude's shoulder, and began telling how she and Jennifer had met last year in a local boutique. "We fell in love with the same Gucci bag," she explained.

"Dior, not Gucci," Jennifer called from her seat and lifted the satin clutch for all to see.

In a halting voice, Claude advised Pierre to take good care of his Jennikins. "I didn't always get it right in my life, but I tried," he added, wiping his eyes.

"What a shithead," Mack said.

Not to be outdone, Dorothy popped out of her chair before I could stop her. "I lift my glass in a toast to the groom, who is charming," Dorothy said. "I lift my glass to the bride, my granddaughter, who is about to embark into marriage. And, Jennifer, marriage is tough. It's just damn hard. All you can do is take it one day at a time. Sometimes one *hour* at a time."

She sat down with a flourish, then leaned over and asked, "How did I do?"

"Perfect," I told her, squeezing her hand.

. . .

After the toasts, the guests began milling around the ballroom. My cell phone rang five times before I could locate my evening bag under the napkins, and several people from nearby tables glanced in my direction. After I clicked off, I located Mack and asked if he could take Dorothy home.

"Sure, but . . . don't tell me you picked up a fat-cat date tonight?"

"I'll fill you in," Dorothy said, grabbing his arm.

As I walked off, I heard her say, "I'm so proud of Bitsy. Why, *she's just like me.*"

When I stepped into the lobby of the Holiday Inn, Ian was standing next to a metal rack, perusing the colorful brochures. Rock City, Dollywood, White Water Rafting. He was wearing a beige shirt, the sleeves rolled up to the elbow, black wristwatch, tan trousers, and Doc Martens. His thick blond hair tumbled down his forehead. My heart sped up. I suddenly remembered once, during a long, luxurious bubble bath in his narrow tub, wondering aloud if I'd been born in the wrong century. How lovely to have toured Cuba with Hemingway, I'd said, or to have lived in Tahiti with Gauguin. Now I thought to hell with artsy types and exotic locales. Nothing would thrill me more than one night in Crystal Falls with Ian Maitland.

He glanced up, and his lips spread into that wonderful, crooked smile and I ran into his arms. He lifted me, and the Oscar de la Renta hiked up as I locked my legs around his waist. With a laugh, he swung me around. He smelled of tobacco and Acqua di Parma. I kissed his lips, his forehead, his chin until his entire face was marked with lipstick. Then I leaned back and sighed.

"My love," he said. One of his hands clutched my bottom, and the other was cupped behind my neck. Then we kissed slowly, luxuriously.

When we broke apart, gasping for air, the night clerk coughed and held up a key. "Toss it here," said Ian. He raised his hand and made a neat catch.

"Your room is pool side." The clerk grinned. "And please, no skinny dipping. It's against hotel policy."

"We'll bear that in mind," Ian promised. He put me down but we were still kissing when we stepped into the Holidome, a glass bubble encasing the pool and hot tub. Reluctantly I broke away and took a breath. The warm, steamy air smelled faintly of chlorine. The pool area was empty except for an elderly couple sitting at a table and a man swimming laps. The water frothed around him. Dear God, it was Louie. The first time I saw him, he'd been swimming in a hotel pool. I wondered if this was a portent.

Ian held up the key—202. "Shall we?" he said, then he fit the key between his teeth, and he lifted me into his arms again, the purple silk draping around us, falling over our limbs like water.

The next morning, I awakened to the sounds of splashing water. I opened my eyes, confused for a moment. Then I remembered where I was and stretched my hand along the sheet. The bed was empty. I pulled up on one elbow, wondering if I'd dreamed my night with Ian.

He emerged from the bathroom, trailed by wisps of steam, rubbing his head with a towel. "Lovely day," he said, grinning. I had forgotten how cheerful he was in the mornings. "You look positively crestfallen," he added. "What's the matter?"

"I'm worried about tonight. I don't know how I'll get through it."

"The only advice I'm authorized to give is editorial," he said. "But it might behoove you to float above the fray—a distanced, omniscient observer. Actually, I should say limited omniscient."

"That might work." I smiled.

"Say, I do like your hair. Scoot over, I brought you something."

He unzipped his suitcase, reached inside, and lifted out a white box with Spode stamped in red across the lid. He put it in my lap and sat down beside me while I opened it. "Queen's Bird!" I placed the cup in the saucer. "Oh, Ian. How absolutely sweet."

"It's not the same, of course; but still, you might grow fond of it."

"I already am. I'll take it everywhere I go."

"There's one condition," he said, drawing me into his arms, taking care not to dislodge the cup.

"What's that?"

"You must take me, too."

Clancy Jane

Rain picked at the screen in Clancy Jane's bedroom window. Deep in the woods, an animal howled, making the hair stand up on her arms. She'd been lying in bed, eating mangoes, surrounded by a dozen felines, but now she sat up, tilting her head toward the window. She heard the cry again. It didn't sound like a wolf or coyote; in fact, in all the years she'd lived on this mountain she'd never heard such a mournful sound. It frightened her—what if this creature ate cats? It shrieked again, and the kittens stood on their toes and arched their backs. Only Jellybean seemed unalarmed. Her paws were folded beneath her chest, green eyes focused on Clancy Jane's mangoes.

"Maybe it's a banshee," she told the cat. Jellybean closed her eyes and purred. Clancy Jane set the mango dish on the floor, licked her fingertips, and rolled onto her side, dragging a pillow over her ear. From the woods, she heard another cry and wondered if she'd get any sleep. Tomorrow was Jennifer's wedding, and truth be told, she'd rather stay home, all comfy in her cotton pajamas, her cats perched all around her, waiting for her to open the bedside drawer and pull out the small tin of liver treats. She used to believe that her cats adored her, but now she had their number. Cats were in it for the food.

From the bedside table, the phone rang. No one but her daughter ever called this late, so Clancy Jane flung off the pillow and groped to pick up the receiver. "'Lo," she whispered.

"Hi, Mama," said Violet. "Hope I didn't wake you."

"No, I've got insomnia."

"Drink some hot milk and you'll feel better."

"I'd rather have a Valium."

"Too addictive." Violet laughed. "Listen, I didn't tell you before because I wasn't sure I could make it, but I'm coming to Jennifer's wedding. My flight arrives in Nashville at two o'clock tomorrow, barring unforeseen complications."

"When you were little, I never dreamed you'd grow up and say things like that."

"I'm sorry. I'm still in my therapeutic mode."

"Well, lose it quick. I can't wait to see you, baby. I haven't driven to Nashville in years, but I'm sure I can find the airport. What time does your flight get in?"

"No, that's okay. I've rented a car, and—please don't get mad—I'll be staying at the Holiday Inn."

"You're staying at a motel?" Clancy Jane swallowed. "But I've got plenty of room."

"Stop trying to make me feel guilty."

"Then stop shrinking me." Clancy Jane twirled the phone cord. She knew this was Violet's way of saying that she could end up staying at Cat Crossing, but she'd booked the room as an escape route. "By the way, don't expect a wedding like yours."

"It wouldn't be a Wentworth event if it weren't pretentious."

"Miss Betty wouldn't have it any other way." Clancy Jane laughed. "Will George be coming with you?"

"We're an evolved couple, Mama. I don't need a man to hang on to. Besides, he's fencing our backyard."

"You're getting a dog?"

"No."

"Too evolved for pets, are we?"

"It hurt us too much when Bojangles passed on." Violet paused. "How many cats do you have?"

"Four," Clancy Jane said, her standard answer. No matter how many felines were lolling around the house, she claimed to only own four. Any more than that and people would talk.

"So," Violet said. "When I see you, I'm not going to hear you say, 'Why don't you visit more often?'"

Clancy Jane's put one hand over her eyes. Her fingers were sticky and smelled of mangoes. "Stay where you want. Visit when the spirit moves you to visit. It's your life, not mine."

"Thank you. I've waited thirty-nine years to hear you say that."

"Besides, there's a banshee howling in my backyard, and it'll just keep you awake."

"A banshee?"

"It could be a coyote." Clancy Jane peered out the window. The sky was packed with clouds, and she couldn't see the stars. The rain had slacked off, but the Channel 5 radar map had shown a jagged green patch moving over Kansas, Arkansas, and most of Oklahoma. The weatherman had predicted a downpour late tomorrow evening, and Clancy Jane hoped it would arrive after Jennifer's nuptials.

"Just because I'm staying at the Holiday Inn doesn't mean that I don't love you," Violet said.

"Are you still harping on that?" Clancy Jane bit her lips. "I know you love me."

After Clancy Jane hung up the phone, she snuggled beneath the down coverlet. The banshee cried again. It sounded a bit farther away this time. Perhaps it was on the move, bad luck in transit. Only God knew where it would go next.

Bitsy and Jennifer

The late-afternoon sun dipped behind a cloud, throwing Hammersmith Farm into shadow. Just off the main road, five teenage boys sullenly directed traffic into the pasture: Mercedes, Jaguars, BMWs, Cadillacs, and Lincolns. After parking their cars, the men strode forward, but the women picked their way around the cow flops, their gowns held above their ankles. They headed toward a path outlined with hundreds of white balloons, each printed with Jennifer & Pierre.

"I don't like outdoor events," Dorothy said as Bitsy angled the Jeep under the banner that read *Wentworth-Tournear Nuptials*, as if to differentiate it from the hundreds of other weddings taking place on this mountain, and parked next to a black Lincoln. Ian was riding shotgun, looking elegant in his tuxedo. Dorothy leaned forward from the backseat, edging between them. "Did you talk my sister into coming?" she asked.

Bitsy turned to Ian. "My aunt Clancy isn't family-oriented."

"And you are?" Dorothy cocked her eyebrow, which had been drawn in brown pencil—Mocha Frost by L'Oréal. Bitsy didn't respond, so Dorothy reached inside her jacket, where she'd safety-pinned a ten-dollar bill to her slip—her just-in-case-there's-trouble money.

"We could get bitten by ticks and come down with Rocky Mountain spotted fever," she said. "The bride and groom could get bitten."

"Now there's an idea," Bitsy said.

"I wish Mack had come with us." Dorothy sighed.

"He'll be here," Bitsy told her. "He's picking up his date."

"You said the keywords—pick up." Dorothy sighed. "I hate to see what *this* one looks like." She sighed again and brushed lint from her jacket. Dorothy watched as Ian helped Bitsy out of the Jeep and wondered if he had any uncles. She looked damn good in this Chanel suit.

She just hoped that Ian didn't know where she'd gotten it, or about her time in the asylum.

Ian turned to Dorothy and offered his hand. She took her time easing out of the Jeep, thanked him, then steadied herself and watched him turn back to Bitsy. The way they looked at each other made Dorothy's heart lurch. If only a man had ever looked at her like that . . . well, it might have helped if she'd had an hourglass figure and nicer features. Maybe then her life would have been different.

"Well," she said, "we'd best get a move on. We don't want to be unfashionably late. Speaking of which, let's pray that Bitsy hasn't overdressed."

Bitsy was wearing a black, off-the-shoulder top with a long pewter-and-cream skirt. Dorothy reached out, as if to pat her daughter's shoulder, but slid her hand down Bitsy's blouse and grabbed the tag.

"Chetta B?" she said, mimicking Jennifer's voice. She released the tag, feigning disgust. "What kind of no-name designer is *that*?"

They looked at each other and laughed. Bitsy grabbed a handful of tulle and lifted her skirt. Ian took one look at her silver evening shoes, then lifted her into his arms again and carried her across the pasture to the path. It was damp because of last night's rain—and more was expected tonight—but Claude's hired hands had laid down clear rubber mats.

At the top of the path, six little girls were holding hands and running in a clockwise circle. "Ashes, ashes," they sang. "All fall down." A few yards away, two little boys were juggling lemons. Smoke curled up from behind a lattice screen, giving off the scent of grilled steak and shrimp. A telephone pole stood near the edge of the hill, with wires running to the tent and to the Porta-Johns, each one the size of a caboose. Claude had electrified the mountain. He probably would have moved it if Jennifer had asked, Dorothy thought. They passed the Porta-Johns and one door stood ajar, showing black-and-white marble tile floors, gold faucets, marble sinks, glittering chandeliers. Two men hurried by, carrying a board—a giant ice carving surrounded by curly endive. The carving appeared to be a chipmunk.

"What is the significance of the rodent sculpture?" Ian asked.

"It was supposed to be a heart," Dorothy told him.

"Perhaps they'll sort it out." Ian watched the two men disappear behind the lattice screen into the catering area. Waiters were rushing around with trays, sidestepping the children. Inside the tent, more chandeliers hung from the pleated ceiling. Tear-shaped bulbs cast light on the black-and-white marble dance floor and the makeshift stage. The tables, each one with an elaborate floral arrangement, formed a C around the checkerboard floor.

As Dorothy wove among the tables, looking at the place cards, the violinist followed behind her playing "Evergreen." Ian and Bitsy followed her. Beyond the tent, on the fescue, white wooden chairs were laid out in a symmetrical pattern reminiscent of the white marble crosses in St.-Laurent-sur-Mer, the hilltop cemetery in Normandy overlooking the sea.

Over by the fountain, the groomsmen were jostling each other. Tonya stood near them, patting her huge white corsage. Resembling a tidal wave in her silk seafoam suit, she stepped over to Pierre and straightened his bow tie in a proprietary way. Claude, looking pale and haggard in white tie and tails, stood off to the side, hands clasped behind his back. Behind him, leaning over the bar was Chick, watching the bartender mix a scotch and soda. He wore a glossy black tuxedo, and a massive cummerbund was stretched over his abdomen like a surgical bandage.

"Chick's got mud on his shoes," Dorothy said with a sniff. "They're Gucci, I'll bet. I've seen his old ones at the thrift store. Is he jaundiced, or is the light too harsh? They *say* he needs a liver transplant. But it could be a rumor. Look—there's Miss Betty."

Holding her ever-present glass of wine, Miss Betty struck a regal pose. She wore a long beige taffeta dress—a traditional color for the mother of the bride. Her corsage was askew—white sweetheart roses mingled with orchids and satin ribbons. Emerald-cut diamond earrings peeked through her chin-length, lacquered hair. And she was wearing tinted sunglasses, even though the sky was rapidly filling with clouds.

"What, no corsages for us?" Dorothy whispered.

"An oversight, no doubt," Bitsy whispered back. "Shhh, she's coming this way."

"Well, hello again," Miss Betty said in a grand voice. She appeared sober and had no trouble recognizing Bitsy this time. "You look younger than springtime with that choppy hair. I'm sure it's the latest style in . . . where are you living now?"

"England," Dorothy said. "She lives in London, England."

"Yes, I believe Jennifer mentioned that you'd moved. She said you were running away from another husband."

"She left right after his funeral," Dorothy said. "The poor dear."

Ian laughed, and Miss Betty gave him a sharp look. She lifted her glass, tossed down the wine, then said, "I don't believe we've met. You're Bitsy's parole officer?"

"Indeed I am," said Ian in his crisp, British accent.

"He's her boyfriend," Dorothy said. "And he's a real famous editor."

"Well, I'd be careful if I were you," Miss Betty said in a flat voice. She started to take another sip of wine then realized her glass was empty. "Have either of you seen Jennifer? I suppose Samantha's helping her get ready. You *do* know Samantha, don't you, Bitsy?"

"We met last night," Bitsy said. And thought, *You old bitch.*

"Yes, yes. That's right. You all met at the rehearsal dinner." Miss Betty turned to Ian. "You missed the gorgeous dress that Bitsy wore last night. Why, I've never seen *any*thing quite that purple, except in a lingerie store."

"No, I saw it," Ian said, reaching for Bitsy's hand, giving it a squeeze.

"It's an Oscar de la Renta," Dorothy said.

"Dorothy, I've got to give you credit," said Miss Betty. "You might be insane, but you have a great sense of style. By the way, your suit is gorgeous."

"It ought to be, it was *yours.*" Dorothy flashed a triumphant grin. Miss Betty seemed dumbstruck. She took off her sunglasses, and glared at the suit. But before she could speak, Dorothy put one hand on Ian's elbow, her other hand on Bitsy's and steered them toward the opposite side of the tent. Behind them, the violinist closed in on Miss Betty and began to play "We've Only Just Begun."

After Ian took off toward the nearest bar with their drink orders, Dorothy nudged her daughter. "There's your brother. And just look at that *thing* hanging on his arm."

"What thing?" Bitsy thought Mack looked stunning in his rental tuxedo. He was standing at the opposite end of the tent, near another bar, holding hands with a tall redhead in a slinky orange dress.

"Don't ask me her name," said Dorothy, "but she works at the Kroger deli. And she has three children—each one by a different husband. At least I think they were husbands. I hope she doesn't try to trap Mack."

The wedding planner hurried by, wearing a whispery beige gown, the hem already stained by the grass. She clutched a sheaf of papers, and her forehead was creased with a deep, V-shaped wrinkle. When she saw

Dorothy and Bitsy, she stopped. "The most terrible thing has happened," she said. "The ushers' tailcoats don't match." The woman looked up into the tent's puckered ceiling, shaking her head. The huge beige bow at the back of her head wobbled. "How can this be?"

"I didn't even notice," Bitsy said.

"I hope Jennifer doesn't," said the wedding planner, her eyes growing wide with alarm.

"She probably will," Dorothy said. "She made me order Mack's tux months ago."

"What about the ice sculpture?" Bitsy asked. "Has Jennifer seen the chipmunk?"

"What chipmunk?" The wedding planner froze.

Bitsy started to explain, but the woman rushed off, pushing her way through the crowded tent. Over by the bar, Bitsy caught sight of a woman in an electric blue dress, the fabric stretched over an enormous stomach. Dorothy saw her at the same time. "That can't be Violet," she squinted. "Lord, she's gotten hefty."

"She's pregnant," Bitsy said.

"Don't be silly." Dorothy punched Bitsy's arm. "Violet's too old. I bet she has gray pubic hairs."

In the distance, Clancy Jane trudged up the path. Perspiration slid down her face, and her long silver-blond hair had stuck to her neck. She was trailed by three little girls in white organdy dresses.

"Good lord, it's my sister. And look how she's sweating." Dorothy shook her head. Then, in a singsong voice, she said, "She's *melting*, Auntie Em."

"Keep your voice down." Bitsy shook her mother's arm, and the upper flesh jiggled. "Just for today. Just for me."

"I'll try." Dorothy sighed. "But I can't give a guarantee."

Clancy Jane and the children moved across the field, pausing beside the buffet. She snatched up a handful of green mints, causing the caterer to scream. "Oh, don't be so anal," yelled Clancy Jane, throwing candy to the little girls.

Dorothy raised her eyebrows. "And you're telling *me* to keep *my* voice down?"

"I want to see Violet," Bitsy said.

"No fair. I saw her first," Dorothy cried, scuttling forward. She caught up with Violet at the bar and let out a whoop. She grabbed her niece's arm and pulled her into an awkward embrace. Violet barely had time to shift her massive stomach out of the way.

"Nice to see you, too, Aunt Dorothy." Violet laughed. "Is Bitsy here?"

"She's right behind me."

"I suppose she looks wonderful—as always."

"Better than wonderful," said Dorothy. "I suspect plastic surgery, but she denies it. Maybe you can tell if she's lying. Although she could be a witch. Witches never age."

Bitsy rushed past Dorothy and threw her arms around her cousin. Dorothy drew back, as if scrutinizing Violet's shape. Bitsy could almost read her mother's thoughts, *It could be a tumor, Or middle-age spread gone haywire.* She knew she'd been right when Dorothy blurted, "Violet, have you gained a little weight?"

"Thirty pounds." Violet placed her hand on the curve of her abdomen, staring at it reverently. "Eight is baby weight, I'm guessing. But I'm afraid the rest is fat."

"I *knew* it," Dorothy said.

"Say hello to Mariah," said Violet.

"Mariah Carey is *here?*" Dorothy's head swiveled, looking at the crowd.

"No, my baby's name is Mariah. I'm having a girl."

"Does Clancy Jane know? I sure hope you've prepared her, because she just arrived." Dorothy pointed to the far end of the tent, where her sister had set up court with the little girls, feeding them mints and dancing in circles. Acting demented, in Dorothy's opinion.

"Not yet." Violet turned to stare at her mother. "That's the reason I kept waffling about coming home. I knew I'd have some explaining to do."

"Go on, I'm listening," said Dorothy. "But first, tell me why you and George waited so long to get pregnant."

"Aunt Dorothy, you haven't changed at all." Violet laughed. "You're still nosy."

"Quit changing the subject. Why did you wait so long?"

"It wasn't intentional." Violet leaned forward. "It's sort of a virgin birth."

Dorothy's eyes widened. "I'm afraid I don't understand."

"George isn't the father," Violet said.

"You had an affair?" Dorothy's hand rose to her throat. Like mother, like daughter, she thought. When those two wanted a man, they just *took* him.

"God, no." Violet shook her head. "I'd never cheat on George."

Bitsy gestured at her cousin's stomach. "If he isn't the daddy, then who?"

"A stranger," Violet said.

"Oh, my lord!" Dorothy clapped her hand over her mouth. In a whisper, she said, "You were attacked?"

"God forbid." Violet shut her eyes. "That's too awful to contemplate."

"Then . . . how?" Dorothy's eyes wobbled.

"Artificial insemination." Violet smiled down at her stomach.

"Now why would you go and do that?" Dorothy cried. "Why didn't you get old what's-his-name to inseminate you?"

"George? Well, he tried his best," said Violet in an offhand voice. "But time was running out, and we wanted a baby."

"Well, don't feel bad. All the movie stars do it." Dorothy's hand moved toward Violet's stomach. "Would you mind if I touch it?"

Chick Wentworth passed by, ice tinkling in his glass. His eyes bugged when he saw Dorothy's hand on Violet's belly. His cummerbund had slipped a notch, riding low on his hips. Then he turned away, and Bitsy saw that he was going bald.

"A sperm donor might be the way to go," Dorothy said, shaking her head at Chick. "Some men just shouldn't breed."

The women turned to look across the tent, past the tables and chairs, toward Claude, who was milling through the crowd, shaking hands and smiling. "Where is Jennifer?" Violet asked.

"She's in a tent somewhere, getting ready," Bitsy said, looking over her shoulder.

"Why aren't you with her?"

"Haven't you heard? The Wentworths have worked it all out," said Dorothy. "Yes, Bitsy should be with Jennifer right now. Helping her daughter get ready. Fluffing her veil, making sure she has something borrowed and something blue. Instead, Claude's g.d. gal pal is helping. Miss Betty couldn't wait to rub that in."

The violinist was now following some teenage girls, playing the theme song from *The Thomas Crown Affair,* Claude's favorite movie. He and Bitsy had seen it at the Princess Theater in 1971, and its lusty scenes had ultimately led to Jennifer's conception.

"There are four mothers of the bride here tonight," Dorothy told Violet.

"You know, I'm a psychiatrist, but I never understood Claude's hold on Jennifer," Violet said.

"Just look around." Dorothy raised her hand. "A fabric tent. Chandeliers. Porta-Johns with marble floors. A fountain spurting out champagne."

Violet looked through the tent, into the field, at the enormous fountain. Guests were bending toward its arcs, holding out their glasses.

"Although it could be piss," added Dorothy.

The musicians took their seats in a roped-off area and began tuning their instruments. The ushers had gathered beneath a canopy that jutted from the center of the tent. Beyond the canopy were the white chairs, where a few elderly guests had already been seated.

"This music is making me ill," Violet said. "I'm not used to the horrors of light FM."

Bitsy tried not to smile. She loved the music. She needed it. Sometimes she even sang it when she was all alone.

"Aww, I know you like that song." Violet put her arm around Bitsy. "But it's too sad for wedding music."

"You should've been here earlier," Dorothy said. "They were playing something from the *American Tail* soundtrack."

"Wedding music should be symbolic," Violet said. "They could at least play Midler. Maybe something from the Bathhouse Bette CD. Like 'That's How Love Moves.'"

"I wasn't exactly consulted." Bitsy smiled.

"Toughen up, kid." Violet made a fist and gently touched her cousin's chin. "If you can get through this wedding, you can get through anything."

"You'd better toughen up yourself," Bitsy said. "Here comes your mother."

But Violet was following Dorothy's gaze, toward the fountain, where an unruly mob had gathered. In their midst was Louie DeChavannes—dashing in cream trousers, a crisp Zegna shirt, blue-gray silk tie, and a pink cashmere jacket. A linen handkerchief was artfully arranged in its front left pocket. On his lapel was a pink tiger lily. And he was wearing mirrored sunglasses.

"All that *pink*," gasped Dorothy. "Jennifer will die."

"I like it," said Violet, then she hummed a few bars from "Hotel California," about pretty boys.

"At least he isn't wearing matching trousers," said Dorothy. "Knowing him, that jacket probably cost a small fortune."

"It did," Bitsy told her. "I helped him buy it."

"Gad, that was years ago," said Violet.

"What were you thinking, honey?" Dorothy's forehead puckered as she turned to Bitsy. "I know you like pink, but *on a man?*"

Just then Louie saw Bitsy and did a double take. When he smiled, Bitsy couldn't help but smile back. He was still handsome, but he didn't look healthy. Under the tan his complexion was gray and chalky. He took off his sunglasses and saluted the women with his empty champagne glass.

I wish he'd—Bitsy stopped herself. Wish what? That he'd shrivel up and die? That she'd never met him? She began looking for Ian. He was standing close to the bar, talking to Mack and the redhead. The musicians started playing "Greensleeves," and Bitsy stole one more glance at Louie. He had put the sunglasses back on, and was leaning over the fountain, extending his champagne glass beneath a sparkling arc.

Let's get this over with, she thought, and squeezed through the crowd. When he saw her coming, he raised his champagne glass in another silent toast.

"Beauty," he said, bowing over her hand. His grip tightened, and he rhythmically squeezed her fingers. She knew the code by heart. *Let's get out of here,* the code said. Her limp hand sent back a terse reply: *No.* A waiter passed, balancing a tray of champagne, and Bitsy let go of Louie's hand and reached for a glass.

"It was kind of you to come," she told him. "It means a lot."

"To whom?" He took a sip of champagne. "Jennifer? *You?*"

She didn't answer. If only he'd take off those goddamn sunglasses. She remembered his last letter. *This is it, kid.*

Over Louie's shoulder, she saw her mother pushing through the guests, a panicky look on her face as she approached. On the other side of the tent, the musicians started playing "Ode to Joy."

"Dorothy!" Louie's voice boomed. "Get over here and give me a hug."

"You haven't changed one bit," Dorothy said in a girlish voice. She reached her chubby arms around his neck.

"Nor you," he said, smiling.

"Flatterer." Dorothy's eyelashes fluttered.

Louie turned to Bitsy. "I hope your mother warned you I was coming."

"I did," Dorothy said.

"Bitsy, I—" He faltered, and his lovely eyebrows came together. Dorothy leaned forward, too. Her heart began to flutter beneath the Chanel suit. Why, he's going to tell her that he still loves her, Dorothy thought. Oh, this was more exciting than the star-crossed romances on *Guiding Light.* His lips were moving rather frantically, but the words seemed lodged in his throat.

Say it, Dorothy thought. Just spit it out. Then Louie's eyes rounded. He looked past Bitsy and stepped backward. Dorothy turned and saw Ian squeezing through the crowd, holding three champagne flutes—quite a neat trick. She almost said, Shoo, Ian! Not that she had anything against the man, except for his U.K. address. She held her breath and tried to shove her thoughts in her daughter's direction. *Bitsy, you belong with Louie.* True, he was limited, but what man wasn't? Then she saw how her daughter was looking at the Englishman, and Dorothy knew the moment had passed.

Ian walked up and held out the flutes. Bitsy put down the untouched glass she'd been holding, then accepted the new one from Ian. A veil fell over Louie's eyes. Then he seemed to collect himself. His smile was automatic, his manners polished and cordial. Bitsy made the introductions, and Louie took off his sunglasses and extended his hand. "Looks like rain," he said, glancing up at the sky. "It could be a portent. Did you see the ice sculpture?"

He raised his eyebrows and grinned. This was part of the famous DeChavannes charm, inserting levity at the precise moment it was needed. "I witnessed the catfight between the delivery men and some blonde—"

"The wedding planner," Bitsy supplied helpfully.

"She was going wild." Louie's grin widened. "Apparently the heart Jennifer ordered went to a reception for a naturalist who specializes in squirrel photography."

"But the sculpture is a chipmunk."

"It seems the sculptor sneezed at a critical moment and lopped off the damn thing's tail."

"Well, it's a warm night." Bitsy laughed. "It won't be a chipmunk for long."

• • •

While the violinist played "Isn't She Lovely," several young men lurched toward the Porta-Johns, but were deterred by the long lines. They reeled toward the pine-strewn path, looking for a private place to urinate. One fellow stumbled down the hill. His friends went after him, and when they returned, their suits were coated in beggar lice.

"We're almost ready," the wedding planner said. "You'll walk down first, Bitsy. Followed by Samantha. Let's just get lined up. Todd? You need to get over here with Jennifer's mother."

Mothers, Bitsy thought. The music segued into Vivaldi's "Spring." She slipped her hand into the crook of her usher's arm. He laid his hand over hers and winked.

"You're one fine-looking mama," he said. "What you doing later tonight?"

"Hush, y'all!" The wedding planner snapped her fingers. Her young assistant rushed up to her, whispered urgently into her ear. "Oh, for heaven's sake," said the planner, and dashed off into the crowd, pausing to glance over her shoulder at the wedding party.

"I'll be right back. Don't anyone move," she ordered.

From the corner of Bitsy's eye she saw a flash of white satin tulle—Jennifer was riding piggyback up the path on a bearded usher. Her hitched-up mermaid dress showed trim, tanned thighs, dainty ankles, and white pumps. In her right hand she was holding a bottle of champagne. The bridesmaids surrounded her, their blood-colored gowns skimming lightly over the damp grass. They resembled ballerinas, tall, anorexic sugarplum fairies. Each girl was wearing pearl studs and a pearl choker, and their hair had been styled into identical French twists. The maid of honor had white powder on her nose and upper lip, as if she'd been eating self-rising flour. She was obviously wired, giggly and electrified. The groom was nowhere in sight. Trailing behind the wedding party was Samantha, holding up the hem of her baby-pink gown—it was the color of the sugar roses on Jennifer's seven-layer wedding cake.

"Okay, I've had enough," Jennifer told the usher. "Put me down, Christopher."

"No!" squealed Samantha, throwing out one manicured hand. "Keep holding her, Christopher. The grass will ruin her dress, and it's a Vera Wang."

The bridesmaids began to twitter, "The bride wore Wang."

"Vera Twang," said one.

"Vera Wrong," said another.

"Vera Wang Wang Blues."

"Y'all shut up." Jennifer slid down the boy's back, and the satin dress made a scratchy noise. Her spiked heels sank into the ground. "I've got to walk sooner or later, and besides, my butt was getting numb."

"Don't smudge your dress," Samantha called.

"Why, do you plan to wear it next?" Jennifer fluffed the veil, which she'd somehow affixed to her short, spiky hair. Her bangs stuck out, the color of oakwood, darker than Bitsy's. Then she lifted the bottle of champagne and took a sip. Bitsy noticed it was Moët, not Dom Perignon or Five Star.

"I resent that. I'm only trying to help." Samantha's cheeks turned pink.

"Oh, don't get your panties in a wad," said Jennifer. "I don't mind if you borrow it. And I've resigned myself to far worse than grass stains."

She glanced down the length of the field, past the white tent, past the musicians, who were playing "Beau Soir" by Debussy. Then she took a step forward, her gown skimming over grass. Lifting her eyes, she looked straight into Bitsy's face. Apparently Samantha saw, too, and tried to position herself between the two women, but Jennifer threw out her arm.

Bitsy stepped hesitantly forward, thinking that her daughter had indeed made a beautiful bride. She started to tell her, but the wind caught the veil, lace and tulle floating around Jennifer's head, who cursed and swatted it down. The wedding planner came rushing up, gripping her sheaf of papers.

"You aren't supposed to be out here," the woman told Jennifer. "Get behind the curtain this instant."

"What does it matter?" Jennifer shrugged.

"Go!" The wedding planner held out one arm, pointing at the tent. She looked just like a bouffant munchkin, shouting at the Wizard of Oz. The musicians began to play "The Arrival of the Queen of Sheba."

"God, those *fools*!" The wedding planner grimaced. "That's a recessional. And it's not even the one we picked. They're supposed to be playing Canon in D. Dammit, what else can go wrong?"

· · ·

When Jennifer finally started down the aisle with Claude, lightning zigzagged behind them. They marched on, oblivious to the disturbance. As they passed the grandmothers' row, Jennifer nodded at both sets of relatives. Miss Betty always called Dorothy "that nut," and Dorothy always referred to Miss Betty as "hoity-toity." But they'd called a truce today. Taking another step forward, Jennifer glanced furtively at her mother, thinking that grace and good looks were inherited. She couldn't help but wonder if she had misjudged the woman. Last night she had found letters stuffed inside the Fitz & Floyd tureen, and she'd stayed up past midnight reading them. And when she returned from her honeymoon, she planned to read them again and have a long talk with her mother.

Claude and Jennifer stepped up to the lattice altar. Her father answered the minister's question about who gave this woman, with "I do," emphasis on the *I*, and handed her over to Pierre. As the minister opened his Bible, the wind began to rise. "And now I shall read from Paul in the book of Corinthians," said the preacher. "'Although I speak in tongues of men and angels, I'm just sounding brass and tinkling cymbals without love. Love suffers long, love is kind, enduring all things.'"

Is it really all those things? Jennifer wondered, then chastised herself for being cynical. As the rain started to fall, a breeze swept through the tent and snapped the canvas panels. The minister asked Pierre if he would take Jennifer to be his wife. Pierre tilted to the right, looking around Jennifer, and gazed at the wedding party. The minister's words trailed off. He wiped the rain from his face and waited patiently for the groom's answer. Jennifer craned her neck, trying to see what had captured Pierre's attention.

"Pierre?" she said.

The groom turned back to the minister and said, "I will, I mean, I guess I do."

Laughter scattered through the younger guests. Jennifer's breasts rose and fell beneath the Vera Wang. When she'd been a small girl, her mother had told her, "You were inside me right *here*." She'd pressed Jennifer's hand against her flat stomach. "You were a baby mermaid, and you kicked like crazy. So much élan! I just knew you'd be born with fins and a tail."

"Better than horns," Aunt Violet had said.

·   ·   ·

After the five-course dinner, the orchestra began playing songs from the seventies and eighties, with a few standards squeezed in for the old-timers. Ian raised his champagne glass and said, "Here's to love."

"To love," said Bitsy, touching her glass to his.

The others joined in, clinking their glasses. A waiter passed a tray of mints. Dorothy rose from her seat and grabbed a handful, then she sat down, offered one to her sister. Clancy Jane started to take it, then saw Byron walking over to the table. He put his arm around the back of her chair. "I was hoping to see you tonight," he said. When she didn't answer, he added, "Your dress is pretty."

She murmured a demure thank you, then looked up at him and smiled. "So, Byron, how did you manage to crack the guest list?"

"Dorothy pulled a string." He winked at his former sister-in-law. She giggled, then gulped down a mint.

"She's pulled more than one." Clancy Jane pointed to Louie, who was dancing with Violet, her enormous stomach shifted to the side. Dorothy rolled her eyes, then ate another mint. In her next life, she thought, she wasn't having any children, and she wasn't breeding Pomeranians, either. She was going to work in a candy shop.

From the stage, the band started playing "Silver Springs."

"At last," Clancy Jane said. "A decent song. Even if the singer is no Stevie Nicks."

"Let's dance," Byron said, extending his hand. Clancy Jane took it and got up from her chair. Across the table, Ian dropped to one knee and smiled up at Bitsy. "Will you dance with me?"

Bitsy studied his face. He seemed to be asking another question, but first she wanted him to know what a long way she'd come, across all the foolish years of her life to reach this calm, contented moment. Then she took his hand. "I would love to dance with you," she said.

They got up, walked over to the checkerboard floor, and leaned against each other. He took one of his beautiful hands and enveloped both of hers, pressing them to his chest. She lifted her chin. He touched her face but didn't say a word.

Several feet away, Louie and Violet were watching. They were still watching when the song ended and a lanky girl swaggered up to the microphone and started singing Poco's "Crazy Love."

"She's never coming back, Louie," Violet told him.

"Doesn't look like it." He drew in a ragged breath. "I really messed up, didn't I?"

"Yes, you did," Violet said in a stern voice, then she softened. "But you're still the only man I know who looks rugged in pink."

The song ended and two new singers launched into a duet, "Ever Changing Times." Clancy Jane and Byron were talking about her cats. She told him point-blank how many she owned and he threw back his head and laughed. Then he hugged her closer.

"Where do they dredge up these songs?" Clancy Jane sighed. "I keep waiting for them to play New Kids on the Block."

"I've missed you." Byron inched closer. Outside the tent, lightning briefly illuminated the hillside. The rain began falling harder.

A woman with bright red fingernails danced by, steering a burly man in a damp tuxedo. "Well, hello, Dr. Falk," the woman said to Byron. Then she turned to Clancy Jane. "Isn't he the most marvelous dancer?"

"He ought to be," Clancy Jane said. "I taught him."

• • •

Dorothy's head was spinning, and it wasn't because Mack had brought that floozy to the wedding—it was the champagne. She sat at the table, her chin in her hands, watching the guests act like pure-dee idiots. She didn't know what it was about weddings, but they seemed to bring out the worst in people. The ushers, oblivious to the downpour, were crowded around the fountain, guzzling champagne. And that damn Chick was out there with them, matching the boys drink for drink. His wet tuxedo was plastered to his body. Miss Betty was standing at the edge of the tent, arguing with the caterer, who was breathing into a brown paper bag. God only knew what this gala had cost. The next time Jennifer got married—and she probably would, considering her age and gene pool—Dorothy hoped the girl would find a chapel in Gatlinburg and skip the high-priced hoopla. For under a hundred dollars, Jennifer could get married, play goofy golf, and have a pancake supper. And for just a little bit more, she could bungee jump.

• • •

Around ten o'clock, the rain stopped falling, and Dorothy wandered out to one of the Porta-Johns. The door of one flung open, and two bridesmaids ran out, their faces swollen and mottled. They looked as if they had been weeping or vomiting, possibly both. Dorothy followed them toward the dressing tent, where a diaphanous curtain drifted in the wind. The girls walked past it, but Dorothy stopped. Inside the tent, she recognized Pierre's voice. She heard groaning. The breeze lifted the curtain several inches, showing tuxedo pants dropping down into a heap around Pierre's ankles. The maid of honor was holding armfuls of her red dress. She was bent at the waist. Pierre moaned again, his eyes halfway closed. The wind died, and the curtain fell, and Dorothy could only see vague shapes behind the cloth; but grunting sounds continued.

My God, Dorothy thought, covering her mouth with one hand. She had to find Bitsy. No, she had to find Jennifer. She couldn't let her granddaughter go on a honeymoon with that little cheater. The marriage was less than two hours old, and already he'd turned into an infidel.

Thunder cracked in the distance, and rain began to patter again. Dorothy hurried back to the tent and sat down in her chair, trying to catch her breath. Jennifer was dancing with her father, laughing at something he was saying. She looked so happy. Pierre's mother stepped out into the center of the marble floor, and began shaking her hips. They looked like lethal weapons, Dorothy thought. She turned away in disgust and saw the maid of honor running around the far edge of the tent, mascara dripping down her cheeks. She lifted her red dress and jumped over a man who was lying in the middle of the field, an empty bottle of champagne cradled in his arms, his body illuminated by a floodlight. With a jolt, Dorothy recognized the body. The redhead appeared to have gone, which just tickled Dorothy to pieces. She started to move toward her baby boy, thinking she needed to fetch him before he caught pneumonia. Then she saw Pierre standing at the edge of the dance floor. He lunged forward, banging into Louie's shoulder, then stumbled around Violet. Jennifer and Claude stopped dancing to watch as Pierre mounted the stage and pushed aside the musicians. He grabbed the microphone and his eyes swept the crowded tent. Then he screamed, "Tiffany!"

The music broke off. A few couples kept on dancing, but everyone else was looking at Pierre. The guests began to whisper. "Who's Tiffany? Tiffany who?"

"The maid of honor," someone said.

Turning to face the stage, Bitsy wondered if Pierre had caught the girl tying condoms and orange juice cans onto the bumper of the bridal limousine and was yelling for her to stop. From the stage, Pierre kept calling the name, and Bitsy finally understood. Miss Betty, who was standing several feet from Dorothy, appeared to have understood, too, and in a loud voice began explaining that Tiffany owed Pierre and Jennifer a great deal of money.

"Tiffany!" Pierre cried again in a hoarse voice.

"*Lots* of money," Miss Betty told a guest.

"TIFF-FANY!"

One of the musicians shook Pierre's arm, but the groom stood rooted. Then someone in the audience clapped, and Pierre took a bow. His father climbed onto the stage, followed by Claude. They grabbed the boy and reeled sideways. For a moment the trio appeared to be dancing, their arms locked together, weaving back and forth. Finally they dragged Pierre off the stage, out onto the lawn, into the pouring rain, next to the fountain.

Jennifer stood motionless in the center of the dance floor. Claude staggered back inside the tent, toward the stage. "Start playing again," he told the band. "And keep on playing, no matter what happens. Just pretend that you're on the *Titanic*."

The musicians grabbed their instruments and began "Addicted to Love," an unfortunate choice. But once they started, they couldn't seem to quit. Jennifer stomped off the dance floor, past Miss Betty, who reached out to grab the girl's arm.

"Your lovely dress," gasped Miss Betty. "You've ruined it."

"Take it to the thrift shop," said Jennifer, pulling away. She ran out of the tent, into the rain. Samantha shot out of her chair and tried to follow, but the marble dance floor was slick from people tramping in and out of the tent, and the tiles were speckled with grass. Halfway across the floor, her feet flew out from beneath her and she landed hard on her hip. The music never stopped playing. Several people rushed over, asking if she was hurt. She sat motionless on the marble, legs bent into a W. She only responded when Louie DeChavannes helped her to her feet.

"I'm a doctor," he said. "Are you hurting anywhere?"

She started to shake her head, then she apparently changed her mind, and vigorously nodded. "I-I might need an examination," she told him.

Next to the fountain, in the rain, Jennifer was yelling at Pierre. He yelled back, and she lifted her bouquet and started beating him over the head. Petals spun into the air. Dorothy stood up, then sat back down. If she made a scene, she'd never forgive herself. She had spent the last few years minding her own business, trying to repair her damaged reputation.

Her theme song was "Smile," even though in real life, she was careful about smiling because it caused unnecessary wrinkles. Lyle Lovett sang that song so pretty, Dorothy just loved him, even though she would never have married him like Julia Roberts had. But maybe Julia had fallen in love with that voice. Lyle had cheated on Julia, too, if you believed the *Enquirer*.

Dorothy believed it.

While Jennifer pummeled the groom, he crouched down, his hands folded over his curly head the way criminals did when the police led them past the press. She turned and saw her bridesmaids lined up and staring. The maid of honor was not among them. Jennifer took a deep breath and threw her bouquet into the air not toward the bridesmaids, but into the fountain. It listed onto its side for a moment, then finally drifted to the bottom.

"Goddammit, Jen," Pierre said, staring down at the flowers. "You didn't have to do that."

"Oh, shut up." She hiked up her dress and started to walk off, then stopped. "You asshole."

"You fucking destroyed it," he cried. Then he turned and leaned over the fountain reaching for the bouquet, but he lost his balance and fell in, face first. A wave of champagne surged over the sides, onto the grass. The bouquet bobbed away, pushed forward by the ripples, sliding along the bottom, only inches away from his grasp.

The rain was falling harder now, beating against Jennifer's shoulders. As she neared the tent she saw her mother, and a memory floated up, of the way they had danced in the front yard. It supposedly had been to bring rain, but suddenly Jennifer wondered if the dance had a deeper purpose, to grant wishes, answer fervent prayers. She turned her face up at the sky, her eyelashes spangled with rain and tears, and made a wish.

Guests had gathered at the edge of the tent. Dorothy didn't like how they were staring at Jennifer, so she began to herd people toward the checkerboard floor. Thank goodness the musicians hadn't stopped. "Please, dance!" she cried in an exuberant, take-charge voice. "Everybody dance!"

The violinist stepped around the fountain and began to play "She Moves Through the Fair." Some of the notes were drowned out by the band—they were singing another Fleetwood Mac song—but the violinist continued undaunted. Bitsy whispered into Ian's ear and squeezed his arm, then walked past Chick and Miss Betty, into the rain. In seconds she was drenched. Lightning cracked overhead, but she didn't seem to notice. Jennifer and Bitsy walked toward each other. The violinist kept playing, and music floated up, past the clouds, rising all the way to the constellations and beyond. Jennifer squeezed her mother's hand and made another wish: *Let me be just like this woman.*

BOOKS BY MICHAEL LEE WEST

MAD GIRLS IN LOVE
A Novel

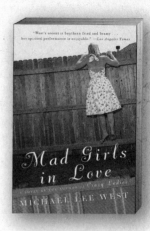

ISBN 0-06-098506-2 (paperback)

Michael Lee West writes about the women of Crystal Falls, Tennessee, and their men with the expertise of a down-home cook who knows just how much hot sauce to add so the cornbread isn't too sweet. Reading *Mad Girls in Love* is like settling into a chair on a porch or at the Utopian Beauty Salon—only much better.

AMERICAN PIE
A Novel

ISBN 0-06-098433-3 (paperback)

"Colorful, larger-than-life characters strut and stew with zest across an equally colorful terrain . . ."
—*Kirkus Reviews*

"West is a major talent, and *American Pie* serves as proof . . . West's writing is a 'Discovery Channel' for and about people." —*Nashville Life*

CRAZY LADIES
A Novel

ISBN 0-06-097774-4 (paperback)

Though she was born in Tennessee, Miss Gussie is no country fool. A woman who can handle any situation, she has her hands full with two headstrong daughters who happen to be complete opposites. From the author of *Mad Girls in Love* comes this lively multigenerational tale of six charming, unforgettable Southern women—a novel of love and laughter, pain and redemption.

SHE FLEW THE COOP
A Novel Concerning Life, Death, Sex and Recipes in Limoges, Louisiana

ISBN 0-06-092620-1 (paperback)

Brilliantly interweaves dark calamity with comedy to depict everyday life in tiny Limoges, Louisiana, in 1952. Told through the voices of its richly eccentric characters, *She Flew the Coop* is an entrancing picture of Limoges's gossipmongering citizens and a beautifully rendered picture of small-town life, filled with wry humor and humanity.

CONSUMING PASSIONS
A Food-Obsessed Life

ISBN 0-06-098442-2 (paperback)

Laced with delicious secret recipes passed from generation to generation, *Consuming Passions* is West's delightfully quirky memoir of an adventurous food-obsessed life. By watching a multitude of relatives cook, squabble, and carry on tradition, West went from a noncooking student to a full-on gourmet of food and words. Throughout, she lends her distinctive humor and often hilarious insights to stories about her trials and tribulations as a Southern woman who became an "accidental gourmet."

"A scrumptiously witty memoir about family, food, and the American South." —*People*

"A must-read. . . . Everything about *Consuming Passions*—from the title to the recipes—just drips with Southern charm." —*Denver Post*